An Albert Payson Terhune Reader

Volume III

An Albert Payson Terhune Reader Volume III
ISBN: 978-1-945307-09-6

Book compilation and design by Rodney Schroeter.

The Silver Creek Press
PO Box 334
Random Lake WI 53075-0334

rschroeter@silentreels.com

An *Albert Payson Terhune* Reader

Volume III

With the original illustrations from the source publications

Compiled by Rodney Schroeter

Silver Creek Press

2018

Table

of

Contents

A Lightning Change

Who was Keith?

That was the mystery.

Columbia University to-day crowns Morningside Heights,—roomy, beautiful halls, scattered through grounds that compare with the famed precincts of Yale, Princeton, or even the University of Pennsylvania.

The Columbia of yesterday (for the dear old University is still glaringly ill at ease in her new home) was confined to one small city block, bounded east and west by Park and Madison Avenues, north and south by Fiftieth and Forty-ninth Streets.

Owing, probably, to urban surroundings, Columbia contained more aspirants to so-called social recognition than do out-of-town colleges, where boys give less time to such diversions and more to athletics.

Especially were these social aspirations strong in the senior class, whose members insisted that they were men and not boys to a far more vehement degree than would those same "men" to-day.

A dozen or so of these seniors (most of them Psi-Upsilon men, with a sprinkling of "Deaks") were banded into a sort of clique, whose sole pride rested on its exclusiveness.

And into this clique Bernard Keith had penetrated.

Keith had entered Columbia at the beginning of senior year. He was not a regular student, but a "special." In other words, he was not working for a degree, but was merely taking a few elective courses of lectures with the senior class.

He was older than most men in the class,—just how old no one could guess. His smooth-shaven, clear-cut face, hard, well-shaped mouth, and quiet eyes might belong equally well to twenty or to thirty.

Thus it was that the dozen exclusive seniors opened not only their ranks, but their homes to the stranger. Having done which, they began to ask who he was.

So long as Keith was looked on merely as a decidedly handsome, well-groomed outsider, whose manners were good and whose wit made him a welcome addition to any crowd, no questions were asked. When, however, he became a probable fixture in the set, an idle query or two as to his antecedents and profession were framed. A dead silence followed. Then came a buzz of conjecture, rumor, and contradiction; and Keith's position as a mystery was established.

An impression, foundationless but strong, that he was the son of an English nobleman sent to America incog. to be educated, at length supplanted these theories. Then the seniors and their families suddenly ceased asking questions, tacitly agreed he was a sprig of English nobility worth cultivating for the sake of future invitations to his country-seat or to his Scottish moor, and stopped talking about him.

Money, a good presence, and decided cleverness had won the day. The sacred circle was once more solid as wrought steel. And Bernard Keith, '93, Arts, was safe inside.

But there was one person who refused to take Keith at the rest of the set's valuation.

Perhaps this was because she had put upon him a fictitious valuation of her own. While implicitly believing the English nobleman story, she yearned for particulars.

Mae Ward found Keith a more than welcome change from the ranks of callow college boys, heavy business men, and conceited litterati who had knelt at her shrine ever since she "came out," six months before.

She and Keith had met at one of Mrs. Meredith's "at homes" three months ago. Van Deusen Meredith was one of the senior "dozen." Mrs. Meredith was his mother.

Three hundred people were squeezed into a space where eighty might possibly have had comfortable elbow-room. The thermometer stood at ninety-four indoors and at twenty-one in the street.

Keith's collar had remained unwilted and he had looked neither cross nor bored. Mae was attracted to him from that minute.

He was presented to her.

"It's very warm in here," Keith had murmured amid the hubbub of voices, and she replied,—

"Yes, she *is* a charming hostess, isn't she?" And the next moment a crowd three hundred strong had wrested them apart.

The next evening he had found himself commanded to take her in to dinner at the Varnum's dinner-dance, given in honor of the just-achieved majority of Willie Varnum, '93, Arts. During the dance they sat together for thirty-five minutes on a red divan at the turn of the stairs. This landing was equipped for the occasion with two rubber-plants, a palm, a cloissonné vase, and three mildly pink Chinese lanterns.

Before the evening ended Mae Ward had made divers remarkable discoveries: notably that Keith possessed the pleasantest voice she had ever heard, that he had nice eyes, that he did not bore her by talking about himself, and that he neither boasted about his family, his athletic achievements, his pointless escapades at college, nor of the houses to which he had been invited.

And now came a new development that started tongues to wagging:

Dicky Long, '93, made the discovery that Keith always had an engagement of some sort between nine-thirty and ten-thirty P.M.

Long and Little Benton dropped in at his rooms one night after he had made study his excuse for departure. Although they hammered and shouted, his door remained locked, the rooms within silent.

And so the mystery remained, until by and by people grew tired of conjectures,—all except Mae Ward.

Miss Ward's father was an eminent lawyer. Her ancestors came to America in that elastic but sadly overcrowded craft, the Mayflower.

Along with a hypertrophated pride of birth she inherited a legal love for ferreting out mysteries and a Puritanical tenacity of purpose.

Moreover, she had so far forgotten all wise parental teachings as to fall in love with Bernard Keith, '93, Arts, and this served to keep up her interest in the man's movements.

Things had reached this stage when one evening Keith called to take her mother and herself to the Junior Ball.

"You are late, Mr. Keith," said Mrs. Ward. "I thought we were to be there by ten. It's nearly half-past ten now."

"I'm so sorry," he pleaded, "but I couldn't get away any earlier. A—lot of things prevented me."

His evident repentance softened the chaperon's heart, and she gave the matter no more thought. But with Mae it was different. This was the fifth time that she had had proof that the tale of Keith's regular nine-thirty to ten-thirty P.M. disappearance was true.

The Junior Ball is Columbia's one grand Social Event (with the largest sort of capital S and E) of the whole year. Then alone it is that class-lines give way to social precedence; when the freshman of good connections and with a reasonably pretty girl on his arm may outrank the haughtiest senior; when the "grind" and the boy who is shy in the presence of women will be wise to save the price of a five-dollar ticket by staying away; when the exclusive set of seniors are in their glory.

Barnard Keith and Mae Ward were sitting out a waltz in an alcove behind the lower gallery, where they could overlook the noisy, pretty scene below, and where a convenient palm shielded them from observation.

"Mr. Stanford tells me you do most of your studying between half-past nine and half-past ten at night," remarked the girl innocently. "Do you?"

The man glanced at her quickly, and as quickly glanced down before replying indifferently,—

"I often study in the evening."

"Oh! that's where Mr. Stanford probably got his idea about your being busy from nine-thirty to ten-thirty every night."

"Probably. You see, in a college like this, where we have no dormitory system, the men know little about each other's actions outside of lecture and recitation hours. In the warm spring evenings I believe there are often singing and general good times on the campus, but there our college life ends."

"How about the 'Strollers'? Don't their performances help on college spirit?"

"They advertise the college by their shows in different cities, rather than promote any particular brotherly feeling here."

"By the way, I'm to be the accompanist, you know, at the vaudeville show they're going to give for the Cherry Hill Mission next week at the Waldorf. Mamma objected at first; but it's only a drawing-room performance, and tickets are ten dollars each. And it's for the same old 'Sweet Charity.' So she gave in at last. By the way, are you a member of the 'Strollers'? or don't your talents lie in the direction of vaudeville?"

Mae fancied a barely perceptible tremor, as of contempt, ran through the man as he answered curtly, almost rudely:

"No. I have no tricks."

"I'm sorry," she answered. "It would have been rather jolly if you were in the troupe. Nowadays I spend most of my time practising on those silly songs."

Mae Ward was in the midst of this practising the following evening when Keith was announced.

"Are the songs good for anything?" he asked idly, picking up one or two sheets.

"Most of it is the same eternal old bore," she replied. "The so-called negro songs, such as no negro ever sang, and some tin-pan skirt-dance music. There's one good air among them, though," she added, taking a sheet of music from the rack, "and the words are rather clever—for that sort of thing. Mr. Hammond is going to sing it—in costume. He is coming around here some night soon to rehearse it with me. I never like to play the accompaniment to a song in public until I've gone over it beforehand with the singer."

"What is the song?" asked Keith.

"It is called 'The Song of the Wanderer.'"

"Is that song published?" exclaimed the man. "I thought it wasn't out yet!"

"Yes; it's quite new, though, I believe. Do you know it?"

"I—I've heard it once. Would it be any help to you to go over it with me? Then it will be easier for you when you and Hammond come to practise it."

"Can you sing it after having heard it only once?"

"I think so. I pick up airs easily, and I can get the words from the page before me."

"Where did you hear it?" asked Mae as she sat down to the piano.

"Oh, at one of the variety houses, I believe," responded Keith carelessly. "An old chap made up like Stanley, with a pith helmet and a green umbrella, sang it."

The girl played a rollicking overture and Keith began the song:

> "I have crossed through lands Hebraic,
> I have cursed in tongues archaic,
> I have met the gentle heathen and Circassion maidens fair;
> Through bazaars Damascene wandered
> (Where my scanty cash I squandered);
> I have seen the merry leper; I have heard the call to prayer.
>
> "I have crossed from Asian mountains
> Unto Afric's sunny fountains;
> I have had a swim in Jordan; I have drunk of Father Nile;
> I have seen Egyptians raggéd
> And a Moslem Imam jaggéd,
> Who discoursed on worldly matters in a most unseemly style.
>
> "Up the Pyramids I've scrambled,
> Through Saharan deserts ambled;
> I have jollied ancient mummies; I have gazed upon the Sphinx;
> I have yellowed every dental
> With tobacco Oriental,
> And I've queered my constitution with unholy Eastern drinks.
>
> "Lacking better occupation,
> I've composed (in adulation
> Of my prowess in such matters) this inspiring little lay;
> You can bet your bottom dollar
> That my number sixteen collar
> Now supports a head whose magnitude you don't see every day."

"I thought you said you had only heard that song once," commented Mae at the close.

"Well?" asked Keith.

"Yet you sang it from memory. After the first verse you never even glanced at words or music."

"I've a knack for remembering silly things."

"Where is your home, Mr. Keith?" inquired Mae suddenly. "I don't mean your bachelor rooms here in town, but your real home."

"My home?" echoed Keith, his half-shut eyes alone giving token that he was on guard. "My home is wherever I chance to be among thoroughly delightful people for a half-hour. For instance, I am very much at home now."

"That was just a trifle heavy, wasn't it?" asked Mae.

"How about the question that led to it?" retorted Keith laughingly.

The girl laughed too, but there was a note of vexation in her laughter.

"Mr. Keith," she said, "do you know you have been the object of a great many conjectures during the past winter?"

"Thank you. Give me anything but indifference."

"But people are saying—"

"They are very kind to take so much trouble. After all, what does it amount to?"

"But you never speak of your personal affairs, of yourself or of your people."

"Why should I bore myself with uninteresting themes? Still, if it will really give you any pleasure, I will gladly tell you the story of my life in words of one syllable and in language fitted for the ears of the young. I was born of poor but honest parents—"

"I don't like to have people make fun of me," interrupted Mae somewhat stiffly.

"But they *were* honest, Miss Ward," Keith protested with mock solemnity, "and poverty has run in the family for generations. Really, you can't expect me to clear up mysteries if you begin by accusing me of making fun of you."

"Then," pursued the girl, ignoring his last speech, "there is a lot of curiosity about your disappearing in that Cinderella-like fashion each night at exactly nine-thirty. You will pardon my rudeness in repeating all this, won't you? You know that I am inquisitive by nature."

"So were Psyche and Elsa and Mrs. Bluebeard; but I never heard that any of them was the happier for having her curiosity gratified," rejoined Keith.

Mae felt a hot flush rise to her face. She could not explain it, except possibly by the troubled look that accompanied Keith's words.

An old engraving of the "Parting between Lohengrin and Elsa" hung in Judge Ward's study. Mae remembered that the Swan-Knight's eyes had worn such a look as they bent upon the woman whose curiosity had cost her his love.

The full strength of the simile dawned on Mae, and she could not raise her eyes to the tall, knightly figure before her.

"Forgive me," she murmured; "I have been very, *very* rude."

"Please don't say that," urged the man. "You were perfectly right to ask, and I answered you like a brute. Some day,—it's a wild, futile hope, I know,—but some day I may have the right to tell you all about myself—and to tell you something else that means far more to me. If—"

The tiny cathedral chime of the clock in the adjoining library interrupted him.

"Half-past nine," he muttered. "Good-night, Miss Ward. You are to be at the Meredith dinner to-morrow evening? So am I. May the fates incite Mrs. Meredith to send me in to dinner with you!"

The fates incited Mrs. Meredith to place Keith and Mae at opposite sides of the table.

Mae was not sorry to be placed so far away from Keith. She now made no secret to herself of her love for the mysterious senior. From his broken words of the preceding night she knew he cared for her. Anxious as she had been to see him again, a certain onwonted shyness now made her glad that the table separated them.

The dinner was strictly informal. Mrs. Meredith prided herself on doing things with Bohemian informality, and was always leading her coteri through a dreary succession of welsh-rarebit suppers, impromptu excursions to Chinatown, "at homes" where men were allowed to smoke, and a dozen other abominations of the sort without which no rich man (or woman) may enter the Kingdom of Bohemia.

"Please hurry over the cigars," she enjoined her husband, as she and the other women rose from the table. "We are all going somewhere this evening. We haven't decided where. We're going to wait till you men come in before voting on it. Mr. Keith tells me he has an engagement at half-after nine, but I count on having all the rest of you join us."

When Keith took his leave at nine-thirty the question as to where the remainder of the evening should be spent was still in doubt. Two factions were hotly discussing the rival claims of Koster & Bial's and of Proctor's.

As Keith left the drawing-room his eyes rested for one moment on Mae Ward,—he had had no opportunity of speaking alone with her that evening,—and he surprised on her face a look that told him more than any words could have expressed. Angered that her heart could be so easily read, she turned with assumed interest to the discussion in hand.

Little Benton a minute later settled the dispute.

"I've got a better idea than going to Proctor's or Koster's," he declared. "What's the matter with doing some slumming? Let's go down to the Bowery Music Hall. It's somewhere near Rivington Street, I believe. We can get a couple of boxes and be guyed by the actors. There'll be a rank show, of course; but it'll be fun to watch the gentle Bowery Boy at play."

"Besides," cut in Hammond, "about fifty of our freshmen have gotten up a slumming party for to-night. They're almost sure to drop in there for a few minutes sometime during the evening, and when they do, look out for fun. There'll be a regular 'Town and Gown' row when the Boweryites resent the Columbia cheers breaking in on the show. Our boxes will be first-rate arena seats. I, for one, vote for the Bowery Music Hall scheme. It's a bird."

The idea took like wildfire. Five minutes later the party were on their way down town.

At the Bowery Music Hall a stout man whose hair smelt like a team of musk-oxen ushered the Meredith party into two stage-boxes. The stage was occupied by a lady of obese build and very yellow hair, and by a man with Dutch make-up and a red-and-green checked suit.

Soon the stage was cleared for the next "specialty."

"Let's see," mused Hammond, consulting his programme. "That was number six—'McGibben and Cohen, side-splitting sketch team!' The next is 'The Great Millicent!' I wonder if the great Millicent is a dog, a bird, or a patent medicine. Whoever it is, he or she is evidently a favorite. See, the name is in letters twice as big as any of the others on the programme, and the crowd is clapping itself black in the face in anticipation."

The piano which served as an orchestra struck up a lively air, and "The Great Millicent" hopped lightly on the stage amid a salvo of applause.

He was dressed in a coarse travesty of an African explorer's costume.

A huge green umbrella hid the upper half of his body. Capacious boots reached almost up to his waist.

He tossed the umbrella, whirling, upward towards the flies. As it came down it turned over, and the Great Millicent caught the point deftly on the tip of his nose. Spinning the umbrella about on this some-what unusual base and tossing his pith helmet into the wings, he began to sing,—

> "I have crossed through lands Hebraic,
> I have cursed in tongues archaic."

Mae Ward, who had watched the stage with growing disgust from the back of the box, now leaned forward, her face set and blanched, and her eyes fixed on the performer with questioning horror.

The lower part of the Great Millicent's face was hidden in bushy scarlet whiskers. A pair of huge smoked goggles covered his eyes. A fiery nose six inches long further disguised him. But to the eyes of love efficient disguises are few.

As Bernard Keith reached the middle of the third stanza his glance fell on the box party, and at last met that of Mae Ward.

The recognition was mutual, but there was scarce a break in Keith's voice as they went on to the end of the song.

"They say that Millicent feller gets seventy-five dollars a week just for singin' a song or two down here every night," commented a Bowery youth to his gaudy "ladifriend" so audibly that Mae Ward in the box just above their heads heard him plainly.

A shout of applause followed the song, and would not die down until the pianist recommenced the prelude.

Mingled with the clapping, yells, and approving whistles rose a sound that brought the men in the box party to their feet.

It was the sharp, barking cheer,—

"'RAY! 'RAY! 'RAY! C-O-L-U-M-B-I-A!" followed by the name, "MILLICENT!"

The college cry, coming in unison from fifty trained throats, cut through the looser volume of applause like a knife.

The whole audience turned to see whence it came.

There, at the back of the house, were massed the body of slumming freshmen, with a mingling of upper-class men. They had entered while Keith was singing.

"The Great Millicent" had opened his mouth to begin his encore selection. At sound of the familiar cheer he started as though shot.

He had again thrown his umbrella high into the flies and was awaiting its descent as Columbians' greeting reached his ears.

Unnoted by him, the huge umbrella fell. Before he could recover himself its ribs raked his face. The umbrella fell to the stage and rolled to the footlights, carrying on its steel rib-points the singer's false beard. Smoked glasses and red nose were alike knocked off by the blow.

Keith whirled about, facing the back of the stage, but not before a voice from among the mass of Columbians shouted in amazement:

"Good Lord! It's Keith, '93!"

"It's Keith!" echoed Hammond from the stage-box.

"Ah, g'wan!" snarled a tough from the centre of the house. "Dat's de Great Millicent."

But his interruption went unheard. The collegians had broken into a yell of astonishment mingled with derision.

The great asbestos curtain, with its gaudily painted advertisements, swept downward with a rattle and swish, shutting off all view of the stage and its occupant.

In the two boxes holding the Meredith party not a word had been spoken since Hammond's involuntary exclamation. For a full minute silence lasted. Then Mrs. Meredith said constrainedly,—

"So the 'mystery' is explained!"

"I'm afraid I can't agree with you," answered little Long. "To me the real mystery is just beginning."

"I don't understand," said Mrs. Meredith. "What is the mystery now?"

"Simply this: Keith is the whitest, best chap I ever knew. If he were a common music-hall singer and had imposed himself on us he'd have been a cad of the first water. And that's just what Bernard Keith is not. What is he, then, and why has he done this? There's the mystery."

"It's a mystery I'm going to unravel, then," announced Hammond, rising.

"What are you going to do?" asked Mrs. Meredith.

"I'm going 'behind' to speak to him. I'm going to hear his own version of the story."

"I'll go with you," said Long and Varian in a breath.

"I don't think we'll stay here any longer," remarked Mrs. Meredith, dusting her wrap with one gloved hand. "We spoke of going up to Sherry's for supper. Will you join us there when you've had your interview with Mr. Keith?"

"And if I was right in my estimate of him, may I bring him along?" asked little Long.

Mrs. Meredith hesitated.

"Mr. Long," said Mae Ward, speaking for the first time, "when you see Mr. Keith would you mind reminding him that he has promised to call on me to-morrow night, to help me on those songs for the 'Strollers'?"

Long, Hammond, and Varian paid an usher a dollar to take their names to Keith.

They found him seated on the one stool of his grimy little dressing-room. It was a six-by-eight apartment. Its furniture, besides the stool, consisted of a table covered with "make-up" appliances, a cracked mirror, a row of clothes-hooks, and a gas-jet shrouded in wire. Keith had removed his make-up and wig. His calm, classic face crowned oddly the grotesque dress which he still wore.

"Well," he said curtly, "what do you want?"

"A lot of things," answered Long easily. "First of all, we want to congratulate you on your performance. It was great."

The anger in Keith's face changed to puzzled suspicion. He made no reply.

"Look here, old chap," said Varian, "we haven't come here like Job's comforters, or to spy, or anything like that. We're your friends. You owe us the truth, you know."

"The debt will be outlawed, I'm afraid, before you can collect it," returned Keith. "And now, if you've nothing more to say—"

"But I have something more to say," interposed Long, calmly refusing to take the hint implied in Keith's last words. "I've a message for you."

"Oh, I can take my congè for granted," said Keith wearily. "You needn't put it in words."

"It was scarcely a congè," answered little Long. "It was from Miss Ward. Do you want to hear it?"

Keith nodded sullenly.

"She wished me to remind you that you had promised to call on her to-morrow night," said Long.

Keith rose abruptly and began to arrange some of the clothing on the hooks. His back was to his classmates.

"I was a boor," he said presently. "Excuse me, won't you? Sit down. Oh, I forgot, you can't,—there's only one stool. Never mind, you won't object to standing. I'm sorry I was such a brute when you fellows came in. I had an idea you came from curiosity, and I was sore. If you want the truth I'm ready to give it to you."

"Wait a second," interposed Varian. "Before you begin I want to tell you that we all three believe in you, and that we only ask an explanation for the sake of the rest of the people who have learned to like you this last year."

"Thank you," said Keith simply.

"Let her go," adjured little Long. "We're listening."

"I'll make it as short as I can," began Keith. "In the first place, my name isn't Keith at all. It's Bernard Fairfax."

"Any relation to General Bernard Fairfax, the Boston railroad king?" interrupted Hammond.

"He's my father," replied Keith. "I was in my junior year at Harvard. My father had ideas about college extravagance and kept me on what I chose to think was a meagre allowance. I wanted more money. I was a member of the Glee Club, and I'd been in some of their vaudeville shows. I had made a hit, and it struck me I might earn extra money that way. I went to the manager of the Lyceum Music Hall in Boston. He liked my work and promised me an engagement. The papers learned my real name and there was a big sensation. Some papers took the line that a scion of Mayflower stock had broken the bonds of society and had struck out for himself. Others published sensational stories of how my father's annual income was over one million dollars, and yet he was so stingy that his only son must seek a living on the vaudeville stage."

"Must have pleased General Fairfax!" commented Hammond.

"He was furious," answered Keith, "as he had a right to be. I think it was the slur about his so-called meanness that hurt him most; but the stain on the family name was a fearful blow too. We had a scene I shall never forget. At the end of it I left home. My father's will was law in our set, and society cut me dead. I drifted to New York, disgusted with society and with everything else. I had to make a living somehow. The only thing I could do was vaudeville. I got an engagement down here and somehow made a hit. But I hated it. I longed for my own sphere again, and wanted to study some profession. With that idea I went to Columbia. You fellows were good to me. You took me in. You asked me to your homes. I ought to have confessed then. But I imagined if I did I'd get the same treatment I had after my break with my father."

"You were dead wrong!" broke in little Long.

"Perhaps. But I dared not risk it."

"But your father?"

"I hear of him now and then. In fact, he is an intimate friend of Judge Ward, Miss Ward's father. He always stays at their house when he is in New York. I almost met him there once. From what I know of him he'll never forgive me. So why should I think about him any more? And yet," he finished, under his breath, "I do."

The three visitors glanced at each other in silence.

"Miss Ward told me this evening," Keith went on, "that General Fairfax is coming to New York to-morrow to visit them for a week. So you see, Long, why I can't call there."

"Look here," broke out Varian, "I've got an idea. Will you leave this business in our hands?"

"But what can you do?"

"Never mind what I can do. Will you put yourself in our hands?"

"Yes. But—"

"Then go to Miss Ward's to-morrow night,—unless you hear from me to the contrary before then."

"I can't. I'd—"

"You've promised."

"Well, I'm in you hands, I suppose. But—"

"Never mind the 'buts.' Good-night old man."

Hammond took Miss Ward home that evening. Late as it was, he had gone into the house, and for a solid hour was closeted with Judge Ward and herself.

General Fairfax reached the Ward house just in time for lunch. Judge and General were enjoying a post-prandial smoke in the former's study an hour or so later, when a little sheaf of cards was brought up.

"Show them in here," ordered the Judge. "No, Fairfax, don't go. I particularly want you to stay." Puzzled, the General sank back in his big leather chair as four young men filed into the room.

They were the trio who had visited Keith, and Harry Stanford, '93, Arts.

One by one they were introduced to the General. Then they stood hesitating, silent.

"You wished to see me, gentlemen?" said the Judge pleasantly. "Sit down, please. What can I do for you?"

"We want to consult you, sir, on a matter where your legal skill may help us," said Long. "It's about young Keith, '93. You know him, I think?"

"Very well indeed. What about him?"

"He's in a good bit of trouble," said Hammond. "You know Keith is the best fellow living. He is a splendid student, an honorable, straight-forward fellow in every way. It seems his mother and he had words on some point they'd probably have laughed at another time,—one that hurt the pride more than the honor. The son, smarting under what he thought was injustice, left home. Everybody he knew gave him the cold shoulder. He was literally cast on the world without a dollar, without a friend. Now, that's where another man would have gone to pieces, but Keith was made of different stuff. He found work—not, perhaps, such work as his family would have approved, but honest, clean employ-ment, for all that. Then he set about finishing his college course. He worked his way to the very head of his class by sheer pluck and hard study, keeping up his other employment at the same time. Why, I've known times, around examination week, when that man has worked twenty hours out of the twenty-four; and through it all, no word of complaint at the mother who cast him off; no railing at his hard luck. I tell you that's the stuff they make heroes of! Don't you agree with me, General?"

"I do indeed!" responded Fairfax emphatically.

"Now, here's the point," cut in Stanford, taking up the tale. "Keith has shown what he is made of; he's proved he can make his own living and go through college at the same time,—not an easy job, by the way,—and, in short, he's shown he's independent. But down in his heart he has a great big homesickness for his mother, for the family he was forced to leave because of a silly college prank. He wants to be reconciled to his mother. He wants to go home. He's proved it isn't her money or social position he wants, but just herself. We, who are interested in him, came to you to see if you can't advise us—to see if you can't suggest some way to reconcile them. Can't you?"

"I'm afraid not," said the Judge harshly. "A man who breaks loose from his family—who by some piece of wanton folly grieves a parent to the extent you say young Keith did—deserves all the loneliness and hardship he gets. He need not hope—he has no right to hope—for a reconciliation. General Fairfax here will agree with me."

"I will not!" rapped out the General. "I most assuredly will not! If a legal training gives a man that view of life, then I thank Heaven I never went into the law! Do you mean, sir, to say that any mother could hear such an account of her boy as these young men have just given without a thrill of pride that God had blessed her with such a son? Whatever his early offence, he has atoned for it. I beg, Judge, that you will use all your power to bring about this reconciliation."

"I'll do my best," assented the Judge, "but I doubt if I can succeed."

"I am certain you will," rejoined the General, "and if this young— what did you say his name was?"

"His name is Fairfax, General," said little Long,—"Bernard Fairfax."

The General sprang to his feet in anger. Then he sat down again and, with one hand shading his eyes, rested his elbow on the chair-arm and looked long into the blazing grate-fire.

The Judge and the Columbians were mute.

At length the General raised his head.

"Where is he?" he asked.

"He will call here this evening," said Judge Ward gently.

"This evening!" echoed the General, once more on his feet. "Do you think I am going to wait five mortal hours before seeing my boy? Take me to his rooms at once, gentlemen," turning almost fiercely to the four collegians.

When Bernard Fairfax called that evening his father's arm was linked in his.

But when, a little later, Bernard finished asking the question he had begun when he had called on Mae Ward two nights before, his father was in another room, quite out of hearing.

And her reply delighted the questioner's father almost as much as it did Bernard himself.

A Park Row Galahad

Monday morning is not a pleasant time in the office of an evening newspaper.

The staff, who have spent Sunday as Providence gave them wisdom, or the lack thereof, are cross and tired. A lot of news has piled up during the past thirty-six hours, which means extra work. Add to this the gloom that accompanies Monday morning the world over, and you will have a fair idea of the atmosphere pervading the city room of the New York *Evening Planet* on the forenoon of a certain Monday in the year of Our Lord 1897.

The big apartment, light on three sides, was dotted with a miscellaneous collection of tables, roll-top desks, reporters' table-desks, and chairs in varying stages of disrepair. The high ceiling was criss-crossed with green-coated electric wires, from which hung shaded arc-lights. Other wires, painted yellow like walls and ceilings, ran blindly to and from telephone boxes and telegraph instruments.

The floor was thickly strewn with trampled, torn newspapers, crushed sheets of "flimsy" and "copy-paper," cigarette-stumps, matches, ashes, and letters.

Four copy-readers bent over their desks, editing early morning stories or putting "c. l. c." heads and "agate" marks on police headquarters slips.

The assistant city editor, a pleasant-faced man with a long blond mustache and childlike blue eyes, had finished making out the assignment schedule for the day and was handing clippings to reporters.

A clump of office-boys, their real work for the day not yet begun, loafed about the pneumatic tubes. A discontented reporter in one of the booths was taking down a story dictated over the telephone by the man in charge of the Brooklyn office. Three other reporters sat smoking, too cross to talk.

And over all the scene rested the aforesaid cloud of Monday-morning gloom.

This dreary aspect would be dispelled three hours later by the rush and bustle incident on "going to press." The *Planet,* being an evening paper, went to press for the first edition at eleven-thirty A.M. This was before the days when war exigencies enabled the public at large to buy "evening" papers at eight-thirty in the morning.

The city editor took the assignment schedule from his assistant and glanced over it.

"I see you have Brooke down for the Enfield embezzlement case," he remarked. "That's the star story of the day, if it pans out. Hadn't you better give it to some more reliable man?"

"Brooke's the best reporter we have, Mr. Curtis," replied the assistant, "if he's only sober."

"Is he ever sober?" retorted the city editor. "Look here, Wilton, I know Brooke's a friend of yours, and I appreciate all you've done for him. If you hadn't shielded and helped him along he'd have been fired long ago. But I've stood his drunkenness as long as I can. He's made us lose half a dozen good stories, and he's utterly untrustworthy. The man's been on a spree for four days, and I've decided to discharge him as soon as he comes back."

"He'll be back this morning, Mr. Curtis," interposed the assistant city editor. "I stopped at his rooms on my way down-town. He's sobering up, and he's thoroughly ashamed of himself. Would you mind giving him one more chance? Remember, he's one of the cleverest men in the business—when he's himself."

The city editor's face relaxed at the other's earnest manner.

"Well," he agreed after a pause, "if he shows up this morning and covers this assignment decently, I'll give him another show. But—There he is now."

Curtis broke off as a man entered the room and slouched across to the city editor's desk.

The new-comer's eyes were red and swollen, his breath was reminiscent, and his face had a pasty, unhealthy look.

His voice alone, when he addressed Curtis, showed him to be a man of breeding.

"I wish to report for work, sir," he said.

The city editor's eye took in all the details of Brooke's appearance.

"Are you fit for work, Mr. Brooke?" he asked.

The reporter flushed, but bowed without speaking.

"You've been ill, I suppose," said Curtis sarcastically.

"No, sir," responded Brooke simply; "I've been drunk for three days. There is no use in lying about it."

Curtis turned aside to hide a smile. He loved his staff, and was one of those extremely rare beings, a justly popular city editor. He was pleased with Brooke's answer, having been prepared for a whining tale of sickness.

"Mr. Brooke," he said more pleasantly, "do you know I intended to discharge you this morning?"

Brooke tried to look surprised.

"But," Curtis went on, "I've decided to give you another chance. If you succeed with the assignment I'm going to give you, and keep straight after this, you may stay on here. If you fail on this assignment through any blunder of your own, or if you are drunk again, I shall discharge you on the spot. It is your last chance in this office. Do you understand?"

Brooke understood. He knew Curtis to be a man of his word.

"What is the assignment, sir?" he asked, his bloodshot eyes resting a moment on this chief's clear-cut features.

"While you were away, Saturday," answered Curtis, picking up a handful of clippings, "young Sydney Enfield, of Carew & Enfield, brokers, was arrested on a charge of embezzling two hundred thousand dollars from the firm of which he is junior partner. There's very little evidence against him, and he'll get off without any trouble. The police themselves look on the whole thing as a silly legal blunder. But here's what I want: I want you to go up to young Enfield's house—he lives somewhere in the early Forties—and get an interview with his wife. She's a mere girl. They were only married last year. I want you to get a good 'human interest' story there. You know the sort,—wifely indignation at her darling husband's unjust arrest, and all that sort of rot. If she won't see you, try to get a statement of some kind from

Enfield's lawyers. They are Porter & Jackson, 992 Nassau Street."

"A nice sort of assignment to send a man on when it's his one hope of holding his job," Brooke growled as he boarded a Third Avenue Elevated train. "The woman will never consent to see me; and as for the lawyers, of course they're under honor not to discuss their client's case with outsiders. Any fool knows that."

The drink-mists gradually cleared from Jack Brooke's brain as he glanced over the clippings Curtis had given him. He was a born reporter, and his professional interest in the case was awakening. Hurriedly he mastered each detail and mapped out to himself the line of questions he would ask should Mrs. Enfield by any rare chance give him an interview.

The hope of keeping his position on the *Planet* too went far towards sobering Brooke. He felt, somehow, that if he were thrown out of work at this crisis there would be no more stoppages on his path to tramp-hood. His "grip" would be lost for good and all.

That he would be able to turn over a new leaf and remain sober, in case he kept his position, was a question on which he was far more doubtful.

Still, he felt, stranger things had happened. A boyish stride replaced his former slouching gait as he walked up Forty-seventh Street towards the Enfield house.

"Is Mrs. Enfield at home?" he asked of the trim maid at the door.

The servant looked distrustfully at him, and Brooke's heart sank.

"Please tell her a reporter would like to speak to her for a few minutes," he went on, his voice growing so husky as to be almost unintelligible.

The maid's face cleared. She went up stairs with the message, leaving Brooke, hat in hand, in the lower hall.

A moment later she reappeared.

"Mrs. Enfield will be down in a few moments, sir," she said with a marked change of manner. "Will you step into the drawing-room, please?"

Brooke laughed grimly as he paced the deserted drawing-room.

"If she'll see me, that's all I ask," he mused. "Trust me to get any story I choose out of a woman; if she'll only consent to speak to me. All any reporter who knows his business has to do is to keep his mouth shut, and in ten minutes a woman will tell all she knows. They begin by swearing they've nothing to say to the press. Then, if a man holds his tongue, they'll talk on till the cat's out of the bag and the story's told."

Brooke stopped short in his walk. Ascending the front steps was a very youthful man with a pad clutched in one hand and a pencil in the other.

"A new reporter from some paper or other," Brooke soliloquized. "Since these people seem so willing to see reporters, I may as well head him off and get an exclusive story on this. He's only a kid; probably his first month in the business. An older reporter doesn't flash a pad and pencil on the public, like a census man. Any old gag will work with him."

Brooke glanced to and fro. The entire lower floor was deserted. He stepped to the front door and opened it before the new-comer could ring.

The second reporter was thus confronted on the doorstep by a solemn-visaged being, who, from his hatless status, was apparently some member of the Enfield family.

"Good-morning, sir," said the youth. "I represent the New York *Dispatch*."

"I knew he was a cut reporter," mused Brooke. "Who ever says 'I represent,' except in detective novels?"

"I should like," went on the new-comer, "to interview Mrs. Enfield on this unfortunate embezzlement case."

"Ah, yes," Brooke broke in, his face assuming an undertaker-like air, "to be sure. But my poor sister cannot see you, sir. Remember what a blow this unmerited disgrace is to her. She is quite prostrated. Indeed, she has not even seen me. But any information I can give you—"

The cub reporter's face brightened.

Brief as was his newspaper experience, he had sense enough to know how unlikely he would be to get a word out of any member of the Enfield family. Yet here was the stricken wife's own brother, willing and even eager to talk. It seemed too good to be true. The *Dispatch* man scarce knew where to begin.

Brooke saved him the trouble. Every moment counted. He must

get rid of the cub before Mrs. Enfield appeared.

"You see," he began in sepulchral voice, "my poor dear brother-in-law is the victim of a conspiracy. We suspect that the magnates of Wall Street—perhaps a syndicate of financiers from all over the world—have become jealous of his rapid rise, and have plotted to ruin him. I am not at liberty to give my reasons for this theory. But take my word that it is the truth. I intend to make a family matter of this, and shall probably challenge either Russell Sarge or J. Pierpont Morgan to meet me on the field of honor to redress my brother-in-law's wrongs."

The *Dispatch* man's eyes opened wide. Here was news indeed!

"And now," resumed Brooke, "I must ask you to excuse me. I fear I should break down were I to speak further of this calamity. I did not mean to say so much; but you gentlemen of the press are so clever; you manage to worm out the best-kept secrets."

Hastily retreating into the hallway, he cut short the *Dispatch* man's condolences by shutting the door in his face.

"I'd like to be in the office," he muttered half aloud, "when that cub carries the story of my duel and the conspiracy to the city editor of the *Dispatch*. But then the *Dispatch* is just the paper to print a story like that in good faith. There'll be a hot time in Park Row when their next edition gets on the street."

The delight of this thought caused Brooke to execute a little pas seul on the fox-skin rug. His saltatory performance stopped abruptly at the sound of a light step on the upper stair.

The next moment a slender, graceful girl, wan and heavy-eyed, entered the room.

She advanced towards the reporter with eager, outstretched hand and a piteous little attempt at a smile.

"It was good of you to come so soon," she said gratefully.

Brooke looked askance.

"I should have sent for you yesterday, but I could not trust myself then to talk calmly," she continued. "To-day I will try to be more reasonable. But you will pardon me, I know, if I'm incoherent. I'll do my best. I will indeed."

Still more mystified, Brooke seated himself and looked dumbly at her. For the first time in his life he was at a loss for words.

This big-eyed little woman, with her dainty, grief-stained face, seemed such a mere child, and withal such a thoroughbred. Why should she not only want to talk the matter over with him, but beg his forbearance?

"It's a long story. I'll make it as short as I can. It's best to be perfectly frank, isn't it?"

Brooke nodded.

"I will go back to the beginning. Don't stop me. I need all my courage. Sydney and I were married a year ago. Papa was wealthy, and I never knew, or even dreamed, the real value of money. So when I became Sydney's wife I supposed he was rich enough for us to live as I had lived at home. He never undeceived me; never refused or grudged one single request I made. When I suggested that I liked this house he bought it. I liked yachting, and asked him to buy a steam yacht last season. He bought it for me. These are only two out of a hundred such instances. I could not express a wish that he didn't gratify. And I—miserable, childish fool that I was!—never dreamed that money for all this couldn't be picked up like so much grass."

The girl choked, paused, and went on.

Brooke watched her dully, in no way understanding.

"Then," she said, "came the end—the horrible end."

The reporter pricked up his ears. The news-gathering instinct told him this was going to be a big story after all.

"For weeks," went on Mrs. Enfield, "Sydney would pace his study floor all night. He grew silent. He seemed to have some awful secret. I was wicked and thoughtless enough to believe he was growing tired of me, and—God forgive me—I reproached him with it. Oh, if I could only stop seeing his look when I said that!"

She shuddered and buried her face in her hands.

Brooke, coldly watching her, noticed how tiny and slender the fingers were, and speculated as to the karats of the solitaire that blazed above the plain gold band.

His foot tapped the floor lightly. Mrs. Enfield raised her head and continued:

"Yes, yes! I'll make it as short as I can. But can't you see—oh, *can't* you—what it costs me to speak of it at all? He came to me last Thursday night and told me everything."

Brooke was all attention now.

"He told me the whole pitiful story. My poor, misunderstood, unhappy boy! He had been admitted as junior partner in the firm just before our marriage. His profits were small, but enough to keep us comfortably if it hadn't been for my wicked extravagance. Then came my requests for more money, more style in living, and all the expenses that in my foolish blindness I looked on as a matter of course. He loved me, and he couldn't refuse me. How could he? Don't dare think it weak in him! It was noble, splendid! But each demand I made took more and more of his money. Soon his savings were gone,—the savings he had worked so hard to lay aside. Then he borrowed money. At last—at last he raised money on the firm's securities."

Brooke's dull, bloodshot eyes were ablaze now. This was luck such as never comes twice in a lifetime. No one really believed Enfield guilty. Newspapers and police alike thought his arrest a stupid mistake. There was practically no evidence against him. He would have gotten off scot-free.

And here the true story of the monstrous defalcation was told exclusively to a *Planet* reporter—told by the guilty man's own wife.

But was it exclusive? If she talked thus freely to him, might not some earlier reporter have been equally fortunate. Might not the story even now be in Park Row. The dread turned Brooke faint.

"Have you told this story to any newspaper men, Mrs. Enfield?" he asked.

"Newspaper men?" gasped the girl. "Great Heaven, no! How could you imagine that I would spread the story of my darling's disgrace to the world?"

Brooke muttered a word or so of apology and breathed again.

"Sydney took—borrowed the securities in such a clever way that no jury in the land could convict him. His arrest is a silly blunder, caused by men who are on altogether the wrong track. The true story, which I've just told you, will never be known. Why, your partner says the case won't even come to trial."

"My partner?"

"Yes, Mr. Jackson, of your firm."

Brooke did some lightning brain work. Who was Jackson? And who, in the name of all the mysteries, was he supposed to be? He remembered now; Curtis had told him that Porter & Jackson were

Enfield's lawyers.

But could that be the Jackson of whom she spoke? And if so, why did she refer to him as Brooke's partner? She had said five minutes before that no newspaper men should know the story. Why, then, had she told it to him?

The man began to see that Mrs. Enfield had mistaken him for some one else. But for whom?

"I know you can help us," the woman resumed. "When the maid said to me this morning, 'Mr. Porter would like to speak to you,' I felt that you had come to our aid and you would save Sydney."

So he was supposed to be Porter, of Porter & Jackson. He remembered now how husky and indistinct his voice had sounded, even to himself, as he had bade the maid tell Mrs. Enfield "a reporter would like to speak to her." The maid, doubtless on the lookout for the lawyer, had naturally misunderstood the word "reporter."

Such an idea seemed like a farce-comedy situation, yet it was the only way in which Brooke could solve the mystery.

Mrs. Enfield continued:

"My husband told me, when he left, that you and he went to Columbia together, Mr. Porter. He went to see you Saturday about this matter; but you were out of town, you know. So he had to consult Mr. Jackson. He told me he'd left word asking you to come here the minute you reached New York. He said you were his oldest, dearest friend, and that I must tell you the whole story. You would help us if any one could, Sydney said. So I gave orders that you, and you alone, should be admitted when you called."

"So much to the good!" Brooke laughed to himself. "This is too easy! And it's just horse-luck."

"You see, Mr. Porter," the girl went on, choking back sobs that would not be silenced, "I've told you everything. Sydney says you're his best friend. Everyone who knows Sydney must love him. You see, don't you, that it was all my own wickedness, and that he was not really wrong? Don't you understand that? He's so good, so gentle, so generous."

But Brooke did not answer. He was mentally mapping out the exclusive embezzlement story that should reinstate him in his old place as the *Planet's* crack reporter.

"I can see from your face," cried Mrs. Enfield impetuously, "how this sorrow of your friend's has wounded you. And now that I've told you all about it I feel almost happy again, for I know he's safe in your hands. And I want you to help me in something else. I'm going to sell this house and the yacht and all the rest of the extravagances, and he and I are going to work hard till we've paid every penny of this debt. Then we'll settle somewhere in the country, and I'll prove to Sydney that his wife isn't really the wicked little fool whose habit of throwing away money so nearly ruined him. You'll help me sell it, won't you? And oh, you *will* see his partners to-day and get him released? He wouldn't consent to be bailed, and said he'd only leave jail a free man. You'll bring him back to me? Promise, *please* promise! I love him so."

Half unconsciously she had caught both Brooke's hands in her own and knelt, looking pleadingly up into his bloated face.

Brooke tried to avoid the eager eyes, and to be oblivious of the trembling, childlike lips.

"I've shunned everyone since this happened," she murmured. "I couldn't face old friends or bear their pity. But with you it's so different. You seem to understand it all; and your friendship for Sydney makes it easy for me to speak to you about his trouble. You can never know all your visit has meant to me."

Brooke disengaged his hands and rose to his feet.

"Mrs. Enfield," he said harshly, without glancing at her, "you have made a mistake. It is your own blunder, and no trick of mine. I am not Mr. Porter, your husband's friend,—I am a New York *Planet* reporter. I came her to interview you about this embezzlement story. It is my duty to my paper and to myself to publish what you have told me."

Then, for the first time since he began to speak, he looked at her.

In an East Side street one day Brooke had seen a brutal 'longshoreman knock down a laughing, three-year-old child that in an ecstasy of babyish affection for the world at large had embraced the man's knees. He had seen the look of blank, horrified surprise on the baby face as the blow fell. Incidentally he had interviewed the 'longshoreman to such effect that the man did not leave the hospital for six weeks.

The same look was in Mrs. Enfield's eyes as she gazed dumbly at him. The same white horror left her childish face drawn and old.

Without a word she sank lightly to the polished floor, and lay there face downward, the fresh morning sunshine pouring in on her.

She had not fainted: the blow had merely robbed her of all speech and power. She lay at Brooke's feet, quivering all over like a beaten dog.

The reporter gazed down on the slender, girlish figure, dully noting how the sunbeams played in her gold-brown hair.

"This would make a good situation in a story," was the thought that years of the writing-habit forced on the reporter's brain. The thought was as unconscious as are a sleep-talker's words.

The woman lay motionless. The quiver had passed. At length a low, wordless moan broke from her lips.

A clock somewhere was striking ten.

Brooke lifted his eyes and looked wearily about the room. Then he walked out into the hall, picked up his hat and stick, mechanically adjusted his tie at the long mirror, and left the house.

The Monday morning gloom was gone from the *Planet's* city room. In its stead an orderly babel reigned.

The paper was going to press.

Curtis, the city editor, stood beside his desk, a frown on his handsome face. In his hand was a copy of the *Dispatch.*

On the first page, in glaring headlines, Curtis read:

"WILL CHALLENGE RUSSELL SAGE!
"SYDNEY ENFIELD'S BROTHER-IN-LAW SAYS HE WILL FIGHT
SAGE ON J. P. MORGAN.
"ENFIELD FAMILY DECLARE THE ALLEGED EMBEZZLER'S ARREST
TO BE A CONSPIRACY.
"MRS. ENFIELD PROSTRATED!"

Then followed a column of weird idiocy that is remembered on Park Row unto this day. The story was an enlargement of the cub reporter's interview with Brooke. The latter was therein described as "pale and tear-stained, his eyes read from long weeping."

"Of course, this brother-in-law is a crank," remarked Curtis; "but Brooke ought to have made a great story out of this. Didn't he send down anything at all?"

"No, sir," answered the assistant city editor reluctantly, "not a word. I don't understand it. He should have telephoned the story to us by ten-thirty. It's twelve o'clock now."

"We've gone to press, and the *Dispatch* has beaten us on the only good story of the day," said the city editor. "I was a fool to trust Brooke. Yet the man seemed sincere in his wish to do better. Perhaps he'll have something about it for the next edition. If not—"

Curtis did not need to finish the sentence. His assistant remembered the chief's warning promise to Brooke, and knew it would be kept.

An office boy bearing a sheaf of papers—first editions of the *Planet,* still damp from the press—burst into the room and began laying copies on the various editors' desks.

Before the door could close behind him some one else entered.

It was Brooke.

Curtis met him in the middle of the floor.

"Well, Mr. Brooke," he cried, "where have you been all this time? Did you get the story?"

Brooke breathed a heavy sigh, redolent of freshly-swallowed whiskey.

"I didn't get any story at all," he muttered thickly. "I—I forgot to go there."

His voice trailed off into a sheepish laugh, and, turning on his heel, he slouched out of the office.

Drunk Or Crazy?

"I CAN'T see," argued Goward, "why you object to taking me into the firm. I'm the only nephew you've got."

"That's my only bit of good luck in the whole affair," retorted Croxley. I've worked thirty-four years to build up this real-estate business. I've done it under a lot of handicaps. Why should I split my profits now, and take only half the glory, by letting *you* in as a partner? Tell me that. What have you to offer that will make it worth my while?"

"What had I to offer that would make it worth May Lowry's while to take me as equal partner?" argued Goward. "Yet that's just what she's promised to do. She promised last night. Not for a term of years either. For life. Are you going to let yourself be beaten in generosity by a little flower-faced girl of nineteen?"

"Generosity," grunted Croxley, "is the one thing I'm willing to be beaten in. Don't think you can coax me into making a fool of myself just because a fluffy-brained girl has consented to take you at your own valuation. So *you're* engaged!" he snorted. "On what prospects, I'd like to know?"

"In the first place," replied Goward sweetly, "I've been your chief clerk for three years. And any man who could get along with Peter Joseph Croxley for that length of time ought to be an ideal life partner for a normal person. Secondly, as you yourself admit, I know the real-estate business from A to building laws. In the third, I've an inherited capital of $2,700. Fourth, as your partner, I'm going to be worth fully $6,000 a year."

"As my partner!" stormed Croxley. "I keep telling you, you young idiot, that you're not going to be my partner."

"And I keep repeating, in firm yet gently respectful tones, that I *am*," smiled Goward. "In fact, if I hadn't believed I was going to, I'd never have had the nerve to ask May to marry me."

"I've faith to believe you'd have the 'nerve' to ask Taft for his job. But you can go back and tell her it is all off."

"Look here," argued Goward. "You'd lose nothing by taking me in as partner. I'd wake this old business up till—"

"Till the receivers held a wake on it," suggested Croxley with elephantine wit. "But I—"

"I've put you on to some of the biggest deals you ever made," protested Goward. "For instance, the Jewelers' Block is the best paying investment of your career. But for the rents those eighty big and little jewelers pay you, where would the Croxley Company be? And I put through the whole negotiation which got you the block."

"Son," observed the older man, "we business men don't reward a fellow for what he *has* done, but for what he *will* do. Jewelers' Block was bought by me two years ago. Now get down to work and stop pestering me. I've no more time to waste talking to cheeky youngsters."

"No," retorted Goward mildly, "I don't think I care to work to-day. I've something more important on hand."

"Notifying Miss Lowry that both partnerships are off?"

"Neither is off," corrected Goward. "One of them is just postponed for a few days. No, I'm going to buy her an engagement ring."

"To tear a hole in that $2,700?"

"Why not? As your partner I'll soon patch it up."

Slipping out of the office in time to escape his uncle's new roar of protest, Clyde Goward strode into the bright springtime street.

In spite of his air of confidence, the young man was decidedly miserable. He knew that he could not support a wife on his salary as chief clerk. He had staked everything on that partnership. And now—

To forget his woes, he turned his steps toward Jewelers' Block, the little district where all the foremost jewel dealers of the city were massed.

There, in the midst of a rather narrow, winding thoroughfare, stood a crescent-shaped block of high buildings owned by the Croxley Company.

The ground floor of each edifice was filled with plate-glass windows in which glittering gems were strewn lavishly upon white or blue velvet. On the upper floors were offices of wholesale jewelers.

There was more actual wealth in precious stones in that one block, so a newspaper had once estimated, than in any other ten blocks in all the city.

To-day a curious little crowd was gathered on the sidewalk front of the block. All were gazing with idle interest at a big, old-fashioned, four-story gray building across the street.

This structure, formerly used as a warehouse and now occupied by business lofts, stood in an odd position. As the crescent curves about the star in its center, so did Jewelers' Block, on the opposite side of the street, face this great, ramshackle old house.

"What's the row?" asked Goward.

"Don't you ever read the papers?" answered the lad. "It was in all of 'em this mornin'. The old Myles Buildin's just been condemned as rotten an' unsafe. An' all the tenants has got to clear their truck out of the lofts before five o'clock."

The news did not interest Goward, and he strolled on to one of the jewelers' shops. There, for the next ten minutes, he occupied himself in sorting over a collection of diamond solitaires. Finally, he chose one and paid $250 for it.

The stone, as the jeweler held it up to the light for Goward's inspection, shone like a sun-kissed dewdrop. Singularly pure and flawless, it reflected back ten thousand rays of dancing sunbeams from its countless little facets.

It was a ring to dream of. Goward paid the money without a sigh.

II.

AT the Lowry home a half-hour afterward the blue velvet box was unwrapped by May's white, quick fingers. There, in its nest of snowy satin, flashed the ring.

The girl snatched it up with a little cry of delight and held it in a bar of sunlight that flooded the room.

Clyde, watching her, saw the glowing joy in her big eyes suddenly give place to a puzzled frown. From her face his gaze shifted to the ring, and an exclamation of angry amazement broke from him.

The diamond seemed dull, muddy, yellowish—the sort of stone that would disgrace an actress's paste tiara!

"What—what does it mean?" he gasped. "Some one has changed it! It was a beauty when I saw it at the shop."

The girl bravely sought to praise the stone, the setting, the shaping of the facets. But Clyde broke in:

"No use, dear heart! There's a horrible mistake somewhere. I wouldn't have had you so disappointed for all the world. Here—give it to me, and I'll take it right back and—"

He broke off as a fresh surprise greeted him.

Restored to its white-satin cushion in the less sunshiny part of the table, the diamond once more blazed forth with all its old radiance.

"The ring's bewitched!" exclaimed May in wonder.

"No," he stoutly declared, "it's a trick. Something about the box makes it shine so."

He picked up the ring, box and all, for closer inspection. As his hand moved into the sunlight, the stone all at once settled back into its former hideous discolorment.

"Perhaps," ventured May, "it's the sunshine that—"

"No," he corrected. "At the shop I held it in bright beams, and it was perfect. I—I don't understand."

"Wait!" commanded May, taking the box from him and moving close to the window, where the full force of the sun beat in through the open sash. "See?"

The diamond flared forth, crystal pure, and in almost blinding glory.

"You were right," he muttered. "It *is* bewitched!"

"You silly boy!" she laughed. "Don't you understand?"

And thereupon she gave him a little synopsis of certain facts in physics she had learned at Barnard.

"*Now,* do you see?" she exclaimed in triumph when she had finished.

"Y-e-s," he drawled absent-mindedly, "I—I see."

But his brows were knit, and his mind seemed far away.

"Tell me," she went on, to rouse him from his odd reverie, "did your uncle agree to take you into the firm? You said you were going to ask him to-day."

Her words brought Goward back to earth with startling suddenness.

"Yes!" he cried excitedly. "He'll take me into the firm all right, inside of a week."

"Oh, how good of him!" she cried. "He must be—"

"He is! You'll like him. He's a dear, generous old customer. And now I've got to run on. I'm liable to have a pretty wakeful day."

Scarce stopping to kiss May good-by, Clyde Goward snatched up his hat and bolted from the house.

His next visit on this "wakeful day" was to a down-town office. There he made a proposition that led the senior partner to eye him suspiciously and edge toward the bell. Only the sight of a fat check induced him to continue negotiations with so palpably insane a customer. Leaving the place at last, with a long strip of legal paper in his pocket, Clyde hurried on to a big, odd-smelling store, and there left a second order and a check—and a fresh impression of his insanity.

<h1 style="text-align:center">III.</h1>

IT was noon on the following day.

Croxley, returning from lunch, stumped over to the desk where his head clerk was quietly working.

"Are you clean crazy?" he demanded, glowering down on Clyde.

"I've been told so, from time to time," assented Goward pleasantly. "What is my latest sign of it—the fact that I still work for you?"

"At the Lunch Club this noon," sputtered Croxley, "they were all laughing about it. And they made fun of me—of me, mind you—for having a lunatic for a nephew! What d'ye think of that?"

"I think they needn't have dipped into the second generation to find something about you to laugh at. But of course you know best."

The irate old man paid no heed, but thundered on:

"They say—they say down there—that you've taken a six months' lease on the Myles Building; that—"

"Quite true," answered Clyde. "Here is my lease. A good bargain it was, too. I picked it up for a song. Only one thousand two hundred dollars for six months' lease. Think of that! And right opposite Jewelers' Block, too. One of the best locations in town."

"You idiot!" roared his uncle. "Don't you know the Myles Building has just been condemned? Not a tenant is allowed to stay in it."

"So I heard. So I heard. In fact, that's why I got it so cheap. I saw the owner yesterday. He was going to tear it down at once. But I persuaded him to let me have it on a six months' lease. You see, I—"

"I see you're stark-staring mad! You had only $2,700 in the world and—"

"No, $2,450," amended Goward; "I spent $250 on an engagement ring for May. And now this $1,200 rent money cuts my capital down to $1,250. Or did, till I spent—"

"You spent still more? Why—"

"Yes. You see I'll get plenty of cash when our partnership deal goes through. As junior partner of the Croxley Company, I will—"

"The partnership!" gasped Croxley.

He could say no more, but glared, gulping and speechless, at the calm young man before him.

"The Myles Building," resumed Goward, "is an ugly, ramshackle old ruin. Its gray front-wall is so discolored that it's a disgrace. I'm having it freshened up a bit. The painters were to begin work early this morning, and—"

"*Painters?* You're having that useless condemned building *painted*—at your own expense—on a six months' lease?"

"It'll liven up the tone of the street. A man should think of his neighbors. Besides, it doesn't cost so much. I get it done at bargain rates. The whole job only costs me two hundred and fifty dollars. That leaves me with a clear one thousand dollars."

"You've spent $1,700 in a single day on—on *idiocy?*"

"No. As an investment. As I told you a few moments ago, I'll get it all back—and more—when I'm your partner."

A buzzing, imperative ring at Croxley's private telephone cut short the old man's apoplectic retort. He bustled into the inner room; returning a little later, growling like a sick bear.

"A pretty mess you've got me into!" he snarled. "Here was Mawley, of Mawley & Greet, on the phone. They're my biggest rent payers on all Jewelers' Block. He's kicking because part of the first coat of paint on your crazy Myles Building is such a glaring color that—"

"That is no concern of mine," interrupted Clyde with simple dignity. "Mr. Mawley's nose is a very unbecoming shade of red. Yet *I* never complain. I can't see what cause for complaint he has when I choose to paint my own leased building. I do not care to hear any further reports of that kind. Please keep them to yourself. I've taken the trouble to look up the law on such matters. And I find that (except in 'restricted neighborhoods'—which Jewelers' Block certainly is *not)*, a man has a legal right to paint his house any color he chooses."

Croxley groaned aloud, tapped his forehead, and slouched back into his own office.

"Mad or drunk! Mad or drunk!" he muttered. "Or *both!*"

IV.

FOR the next two days Clyde Goward did not return to work. Yet his name was on hundreds of mouths in the business district. Every half-hour the police were forced to clear the street before Jewelers' Block of the dense, gaping crowds that lined the thoroughfare.

Under constant work by a double shift of painters, the once dingy front of the Myles Building had assumed a truly marvelous aspect.

The dirty, gray cracked stucco had given place to colors that would have shamed Joseph's coat. Wide stripes of fiery vermilion red and flaring, poisonous yellow were joined by lines of glowing marsh-green.

The building was on the south side of the street, where the sun played lovingly upon its horribly vivid hues. One newspaper called it "The Rainbow House." And the name stuck.

But the debasing notoriety to an old and ultra-respectable neighborhood was the very tiniest of Jewelers' Block's grievances. These same grievances promptly swelled into something very like a riot.

The storm was at its most sulfurous height when, on the morning of the third day, Clyde Goward came back to the Croxley Company's offices.

"Where on earth have you been?" shrieked his uncle, literally hurling himself upon the youth. "I've hunted and telephoned and telegraphed everywhere for you. I—"

"I ran out into the country," replied Clyde blandly. "I thought a couple of days' rest might cure my insanity. And I really believe I'm quite well again. I—"

"Here!" interrupted Croxley. "Jump to the telephone and order that awful building of yours repainted at once in gray or some other quiet color. I'll pay for it. Have sheets and canvas draped over it at once. In a rush!"

"I don't understand you," protested Clyde. "What building are you talking about?

"The Myles Building, of course. You've no idea what awful trouble you've got me into. The place glares out in that fearsome red and yellow and green, and throws such a reflection across the street that it's ruining every man's business on Jewelers' Block."

"But how? If—"

"I don't know! But it seems the light spoils the looks of their precious stones. And they've telephoned me and called on me, and sent swearing committees to me, and tried to get injunctions and—I don't know what not. You must have those terrible colors covered up *at once!* This is ruining me!"

"Dear old uncle," exclaimed Clyde, "what nonsense you are talking! As if the color of a house half a mile away from here could ruin you!"

"I tell you it *is* ruining me!" almost wept the desperate old man. "Nearly all the Jewelers' Block leases expire within the next six months. Not a man will renew when his business is being spoiled. Every mother's son of 'em will leave, and go to some neighborhood where there's no 'Rainbow House' to make their jewels look like yellow paste. I'll have eighty vacant offices and stores on my hands in place of the block that brought me my chief income."

"How strangely you speak," murmured Clyde. "I gather from all this that while I was insane I must have painted the Myles Building some most unfortunate color. Odd that I can't remember it. But I probably had some very good reason for doing it. So I'll just leave it as it is."

"You *can't!* You *won't?*" howled Croxley. "Why, man, it would be the ruin of me! There's *another* of those rabid jewelers at the phone now! I—I—"

"What odd freaks an insane man's brain takes at times!" philosophized Clyde. "For instance, during my attack I had an hallucination that you refused to take me into partnership. *I,* who am your only living relative, and the man who has built up your business to what it is! Wasn't it a very strange delusion of mine?"

Croxley paused, midway in an outburst. Long and wonderingly he eyed his gently smiling nephew. At last he slowly said:

"The papers shall be made out this afternoon, my boy. Understand, though," he went on with some of his old roughness, "you didn't *trick* me into this. I only do it because the brain that could create the Rainbow House will be worth a lot to me in the business. Now go and telephone the painters to cover up that red-and-yellow monstrosity."

"In a moment," assented Clyde. "First, I'd like to use your private phone to call up May Lowry. You see, I forgot to ask her to set the wedding-day. Thanks, partner!"

But it was not till that evening that he told her he had her to thank for the whole brilliant idea.

He then recalled to her how, in her exposition of her physics lore, she had placed the diamond over a gaudy oriental scrap on the table. Its chief colors were red and yellow in wide stripes, joined with narrower ones of vivid green. The sunlight, reflected back from this atrocity, had made the stone seem lifeless, and given to Goward his very fortunate inspiration.

Back to the Wickiup

By Albert Payson Terhune

WHEN John Pine, Yale, 1906, and more or less rising lawyer, stepped down from the dusty train to the dustier water-tank platform at Prairie Rose, he ceased to be John Pine.

At the first big breath of sage-brush zone that displaced the Pullman smoke and cinders, the East and civilization all at once seemed far away; like the memory of a troubled dream.

As an obese Sioux rose clumsily from a huddle of blankets in the lee of the tank and waddled toward him grunting, *"Hu-hu-kola!"* John Pine, in replying *"Hu-hu-kola-wash-ti!"* not only ceased to be John Pine, but all at once he became again Et-i-Wa ("the Pine Tree"), member in good and regular standing of the Brulé clan of the Sioux nation.

Fat Bear, who had been his chosen comrade, and more than brother since babyhood, and who had for weeks been checking off the days until Pine should return from the East, showed in his broad, brown face no sign of emotion at seeing his beloved friend. Nor did the two shake hands.

Beyond that guttural *"Hu-hu-kola"* they spoke no word and gave no indication of pleasure at the meeting, but moved side by side toward the rattletrap buckboard hitched to the far side of the tank. A ewe-necked, rat-tailed pinto pony, branded and lean, stood between the shafts, head adroop. As Fat Bear unhitched the little horse, Pine slung his suit-case into the buggy and climbed in after it. Already his eyes were straining across the hazy miles of prairie in search of the far-off reservation village of his clan.

Arrived at the village after a fifteen-mile breakbone ride, Et-i-Wa was received by the whole population of ninety, who had turned out to do honor to his arrival. No one smiled. No one offered to shake hands.

From all outward appearances the home-comer might readily have been a total stranger of unsavory repute, whose designs on their welfare the villagers strongly suspected.

In the East a dozen hands would have been extended as John Pine stepped from the buckboard. A dozen voices would have been raised in cheery welcome. Here a few grunts and placid stares alone attested that his people were glad to see the far-wandering Et-i-Wa at home again.

Then the man who had been to Yale, who had practised law, who had moved in pleasant society in New York, unemotionally took up his life as a brave of the once terrible Brulé clan.

His Eastern clothes, which he so easily wore when in the haunts of the white man, were discarded for the garb of the Sioux. His face—dark in spite of long confinement in office and between city walls—grew daily more bronzed by contact with sun and wind.

His muscles tautened and his flesh vanished under a rigid course of horsemanship, whether in the quest of such scanty "big game" as remained in the district, or in "riding herd" on his people's great cattle-bunches.

Altogether, at the end of a month or so, few casual observers would have recognized the tanned, blanketed Et-i-Wa as the well-groomed, swarthy John Pine.

Then the girl came.

A little party of tourists from New York were traveling by lazy stages through the Northwest, enjoying the odd experience of leaving the train for a week or two at a time and camping on hill-ridge or among the prairie flatnesses.

This form of outing has gained in popularity of late years. The man who "personally conducted" the party—Frank Whitman, an ex-guide and pioneer—saved enough money through the venture to stay drunk all winter.

And, in due course, he brought his tourists to Prairie Rose, debarked the tenting outfit, and pitched camp not a mile upstream from the Brulé village.

To this same village, in quest of local color, on the evening after their arrival, Whitman brought several of the party.

They threaded their way through tents and picket ropes to where the camp-fire winked its red eye in the center of the settlement.

Around the blaze sat or sprawled a score of blanket-wrapped Indians, for the evening was cold.

"Here," announced Whitman, with an explanatory wave of a not overclean hand, "here, ladies and gents, you see the noble red man in his native wilds. He ain't so impressive to look at as he used to be in the old days, when he'd go pirootin' over the plains on the war-path or maybe was settin' out on a scalpin' bee. I rec'lect once, over in the Sweetwater country, back in sixty-nine—"

"And these," loudly observed old Judge Torrey, surveying the seated and totally indifferent Indians, "these are Uncle Sam's wards, hey? The terrors of the plains that I used to read about in the dime novels? They look about as terrible as so many picked chickens."

"Hush, father!" begged the girl, "they may understand English."

"Not them, miss," Whitman reassured her. "They can grunt and ask 'How much it cost?' and 'Give poor Indian fire-water,' and a few fancy phrases like that. But that's about all. They're too stupid to learn more."

"But they're cleaner than I expected," said the judge. "They aren't even as picturesque as when I saw them in the Buffalo Bill show."

"An actor ain't so picturesque in his smokin'-jacket as when he's playin' *Hamlet*," answered Whitman. "In the Bill show, they're represented burnin' settlements and scalpin' settlers an' holdin' up the Deadwood coach an' such like parlor tricks. You'd better be glad they ain't handin' out that line of 'picturesque' action now. They're safer to watch, with their peace-blankets around them."

"A sorry lot!" commented Rotter, a New York commission merchant, who was standing somewhat close to the girl. "Wait till I see if I can't get a rise out of one of 'em."

"Oh, don't!" begged the girl.

But Rotter was a forceful young fellow, the sort to whom feminine opposition is a signal to keep on. Singling out the nearest and most stolid-looking of the blanket-wrapped forms, he strode up and tapped it on the shoulder.

"How?" he grunted in his best conception of Indian patois. "How, red brother! Me paleface, who come from land of rising sun; from Eastern land where Great White Father lives. Red brother ever hear of Great White Father at Washington?"

Slowly the shapeless, blanketed one answered:

"If you are referring to President Taft, I've heard of him, of course. And I have had the honor of meeting him. We are graduates of the same university, he and I. I met him at commencement-time last year."

Had the red brother cast a bomb into the tourist group he could not have caused much more amazement than by his quietly modulated reply.

"He—they—understand!" gasped Mr. Torrey. "And we've been talking about them as if they were natural history specimens!"

"Whoever taught you to talk?" sputtered Rotter, staring as if at a speaking doll.

"My parents," returned the red brother. "And at the same time they taught me the rudeness of intruding uninvited into other people's homes and making uncivil speeches about them."

"But we're sorry!" pleaded the girl, stepping forward, impulsively. "Please forgive us. All of you."

She had been in the rear of the group; unseen, unheard by the red brother, who had not turned nor looked up at the advent of the tourists.

But now, at her first audibly spoken word, the blanketed form had sprung to its feet and was facing her, dumfounded.

"Miss Torrey!" he cried, in crass astonishment.

For a full ten seconds she stared, wide-eyed, at the tall, lean figure before her; at the moccasined feet, the buckskin hunting suit, the gaudy blanket; the straight, rather long hair; the bronzed, high cheek-boned face, with its dark, staring eyes. Then—

"Mr. Pine!" she exclaimed, in total disbelief. "Or—"

"Your eyes are good," he said, "but your memory for names is at fault. Here I am Et-i-Wa. It is a prettier name than Pine, and more in keeping with my surroundings."

"But what on earth—"

"Am I doing here?" he finished. "I am at home. Among the people of my childhood. You are surprised? The world is a small place. But it is a very delightful place, since *you* have happened to drift here. You are with the tourists who arrived to-day? You will let me come to see you in the morning, won't you?"

"Yes. Oh, yes," babbled the girl, scarce knowing what she said.

"Father," she added, turning to Judge Torrey, "you remember Mr. Pine?"

"How?" said the confused judge, in doubtful salutation, trying to remember what the peace sign was like and wishing he knew how to make it.

But Et-i-Wa's hand was outstretched in cordial greeting.

"It's good of you to remember me, sir," he said pleasantly. "The last time we met you were on the bench, and I had the bad luck to lose a case before you."

"My decision—" stammered the judge, wondering vaguely if the Indian would try to scalp him through vengeance, "my decision was—"

"Was just. It is good to see you again, I hope you will let me be your guide, and Miss Torrey's, to some of the beautiful places around here. A stranger can't expect to see half of them. May I ride over to-morrow?"

"Of course—yes, of course!" answered the judge, his scalp settling back to its normal condition. "Come, my dear," he went on, turning to the girl. "It's getting chilly. I think we'd all better be starting for camp. Good night, Mr.—Mr.—"

"Et-i-Wa," prompted the girl in a whisper.

"Sounds like a breakfast food!" snickered Rotter.

On the way back to Whitman's camp the judge and his daughter fell a little behind the others.

"Of all things!" Torrey was saying, over and over. "An Indian! A blanket *Indian!* John Pine! And we've actually had him at our house!"

The girl made no reply.

"I wonder though," went on the judge, bringing his judicial faculties into play, "I wonder we never thought of it. He's so dark. And his hair so straight and black. And his cheek-bones are high. But I've seen dozens of white men who looked almost as much like Indians. H-m! Gone back to his blankets! They all do, sooner or later, I've heard. But he seemed such a fine fellow. And he had a promising law career in New York. He'd risen fast. Just think of this throwing all that away to wear a blanket and eat dog-soup or whatever it is that Indians eat! Isn't it wonderful, daughter, how heredity will overcome environment?"

Again the girl did not answer.

"That's the way it goes!" pursued the judge. "It happens all the time. A tribe will send its chief's son East to go to school and learn the white man's magic, or whatever they call it. And, nine times out of ten, that is all the good it does. I saw a play on the same theme a year or two ago. It was called 'Strongheart,' or something like that. About a chief's son who went to college in New York and was made much of in society, and had the audacity to fall in love with a white girl. He—Why, little girl!" he broke off in alarm. "What's the matter, dear?"

For the girl had broken into a fit of unrestrained weeping. She buried her face in her father's shoulder and sobbed convulsively.

"You don't mean—" gasped the judge, at last.

"Don't!" she begged, hysterically. "He never knew or guessed. It was only a dream. A foolish dream of mine. I'm wide awake now. Horribly wide awake. Please don't let's speak of it again!"

"He is coming over in the morning," hesitated Torrey. "Shall I send him word not to?"

"No! You mustn't. We must meet him just as we always have. I'm sorry I was so foolish just now. I won't be, again. It isn't Mr. Pine's fault that he's not one of us. And it would be cruelly rude to show him we notice the difference. At most, we'll only be here a week or two. And after that we are never likely to meet him again. Now let's talk about something else."

II.

"No," said Et-i-Wa. "They don't call him 'Fat Bear' because he looks like one. It's because a huge, tub-shaped grizzly blundered into camp the day he was born."

"And," queried the girl, "they named him for a *bear?*"

"It is the custom in many of the tribes. A boy is named for the first object on which his mother's eye falls after he is born. For example: A bull buffalo charged into a Sioux camp one day, a good many years ago. A rifle-shot stopped his rush. Instead of tumbling over, he crouched down for a moment in a sitting posture, right in front of a lodge where a new-born baby lay. And the child was henceforth known as 'Sitting Bull.'"

"Not the great—?"

"That is how he is said to have got his name. Again, a mustang, that had been sunstruck, once ran amuck in an Indian camp. And a child, whose mother chanced to see the plunging brute, was named 'Crazy Horse.' Another child was born out on the open prairie in a rain-storm that beat blindingly into his mother's face. And the child became 'Rain-in-the-Face.' The custom sounds senseless to outsiders, but it is interesting. And it is just as worthy as to name a boy for a rich relative, in the hope of getting into the namesake's will."

"You have made Indian customs so clear and so interesting to me this past fortnight," mused the girl. "And you have made me understand your people as I never dreamed I could. To understand and sympathize with them. Until I came out here, I thought of them as—"

"As Buffalo Bill dime novel demons, or else as unkempt, unwashed brutes," he finished. "Most people do. But you have seen our camp. You have seen how clean it is and how sanely governed. The Indian puts on war-paint and dances the ghost-dance; and people laugh at him. Does he look or behave more ridiculously than the whites who rouge and powder their faces, put rings in their ears, on their fingers, and around their necks, and dance the Turkey Trot in ball costume? Would a man, who had never before seen either, think one more ridiculous than the other?"

"I never—I never thought of it that way before."

"In New York one spends three-fourths of the time between walls and under roofs, in air not fit to breathe. From toe-tip to head-crown, one's body is swathed and cramped and twisted and choked by tight, heavy clothes. One stays awake during the hours when sleep is most refreshing and lies asleep during the hours when day is most beautiful. One eats when one is not hungry, drinks when one is not thirsty, and talks when there is nothing to say. All in the holy name of Civilization."

"But—"

"Out here," he continued, "one sleeps when Mother Nature whispers 'sleep,' wakes when she say 'wake,' eats and drinks only when she says 'you hunger' or 'you thirst'; wears clothes that spell comfort, is silent when speech becomes folly; and lives under God's broad heaven, under His white sun and wonderful stars. Wherefore, white men declare Indians to be 'savages,' and little better than the beasts. But I bore you with my endless lectures. I am sorry."

"You don't bore me," she returned; and under her breath she instinctively murmured, "I wish you did."

He said nothing in immediate reply; and she was gratefully certain he had not heard.

They were seated on a cliff-edge overlooking miles of billowy, flower-strewn prairie. A little behind them, Whitman and his subordinates, impeded by the proffered help of the rest of the party, were pitching camp.

On the morrow the tourists were to depart eastward. And they had arranged a "mountain picnic" for the last day and night of their stay.

"Bison Nose" was a precipitous, flat-topped, wooded mountain that rose abruptly from the prairie. In the midst of a clearing on its summit was a clump of hunters' huts, surrounding a well, and this summit had been chosen as the scene of the twenty-four-hour picnic.

The luggage and provisions had been "packed" up the narrow, twisting trail from the lower ground, and the picnickers had followed pantingly up the steep incline.

For the past fortnight Et-i-Wa and the girl had been together almost daily. They had ridden, tramped, and hunted in each other's company.

Judge Torrey, remembering the talk with his daughter that first night, had made no objection. He knew, as did the girl, that the intimacy could be but temporary; and for her sake he had not the heart to interfere.

Et-i-Wa now sat for a minute, his dark eyes resting in brooding uneasiness upon the vast panorama before him. Then, very quietly, he asked:

"Why?"

"I—I don't understand," she answered perplexed.

"You said you 'wished I bored you,'" he answered. "Why?"

She could not frame the answer she wished, but lowered her gaze and became all at once very busy tearing to pieces a flower at her belt.

"Why?" he insisted.

Without waiting this time for a reply, he went on:

"Is it because you don't *want* to—to like me?"

She looked up, met his commanding gaze, and could not lie.

"Yes," she said.

"Why not?"

"Oh, can't you understand?" she pleaded. *"Don't* make me say it!"

"You know, of course," he pursued calmly, "that I love you. They say a woman always knows. If that is true you must have known it long ago—in the days back there in New York. I dared to hope, even then, that *you* had learned to care, just a little. But I didn't have the courage to ask. Out here it all seems different. And I *do* ask. Tell me!"

She could not speak.

"Tell me, dear!" he insisted.

Below them, along the prairie trail, passed in single file a line of mounted Indians returning to the Brulé village from a visit to another part of the reservation. The squaws, who brought up the rear, were squat, hideous, shapeless. They sat their ponies like meal-bags.

Their faces were blistered by cooking for "braves," who deemed it debasing for a man to cook. Their hands were calloused and their shoulders were stooped from bearing burdens that their husbands might loaf.

The girl looked at the patient, ugly creatures, and a vision of their life rose before her.

"No!" she cried as if in sudden pain. "No! Oh, *no!*"

He had been leaning toward her, his eyes alight with longing. Now, with a sharp intake of breath, he drew back as if she had struck him across his bronzed face.

"I am sorry to have distressed you," he said very gently, as he noted the tears in her eyes. "Please don't give it another thought. Shall we go back to the rest now?"

Silently she rose and followed him.

III.

THE camp-fire was smoldering low. The guide whose duty it was to replenish it with fuel sat snoring, his back to a hut-wall. Midnight had passed. The campers, one and all, were sleeping the heavy, dreamless sleep that follows on an active outdoor day in high altitudes. And they had slept for hours, as had the guide whose duty it was to guard them.

It was Et-i-Wa who first awoke. He came to himself with a sick feeling of utter misery—the same with which he had fallen asleep in the midst of his crumbled air-castle.

But, keen as that grief was, he knew something more palpable must have shaken him from his deep slumber. And he lay now wondering what it might have been.

It was not the music of Rotter's snoring at one side of him, nor the breathing of the other sleepers about him. He was certain of that. Then, all at once, he knew. It was a stifled sob from somewhere out in the night.

Silently he threw on the few clothes he had removed and slipped out into the clearing in front of the men's sleeping-hut.

At the side of the dying fire, in the center of the open space, a little, unhappy-looking figure sat huddled on a fallen log. He knew it at a glance, and after a moment of hesitation went toward it.

The girl lifted her head from between her hands at his approach. Her face was tear-streaked, but she spoke without a tremor.

"I woke up," she whispered, "and I couldn't get to sleep again. So I dressed and came out here. I—"

But he was not heeding. Suddenly, even as he bent to hear her whispered words, he had sprung to his full height and began to sniff the air.

"What is it?" she asked, wondering at the look that leaped into the other's face.

"Fire!" he answered shortly. "Not camp-fire, either. Burning grass!"

The girl sprang to her feet, startled by the excitement that rang through his quiet, deep voice. A lurid glow hung about the tree-trunks on the steep slopes of the hill.

A crackling sound as of myriad tiny torpedoes exploding far

away, suddenly rose to them on the still air. And now, even the girl's untrained nostrils could detect the acrid smoke reek.

Without another word Et-i-Wa ran to the cliff-edge at the far end of the enclosure. She kept breathlessly at his side.

Arrived at the brink they looked down. Below them the miles of prairie were aglow and dazzling with sheets of fire.

A wave of flame seemed to sweep up to the very base of the hill, to part at its stony foot like waters about a boulder, and to swirl on to either side.

"A prairie-fire!" cried the girl.

"Yes. And it came on us as quickly as a thunder-storm. And with less warning."

"Are—are we safe up here?"

"Perfectly. This hill has withstood a hundred prairie-fires. Otherwise its trees would never have lived to be so large. That stratum of broken rock all around the base protects us. So do the green of the trees and the lack of undergrowth on the lower slopes. But when the smoke begins to rise we will be half strangled. Come, let's wake up the others."

"Can't we escape?"

"It will be a good many hours before the fire dies out enough for our bases to travel over any part of the prairie. But we'll be all right up here, except for the smoke. Come."

They started back toward the camp. But cries and confused queries from the clearing, and a general exodus from the sleeping-huts showed them that the alarm had already been given.

The glare of the fire below had now begun to make the clearing bright. Every stick and stone was visible.

The girl, walking a step or two in advance, halted suddenly with a little cry of fright and stepped back, catching Et-i-Wa by the arm. For, from the dense thicket that ran from half-way down the mountain to the summit, out into the light sprang a yellow, tawny thing, that flashed past them like a great streak of flame and was lost in the bushes at the farther end of the clearing.

"A mountain-lion," whispered Et-i-Wa. "Don't be frightened. It will not harm you."

"Oh! It—"

"Every beast for miles around," he added, "has sought this mountain, by instinct, as a place of refuge. As the flames below grow hotter, they will come higher up, for greater safety. They will not hurt you."

He spoke as might a mother who soothes her child's fear of a big but perfectly harmless dog.

Judge Torrey ran to meet them.

"Hurry!" cried the old man, "Frank Whitman says we must get indoors. He says there will be dangerous wild animals up here before long. Oh, isn't this terrible?"

"Don't worry, sir," said Et-i-Wa; "we are perfectly safe."

Nevertheless Whitman herded his charges unceremoniously into the mess-cabin—largest of the trio of huts. No artificial light was needed, for the flickering red glow from the sea of fire beneath them illumined each corner of the log-room with an unearthly gleam.

The heat, too, grew more and more intense; and blurs of smoke began to sting nostrils and eyes. From the low, wide windows the tourists gazed out at the odd scene. But scarcely had they taken their places at the rough casements when an exclamation from one of the guides drew all eyes to the head of the path by which they had climbed to the summit. There they beheld a huge, furry head swaying angrily from side to side—two wrathful little eyes, an unwieldy bulk wherein red sparks still sputtered.

Then, out into the clearing rolled the newcomer—a bear—big, awkward, awesome. Into the open it plunged, sadly out of breath as from a long run and hard climb; then paused as though aware it was in momentary security from the fire.

And an instant later a black-tail buck came crashing upward through the thicket, head back, soft eyes wide with terror, and crouched shivering in the open space before the cabin.

"Oh, for a gun! muttered Rotter. "Here, Whitman! Lend me your six-shooter."

Without waiting for leave he snatched the ornamental, ivory-headed revolver from Whitman's holster, and leveled it at the crouching, trembling deer.

Before he could pull trigger, before any one else could interfere, Et-i-Wa by a single swift gesture had struck the weapon from his hand.

"My friend," he drawled, picking up the revolver from the floor and handing it back to Whitman, then turning to face the discomfited Rotter, "you seem to forget those beasts are here for *sanctuary*. It's about as sportsmanlike to shoot that poor deer just now as to horse-whip a sleeping baby."

"Moreover, young fellow," snarled Whitman, with the plainsman's true hatred for any sort of interference with his weapons or gear, "I'll thank you to remember it's manners out here for a gent to keep his hands off'n another gent's hardware. You yank my gun away from my holster again and I'll sure be obliged to slap them wrists of your'n good and hard. Oh, gee!" he broke off with a gasp, "do look, every one! It's a whole Noah's ark!"

No one spoke. All were gazing thunderstruck at a sight surely never before seen save by some frontiersman in like predicament.

From the path ahead, from the copses, from the thickets, and especially from the gentler slope of the low mountain on the nearer side, a steady, panting, rustling, growling, stamping, padding stream of animals were pouring up onto the little plateau.

From miles away on every side they had flocked at the first breath of the oncoming flames to this one fire-break. And, as Et-i-Wa had predicted, when the heat in the dense hiding-places on the lower slope grew too intense for comfort they had stampeded upward toward the comparatively cool summit.

Rocking-gaited bears with whimpering cubs; black-tail deer and antelope—from stately and horned bucks to stumbling little fawns; snarling, cringing coyotes; a gray wolf or so, with bushy tail clamped between legs; several gliding, stealthy, gold-coated catamounts with ears flat and eyes blazing green; one or two bellowing steers that had strayed from the herds—and, here and there, twisting and wriggling along the outskirts, the bodies of scared rattlesnakes.

In less than ten minutes the clearing was full—full of such an assortment of northwestern mammalia as surely was never before gathered together by mortal collector.

It was less like a scene from Noah's ark than from some opium-crazed Doré's pencil. In and out they weaved, shoving, moaning, padding about the narrow confines of the summit.

Mountain-lion justled against blackbuck fawn, and slunk aside, growling harmlessly. Wolf and bleating calf cowered side by side, each regardless of the other. Bear and antelope rubbed shoulders in that general swaying and involuntarily grinding movement of the thronged creatures.

A common terror—a common and terrible foe—had robbed them, one and all, of every emotion save fear.

"Say!" chattered Rotter, "what a fortune for a menagerie man if he could catch the lot for his 'Happy Family' cage."

No one answered. Indeed, speech was becoming difficult. The air was suffocatingly hot. It parched the lips and swelled the tongue. The smoke reek, too, caught and propelled by some vagrant breeze, was filling the cabin.

Its fumes turned the eyes into hot marbles, tortured the dry throat with paroxysms of coughing and threatened to burst the anguished lungs.

"Where's the drinking-water?" Rotter croaked thickly to Whitman.

The guide pointed toward the big oaken pail in the corner. Rotter crossed hastily to it and snatched it up.

"Empty!" he groaned.

"Not quite," corrected Et-i-Wa, taking the pail from him and passing a handkerchief around its inner bottom and edges.

He drew out the handkerchief slightly moist from such drops as had adhered to the inside surface.

"Take this," he said in quiet command to the girl. "Hold it doubled across your mouth and nose when you inhale; it will make breathing easier and cool your throat."

To her own surprise the girl found herself obeying him. And the first breath through the water-cooled linen brought so much relief to her burning throat that she glanced at him with involuntary gratitude.

But Et-i-Wa was not looking at her. His eyes were fixed anxiously upon Judge Torrey. And before the girl could follow his glance he had leaped forward and caught the old man in his arms just as the latter collapsed in a swoon.

"It is his heart! It's his heart!" cried the girl in keen distress. "The doctor warned us."

Et-i-Wa had already laid the judge carefully upon the floor and was opening his collar and the neck of his shirt.

"It is not dangerous," he said, as he worked over the unconscious man. "He is old and not strong. That is all. And the suffocation and the pain made him faint. We could bring him around easily enough if we had—"

He paused and glanced at the empty water-pail.

"But it is the *heart*," explained the girl, "and that is always dangerous. The doctor said if he should faint again, and we had none of the regular stimulant at hand, a dash of cold water in his face would—"

"H-m!" interrupted Whitman, "might as well ask for a dash of radium. It'd be just as easy to get. Yonder's a well, out there, with enough water in it for an army. And here we are. And between us and the well is a whole passel of varmints. Enough to scare all the lion-tamers that ever came down the pike. I'm sorry, miss, but I'm afraid the old gentleman will have to take his chances."

"But," wailed the girl, "the doctor said if he were allowed to remain in one of these fainting fits for any length of time he might—"

"He won't be," broke in Et-i-Wa; "please don't be frightened, Miss Torrey."

As indifferently as a country boy going to water the cows, he picked up the big pail and started for the door. He had all but reached the threshold before any one guessed his intent.

"Well!" exclaimed Whitman, "of all the wall-eyed idiots! Son, them varmints will—"

"It's—it's suicide!" croaked Rotter hoarsely.

But the girl alone made a move to stop Et-i-Wa.

She flung herself between him and the door.

"You shall not!" she blazed.

"Please—" he began.

But she cried again:

"You shall not! It is certain death. Stop, I say!"

Shifting the pail's handle to the crook of his arm, and speaking no word, Et-i-Wa very gently lifted her from before him and set her down on her feet at some distance back in the room.

Then, with almost incredible swiftness he had unbarred and opened the door, slipped out and closed it behind him.

The cowed wild beasts gave no heed to his presence. On the threshold he all but stepped on a cringing jack-rabbit. It did not stir nor note the brushing of his moccasined foot. A rattlesnake, a few feet farther on, did not so much as coil itself or sound its harsh note as he accidentally touched it with his toe.

Twisting his way among bulky, cowering, slow-moving forms, sometimes obliged by the very denseness of the press to push a path forcibly between two big carnivora, Et-i-Wa reached the well.

Here the throng was thickest. For the beasts smelled the water. And they were as sore athirst as their human fellow captives of the fire.

Up from the cool wet depths, hand over hand, Et-i-Wa drew the bucket. Splash! into the four-gallon pail he poured its precious contents.

And on the instant he became the vortex of a maddened, jostling, roaring, bellowing mass; carnivora and cattle alike smelled and heard and saw the blessed water for whose lack they were so cruelly suffering. And they stampeded for it.

Terror was still their master. Wherefore claws remained sheathed and teeth lip-hidden. But with pathetic earnestness they closed in upon the man in a solid phalanx.

The girl, from within the cabin, saw the surge of furry bodies that eddied and crowded about Et-i-Wa. With a cry she ran toward the door. But Whitman caught and detained her.

Had the thirst-crazed brutes not also been fear-crazed, and had there been scope in that confined space for a concerted rush, the man must have been overborne and crushed to death in a second.

But, holding the dripping pail high in the air, he made shift to stand for an instant protected by the angle of the well, while, with his free hand he drew up a second bucket.

Then, with full force, he hurled the contents of the pail as far to one side of him as he could.

With a swash and gurgle the cascade of water struck the ground fifteen feet away, sending little rivulets in every direction.

And, as Et-i-Wa had foreseen, the sound and scent of the running water was too much for the half-numbed senses of the animals. They stampeded for the area where the precious fluid was already soaking into the earth.

Before the flood had struck ground Et-i-Wa was busy dashing the second bucket's contents into the pail.

Now, pail in hand, he was running for dear life toward the cabin, through the straggling rear-guard of the animals which were already massing around the water-soaked space of earth.

Almost unimpeded, he reached his goal before the parched-tongued brutes could catch up with him.

Over the threshold he bounded, as Whitman flung open the door to admit him.

The door banged shut again in the very faces of two lunging bears and a mountain-lion, and pinched the forepaw of a timber-wolf between jamb and portal.

At the same instant Et-i-Wa had reached Judge Torrey's side and had splashed half the contents of the pail over the senseless man's face and throat.

As though his act were a preconcerted signal, a splitting reverberation shook the cabin. In the next breath the brightness of the fire-glow paled before a vivid glare of lightning. A tall tree at the clearing's edge shattered with a splitting, rending sound, and toppled outward over the incline.

And before the lightning-riven trunk could crash to earth, the rain had begun, a cloudburst that beat down the nearer flames and hissed into the parched ground.

Judge Torrey gasped, caught his breath, and opened his eyes. Leaving the recovering man to his daughter's ministrations, Et-i-Wa crossed the room and, alone, at a far window, stood gazing out unseeingly at the gushing volume of rain.

He had not known whether he had stood there for a minute or for fifteen, when a light, timid touch on his arm made him turn.

The girl was at his elbow. The rest of the tourists were still grouped about the opposite windows looking out at the storm; except for Whitman, who was talking with the judge, who was rapidly recovering from his faint.

"Your father is better?" asked Et-i-Wa.

"Yes," answered the girl, "he is out of danger now. Thanks to your—"

"I'm very glad," he interrupted, embarrassed and seeking to stave off her praise. "It was good of you to come and tell me."

"That wasn't why I came now," she hurried on, not daring to look at him. "I—I came to tell you that what I said this afternoon wasn't true! I *do* care. I have always cared. Always. From the first. I—”

“Don’t!” he rasped out, “you have no right to hurt me like this. You think you owe me gratitude for the trifling service I did your father. And you are trying to repay it by—”

“Gratitude? Repay? Yes, I do feel gratitude—all the gratitude in the world. And neither of us can ever repay you. But—”

“Then—”

“But I wouldn’t marry any man through ‘gratitude.’ It would be the cruelest way to injure him. I—I love you. Can’t you understand? I love you. And I have always loved you. But I felt I couldn’t stand all the things that marriage to you must mean. Then, to-night, when I saw you go out there and move among those horrible beasts like a shepherd through a drove of sheep, I knew that nothing in all life counted or even could count—except *you!* I can stand the hardships, the—”

“Hardships?” he repeated in perplexity, “why must there be hardships? I am not rich. But I am making a fair income. And it is larger every year. I—”

“It isn’t that,” she murmured confusedly.

“What is it, then? If there is something about me that makes it a hardship to be my wife, I can’t let you sacrifice—”

“I *want* to!” she declared, “and I’m going to. I’d rather marry such an Indian as you than any white man.”

“Indian?”

He spoke with an amazement whose genuineness she could not doubt.

“Indian?” he repeated, “what do you mean?”

At the dazed wonder in her eyes a light broke in on him.

“Good Lord!” he gasped, “you thought *I* was an Indian? Why? Who ever told you such a thing? My father was a Boston man by birth and my mother was English.”

“But—but—”

“My father was a missionary to the Sioux,” he went on, “and I lived at the mission out here until I was twelve. The Brulés adopted me and treated me like one of themselves, because they loved my father. And every year I run out here for a month or two, on vacation, because I enjoy the change. When I come here I adopt their customs. Just for extra comfort, and because it pleases them. And they call me ‘Et-i-

Wa,' which means Pine Tree; because that's the nearest they can get to my real name—John Pine."

"Oh!" she panted, "I'm *so* glad! So *glad!*"

"And you loved me enough to marry me and become a squaw. Oh, darling! I—"

"I wish to thank you, Et-i-Wa, with all my heart, for your great service to me," interrupted Judge Torrey, crossing totteringly to where the two stood very close together in the far corner of the room.

"We will call it square," laughed John Pine, "if you'll forget that name 'Et-i-Wa!' I'm going to drop it. It's an unlucky one. It—it almost lost me the only sweetheart I ever had!"

Chapter I.
The Costliest Taxi Ride.

DOWN Broadway from north of the Circle came the solemn line of taxicabs. Twenty of them formed the procession as Fifty-seventh Street was passed. At Times Square the number had swelled to thirty. At Twenty-eighth Street there were forty of the buzzing little vehicles—black, yellow, green, red—all dutifully following one wherein sat a pleasant-faced, well-dressed man of twenty-five.

The occupant of the first taxi was the only passenger in the whole forty. He kept a sharp alternate lookout from each of the side windows. And whenever he could catch the eye of a waiting taxicab's chauffeur along the curb anywhere, he beckoned him to fall into line at the end of the procession. And usually the chauffeur obeyed, catching inklings of the parade's meaning from the drivers of its various motors as they chugged past him.

At a decorous pace went the forty. Yet even to jaded Broadway the spectacle of two score empty taxicabs following each other in close alignment caused several thousand pedestrians to pause and stare in amazement.

"It's a strike," hazarded one onlooker. "They're making what they call a demonstration."

"It's an 'ad,'" contradicted another.

"Of what?"

"I don't know. But in New York it's a safe bet to call everything you don't understand an 'ad.'"

Traffic Policeman Dever was a wise man. At least, he was New York wise. He had the needful sixth sense that warned him of anything out of the ordinary that might be transpiring fully a half mile away. And now that sixth sense was working overtime. He glanced nervously down the busy street, then up; and he saw why he had felt a coming matter of interest. Down upon him was bearing the strong, single-file procession.

Traffic Policeman Dever strode into the middle of the street, waving back trucks and autos as a lesser man might brush aside flies. And he planted himself straight in the path of the leading taxicab. One uplifted finger brought it, and, necessarily, all of its thirty-nine followers, to a halt.

"What's the meaning of this?" he demanded of the chauffeur.

Before the latter could reply, his solitary passenger opened the cab door and leaned out.

"What's the matter?" he asked the policeman peremptorily. "Why do you stop us? We were not exceeding the speed limit."

"Are—are you in charge of all this?" queried the bluecoat, indicating with an indignant wave of his hand the chain of halted taxis.

"I am," coolly replied the passenger.

"What's it all mean?"

"Since when has an officer of the law acquired the right to stop a law-abiding citizen with a question like that?" asked the passenger sharply.

"Have you got a license for this parade?"

"This is not a parade."

"Isn't, hey? I'd like to know what it is, then! And if you haven't got a license from city hall to—"

"This is not a parade," gravely repeated the young man. "It is a private taxicab ride I am taking."

"Oh, beg pardon. I supposed all them other taxis was with you."

"Hold on!" said the passenger, as the policeman started toward the second taxicab to continue his inquiries. "They *are* with me. In fact, they are part of my ride."

"Part of your ride! Are you drunk or batty?"

"I take it you've been on the force long enough to size up a man who is in either of those conditions. Do I appear anything but sober and sane?"

"What the blue blazes is it all, then?"

"It's just what I told you: A private pleasure ride I am taking down Broadway from Seventy-second Street to Twenty-third. And, I may add, it is probably about the costliest taxi ride on record. And you are unconsciously adding to the expense by keeping me waiting here while all the indicators are piling up time charges."

"A private taxi ride!" babbled the traffic policeman. "And with forty taxis! Oh!" A light was breaking in on him. "It's a bet you're paying?"

"It's anything you choose. I wanted the costliest taxi ride possible. I could occupy only one taxi at once, so I chose the others as an escort. Now, if you are quite satisfied, we'll—"

"I am *not* satisfied! You can't do a thing like that. It's against the law."

"Against what law? Kindly cite the statute I am violating."

"Don't go getting gay now," blustered the officer, "or—"

"One moment. I am a lawyer. Here is my card: 'Ralph Mohun, Attorney at Law, 174 Nassau Street.' I know as well as you do that a policeman is forced to cite the charge he makes. What is that charge, please?"

"Disorderly conduct," answered the policeman, falling back readily upon that never-failing prop of the law enforcer.

"Disorderly?" echoed Mohun politely. "In what way? What disorderly act have I committed or incited? I and my taxicabs were moving along quietly and minding our own business when you butted in on us. Where does the disorderly conduct come in?"

Traffic Policeman Dever glowered about him. His eye fell on a growing knot of people and on several trucks whose drivers had drawn in to see the fun. Also, as the line of taxis was on the downtown trolley tracks, the cars began lining up behind.

Mohun glanced at his watch; then repeated:

"How is my conduct disorderly?"

"Impeding traffic and causing a crowd to collect," glibly recited the policeman.

"It is *you* who have done both things—not I. We kept on from Seventy-second Street to Twenty-eighth, and never impeded the movements of so much as a pushcart. Until you stopped us, there was no block of traffic. As to causing a crowd to collect, we've been traveling at a uniform speed of twelve miles an hour—quite within the speed limit, but far too fast to allow a crowd to gather at any given point. You'll admit a crowd can't travel, as a crowd, at twelve miles an hour, along a city street?"

Policeman Dever looked doubtful. The papers of late had been hammering the police for officiousness in minor cases, and for laxity in detecting crime. So had the city magistrates. This young fellow was a lawyer. He seemed decidedly ready to stand up for his rights, and to have a clear technical knowledge of what those rights were.

The policeman's ears still tingled with rebukes lavished upon him that very morning by a magistrate before whom he had haled a youth for auto speeding. The youth had proved by four witnesses that he was just within the regulation limits. Traffic Policeman Dever had no desire whatever to repeat that experience. Moreover, he would be off duty in another hour, unless some arrest should force him to attend afternoon court.

"G'wan!" he commanded majestically, stepping back from the path of the leading taxicab.

The chauffeur started on, and the obedient thirty-nine—now reenforced by at least six more—followed suit.

One trifling incident—at least, to all appearances, trifling—occurred just as the procession got under way: A theatrical billposter, diverted from his task of decorating ash cans with notices of a new play, had stopped to watch the halted line. Acting under sublime inspiration, he had darted forward, unobserved by the chauffeur, just as the procession was about to start again, and had slapped a freshly pasted "two-sheet poster" of the play upon the glass of the hindmost taxicab.

A trifling occurrence truly to change the trend of at least two lives and to rob the waiting public of a decidedly amusing item in their daily newspapers!

Chapter II.
A Man, a Maid, and a Race.

RALPH MOHUN'S triumphal and vicarious private joy ride in forty odd taxicabs was not done with its interruptions. At Twenty-third Street an "extension team" of eight horses was crossing Broadway, drawing a sixty-foot iron girder, suspended by chains from massive beams of a huge truck.

The team was bound eastward toward a new skyscraper. Half across Broadway one of the chains supporting the swinging girder parted. The damage was not sufficient to let the girder fall, but it loosened the supports so perilously that both men on the truck's seat leaped down to hook the chain in place again. Meantime the girder and the horses blocked the whole width of Broadway. And once more, perforce, the taxi procession jarred to a halt.

Then it was that the girl came into the story. When first Mohun saw her she was standing on the curb, frantically signaling to the few foremost taxis. As their chauffeurs paid no heed to her, she ran out into the street and said something to the chauffeur of the taxicab directly behind Mohun's.

Mohun, through the glass at the back, watched her. He saw the chauffeur say something, shake his head, grin, and point forward to Mohun's cab. The next moment she was at the window beside Mohun.

"Pardon me," she said hurriedly. "Is it true all that line of taxis has been hired by you?"

Mohun beamed with pleasure. "It is," he admitted. "And if you are a reporter, my name is —"

"I am not a reporter!" she interrupted. "I am a stenographer."

"Oh!" ejaculated Mohun, in dire disappointment. "Then—"

"I am stenographer for the law firm of Warburton & Spogg. I have a will here they have drawn for a client. They just got word by telephone that he is dying, and must sign it at once or not at all. They told me to take it to him. Mr. Spogg told me to take a taxi, as I might not get there on time if I waited for all the changes of cars. Our office is across the street here. Can't you let me have one of your taxis? It is a matter of life and death."

Her tense earnestness and the frightened, pleading light in her big eyes appealed to Ralph Mohun far more strongly than did her mere words.

"Of course!" he exclaimed impulsively. "Jump in here. What's the address?"

"Lexington Avenue," she announced, "next to the corner of Ninety-first Street."

Mohun was already out of the taxicab and helping her in.

"Lexington Avenue and Ninety-first Street," he called to his chauffeur. "Go as fast as you can without getting pinched."

The team had just hauled the girder out of the way. Mohun stepped into the taxi, and seated himself beside the girl. It did not occur to him until long afterward that she could have made the trip quite as well without him, and that perhaps she might not wholly relish the unasked companionship of a stranger.

She glanced quickly at him as he slammed shut the door behind him. Then, evidently reassured, she said:

"I thank you very, very much. I hope I haven't interfered seriously with your plans?"

"Not at all. I was going downtown only as far as Twenty-third Street, anyhow. I'm sorry my foolish stunt came so near delaying you."

On two wheels the taxi had rounded the Twenty-sixth Street corner and plunged eastward along the north side of Madison Square. Before Mohun could speak again, it had spun around the corner into Madison Avenue and was shooting northward.

Behind—though neither of the leading taxi's occupants thought of it at that moment—followed the rest of the procession. The chauffeurs had had orders to follow their leader. These orders had not been changed. Therefore, not at all averse to getting extra money, they streamed up Madison Avenue in the wake of the first cab.

It was no longer a decorous, but puzzling, parade; it was much like a race. The leading chauffeur was keeping within the speed limit whenever a policeman chanced to be in sight, but he was keeping so little within the narrow legal margin as to cause the sensation of flying; and the forty odd pursuers were close behind.

Seldom has sedate Madison Avenue witnessed such a spectacle. People halted agape. Then, as the fluttering play bill on the window of the rearmost taxicab met their gaze, they grunted, with the air of a man who has fallen victim to a trick question, and growled:

"H'm! What crazy trick will they sink to next to advertise their silly shows?"

The girl glanced back through the glass at the flying, serpentine line of taxis. Then she turned to Mohun, her pretty face alight with curiosity.

"Would you mind," she asked, "telling me why you did it?"

"Did what?"

"Hired all the taxicabs in sight. Is my question impertinent?"

"Not at all," he answered. "I did it to get my name in print."

Chapter III.
Two Mere Details.

THERE was a world of disappointment in the monosyllable that the girl uttered in reply to Mohun's explanation. As she exclaimed "Oh!" he fancied there was expressed not a little contempt as well. Somehow, her tone hurt him. He found himself all at once unaccountably anxious to stand well in the opinion of this big-eyed girl who had so oddly entered his life.

"Please don't think I'm the ordinary notoriety seeker," he begged. "I don't think I am. As a rule, I'm no more anxious to make myself conspicuous and ridiculous than any other normal New Yorker is. But this is a different matter."

"Then why, if I may ask it, do you want to get your name in print by doing such an absurd thing as this?"

"To gain notoriety as a spendthrift. To have the newspapers publish articles about my taking the most expensive taxi ride in the history of motor vehicles. To have them make fun of me."

"Yes?"

The clear tone still held more than a hint of contempt. And this stirred him to resentment.

"I want the papers to print this story," said he, "and I want to send every account of it out to Detroit to my former guardian, Judge Estler."

"He will be pleased at such—"

"He will be furious. He will despise me. If there is one thing he hates worse than a spendthrift, it is a notoriety seeker."

"I see. You have a grudge against him? You want to make him suffer?"

"Make the dear old judge suffer? I'd sooner cut off my right hand than cause him needless pain! He's like a father to me. In fact, he's the only father I've ever known. He'll be furious, as I say. I can't help that. And he'll disinherit me."

"For the sake of a senseless prank, you are willing to risk disinheritance?"

"That's why I'm doing it."

"I wonder," mused the girl, "if you are *quite* insane, or if you are only trying to amuse yourself at my expense?"

"I don't blame you for being puzzled. May I tell you a little about it, or would it bore you?"

"You have made me very curious. And curiosity and boredom don't go together."

"You see," he said, forgetting the girl was a stranger, and knowing only that a strange, new impulse drew him to her and made him long to confide in her, "Judge Estler was my guardian. He and my father were chums. He brought me up and gave me my legal education, and sent me here to New York to practice law. He gives me a big allowance, too, because he says he can trust me to live wisely on it without being extravagant."

"And yet—"

"The other day I learned through a friend of his that the judge has a niece living. I thought he hadn't a relative left on earth. It seems he quarreled with his only brother. They hated each other. I knew that. But I didn't know that the brother, who died poor, left a daughter. She would be about my own age now—oh, no, she would be younger. According to this friend of the judge's, she is somewhere in or around New York."

"Well?" came the quiet reminder, as he paused.

"I wrote to the judge," resumed Mohun, "and told him I had no right to be receiving his money, and to be heir to his estate, while his own niece was still alive and probably living in poverty. I asked him to let me find her if I could. And I insisted that she inherit his property."

"That was fine of you!" said the girl. "Splendid!"

"No," he returned, embarrassed at her sudden warmth of praise. "It was the only thing a tolerably white man could do. I am grown. I am making a fair living on my own account in the law, and I am going to keep on making more and more. Why should I live on Judge Estler's bounty while his niece may be starving?"

"What does the judge say to all this? Or hasn't he answered your letter yet?"

"He answered it. I got his letter this morning. He says, in brief, that, as he hated his brother, he has no particular interest in hunting for the latter's daughter, and that he is quite content to let me be his heir. He says a lot of very kind things about me, and winds up by saying that if it were not for me and the fact that he is so fond and proud of me, he would look up his niece's whereabouts sooner than leave his estate to charity, as he would then have to do. He finishes by telling me that if I had turned out to be in any way unworthy he would have left me to shift for myself, and would have provided for his dead brother's child—if he could find her. It's a characteristic letter all through."

"And so—"

"And so I'm going to take him at his word."

"I don't understand."

"He says, in effect, that if I were unworthy, he'd find Claire and take care of her. As I told you, I'm earning a good living on my own account. I don't want to get big checks all the time from Judge Estler, while his only niece is, perhaps, working at starvation pay in some store, or wearing out her youth and her health in a factory. I couldn't look myself in the face in my shaving glass if I did a thing like that."

Encouraged by the girl's smile of strong approval, he added:

"No arguments of mine would shake the judge. I know him well enough for that. So I'm going to force his hand. He'd drop me for her if I were unworthy. Very good! I'm trying to be unworthy."

Despite his earnestness, she could not stifle a laugh.

"I was puzzled how to set about it," he explained. "You see, I don't care for any of the dozens of dissipations that prove men unworthy. I don't drink, I don't gamble, I don't want to rob a bank. What was left? To play on the judge's two weaknesses—his hatred for foolish extravagance and for notoriety. I resolved to do both."

"And—"

"I drew a whole lot of money out of the bank this morning. But I couldn't decide what to do with it to get myself into print in a way that would shock him. Then a taxicab passed me—and my great idea arrived."

"So that is why you have all these taxicabs flying after you now?"

"Great Scott! I'd forgotten them for the moment," he exclaimed, staring back through the glass. "There they are! Oh, every paper in New York will have a big, funny story on this. That's why I hoped you were a reporter. I wanted them all to get my name. I told it to my chauffeur, and I told him to pass it back to the others. Some reporter is bound to ask one of them."

"We are nearly at Ninetieth Street already," she broke in. "Oh, dear! Now I'll *never* know how the venture comes out! It's like missing the last installment of a serial."

"Not necessarily," he corrected. "Won't—I know it's a fresh thing to ask on such short, informal acquaintance—but won't you let me call and tell you the rest, from time to time, as new developments come up?"

Again she looked closely at his eager face. And once more what she saw there seemed to answer her unspoken query.

"Yes," she said, "I shall be glad to see you if you care to call. You have been very kind in helping me get uptown so quickly. I live on Stuyvesant Square; I'll give you my card, Mr.— Mr.—"

"Ralph Mohun," he supplied.

"My name is Ruth Gray," she said.

"Ruth Gray," he repeated slowly, as if enjoying the beauty of the name.

"I wonder," she mused laughingly, "what my cousins will think of my telling a man he could call when I didn't even know his name? Please don't think I'm too unconventional. Really I'm not. But somehow, after your kindness in giving me this lift, and in honoring me with such a confidence, I don't quite feel as if you were a stranger. Besides"—with a childlike laugh—"I'm tremendously curious to know how you will come out in your efforts to get disinherited. By the way, does it occur to you that Miss Claire Estler may not *care* to be found?"

"Not care to? When she sees an advertisement asking her to come and qualify as heiress to a rich man? Impossible!"

"Here we are!" said Ruth Gray, as the taxicab drew to a halt. "Thank you again, a thousand times. Good-by, and—good luck to your venture!"

Chapter IV.
"Conspicuous By Its Absence."

RALPH MOHUN was up at dawn next day. He hurried out and bought a copy of every New York newspaper. Then, carrying them back to his room, he prepared to revel in a series of lurid accounts of his taxicab adventure.

Every page of every newspaper he searched diligently and without avail. Not one word of the wondrous procession which had electrified Broadway and Madison Avenue could he find in any of the papers. Mohun dropped the last sheet to the floor and leaned back in sheer bewilderment.

He would have felt less astonished had he overheard, the day before, a certain telephone conversation between the city editor of the *Planet* and a tipster who was wont to pick up a living by sending in to the papers such bits of news as he happened upon, or managed to nose out—a recognized industry, by which many a man keeps alive in New York.

"Mr. Casey," phoned this tipster, "a procession of forty-three taxis just went down Broadway and turned into Twenty-sixth Street, and went buzzing up Madison Avenue. Forty-three of them, I counted. And no one in any of them except the first. One man in that. Well-dressed, good-looking chap. They were held up at Twenty-eighth Street by Traffic Cop Dever. The young fellow told Dever he was taking the costliest taxi ride on record. Gave him his card. Ralph Mohun's the name—one-seventy-four Nassau Street—a lawyer."

The editor's "nose for news" dilated. "Good!" he said. "No one in any of the other taxis, you say?"

"Not a soul in the whole forty-three but this Mohun," the tipster assured him then, walking blindly to destruction, he added: "Some billposter got gay with the last taxi of the line, I guess. There was a placard on the window of it that said: 'Don't miss "My Lady of Mystery," at the Hyperion Theater,' and—"

"Say, you!" roared the city editor. "You try to put over another advertising freak on us as a straight-news story; and we'll can you for keeps!"

Whereat he hung up the receiver and growled to his assistant:

"Look out for any more tips Weiman sends in. He's getting crooked. Tried to land a Hyperion Theater press-agent story on me just now."

With unimportant variations, a similar scene was enacted in the city rooms of other daily newspapers. Several actual reporters had witnessed the taxi parade of the previous day, and had scanned it with keen and delighted interest until they chanced to view that luckless playbill.

The outside world may or may not know that each theater or other amusement enterprise hires a man—usually a former reporter—at forty dollars to one hundred dollars a week for no other purpose than to secure the insertion of press notices of their particular productions in the newspapers. These press agents fight a steady and often winning battle with the city editors of the papers, continuously striving to dress up some fact concerning their theater, or its actors, in such manner as to make it read like a straight-news story.

Of old they often succeeded. News that a prima donna's jewels had been stolen, that an actress took milk baths, that a hotel had barred her pet dog from the dining room—these and so many more stories of the sort crept into print that to-day editors are forever on the lookout to balk such schemes of unpaid advertising.

Hence to these editors the tidings that forty odd taxicabs had paraded Broadway and Madison Avenue, setting forth the attractions of "My Lady of Mystery," were as the hackneyed red rag to the bull. And naturally, as every newspaper man will understand, no word of that same "costliest taxi ride on record" broke into type.

Ralph Mohun, ignorant of all this, sat in dire perplexity. He had spent several hundred perfectly good dollars for nothing.

"No," he contradicted himself, "not for nothing. I met Her!"

Already he had come mentally to refer to Ruth Gray as Her, with the largest sort of a capital H. Now the thought of the girl roused him from his frowning reverie. He had boasted to her of his intent. He had told her why he was taking that odd ride. And evidently she had approved his motive. She, too, doubtless would scan the morning papers for an account of the parade. Failing to find it, might she not doubt the truth of all he had told her?

"I don't know why it fell through," he muttered to himself. "But it's up to me to find something that will go. I can't give up like this, especially after what I said to her."

His eye wandered about the room in search of inspiration. Then, still searching, his gaze swept the floor at his feet, and at last focused itself upon something. First he glanced idly; then with sudden interest. Next he sprang up, exclaiming aloud:

"I've got it! The greatest idea yet! And this time they'll *have* to notice it in the papers. I'll get columns and columns printed about it!"

Chapter V.
A Feast for an Emperor.

THE object that had given birth to Ralph Mohun's inspiration was not, at first sight, of an especially inspiring sort. In fact, it was nothing more than an advertisement in one of the several newspapers that lay cluttered about the floor.

The advertisement contained a picture of a huge and particularly garish-looking building; also the information, in display type, that this edifice was none other than the new and resplendent St. Crœsus Hotel, which, having just reached completion, would be opened to the eagerly waiting world at large on October 14th.

Mohun picked up the paper and read the advertisement all over again, including the smaller-type announcement that the St. Crœsus was the largest, most expensively decorated, most luxurious hotel ever built in America or any other country.

He cut out the advertisement and went straight to the man whose name appeared thereon as manager of the new hostelry. The manager turned out to be a foreign-looking personage with the bearing and the beard of a traditional French marquis of the old school. He rejoiced in the name Querouaille—and he looked it.

Mohun introduced himself, and came straight to the point.

"Mr. Querouaille," he began, making sad hash of his pronunciation of the name, "I understand from your advertisement that you are to open the St. Crœsus Hotel on October fourteenth."

"Yes," answered the manager uneasily, "that is our intention; but—"

"How much would you charge," queried Mohun, "to postpone the formal opening until October fifteenth?"

The manager stared at him in blank wonder. Many and conflicting thoughts and conjectures and hopes went tumbling over each other in the managerial brain, all started into action by that strange question. That very morning he had experienced a disagreeable shock in reference to that same widely and loudly advertised opening. The water had been turned on, the previous day, in the upper floors of the St. Crœsus, and, as chief expense of construction had gone to splendor rather than to mere plumbing, four water pipes had promptly burst. The decorated ceilings of three stories had been utterly ruined thereby; so had the hangings of the upper corridors, and a large area of ballroom flooring.

Men were already hard at work remedying these defects, but his superintendent had just told him that the work of repairing could not possibly be finished before October 15th, at the very earliest. Therefore Mr. Querouaille had ever since been casting about in his fertile mind for some good and lucrative excuse for announcing a day's postponement of the grand opening. To say the delay was due to defective plumbing would be to ruin in a moment the hotel's vaunted reputation for perfect appointments and fixtures. And here, out of nowhere, came a man who actually hinted at *paying* him for delaying what must perforce be delayed.

The manager was a good poker player. As soon as he could arrange his tangled sensations, he coolly said:

"This is a very strange question, Mr. Mohun. I fear I do not quite understand you. Will you please explain?"

"Certainly," replied Mohun. "You advertise that this hotel—the most expensive and finest in the world, according to your statement—will be formally opened on the fourteenth of October. I wish to give a dinner there on the evening of the fourteenth."

"Oh!" grunted the manager, in dire disappointment. "I have no doubt that it can be arranged. I will refer you to my steward. Those details are not in my province. I—"

"I think they are," put in Mohun. "I wish to give a dinner—a dinner of six covers."

The managerial face fell still farther. A dinner for six—not even a banquet! He rose to end the useless, profitless interview; but Mohun stayed him.

"Look here," went on Ralph, "I want the entire hotel for this dinner."

The manager fidgeted nervously, and glanced toward the bell.

"No," said Mohun patiently, "I'm not a crank; or, if I am, I can pay well for the privilege of being one. Here is my proposition in a nutshell: I want to give a dinner that will be the talk of the whole city and country. Many people have tried to do that, I know. But I am going to outdo them all. There have been monkey dinners and horseback dinners and dinners where dancers have been brought in on a big pie. But I intend to improve on that."

"Yes?" said the manager doubtfully.

"I care little about the menu or decorations," explained Mohun. "A good dinner, at twelve or fifteen dollars a head, will suit me. But, as I said before, I want the whole hotel in which to give it. I don't want any other guests in the house but my own. I want my party to enlist the undivided service and attention of every employee in the St. Crœsus, from steward to hat boy. Do you get my idea?"

"Partly—I think," stammered Querouaille.

"In brief, I wish to rent the entire hotel for that night. How much?"

Chapter VI.
A Libel-Shy Press.

THE manager sat silent for a space, thinking fast and cleverly. He had once been a Broadway waiter, and if there is any kind of man a Broadway waiter cannot size up at a glance, that man has never yet been on Broadway. So the manager realized that Mohun was neither a crank nor a political joker, but was in sober earnest in making his amazing proposal. And Querouaille's heart rejoiced. Here at last was the solution of his problem. Here was not only an excuse for postponing the grand opening by one day, but an excuse that would advertise the hotel from one end of the land to the other. His efforts at free advertising had not, up to this point, been wholly successful. And now, behold, a golden opportunity was at hand. Yet again he showed no emotion.

"The difficulties are great," he said; "almost insuperable. At first glance, I should be forced to refuse. If you care to give me a day in which to consider your remarkable request and to confer with—"

"I will give you five minutes!" declared Mohun.

"H'm! You American millionaires are so impatient! You are willing to pay fortunes to save yourselves one second of time. May I ask if you would wish your guests to go over the whole hotel?"

"No. I just want to be certain that there are no guests in it but mine. We shall use only one private dining room and a lounging room. But it must be understood that I have technically the control of the whole place for that evening."

The manager sighed with relief. His one difficulty vanished. Had Mohun insisted on making some sort of use of the dismantled upper floors, the deal must have fallen through. For a glance would have shown the place's unreadiness for occupation. But the floor on which the rooms he would use were situated was wholly undamaged, and while the six guests dined belowstairs the men making the repairs could be hard at work above.

"Come!" urged Mohun. "The five minutes are up. I'm waiting for your answer."

"I accept," said Querouaille. "It is unusual, unprecedented, but I accept."

"Good! And your terms?"

"I will think them over, and—"

"Your terms?" insisted Mohun.

"Shall—shall we say twenty-five thousand dollars?" suggested the manager airily.

"No," replied Mohun, "we shall not! You have quite misunderstood me, I see. I want to rent the use of the hotel for one evening. I do not wish to buy it. Good day!"

"One moment!" shrilled the manager. "Let us talk this over calmly."

"Yes," agreed Mohun, "let's talk it over. And let me begin the talking. In the first place, I am willing to spend a large sum of money for the sake of the notoriety this dinner will bring me. That is understood. And for that I shall be called a fool; perhaps rightly. Yet I am not the sort of a fool who pays ten dollars cash for one dollar's worth of value."

"But—"

"But this dinner will be the greatest advertisement your hotel could get. The advertisement alone will be worth thousands of dollars to you. And if you can earn a little extra money on the side it will be so much clear gain. Now that I have set forth the situation clearly, let me hear what you have to say."

Mohun was playing wholly in the dark. Had he made the same proposal to Querouaille under ordinary circumstances, the hotel being ready for guests at the time announced, he would have had no earthly chance of carrying through the deal. But now, quite unknown to himself, he held all the winning cards.

The upshot of the contest was that, a half hour later, he had closed a bargain that was far more nearly equitable than he had any right to expect. He wrote a check to bind the bargain, and was departing when Querouaille said:

"Since you say you wish publicity, Mr. Mohun, let me ring for our publicity agent. He will have entire charge of apprising the newspapers of this remarkable dinner. Perhaps if you could give him any views on the subject that you may have, and could in return act on some of his suggestions, it might be beneficial to all parties."

He turned to his desk telephone and gave an order. A few minutes later the hotel's press agent came in. Querouaille introduced him as Mr. Luther Mack.

Mr. Mack was a smallish man, with truly wonderful clothes. He had an air of one to whom millions are but baubles. Always afterward when Mohun recalled him, he did so in a vague connection with a rather tainted dollar sign.

Mr. Mack greeted Mohun effusively when his business was made known. At once he launched forth in a verbal sketch of such a campaign of publicity as should send the names of Mohun and St. Crœsus hustling endlessly down the corridors of time, hand in hand. Drawing forth an exquisite little gold-handled knife, he sharpened a gold-mounted pencil, and made rapid notes on a gold-bordered set of pocket tablets.

"A feast for an emperor!" he rhapsodized. "That's a good line to start with."

Mohun stared fascinated at the wondrous being. He looked from Mack to Querouaille and back again in a trance of bewilderment. One thing alone was clear: These two geniuses were going to launch him on a sea of publicity that must triumphantly wash every dollar of Judge Estler's fortune from his pockets into Claire Estler's.

He departed from the dual presence feeling his end was at last firmly accomplished. The next move was to secure his handful of guests. This was an easy matter, for he was popular and knew how to order a good dinner. Every invitation was accepted.

Daily Mohun scanned the newspapers for some advance notice of his dinner; and, as before, he scanned them in vain.

The great evening of October fourteenth arrived. The dinner was a success. Everybody had the jolliest sort of a time.

Next morning Mohun bought all the New York papers to reread the tale of the banquet. To "reread" it. For he had read it before—in typewritten form—a matter of five thousand words, hammered out industriously by Mr. Luther Mack, "manifolded," and sent to every newspaper.

But, as before, not one line about the dinner appeared in print anywhere. So far as publicity was concerned, Ralph Mohun might as well have thrown his money into the East River.

The mystery of it dumfounded him. He called up Mack on the telephone, and found that worthy man equally dumfounded.

"It's a mystery to *me!*" moaned the press agent. "The biggest story

I ever handled. And not one of 'em would touch it—not even the preliminary dope—the 'come-on' stuff. When they passed that up, I thought they'd sure fall for the main story itself. Old Querouaille's mad as a wet hen. I'm afraid to go within a mile of him. Yes, it's sure a mystery to me."

But it was not a mystery to the newspapers. Here, in brief, is the secret: While the Hotel St. Croesus had been in process of building, Mr. Mack had "framed up" several more or less dubious press-agent yarns concerning it. And as the papers regarded the erecting of a new hotel as a matter of public interest, some of these stories had been printed.

This had so encouraged Mr. Luther Mack that he had at last launched a St. Croesus story that was not only a cleverly disguised fake, but which also involved a well-known banker. The story had been printed. The banker denounced the use of his name as unauthorized, fraudulent, and damaging, and brought suit in criminal libel against the papers that had printed the tale.

From that moment no city editor in New York would have touched one of Mack's stories with a twenty-foot pole. Thus it fell out that when he sent them an account of a reputable lawyer's hiring the whole hotel for the purpose of dining six guests, they once more scented a possible libel suit from the lawyer in question, and, with one accord, refused to print the highly entertaining and—for once—entirely true narrative.

"What am I going to do?" Mohun demanded of himself, in stark desperation. "The whole world seems conspiring to keep out of the newspapers the fact that I'm a fool."

Then came his third and most spectacular idea.

Chapter VII.
A Central Park Knight-Errant.

SO keenly did this new plan appeal to Mohun that he resolved to delay putting it into effect until he could tell it to Ruth Gray. Somehow, of late he had formed the habit of consulting Ruth about nearly everything. Nor did she seem to object to his taking up so much of her time. He had got into the way of calling on her two or three evenings a week. He now called her up on the telephone to ask if she were to be at home that evening.

"No," she answered; "I'm sorry, but I have to work late at the office tonight."

"What a shame!" he ejaculated. "I had something wonderful to tell you."

"Not that Judge Estler has changed his mind?"

"No; but—"

"You haven't found Claire Estler? But that's a foolish question. I know you haven't."

"I haven't even looked for her. What's the use until I can make her uncle acknowledge her rights? It would be cruel to find her and raise hopes that the judge might not consent to fulfill. If everything else fails, I will trace her whereabouts and turn over to her secretly the money he sends me. But there'll be time enough to do that if I find I have to. And I won't have to. For the plan I have now will make Judge Estler look on me as the most notorious idiot of the century."

"Oh, dear! Another of those horrible pieces of useless extravagance!"

"Not at all. It will cost me almost nothing. But it will get my name in print in every paper. And it may land me in a police station."

"In a police station?" she gasped.

"Oh, don't worry. I'm not going to commit any crime. Here's my plan: You've read some of the old-time stories of knight-errantry, of course?"

"Yes. What about it?"

"You remember how the knights of old used to stand guard at some spot in the highroad and bar the way against all comers?"

"Yes."

"Well, that's what I'm going to do to-morrow morning."

"What?"

"You know, I ride horseback in Central Park early nearly every morning. So do dozens of men—supposed-to-be rich men of leisure whose doctors have ordered them to take easy outdoor exercise. Some of them make a very sad job of trying to look the part. There are cut rates in saddle-horse tickets, you know, just as there are in drugs and theater tickets. If you want to see some funny stunts on horseback, just stand on the stone bridge some day and see them jounce by. Now and then there is a star rider who can control his horse, but usually the nag chooses his own pace—trots or canters, just as the whim strikes him. Come along some morning and see the fun. Beats the clown riders in the circus. Some one called them the hobbyhorse cavalry, and you'd agree they were well named if you could see them with their stirrups strapped up near the horse's mane. Why, a rocking-chair isn't—"

"Look here," broke in Ruth, "do you know I am a very busy person? Besides, I know you are only killing time. Come, tell me about your new plan."

"All right. Well, I am going to stand guard, on horseback, directly under the stone bridge, near the south end of the bridle path. You know the place—where bad boys toss peanut shells down on the riders. I'm going to wait there and turn back every rider who comes along. It won't be long before there'll be such a crowd of angry equestrians there as never before gathered in New York. Then will come a mounted policeman, and—oh, joy, at last!—all the papers will be full of the 'eccentric holdup in the park,' with my name spread all over the front page."

"Did you ever? Of all the insane folly! I—"

Central cut in and broke the connection.

Mohun glanced at his watch. The hour was still early—only a little after nine. While it was later than his usual time for horseback exercise, he decided, on impulse, to put the idea into effect without waiting another day. Privately he feared lest the girl's sane disapproval would turn him from his mad purpose if he should wait for another talk with her. So, telephoning for his horse, he proceeded to don his riding clothes.

A half hour later he was posting through the plaza entrance of Central Park. As his powerful roan horse felt the soft soil of the bridle path under his hoofs, he curvetted and tugged at the bit, eager for a gallop. But Mohun sternly reined him in, and headed the roan toward the stone arch which he had resolved to make the scene of his strange operations. Horse and rider were both fine, strong specimens of their kind, and as they moved along they drew admiring glances from men and women on the walk.

The park was in the full glory of autumn beauty. Several riders galloped or posted past Mohun as he neared his destination. To these he gave no heed. There would be more.

He halted under the arch and reined his mount sideways across the narrow road. Scarce had he waited twenty seconds before a youth in English riding clothes came jockeying awkwardly along upon a bobtail, hard-trotting chestnut.

As the newcomer neared Mohun, he turned aside to pass through the narrow space left by the roan's barricading body.

"Pardon me," said Ralph, pushing his horse forward to intercept the other, "but you'll have to go back. I'm holding this pass against all comers."

The youth reined in, looked stupidly at Mohun, then said:

"Oh, this part of the path's closed for repairs, I suppose? Thanks for telling me."

He turned and trotted meekly back.

Chapter VIII.
Somewhat Different.

"WELL, of all the sheep!" Ralph exclaimed. "Isn't that just like a New Yorker? We're so used to being bossed and ordered around that we obey every stranger. If I stood at the top of the subway steps and said 'No trains running to-day,' not a soul would doubt I was telling the truth. I ought to have worn a mask and carried an old-fashioned horse pistol, and growled 'Stand and deliver!' "

The sharp thud of cantering hoofs around the curve just beyond caused him to turn from his cross reflections. Around the bend came a square-jawed little man, evidently a groom, riding one stocky cob and leading another.

"Go back!" ordered Mohun sternly.

"Why?" asked the groom, coming to a halt and looking in wonder at the young man with the authoritative voice.

Mohun vouchsafed no reply, but maintained his forbidding position across the road. Before the hesitating groom could speak again, two men trotted around the bend, and slackened their pace at sight of the three horses in front of them.

"What's wrong?" asked one of them.

"I dunno," answered the groom. "This gentleman says—"

"This gentleman says," interrupted Mohun suavely, "that you can't pass. Go back!"

"What's the reason we can't pass?" truculently demanded one of the two late arrivals.

"Because I say so," gently explained Mohun. "I am holding this archway against all comers. Go back!"

"Back nothing!" retorted the man. "You're daffy! We haven't got all day to wait."

He touched his horse with the spur. But instantly Mohun, by a skillful move of the roan, barred the path before him.

Around the curve at that moment jogged a riding master with six pupils at his heels. Seeing the little crowd in front, and supposing there had been an accident, they reined in.

"Good!" approved Mohun. "Now there are—let's see—ten—no, twelve horses and eleven men. The mounted police can come as soon as they are ready. The crowd is big enough."

A babel of excited queries, replies, objurgations, and demands beat pleasantly about his ears. To all he returned a bland smile, and quietly maneuvered his splendid roan from spot to spot of the narrow way to block all passage. And three more riders came up during the brief moment of excitement.

Mohun was an expert rider, and his horse apparently understood and enjoyed the fun. Mohun knew he could hold control of the situation barely a minute longer at most. But in that time he was certain a policeman would appear.

Already on the bridge above the path a throng of park pedestrians had collected and were staring down in delighted perplexity at the growing knot of passaging, uneasy horses and angry men.

Then, above the looser volume of noise, Ralph Mohun heard the sound for which he had been waiting: The thunderous pad, pad, pad of a fast-running horse. Evidently a mounted policeman was bearing down on them at top speed.

Mohun rose in his stirrups to catch the first glimpse of the rider as the latter should round the curve. And now his ears told him there was not one horse approaching, but two—one evidently somewhat in advance of the other.

Around the bend dashed the foremost horse, and Mohun gasped, for here was no blue-clad park guardian hastening to the chastisement of a lawless knight-errant. The rider was a woman—young, good-looking. Her hat had fallen off. Her hair was streaming loose. Her pretty face was white and terror-stricken.

And her horse evidently was running away with her. Behind, hopelessly trying to overtake the fear-maddened animal, galloped a baldheaded, elderly man.

Chapter IX.
The Runaway.

THE woman was tugging furiously but helplessly at the reins. Her big black horse, his head down, had taken the bit between his teeth, and was bolting.

Into and through the scattered group of riders the runaway plunged. He was upon them before they knew it; he burst his way through them unchecked.

A cry from his rider, a shout from the baldheaded man in pursuit, a chorus of yells from the "held-up" equestrians, and the runaway had burst his way through the group and was thundering under the arch-way, with no obstacle to check him.

Ralph Mohun could never afterward clearly define his thoughts or his action at that particular moment. From the time the woman appeared around the bend, ghastly pale and helpless, up to the time when she tore through the amazed group of riders in front of the arch, a bare second had elapsed.

Yet that single second had sufficed to make Mohun do a thing that was prompted solely by his subconscious mind. Acting on sheer instinct, he had wheeled his horse and driven spurs into him. The same cool, clear instinct that had prompted the action also guided it aright. He had not dashed forward to meet the runaway; he had not even thrown his horse in the black's path. Instead, he had driven his horse forward at full speed in the same direction that the black horse was running.

It takes a perceptible space of time for any starting object to gather headway. And, though Mohun started a second ahead of her, the girl was alongside of him and past him before his roan could gather headway.

Ralph made an ineffectual snatch at the black's rein as the runaway tore past him. Then he settled down in the saddle for a chase.

On thundered the black, his panic-stricken rider swaying in the saddle and still making futile efforts to stop him. She might as well have tugged with her frail strength against the Empire State Express.

On flew Mohun's roan in pursuit—his wonderful, long, easy stride tireless and incredibly swift; and behind him the yelling group of riders Mohun had held up. They were led by the baldheaded man, whose face was yellow with dread. A mounted policeman brought up the rear.

It was a spectacle such as Central Park had not witnessed in many a day, but the spectators were few, for by the time some pedestrian had paused, attracted by the multitude of hurrying hoofbeats of horses hard ridden, the strange cavalcade had flashed past.

Mohun, dimly aware of the cries and the drill beat of hoofs behind him, was riding as never had he ridden before. He was urging every atom of speed from his gallant roan, and the horse responded bravely to voice, hand, and spur. Inch by inch, he drew in upon the flying black. He felt that soon or late he would come alongside.

It is an odd fact that a cleverly guided horse is usually capable of greater speed than one that is running wild, even if the latter happens to be carrying a lighter weight. For instance, when a jockey in a horse race is thrown and his mount gallops on unridden, the riderless horse seldom reaches the wire as soon as do his competitors.

Little by little, Mohun was cutting down the distance between himself and the girl. Now his horse's head was at the black's sweating flank; now the red-nostriled roan nose was creeping forward and forward to the other's saddle girths.

Around a turn in the path they swept, and the shortness of the curve gave the roan, which was on the inner side, an advantage that brought him close to the black.

The latter was panting noisily now, and his once glossy neck was areek with foam flecks; but he showed little slackening of speed. Nevertheless, as Mohun well knew, the race would not last much longer. In twenty strides Ralph would be far enough ahead to seize the black's bridle close to the bit and stop him after the fashion which mounted policemen have reduced to a science.

At best, however, this would be ticklish work. And Mohun involuntarily glanced ahead, to see what kind of roadway was before him. For at a turn on the edge of a declivity such a maneuver would be dangerous.

And as he looked, an involuntary cry burst from his tense lips. It was echoed by a scream from the woman. Across the path a plank had been laid, on two trestles. And just beyond this stood a couple of pushcarts, heaped high with earth, with which several laborers were mending the roadway.

Now Ralph understood why all the pedestrians he had met under the archway had come from the opposite direction. He also understood that he could not hope to reach the black's bridle and jerk him back to a slow pace before the maddened horse must crash headlong into plank and carts. And such a crash meant certain maiming and probable death to the runaway's rider.

Chapter X.
At the Wrong Time.

THERE was less than a second in which to think. And again Mohun's alert brain acted without his conscious volition.

"Kick your foot free from the stirrup, and drop the reins!" he shouted to the imperiled woman.

And even as he roared the command, he braced himself, gripped the roan tighter with his knees, and flung his free arm around the woman's waist.

With a mighty heave, he lifted her clear of the saddle, as horseback wrestlers do the trick in cavalry "armory maneuvers." At the same time, he drew in the roan so suddenly that the fast-flying horse fell back on his haunches and was well-nigh thrown.

The roan came to a sliding, snorting halt, with his knees touching one of the trestles. The black, bursting past the plank barrier, crashed full into the nearest cart, upset it, and tumbled to the ground with a broken neck.

The woman gave a weak cry at the sight, fainted, and lay a dead weight on Mohun's arm and shoulder. Ralph lowered his insensible burden and himself to the ground, and laid her on the grass alongside the path. He felt weak and dizzy. His head swam. Now that the peril was over, reaction set in. But he had neither desire nor opportunity to yield to it.

Scarce had he laid the fainting woman down when two mounted policemen reached the spot. They had outstripped their less-expert and worse-mounted fellows; the rest of the pursuers streamed up a moment later. In the van of the strung-out procession galloped the baldheaded man. He leaped to the ground and bent over the woman. Already she was recovering consciousness. Supported by her elderly escort, she sat up and looked wildly around.

Her glance fell on Ralph Mohun, who was leaning wearily against his panting, sweat-drenched horse.

"You—you saved me—from—from *that!*" she murmured brokenly, pointing to the dead runaway and the overturned dirt wagon.

The elderly man rose from beside her and came toward Mohun.

"I can never thank you," said he. "Words are too weak. But for your pluck and skill my wife would—" he broke off, with an uncontrollable shudder.

"Please don't say any more about it," begged Mohun, in embarrassment. "It was lucky my horse happened to have the speed and the sense needed for such a feat. That was all. And now, if I can be of no further service—"

"Say, officer," piped the groom, turning to one of the several mounted policemen who by this time had joined the crowd, "that man held me up, back there by the arch bridge, and he—"

The complainant got no farther. Half a dozen of the other men whom Ralph's prank had inconvenienced closed about the groom with a common, tacit impulse, and hustled him back out of the group.

The policemen, who had no idea what the complaint was about, did not interfere.

"You idiot!" growled one of the riders, giving a bill to the groom as they hustled him out of earshot of the police. "Haven't you any better sense than to try to get a man into trouble when he's played ducks and drakes with his own life to save a woman from being killed? Clear out! None of us know what that fellow meant by holding us up, and none of us care. He's just bought the right to do worse than that and get away with it."

Meantime, the elderly man had again brushed aside Mohun's admirers and was pressing eager gratitude upon him. "I am J. H. Bryce," he was saying. "You may perhaps have heard of me. May I ask the name of the man to whom I owe so much?"

J. H. Bryce! The name was known in New York and all over America as that of the newest and most spectacularly rich of the trust magnates. In Ralph's heart arose the wild thought:

"Oh, if I could have held *him* up at the arch, it would have got on the front page of every paper in town! Just my luck!"

"May I ask your name, sir?" repeated Bryce.

A policeman, who was making official notes of the affair, and who had dutifully and impressedly taken down the trust magnate's name and address, turned with waiting pad and pencil to hear the rescuer's name.

Mohun was conscious of an absurd desire to laugh. Here for weeks he had striven vainly and with infinite effort and expense to get his name in print. And every time, for some reason unknown to him, he had failed. Now, by merely mentioning that name, he could be featured as a hero in all the newspapers. His name and picture would appear. He would be hailed as the gallant rider who rescued the beautiful and fabulously rich young Mrs. J. H. Bryce from death.

And all this was exactly what Ralph Mohun most wished to avoid. He had a horror of notoriety for notoriety's sake. In order to restore to a girl the heritage of which she had been wrongfully deprived, he had been willing to pose in the newspapers as a spendthrift fool. That had been a sacrifice, and he had been prepared to make it, for principle's sake, at whatever cost to himself. He had been mysteriously denied such a chance.

Now it was quite different. The notoriety would not accomplish the ends he sought. In fact, it would defeat them. Apart from his distaste for appearing as a grand-stand hero, he knew that Judge Estler, on reading the story of his heroism, would but think the more highly of him, and would be all the more set in his refusal to disinherit him for an unknown niece. All this flashed through Mohun's brain as Bryce asked the question, and as the policeman stood with notebook ready to take down the answer.

"If I have been of any service to you, or to Mrs. Bryce," said Ralph, "I hope you will square the debt by letting the whole affair drop right here and now. I greatly prefer that my name should not appear in the matter."

"But," interrupted the recording blue-coat, "I've got to make a report of this to be sent to headquarters. I've got to have the names, and—"

"As I understand it," interrupted Mohun, "Mr. Bryce does not intend to bring suit against the city?"

"Certainly not," answered Bryce. "It was nobody's fault. My wife was trying out a new horse that had caught her fancy. A newspaper blew across the brute's face, and he bolted. That was all. I—"

"And no one has been injured?" pursued Mohun.

"No," replied the policeman.

"Then," said Ralph, "you are perfectly aware that you've no legal right to insist on knowing my name."

"I—I suppose not," admitted the bluecoat; "but—"

"I don't wish to intrude on your privacy, sir," said Bryce courteously, "or seem ungrateful by pressing you for a name you prefer not to give. But you have rendered me the greatest service to-day that one man can render another. And I wish I might—"

"I trust Mrs. Bryce will be none the worse for the shock," interposed Ralph, "and I hope you'll both pardon my discourtesy in not granting your very simple request."

He vaulted into the saddle and cantered away. Bryce turned excitedly to one of the policemen.

"Here's my card," said he. "Bring me that man's name and address, without letting him know what you're after, and it will be the best-paying day's work of your life. Hurry!"

The policeman mounted and vanished in a cloud of dust.

Chapter XI.
Fate's Last Throw.

FORTUNE became lavish, as if resenting Mohun's efforts to impoverish himself. The day after the park runaway he was engaged as associate counsel in a great corporation suit, with a retainer of fifteen hundred dollars. And during the next fortnight business fairly surged in from all sides.

"Pull" and chance will do much for a man, but only if he has the ability to take fullest advantage of them. And Mohun had that ability. Day and night he toiled on this new influx of legal work—and he made good.

In his first moment of leisure, he turned back with bulldog tenacity to his effort to make Judge Estler recognize his niece. He wrote the judge a long letter. After telling of his own recently improved finances, he repeated his plea that the judge find his niece and give her the wealth that was rightly hers. He continued:

> You said that if I should prove unworthy, you would make her your heiress. I have proved unworthy. Here is a brief list of several misdeeds of mine, committed during the past month or two:
>
> Wishing to enjoy a really expensive joy ride, I hired nearly fifty taxicabs and rode at the head of them for nearly six miles. You can figure out for yourself what the useless cost of that ride was. Also the unpleasant notoriety it occasioned.
>
> Next, in order to give such a dinner that for senseless extravagance would be unequaled in New York annals, I hired the entire St. Crœsus for a day and evening. There I and five guests dined. We had the hotel to ourselves, the entire working staff being at our service. You can fancy the cost of that.
>
> A day later it occurred to me to seek further notoriety by holding up every rider who chanced to pass a certain point on the Central Park bridle path. I held up a dozen or so, and finished the performance by lifting a lady—a perfect stranger—out of the saddle.
>
> It rests with you to decide whether you care to send an allowance to such a man as the foregoing confession shows me to be, or to make me your heir.

Four days later Judge Estler's reply came. It was characteristic and to the point. It read:

> MY DEAR BOY: Will you kindly stop interfering with my affairs? I shall do what I please with my money, and no argument of yours can turn me from what I know to be right. Your statements about leading forty or fifty taxicabs all over New York, and hiring a whole hotel to dine six people, and holding up equestrians in Central Park do not interest me at all. I understand the motives of all three of those amazing but commendable lies.
>
> You know how I hate foolish extravagance and cheap notoriety, and you pretend to have done all these things in the hope of disgusting me with you and of turning my money from yourself to my niece. It was a kindly thought on your part, but a crazily silly one—not worthy of your brains. You might have known I would not believe such an awkward tissue of lies. Especially from you. You have always been so truthful that now when you try to lie you can't even do it cleverly.
>
> Does it occur to you, Ralph, that if you had done any one of those three things you say you did, the newspapers would have been full of the accounts of your antics? I see the New York papers every day. And not one of them mentioned any of the three, although I am enough of a man of the world to recognize that all three stories would have afforded the papers a splendid opportunity for a sensation. Your name would have been featured in a most unpleasant fashion. Whereas there has been not a word about you in any such connection, nor even a mention of the joy ride, the dinner, or the holdup.
>
> I am proud of you, lad, for the advance you are making in the law and you can't make me ashamed of you if you try. I rejoice in your growing success. Soon I want to hear that you have chosen some suitable wife.

"Suitable wife!" exclaimed Mohun, as he finished reading the letter. "Nice way to write to a man who wants to be disinherited! Was there ever such luck as mine? I hear every day about men and women who work and plan and toil to keep in the good graces of some rich relative. Yet when I throw Fortune bodily out of the door, she climbs back through the window! Men who try to keep out of print fall into it. While I—Well, I'll hunt for Claire Estler myself."

He mused for a minute, then muttered, in elation:

"I have it! The best idea yet! He wants me to find a suitable wife. I suppose that means some woman with all the money fit to print, or else a big social position. It will make him furious if I can tell him I've married a girl who has neither. And I *can* tell him that—if—if Ruth will let me."

He no longer ever sought to disguise from himself the fact that he cared a lot for Ruth Gray. A dozen times when he had been with her an avowal had trembled on his lips. But always the man who was fearless in other matters had lost courage when he looked into this particular girl's clear eyes.

Now, forcing his courage to the sticking point, he went to the telephone.

"Are you still working at the office in the evenings?" he asked Miss Gray, over the wire.

"Yes, but only this week. After that I will—"

" 'After that' is too far away. May I call at your office in twenty minutes, with any chance of seeing you alone?"

"Why—it's in business hours—"

"But it's terribly important. *Please!*"

"Do you suppose a law office employs stenographers," she laughed, "to give terribly important personal interviews to outsiders during work time?"

"Don't joke about it," he pleaded. "It's really the most important business I've ever had to transact."

"Very well," she sighed, in mock resignation. "Mr. Warburton is out of town, and Mr. Spogg is in court. Perhaps I can steal ten minutes, if you insist on it, but—"

"Don't spoil it with any 'buts'!" he interposed. "I'll be there as fast as the subway will carry me."

He left his office in a rush, crossed to John Street, and took the subway northward to Twenty-third. Never had the local trains seemed to crawl with such maddening slowness. Arrived at Twenty-third Street and Fourth Avenue, he hastened westward, then cut across Madison Square toward his destination.

Two minutes later he was entering the little, partitioned room in the law office of Warburton & Spogg, where Ruth Gray presided at the typewriter.

"If it's Mr. Spogg or Mr. Warburton you're looking for," began the boy in the outer office, "they're—"

"I know they are. I've an appointment—"

"I'm on!" interrupted the boy. "It's appointments like yours that help the marriage-license clerks earn their twenty-five per. Don't let me stop you. There's the door of her room over there. I'll try to steer the boss off if he comes in while you're here."

The boy dodged as Mohun made a gesture toward him. Then he beamed. For Ralph's outstretched hand had a two-dollar bill in it.

"Easy money!" exulted the boy. "Cupid forever!"

Chapter XII.
A Proposal and a Discovery.

"YOU said the business was terribly important," observed Ruth Gray. "Yet you've stood there looking at me, without a word, for two whole minutes."

She spoke with a forced lightness to hide her own nervous state. For, womanlike, she read his eyes, and what she saw written there set her heart to healing unaccountably fast.

"It's hard to say," stammered Mohun. "Still," he added, with a momentary return of courage, "it can be said in three words." And he spoke the words fervidly.

He paused, scared at his own temerity. The light in her big eyes checked him. Less gifted than she at reading such signs, he knew not whether what he saw there was love, or mere surprise, or even disfavor. But, to his joy, she, too, spoke three words, and precisely the same ones he had uttered.

Then he moved impulsively toward her, but her upraised hand halted him.

"One moment," she said. "There is something I must understand. You have told me several times that Judge Estler has set his heart on your making a brilliant match. Is—is what you have just said to me a part of your campaign to anger him?"

To Ralph Mohun this simple deduction, backed by feminine intuition, seemed little short of miraculous. He was sore tempted to lie, for he could now read the look in those dark eyes of hers as a desire to believe him—to be freed of the suspicion she had voiced. But to this girl, above all the world, he could not lie. So he made haste to tell the awkward truth as awkwardly as possible.

"It *is* part of my 'campaign,' as you call it," said he haltingly; "but I—"

"Ah!"

The monosyllable was almost a cry of pain. It seared Mohun's heart like white-hot iron.

"You don't understand!" he exclaimed. "You don't understand! Let me explain. I—"

"I understand only too well," she answered, "and there is nothing to explain."

"But—"

"Wait! I understood even better than you seem to. It is I who must explain your actions to you. You have tried to turn Judge Estler's bounty from yourself to a woman you do not know, and you were willing to sacrifice yourself to do it. That was quixotic, yet it was worthy, and I honored you for it. But now you have tried to sacrifice me as well—"

"No, no!"

"Yes!" she contradicted, her eyes blazing, her cheeks aflame. "You would marry me to give this unknown girl a fortune. You would—"

"I would not! I would marry no woman on earth if I didn't love her! And I—"

"For the sake of another woman, you would make my life miserable. You thought out your plan, and then came here smugly to make me a party to it. What must you have thought of me, to believe I would fall in with such a scheme?"

"You have no right to say that! There is not a word of truth in it! I confess I hoped Judge Estler would be angry at me for such a marriage, and I see now, for the first time, how contemptible it was for me to think of you in such a connection. I ask your forgiveness for it. But you are wrong to disbelieve me when I tell you I love you, Ruth, for that is the truth. And I'm going to make you learn to care for me. Do you understand? This isn't stage love talk, perhaps, but it's the truth. And you've got to believe it!"

Carried away, far past the point of fear, by his love for her and his indignation and self-contempt, Mohun hurried on:

"I love you! And I believed—I dared to believe—you were beginning to care for me. That shows what a presumptuous fool I was, perhaps. But I'm going to make you care. And as for Judge Estler and his niece, they can find each other or not—I'm done with my quixotic venture. All that matters now is you. And I mean to win you. Soon or late, I'll do it!"

Her face was averted. Her moment of righteous wrath was past, swept away by his tide of emotion.

"Look at me!" he commanded. "Look in my eyes, and then tell me if you can doubt I'm telling the truth. Look! I—"

The door of the other office opened unceremoniously. A man and a woman entered.

"Good morning, Miss Gray," said the man. "My wife and I have come to sign the Brierdale real-estate transfer. Mr. Warburton said he or his partner would be here at this—"

He halted abruptly as his eyes fell on Ralph Mohun. The recognition was mutual. The newcomer was Bryce, and the woman at his side was the woman whom Mohun had rescued. Bryce came forward with eager welcome.

"Mr. Mohun," he began, "I am more glad than I can say to meet you again."

"You—you know my name?" faltered Ralph.

Bryce blushed guiltily.

"I—I happened to learn it," he evaded.

He did not say how he had "happened" upon the knowledge, nor did he add that it was he who had ever since been directing the steady stream of law business into Mohun's hands.

Now Mrs. Bryce had come forward, and, with a smile of pleasure, was offering Ralph a very much ringed hand.

"You never even gave me a chance to thank you," said she. "And it was only by accident I found out who you were."

"How did you find it out?" asked Ralph, eager to shift the talk away from gratitude to safer channels, and, above all, wishing these supergrateful and tremendously rich people would take themselves away and leave him alone with Ruth.

"I—I just happened to learn about it," stammered Mrs. Bryce. "You see," she went on, equally eager to change the topic, "we come from the same city, you and I, and—"

"You came from Detroit?" asked Ralph.

"Yes; but I left there when I was a baby. My father knew your father, Colonel Mohun, years ago. I've heard father speak about him. Then—"

"So? What was his name?"

"Clark Estler."

"What! You are Claire Estler?"

"I *was*. I'm Claire Bryce now. And—why, what's the matter?"

Mohun had collapsed in a chair, and was in a spasm of laughter.

"Oh!" he panted. "To think of it! For months I've been trying to ruin my prospects in life by finding Clark Estler's half-starved, lonely daughter, so that she might have Judge Estler's fortune. And here I find you married to a man who has a dollar for every penny Judge Estler possesses! But, thank Heaven, my mission is over! I can write to the judge that his poor, lonely niece is wealthy enough to buy him and half of Detroit. It strikes me that I have been some lunatic."

"Judge Estler knows all about it," said Mr. Bryce. "A month or two ago he wrote to Warburton & Spogg—they're his attorneys here, you know—asking them to trace his niece. And, as they are our attorneys, too, the search was not difficult. We expect the judge in New York on a visit to us next week."

"Isn't that like him!" ejaculated Ralph. "Here I stirred up the dear old fellow's conscience about his niece, and he wouldn't give me the satisfaction of knowing I'd done it. So he gets other lawyers to make the search, and never says a word to me about it. Now—oh, by the way," he interrupted himself, "will you excuse me a second?"

He stepped into the vacant adjoining office, and beckoned to Ruth Gray.

"Ruth," he said, as she came half reluctantly in response to his gesture and the appeal in his eyes, "you know now, don't you, that what I said is true—that I'm not trying to help Claire Estler by asking you to be my wife?"

"Yes," she whispered. Their hands met in a long pressure as she looked up into his eyes. "Yes, I know."

"I'm going to get into print at last!" he said. "In the 'Married' column!"

The Sights They Missed~

By Alfred Payson Terhune.

Chapter I.
On the Front Seat.

TIVERTON stepped back just in time to score a clean miss for a whizzing automobile. And in so doing he backed so close to a trolley car that was rounding the Twenty-third Street curve into Broadway that he began an involuntary forward jump—one that landed him a few feet from the sidewalk, close to a large object that was long and low and wide and pale green. In appearance it was something between an auto truck and a royal barge; a sort of circus float on pneumatic wheels.

Tiverton would not have given the thing a second glance—a sight-seeing bus being no novelty to him, after three hustling years in New York—but for two faces whose gaze he chanced to catch fixed on himself as he looked upward. The observing faces belonged to two people sitting each on the end of one of the bus' sitting seats—on the end nearest Tiverton.

One of the two watching passengers was a man; the other, in the seat directly in front of him, a woman. The man's face was of a deathly white hue; a long black mustache split it transversely. The woman's cheeks were flushed, radiantly bright by contrast to the man's, and her eyes were still big and startled at what she seemed to consider Tiverton's narrow escape from injury, or worse. The man, on the contrary, was laughing at the auto dodger's mishap; and the laugh gave Tiverton an acute sense of having made himself ridiculous by his self-preservative jump backward and forward. He was aware of a growing desire to punch the laugher's white face.

But a second look at the girl turned the current of his thoughts from anger to frank admiration. She was still looking at him, neither boldly nor coyly, but with a dawning quiet interest that seemed to appraise and to approve his deep chest and thick shoulders as well as his square-jawed, erect head. It evidently occurred to her that her gaze might be open to misconstruction; for she shifted her glance and, turning half around, said something to the grinning man behind her. The latter answered with a total lack of surprise that argued acquaintance.

Arthur Tiverton was aware once more of a little gust of anger somewhere in the recesses of his brain. It was preposterous that there could be anything in common between so altogether lovely a girl and that laughing death's-head of a fellow! And yet—

The seat next to the girl, as Tiverton could see, was vacant. An impulse possessed him. Hurrying around to the ticket seller he laid down a dollar bill and bought a seat for the bus' forthcoming trip. Then he turned back to the vehicle and prepared to take the vacant seat alongside the girl. It was all a matter of impulse. Tiverton had no intention whatever of scraping acquaintanceship. It was not his way to pursue unknown women with attentions. But, having an hour or more to kill in as painless a fashion as possible, he had suddenly decided that the time could not be slain in any other way half so pleasantly as in sitting where, unobtrusively, he could look now and then at the prettiest girl he had ever seen.

His ruse, if unworthy, met with the failure it merited. For, just as he was about to mount the footboard, two men and two women, who had bought tickets a half minute ahead of him, filed solemnly into the four vacant places in the seat which the girl had hitherto occupied alone.

Tiverton thought of taking a place in the seat just behind—the one whose far end was occupied by the white-faced man. But alongside the latter sat three other men, all fairly well dressed and with an indescribably "out-of-town" air. And as Tiverton moved toward the fifth place it was preempted by a stout woman in black carrying a bulky umbrella.

He was half minded to give up his silly scheme of riding on the same bus with the girl, now that he could not sit where he could see her; besides he had learned from the sign that the bus was bound for a tour of the downtown business section—a part of the city where he himself worked every day from nine to five. But he had bought his ticket. He would at least be on the same bus with the girl. And perhaps he might yet maneuver to catch a glimpse or two of her during the journey.

As he stood, uncertain, the bus was fast filling. Nearly every seat was taken. Half ashamed of his folly, Tiverton moved toward what seemed to him the most desirable of the few places still unoccupied— that next to the chauffeur. It was in the seat just in front of where the girl sat. He made his way thither, and as he sat down he glanced back as though merely seeking to size up his fellow passengers on the five rows of seats.

Again his simple ruse failed. The girl was still sitting sideways, her shoulders to him, talking with the white-faced man. Tiverton could not see her face at all, except for one pink ear and a quarter segment of cheek. But he saw something else that mildly puzzled him. Her position brought into Tiverton's line of vision part of the figure of the man with whom she was chatting; and the man's fingers were absently toying with a bit of paper. At a twist that he gave to it Tiverton could see that the paper appeared to be a ten-dollar bill. No, a slight flourish of the yellow-backed slip showed him that his guess was not quite correct. It was not a whole bank note that the man was manipulating. It was only *half* of a ten-dollar bill. From the man's handling of it Tiverton could almost fancy he was making signals or trying to attract some unseen person's attention.

Chapter II.
A Queer Mistake.

EVEN as Arthur looked the girl pointed toward the bill and said something. Again the man laughed, made a reply, and stuffed the bisected piece of currency into his vest pocket.

A slight jar and the bus was in motion. The chauffeur piloted it deftly into its proper position in the sluggish stream of downtown traffic. The announcer—a large, bored-looking functionary—rose from his lounging position against the dashboard and, lifting his short megaphone, faced the passengers.

It was a scene Tiverton had witnessed a hundred times—usually with the smile of amusement that New Yorkers are apt to bestow on the out-of-town visitors who choose this way of getting a comprehensive idea of the city. But it was his first experience as part of the spectacle.

"Great old burg, hey?" remarked the chauffeur gruffly, under cover of the announcer's megaphoned speech.

"Yes," returned Tiverton, amused at the other's apparent belief that this passenger, too, was an out-of-towner who must be entertained.

"Beats Paris or London or Chicago or Denver, folks tell me," pursued the chauffeur. "There's even one or two folks that's so enthoosiastic they declare, right out in meetin', that it beats North Wilbr'm, Mass."

"What's that?" asked Tiverton, all attention. It startled him somewhat that a stranger could have hit upon the name of his home village seemingly by sheer accident. He looked for the first time at the chauffeur. The latter was leaning in an absorbed manner over his wheel. Under the low-drawn cap Tiverton caught an impression of fiery red hair, freckled skin, and a combative profile.

"What in blazes do *you* know about North Wilbraham?" he asked.

"Well," drawled the chauffeur, "I remember readin' a lot of stories in the New York papers about three years ago that began something like 'Ex-try! Latest War News from North Wilbr'm! Arthur Tiverton Starts Today for New York to Make John D. Look Like a Piker!' "

The chauffeur turned a grinning face of welcome toward his passenger as he spoke, and ended his mock quotation by sticking out a gauntleted hand.

"Hello, Art!" he exclaimed.

"Denny! Good old Denny Cross!" responded Tiverton, meeting the outstretched hand with a hearty pressure. "What on earth are you doing here?"

"Savin' twenty-five lives," answered Cross. "If you don't believe me I'll be glad to prove it by letting this Noah's Ark run into a trolley car or climb up the side of a skyscraper."

"But—"

"That's the answer to Foolish Question Seven Hundred and Eleven. What did I look as if I was doing? Pickin' roses along the subway tracks? I'm a rubberneck buggy's pilot. I've been on this job, man and boy, for pretty near two months. And, till you swarmed up onto the quarter-deck a few minutes ago, I hadn't seen an old-home face in five years. Gee, but it's good to see you, Art! The folks wrote to me, three years back, that you'd come to New York. And I've been looking for you. But in this village there's apt to be quite a lot of faces sauntering along Main Street or at the post office or around the grocery store. So somehow I missed you."

"To think of our running across each other here!" cried Tiverton. "I mustn't lose sight of you again. Drop in at my place some evening. Here's my address." He handed the chauffeur a card. "Don't forget. We'll have dinner and go to a show and talk over North Wilbraham."

"H'm!" muttered Denny, trying, New Englandlike, to mask gratification under ungraciousness. "You're all togged up like ready money. I guess you'd be ashamed to be seen with a yap like me tagging along after you."

"Drop it!" said Tiverton. "I guess you've forgotten how I used to duck you in the Scantic when you got too fresh back in the days when we were kids. Well, you're none too big to be ducked now if you talk that way."

"Why, you big bluff!" bristled Denny. "You never saw the day you could duck me. But we'll let it go at that. I was only thinkin' you'd be ashamed to be seen with me. I might 'a' known better."

"You certainly might. How has New York used you?"

"It's let me live. For two years as a subway guard, for three more as a taxi shover. Then came the strike, and—well, I got this job."

"Like it?"

"Sure. I like anything; only some things more'n others. And Sam Tubbs—that's the leather lung-man chap megaphoning—least of all. He's sure a gloom, even at his best. And I've been brought up too careful to tell you what he is at his worst."

"These sight-seeing busses do a pretty good business, don't they?"

Without a pause for breath, or cracking a smile, Denny delivered himself as follows:

"With our specially constructed automobiles of large carrying capacity all interesting parts of New York may actually be seen between sunset and sundown and at a lower rate than would be possible by private vehicle. Passengers are taken whirling through the streets, wonder after wonder piled upon their bewildered gaze, while expert guides and lecturers eloocidate in detail each point under observation. Previously, strangers in New York, lacking knowledge of how to reach points of interest, have had fatiguing and arduous experience. But now, by using our—"

"Help!" cried Tiverton. "For Heaven's sake, Denny, what has happened to your brain?"

"I learned that by heart from one of our booklets," explained the driver. "I know more of it—plenty. Want to hear—"

"No! Leave it to the announcer. What—"

"See that little chap crossing the street over there?" cut in Denny. "Pal of mine. Born and bred in Doyers Street. In the heart of Chinatown. Lived there till he was forty. Then moved up to Greenwich Village. Next day he planks down a dollar to ride on a 'seeing Chinatown' tour of ours."

"But these seeing New York busses—"

"Don't call 'em that any more! 'Tisn't the monaker. 'Touring New York automobiles' is the name now. Folks got guyed for riding on 'em under the old name. So it was switched. These little five-seated-cars are too slow for me. I want a job in the pilot house of one of our eight-seaters. Then—What's the matter?"

Tiverton had started in surprise. Denny saw his friend was no longer looking at him, but staring in wonder at Samuel Tubbs, the announcer. That worthy had just pointed out a particularly large and hideous skyscraper, and was intoning loudly:

"The Whitelawn Building! Erected in nineteen hundred and six. Celebrated as containing the palatial suite of offices of Cyrus Q. Buchanan, the mining king."

"That's wrong!" declared Tiverton to the driver.

"No," said Cross, "I'm flattering Tubbs when I say I hate him. But he's the best announcer we've got. He never makes mistakes. And he knows this route with his eyes shut. What gave you the idea he was mixed up?"

"Because," answered Tiverton, "I happen to be Mr. Buchanan's private secretary. And his office isn't in the Whitelawn Building, or anywhere near it. This looks queer to me."

Chapter III.
Half of a Ten-Dollar Bill.

TO Tiverton's bewilderment, Denny showed no surprise. "I knew there was something phony," said the chauffeur. "I piped 'em for a second, before we started."

As he did not specify who "'em" might be, Tiverton glanced back over the serried rows of passengers. He was just in time to witness a true case of "rubbernecking." The white-faced man had half risen in his seat and was looking back at the Whitelawn Building, talking and gesticulating. The three rural-looking men at his side were following his words and the direction of his gaze with keen interest; so, Arthur noted, was the girl.

"What's the idea, I wonder?" said Tiverton, as he turned again to Denny.

"The idea," returned Cross, "is that Sam Tubbs is so crooked he could hide behind a corkscrew. That's the main idea. The other end of it is that a man back yonder made Tubbs a mighty funny present a while ago, just before he took his seat. Tubbs and he were around at the far end of the car, and I suppose they thought no one could see. The starter didn't; but I did. It's a way I've got."

"A present? Cash?"

"No, cash divided by two—one-half of a ten-dollar bill. Can't buy much with that. But Tubbs seemed real tickled. I don't see the point; yet I'm wondering if that near-tip had anything to do with Sam's phony announcement just now."

"Why should it? What's the connection?"

"I've been for weeks on the same bus with Sam, and I never heard him make a slip. I never saw him get a tip, either; touring-bus patrons don't often give 'em. So when I hear the slip and see the tip on the same ride, I put them together. What?"

Tiverton recalled the white-faced man's behavior when the bus was passing the Whitelawn Building; and Denny's mention of the torn bill recalled at once the similar section that had fluttered in the man's fingers.

"The fellow who gave your friend Tubbs the half bill was very pale, wasn't he—with a wild-West black mustache?" queried Tiverton.

"That's the chap! Mind readin', are you?"

"No; but I'm going to. This whole thing looks funny to me. I mean to find out if I can—wait a second. There's the Cogghall Building just in front. Cyrus O. Buchanan's offices are there. I want to see if Tubbs will mention him among the Cogghall's tenants."

"He's got to," declared Denny. "He does, every time. Buchanan's the biggest face card in the Cogghall deck. And it's a deck with mighty few two-spots in it, at that. Listen!"

The announcer pointed to the building. Through his horn he droned a list of renowned financiers who had offices there. The list, as Tiverton recognized, was accurate save for one omission—it did not contain Cyrus Q. Buchanan's name. Arthur leaned nearer to Cross and spoke in a voice even lower than the low pitch in which their talk had been conducted.

"I'm going to find out the point of this joke," said he, "if it takes me a week to do it. A week is all the time I have, for Mr. Buchanan comes back from his Western trip a week from to-day. And when he's in town there's no loafing for his secretary."

"If he keeps you so busy how do you happen to be eating up the busiest hour in the day on a low-power joy ride like this?"

"When he goes away he either takes me along or leaves me with only half work while he is gone, so that I may rest up and be ready to put in twenty-four hours on a stretch, if necessary, when he gets back. That's why I find myself with time on my hands, this week. I'm going to use up a lot of that time in digging out a fact or two in this queer puzzle. It's probably a trivial matter—a joke or something; but it brings in my employer's name. And his name has too big a face value to serve in a joke."

"Likewise," dreamily observed Denny Cross, looking anywhere rather than at his companion, "there was a girl—a mighty pretty girl, at that—who got on the bus with this white-faced chap's party. Not that you'd be at all int'rested in anything so trivial as that; for all you stared so admiring at her before you climbed aboard here. That wouldn't have anything to do with your follerin' up the joke."

"If it's just the same to you, Denny," said Tiverton pleasantly, though he reddened as he spoke, "we won't discuss girls we neither of us know. It isn't—"

"That's right!" solemnly admitted Denny. "It isn't. It says so in a book I read once—a book all about folks who wore di'monds to breakfast and looked on a one-million-power plootocrat as a piker. But I'm not jumping over the bars in speaking, respectful-like, of that lady back there; for she isn't some one 'we neither of us know.' It's a lady I had the pleasure of workin' for more'n once last year. She remembers it. An' she was kind enough to nod to me, real pleasant, when she got aboard. Blest if I don't believe she'd have come over an' said 'Howdy' to me if she'd had a chance. There's nothing stuck up about her; there never is about the real first-class ones. It's only the second-raters that treat their work-folks like dogs."

"You—you say you worked for her?" exclaimed Tiverton.

"Sure—in a way. She stopped for a month at the Idler—a little quiet apartment hotel up on the West Side—last year. My taxi was in the rank there. She liked my careful driving, she said. So she hired me pretty near every day. Once I got back a pocketbook one of the chauffeurs had swiped from her, and when she went away she slipped me a brace of iron men and thanked me for taking such nice care of her."

"Who—"

"I don't know. I take it she lives somewhere up State or out West, or maybe in Jersey, and just comes to the big town once a year or so. Seems to have enough cash to keep the wolf in the offing. Her name is Wesley—Miss Florida Wesley."

The car was on its return trip from the Wall Street district; and as Denny spoke he steered it deftly into its harborage. The passengers descended awkwardly to earth. Among the first was Arthur Tiverton. Standing idly to one side, he watched the party of five headed by the white-faced man. As the man stepped down, he brushed past Tubbs, the announcer. The momentary contact was elaborately accidental. But Tiverton, watching from between half-closed eyes, saw a quick, furtive interchange of gestures—a double move that transferred from the passenger's hand to Tubbs' the neatly torn half of a ten-dollar bill.

Denny had come down from his seat at the steering wheel, and was glancing about him as though to find some one. Tiverton stepped up to him.

"Tubbs has the whole bill now," said he.

"Yes," said Denny, "I saw. It's an old trick. Paste the two halves together and the bill's as good as new. It's torn to make sure the job's done and to make sure of fair play on both sides. I saw it fail once, though. A taxi chauffeur that I knew got half of a five-dollar bill beforehand as a tip for driving a farmer all over the city. It was a half-day trip, and the chauffeur sure did his best to earn the rest of that five. At the end of the ride the farmer says to him: 'That 'ere half a bill ain't no use to you as it stands. I'll give ye ten cents and a seegar fer it.' But say, Art, did you catch what our snow-faced friend says to Tubbs as he handed out the second half?"

"No, I was too far away."

"I wasn't. He whispers: 'To-morrow. Same time.' An'—"

"I'm glad to see you again, Cross," said some one at Denny's elbow, in a pleasant voice.

Both men turned. It was Miss Wesley who had made her way to the chauffeur's side.

"You are doing well here?" she went on.

"Yes'm. Thanks. Same to you!" sputtered the embarrassed but delighted Denny. "An'—please, would you think me fresh if I took the liberty to make you acquainted with an old schoolmate of mine? Mr. Arthur Tiverton, Miss Wesley."

Chapter IV.
The Girl.

DENNY CROSS confessed later to Tiverton: "I know it was a bone-head play to introduce a side-kicker of mine to a dame of her class; but I was so fazed at her coming up to us, unexpectedlike, that I said the first thing that seemed to fit in."

Though Miss Wesley looked somewhat taken aback at the unexpected introduction, she inclined her pretty head in civil acknowledgment of Tiverton's bow. Then she nodded a good-by to Denny and turned away, just as the white-faced man with his three rural-looking companions bore down upon her.

The man said something to her that Tiverton could not catch. But he heard her reply in a clear voice:

"Thank you, Mr. Devereux; but I think I'll take a street car up to Thirty-fourth Street. I have some shopping to do."

They melted away in the Broadway and crosstown crowd.

"Devereux," repeated Tiverton, half aloud.

"Fancy monaker," said Cross. "Puts it all over a name like Tubbs, no? Well, I've got to hustle. I s'pose you meant what you said 'bout my dropping in on you at your rooms?"

"Of course I did. It'll be good to have an old-time chat with you. By the bye, are you sure it was 'to-morrow' that Devereux whispered to your friend Tubbs?"

"Dead sure. Why?"

"Because," said Tiverton, "I'm going to be here at the same time to-morrow on the chance that some other 'mistake' will be made by the announcer—a mistake possibly like that of to-day. It may be none of my business, but unraveling even a silly little mystery like this is mildly amusing. Save me a seat beside you if you can; in case the 'tomorrow' should mean an appointment like this afternoon's. Good-by."

The following morning, Tiverton was early at his employer's office in the Cogghall Building, and in a short time he wound up his routine business for the day. He was annoyed at himself for being unable to shake from his mind a hundred buzzing conjectures as to the meaning of the seemingly trifling Devereux-Tubbs mystery. He looked at it from a dozen different angles, but from none could he gain a viewpoint that satisfied him.

That any sane man should pay a touring automobile announcer ten dollars to say that a certain financier had an office in a building half a mile north of that financier's actual office, seemed an absurdity. But, remembering the giving of the halved bank note and Devereux's odd behavior when Tubbs made the announcement, he could come to no other conclusion than that the incident had some interesting significance.

Between moments of fruitless puzzling, Tiverton found himself indulging in the pleasanter, but equally futile, recreation of bringing back to his mental vision the face and the voice of Florida Wesley. He recalled also what Denny had said of her having stopped a year earlier at the Idler apartment hotel. He wondered whether she was staying there now. He supposed so, since out-of-town people have a way of making some one hotel their invariable headquarters when they are in New York.

Then Tiverton laughed at himself for a sentimental fool, for wasting so much thought on a girl whom he had seen but once, and who, in all human probability, he would never see again. Whereat, he went right on thinking about her, intermitting his roseate thoughts with further conjectures as to Devereux and Tubbs.

At half past twelve his office work was done; the rest of the day was his. He had planned to run down to Coney Island for an early-season swim and for dinner. But, with a grunt of self-contempt at his own folly, he found himself walking northward, in the direction of the Whitelawn Building.

Arrived at the garish front of that particularly aggressive skyscraper, he hesitated again; then turned in at the doorway. In the big entrance hall he glanced about till his eye fell on a square black slab in the wall with raised white letters. "Office Directory" was printed at the top of the slab, and beneath, in much smaller type, were the names and room numbers of the Whitelawn's several hundred tenants.

Tiverton glanced along the list headed "B." He knew perfectly well that Cyrus Q. Buchanan had no office in this building. But it occurred to him that some other man named Buchanan might have one, and that this might account for Tubbs' announcement; either that or some fly-by-night crook might have assumed the name of Cyrus Q. Buchanan for the purpose of fleecing the unwary. This, he realized, would be a dangerous trick and one almost certain of quick detection. No swindler was likely to risk it. Yet it was worth a look; if only to safeguard his employer's interests. But, as he had foreseen, no "Buchanan" appeared on the board. After a second look, Tiverton walked down the hall to where the uniformed elevator starter was standing.

"I'm looking," explained Arthur, "for Mr. Buchanan's office—Cyrus Q. Buchanan's. I can't find it on the directory list, and—"

"And you can't find it in the building," snapped the starter, with scant courtesy. "Cyrus Q. Buchanan's got no office in the Whitelawn Building. I tell 'em all that. And some of 'em want to argue it out and prove to me I don't know who our own tenants are."

"So I'm not the only one to bother you with such a fool question?" queried Arthur, the joy of the hunt quickening his pulses.

"No; two others in the last three days. But they looked like dressed-up rubes, and you don't. When I told one of 'em there was no Buchanan here he asked for Mr. Devereux's office."

"Devereux?"

"Yes. Twelfth floor—twelve hundred and four to twelve hundred and seven. The rube went up there, and when he came back he gave me a wink and said he 'guessed I knew how to keep a secret,' whatever he may have meant by that."

Tiverton drifted away from the loquacious starter and back to the directory. There, under the heading of "D" he read:

"Devereux, R. T. 1204-7."

Arthur went across to an elevator labeled "Express to 11th Floor" and was shot upward. At the twelfth floor he alighted and made his way along the corridor until he faced a ground-glass door on which was lettered in gilt:

1204

R. T. DEVEREUX & CO.

Mining Properties.

Entrance 1205.

To Room 1205 Tiverton went, and, opening the door, walked into a small and rather overfurnished waiting room. The only occupant there was an office boy who nodded drowsily over a corner desk.

"It must have been a great night," remarked Tiverton cheerily. "Will you wake up long enough to tell me if the boss is in?"

The boy rose, blinking. "Friend of his?" he queried, visibly impressed by the intentional familiarity of Tiverton's manner.

"No," Tiverton answered, laughing, "an enemy. Is he in?"

"He's out to lunch," was the reply; "and he's got a date uptown in the afternoon, but—"

"I know," said Tiverton, "but he isn't due uptown till two. So—"

"Oh, maybe he'll be back then before he goes up there." The boy yawned. "If you're one of his crowd you can wait in the reception room in there, if you want to."

"Thanks, I will," said Arthur. "Pleasant dreams."

He passed on into a large inner room, and the spring door swung shut behind him. He found himself in a showy apartment—half office, half lounging room—with doors opening out on either side. It was not Tiverton's first glimpse of such places, and he wasted no time in idle staring, but walked straight over to the flat-topped desk that stood between two windows.

The desk top's only contents were a dozen loose sheets of paper, a rack of envelopes, a silver inkstand, and some pens. It was the paper that interested Tiverton. He picked up the nearest sheet of it, and at the top read the strong black letter heading:

DEVEREUX & CO.,
Mining Properties.
R. T. Devereux.   Cyrus Q. Buchanan.

Tiverton was not surprised. He understood the game now. It was not new in the financial district, and several of its former players were even then enjoying the State's hospitality at Sing Sing, Auburn, and Clinton.

He had often heard of the old scheme, on the part of some crook promoter, to pretend that a financier of note was the "company" or the silent partner in his concern; and by the conjuring power of such a name to reap a goodly shearing of wool from the lambs.

The necessary stationery involved merely the aid of a dishonest or ignorant engraver. The use of paper thus engraved, in the United States mails, had often set the government on the track of such crooks. But Tiverton knew that the mere presence of such stationery on a promoter's desk was no violation of law, so that it was safe for the rascals to leave it there for the purpose of impressing their intended victims. Nor was he astonished to see several stamped and postmarked enveloped flung with elaborate carelessness at one end of the desk, and all addressed "Cyrus Q. Buchanan, care of Devereux & Co., Whitelawn Building."

It was a very pretty little booby trap as it stood—the whole place. Yet Tiverton marveled at the daring use of a name so high in the financial world as Buchanan's.

"A case of quick touch-and-go work," Arthur decided; "a scheme with a sudden punch in it, and then a getaway. But what, in the name of all that's wonderful, has the rubberneck coach to do with it?"

He had seen all he needed to show him the misuse to which his employer's name had been put. It remained only to apprise Buchanan by telegraph, and to await the latter's action. Action, with Cyrus O. Buchanan, was seldom long delayed, nor was it apt to be over-gentle.

Tiverton turned from the desk between the two windows, and took a step toward the door. Then he halted, for the door opened and some one entered. The newcomer was Florida Wesley, the girl of the touring automobile. She came into the room a little way, caught sight of Tiverton silhouetted against the sunshine of the window, and paused. It was clear that with the strong light at his back she did not recognize him.

"Pardon me," she said, "but Mr. Devereux is out, and probably won't be back before four o'clock at the earliest. If you are a client—"

She checked herself, for, as she spoke, Tiverton moved forward. She saw his face, and recognition dawned in her own—recognition, and something that seemed to him akin to panic.

Nor was Tiverton as calm and nerve steady as was his wont. He was saying to himself in a sort of daze:

"She came in here as if she *belonged;* and she spoke to me as though she were one of the firm. A crook company for fleecing silly sheep. And—Oh, a girl with eyes like those!"

Chapter V.
The Second Ride.

"MR. TIVERTON?" said the girl, hesitating, as if undecided whether to say more.

"It's good of you to remember me," he said. "Are you waiting for Mr. Devereux, too?"

"Yes," she answered uneasily. "The boy in the anteroom was asleep, so I came in. I thought he might be—"

She stopped, perhaps remembering, as did Arthur, that she had just said Devereux was not likely to return until late afternoon. They looked uncomfortably at each other. Then Arthur, offering her a chair, said: "Do you mind if I wait with you?"

"Not at all," she assured him, still apparently ill at ease. And she took the proffered chair.

"You are a friend of Mr. Devereux?" she asked suddenly.

"A friend of one of your far humbler admirers," he answered evasively; "of Denny Cross."

"He is a character, isn't he?" She laughed. "He was the best chauffeur at the hotel where I stopped last year, and he restored a stolen pocketbook to me."

"He was the son of our farmer up at North Wilbraham," said Tiverton, "and he and I played together as boys. I had lost track of him till yesterday."

They drifted into pleasant talk on indifferent topics, and for half an hour or more they chatted, while the office boy snored softly at the anteroom desk outside. Tiverton found Miss Wesley altogether delightful. For the moment he quite forgot his suspicions of her. The two found each other wonderfully congenial. At the end of a half hour they felt almost like old acquaintances. It was with real regret that Arthur noted the passing of time, by the wall clock, and recalled his plan to be at the corner of Broadway and Twenty-third Street for the seeing New York bus' two-o'clock trip.

He rose, with something like a sigh on his lips, and held out his hand.

"It has been good to meet you," he said simply. "I wonder if you will think I am impertinent if I ask leave to call. You see," he blundered on, "I know so few people in New York, and you—"

He stopped. She was looking at him not in wonder or displeasure, but with an expression he could not quite fathom. It seemed to him almost one of sorrow.

"Yes," she said at last. "Please come. I shall be very glad to see you."

"Oh, thank you!" he exclaimed impulsively. "And when am I likely to find you home? May I call to-morrow evening—early? Is that too soon? Or have you an engagement?"

"No, I have no engagements for tomorrow evening. I shall be at home. I am stopping at—"

"The Idler?" he asked.

His repetition of what Denny Cross had told him of her former New York headquarters produced a remarkable effect on the girl. The soft lights in her big eyes grew hard. And her full lips compressed, then parted as if for hasty speech. But she closed them again, and, after a long look of scrutiny, said coldly:

"Yes. I am at the Idler. Good afternoon."

"To-morrow evening, then?" he rejoined, as he started for the door, marveling at the odd change in her manner.

"Yes," said Miss Wesley, in a tired voice; "to-morrow evening."

"Now," mused Tiverton, as he rattled uptown on the subway, "what the deuce could I have said or done to make her look at me like that? It was almost as if I'd sworn at her. And—and why did she wait at Devereux's office after I left? She had said he probably wouldn't be back. Does she belong there? Did Providence bestow such eyes upon a girl who is the accomplice of a crook?"

At Twenty-third Street he left the subway, and went to the nearest telegraph office, where he wrote out a long message in cipher, which he dispatched to Buchanan. It explained the whole Devereux affair as far as he himself understood it, and asked for instructions. Then Tiverton made his way westward to the starting point of the sight-seeing automobiles. The telegrams had taken somewhat longer to write than he had expected, and on his arrival he found the "downtown-trip" bus almost full.

A single glance showed him R. T. Devereux at the extreme end of the third seat, as before—on the side that would be nearest to the Whitelawn Building on the southward journey. Next to Devereux and in conversation with him were three men. They were not the three he had talked with on the preceding day, but they bore the same general air of prosperity and of a rural tailor's handiwork.

Devereux, as he talked, was glancing furtively to left and right, as though in search of something or some one. As he caught sight of Tiverton it was plain from his expression that he had discovered the object of his covert search. His ashy face went a trifle ashier, his eyes narrowed to slits, and he followed every motion of the new arrival.

Tiverton affected to notice nothing of this, but went forward to the front seat, where Denny hailed him with a grin of welcome, and made room for him in the place next to the wheel.

"I was afraid you wouldn't make it," said Cross. "Listen quick, now, before Sam Tubbs gets aboard; there won't be any time afterward for a private chin. We talked pretty soft yesterday, you and me. But Tubbs' ears are so sharp he could use 'em to shave with. He caught a word or two between megaphone spiels, and some time between yesterday and now he must 'a' got to thinking. For the minute Devereux shows up to-day Tubbs runs up to him with a line of whispered talk and then they both rubbers at me. Keep the soft pedal on to-day. Cheese it! Here's Tubbs."

The announcer climbed on, off went the bus, and Tubbs, megaphone to lips, began his "lecture." Neither Tiverton nor Cross spoke, but they could note the announcer's occasional glance at them.

As the bus neared the Whitelawn Building Tiverton riveted his gaze on the announcer. The latter looked at him, then at Devereux, and, in a voice that shook, he repeated his speech of the previous day, naming among the well-known tenants of the building Cyrus Q. Buchanan.

Tiverton looked back over his shoulder at Devereux. The white-faced man was pointing out the building as before, and his three companions were evincing great interest in it. Devereux's eyes shifted from the skyscraper and met Arthur's. In them Tiverton could read both fear and hatred.

"He looks at me as if I were a melodrama hero, and he the heavy villain," remarked Arthur to Denny, under cover of the badly rattled Tubbs' next announcement. "Why, I wonder?"

"Same reason Sam Tubbs is leery of you," decided Cross. "They're up to something, and they're wise that you're tabbing their game. Tubbs is afraid you'll report him and get him fired, and maybe prosecuted, too! The other chap's game may be so crooked that it spells jail. So both of 'em have cause to shy at you."

"I know what one of Devereux's games is," said Arthur. "But he doesn't know I know that. This much is plain: He bribes Tubbs every day to tell a lie about the tenancy list of the White-lawn Building. It remains to be seen exactly what use he makes of a sightseeing bus man's misstatement. Whatever the scheme is, it's serious enough to scare them both to know I'm watching it."

"And it's plainer still that you'd better look out for yourself," said Cross. "It's dangerous enough to have such men sore on you; but when they're scared of you besides—well, they're apt to do things."

Chapter VI.
A Puzzling Experience.

AT an unpardonably early hour next evening Tiverton called at the little Idler Hotel on the upper West Side. He had not realized how early it was until, after sending up his name to Miss Wesley, and going into a little reception room off the foyer, he saw that the mantel clock registered ten minutes to eight.

Tiverton was still framing an apology for his unseasonable call, and comforting himself with the possibility that a girl from the country might be used to receiving visits so soon after dinner, when some one came into the room. Tiverton turned, and beheld not Florida Wesley, but a tall man in evening dress. And the man was R. T. Devereux. If that white-faced person of mystery had looked like a melodrama villain in the prosaic surroundings of a seeing New York bus, he looked now like a stage Russian prince in his severely faultless evening attire. Tiverton was forced into reluctant admiration of the man's aspect and bearing.

Becoming aware of Tiverton's presence in the room, Devereux drew himself up stiffly. Into his white face came again that look of fear, mingled with sharp malice. But, with rare self-control, he recovered his composure; so quickly, indeed, that a casual observer could not have noted on his face any expression save of bored indifference.

He glanced carelessly at Tiverton, then moved toward a chair at the far end of the reception room. But Arthur was not content to let the chance slip by.

"Mr. Devereux?" he said civilly.

Devereux rose from the chair in which he was just seating himself, and faced about. His features were unmoved. But Tiverton, thanks to long training in the school of Cyrus Q. Buchanan, was too shrewd to judge any trained man's emotions from the expression—or lack of expression—of the face. His glance went at once to the white-gloved hands that hung inert at Devereux's sides. He saw that the fists were clenched in nervous tension.

"Mr. Devereux," he repeated. "May I introduce myself? I am—"

"Mr. Arthur Tiverton," interrupted Devereux, with cool and purposed insolence, "of nine-ninety-nine West Eighty-fifth Street. I know. So you can spare yourself the trouble of inventing an alias for my benefit."

"I don't indulge in the luxury of an alias," retorted Arthur, in perfect good humor, marveling none the less at the other's knowledge of his name and address; "any more than I can afford to claim as my partner a man who does not even know me by sight. Both those little extravagances cost too much for a poor chap like myself. Criminal trials are so expensive—as perhaps experience has taught you?"

The tone of the daring query was quite civil, and Devereux met it without flinching.

"There is probably a point in what you say," said he, "if only I could understand. I am not good at jokes."

"Oh!" Arthur laughed. "All jokes have points. Even ten-dollar witticisms at the expense of sight-seeing auto passengers who are told that Cyrus Q. Buchanan occupies an office he has never even heard of."

Devereux raised his eyebrows noncommittally.

"Does it cost more, Mr. Devereux," went on Arthur, in the same tone of pleasant impersonality, "to have a fake letterhead engraved than a genuine one? I mean, does one have to tear a bill in two before the stationer will consent to—"

A swish of skirts at the door interrupted him. Florida Wesley came in. Arthur advanced, hand outstretched, toward her. It had occurred to him from the moment of Devereux's appearance on the scene that the man, like himself, was at the Idler to call on Miss Wesley. And, with a glow of battle in his veins, Tiverton resolved to "cut him out." If it were to be a contest of assurance, of wit, of power to entertain, he was determined to monopolize the girl's attention.

She replied graciously, even cordially, to Tiverton's greeting. Then she turned to Devereux, who was bowing before her.

"I tried to get you on the phone," said Devereux, "but you hadn't come in yet. I have a box for 'Robin Hood' at the Casino to-night—the revival you said yesterday you wanted to hear before you leave town. I wonder if you would care to go there with me?"

She hesitated. Before she could make answer, Tiverton said, with ready ease:

"It's too bad, Mr. Devereux. Miss Wesley was kind enough to say I might call this evening, and to stay at home for me. I was hoping, Miss Wesley, on the way here, that you might like to go with me to the Olympic Roof Garden. It opens to-night. And they say the show is better than most of its sort. So I came early to ask—"

"I'm so sorry," said Devereux. "I planned such a jolly evening for you, Miss Wesley. Perhaps another time I may be luckier."

The man's graceful withdrawal from the competition made Tiverton half ashamed of his own aggressiveness. He felt instinctively that he was not shining by comparison with this well-mannered enemy of his. And he sought to make amends.

"If you'd care to see the show at the Casino, Miss Wesley," said he, "I don't want for a minute to stand in the way of your having a good time. I can call another evening, and—"

"If you really don't mind," she said

It was the first time she had spoken, or had a chance to speak, since she had entered the room. Tiverton could not believe his ears. He had made the renunciatory offer out of the merest courtesy, and with not the faintest idea that she would accept it.

"If you are quite sure you don't mind, Mr. Tiverton," she went on, in sweet apology, "I think I'll take you at your word. I do so much want to hear 'Robin Hood.' And this may be my last chance. I hear it is to be taken off in a day or two."

"Why, of course. I—"

"And since Mr. Devereux has gone to the trouble of getting a box for it," she hurried on, still apologetically, "it would be a shame not to—"

"Naturally," agreed Tiverton, with the best grace he could summon up.

"And you will call again?"

"Thank you!" he answered noncommittally. "It is good of you to ask me. I hope you'll enjoy the opera very much. Good night, Miss Wesley—Mr. Devereux."

"Good night, Mr. Tiverton," the latter called after the departing Arthur.

As he passed out Tiverton fancied that he heard a man's laugh—pleasant and well modulated, full of genuine amusement; and he made his way to the street in a white rage. He could not understand Florida Wesley's uncivil action in dismissing him for the sake of a much later invitation. She had not seemed to him the sort of girl to do so rude a thing, and her behavior puzzled him almost as keenly as it hurt him.

His brain hot with angry mortification, and his heart heavy with disillusion, Tiverton walked aimlessly from street to street for hours, rehearsing the scene at the Idler, and nursing his wrath and heart-ache. At last he steadied down to his normal state, and realized that the hour was late, and he was a mile or two from home. Quickening his pace, he trudged down West End Avenue to Eighty-fifth Street. Then he turned into the latter street—his footsteps echoing through its deserted width—and made for the house where he had his bachelor quarters. A few doors away from his destination a man rose from behind an area railing, and, with some dimly seen weapon, struck heavily at Tiverton's head.

Chapter VII.
"In the Day of Battle."

THE man had risen noiselessly from his hiding place; nor, in springing forward, had he made any sound. Like a dim-seen specter of the night he sprang and struck. So swift and silent were his advent and attack that they had taken Tiverton wholly by surprise; he had been walking rapidly, and had almost passed the areaway when his assailant appeared. Yet instinctively he ducked to one side just as the blow fell. This half-unconscious shift, coupled with the uncertain light and the speed at which his victim had been walking, served to mar the thug's aim.

The blackjack struck glancingly. It caught and smashed Tiverton's stiff hat crown in its passage, but barely grazed his head. Arthur whirled, before the other could raise his arm for a second blow, and grappled him. But even as he did so two men who, unobserved by him, had walked close behind ever since he turned in from West End Avenue, threw themselves on him. None of the trio spoke. Nor did Tiverton cry for help. Thus, the voiceless struggle of the four, there on that half-lit pavement of the deserted side street, failed to attract, at first, any attention from the slumbering inmates of the adjoining houses or from such few people as chanced still to be abroad on either of the block's intersecting avenues.

If the first man had bungled through nervousness or miscalculation of distance, his two allies showed more precision. As Tiverton closed with the blackjack wielder, one of the other two caught him deftly by either arm, jerking him sharply backward. The first man, freed, swung his weapon once more in air, poising it for a second and more accurate blow.

Tiverton, the primal fight lust springing to life in every fiber, did not think of shouting for assistance; nor did he so much as realize that before such a cry could bring help, the trio might finish him and make good their escape. Instead, he flung himself with all his force forward and downward in one swift move of his whole muscular body. The maneuver was so quick, diametrically opposite in direction from that against which his two captors had braced themselves, that he broke momentarily free from their double grip, leaving part of a coat sleeve in the hands of one of them. And the blackjack blow whizzed harmless above him. At the same moment Tiverton caught the striker about the knees, drawing inward and putting all his force into a jerking upward heave. It was a simple "rough-house" trick he had learned as a boy at school. And it served.

Up went the tough's feet, and down came the rest of his body. He struck the pavement square on his shoulders and the back of his head. The impact knocked the breath out of him, and half stunned him. The blackjack flew from his hand. But before Tiverton could regain his feet the two others were upon him, bearing him down by sheer weight, cramping his movements—kicking, striking, gouging, employing every trick of the underworld street fighter. Their victim's activity and the uncertainty of the light prevented them from working with the wonted swift, deadly effect of their class. Moreover, in the scrimmage, Tiverton had become so "mixed up" with the fallen thug, who was trying to scramble to his feet, that they were hampered.

Tiverton dodged one blow, countered another, and hurled himself to one side just in time to avoid a heavy boot's swinging kick—which found sonorous lodgment in the ribs of his half-prostrate first assailant. He struck out, in intervals between blocking the showering blows, with fierce precision and with all the speed he could muster. Sometimes his fists encountered empty air. Oftener they thudded against clothing or flesh, with a numbing smash that gave him vague delight.

For less than thirty seconds this rough-and-tumble endured. Then, bruised and battered, Tiverton managed to stagger to his feet. He grappled with the nearer of his two upright antagonists, driving his left forearm under the latter's chin and at the same time hammering short-arm blows to his face. Both men now set upon him, showering blows with greater force than science at every part of his anatomy within reach. Hard pressed to counter and to duck, he yet was able to return with interest more than one of these blows. But at this juncture the tough whom Tiverton had first thrown feet upward, and whom his accomplice's ill-directed kick had further incapacitated, recovered his wits and his strength sufficiently at the same instant to reach forward from his semirecumbent posture and catch Tiverton's ankles.

Down came the man who was making such a brave fight against hopeless odds. Then one of his assailants stooped down, seized the blackjack, and, taking lightning aim, struck. As he did so, two things happened—a white-clad woman in an upper window of a house across the way began to scream "Murder!" to the accompaniment of upflinging windows and sleepy questions. And the blackjack wielder found himself caught around the neck from behind and jerked backward off his feet.

Tiverton, at the same time freeing his ankles from their imprisonment, jumped up. He was just in time to see his two fallen assailants getting shakily to their feet; while the third, in the tight grip of a new hand in the fray, was being carelessly and hastily deposited in a heap in the gutter.

From West End Avenue came running footsteps, punctuated by the recurrent beat of a police club on the pavement. And that sound was the elixir of life to the three toughs. The two who had regained their feet made off at a shambling run in the opposite direction from the oncoming patrolman. The man in the gutter scuttled along for a yard or so on all fours like a lame jack rabbit, then lurched up to a crouching position, and ran for his life in the wake of his fellows.

Tiverton made after the last fugitive, and the newcomer in turn made after him. As they reached the door of the house where Tiverton lived, the other man adroitly caught him by the arm and brought the pursuit to a sudden halt.

"In here!" said he. "Quick's the word!"

Chapter VIII.
A Ray of Light.

AT the restraining touch on his arm, Tiverton had pulled free, still too inflamed with battle to tell friend from foe, and eagerly ready to try conclusions with this possible fresh antagonist. But at sound of the other's voice his clenched fists relaxed. "Denny!" he panted. "Denny Cross!"

"In here!" repeated Denny, dragging him forcibly up the short flight of brownstone steps into the vestibule. "Quick!"

"But—"

"Cut out the buts. Do as I say, unless you want more trouble."

He fairly hauled the tired man inside the vestibule, and closed the outer door after them, just as the patrolman trotted past in pursuit of his already vanishing triple quarry.

"Where's your keys?" asked Cross. "We're goin' up to your rooms before that cop stops running and comes back to listen to what the nightgown chorus from the windows has to say."

With fingers that shook from reaction and overstrain, Tiverton drew out his bunch of keys. Denny took them from him, tried two or three in the inner door's keyhole, found the right one, and let them into the hall. Two minutes later they were in Tiverton's sitting room, and Denny had turned the electric key, flooding the place with light.

"Sit down there!" he said to his panting host. "I'm going to look you over for a list of the damages. So! Now, work all your joints one after the other. Never mind if some of them hurt. That won't mean much. I want to see if anything's broke. All in working order? Good! Now, draw a long, slow breath, if you can sidetrack the panting long enough. Hurt? Sure it doesn't? Good! That means no ribs smashed. I guess you've got what the hospital reports call 'abrasions and contusions, but no fractures or internal injuries.' That's French for 'paint scratched, but cylinders all right.' Now, get off what's left of your coat and vest and collar, and I'll wash some of that dust from your face. Gee, man! You sure played in luck! Not a black eye! But you've got a few dandy bruises on your arms and throat."

As he talked, Denny was ministering to his friend with the quick skill of a prize-ring second—manipulating, fanning, sponging. Tiverton was content for a few minutes to submit to the kind ministrations of his friend. Then, with renewed vitality, curiosity came to the fore.

"How did you happen to get in on this holdup, Denny?" he asked.

"Holdup? Say, if you don't know a holdup from a smash-up, it's a pity I didn't give you a minute longer before I butted in. You'd have found out all about it by now."

"What do you mean?"

"Lots of folks get held up, in the course of the year, in these quiet side streets, late at night," explained Denny. "And the guys that do the work generally make a get-away a good many jumps ahead of the cops. But they don't work it the way these lads did to-night. It's a come-up from behind, an arm around the neck, or a coat over the head, or a leveled gun; then a quick frisk and a fade; while the mark is still wondering what ran over him."

"But—"

"This was a smash-up party. When holdups find a man will fight—

and can fight—they don't keep on slugging. They move out—if the street's as civilized as this one. No, son. These fellows were out to get *you,* not your cash or your ten-dollar watch and chain that you won at the raffle."

"To kill me?" gasped Arthur, unbelieving.

"No; I guess not as bad as that. They'd 'a' used a knife or even taken a chance with a gun and an automobile skip if they'd wanted to kill you. But they most likely planned to give you a few days' or weeks' rest at a nice hospital, with a few broken bones or maybe a concussed brain or a cracked skull. Murder's too risky; the other way's a lot safer."

"What object could any one have in—"

"In getting you out of the way for a week or two, so that some game could be run off without your butting in?"

"Do you mean—" cried Tiverton.

"I sure do; and then some."

"Nonsense! We're not living in the Middle Ages."

"Of course we ain't. Rubberneck coaches weren't hatched yet in the Middle Ages."

"What have—"

"What have touring New York autos got to do with your being beaten up? They've got this much to do with it."

Denny pulled from his deep inner coat pocket an object from which the remnants of a wad of grimy cotton waste were still trailing.

"I picked this up," said he. "I back-heeled the man who was just going to bounce it off your bean. He dropped it when he fell. I picked it up when we all began our little Marathon with the cop as scratch man."

"It's a monkey wrench."

"It was used as a blackjack. But as we came in I unwound most of the cotton from around it. If they'd wanted to croak you outright, they'd never have bundled it up at all. I took a good look at it as we came up the stairs. This wrench is an old acquaintance of mine. See?"

He pointed to a sort of trade-mark branded into the wood of the handle—a circle with several letters around it.

"That mark's on all the tools in our emergency kit on the benzine buggies that take folks on seeing New York trips," went on Denny. "It's the company's brand. Some one who has the right to go to one of our kits picked this toy for to-night's merry-making."

"Tubbs!"

"Well, it's more likely Tubbs than the Czar of Ireland or the Mayor of Turkey. That is, unless you've been riding around on other cars than mine, giving 'lecturers' reason to be so scared of you that they want to put you out of commission for a while. Have you? If not, we're safe in placing a small bet that it's good old Mister Sam'l Tubbs, esquire. I warned you—"

"Denny," broke in Tiverton, "I haven't thanked you. But I do, from the bottom of my heart. If you hadn't happened to come along just when you did—and I still don't see how you did happen to—I'd have been—"

"Happened, hey? Son, them things don't happen outside of stories and plays. I told you yesterday to look out. I told you it was more dangerous to have folks scared of you than sore on you. You wouldn't listen."

"You were right."

"It's a way I've got. I come around here to see you to-night, after supper—just as you asked me to—to have a North Wilbr'm chat. And—"

"I'm sorry I wasn't home. I—"

"You weren't far from it. As I came up to this house you were just leaving it. And it struck me how dead easy it would be for anybody to knock you in the head from behind. So I trailed along. You went to a hotel. Pretty soon out you came, looking like you'd lost nineteen dollars, and had a toothache to boot. You were so rattled you almost got run over by a dozen taxis. I saw you weren't fit to be left at large. So, just for the fun of it I kept on trailing."

"But why didn't you come up and speak to me?"

"Why should I? You looked about as friendly as a convention of hornets. I kept on. And a nice fool walk you led me. I was for giving it up once or twice. But I got curious, so I didn't quit. At last you hit up the pace, and somehow I lost you. But you seemed to be heading for home here. So I took a chance, and came to Eighty-fifth Street. I got to the corner just in time to see you in the middle of that mix-up. The whole thing couldn't have lasted two minutes. But I kind of wish I'd been two minutes earlier."

"Denny Cross! You spent a whole evening, after a hard day's work, acting as bodyguard to me, to save me from being hurt?"

"Well, if you like to put it that way—You see, we're both from North Wilbr'm, and—"

"Denny, you're white clear down to the ground. I won't try to thank you any more, because I don't know the right words; but I think you know how grateful I am."

"Aw, can it!" muttered Denny. "And after this keep out of mischief. Quit butting in on crooked folks' games."

"I can't. I'm going to see this thing to a finish. I've got to. The fight is only just beginning. Tubbs and the others are nothing more than Devereux's tools. He's the man I've got to fight. It's plain enough now. He must have set some one to follow me, the last time I left the sight-seeing car, for he knows my name and where I live. I found that out this evening. And he set these men to get me to-night. They were waiting for me to come home. It's all clear. And to-morrow—I'll have it out with him."

"Artie," drawled Denny Cross, "you're more kinds of a fool than I thought you were; but you're as many kinds of a man, too!"

Chapter IX.
In the House of the Enemy.

WORK claimed Tiverton until nearly three o'clock the next afternoon; then, as he rose from his desk, a telegram was handed to him. It was from Cyrus Buchanan, and said, with characteristic terseness:

Meet me at office, four p. m.

Tiverton had not expected his employer to return from the West for another three days, and on the strength of that belief he had invited Denny Cross to dine with him that evening. Before he and Denny had parted on the preceding night he had told Denny what he had learned concerning Devereux, omitting only all reference to Miss Wesley, and the chauffeur had been keenly interested.

Now Tiverton would probably have to spend his first evening of Buchanan's return in going over a quantity of piled-up correspondence. His first move was to call up Denny at the touring New York company's stand in Fifth Avenue. He was lucky enough to catch Denny just returning from the two-o'clock downtown trip.

"Too bad," was Cross' comment on his news. "Better luck another evening. But it'll keep you out of mischief, maybe, to have your boss back. Now maybe you'll have to steer clear of Devereux for a while."

"Not exactly," said Tiverton, with a laugh. "I've nearly an hour on my hands before I'm due back here at four o'clock. And I'm going to run over to the Whitelawn Building."

"What for?"

"To have a little friendly talk with R. T. Devereux. I've had it on my mind all day, but I've been too busy until now."

"What the blazes are you going there for?" asked Cross in disgust. "Aren't you content with one beating up?"

"No; I'm still hungry. I'm going to have a settlement with R. T. Devereux, and find out what he means by hiring gorillas to attack me."

"If you've got to be a plumb idiot," grunted Cross, his voice rough and blurred across the telephone, "wait for me. I'm off for the day, and I'll come down and—"

"Thank you, old man. But I haven't time. I'm due back here to meet Mr. Buchanan at four sharp, and he's not the sort to be kept waiting. I've barely time now to get up there in a hurry, and have my settlement with Brother Devereux. Thank you just as much; and good-by."

He forestalled a rising storm of protests from Denny by hanging up the receiver. Ten minutes later he was at the Whitelawn Building. As he walked down the gilt-and-onyx hall of the skyscraper toward the line of elevators, he saw ahead of him a graceful figure in a tailored suit. He recognized Florida Wesley at a glance, even though her back was turned to him. Instinctively he quickened his pace. But before he had lessened by half the distance between them, Miss Wesley had entered an express elevator, and was shot upward in it.

There was no other express ready to start, and Tiverton was forced to take a drearily slow local that stopped at almost every floor between the first and the twelfth; he had ample time to consider the impulse that had prompted him to try to overtake the girl. He remembered her rudeness of the evening before, and his resolve to see no more of her. And at the thought, he was glad he had not caught up with her. He even berated himself for courting the first humiliation at her hands.

Then came reaction and a more worthy thought. He had been wrong in suspecting Florida of any connection with Devereux's swindling schemes. Ever since last night he had realized that a man does not treat his business partner or his confederate with the formal courtesy shown by Devereux toward Miss Wesley in that brief three-cornered interview at the Idler. Her behavior toward him then, and his toward her, had been that of two people whose acquaintanceship is still in the earlier stage. Therefore, Tiverton concluded, her visits to this office were unquestionably on business. What business? She lived up State somewhere. Presumably, as she stopped at the high-priced Idler during her stays in New York, and made daily use of taxicabs, she was a woman of means. Tiverton knew that on the gullibility of well-to-do single women the swindler often thrives.

In a flash the whole matter was clear to Tiverton—Miss Wesley's calls at the office, Devereux's attentions to her, and all. He was "roping" her into one of his swindling schemes; a scheme to rob her of such funds as the crook might cajole her into putting into some wildcat venture or raw fake. At once, on this reflection, Tiverton's mortification and his grievance against Florida Wesley vanished. He forgot the slight she had put upon him. He forgot everything except that an innocent girl whom he cared for was about to become the victim of a cheat; was about to be defrauded perhaps of her livelihood, to fatten the bank account of a thief.

Before his slow-moving car reached the twelfth floor his purpose in going to Devereux's office had shifted. He would leave the settlement of his personal account with Devereux till another time. To-day he would merely demand an interview with Florida, and would tell her of the trap into which she had been lured. To Devereux's face, if need be, he would tell how she was being victimized and defrauded, and what sort of concern "R. T. Devereux & Co." really was. Full of his resolution, he left the elevator, and hastened down the hall, to Suite 1204-1207. Entering the waiting room, he accosted the office boy, who this time chanced to be quite wide awake.

"I want to see Miss Wesley—the lady who just came in here," said he.

The boy eyed him, perplexed; then slouched into a room to the left of the inner reception room—a room marked "Mr. Devereux, Private."

Tiverton judged that the boy had gone to notify his employer; and as he preferred to see Florida in person before Devereux could interfere, he took a step toward the reception room. As he did so, the boy issued from the private office.

"Miss Wesley's in there," he said, his thumb over his shoulder in the office's direction. He resumed his seat at the desk.

Tiverton crossed to the private office, and, as the boy had left its door ajar, entered without knocking. The room had but one occupant. Devereux was standing in the middle of it, visibly flustered.

"What do you want?" he demanded nervously.

"I want to speak with Miss Wesley," replied Tiverton; "at another time with you, but just now with her. The boy said she was in here."

"I told him to say so," said Devereux, glancing guiltily over his shoulder to the closed door of what was evidently an inner room, and lowering his voice a little. "What do you want of her?"

"That is my affair. Please tell her that—"

"Not so loud!" muttered Devereux, with another scared glance at the door of the inner room. "She—she isn't here."

"She is!" contradicted Tiverton, advancing. "She is in that room behind you. Let me go in there, or—"

"This is my office," weakly blustered Devereux, hurriedly backing against the door of the room toward which his guilty, furtive glances had been straying. "Get out of here! Miss Wesley is not—"

Tiverton did not let him finish the sentence. His own time was short. He was not minded to waste any of it in arguing with a man who, he was convinced, was lying to him.

"She is in that room behind you!" he declared. "Move aside and let me get in there."

"No!" expostulated Devereux, still guarding the door with his body. "I tell you there's no one in that room. You'll enter it at your peril. I—"

He got no further. Arthur's out-flung hand caught him by the chest, gripping both lapels of his coat at their juncture, and, with one swift wrench, threw him aside, clearing the door of the living obstacle that had stood trembling before it. Without waiting to see if Devereux would retaliate or even defend himself, Tiverton, in almost the same move, snatched open the heavy wooden door and sprang into the room. Before he could turn the door was slammed shut behind him. He heard the rattle of a lock, then the click of a bolt. At the same instant he realized that there was no one in the room but himself. He was locked in; as neatly caught as was ever hare in a poacher's trap.

Chapter X.
A Call for Nerve.

TIVERTON stood stock-still a moment, staring about him, taking stock of his position and his surroundings. He was in one of those "inside rooms" common to many office suites—rooms usually devoted to storage or to files. There was but one window—about two feet square, and at a height of five feet from the concrete floor.

The only door was that through which he had passed. It had no ground-glass upper half; it was massive, thick-paneled, of a type that probably would withstand the assault of two or three men.

Tiverton understood on the instant the simple trick that had been played on him; and he was philosopher enough to smile grimly at thought of the ease wherewith he had succumbed to Devereux's ruse. Had his mind not been full of Florida Wesley and of his plans to save her from being swindled, he knew he must have detected at once the false note in the man's manner, and have known that so cool and practiced a sharper would not cringe and betray weak nervousness as Devereux had pretended to. He was trapped, and he felt that nothing was to be gained by fuming or fretting or by useless repining.

The next move was to get out. Wrapping his handkerchief round his right hand's knuckles for protection, he drew back his arm, and, putting his shoulder and every atom of his strength and weight behind the blow, he smote one of the long upper panels of the door. The net result of this move was to numb his right arm to the elbow. Next, taking as careful aim as if on the football field, he swung back his right leg, braced himself, and kicked with all his might at the short bottom panel. The impact of the kick resounded through the little room, but the door held as firm as the eternal hills. He had heard a bolt, as well as a key, when the door was fastened behind him by Devereux. Hence he knew nothing was to be gained through trying to snap the lock by the old device of driving his heel at the keyhole.

He stood moveless, trying to work out the next step. He was puzzled not only as to how he should get out, but why he had been locked in. He remembered Denny Cross and the attack uptown, and knew that this latest action of Devereux was only another move in that rascal's game.

His eye was attracted to a slip of paper that lay under the door just across the threshold. He had not noticed it thrust there. And he was very certain it had not been there when he came into the room.

"Must have been shoved under while I was too busy hammering the door to notice it," he decided.

It was a folded scrap of note paper with a "Devereux & Co." head. On it this was hastily scrawled in pencil:

> Don't be fool enough to try knocking the door down. You can't. If you'll behave yourself I'll send in a couple of hours or so to let you out.

There was no signature; the note needed none. But its contents served to increase tenfold Tiverton's bewilderment. But with a shrug of the shoulders, he gave up the riddle, and prepared to wait with what patience he might, since waiting was apparently the one thing left for him to do. Nothing was to be gained by losing his head or going into paroxysms of rage.

It occurred to him to shout, but he dismissed the thought. His voice probably would penetrate to the outer office of the suite, but scarcely to the main corridor beyond; and the man who had locked him in was not likely to permit any subordinate in the suite to let him out.

There was not a stick of furniture of any description in the little cubbyhole of a room. But the window sill was rather deep. The prisoner drew himself up to it, and looked out on the chance of attracting by his gestures somebody in one of the windows of the opposite building. But he found there was no "opposite building"; at least that the building just across the street from the Whitelawn was several stories lower, and that none of its windows commanded a view of his.

He opened the sliding window and looked out. The report of a cannon, much less a human voice, at that height, could not have penetrated the roar of lower Broadway. He dropped back to the floor and stood there.

"It's checkmate," he admitted to himself. "I lose."

He walked back and forth to relieve the tedium of standing. Then he read over the letters in his pockets. After which he went to the door and called:

"Devereux!"

There was no answer. No sound came from the adjoining "private office." He remembered Buchanan's injunction to him to be at the financier's office promptly at four, and looked at his watch. The time now was four-five. He recalled Buchanan's intolerance of a tardy employee. There would be a scene. But at the moment this bothered him little. For, if ever man had a legitimate excuse for lateness, he assuredly was the man. He found two more letters in an inner pocket, and destroyed a little more time in their dry perusal.

Then a new reflection came to him. And with it fled his philosophic calm. While he was standing there inert, Florida Wesley was perhaps being cheated of her money. He had come thither, post haste, to warn her. And he was doing nothing.

He went again to the window, drew himself up into its open casement, and looked out once more. The coping outside was perhaps eighteen inches in width. It was of corrugated stucco, sloped slightly downward, to shed rain. The sight gave Tiverton a thrill of inspiration. Wriggling his shoulders obliquely through the narrow window until half his body was outside, he looked to right and to left.

The coping apparently ran the whole length of the building. The nearest window to his own was perhaps fifteen feet to the left of him. And that window, he calculated, spelled escape. He crawled wholly out, so that he sat in the open window of his cell, his feet resting on the coping. He looked down. Two hundred feet below Broadway hummed and throbbed. Its scurrying pedestrians were little black beetles; its automobiles were rushing blurs; its trolley cars small rhomboids of motion. The sense of great height and its accompanying dizziness came over Tiverton. He shook off the feeling.

"I could walk for miles on an eighteen inch plank laid on the ground," he told himself, "even if the plank sloped a little, as this coping does. I could walk it forever, and not once lose my balance. Any one could. Well, there's not an atom of difference between walking a plank on the ground and a coping two hundred feet in the air. It's all in the imagination. It's a question of nerve and of simple pluck."

He slowly brought himself to a standing posture on the ledge. Then, shutting out from his mind all thought of the sheer and awful drop to one side, and the two hundred feet of empty air that lay between him and the street below, he began to work toward the window that was his destination.

A stiff breeze was blowing at that height, and it tugged at him as with sentient fingers, seeking to destroy his doggedly maintained balance. With tight lips he choked back the unreasoning dread which so often attacks even the coolest man at such a dizzy elevation. He leaned inward against the wall, and in six steps he was at the window. He fumbled with the lower sash's thin top line.

Chapter XI.
In the Sound-Proof Booth.

AS usual, in upper stories of office buildings, the window was unlocked. It yielded to his upward pressure. He raised it an inch; then, stooping, put his fingers under the bottom of the sash and lifted it far enough to admit himself. He worked swiftly, lest any one within should seek to bar him from entering. In ten seconds from the time he reached the window he had stepped down into the room it lighted. It was empty. Also it was totally unfurnished, as had been his temporary prison. This struck Tiverton as strange. That two rooms in a single suite should be allowed to go to waste, where room rents were proverbially high, was incomprehensible. A smaller suite would have saved Devereux much money, and apparently would have served his purpose quite as well.

The only break in the four walls' blank space—except for a door—

was made by a sound-proof telephone booth. This Tiverton supposed was a relic of some broker or bucket shop's occupancy of the suite. But a second glance showed him a telephone directory hanging on a nail outside the booth. The book's date was that of the current month.

"Why does Devereux do his telephoning in an unfurnished room instead of using the phone at his office desk?" wondered Tiverton.

Then a second oddity came to his notice. On the rather dusty floor were several darker squares and oblongs. He had seen newly vacated offices before, and knew the marks left on parts of floors whence desks, tables, and rugs have just been removed, and when the room has not yet been swept since such removal.

"He's planning a get-away!" Tiverton told himself. "He's moving out his furniture room by room. The suite most likely is an empty shell by now, with just an office or two left furnished to fool customers."

He started for the door, tried it, and found it locked. This door, like the one of his cell, was of solid wood instead of having a glass upper half. Tiverton knew by recent experience the folly of trying to force such a structure.

He turned hastily to the telephone booth, whose door stood wide. As he crossed the room he was aware for the first time of the murmur of talking voices. He located the sound as coming through a thin partition wall to the right of the room in which he was now locked. Entering the booth, he closed the door behind him, and reached for the receiver. As he touched it, and before he could lift it from the hook, the telephone bell rang. He hesitated, then lifted the receiver, and said:

"Hello!"

"That you, Rolf?" came a somewhat excited voice from the other end of the line.

Tiverton puzzled for a fraction of a second. Then he recalled that among the decoy envelopes he had seen on the reception-room desk the day of his former visit to the office was one addressed to "Cyrus Q. Buchanan, or Rolf T. Devereux."

"No," he answered, anxious to use the telephone himself. "He's busy. Hang up, please."

"I've got to speak to him," came the excited voice. "Tell him to drop everything and jump to the phone."

"If you want him in such a hurry," said Arthur, resolved not to lose his chance of using the wire, and noting that the number on the instrument did not bear a party letter, "why don't you call him up on his other phone?"

"He told me not to trust the switchboard for private business; you know that, if you're with him," was the retort. "He keeps this number for such calls."

"I'll tell him you want to speak to him," drawled Tiverton lazily. "Who shall I say?"

"Belden. Henry Belden. Quick!"

Tiverton set down the receiver. It occurred to him that a little delay in arranging his own escape might be used to good purpose. He counted twenty, then lifted the receiver again. With as near an imitation as he could give of the marked rasp in Devereux's voice, and speaking low and hurriedly, as if in perturbation, he called:

"Hello, Harry! What's wrong?"

"You sound as though things weren't oversmooth at your own end," was the answer. "Listen, Rolf! Don't fail on the clean-up this afternoon. And rush it. We're smashed if you don't. Buchanan got back to town half an hour ago two days ahead of time. Rush things! If he ever gets wind of—"

Tiverton drew in his breath sharply between his teeth, as if in dire consternation—a conservative noise, and one that saved the need of verbal reply.

"I didn't get the tip till a minute ago," went on the speaker, "and I've let you know as soon as I could. I won't keep you. Chase back to the meeting. I suppose it's in full blast now, isn't it? I judge from your voice you're het up over it. Keep cool. It's a sure thing. And *rush!*"

With a grunt that might have expressed to his hearer almost anything except its utterer's identity, Tiverton hung up the receiver. Then, a few seconds later, giving the wire time to be cleared, he took it down again and called up Cyrus O. Buchanan's private office. His employer answered him. In a dozen quick sentences Tiverton outlined the situation, and his own plight. To his wonder, the mining king showed no surprise, but said calmly:

"Stay where you are till I come."

Tiverton left the phone booth, closing its door lest some new summons of the bell reach the next room. Then he went to the partition and stood there. For fifteen minutes he stood thus, two-thirds of the speech on its far side plainly audible to him.

Then a faint rattling noise caused him to turn. He looked around in time to see the door swing slowly open. On the threshold stood the burly, rugged figure of Mr. Buchanan. Tiverton was about to speak to his employer, but the latter, with a warning gesture, checked him and beckoned. Marveling, Arthur followed the mining king into the waiting room that opened into the main corridor, and out of the room in which Tiverton had been standing.

At he corner desk sat the office boy, vastly cowed and wide-eyed. Over him, a menacing sentry, stood Denny Cross. Buchanan held a bunch of office keys, with one of which he had evidently just unlocked the door of Tiverton's room. The turned-out pocket of the scared boy hinted how the keys had been obtained.

Chapter XII.
The Booby Trap.

"DENNY!" exclaimed Tiverton, scarcely above a whisper, in deference to Buchanan's wordless warning. "Glad to see you. But what the dickens you doing here?"

"Butting in," cheerily replied the chauffeur. "I got worried about you, Art, so I took a run down to your office. You didn't show up at four, so I got a message in to Mr. Buchanan. Just then you phoned him, and he let me come along. There's others coming, too," he went on, with a delightful air of mystery. "He phoned 'em, too, but he wouldn't wait for 'em. So—"

"Come on, Tiverton," interrupted Buchanan. "From the voices I suppose they're in there?"

He nodded toward the door of the reception room, and added: "Cross, stay here and keep that boy from giving the alarm. Let in the others when they come, and get rid of any chance callers."

"Sure," said Denny, with a grin. "I'm one of your dandiest little doorkeepers; but I never thought I'd get a chance to hold down the job even for five minutes under the direct orders of Cyrus Q. Buchanan."

"Come to my office to-morrow," said Mr. Buchanan, with a grim smile at the pleasantry, "and I'll give you a better job. I like your type of man. Come along, Tiverton."

"One moment, sir," said Arthur. "While I was waiting for you I heard enough through the partition to give me the hang of the game, I think. It is the same old trick—using a big man's name to lure a group of rural investors into getting in on the ground floor of a company that doesn't exist, taking up shares, and paying outright for them. Devereux is holding the subscription meeting in there now. He'll cash a dozen big checks to-morrow when the banks open; and an hour later he'll be hard to find."

"I think you're wrong," said Mr. Buchanan. "He'll be one of the easiest men in New York to find. The Tombs' ledger will be the only directory any one will need to consult for his address. Come!"

He walked to the reception-room door, opened it quietly, and walked in, Tiverton at his heels. The spring on the door closed it behind them.

Twelve or fifteen persons were seated in the room facing the desk at which sat Devereux. Among them were Florida Wesley—the only woman present—and the men whom Tiverton had seen as Devereux's fellow passengers on the two trips aboard the sightseeing automobile. The others were of a like type—men whose looks bespoke prosperity, and whose bearing and mode of dress spoke rather of the village than of the city.

Devereux was speaking as the two newcomers entered. For the moment he did not see them, as he was facing obliquely away from the door.

"That, I think, is all," he was saying. "As I said, I am sorry Mr. Buchanan is detained in the West longer than he expected to be, and cannot keep his appointment to attend our meeting. But as his letter, that I've just read, tells us, it is on *our* business that he is there, and to clinch the consolidation that will nearly treble the value of our stock. And now," producing a packet, a typewritten list, and a fountain pen, "though it is a trifle informal, perhaps, I will receive your checks and issue the shares. Make them out to R. T. Devereux & Co., please. Not to me or to Mr. Buchanan. We—"

"Why not to Mr. Buchanan?" cut in the mine king. "I like to get all the easy money I can."

Every one turned. The up Staters frowned heavily at the intrusion. Florida Wesley started to her feet. Devereux sat moveless, tense, his eyes riveted on the newcomers. His face did not change a muscle. His self-control was superb.

"My old friend, Rolf Devereux," purred Buchanan. "How are you? Still under your own name, I see? Well, that's one point in your favor, and, I'm afraid, the only one. We haven't met, I think, since I had to discharge you six years ago for taking a more than neighborly interest in our customers' accounts."

Devereux made no reply. The herd of sheep, ripe for the shearing, looked from him to Buchanan, and back again in bewilderment.

"And now, it seems," went on Buchanan genially, "we're re-partners, you and I, in a mining deal, eh? And I'm just in time to get my share of the profits in a mine commodiously situated on a fake map? Fine! But best of all is that touch of yours in having a sight-seeing auto lecturer announce to your clients that my office is here instead of in the Cogghall Building. That was a real stroke of genius, my friend. Genius! For no out-of-towner would doubt the announcement of a public servant like a seeing New York lecturer. *He* couldn't possibly be in on the plot. You couldn't safely put my name on your door or on the directory board; but a rubberneck-coach announcer served quite as well. And it clinched these people's belief in you. So you gave them free rides, and the lecturer gave them false information—and in return they were going to give you good money. Well played!"

"Who is this man?" angrily demanded a fat country banker with a short, gray chin beard. "What is he driving at?"

"He's trying to explain," said Buchanan, laughing, "that Mr. Devereux is going to start in a few minutes for jail."

"You are mistaken," said Devereux coolly. "I must be caught before I can be jailed; and I've a fair start. Clear a way there, please." He drew from a desk drawer a blue-barreled revolver, and, swinging to his feet, raised it. "Clear the way to the door!" he commanded.

Two investors dived under chairs. A third yelled "Police!"

"Drop that just where you are, Mr. Devereux," said Florida Wesley, who stood a little to one side of the swindler. "Drop it, and don't shift your aim this way. If you do I'll get you first."

Her voice was sweet and low-pitched. Yet as Devereux involuntarily shifted his gaze in her direction he let the weapon fall from his hand. Miss Wesley had taken unobtrusively from a hand bag at her wrist a small but very businesslike automatic pistol; and its muzzle was in an uncomfortably direct line with Devereux's head.

In her big eyes there was a quiet intensity of meaning that no one could mistake. Wherefore Devereux, whose own revolver muzzle was not leveled in her direction, but on those who had stood between him and the door, thought it wise to obey her modest request. He stood disarmed, helpless, staring at her.

"Miss Wesley!" he gasped, his monumental calm for once utterly deserting him.

"Yes," she said, lowering her weapon, but still keeping him covered. "Miss Wesley—the girl from Cazenovia, Madison County, who came into her property last month, when she was twenty-one, and wrote a letter of inquiry about one of your circulars she chanced to see. Stand still, please, Mr. Devereux. Mr. Tiverton, may I trouble you to telephone for me to—"

"Miss Wesley!" again gasped Devereux incredulously.

"Of the United States secret service—and incidentally at your own," acknowledged the girl. "We have been at work over your doubtful use of the mails for some months, Mr. Devereux. And I think at last I have made the case complete. You would have been arrested by my associates anyway, as you left the building. But as they weren't to arrive for half an hour yet, I'll ask Mr. Tiverton to telephone to—"

"It isn't necessary," put in Mr. Buchanan, indicating two men that Denny Cross was ushering into the room. "Here are a couple of men I've had on this case. I phoned for them to come here just before I started. It is odd we both planned to make the arrest to-day, Miss Wesley, for to-morrow would have been too late. I judge so from the fact that Devereux locked up this secretary of mine, whom he seems to have taken for a secret-service man, and whom he wanted to keep from bringing down the law on him until he could get clear with the checks. There's your man, officers."

"Yes," said Miss Wesley to Tiverton, on their way uptown, "I did think you were one of his confederates, when I found you knew where

I lived; and I tested the belief by seeing what you'd do when I broke an appointment with you and went to the theater with him. But your face when I accepted his invitation told me how wretchedly mistaken I'd been. And, oh, I was so sorry!"

"But this evening I may call?" said Tiverton.

"This evening," she assented.

"And other evenings?"

"It is quite likely," said Miss Wesley, and they both laughed.

Cephas the Paladin

CEPHAS was his name. He was a pig. But he was, none the less, a paladin. A porcine St. George when fate at last sounded the call for his great adventure.

Byram owned him. Byram was the man who had mortgaged his up-State farm to buy a half share in the "Trip to Mars" concession at the Pan-Universal Exposition.

Most expositions, or world's fairs, are financial failures. But most of their side-show attractions make money. And—thanks to Cephas—the Trip to Mars was one of these money-makers. Through its gingerbread-gilt gateway on the Street of a Thousand Laughs trickled a goodly stream of sight-seers, and of dimes, throughout that long, hot summer.

Byram, exiled for the season from his beloved farm in order to make ten times as much money at the exposition, was acting as his own ballyhoo man to draw trade to the Trip to Mars. And on the third day of the season his raucous cries of "Greatest, most *ree*-fined, most side-splitting show of the century," were suddenly punctuated by a squeal that split the looser volume of his clamor as a sword blade might cleave past-worthy melon.

And at that imperative insult to the eardrum, full a thousand hurrying, babbling people stopped and, for a flash of time, were silent. The sound had wafted Byram momentarily back to his farm. It carried the memory of many another listener to a similar starting point.

Byram sought to locate the cause, and at a glance he found it. Down the narrow Street of a Thousand Laughs rumbled a big market wagon, taking this short cut to the heart of the city. The wagon was loaded high with crated poultry, calves, and pigs.

An insecurely fastened crate at the very back of the pile had shaken loose, and had fallen to the ground, where, from the tumble, it promptly disintegrated. Its late occupant stood free, dazed, indignant, in the middle of the thronged street; giving forth squeal after squeal, that filled the whole walled space with a series of shrill and unlovely echoes.

The vocalist was a very small, very thin, very youthful pig. For scarce a month of time at most could he have been on earth. And during that brief month he had apparently cultivated his voice at the expense of his anatomy. For, seldom has so much leanness been seen in conjunction with so much youth. Indeed, only the most optimistic of farmers could have hoped to sell such a rawboned and stunted baby porker at any market.

The wagon vanished around a corner, leaving the baby pig stranded and deserted; a bit of noisy jetsam on the shores of the Street of a Thousand Laughs. Byram gazed. So did every one. And a Homeric guffaw arose. The Street was for once living up to its name. The piglet retorted with an ear-racking squeal.

A long-legged, rangy dog dashed from the crowd and charged the waif. The baby pig, no whit daunted, wheeled to meet the charge. Yes, to meet it halfway. His pink lips drawn back over tiny, white milk tusks, his scant spine hairs a-bristle, his vocal cords throbbing with a long-drawn squeal of glad challenge, the pig scampered toward his thrice-larger foe.

Whereat, the dog, which was of many breeds, checked its attack in mid-course, tucked a grubby tail between its flanks, and wheeled in flight; turning piggy's solo squeals into close harmony by the addition of a long, fear-stricken howl.

The baby paused, blinking his nearsighted little red-rimmed eyes in search of his flying foe. And at that moment Byram was mastered by one of the inspirations that had lifted him at thirty from farm hand to rising showman.

He strode forth and snatched up the valiant little porker. The latter seemed to know from the way he was handled that Byram was accustomed to pigs. So, unresisting, he allowed himself to be tucked under the man's arm and carried into the cubby-hole office of the Trip to

Mars building.

A boy was sent on the run for a half-gallon can of buttermilk, and with further orders to hunt up the market man from whose wagon the pig had been jolted, and to pay him two dollars for the attenuated prize. Just then Byram's partner, Bud Crane, happened in.

"We aren't showing freaks," was Bud's comment, at sight of the Little Stranger. "What good is a living skeleton to us?"

"But we're selling the dear public," gently corrected Byram. "And I've just bought for two dollars the best barker on the Street. I'm going to tie this pig to a six-foot cord alongside of my ballyhoo bench outside there. His squeals will make every mother's son in earshot stop and listen to me."

But Crane was dubious. Byram expounded his theory of the farm memory that lurks in the back of every one's brain. And he told how the crowd had waxed silent, and had turned, as one man, at piggy's unrehearsed recital.

"But won't the S. P. C. A. butt-ins get after us?" objected Bud, "for—for torturing a dumb animal—or something?"

"This animal's worst enemy couldn't call him dumb," retorted Byram. "And, besides, nobody's going to torture him."

"Then how'll we make him squeal?"

"We'd have harder work to stop him. A pig of that age and breed squeals every few seconds, anyway. Just as he's doing now. He'll be a dandy card. Folks'll get talking about it, too. And then—"

"All right," conceded Bud comfortably. "And say! I've got a corking idea for a name for him. 'Spareribs!' How's that? Look at his sides. You see, he's—"

"His name," coldly decided Byram, "is Cephas."

"Cephas?" echoed Crane, in blank wonder. "Why Cephas?"

"Why *not* Cephas?"

This argument could not be parried. It could only be ignored. Crane protested feebly:

"It's a fool name."

"It's my father-in-law's name," rebuked Byram, with icy dignity.

"Oh, I see. The old man's the one who's got the mortgage on your farm, isn't he? I remember. All right. Let it go at Cephas.'"

And Cephas it was; thenceforth and for the season.

Through the torrid, sticky summer, Byram, from his ballyhoo bench, extolled the marvels of a Trip to Mars. From noon to midnight he added his ever-hoarsening shouts of praise to the clamor of the Street of a Thousand Laughs.

And on the sidewalk beside Byram, every week day, from noon to midnight, stood, or sprawled, or trotted Cephas; ever and anon lifting to high heaven a squeal or a succession of squeals that tore the busily humming summer air into shreds.

Never did Cephas squeal without drawing as much attention as did all the Street's human barkers combined. City folk would jump in amaze and turn to see whence emanated the fearsome sound. Memories awoke in most passers-by, and curiosity in all. And the Trip to Mars speedily became the best-advertised show at the exposition.

Cephas, with a brazen collar about his brazen throat, and a long brass chain connecting him with Byram's bench leg, went through the business of the day with undying spirit.

Sometimes he would pace or gallop from one end of his tether to the other; shrieking in drawn-out fervor at every step. Again he would stand and survey the passing hundreds with the impersonally curious eye of a philosopher, squealing only occasionally and in a dispassionate tone, as one with a dull but needful duty to perform. When rain pelted heavily, or the August sun fell like a fiery scourge on the cement pavement, Cephas would lie at ease in the sparse shadows under the bench, squealing with a somnolent but racking dreaminess.

Thanks to the new ballyhoo, the Trip to Mars did unparalleled business. It drew quarters when equally meritorious shows drew nickels. It paid the mortgage off Byram's farm, and started a plump little bank account for him. It earned for Bud Crane a pale-yellow diamond, with crinkly depths and of unbelievable area.

Cephas toiled on; sleeping in the mornings to an hour that would have brought a flush of shame to his farm ancestors; and sitting up till every other pig in America had finished half its night's sleep. He ate in large quantities and at frequent intervals. Beyond his regular diet, there were many and heterogeneous contributions—ranging from apple cores to crack-jack—from passing admirers. And his physical exercise was limited and spasmodic. Yet he gained no flesh. Perhaps nature did not intend that he should. Perhaps squealing for a livelihood twelve hours a day on a crowded, hot, ill-savored cement pavement, and sitting up until midnight do not tend to put flesh on little pigs. In any case, Cephas remained svelte; not to say bony. And his general size increased so imperceptibly that he was scarce three inches longer, or an inch taller, in September than he had been in June.

Cephas' lack of growth, and his perpetual thinness, worried Byram. Yet he could see nothing amiss with the squealer's appetite or general health. He had grown genuinely fond of the queer little fellow during their months of jointly haranguing the multitudes. And Cephas reciprocated the man's affection.

Cephas was not demonstrative. But on such rare intervals as he was loose he would always seek out Byram and trot gravely at his heels, or lie curled in an angular bunch at his feet. Bud Crane the pig openly and throatily disliked. And Bud regarded Cephas merely as an unlovely, but paying, adjunct to the show.

Strewn through the summer there were several happenings to lighten the monotony of Cephas' life. Once, for example, he was stolen. And his squeals of wrath furnished a running clew to his negro captor's movements, until Byram and a patrolman could overhaul the fugitive in the crowd.

Again, the shed wherein Cephas slept, at the back of the Trip to Mars building, took fire just before dawn one day. And the flame-defying squeals of fearless Cephas awakened Byram and other sleepers barely in time to save the pig's bacon from more than a superficial, if painful, scorching; as well as to save the building, and probably the entire flimsy Street of a Thousand Laughs.

An exposition newspaper published a story of the scant-averted holocaust; heading it, "PIG TURNS IN A SQUEAL ALARM," and running a picture of Cephas, the hero of the account. (Cephas never having been photographed, a "stock cut" of a prize Berkshire boar was printed as substitute.)

Then, dog fights were matters of such frequency that they hardly called for comment. It was a favorite amusement for the Street's youthful hangers-on to catch some large or small stray cur, haul him to the space in front of the Trip to Mars, and then gleefully "sick him onto" Cephas.

The baby pig met all canine comers. Yes, met and routed them.

Such few dogs as withstood his first indignant rush found his teeth amazingly sharp, and his skin incredibly tough. And the assailants seldom wasted time over the useless combat; but withdrew as early in the action as they could tear themselves free.

Thus—fighting, squealing, half baking, singed, stolen, stared at, the butt of inextinguishable laughter—Cephas wore out the red summer and shrilled a gallant greeting to the purple-and-gold autumn.

The exposition was at its last gasp. The Street of a Thousand Laughs prepared to put up the shutters. The crowds had dwindled. Summer and shows were past; winter and work were at hand.

Byram and Crane on the first of October, counted up their comfortable profits, divided a good sum of money, and rejoiced. Byram next day was going back to his worshiped farm, to make ready for a record agricultural year, wherein labor should for once be reënforced by capital. Crane, buying out his partner's interest in the Trip to Mars, prepared to take the show to New Orleans for the winter.

Byram went over to the Agriculture Building, on the Street's last day, to buy some farm implements at end-of-season rates. Crane was packing some of the Trip's paraphernalia. Cephas, his position now a sinecure, was snoring shrilly under the vacated ballyhoo bench. The show was closed.

Then it was that Ophido, the Cobra King, from the Hindu Village across the Street, honored Mr. Bud Crane with a morning call; Ophido, in private life, bore the more reasonable cognomen of Murtha. And Bud had known him in the olden years before ever Ophido was a Hindu. The Cobra King's visit was of a business nature. His star python, Brahma—second largest of its species in captivity—was ready to be fed. Brahma, python fashion, ate but once in seven or eight months. And he always evinced his periodic desire for food by an increased liveliness. Such liveliness, Ophido told Crane, had now obsessed Brahma. Nor would the reptile quiet down sufficiently for transportation, or for safe handling in public, until hunger should have been appeased, and sweet reflection should bring back the snake's wonted laziness.

Pythons, Ophido prattled on carelessly, will eat nothing but live food. A half dozen kicking rabbits, a month-old kid whose horns have not yet sprouted, a lamb, or even a small dog, will serve amply for the semiyearly banquet. Or—here Ophido coughed discreetly—at a pinch a young pig might do.

Crane pricked up his ears. Ophido dropped glittering generalities and went further into details.

"Business is dead," he explained. "Here's the last day; and the only way we could get a handful of boobs into the Village was by advertising that Brahma's to be fed. Now, that squealing pig of yours is pretty well known about here. If I could send word around the Street that he's the dinner picked out for Brahma, it ought to draw a whole bunch of folks. Get the idea?"

"Yes," said Crane doubtfully.

"The feeding's advertised for an hour from now," went on Ophido, "and I could get the news around before then. How about it?"

"No," decided Crane, after a moment's wistful thought—during which he covertly surveyed a half-healed scar on his thumb, the imprint of Cephas' tusks on an occasion when Bud had tried to slap the pig into louder squeals. "No. It won't do. Byram would never stand for it. He's fond of the measly little cuss."

"I thought you'd bought out Byram."

"I have."

"Then the pig's yours. He's part of the show, isn't he?"

"Why, I s'pose that's so," admitted Crane, hope dawning in his voice. "But," he added, "Byram would raise an awful kick just the same."

"Afraid of him. I see."

"No," glumly denied Crane, "I ain't afraid of anybody. Besides, he's away for the morning. And the pig's no use to me down South. He'd cost more to transport than he's worth. What'll you gimme for him?"

After some slight dicker, five dollars and Cephas changed hands. And Ophido-Murtha, the Cobra King, departed for his Hindu Village, bearing with him the indignantly protesting Cephas.

"'Twon't hurt him? Not so very much?" queried the conscious-twinged Crane, as he escorted his guest across the Street.

"Not a bit!" Ophido assured him. "When a python looks at the critters that's put in his cage, they just get paralyzed, all at once, with fear. Kind of hypnotized. And they don't move a muscle, but only crouch there, with their eyes popping while he gets 'em ready to eat.

It's a painless death. The S. P. C. A. folks themselves says so. Some of 'em."

An hour later the Serpent House of the Hindu Village was full to overcrowding with eagerly morbid sightseers, who had paid double rates for the dual privilege of seeing Brahma feed and Cephas die.

"Ladies'n gentlemen," began the hirsute lecturer, mounting a box beside a glass-faced cage that filled one end of the narrow hall, "you will now be treated to one of the most instructive sights in the fascinatin' domain of Ophidian natural history. Brahma, the mammoth python, second largest snake in captivity, will proceed to break his eight-month fast, before your very eyes, by devouring a large and livin' pig. Please keep as quiet as you can, ladies'n gentlemen, until this wonderful exhibition is over. For pythons is very dainty about their eatin'. And if they're disturbed or distracted, why, they won't eat at all. Ready, Mr. Ophido?"

Ophido advanced from behind a screen, carrying at arm's length between his hands the struggling Cephas, whose presence had been audible throughout the entire brief "lecture." The Cobra King went to the rear of the cage; an attendant with him. The audience sat mute; every eye glued to the interior of the glass-fronted inclosure.

There, on the floor, before a painted backdrop supposedly depicting an India jungle at sunrise, moved something—enormous, sinuous, hideously beautiful. Fold on fold the python had assembled together his squirming length; the satin pattern of red-brown and black widening, as the body expanded in process of coiling, to the girth of a human thigh. Then, untangling his massed convolutions, Brahma flattened out to almost the full depth of the huge cage; and glided restlessly from end to end, from corner to corner of it; running his head and neck man-high along the slimy surface of the glass.

Nothing short of famine or intense pain could rouse a captive snake to such unwonted activity. Clearly, Brahma was hungry. He could not stay quiet. His habitual dead-and-alive lethargy was shed like last year's skin. He nosed in corners; and, coiling himself once more, gazed at the spectators in expressionless malignity from lidless bead eyes set in a triangular head as large as a dog's.

Uncoiling again into a thick, sinuous bar, he recommenced his undulating tour of the cage. Suddenly he halted, slithering to one side of the inclosure, and raising his three-cornered head as though in preparation for attack.

At the same instant a panel in the back of the cage was shot open, and then shut. In the momentary interval the gaping spectators caught a glimpse of two hands that tossed an object through the aperture.

And Cephas stood in the cage's cleared central space.

The pig's little white-lashed eyes blinked with a fleeting look of bewilderment—none who knew him could call it fear—at his strange surroundings. He gazed beyond the sheet of glass, and beheld the staring audience. Professional instincts seemed to tell him that here was a show of some kind, and that it was incumbent upon him to squeal.

The pink mouth opened for a vocal effort. Then, evidently, a swift, rustling sound distracted his attention, and showed him he was not the cage's only occupant. He wheeled abruptly. And Brahma came into his blinking line of vision.

The python, at sight of his prey, had coiled tight, and was now thrusting forth and drawing back his three-sided head, almost on a level with the floor; to gauge the distance for a strike.

"Yes, ladies'n' gentlemen," the lecturer had resumed in a carefully subdued voice, "the first glance from the python's mysterious hypnotic eye charms the trembling prey into a sort of stoopor. And—"

He got no further. Just then Brahma, having satisfactorily measured the distance, struck, flashing forward his head and ten feet of his mighty length with a speed that the eye could not follow.

At that juncture, Cephas had caught for the first time a full and comprehensive view of his horrible cagemate.

The python struck. But Cephas was not there. With a squeal whose shrill fury paled all his life's former attempts at song or at displeasure, the pig sprang forward to meet the assault.

Yes, and he launched himself into the fray a fraction of a second sooner than did Brahma. High in air leaped Cephas, above the swift-darting triangular head.

And down he came, all four pointed trotters bunched together on the neck scales of his adversary. His sharp little white tusks promptly buried themselves to their entire short length in the flesh at the very base of Brahma's skull.

With one convulsive start the giant snake upreared; until his head, and the neck in whose nape Cephas' teeth were sunk, smote resound-ingly against the cage roof.

The impact was terrific. It shook the cage like a miniature earth-quake. But it did not shake loose the hold of Cephas.

Dearly, no doubt, would the pig have loved to exhaust in a battle squeal such little breath as the blow against the roof had left him. But, to squeal, a pig must open wide his jaws. And Cephas' long, narrow jaws were otherwise engaged. So, in his hour of mortal stress, this one beloved expression of emotion was denied. He must fight without the inspiring thrill of music.

The python dashed himself against the painted walls and the floor, striving in growing panic to shake free and to strike. Each smashing beat of the flail head and neck seemed more than enough to flatten Cephas into shapelessness.

But he was a hard, gristly little fellow, this sacrificed pig; as resilient as a rubber ball, and bothered by no easily crushed flesh. Also, he had the heart of a paladin: zealous, flamboyant, unafraid. D'Artagnan's, at the Gascon's glowing best; even if swathed in porcine skin.

Finding the puny foe refused to die, the python resorted to the constrictor tactics of his race. Around the bristling, tense body of the pig he swept his giant folds.

Coil upon coil Brahma cast around his enemy; hampered vastly, it is true, by the fact that Cephas was behind, instead of in front, of him; but none the less managing to secure a fairly close grip on the tiny hero. Then the python proceeded to "constrict."

Had Brahma been able to coil himself in his customary way, around the pig, the end might have come quickly. But Cephas' posi-tion made this impracticable. So the python merely held such hold as he had caught.

Ophido, and the lecturer, and the attendants, and every one else remained almost as moveless as the combatants; powerless to shake off the primitive spell of battle.

That was the situation when Byram—a rumor of the intended slaughter spectacle having reached him in the distant Agriculture Building—elbowed his way into the hall.

Byram was as dangerously angry as only an even-tempered man may become. He was yellow-white, and there were gray dents on either sides of a mouth that was clenched as tight shut as Cephas' own.

He went through the packed crowd without causing the remotest inconvenience—to himself—and made straight for the glass-fronted cage. He stopped only once, and then but momentarily, in his swerveless progress. That was when Crane, as Byram pushed past him, tried to say something by way of excuse or explanation. Byram halted only long enough to aim—and land—a left hook that reached Bud's jaw, and caused him to sit down with great force and promptitude.

Byram, not even troubling to look back, continued his way to the cage. In his right hand was the thick blackthorn stick he always carried.

He had nearly reached the cage before he was first able to see, through the press, the motionless duelists on its floor. Another step brought him to the glass. And he smote its polished surface with the full swinging force of his stick.

At the first blow of the blackthorn knob, the thick glass split in five directions like so much skin ice under a boy's toe. The second, third, and fourth, delivered with a speed that seemed to make them but a single stroke, shivered the entire glass front, leaving a huge, ragged gap in the center.

Through this gap, Byram stepped; the jutting point of glass tearing his clothes and his hands as he went.

Above the two fighters he towered, his stick upraised, seeking the most vulnerable section of the snake's anatomy. The smash of glass had broken the spell that had gripped the crowd. Silence was replaced by confused shouts and babbling; through which boomed the quite unheeded imprecations of Ophido-Murtha, the Cobra King. There was a surge and a scramble in every direction, too; with much scuffing of feet. No one greatly cared to be so near the abode of the second largest python in captivity, when that captivity was lessened by a broken cage front.

But the incipient panic was wholly groundless. Nor did Byram's upraised blackthorn descend upon the snake. For, even as the man poised the stick for the blow, there was a sudden movement in the mountainous mass of coils, from tail to head. Then, very slowly, the thirty-foot body unwound; twisted feebly over on its hack; exposing an endless stretch of white, scaly underside; and lay there. The python's neck was quite scientifically broken; by the incessant and ever-fiercer grinding of a double row of white little tushes.

Beside his huge foe lay Cephas; a small, crumpled heap, curiously awkward and twisted in pose.

Ophido strode vengefully toward the wrecked cage, chanced to observe Bud Crane scrambling up dazedly from a sitting posture on the floor; paused, and reconsidered his planned onslaught.

"If I'd charged ten dollars a head for admittance to this fight," half blubbered the Cobra King to nobody in particular, "it wouldn't half 'a' paid me for losing that python!"

Byram did not hear. He was kneeling beside Cephas, running a tender hand over the limp body, and straightening out the cramped limbs and back.

"Somebody's going to get the licking of his life for this!' he announced to all and sundry, as he gently lifted the small hero in his arms.

Cephas the Unafraid opened one white-lashed, red-rimmed eye, and contributed to the babel of surrounding din a feeble but dauntless squeal. Byram, in incredulous joy, fanned the half-swooning warrior with his hat, and once more ran practiced fingers over Cephas' battered anatomy.

"A rib bashed in, and shoulder 'way out of joint," was his half-audible diagnosis. "But he's beginning to breathe free. And his heart's going. It doesn't hurt him when I punch him anywhere but on the shoulder and the rib. No inside injuries. He'll live—the gaudy little scrapper."

"Say, Byram!" hailed a freak-show manager as the rescuer bore his wounded pet, unopposed, through the excited crowd, out of the Serpent House, "I'll give you fifty dollars for that pig, for my mu-see-um. I'll bill him as the Porcine Paladin and Python Killer, and he'll be—"

"You'll buy me as easy as you'll buy Cephas," growled Byram. "He goes back to the farm with me to-morrow, after the vet has fixed him up. And there he stays forever and ever. In clover. As Providence meant a pig to. Not ballyhooing and killing pythons for breakfast. Hey, Cephas?"

And Cephas, the porcine paladin, gave assent, in a muffled but defiantly happy squeal.

The- Fate Chaser

"NOW," intoned the bazaar minstrel, right whiningly, "it was granted unto Rustun Ali, the sheik, to see in a dream the throne of Allah the just.

"And he beheld and saw Allah call unto him Azrael, the angel of death.

"And Allah spake unto Azrael, the angel of death, saying:

"'Arise and gird on thy sword; and, on the eighth day, smite Rustun Ali, the sheik. And thou shalt—'

"But Rustun Ali, the sheik, did abide to hear no more. He awoke in icy fear.

"And he delayed not to set his house in order, but cast his garment over his head and fled northward into the wilderness from the city of Helron; wherein was his dwelling.

"For eight days ran he northward and stayed not; fleeing ever to escape the sword of Azrael, the angel of death.

"And on the eighth day he came unto the city of Damascus. And he was sore spent. Yet he was glad of heart. For oft had he looked behind him. And not once had he seen Azrael, the angel of death, pursuing.

"And as Rustun Ali, the sheik, entered the city of Damascus, lo! before him in the southern gateway stood Azrael, the angel of death. And Azrael said unto him:

"'Oh, Rustun Ali, the sheik, it is well that you are come hither at the appointed hour. For it was here, at the gateway of Damascus, that Allah the just bade me smite thee.'

"Which sheweth, O illustrious ones," concluded the minstrel, "that no man may—"

But Halil Ben Ismaïl did not wait to hear the neatly pointed moral of the chant. He strode out from the cool shade of the bazaar street; his scarlet slippers slopping, unheeded, through the muck of the narrow roadway.

Fear was at Halil Ben Ismaïl's heart. And the singsong tale he had just heard had set his dread to throbbing; as a bit of barley sugar might stir to fresh anguish an aching tooth.

Three days earlier—yes, and for as many years before that as he had lived—Halil had deemed himself the luckiest of men. From the terrace of his house on the hillside that overlooked the busy harbor of Jaffa he had gazed forth across the blue waters daily; toward far-off Europe, land of barbarian and infidel; and had felt that no man in Jaffa or in that unknown world beyond the west was more fortunate than he.

For he had youth and moderate wealth and an ancient name; and he had made the pilgrimage and—so far as a grown man and a shereef might deign to be—he was very much in love.

He loved the maid whose father's gardens adjoined his own: Ayesha, daughter of Ilderim, the banker. She was fair and she was wise. She had gone to school at the Christian mission for two entire years; albeit the Prophet, in the second chapter of Al-Koran, cautions believers against permitting women to learn the written word.

And, once as Ayesha had walked in the walled garden at sunset, Halil had heard her sing. Braving death were he discovered, he had climbed the olive tree that grew against the wall and he had dropped down upon the far side. Not once but three times had he and Ayesha spoken face to face; there in her father's garden.

A shameless and brazen procedure, forsooth—even though Halil had not so much as touched the hem of her *Kumbaz*—and one that the well-born maid could never have permitted had not the wicked mission taught its pupils that women have souls and rights.

For which Halil Ben Ismaïl blessed the mission; albeit he feared lest so impious a blessing might carry in its wake a curse from Allah, the just, to himself.

And, now—

Two days earlier, Halil had summoned a wekeel—official

go-between—to beg of Ilderim, the banker, the hand of Ayesha. And, after a scant twelve hours of bargaining, the banker—who knew and honored the family of Halil—had given consent.

Moreover—not aware that the twain had met and spoken by stealth—he had fixed the dower at a mere eighteen hundred medji-die. And in that land, where the groom, not the bride, pays dowry, so reasonable a sum for so fair a maid was true generosity.

Halil in his first boundless joy had wandered forth under the stars, that he might be alone for a space with this great, deep happiness of his. Far had he walked; the night wind in his face, the white stars above him. Far out among the olive hills that lie behind Jaffa.

And there, at midnight, he had chanced upon a man who was riding, and riding hard, to the city. The man, seeing Halil alone and far from the walls, and noting in the starlight his rich dress, had drawn a bell-mouthed pistol and had demanded the lover's purse and his rings.

And Halil, angered that his gold dreams should be so roughly interrupted, had in a gust of rage cast caution to the dogs and had struck out full fiercely with the stout *nabout* staff he carried.

The blow had taken the robber by surprise; so that he had had time neither to pull trigger nor to dodge. Full on his frontal bone the *nabout's* knob had crashed. And down from the saddle into the white road he had pitched, like a tossed grain bag.

Then, by light of tinder box and steel, Halil had looked to see what manner of thief this might be who had attacked him on the open way. He had pushed back the concealing Kaffiyeh folds from the robber's face. And then the tinder box had fallen forgotten into the white dust.

For the man was a Bedouin. A Bedouin, too, from his dress, of the Beyt Ammah, a tribe that feared neither Allah nor Allah's mortal children. Moreover, the Bedouin was very evidently slain. For his jaw was dropped and his breath was sped.

The fact that he had slain a thief who would blithely have slain him had not at all troubled Halil Ben Ismaïl. But that the victim chanced to be of Beyt Ammah had set his heart aquiver like jelly. For, even more than usual among the Bedouins, did the Beyt Ammah men hold fiercely sacred the blood atonement law of their ancestors.

When a man of their tribe fell, in time of peace, and at the hand of an outsider, it was the sworn duty of every man, woman, and child of the Bey Ammah to avenge that death. Yes, even to tracing the slayer, if need be, a hundred miles or more. By the score were piled up the windy chronicles of such vengeance hunts. And in all the roster there was scarce one record of failure to secure the blood atonement

Wherefore, Halil Ben Ismaïl had gone sick and trembled; though commonly he was a brave man. He had laid his hand above the bare heart of the Bedouin. To his shaking touch the body already seemed to be cooling. Assuredly Halil could catch no feeling of heartbeat. The head, too, was bent oddly far to one side. The neck—

In panic, Halil had fled down the road whence he had come.

For a full mile he had run. There was a chance, perhaps, that the killing might not be traced to him. But seldom did a Bedouin ride alone on so long a journey as from the Beyt Ammah country to Jaffa. And doubtless the others of the dead man's tribe were not far behind. Soon they would come upon their comrade's body. Halil must be safe at home, with no trace of his passing, before they could come up with him. And his run had become a frenzied rush.

Suddenly he had halted and had turned back upon his tracks, still at top speed. For he remembered.

He had remembered the tinder box. The embossed silver-and-shell box on whose cover was graven the characters of his name; a name known well throughout Jaffa.

He had dropped it from his nerveless fingers when he had seen who his victim was. He had dropped it then in the road beside the body, and—fool of a thousand fools!—he had given it no second thought.

Had he written out his name or parchment and pinned it to the dead Bedouin's chest, he could scarce have left a stronger clew for the next-of-kin avengers to follow.

They had but to ride into Jaffa an ask at the first shop: "Who is Halil Ben Ismaïl and where abides he?" Unless—unless—

There had been one chance in three that the slain man had been riding far enough in advance of his fellows to allow of Halil's reaching his body before they could come up. And that chance Halil had taken.

He had reached the scene of his meeting with the Bedouin. It was the same place. There could be no doubt. For even by the faint starshine Halil could see the imprint of the sprawling body in the dust.

But the body itself was gone. So was the lean desert horse that Halil had left cropping thorn shoots at the roadside.

So was the silver-and-shell tinder box.

All were gone. Halil, on hands and knees, had groped frantically, for a radius of ten yards, for the box. But to no avail.

He dared not wait longer. He understood enough of Bedouin ways to know what had befallen. The dead man's fellows had arrived—a few of them—had found the body in the road; had searched for a clew to the slayer; had found that, too, with ridiculous ease; and, carrying their comrade, had ridden back to meet the others of their party who were coming on more slowly.

Forgetting his fatigue, Halil Ben Ismaïl had gathered up the skirts of his robe and had fled. Nor had he paused until he was within his own hillside house—the house whose rambling garden adjoined Ayesha's.

There, for hours, he had sat—waiting. At dawn they might come. Or, if they feared the pasha's hand in punishment, they would bide their time and come by stealth at an hour when their vengeance could be wreaked in safety. It might be in a minute. It might be in a week.

It was hard to die when one was young and rich. Very hard to die when one loved, and was loved. And Halil had to call on all his Eastern fatalism to sustain him.

But when two days passed, and his foes still waited, the gnawing fear was whipped into action by waxing wrath.

He had done no crime. He had but struck to save his own life. He had not meant to slay. And yet he must crouch in his house, like a felon in his cell, waiting to be killed. It was not fair, nor to be endured.

Halil walked abroad and boldly entered the bazaars as was his morning wont.

Inshallah! Let death meet him in the open, if it would. And in the open, as he paused, attracted by the droning of a minstrel, the song of Rustun Ali, the sheik, was sung into his straining ears. The song of the dreamer who fled to escape death, and who, fleeing, ran upon the death angel's very sword. It was not a chant to put cheer into a doomed man's heart.

Halil strode down the zigzag alleyway leading from the bazaars to the sea. He had no definite aim in view. But fear goaded him onward. Anything was better than to stand still, there in the bazaar shadows; whence at any moment a darker shadow might glide forward and drive a curved Bedouin knife into his back.

Down the steep alley he hurried, toward the patch of shingle at its foot. There he halted. In front of him lay the blue harbor, shark-infested and smilingly treacherous—perhaps the most treacherous, uncertain harbor along all the Syrian coast. A half mile to the left was the long jetty; a half mile out from shore the crazy black breakwater, with its wave-polished mass of rock teeth.

Just within the breakwater lay a big Feringi sail ship; her queer-dressed crew—womanishly beardless for the most part, and with their white skins only slightly tanned—busy on the decks. Some of them were hauling at some meaningless-looking ropes. And as they hauled, they were singing in rough, rumbling voices a still more meaningless Feringi song.

Halil had gone as a lad to Al-Azhar in Cairo and had mastered more than a smattering of the queer Feringi tongue. Yet, though the words came distinct to him across the still water, they made scant sense. He assumed that the chant was a Feringi sea prayer; and fell idly to listening:

> There's tinkers an' tailors an' sojers an' all—
> Weigh ho! Roll a man down!
> What ship as good seamen aboard the Black Ball—
> Give us a chance to roll a man down!

Yes, no doubt a prayer to one of their gods. And Halil grimly hoped the god might understand its sense better than did he.

> Come all ye bold topmen an' listen to me—
> Weigh ho! Roll a—

"Allah, the all merciful, will repay thee, O prince!" interrupted a droning voice at Halil's elbow. "May Allah and His Prophet preserve thee and add to thy hoard! Have pity upon the sufferer! What says the Book?—'To give alms to the afflicted is to receive the key to paradise.' I am afflicted, O rich man who art handsome as Omar. Baksheesh!"

Halil turned; tossed a piaster in the general direction of a fat beggar who, in passing, had made a professional pause to break in on the doomed man's musings; then turned away again. But almost at once he wheeled, gripping his *nabout* more tightly, and faced toward the petitioner. Might not the beggar perhaps be—But no. The plump mendicant had picked up the piaster and was waddling on toward the alley way that led up to the bazaars.

Halil, ashamed of his own fear, turned back toward the ship. It was bitter and shameful to fear thus the face of man. Then, out of stress, was born his idea:

This Feringi vessel was making ready to weigh anchor. Doubtless to cross to some of the barbarous, far-off Feringi lands; distant lands where even the Beyt Ammah's revenge could not hope to follow.

Halil's problem was solved. He ran up the hill as lightly as a boy, and into the stall of his bankers. A half hour later, all his available funds in his belt, he was back at the beach and hailing a passing rowboat.

Along the Street of a Thousand Laughs strolled Halil Ben Ismaïl. He liked the Street of a Thousand Laughs better than any other section of the Pan-Universal Exposition. For sometimes when night had risen—not fallen, but *risen,* in the flare of a myriad flaring lights, to an accompaniment of fifty bands—sometimes when night had risen, especially Saturday night, the Street of a Thousand Laughs reminded him of the busiest of Jaffa bazaar days.

The noise, the jostling, the numberless shuffling feet, the uncountable odors, the babel of joy-rough voices, the raucous yells of the barkers—all blended into a single mighty chord. A chord hideous to the Occidental non-reveler's senses; inexpressibly homelike to this exile from the land where noise and multitudinous smells are synonyms for gayety.

From soap boxes and stands in front of gilt-and-electric-light "attractions," brass-lunged men were roaring the marvels of their shows. In an elevated cage in front of a canvas-front booth, a hairy wild man, burrowed in straw, clanked his chains and gibbered with a southern Louisiana accent.

Hot dog, popcorn, and salt-water taffy scented the air. Ball-throwing stands and shooting galleries lent the babel chorus a continuous staccato sub-tone. Ghastly green-lit photo galleries, red-bulbed dance pavilions, blue-windowed concert halls added color to the eternal glare of white lights.

City folk, country folk, shopgirls, boys of all sizes and costumes— every sort of seeker for cheap and loud fun—jammed the sidewalks and the narrow middle way.

Over all brooded the solemn, stifling night of summer, that made people stop every now and then and gasp for air; that transformed stiff collars, at a moistly magic touch, to limp cloths.

To Halil Ben Ismaïl, official interpreter for the Cairo quarter, a furlong distant, the air was but balmy; the racket was pleasingly reminiscent; the indescribable reek of odors was a trifle insipid.

But on the whole Halil rather liked the Street of a Thousand Laughs. Of a certainty he disliked it infinitely less than anything else in this bleak, barbarous, gray-lived America which had become his unloving and unloved land of refuge.

America contained and represented everything Halil did not like. But at least it was the last spot on the face of the earth whither the Bedouins of the Beyt Ammah might be reasonably expected to wander in pursuit of a blood quest.

It was hard to imagine such a possibility. And Fear no longer crept whispering at Halil Ben Ismaïl's elbow; nor, sharing his pillow, mouthed its bugaboo horror in his ear, through the long nights.

In fact, his dread was just strong enough, together with its twin sister Prudence, to make bearable his homesick hatred for the Western World and to hold in leash his craving to go back to his house on the Jaffa hillside—the pleasant stucco house whose garden adjoined Ayesha's.

But, though the ten months of his absence had been as a century to him, the absentee, yet he knew full well that it was as a mere day in the sum of a Bedouin tribesman's hate. News, in Syria—even in anterailroad, antetelegraph Syria—flew fast. And the Beyt Ammah folk had many friends in Jaffa. Friends who, knowing their blood quest, would be quick to apprise them of the much-sought slayer's return from across the world.

So on stayed Halil in the land of his loathing. Nor did he dare make known his whereabouts by sending to his bankers for the accrued boat rents which formed, customarily, his livelihood. He had drawn his ready cash, it is true, when he left Syria. And to him, at the time, the sum had seemed well-nigh enough to keep him at ease for years.

But in this land of pasty faces and growl-deep voices—in this land where even the best-clad men carried no belt knives, and where merchants neglected to shriek in falsetto when they bargained—in this America, money melted like summer snow on Mount Hermon.

At even the lowest inns, a room with a bed could scarce be had for a day and night for less than a half dollar—ten or twelve full piasters, five-eighths of a whole medjidie. A man's meal in a street khan cost no less than five piasters—and for vile, overcooked meat, at that; without a single drop of deliciously greasy oil or one pinch of barley sugar on it.

Then, to ride in one of their horseless rail wagons, for even a scant four miles or so, meant the squandering of another piaster. As for their places of amusement—the cheapest and poorest of their magic picture shows cost more than at home would a long blissful evening of coffee and nargile; brightened by the best tales of a coffeehouse story-teller. As for clothes—ten precious silver dollars had his present outfit cost.

Small wonder that Halil's rich savings had taken wings and that, on the verge of starvation, he had availed himself with tearful joy of the chance to act as interpreter for the aggregation of despised donkey boys and Nile fellahin calling itself the Cairo quarter, at the Pan-Universal!

Twelve dollars a week—prince's wage!—and food and shelter. Already he had laid by enough money to go home—if he dared; which he did not.

Halil Ben Ismaïl sauntered along the Street of a Thousand Laughs on this July Saturday night, comforting his homesick heart with the heat, the noise, the smell. He prided himself, too, that in his new fashionable and well-cut Occidental clothes, he was easily passing muster as an American of wealth, high birth, and even of title.

His frock coat, it is true, had been constructed for a considerably larger man; and his wide-checked white-and-black trousers had been once intended to grace the legs of a man far leaner—a minstrel end man whose show had gone to pieces, as a Pan-Universal attraction, before he could pay his tailor.

The red slippers, too—ever the dress shoe of the Syrian as the frock coat is his ideal of European elegance—were a trifle conspicuous. As were the scarlet flannel vest with its brass buttons and the furry high hat whose sweatband was generously papered to make it fit.

But the general effect, Halil knew, was wholly desirable and up to date. His costume, taken all in all, was such as an American emir's son might be expected to wear. It elicited glances and even smiles from more than one passing shopgirl. Halil settled his sky-blue tie more straight at such moments and swung his rattan cane more jauntily between his yellow-gloved fingers.

It was good to be handsome and to be fashionably attired. It was pleasant to be the recipient of smiles even from these chalk-faced Feringi maids. It momentarily made the yearning for Ayesha a little less bitter.

"Hey, Ismale! Oh, Benny Ismale!" yelled Bogan, half proprietor of the Trip to Mars, as Halil Ben Ismaïl moved past the Martian attraction's doors.

Halil stopped; glad to be hailed by an acquaintance, in this Street of a Thousand Laughs and a Million Strangers. He had a nodding acquaintance with Bogan, who was a friend of the Cairo quarter's manager. So he turned in from the throng to the little semi-enclosed space at one side of the Trip to Mars entrance.

"Salutations, O Bogan," Halil observed, in carefully acquired American idiom. "May peace be to you and to your children's children!"

"Same here," returned Bogan. "Only I'm a bachelor. But thanks just the same. Want to earn half an iron man, Benny? Fifty cents," he translated, as Ben Ismaïl looked puzzled.

"Of a sure," gladly answered Halil.

"I'm sorry to butt in if you're hurrying to fill a date," joshed Bogan, eying the gaudy costume.

"I should become worried!" retorted Halil gayly.

Bogan turned to a stout, very bald man at his side.

"Higgs," said he, "shake hands with my friend, Mr. Benjamin Ismale, of the Cairo quarter. Ismale's the interpreter over there. He can help us out if any one can."

Mr. Higgs acknowledged the introduction and announcement with a courteous grunt.

"You see, Benny," pursued Bogan, "it's like this: Mr. Higgs owns a part interest in our Trip to Mars. He was down to New York yesterday. And over to Ellis Island he come across an Egyptian or a Hindu or some other kind of heathen—no offense to you, Benny—that had come across as a stowaway and had been held up for deporting."

"Of a certainty, O Bogan, effendi," assented Halil as Bogan paused a moment to relight a frayed cigar.

"Well," went on Bogan, "this was a picturesque guy; with his funny brown face and the Oriental dewdads he was wearing, and all that. So Higgs here gets a notion he'd make kind of a hit somewhere in our show. As the Man from Mars, or something like that."

"I perceive," said Halil, who did not at all.

"So Higgs pays his thirty dollars entrance fee to the United States and his four-dollar alien tax, and brings him up here. Now that he's here, we can't make him understand a thing. Naples Mike has tried him in three languages—or lingoes Mike says are languages; they sound more like gargles, to me—and Naowa's tried him on the sign language. No go. No savvy. And he squats inside there in a cubby-hole in the dark, looking about as wise as a stewed tripe and not doing a thing for his board and keep except keening a kind of wurra-wurra dirge in his own tongue. Come in and look him over, won't you, and talk to him in Cairo or Egyptian or something? Maybe you can make him understand what we want him to do."

"He cannot talk words? He possesses no verbiage?" asked Halil as he started obediently toward the gate, convoyed by Bogan and Higgs.

"Oh, he talks all right," Higgs reassured him. "Only he don't say nothin'. He's spent most of the evenin' squattin' there in his corner chantin' that fun'ral march singsong of his."

"A lament. A lamentation," pronounced Halil, as, passing through the gate, he caught muffled fragments of familiar sound from within.

"It's a lamentation, all right," agreed Bogan. "Worse'n any lamentation that seven cats in an alley could make. He's been at it for an hour, now. D'ye s'pose he's sick?"

"No," decided Halil. "But he is far from home. It is the manner of the folk in my world to voice thus their grief. It calms. I myself when first I boarded your heavenlike country—"

He paused. Both in speech and in steps. From around the corner of a partition directly in front of him came in sustained, if husky, tones a minor chant; rising now and again to a sustained howl, only to scale down to a groan. It was the accent of the Lament Song; familiar to every one who has pierced the outer tourist crust of the East.

The joy of hearing once more his own beloved Arabic—purest of Syrian Arabic at that—held Halil Ben Ismaïl spellbound.

"Ohé! Aiai!" came the droning dirge from beyond the partition corner. "Stout of heart as a desert lion, and beauteous of face and form as the angels of Allah and the crest of Hermon, was Nasif Abou-Najib. Proud was he as was Ali, the khaleef, of old. Proud and strong and of noble lineage! *Ohe! Mashallah!* Behold him now!"

"What's the old guy blitherin' about?" demanded Higgs.

Halil translated.

"Who's he talkin' about?" asked Higgs. "Who's the person that's like lions and angels and—"

"It is him himself," explained Halil.

"H'm! He's changed a whole lot, then, since the last time he looked in the glass," was Higgs' comment. "What's he singin' his own charms for, in that fool way? Tryin' to make a hit with himself?"

"No. It is custom. It is portion of the lamentation. It is the manner, universally, of lamentations. Listen! He says—he says: 'Lo, I was as an emir—yea, as a sultan of earth and sky. And I was the—what you call hero—the hero of all the sons of Islam. None was like to me in fame, in wealth, in valor, in beauty.' "

"It's easy to see the old heathen hates himself like poison," observed Bogan. "Listen! He's at it again."

The rumbling voice, after ceasing for an instant, wailed forth raucously once more:

"And on this black day, where is Nasif Abou-Najib, the glorious? Far from his fatherland! Afar in the country of the infidel. A landless man. Lo, Nasif Abou-Najib hath slain a man in his wrath. A lowborn man, whose next of kin swore the blood oath and who pursued, even with the soldiers of the pasha—on whom be the red curse of Gehenna!—so that Abou-Najib fled for his life. Yea, to the land of the Feringi—to the bourne of the red-haired and godless!"

"You see, Mr. Ismale," Higgs was explaining as Halil, a thrill of sympathy for a fellow fear slave gripping him, was about to round the thin partition wall, "you see, it was like this: I picked up a little of his story from the immigration people. He stowed away on an India-bound ship at some port over in Egypt or Syria; pretty near a year ago. The captain dug him out and made him work his passage. First thing when they struck India, he saw a feller from his own land on the wharf; and he wouldn't go ashore. Not even when the ship was laid up for repairs for three or four months. Lived in the hold all the time, and did odd paint jobs and rust pounding for his keep. Seemed to be scared of something."

"Yes," said Halil positively. "He was affrighted. I know."

"Then when the ship stopped at his own port on the way west, the captain had him run ashore. But they'd no sooner got past Port Said than they found he'd stowed away again. So they brought him on and left him at Ellis Island. Chase around to him now, won't you, and do some translating?"

Halil, in three steps, had turned the corner and found himself at the doorless opening of a rubbish cupboard. There, in one end of the closet, half invisible in the dim light of the recess, huddled the robed and ragged figure of a man.

"*Naharak sai'd!*" greeted Halil. "*Aleikum salaam!*"

The figure ceased rocking to and fro and rose from its recumbent posture.

"*Naharak assad!*" duly returned the lament singer. "And may peace be to you multiplied, and may you lie where rose leaves shall fall upon your tomb, O you who in the land of devils speak with the tongue of the Prophet's sons!"

"May the Compassionate ordain a couch of silk and gold for you in paradise, O brother of eagles!" said Halil. "And may your children be sultans! What do you here, far from the home of our fathers?"

"I slew a man and I fled from the avengers," replied Abou-Najib, as simply as if he were recounting the tale of a minor error of judgment. "I fled, for they were strengthened by the pasha's troops, and my tribe could not protect me, nor was the whole desert wide enough to hide me from so many pursuers."

"And that is why—"

"I fled my country. I would I had stayed and perished on the Prophet's soil."

Halil, in silent sympathy, stretched forth a handful of yellow cigarettes. First touching his own breast and forehead with his long fingers, Abou-Najib eagerly accepted the entire handful. Sticking one cigarette in his mouth, he pouched the rest; then, with the universal smoker gesture, he groped in the breast of his robe.

Halil, divining what the man sought, fished out a card of matches. He was vastly proud of his new-found familiarity with so marvelous and intricate a novelty as a safety match. And, as much to air that familiarity as to give the refugee a light, he struck a match on the card's strip of prepared surface.

At the same instant, Abou-Najib found what he had been seeking. The match flare illumined every corner of the tiny cubby-hole. It showed in detail the ragged figure of a desert Bedouin who was just drawing from his robe's bosom a little tarnished box.

A silver-and-shell box of odd workmanship; whereon, in Arabic characters, a name was engraved.

The match fell from Halil's stiffening fingers to the floor, leaving the two men in what seemed a denser darkness than before.

"That box!" croaked Halil, finding voice as the Bedouin struck flint and steel. "How came you by it, O offspring of fifty thousand justly punished grave robbers and murderers?"

Abou-Najib, in no wise resenting the mildly discourteous wording of the query, made chuckling reply.

"In just payment for a cracked head. As I rode in flight to Jaffa from my own country of the Beyt Ammah, to take ship, I met by night a man who looked as though his purse might speed my journey. But when I would have taken it, he smote me to the ground with his staff. I woke to find he had fled. Yea, the fool had not alone fled without robbing me, but had left—this! He—"

"Oh, Nasif Abou-Najib!" broke in Halil, his voice cracked and high-pitched in a delirium of incredulous joy. "Thy rightful tomb will be in the body of hog or vulture! And I would hasten thy journey to that fit resting place! Were it not that thou hast just lifted Azrael's black wing from before mine eye. Knowest thou the tale of Rustun Ali, the sheik, who fled on an eight-day journey to escape the sword of the death angel, and who, at his journey's end, found the angel awaiting him?

"Folk mistell that tale. It should end: 'And the angel was none but a ragged Bedouin murderer who must eke out his days in a far land, while his victim returneth to Allah's most blessed country by the earliest boat.' *Ma-Salaam-i,* O brother to the herd of Gaddarene swine! Many have raced with Fear. But few save Halil Ben Ismaïl have passed him by.

"Farewell—and take the loving blessings of the fool who neglected to rob thee. Ayesha is waiting for me!"

Solemnly but fervently, Halil Ben Ismaïl removed his furry high hat from his head. Yet more solemnly and fervently he placed it on the concrete floor and drove his slippered heel through it. Next he ripped off the frock coat that an hour earlier had seemed to him the desired acme of fashion. Snatching the torn burnoose from Nasif Abou-Najib's shoulders and tossing there his frock coat in its stead, he wound the burnoose folds around his own body and strode forth into the Street of a Thousand Laughs.

"I no longer look so like a native and inhereditary American that none would guess me foreign born," was all he would vouchsafe to the wondering and questioning Bogart and Higgs as he swept past them on his way out. "And as for the half of an iron gentleman that you pledged to give me to interpret, you may lavish it on Nasif Abou-Najib. I grudge it not for him. For, what says your Feringi proverb speech:

"'It is a sick wind that blows when nobody is good. So thieves fall out of it. And honesty becomes the best politics.' I am going *home!*"

The "Other Man"

THE train grunted along the stretches of dead-flat, uninspired country, chewing the miles leisurely, rather than devouring them; stopping with hollow groans of brake and wheel at a myriad hopeless way-stations; starting on again with an optimistic jar, as though to joggle its several hundred passengers out of their journey-born apathy.

The day was torrid. A dry, copper sun hammered down on a parched world. Yellow road-dust mingled lovingly with black cinders, and then sifted through car-sash and screen, stinging noses and eyes, griming faces and hands, making travel a horror.

Horace Steell sat alone in the smoker of his Pullman. It was not a train that catered to the better class of passengers, being an "accommodation" that started at a bad hour and made every stop between the metropolis and the distant group of seashore resorts. Thus it carried but two Pullmans. And this afternoon both of these were nearly deserted, while the day coaches were jammed to the platforms with folk from various villages, homeward bound from an Oddfellows' Excursion. Thus, from the city on, Steell had had the smoking compartment of his Pullman all to himself.

He was a big, comfortable-looking man whose soul had taken on flesh from much prosperity and from dearth of fate-buffets. His struggles had come early; his rewards had been rich. Wherefore, his soul was become not only plump but out of training, and in his face he showed all this, as might a former athlete who has let his muscles soften.

He sat asprawl, in the compartment's best corner, his feet on the seat in front of him, a cigar between his fingers, a magazine open athwart one knee.

He was very comfortable. And it was with something akin to a frown that he glanced up as some one else, passing the door, hailed him.

"Hello, Mr. Steell," called the intruder cheerily, pausing just outside the doorway; "I just drifted through to see if there was anybody aboard that I knew. Where'd *you* drop from?"

Steell accorded the wholly worthless question the reply that seemed its due,—a reply that would be most nearly (and with gross inadequacy) depicted in print as something between "H'm!" and "Ugh!"

Steell accompanied the sound with a barely perceptible nod of greeting.

"Bound for the shore?" queried the other, no whit abashed.

"Yes," said Steell curtly. "Ocean Park. Week end. My family's down there."

"Ocean Park, eh? Queer! I'm going there myself for a fortnight. The Stevenses are having a house party of sorts. I suppose I'll see you at the dance to-night at the Casino? Stevens says it's to be—"

"I'm going down to Ocean Park for *pleasure*," returned Steell gruffly.

"Oh, I forgot. You aren't a dancing man, are you? 'Endurance, rather than speed,' eh? Safety first. Anything worth reading in that magazine?"

"Come in and look it over, if you like," suggested Steell, with much the cordiality he might have bestowed on inviting a mosquito into his bedroom.

"No, thanks," refused the other, still in the doorway. "One thing I could never bring myself to stand is cigar smoke. And this compartment reeks of it. That's why I'm keeping out of range. I'll just be toddling on to my seat. I'm in the car ahead. By the way—anything new in stocks, to-day?"

"The Stock Exchange is closed on Saturdays, Mr. Nevin," replied Steell. "I'm sorry. I suppose they didn't think you'd be asking."

After this ponderous morsel of irony, he returned to his magazine. Nevin lingered for an instant longer in the doorway; then, with a pleasant, "See you later on," he moved away.

A STRANGER, overhearing that short colloquy, would doubtless have set down Horace Steell as a boor. As a matter of fact, it had cost him far more effort to be even thus mildly civil to Nevin than he would have expended in conciliating an entire board of directors.

Nevin was Steell's pet aversion, a man who had eaten his dinners, danced with his pretty wife, ridden in his motors, cruised on his yacht, enjoyed in fifty ways his careless hospitality—and never at Steell's personal invitation. Incidentally, Nevin had eaten the dinners, danced with the pretty wives, ridden in the motors and cruised on the yachts of fully fifty other men—and, never at *their* invitations.

He was the product of the times, vulgarly known as a "tame cat." Having no home ties, a lean income, a deferential and snub-proof presence, an insinuating manner and abundance of leisure, he was a happy little parasite on the gold-leaf hide of Society.

Nevin danced well, talked amusingly, played a tolerable card game, was indefatigably eager to run errands and make himself generally useful, and had far better taste and keener judgment in feminine fashions than any man has a right to.

For these reasons, women petted him, made use of him and let him fetch and carry for them and advise them in matters of dress and entertainment. And they repaid his pretty services by inviting him to their husbands' houses, as filler-in for dinners and as handy-man at house-parties. No one seemed to accept him seriously. And men— real men—did not accept him at all. Hence the gruffness of Horace Steell, who, as a rule, erred on the side of geniality.

Steell was not destined to make much progress in the magazine he was reading. He had scarce turned a page, after Nevin's interruption, when the train jostled its cars to a tired standstill at the junction with a road running from another and farther-inland city.

Several people clambered into Steell's car, and one man, cigarette in mouth, made for the smoking compartment. He was halfway to the seat opposite Steell when the latter chanced to look up and the two men recognized each other.

Steell was on his feet at once, his hand outstretched, his big voice booming a jolly welcome.

The new arrival—a fragile, carefully-groomed man of perhaps thirty, over whose cheekbones tuberculosis had daubed red "no surrender" signals—seemed less pleased at the meeting than did Steell. In fact, he stopped short, in evident and not over-glad astonishment on sight of the compartment's occupant. As an afterthought, he remembered to accept the outstretched hand and to mutter some form of greeting.

"Good old Dicky Ware!" Steell was exclaiming. "This is a dandy surprise. How far down the line are you going?"

"To Ocean Park. I—"

"Good boy! Can't you stop with us? The Missus is down there, you know, and the kids. She'll be delighted to see you."

"I knew she was down there," said Ware, slowly, after a brief pause; "but I didn't know *you* were going to be. I understood you had to stay over in town till next week."

"I did, but I don't. We wound up the deal this noon. So I telegraphed ahead and caught the first train."

They had sat down opposite each other. Steell held out his cigar case. Ware declined the proffer with a word of thanks and lighted a cigarette. Then he leaned back, resting his head on the dusty leather chair-top. There were hollows below his big, restless eyes, and his thin lips were tense. Except for the red cheekbone splashes, his face was dead white. Steell glanced at him with solicitude.

"Dick," he said, "you look all in. What's the matter? Are the lungs worse, or was the ride too much for you? It's beastly hot and dusty."

"Neither the lungs nor the ride," answered Ware, lifelessly, his eyes half shut; "just a big disappointment that's hit me. By the way, I'm starting for Arizona, Monday, to give the desert air another chance to patch up my breathing apparatus. I'll be gone a year or more, if I ever come back. And—"

"Oh, buck up, old man!" exhorted Steell, highly uncomfortable and noisily hopeful. "Arizona'll put you on your feet in no time. You're good for another half century, if you'll take any kind of care of yourself. Why, I knew a chap, once—Dale, it was, Simon P. Dale—you must remember him!—well, he was twice as badly off as you are—doctors had all given him up—and he went out there, to a place called—"

"I know, I know," assented Ware. "They all do. I've heard about them all. That's not what's bothering me. It's the disappointment that's come before I start out. It's caught me rather hard."

"What is it? Can I help?"

"You *could* have helped; but you *can't*. It's too late. At least—I wonder!"

"Wonder what? If there's anything I can do to help you, why, just turn in a still alarm for me. We've been pretty good friends, you and I, Dick, for six years and more. Just put a name to what you want done."

"You can't do anything," said Ware, irritably.

HE lapsed into a moody silence, glancing covertly at Steell once or twice, yet hesitating to encounter his friend's crassly puzzled gaze. At length, on quick impulse, he looked up and spoke. He spoke shortly, decisively:

"After all, what's the use? I'm as good as a dead man. We spend our lives lying to each other; why should we spend our deaths doing it? It would be a luxury to tell the truth, once, in a way. And if ever I'm to enjoy any luxuries, I haven't much time to waste. Besides—there's one chance in a million—"

"Dick, what in blazes are you mumbling about? You don't make

sense. What's the main idea?"

"You asked me to tell you about the disappointment," said Ware, speaking jerkily, his eyes alight with a sudden recklessness. "Why shouldn't I? I can't get more than a thrashing. And I've grown so shaky, anyone can bowl me over."

"Are you drunk, old man?" asked Steell, anxiously catching but fragments of Ware's preamble.

"No such luck," retorted Ware. "Here's the yarn. I'm in love. I—"

"In love? You poor chap!"

Steell spoke with no trace of badinage, but in sympathy as genuine as it was tactless.

"I love a woman," went on Ware, unhearing, and with the light of fierce recklessness growing deeper and deeper in his big eyes. "I love her with all my heart and soul, with all that's good in me, with all that's bad in me. I have loved her ever since I saw her. I shall keep on loving her when this cast-off body of mine is dust. There's nothing for me, here or in heaven or in hell, but *her*—just *her!*"

He stopped to catch the scant breath that he had been wasting so thriftlessly in his vehement outburst. Steell, amazed at the odd confession from a man usually so taciturn, stared agape, trying bewilderedly to make up his mind whether to say something jovial or something consolatory. Presently, Ware resumed in less excitement:

"I love her and she loves me. For a long time I couldn't believe she did—it didn't seem possible. I am a wreck; she is glorious in her strength and health and loveliness. I couldn't believe it, though I'd have given what was left of my life to believe. But, little by little, it dawned on me, clearer and clearer, till at last there was no shadow of room for doubt. I no longer just *believed*—I—I *knew!* And then came the order that I must start for Arizona."

"Good Lord! What rotten luck!"

"I wouldn't have agreed to go, but there is always a shred of a hope. If I go, and if by any miracle I get well, I'll be able to come back and—and claim her."

"All the luck in the world to you, old friend!" exclaimed Steell, a mist springing unbidden to his eyes. "I'll be rooting for you."

A smile that was hideous in its ghastly mirthlessness tortured Ware's pale lips.

"The 'disappointment,'" he hurried on, "is this: I was going to have one insanely happy Sunday, alone with her, before I went—one day whose memory would help me fight off death. She wrote to me to come to her. Her husband—"

"Husband!" shouted Steell in stark amazement. "Why, man, you never told me it was that kind of thing! I supposed—"

"Probably you did. But you won't, any longer. I was to go to her for Sunday. Her husband was to be away. I was to have the whole wonderful day, just with her—we two, alone, before I went out into the dark. And now—now I find her husband is not going to be away. That's all."

Steell was staring at him in dull perplexity.

"That is all," repeated Ware, very simply. "I love your wife. She loves me. And, thanks to you, I'll never see her alone again."

STEELL did not speak. Twice his lips sprang apart, fiercely, but no word issued from them. His florid face purpled. Ware sat, imperturbable, enduring his apoplectic glare, a perfect calm on his own thin features.

And, during the tense moment, Nevin reappeared in the doorway, beaming with kindly patronage on them both.

"Why, how do, Mr. Ware?" he bubbled. "I heard you'd gone out West somewhere. You're looking awfully fit. I haven't seen you in such good shape for a long time.—Mr. Steell, I just trotted back to ask if you'd lend me that magazine to glance over, if you're through with it. It's stupid as the deuce, sitting in there and breathing cinders and looking at a billiard-table landscape."

Steell, moving like an automaton, handed him the magazine. And with profuse and unheard thanks, Nevin vanished. Then, slowly facing Ware again, Steell began to speak, his voice a husky rumble, far down in his throat.

"It's hard to know just what to say to you," he growled. "If I should tell you that you lie in saying Claire loves you, you would try to resent it. And the strain would be bad for you, even if I should keep my hands at my sides. If I smash you, on general principles, for insulting my wife by such a dirty suggestion, I—why, I *can't* hit you, Dick, any more than I could beat up a cripple. You must see that. So what am I to do?"

He spoke in genuine distress. Ware answered with the same dead calm:

"I haven't lied. I have spoken the plain truth. It's a way I have. You ought to know that by now. I love Claire and she loves me. Do whatever you want to."

"Claire—Claire has told you she loves you?" demanded Steell in utter incredulity.

"Yes; with her dear eyes, with every intonation of her voice, with a million indefinable little actions—with everything except her lips."

"H'm! Then she *hasn't* told you!"

"Not in language *you* could understand, but to me in a language that made mere words seem useless. *I* understood."

"That means," decided Steell with judicial acumen, "—that means she doesn't care. She's been kind to you because you're sick, and you've misread her kindness. She's never lowered herself by speaking one single, solitary word of love to you. With an invalid's feverish twist of mind you have imagined the whole thing."

"If you like," said Ware, indifferently, as he groped in his pocket for another cigarette.

"Look here!" blustered Steell: "What do you mean by coming to me with this filthy cock-and-bull story? You take advantage of your condition. You know, well enough, if a man who wasn't an invalid had told me what you've just told me, I'd have broken every bone in his body."

"I'm not hiding behind my illness," said Ware, stiffly.

For a second or two, Steell glowered heavily at him, then started off on another tack.

"Even if you believe she cares for you—and she doesn't—why do you tell *me?* I'm not up on the fine points of extra-marital etiquette, but it seems to me a yellow-dog trick for you to tell me—to tell me— her husband—that she doesn't love me and does love you. What did you say it for?"

"On the one-in-a-million chance that you'd prove a white man instead of a conventional savage. On the bare off-chance that you'd put Claire's happiness ahead of yours and set her free to come to the man she loves."

"What do you mean by that?"

"She loves me; I love her. She does not love you. You have two courses open—you can hold her to her vows and to the rights the law gives you over her; or—you can save her from lifelong misery and slavery and make her happy by setting her free. It is on that chance I said what I did."

When Steell spoke again, the bluster had gone out of his deep voice, the anger out of his eyes.

"I've gotten so in the habit of loving Claire," he began, "that it's come to be like the air or the sunshine or any of the other things we never notice and yet can't live without. We've been mighty happy together, she and I. At least, *I* have. And it's never occurred to me to doubt that she loves me every bit as much as I love her. She likes a good time and she likes lots of attention. But then, it's natural a pretty woman should; and I never kick. I don't object to it at all; but when it comes to her caring for somebody else—"

His words trailed away. He looked fixedly out of the window at the suburbs of the first of the string of seaside resorts through which the train was rattling. Presently he continued:

"Claire doesn't love you or any other man, except me. I know it. But I'll promise you this: If ever you can prove to me that Claire *does* love you and that her happiness lies in getting you and losing me— well, I won't stand in her way. Understand that? I'm no hog—I don't want any woman's body when her heart belongs to another man. If I should find she loves you, I'd step aside. But she doesn't. She—"

THROUGH no volition of his own, Horace Steell started from his seat, flew in midair straight across the compartment and landed with an echoing thump among the leather cushions on the far side.

The screws that held Ware's swivel chair to the floor ripped all at once from their fastenings. The chair hurled itself against the same padded leather buffer that had broken Steell's aërial flight.

Both windows of the compartment shivered simultaneously into countless fragments. The floor buckled, and a length of polished and carved scantling crashed downward, barely missing Ware's head.

In the instant, a rending sound as of splitting planks, magnified a million-fold, filled the air. It was punctuated by grinding metal, a hail of tinkling glass and a ragged chorus of screams.

Steell, the breath knocked clean out of him, scrambled gasping to his feet and lifted the prostrate Ware. The latter, blinking dazedly, held to the big man's arm for support.

"Hurt?" demanded Steell.

"I—I think not," panted Ware. "I seem to be all right. What has—?"

"Then let me help you out of this," said Steell, suiting the deed to the word. "These cars sometimes have a comic way of starting to burn, when there's a wreck."

The car from which they clambered had suffered least of any on the long train. The coaches ahead of them were piled and humped like a broken-backed caterpillar, and those to the rear were derailed.

"Head-on collision!" they heard some one bawl as they emerged into the hell of it all.

The next half hour went as does the first half hour after all bad railroad wrecks. Luckily, the two trains had collided within a furlong of the Sea Bank Railroad station and in the very heart of the thriving resort of Sea Bank itself, a resort where summering doctors were plenty and where hotels and boarding-houses could and would give shelter to the wounded until the hospital train should come up.

Steell, resting at last from his task of volunteer helper in dragging the injured from the tangle of wood and twisted steel, came back to where Ware was sitting.

"Sure you're all right?" he asked.

"Yes," said Ware. "While fifty healthier men are damaged, it hasn't even brought on a fit of coughing. You did good work in there, Steell. I've been watching you. You must be dead tired."

"I didn't get tired," denied Steell. "I didn't have time. Now, I want to find the nearest telegraph office or long-distance 'phone and send word to Claire, at Ocean Park, that I'm all right. Some news of the wreck will get there and she'll be horribly frightened. She knew I was to be on the train that—"

"She knew I was to be on it, too," interrupted Ware. "Listen, Steell; I've been doing some thinking, this last half hour. Were you telling the truth when you said you'd stand aside, if you were convinced Claire loved some one else?"

"Certainly. But this is no time or place to discuss—"

"You are wrong. It's the very time and place, a time and place that couldn't be duplicated once in ten years."

"I don't understand," said Steell, impressed by Ware's strange eagerness.

"It is very simple. Are you willing to put Claire's love for you to the test?"

"It needs no test. I refuse to talk further about—"

"I hold you to your word. Make good! You said you would give Claire up, if she loved me. She *does* love me. And this is the time for my proof that she does."

"If—"

"I asked a man about the hotels here. I got the names of several. One is Mercer Hall. Another is Whitecourt Inn. I take those names at random."

"What is the point of this? I can't wait to listen to any more of your queer ramblings. I must send that telegram to—"

"Yes. You must send her a telegram; so must I."

"You? Where do you come in?"

"I am going to send Claire a telegram saying I was injured in the wreck and that I have been carried to Whitecourt Inn, because I'm too badly hurt to be taken aboard the hospital train."

"You'll send a lie like that? What for? I—"

"Yes, a lie like that; and so will you. Only yours will be dated from Mercer Hall. Don't you get the idea, even yet?" he ended impatiently.

"No," growled Steell, "I don't."

"You say she loves you," impatiently exclaimed Ware, as to some stupid child. "*I* say she loves *me*. Here is the one golden chance to put it to the proof. Let each of us send her such a telegram as I've outlined—you from Mercer Hall, I from Whitecourt Inn. Let each say he is at the address given and that he is lying there dangerously injured, perhaps fatally."

"And frighten her? That's the rottenest—"

"No, to bring her here as fast as train or motor-car can carry her."

"Here?"

"Here. To the man she loves."

"To me? But—"

"No, to *me*—to decide it once and for all. In time of sudden disaster, a woman who really loves doesn't hesitate. She goes straight to the man she loves, she goes to him if it ruins her whole future. Now, if Claire Steell hears that the man she loves is terribly injured—perhaps dying—at a hotel in Sea Bank, she is coming to him, and she is coming with all speed. The only question left is: Who is the man she loves?"

"This rigmarole—"

"You will be at one hotel, I will be at another. She will come to the hotel where she thinks the man she loves is waiting for her. Oh, you begin to understand, at last, do you? Well, are you ready to make the test or are you afraid?"

"It is too abominably cruel—too whimsical—"

"It is not whimsical, at all. It's as exact and infallible a test as any problem in Euclid. As for cruelty—what is it, compared to the cruelty of binding Claire for life to a man she doesn't love—if she loves me? What is it, compared to the cruelty of your own uncertainty, for the rest of your days? For you *will* be uncertain about it, no matter how

hard you pretend to yourself that you aren't. How about the cruelty of sending me away to eat out my heart, alone, there in the desert? The 'cruelty' of the test I offer is as nothing compared to any of those. I ask you, again: Are you ready to make the test, or are you afraid?"

He paused, fighting for breath, and Steell very quietly made reply:

"I am afraid. But I am ready, too. Write the telegrams."

DUSK had sickened into evening, and the evening was waning. From an unlighted room just above the front doors of Whitecourt Inn, Ware peered down into the drive-way below him, scanning the face of every woman who mounted the hotel steps and passed into the glare of the veranda lights. Since afternoon he had sat thus. His eyes throbbed with the strain, and his body was agonizingly cramped. But Claire had not arrived.

Horace Steell, seated in a dark niche of the Mercer Hall veranda, smoked an endless succession of cigars and puckered new lines in his face by squinting through the half-light at every woman who approached the doorway.

At first he smoked with a grim confidence, then with outward stolidity, then with a growing nervousness that he took no pains to conceal. He fell to recalling a thousand little incidents in his home life with Claire that might or might not indicate she cared for anybody but him.

As the hours limped by, his nervousness swelled to frenzy. She had had time to make the ten-mile journey from Ocean Park by the slowest train, by the most wheezy automobile—yes, she had had time to get there on foot, on hands and knees if need be. And she had not come.

Or had she come?

Had she come to Sea Bank and gone directly to Whitecourt Inn— to Ware? Steell cursed himself for a beast and an imbecile for having consented to so insane a test. At the first, he had told himself he had agreed to it in order to prove once and for all to Ware how idiotic were the latter's pretensions. And now—

A church clock tolled midnight. His repeater, there in the dark, confirmed the clanging bell. Midnight! And she must have received the two telegrams by five, seven hours ago—seven hours to travel ten miles—to the man she loved.

All at once, the only possible explanation forced itself on him, with a logic he could no longer resist: She had come to Sea Bank; she had come with frantic, trembling haste; she had come—to Ware!

There was no longer room for the faintest shade of doubt; and Steell squared his mighty shoulders to meet the blow, to remember that he must live up to his agreement.

He left the veranda, clattered down the wooden steps and out into the street—where he well-nigh upset Ware, who was hastening past from the opposite direction on his way to the station.

Ware nodded, formally, and would have passed on. But Steell, a wild thrill of hopes stirring his dead heart at the other's crushed aspect, laid a hand of detention on his shoulder.

"You were right," said Ware, with almost a sob in his voice, as he strove to shake off the tight-gripping hand. "You were right, and I was a presumptuous ass to dream that she cared for me. I don't blame you for lying in wait to gloat over—"

"Gloat?" echoed Steell. "Why, man, *I* haven't seen her! She hasn't been near my hotel."

"What?" croaked Ware, unbelieving. "You—you mean, she—"

"I haven't seen her," grunted Steell, reaction making him surly. "Your silly test has—"

"—Has failed because she didn't get the telegrams," suddenly declared Ware. "It's the only possible explanation. She was out riding and was detained, or else she was sailing or driving somewhere, and she never got the telegrams."

"You're right," assented Steell. "I was stupid not to think of it before. Even if she didn't love me, common decency would have made her send some word of inquiry here during the past seven hours, if she believed I was dying. Yes; she wasn't at home. And if she gets there before I do," he added, ruefully, "I'll have a sweet time explaining those messages."

Side by side, they started down the broad-paved sidewalk toward the station. Neither spoke during the journey, until, passing an electric-lighted hotel porch, on their route, Steell spied a long-distance telephone sign. Halting, he said:

"I'm going in here to call her up. She may get my telegram before I can reach Ocean Park, and if she does, she'll start for here. I must stop her from doing that."

He ran up the steps and into the hotel lobby, Ware close behind him.

"Where's your telephone booth?" he asked of the night clerk.

As the clerk was about to reply, the desk telephone buzzed and he picked up the receiver. After a moment of listening, the clerk said with awkward solemnity:

"Dead, hey? Gee, but that's too bad. Poor guy! Yes, I'll tell the *Bulletin* reporter when he comes back. By the way, Doc, how did he spell his name—the reporter'll want to get it right. Was it Nevin or Nevins? Oh, Nev*in*. Yes, I got the first name—Percival L. Nevin. All right, Doc, I—"

He turned a sorrowfully bovine face from the telephone as the two men in front of the desk started forward simultaneously at sound of the name.

"Percival Nevin!" exclaimed Steell. "Why, good Lord, Dick! Only this afternoon—"

"Did you gentlemen know him?" queried the clerk with unction. "Yes, he was smashed up in the wreck. They brought him here. Doc Owens had charge of him. If anyone could 'a' pulled him through, it would 'a' been Doc. So you knew him, did you? Maybe you could tell me a little something about him, so I could give it to the reporter for our Sea Bank paper when he comes back?"

"And I snubbed him!" Steell was saying remorsefully to Ware, turning a deaf ear on the clerk, "only this afternoon; on the train—snubbed him good and plenty! I wish I could—"

"I don't suppose there's anything we can do," commented Ware. "We weren't close to him in any way, but—"

"Gents," said the clerk with an ideal undertaker inflection, "if you'd care to see him—being old friends—why, he's in 117, down at the end of that corridor—last room to your left."

"No!" cried Ware, shrinking back, with the chronic invalid's instinctive horror of looking on death. "No! No!"

Steell eyed him in open scorn.

"As you please, Dick," said he, "but *I'm* going. I never liked the fellow and I don't pretend I did. But at least I was an acquaintance, and he's dead, here, among strangers. It may be a question of cash, too—he was always broke and so were the few relatives he had. I'm going to see him."

"I'll show you the way," glibly volunteered the clerk.

HE CAME from behind the desk and tiptoed down the corridor with exaggerated noiselessness, waving one arm in sepulchral gesture to Steell to follow. Ware, rankling at the contempt in the big man's tone, defiantly fell into step alongside of Steell. And thus, ushered by the clerk, the two came into the presence of the erstwhile "tame cat."

The room of death was dim-lit. At a table, under a single thick-shaded electric burner, sat a bearded man filling in a certificate. On the bed, only half visible in the gloom, lay something covered by a sheet.

And among the bedside shadows knelt a woman who wept in frightened, strangled sobs.

At sound of the three men's steps, the woman looked up, her white face distorted.

"Claire!" mouthed Steell, his choked voice breaking into an absurd falsetto.

"He had her 'phoned for the minute they brought him here," whispered the clerk, with tragic relish, "—last thing before he went unconscious. Say, gents, I never thought anybody could 'a' got from Ocean Park to here as quick as that lady did. Poor thing!"

A Post-Marital Engagement

STEVE CARLILE had much wealth and scant leisure.

Dick Alton had little leisure and less wealth.

Ceres Carlile had the love of both men.

You see, it starts out like so many other "triangle" stories! But, for that matter, all horse races start alike. So do all human lives, all thunderstorms, all toothaches. But no two of them continue along just the same lines. So, read on, wont you?

Steve Carlile was not the typical plutocrat whose business absorbs his whole mind to the exclusion of his wife —the wife who, neglected, turns for consolation to the sinister man with the black mustache. On the contrary, Steve was very much alive to his wife's loveliness. He was demonstrative, slangy, a good fellow.

His friends called him "Red." They still called him so, even since the thatch which gave him the nickname had vanished prematurely, leaving only a gallant but hopeless little array of scarlet hairs that stood defiantly in a half-moon formation to fight back the further encroachments of shiny baldness. Once, Steve had been an athlete. Now, but for his arms and shoulders, he could have taken off his belt without unbuckling it, by the simple process of shoving it upward over his head.

Dick Alton was a lawyer with more zeal than cash, more breeding than clients. He was good looking, of good family and with a little patrimony that just kept him well groomed and lodged and fed.

He and Carlile were tolerably well acquainted. Indeed, Steve was Alton's only rich client. Ceres met Dick at a dinner and then at a dance and then at another dinner; and then he called on her; after which he kept on calling.

The husband didn't care. He liked Dick, and he had sized him up as wholesome. Moreover, Steve used to say all other men's interest in Ceres was a compliment to himself. He had many compliments, for she was lovely.

To Alton, at first, she was merely a charming woman who talked well, danced well and—crowning glory!—listened well. He found it pleasant to call on her. He found it pleasanter and increasingly pleasant.

THEN it was that Steve Carlile went to Chicago to fight his historic wheat-battle, at close quarters.

And on the evening her husband left New York, Ceres went to a dance. Dick Alton was there. He came home with her. She was just a little blue, because Steve was away. And, because she was blue and lonely, she asked Dick to come in and smoke a good-night cigarette before he started for his bachelor quarters.

The night was bitter cold, and there was a fire in the library. Its warmth went to both their hearts. Ceres looked unwontedly pretty and winsome with the fire-glow in her eyes and her hair. A clump of violets in her shoulder-knot gave off a faint, warm perfume that filled Alton's nostrils and his brain.

How it happened, neither of them ever knew. But all at once the violets were staining Dick's shirt-front, and the fragrance of their crushing made him drunk—that and the fresh-pulsing adorableness of the woman he had caught so impulsively, so fiercely, to his breast.

Of a sudden they stood apart, staring at each other, blankly, almost accusingly. Alton's face was flushed; and a swollen vein on his temple was throbbing visibly. He was shaking from head to heel as with a chill. The woman was white, palpitant, wide-eyed, aghast. And thus for a space they stared. Then:

"How—how *dared* you?" panted Ceres.

"We've—we've done it now!" gasped Alton.

They spoke, both, in the same breath. So neither heard the other. They made a second start; but this time Dick gained the lead. Also, in a measure, he regained his self-possession.

"I love you!" he said, "I *love* you! I didn't mean to—to do what I did. But—but it's done. And—and I—I love you!"

He had moved close to her as he spoke. And his voice came from the very depths of his throat. His breath was hot on her averted face. His tone rather than his words stirred her strangely.

"You mustn't!" she cried. "I—I—"

"You love me!" he answered in a growl of mastery that thrilled and astonished himself as much as it did Ceres.

"I—I don't," she protested feebly. "I—"

"You love me!" he declared, glowing like a young god in his new role of victorious lover.

And he kissed her again.

That was all. And presently he took his leave; treading on air, his head very high, his brain a whirling tumult.

WHEN he was gone, Ceres crouched on the hearth-rug in front of the fire, sobbing hysterically, trying to think, trying to be sorry. She had been happy with Steve Carlile. She had loved him—or so she had thought. But now, in the all-revealing glare of the evening's happenings, she saw their life together had been placid rather than inspiring. They had been jolly comrades rather than true soul-mates. And—Steve was close upon fifty, while she and Dick were still in the divine twenties.

Alton had swept her off her feet by the wild force of his young adoration. Had she known an hour earlier what was coming, she would have been revolted at the idea of other lips than Steve's touching hers. But now—

She was too young, too unversed in the mechanics of infatuation, to recognize at their mere face value the blended forces of midnight, of propinquity, of a warm room in bitter weather, of violets, of firelight, of dance-music echoes, of youth, of unexpectedness, of whirlwind attack. To Ceres' dazzled mind, all these elements were but accessories that enhanced, but had no share in causing, her new dream of love.

She loved Dick Alton. And she was married to Steve Carlile—to Steve Carlile, who trusted her—whom, she had thought till now, she loved dearly. She ought to be ashamed, to hate herself. And—she loved Dick. It was not her fault. She told herself so, over and over again.

It was Fate. She recalled the piteous tales of Paolo and Francesca, of Pelléas and Mélisande, of Lancelot and Guinevere. She saw herself a destiny-driven heroine, Dick as a pre-Rafaelite wooer, Steve Carlile as a medieval ruffian whose dagger would one day cut asunder their happiness.

All night, Ceres Carlile lay awake, seeking to solve the life-problem that had engulfed her. Dawn found her still irresolute, still helpless—one moment vowing never to see Dick Alton again and to telegraph a full confession to Steve, the next instant telling herself she had a right to the new rapture that was hers, and that youth must ever turn to youth. She tried, with some success, to bolster up these latter theories by maxims from long-haired poets and gray-linened amatory philosophers. It was surprising how many criminally asinine encouragements of that type she could recall—from Swinburne's *"To say of Shame: 'What is it?'"* down—or up—to Emerson's counsel, which she misquoted into: *"Desirest thou something, oh Discontented One? Take it and pay the price."*

DICK ALTON slept the sleep usually set apart for the just. His first waking thought was that something very wonderful had happened to him. Then, as he lay staring out at the rain (it usually rains, next morning), his rapture began to cloud.

He was a clean chap, and not addicted to making love to his neighbor's wife. Nor was he over-brilliant. He was just young. As he tried to live over the scene of the previous night, he could not at all understand how he had come to do what he had done. He had been tremendously fond of Ceres, of course—but only in an impersonal way, admiring the prettiness and sweetness and youth of her, never picturing her as his own.

Then had come that moment of insanity, the moment when warmth and perfume and beauty and dangerous nearness had swept him away; and he had found himself vowing deathless love to a wonder-woman who was gripped close to his heart—a woman he had never suspected he loved.

And now, what was to be done?

That afternoon, he called on Ceres. She had written him a note, telling him they must never, *never* meet again and that he must go away somewhere and they must both forget. The note was tear-splashed. Oddly enough, it did not reach Dick—largely because Ceres tore it up after she had read it over for the fifth time.

When she came into the room where he awaited her, she had a speech of dismissal all ready to deliver. He too, after a day of remorse, had prepared two or three approaches to a declaration that the only honorable thing for them to do was to part. But when they saw each other, Ceres forgot her rehearsed lines, and Dick was ashamed to make his renunciatory speech. So there was an awkward pause. And then, not knowing what better to do, he kissed her.

After a time they sat down and undertook to talk over this mighty crisis in their lives. It was a wholly new thing for them both, and so neither had the slightest experience to go on. Yet, given such an unworthy theme, they did not deal with it so very badly.

After much talk, their decision sifted down to this:

That they loved each other; and that while this was very regrettable and very terrible, yet it couldn't be helped; and that heaven-made love was stronger than man-made love. Also, as Steve Carlile was Ceres' husband, they could not with honor continue to meet in Steve Carlile's house; and that Dick must not come there again. Also, that this glorious love of theirs must be *kept* glorious.

THEN began the days of drifting. Ceres and Dick were together every daylight minute he could spare from his work. Their romance's course would have evoked a smile from a man of the world. Yet the smile would have been as kindly as it would have been wondering.

There were clandestine lunches at downtown restaurants; there were taxi drives in the Park; there were long and desultory walks; there was tea, nearly every afternoon, at some hotel. There were presents, too—flowers, candy, bits of not-too-costly jewelry and the like. And there was much love talk.

To a man of average spare time and of average means, there is nothing very extravagant about such a program. But Dick Alton's means barely sufficed for his own rather simple needs. As for time— he had reached the stage in his law practice where minutes are not yet dollars, but where the wasting of them means the certain absence of many future dollars.

And he began to realize several things: One was that a young lawyer does not make very rapid strides in his profession when he dawdles for two hours over the lunch-table, when he daily leaves the office at four in the afternoon or earlier, and when he delays a fuming client's business to talk for a solid half-hour in the middle of the morning to a lovelorn woman who has called him up on the telephone.

Then too, such items as elaborate lunches, teas and dinners, the daily buying of flowers or candy, the constant taxi-extortions, the more than occasional purchase of some trinket whose price scaled from ten to one hundred dollars—these outlays wrought sad havoc upon his slender savings and slenderer income.

Ceres would have been content with him, on a cheese-sandwich lunch and a trolley ride and with the offering of a fifteen-cent bunch of street carnations. But how was he to know that? And how was Ceres—accustomed by Steve to thinking money was as plentiful as trouble and as easy to acquire—to know he was robbing himself in order to stand well with her?

More than once he had to set his teeth and to command himself fiercely to "go ahead and play the game!" Which is not the way an ardent, if illicit, lover is supposed to refer to his newborn love-affair.

Then soon, to both of them,—blotting out money-worries and conscience and a checked law-career and other such light trifles,—came fear.

IT came to Dick the day of their third lunch together. At the next table to them sat a business associate of Steve's. And at sight of this mild-faced old financier, Dick's heart jumped. What if the man should some day chance to mention to Carlile that he had seen the latter's pretty wife lunching alone with Alton? What would Carlile do? Would not his suspicions at once blaze up? Dick did not tell his companion what he dreaded. Nor did he so much as say that the other man knew Steve.

Fear came to Ceres next afternoon. She and Dick were in a dim-lit hotel tea-room, whose every table was occupied by some low-voiced *tête-à-tête* couple. A lank woman who reeked of stephanotis paused at their table on the way out and greeted Ceres gushingly. When the woman had passed on, Ceres turned with tragical intensity to Dick, started to say something, changed her mind and asked if he would have another cup of tea. What she had started to say, and didn't, was:

"That's Steve's dearest friend's sister. He'll be told we were here—here in this half-twilight place where nine-tenths of the men and women are holding one another's hands, under the tables."

So Fear was born. So Fear grew.

EVERY day, the large city's dweller is likely to meet a full dozen people he knows by sight, or more intimately. Every day, he meets them and does not give the meeting a second thought. But when he is bent on business that must be secret, or when he is with some one with whom he should not be, or is aware that there is a smudge on his collar—he recalls every such chance encounter and has not the slightest difficulty in conjuring up memories of suspicious or derisive looks on the faces of those he met.

So with Dick Alton and Ceres. Almost from the beginning they were forever running into somebody that one or both of them knew—somebody who, they were certain, eyed them in cold disapproval or with a gaze of covert and evil imaginings.

At first, they did not speak to each other of this. Both were futilely trying to believe that these people would not, one and all, begin babbling of what they had seen and of what their low minds would lead them to infer from it. But the effort was vain. The two grew to feel they were marked, whispered about, pilloried, that the tale of their affair—magnified, distorted, made hideous—had reached or was reaching the farthest corners of their social universe.

And, finally, they voiced the fear. It was Ceres who broke the tactful silence on the subject. One afternoon, as they were driving home through the Park in a wheezy taxicab, from tea, she said:

"Did you see the man who bowed to me as we got into this taxi? That was one of Steve's clerks. He has been to the house once or twice with papers. Did you notice the queer way he looked at me? I'm—oh, I'm *sure* he suspects something. He'll be certain to speak about it, down at the office; and then—"

"Why, of course, he won't," Dick reassured her, stoutly. "And if he did, what would there be to speak about? That he saw you getting into a taxi, at six o'clock in the afternoon, with a harmless looking man?

There's no great scandal in that. Don't worry, sweetheart!"

"IT isn't only that," she broke out, vaguely irritated at his manner. "It's ever so many things like it. Josephine Chard saw us one day. She'll tell Steve's sister. Harry King saw us walking on the Avenue. He'll tell it at Steve's club. Mary Romer saw us coming out of Thorley's. She'll tell everybody in sight. She always does. Old Mrs. Beasley met us on the way to lunch last week, and she looked at me as if I were a ten-dollar gold-piece she'd found—the cat! She calls every month or two at Steve's office to ask him about some bonds she bought on his advice. Next time, she'll tell him. As for that Parkins woman who spoke to us once at tea—she's a lifelong friend of the family. And then that—"

"But, dearest!" he broke in, albeit less assuredly than before, "we've done nothing wicked. There's nothing any of them could tell that would—"

"Oh, isn't there?" she almost wept. "When Steve hears from a host of different sources that I've been seen everywhere, at lunch, at tea, walking, driving, shopping—all with the same man—"

"But—" he began; then he stopped, for she hurried on:

"The Vynings had a big dance, last night. I wasn't invited. I was invited to the one they gave last year. There were two 'At Homes,' this week, that I expected to be asked to, and—"

"Dear, you're making a mountain of a mole-hill," he soothed, in a tone that would not have deceived a lunatic. "Don't you know that nearly twenty per cent of the card envelopes sent out never get to their address? I've heard that postmen dump them by the hundreds, into ash-cans and—"

"You know I'm right!" she cried in sorry triumph, intuition leaping to life at the false note in his voice. "You *know* it! You've been noticing it, too. You've been thinking just what I've been thinking. You've seen how people stare at us—people we both know, people that *you* know."

He tried to deny it, but the lie jammed crosswise in his throat. He reached out and caught her cold hand in his. She found the touch annoying and drew her hand away. For a space, they sat wordless, fear uniting them far more intimately than ever love had done.

DICK, while Ceres talked, had been recalling a street meeting with an elderly client of his, a few days earlier, when he had been walking with Ceres. The day before that, the same client had written he expected to call soon at Alton's office. He had not come there—nor had another occasional client from whom Dick had expected a visit, a man in business with the first.

"Did you ever read Dumas' 'Antony?'" asked Ceres, suddenly.

"No. I thought Shakespeare—"

"This was a different play, a play about *Antony,* a Frenchman, who loved a woman named *Adèle* and was loved by her. Her husband was years older than she was. And he was away from home for several months. *Antony* and *Adèle* thought nobody suspected anything, till all at once people began cutting her. And somebody wrote to her husband about *Antony;* and the husband hurried home to murder them both."

"Did he?" asked Dick in a tone he tried right valiantly to make careless. "Did he—murder them both?"

"No," said Ceres, "because, to save *Adèle's* reputation, *Antony* killed her. And he said to her husband: '*Elle m' a resistée; Je l'ai assassinée!*' He—"

"B-r-r!" shuddered Dick. "What ghastly rot! It's an impossible situation!"

"It's a situation *we're* beginning to face!"

"Nonsense! We—"

"'The wages of—'"

"There's no sin. It—"

"Will Steve believe that? Will *anyone* believe it?"

"My darling, you sha'n't talk so. You're all overwrought. You're—"
Smash!

THE taxicab was lifted bodily in air for a few seconds, under a heavy impact from behind; then it careened and crashed over on its side. Ceres and Alton found themselves in a squirming and jolted heap, underneath cushions and a shower of broken glass and one of the window-sashes. The chauffeur lay sprawled like a huge straddle-bug on the roadway just in front. The cab's engine raced deafeningly for a moment, then "died." Before Dick could more than realize that he was pressed face downward against one of the taxi doors, with his nose on the ground, and that Ceres was huddled heavily against his backbone, the door above them was yanked open. Amid a clamor of voices, hands reached down and drew the woman's weight away from him. With a wrench, Dick righted himself and, by the help of a police-man, clambered up and out to the road.

There, very white and breathless and dizzy, and leaning on the arm of a traffic policeman, was Ceres. A bit of flying glass had nicked her left cheek; and a little trickle of blood was oozing down her face. Several million people stood around them.

At least, there was still another policeman, and there were four or five pedestrians and the occupants of another taxicab. And, emerging from a big limousine whose lamps were jammed against the rear axle of the overturned cab, were a chauffeur and three passengers.

"You're all right?" a policeman was asking the half-stunned Alton. "Only shook up a little, hey? No bones broke? I saw it, how it happened. That big car tried to pass you, and it skidded and bumped you. It—"

Dick shook himself free and lurched over to Mrs. Carlile.

"Ceres!" he cried. "Sweetheart! Are you very badly hurt? Tell me!"

Even as he spoke, one of the passengers of the offending limou-sine—a woman in a fur coat—exclaimed:

"Why, it's Ceres Carlile! Oh, my dear, I'm so sorry! You must let us take you home. It was all Gavroche's carelessness. I've begged Mr. Herne to discharge him. He takes such chances and—"

THE fur-coated woman's eyes fell on Dick Alton. And at the same time her brain, somewhat belatedly, appeared to catch the import of what Dick had just said to Ceres. And, through her dense furs, the woman appeared gradually to freeze.

"Can we be of any assistance?" she went on, stiffly. "I regret extremely that we should have been the cause—"

"What's the name?" put in a policeman, notebook in hand.

"This is Mr. Francis K. Herne's car," answered the woman. "My address is 400 Riverside Drive. If you wish—"

"H'm! And *your* name, lady?" said the bluecoat, writing busily as he turned to Ceres.

"My name," Ceres faltered, "is—"

"Is not necessary to give," Alton had the sense to interpolate. "We shall not bring suit. So—"

"But I gotta get the names," stormed the officer. "The law—"

"The law requires nothing of the sort," said Dick, sharply. "I am a lawyer. If there is no charge against us and if no civil or criminal suit is proposed, we are at liberty to withhold our names."

"But this poor feller," protested the policeman as the chauffeur came somewhat groggily into the group. "This poor feller may want to sue."

"We were passengers," answered Dick. "We saw nothing. You have the name and address of the limousine's owner. That is all the man needs. Come," he added, to Ceres, "let's go. There is a taxi across the road."

He half led, half supported the dizzy girl to the providentially disengaged taxicab, helped her into its musty interior and in a whisper gave the chauffeur her address. They had left the Park behind them, before Ceres could find her voice. And even then she did not answer any of Dick's frenzied questions as to her injuries. All she said was:

"It's happened. The very worst. Her husband is Steve's best friend. It's all over, now. Well, it's better—it's better than the fear."

WHEN they reached the Carlile house, she spoke again—this time to bid Alton come in. It was the first time he had entered the house since the night, a month earlier, when he had told her of his love. It seemed a century—a century of horribly long days.

"I asked you to come in," she said, as they entered the library, "because I want to tell you what I am going to do."

As she spoke, she sat down and began to dab her cut cheek with a wad of handkerchief. Dick stood over her, puzzled, wondering.

"I can't stand this any longer," she went on, speaking jerkily, like a spent swimmer. "I can't stand it. I can't. I understand now why people who are condemned to die at a certain time, try to kill themselves beforehand. I'm going to do that."

"Ceres!"

"Not the way you mean. I'm going to write to my husband—this evening. I'm going to tell him all about everything. He can divorce me if he wants to. He can kill me if he wants to. But, anyhow, he'll *know*. And it will be a million times better for him to hear it from me than from any of those other people. And there won't be any suspense, then, as to how or when he'll find out. I'm going to tell. That will kill this eternal fear—even if it kills *me, too.*"

SHE looked up at Alton, defiantly, as if challenging him to oppose her. Dick's face had gone pale, and his lips and fists were tightly clenched. Fear was having its final and supreme will with him. He was trying to forecast what a man, of Steve Carlile's sort, might be expected to do to the lover of his wife. And stark terror—not of man for man, but the world-old terror of lover for husband—encompassed him, like a choking smoke-cloud.

He stood to lose so much! He had gained—nothing! The bargain seemed grossly unfair, the punishment inordinate—as probably it has seemed to ten million men, since the birth of time—men caught as was Dick Alton, and with better reason for dread.

His shoulders squared, and he said quietly:

"You are right. It is better. And we can't suffer much worse than we've been suffering. Certainty is better than—"

HE broke off. Steps were coming down the front stairway—heavy, clumping masculine steps, such as could belong to no manservant in a well-appointed house. Then Steve Carlile's big body filled the library doorway. Alton noticed he was wearing housecoat and slippers.

"Hello, good people!" hailed Steve, on sight of the room's two occupants. "Didn't get my letter, hey, Ceres? It was on the hall table, when I got in, half an hour ago. I figured on its reaching you by noon. I found yesterday I could get home a week earlier than I'd—"

He had been crossing the room toward his wife, arms outstretched, as he spoke. Now, as she rose and faced him, he cried:

"Why, what's the matter, old girl? You look as if I was a ghost. And, who's been scratching your face?"

Drawing a deep breath and fending off her husband's embrace, Ceres made breathless answer:

"I was going to write to you. That's why I asked him to come in. I was going to write, this evening, and tell you—"

"One moment," interposed Alton, stepping between Ceres and the bewildered Steve. "Mr. Carlile, your wife has been blameless. The fault is all mine. I love her. She loves me. Now—do whatever you want to."

"It was *my* fault, too, Steve," broke in Ceres. "The whole miserable affair was just as much my fault as his. I—"

"Hold on!" demanded Carlile, speaking with an authority that held no menace in it. "One at a time, please. This is a merry homecoming, to be sure. Let me get things straight. Is it a joke you two are putting up on me, or—"

"No," said Alton, "it is not. After you went away, Ceres and I found out that we cared for each other. That is all."

"All?" echoed Steve, quizzically. "Isn't it almost enough? I'm no glutton. And—oh, let's sit down."

THE monumental calm of his manner—his utter refusal to play up to the situation or to be so much as startled by the uncouth suddenness of the mutual confession, acted upon the two others as a splash of ice-water on an over-hot face. His mode of taking their terrible news left them speechless, jarred, shamed. They felt like naughty children in the presence of a kindly, patronizing schoolmaster. Heroics or coarse fury they could have met and battled. This amused tolerance disarmed them.

"Let's sit down," said Steve again.

Meekly they obeyed his suggestion.

"Now, then," said Carlile, glancing interestedly from one to the other, "I take it I've got the main facts, so we needn't waste time elaborating *those*. I gather from the words of eager welcome you fired at the returned wanderer just now, that you two find you're in love with each other. Well, there's nothing in that worth getting out an 'Extra' on. It happens often enough. So why the heavy tragedy and the glowers of despairing courage? I'm lot going to bite either of you."

"You surely can't understand," began Dick, "or you couldn't take it so—"

"So sanely? Why not? Where's the use of my making war-medicine? The time to do that would have been before the beans were spilled. It's no use afterward. Take it calmly, little people. If *I* can do it, *you* should be able to. Now, let's get down to cases, and we can clear up this muddle in no time and without any mislaying of temper or wasting long words over it. It's a perfectly simple problem. Watch me solve it."

"Steve," said Ceres, almost resentfully, "I don't see how you can bring yourself to—"

"A whole swad of people haven't been able to see how I can 'bring myself' to do things," he replied, cheerily. "That's how I happened to have annexed nearly two million dollars before I was fifty. But the bragging can wait. Alton, you're gone on my wife, and you say she's equally stuck on you—cutting out the fireworks language, that's the United States for it. You want to marry her, of course?"

"Of course!" declared Alton very loudly indeed.

"The noisier, the more convincing," approved Steve. "That's why boys whistle when they go through woods in the dark. How are you fixed?"

"I have an income of about fourteen hundred dollars a year from my practice, if that is what you mean," the bewildered Alton heard himself saying. "And my father left me about thirteen hundred dollars a year more."

"Twenty-seven hundred in all, hey? Not bad, for a boy of twenty-six. In fact, it's pretty near half as much a year as I give Ceres to dress on."

"I am not rich," said Alton, stung into retort, "but—"

"You sure aren't," pleasantly agreed Steve. "Ceres has been having an allowance of something like five hundred dollars a month, just for herself. And during the past year she hasn't overdrawn it more'n twelve times at most. I'll say that for her. It costs me, besides, something like fourteen thousand a year to run this house and the place up on the Sound. We live rather quietly, at that. And then there is the upkeep of the cars and the—"

"I am not competing with you in expenditures!" flashed Dick.

"Why not?" blandly asked Steve. "You're competing with me for my wife. It's only square, for her sake, that you should be able to compete with me in money too. She's never in her life spent less, a month, than you earn in a year; and she'll have a swell time learning how to cut down. But that's her business, and yours—not mine. 'Love in a cottage,' eh, old girl? Some enjoy it. I hope *you* will."

"It isn't a matter of money," said Ceres, unsteadily. "I could—"

"You could live in one room and on one meal, with a fellow you love," supplemented Carlile. "I know the talk. And you love Alton well enough for that, of course. So let's pass on to the next cage."

He glanced genially from one to the other:

"Who's going to get the divorce? And how?" he asked, forestalling a half-tearful interruption from Ceres, "Being a lawyer, Alton, you can save her a lot of money that way. Why, a chap out in Chicago told me it cost him more'n four thousand dollars to work up his divorce case; and at that, it was thrown out of court. Now, of course, I'll let Ceres do the divorcing. That's one of the good old rules in the dirty old game. But on what grounds? I'd like to oblige you, old girl, by giving you 'cause,' here in New York State; but that sort of thing is rather out of my line. It's a bit too much to ask of me. So I'd prefer to have you get it some pleasanter way. How would Desertion do? Or Cruelty?"

"Don't!" she begged. "How can you speak so cold-bloodedly of such—"

"You ought to be thanking me," he chuckled, "because by letting you get the divorce I let you get alimony, too. Be sure you apply for a thundering big alimony for her, Alton. I'll stand for it, whatever it is. And you'll be surprised to see how nicely it'll eke out that little twenty-seven hundred of yours—"

"Stop!" ordered Dick, fiercely. "You have no right to hint that I'm looking for her money. I can support—"

"You can support her—with plenty of economy—just about one month, on your year's income. You don't suppose I'm going to let her starve, do you? Maybe you don't know, even though she's kicking me off at a siding, I'm fonder of her than I am of everything else on earth. And I'm going to see she's well fixed for cash. How would fifteen thousand a year strike you, Ceres? With Dick's stalwart twenty-seven hundred, that would make—"

"Oh, you're a brute—a *brute!*" sobbed his wife, breaking down.

"Me?" queried Steve, amazed. "Good Lord, girl, I didn't mean to be! If I'd gone ranting around, trying my new automatic on Alton and pinning the Big Red Letter on *you,* or giving you both a *Hazel Kirk* shassay out into the snow, I could understand your handing me a pet name like that. But, on the level, aren't I playing the hand pretty square? I'm only trying to put you on Easy Street. Where does the 'brute' part come in?"

But she sobbed hysterically, by way of answer. And he went on:

"Then we'll have to frame up some way, too, for folks to keep from shelving any of the blame off onto you. I don't want women turning up their noses at you. And, for your sake, I don't want Alton to lose friends or clients, either. So we'll—"

"Have *you* no heart?" wailed Ceres. "Does it mean so little to you, that you can talk about incomes—and alimony—and all those things? Doesn't it mean anything to you to lose *me?*"

For an instant the comfortably smiling face grew hard.

"Girl, dear," said Steve, "let's don't talk about that end of it. All my life, I've howled like a freight-whistle whenever I pricked my finger; but I've always tied a grin in front of me when my head was being cut off. It's my way. It's just as easy as the other way round—or it was till to-day—and usually it's a blamed sight nicer for the folks who are with me. Let it go at that. Now, then, Brother Alton, what's the quickest a divorce can be railroaded through, when there's plenty of cash behind it? I ask, so we can arrange all that, and maybe even set the wedding day, before we wind up this little love-feast we're having."

Ceres' sobs had again broken control; and now they almost drowned her husband's jovially businesslike voice.

"There, there, little girl!" crooned Steve, his gigantic hand on her heaving shoulders, in awkward caress. "Don't take on so! There, *there!* I'm trying to make things all smooth for you, Baby. Here, Alton,"—drawing the resisting Dick toward her,—"you take a try at comforting her. She loves you. You can quiet her, better'n a has-been like me."

BY force, he put the lawyer's reluctant hand on Ceres' shoulder. She recoiled from the touch as though it scalded her. And in the recoil she found herself very close to her husband. Steve moved a step farther away.

"Alton," he said, eyeing the glum and hugely embarrassed youth, "if you don't mind my saying so, you aren't giving a very hot imitation of a sighing swain. Look, Ceres! He's as chap-fallen as if a rich relative had left him a Kentucky feud. Is that the way young fellows act, nowadays, when they love some one who loves them?"

Ceres looked, despite herself. And before Alton could mask his expression, she had read it.

"No!" she cried, in tearful jubilance. "It isn't! It's the way they look when they don't 'love some one.' He doesn't love me! He *doesn't*—any more than I love him."

"I—I—" protested Alton; then he mustered strength to say, mechanically:

"I adore you."

"You don't!" she flashed. "Oh, I'm so glad! So *glad!* Steve, I'm so glad."

She was gripping her husband's house-coat by both lapels; and she fairly shouted the words up to him.

"And," she continued, joyously, "I don't love him, either. I've known it all along. But I never knew I *knew* it till you began to talk about my marrying him. Then I—"

"Didn't you know it till then?" asked Steve in surprise. "Why, I knew it long before that, girl. I knew it at the start, when you spoke of your mix-up with him as 'the whole miserable affair.' Women don't talk that way about happy romances—only about scrapes. Want to get out of the scrape, little sweetheart?"

"Want to? *Want* to?" she murmured, in ecstasy. "Oh, *yes*. You know I do. You knew it all along, you brutal old angel. But"—her joy dying out—"you—you can never feel the way you used to, about me, Steve. I'm not fit to stay here with you. I've—I've kissed him. And we've held each other's hands. And we've had tea and lunch and taxicab rides together! Ugh! You won't want—"

"LISTEN to me, Ceres," said Steve: "I want you with all my heart. And I'm going to have you—forever and ever. I wouldn't be jealous, would I, if you'd been engaged to some guy, before ever you met me? I wouldn't be sore about his kisses and all that, would I? Well, we'll just figure out you were engaged to friend Alton this past month. It was broken off. And you're marrying *me*."

"But people have noticed—they're saying things—"

"Girl," he returned, with a new gravity, "nothing in this whole measly world is on the free list—not even post-marital 'engagements.' Everything's got to be paid for. Look close enough, and you're bound to find the price-mark. The foolish things, sometimes, must be paid for more than the bad things. From your own story, you've been plenty foolish, this past month. And you've got to pay—just as much as if you'd been worse. That's only fair. (You don't have to pay *me* anything. That's because there's no balance account between a man and a woman who love each other.) But you'll have to pay other folks—folks who have no right to collect. That's apt to be the way. But are a few snubs and maybe a direct cut or a nasty whisper when you come into a drawing-room—is all that too much to live down? Is it too much to pay for the privilege of having been 'engaged' to a nice young chap after you were married to an old geezer like me? Is it?"

"Yes!" she made muffled answer, from somewhere in the folds of his waistcoat. "It's a million times too much. But—but it isn't one-millionth enough to pay for coming back to a second honeymoon. Oh, Steve, I feel so glad and so ashamed and—and—safe! Dearest, I've been *sick* with fear."

"That ought to have told you you didn't love him, girl. The Book says: 'Perfect love casteth out fear.' Maybe that's why no lawless love can ever be a perfect love. By the way, Alton—why, the earnest young lover has gone! 'Perfect love' seems to have cast *him* out, too—along with fear."

"Along with—fear!" she sighed blissfully, her upstretched arms groping their way about his neck.

Money Makes the Marriage Go

WHEN they married, Royce Churchill had an income of three thousand dollars a year, earned from his law practice. Mavis, his wife, had an income of six hundred dollars a year, inherited from her great-aunt Clara.

When they had been married three years, Royce's income had swelled to five thousand dollars, and Mavis' was still six hundred. When they had been married five years, Royce's income was still about five thousand. Mavis' was thirty-two thousand.

Yes, you read it aright, the first time: thirty-two thousand dollars.

It was brought about by one of the everyday miracles of life. Early in the fourth year of their married life, Royce had to go to Mexico for three months on law business. As there was a revolution or so, brewing and bubbling, in that caloric republic, he did not take Mavis along. She beguiled the time, while he was gone, in scribbling. It was a taste that had always been hers.

When Royce came back to New York she showed him, more or less shamefacedly, what she had written. It was a play—a fluff-brained, inconsequent little play, wherein nothing much happened, but where the scanty stock of happenings was amusingly set forth.

Royce was inordinately proud of the silly playlet. He howled rapturously over its frothy nothings, and gasped aloud at its unconscious daring. Then he vowed it must be produced. It was copied—five times—in blue-bound manuscript books, beautifully typed and with the amateurish stage directions neatly underlined in scarlet. And it read little less inspiredly to Royce in its cold type form than when it had sprawled, crossed-out and interlined, on both sides of the rough-draft pages.

Then came the nerve-sickening weeks, when the blue-bound 'script fluttered gayly forth to one manager after another—to flop back rejected. Each rejection made Mavis more and more profoundly unhappy, until at last Royce could stand her growing despondency no longer.

Without saying a word to her of his intent, he went in person to a second-rate manager and staked his entire store of savings and putative borrowings—some seven thousand dollars in all—on having the play produced at his own expense.

ROYCE knew nothing of theatrical affairs. That was why he dared risk real money on his own novice judgment. He loved Mavis with all his heart and soul. And to lift her from the Slough of Despond in which she was so dejectedly splashing, he would bithely have chanced a far greater sum, if he had possessed it. The only stipulation he made with the manager was that Mavis should not know that her husband had financed the venture. The play, she was to believe, had been accepted on its merits—or their lack.

This is not a theatrical story; and so the climax of this particular part of it may be scaled in a mere mouthful of words.

For seven thousand dollars one does not get a Belasco production. And Mavis Churchill's featherweight play was put on in pitiably sleazy fashion with a decidedly "roady" company. It had its New York opening at a hoodoo theater, after a single appalling week on the road.

And it ran there for three hundred and nine consecutive performances.

You see the idea—or dearth of idea—and the treatment were quite new. The thing chanced to tickle the Manhattanese and the strangers within their (hotel) gates. It was "different,"—not necessarily good, just different,—with the "difference" for which managers are forever clamoring and from which they are so prone to shy in terror.

In any event, Mavis' play was one of the four successes of the theatrical year. And the three-act comedy with which she followed it was almost as successful.

Whereat, Mavis computed that she was clearing something over thirty thousand dollars a year, on royalties.

Now, as all folk know, it is easier for a family to live, in New York, on twelve dollars a week than on twenty-two. The family of the wage-earning laborer thrives. The family of the salary-earning clerk skimps. On Royce's five thousand dollars a year, the Churchills had lived very nicely indeed, but cosily rather than luxuriously.

Their apartment had cost them ninety dollars a month, their maid thirty more, their food another ninety. When clothes and amusements and summer outings had been deducted from the remainder, there was not overmuch left. And that thin surplus went into the savings bank.

The Churchills had not been extravagant. So they had lived right comfortably—for New York. There had always been, it is true, the need for thought, in expenditure. And more than once, Royce—like every other American husband—had longed to give his wife the splendid things that women of her acquaintance owned. It was a natural yearning. And he had been the better for it.

NOW, all at once, that yearning could be gratified. To the man with a million a year, thirty-two thousand dollars is a pittance. To the family that has spent less than five thousand a year, it is a Monte Cristo fortune. There is—for the first few months, at least—nothing it won't buy.

Immediately Mavis launched out, pushing her way vigorously through the royalty-checks that avalanched about her. Like a child with a Christmas dollar, she began to pile up treasures.

The apartment was discarded for a bijou little house on West End Avenue. The solitary maid had three costly colleagues. The occasional taxicab was replaced by a pretty and none too economical town-car. And a chauffeur went with the car—at as much a week as once the lone maid had received per month.

Mavis delighted most to shower gifts on Royce. The fur overcoat he had ever coveted but never could feel able to buy, the Manton shot-gun, the new office furniture, the gold cigar-case with his monogram in tiny rubies—all the things he had craved and never expected—were his, without the asking. And for a time husband and wife were like two deliriously happy youngsters to whom vacation and unlimited spending money have come. There were no sordid trials to look back upon, but that did not lessen the present spree's delights.

Their little circle of old friends had always been a quiet joy to them. Now this circle was instantly and vastly enlarged. For all sorts of new and distinguished people began to troop into the Churchill's lives.

Once they had thrilled on meeting, at a charity dance, the author of a best seller, and a Broadway leading woman. Now, both as guests and hosts, they met scores of people who had hitherto been to them merely illustrious names: theatrical stars of the first magnitude, playwrights of the world-fame, first-flight novelists, painters—and folk, sometimes, whose likenesses smudged the "society" columns and who, through taste or curiosity, sought the companionship of those who were achieving things in the world.

Yes, the Churchills' circle of acquaintances enlarged tremendously. Then, without diminishing in size, it lost one by one of its old-time membership. The friends of other days felt (and were) insignificant, out of place, in the new throng. And gradually, unostentatiously, they dropped away, scarce missed.

ROYCE did not wake from the golden daze for many a long month—not until he chanced to overhear some born humorist refer to him as "Mr. Mavis Churchill." The same day, he read, in a list of guests at a Drama League dinner of the preceding night, "Mavis Churchill and Mr. Churchill." That afternoon at his club he was introduced to some one by a fellow member, who added in explanation, "Mrs. Churchill's husband."

He did not like that sort of thing. He did not like it at all. He decided to tell Mavis about it. He had always told her his troubles, big or small. She would understand how galling it was. And she would ease the annoyance in her own tactful way, by saying something to take the irritation from his memory—just as she had been wont to do in the olden life, when troubles had still existed.

But he reached home to find her busy with a manager who had called by appointment. She heard Royce's step in the hall, but did not ask him to join in the managerial conference. When he walked in, unasked, she greeted him affectionately. The manager, too, was civil. But Royce had a vague sense of being in the way. He felt as he had when, in boyhood, he had stumbled in on some household-finance discussion between his parents.

And he made awkward excuse to leave his wife and the caller to their business talk. He wandered upstairs, feeling almost like an interloper in his own house. "His own house?" No, the house was Mavis'. At least its rent was paid from her royalties. That had never before occurred to him. From her marriage day he had, until now, considered all their possessions as the common property of both.

The manager did not leave until so late that Mavis had barely time to dress for a dinner she was giving that evening, and Royce had no chance to speak to her alone.

AT the dinner, he said little. He realized, all at once, that there was no need for him to exert himself to play the host. He was not the host. He was only the hostess' husband. He saw that now. He railed at himself for a purblind fool for not having seen it before.

These people—these people whom he could never have hoped to meet through his own endeavors—were not in the very least interested in him. They had come hither as guests of the famous Mavis Churchill—the woman who had devised a new angle on the ancient art of play-writing, and who was lionized accordingly.

Royce recalled the few and simple dinner parties they used to give in the old apartment, dinners where at times he had, perhaps, unconsciously dominated the talk, where it had seemed to him that Mavis had played only a charming second to his lead. He remembered how indulgently their friends had been wont to laugh at her occasional queer little irrational witticisms—the same type of verbal oddities which had later made her two plays such a hit, and to which people nowadays listened with such breathless appreciation.

"No, I don't like her," he heard Mavis saying, to-night, at the far end of the table, in answer to a transatlantic actor-baronet's question, "and I'm glad I don't. For, you see, if I liked her, I'd be with her as much as I could. And I'd hate to be."

A ripple of zestful laughter greeted the somewhat slender pleasantry—a pleasantry that would have been almost skeletonian but for the speaker's personal charm.

"Speaking of not liking people," put in Royce, clearing his throat and throwing a "carrying" quality into his voice, "that reminds me of a man I used to know in college. One day, he—"

Royce let his voice trail away. No one was listening. No one had heard. Mavis was telling of an incident that had happened at rehearsal the day before. And everybody at her end of the table was hanging on her quaint diction. Royce settled—or, rather, slumped—lower in his chair, and waxed glum. No one noticed. Nobody so much as sought to rouse him.

People who weren't talking with Mavis were talking with those next to them. They were talking a language of their own, a language Royce did not speak nor understand: the jargon of stage, studio, literature. Even the woman he had taken in to dinner was gayly chatting, with her back to him.

And now Churchill realized that all the dinners and other functions he and Mavis had given or attended had been like this. He had been an outsider. He had been "Mavis Churchill's husband." And never until that night had his eyes been opened to the fact. Up to then, it had all been so new, so exhilarating, so interesting, he had given no thought to his own role in the comedy. But now he was awake, very wide awake indeed.

Looking across at Mavis' pretty face, daintily flushed with the excitement of adulation, Royce felt a thrill of love and pride. He was ashamed of himself for his momentary peevishness. He felt he ought to be glad—he was glad, heartily glad—at his adored wife's success. Was it any fault of hers that these celebrities had the good sense to seek her society, to prefer her talk to his? She was not to blame if—

"I'm not sure, yet," he heard her say to some one. "But I've been thinking it over, lately. And I've almost decided we'll go for a month, to Nantucket—just at first, you know, to rest. It's such a dear, drowsy old place. I'd love it, if it weren't for the whales, offshore. Whales always bore me. They look so disgustingly much like their pictures. But I think we'll go there. We may take a cottage for the month. I'm going to write and make inquiries."

She was forming summer plans, forming them without so much as consulting Royce. She, who of yore had never dreamed of taking such a step without his sanction and help. And again glumness settled over the unnoticed husband.

HE said nothing to Mavis—even after the guests were gone—concerning the resentment that was gnawing at his vanity. But next morning, the smolder was fanned again. On the way to the office he met a former client who was also a school friend.

"Curtis," he said, abruptly, in the midst of a car-strap chat, "would you mind telling me why you took that contract case of yours to Ebbett & Ebbett? I've been doing all your law business for nearly ten years. If my work wasn't satisfactory, why didn't you tell me so, instead of—"

"Satisfaction?" echoed the ex-client in genuine amaze. "What rot! Of course it was 'satisfactory.' Only—"

"Only *what?*" demanded Royce.

"Why," stammered into other man, "now that you've come into all that cash, I didn't suppose you'd want to bother over a measly little piker job like that contract-case of mine. I'd as soon think of asking John D., in person, to sell me a nickel's worth of gasoline."

"I haven't come into any cash," retorted Churchill, hot and sulky. "I'm doing about as well as I was last year. Perhaps a few per cent better. But—"

"I meant your wife's success and all that," explained the man, uncomfortably. "I supposed—"

"That I was living on my wife's money?" flashed Royce. "Thanks. We have an unpleasant little name for men who do that. I'm still in business for myself—though I don't care, in future, to add to that business through you."

Without giving the astounded client a chance to reply, Royce stamped out of the car, mad clear through. So this was the way his downtown acquaintances looked on him, nowadays!

In the weeks that followed, Royce Churchill kept his eyes and ears on the alert and his mouth shut. Thus he saw and heard much, and gave no outward sign of it. He wanted to be just. He wanted to judge fairly, to make certain of his ground. In former times Mavis would have noted at once his change of manner. But rehearsals, and the whipping into shape of her newest play, and a thousand social distractions, and plans for the near future, all kept her mind and body almost hourly engrossed, to the exclusion of such lesser matters as her husband's new reticence.

SO while she worked and planned, Royce watched and planned. And in six weeks came the crisis. To Mavis it came with utter suddenness, to Royce as the result of long preparation.

"I've just had a letter from a house-agent down at Nantucket," she said casually, one morning at breakfast, as she glanced up from a pile of mail at her place. "I'd like you to run down there, to-morrow, if you don't mind, and look at the cottage he writes about. If it and its grounds are half he says they are, then the mystery of the Garden of Eden's site is cleared up at last. We're lucky to get it at all, even for a month. If you'll go there and—"

"I can't," said Royce, briefly. "The Marden trial begins to-morrow. It may drag on for weeks. And in any case, I'm too busy to—"

"You're working too hard," she told him, with a judicial decisiveness that riled him, "much too hard. The one-armed-paper-hanger-with-the-hives was a languorous dreamer compared to you. You're working all the whole time. I don't like it, Royce. There's no need for it."

Instinctively she was adopting a wise-parent tone—she whose pretty deference to his wishes had aforetime been so winsome.

"I don't spend nine hours a day at the office and in court, just for the fun of it," he told her, trying to be reasonable.

"I know you don't," she said. "If you did, I wouldn't mind. I want you to have all the fun there is. But it isn't fun for you and as I just told you, here's no more need for it."

"No more need for it?" he rasped. "At the very time when my years of grinding hustle are beginning to count for something? I'm starting upward, now. If I keep on working like this, another ten years will double my income. If I loaf, there are a hundred lawyers ready to grab what gets past me. 'No need,' eh?"

"Absolutely no need," she repeated, standing placidly to her guns, with that air of gentle superiority he found so maddening. "Absolutely none, Royce. Why should you drudge away all the best years of your life in making ten thousand dollars grow where only five thousand used to blossom? I have more than three times as much as that; and I shall be getting more and more, every year. We can live so beautifully on that. It's absurd for you to waste your time in adding just a silly pittance to the royalties."

"You suggest, then," he asked with chilly calm, "that I live on your money?"

"Of course. Didn't I live on yours, long enough?"

"No," he told her, "you didn't. Not nearly long enough. We'd have been a million times happier if you'd kept on doing it, forever, as God meant a wife to."

"Nonsense!" she laughed. "You old-fashioned Dodo-bird of a family-story-paper husband! You're worse, even, than the inspired members of the Put-Your-Wives-to-Work Club. I—"

"We needn't argue it," he said stiffly. "I'm *not* going to live on your money."

"I was afraid you wouldn't agree to," she sighed. "Men—some men—are so silly that way. So I figured out a perfectly darling plan, in case you wouldn't. (You see I've been thinking it over, the way Napoleon would, if ever he'd had a stubborn husband to outgeneral instead of just a lot of extra-illustrated emperors.) Here's my idea: I'm getting richer and richer all the time. And I haven't any head for business. There's a flower-flecked hollow where my Bump of Finance ought to be. Besides, it takes my mind away from my work to have to think of details. Now, details are your sweetest talent. I want you to take charge of them all for me."

"I'll be very glad to. I'd have offered to, before, only—"

"Good old boy!" she approved, happily. "You're going to be nice and sane, after all! I was so afraid you'd be cranky about it."

"Why should I be? Isn't it a husband's—"

"You see," she continued, eager to air her plan to the full, now that he was so amenable, "—you see, there'll be contracts to argue over and bank-accounts to keep straight and bills to audit and letters to write and callers to see and interviews to arrange and business bothers (like this Nantucket matter) to look after—and—and all that. Oh, it will keep you pretty busy, sometimes; so you won't feel you aren't earning your salary."

"My salary?" he babbled, having listened with growing bewilderment to the list she had so glibly enumerated. "What salary are you talking about?"

"I'm coming to that," she said gleefully. "I was saving it to the last, for a treat. I'm going to give you twelve thousand dollars a year."

"Mavis! I—"

"Just think!" she exulted. "You'll be the highest paid private secretary in captivity! Won't it be simply dandy? *Don't* look so flabbergasted, dear. It's all true. I mean it."

ROYCE CHURCHILL'S collar had all at once waxed too tight for him. He had read of men whose collars suddenly choked them; but hitherto he had put such cases in the same fictional cage as "seeing red" and "white with rage" and other terms dear to strenuous pendrivers. But now he could scarce breathe, for the pressure. He tried twice to speak, but succeeded only in spluttering. His rage sent physical nausea rushing through his whole system. Bad as his forecasts of Mavis' new frame of mind had been, they paled to empty nothingness beside the reality.

"So," she went on in triumph, "you'll be making more than ever you could expect to in the law. You wont have to work half as hard as you do now, and—"

"Mavis!"

Royce fairly spat the word at her. She paused in amazement at the shaking fury of his voice, the glassy fierceness of his eyes.

"Are—are you sick?" she asked in alarm. "What is it?"

"You—you are offering me—*me*—a job as—as *your* private secretary?" he blurted thickly.

"At twelve whole and glittering thousand dollars a year," she answered him, relieved to think his emotion was caused by joyous surprise and not by illness.

"Good Lord!" he groaned. "It's come. Here's where I find the nightmare's the only thing left that's true."

"Why, Royce—"

"You offer me the post of private secretary!" he blazed, his words and his wits coming back to him in a rush. "You want me to give up my career—my life work—for the privilege of being my own wife's servant. You want—"

"Oh, what an idiotic way for a grown man to talk!" she broke in impatiently, vexed also at the failure of her plan. "Wouldn't you rather earn twelve thousand dollars than five thousand dollars? Wouldn't—"

"No!" he shouted. "I wouldn't. I'd rather earn six dollars a week as an office-boy than be the servant of the woman who promised God to 'honor and obey' me."

"That's melodrama," she scoffed.

"Naked fact always is. It's time for a showdown, between us two, Mavis. I've seen it coming, and I've hoped it could be staved off by your coming to your senses. But it can't. I hoped you were only drunk with money. But you aren't. You're stark crazy with it. And you've got to be cured, if I can cure you. If I can't, I'm not going to be your asylum-attendant any longer."

"I'd rather talk to you when you are calmer, Royce!" she said, loftily. "You seem hardly yourself. I don't at all understand the wild things you're saying. When you have quieted down, I'll ask you to explain them."

WITH a supreme effort he forced back his fury of excitement. "I have 'quieted down' now," he said with tense calmness. "And I am ready to explain. I'll put it as briefly as I can. You and I were pretty happy—once. We had all the cash we really needed, and pretty nearly as much as we wanted. I worked hard for it. And I enjoyed the work, because it meant comforts for you. You were content with what I was able to do for you, and you were proud of me for being able to do it. You paid me—and more than paid me—by making my life happy, by making our home a real home, and by all the thousand things a good wife does to offset the little her husband does for her. We had the same friends, the same interests, the same joys, the same sorrows, the same funds, the same lack of funds. It was the partnership Nature intended, a wonderfully beautiful partnership. And now—"

"And now," she said angrily, "we have six times as much money and sixty times as much—"

"As much misery and heartache and humiliation," he supplanted.

"Humiliation?" she echoed, perplexed. "Why—"

"At least, *I* have," he declared. "Is it no humiliation to me to stop being Royce Churchill and to be—'Mavis Churchill's husband?' Is it no humiliation to be a mere unnoticed figurehead—a necessary evil— at my own dinner-table? Is it no humiliation to have my wife offer to make me her paid employee, to fill the house with people who ignore me?"

"If you are finding fault with the people I ask to my house," she began, coldly, "they are—"

"That's just the point," he raged, his forced calm wearing thin. "You speak of it as *'my* house!' And it is. But it shouldn't be. The old home was *our* flat. This is merely *your* house. That is why it is no home at all, either for me or for you. And when home goes, married happiness goes with it."

"Royce," she said in almost impersonal comment, "do you know you're talking just like a man in a mid-Victorian play? People don't talk that way any more, not even on the stage. Can't you be sensible? If—"

"Yes," he answered, cooled by her interpolation, "I think I can. I think what I'm going to say is more sensible than anything you or anyone else has ever yet heard from me. If you'll do me the kindness to hear me out—"

"Oh, dear! A sermon?"

"Perhaps. But as it will be the last, as well as the first, please listen to it. I'll make it brief."

"The last?" she repeated. "What do you mean?"

"YOU are rich," he said, unheeding, "and I am not. That is a wrong condition for a husband and wife. Only a man who is either knave or fool marries into such a condition. In either case he is punished. A man who *steals* money may sometimes escape punishment, but a man who *marries* it never can. I didn't marry it. But I'm the loser, just the same. And I don't like being a loser. It is a new rôle to me, a rôle I'm not going to play any longer. If a man earns more money than his wife, there's the usual chance for happiness. If the wife earns more than he, there's none."

"If you're jealous because—"

"Jealous? Perhaps I am. Jealous of the money that has taken my wife away from me, just as I'd be jealous of the man who did the same thing. And—"

"What utter silliness! I haven't been 'taken away from you!' That's maudlin nonsense. I still live with you, and I—"

"Pardon me," he interposed. "You no longer live with me. I live with *you*. There's all the difference in the world. And it is not right that a husband should live that way."

"I don't see why not," she protested. "It's all the same. If you are going to stick to old-fashioned, worn-out ideas, of course—"

"They are not old-fashioned. They are not worn-out. They are eternal. They have endured from the beginning of the universe. They will endure when this world falls to pieces from old age. *What always has been, always will be.* That applies to everything in life, Mavis, no matter what all the army of crusaders may say."

"It is not true. There has been a tremendous change—"

"There has been no change since the birth of time. And things that have not changed in sixty centuries aren't going to change in sixty years. In the cave days, human nature was naked. Folk fought, schemed, loved and planned. Then, in the course of the centuries, we spread a sort of gloss or veneer over naked human nature, as we spread clothes over naked human bodies. But scratch through the veneer to-day, and you find folk figuring, scheming, loving and planning, just as they did in cave times. Human nature hasn't changed, one jot. Fashions in clothes change, year by year; yet no one claims that the bodies under the clothes are any different from those of six thousand years ago. It's the same with human nature— But I'm boring you."

"FRANKLY," she yawned, behind her slim hand, "you are. What does the sermon lead to?"

"That wasn't the sermon. That was a digression. The point is that, even as human nature in general is the same as it was, so it is in the relations of man and wife. In the cave days, man went forth to hunt food and clothes for his mate. Her share of the partnership was to guard the cave, to prepare the food and skins he brought home and to raise his family. It was an equal division. Being stronger, he did the hard and perilous share of the work. She did the share she was fitted for. The 'share' of both has changed since then, but the relation stays the same. Even as cave-folk must have sneered at a man who sent his wife out to find the family's food while he loafed idle at home, so modern folk sneer and will always sneer at the man who lets his wife do the work and support him. And I don't intend to be sneered at, any longer."

"Cave-man talk is getting to be so bromidic," she sighed,

pathetically.

"A thing can't become bromidic until it's so true that everyone knows it. And this isn't cave-man talk. I'm not complaining that women have careers and that they vote and that they are doing glorious work in the world. Times have changed—thanks to Man's inventions, not to Woman's—so that a woman no longer needs to live in a home-prison or a harem, seeing nothing of life and taking no part in it. But times will never change so that man and wife can live together in any way other than as God planned for them to live. For the wife to be the provider and the husband the dependent is against Nature. And, in all reverence, I believe it's against God as well."

"What are you driving at, please?" she asked him, her affectation of boredom changing to covert anxiety.

"At what I said, at the first," he replied: "that we can't go on as we have been going. I want a wife, not a financial supporter. Are you willing to go back to our old way of living?"

"To give up my career—to—?"

"No, not to give up your career, unless you want to—though you just ordered me to give up mine. Go on with your work, if it amuses you. No one will be prouder of your success than I, or gladder of the luxuries its profits will let you buy for yourself—for *yourself*, not for *me*. But I want you to come back to the life we used to lead, to live in a home I can afford to pay for—to let us entertain such people as are the friends of both of us and who won't look on either of us as uninteresting appendage of the other—to consult me about the family plans and arrangements as a husband has a right to be consulted: to be, in short, my wife, my partner, not my boss. I went into business for myself the day I was admitted to the bar. And for a while I starved, just because I wouldn't be anyone else's understrapper. I don't propose to change my resolve at this late day."

"Oh, how abominably selfish you are!" she flared. "How selfish and—and how like a man! It's men of your type who have made slaves of women!"

"Were you ever a slave when you lived with me?" he asked quietly. "Your every wish was my happy law, then. You are a slave now, I grant—a slave to money, fame, to a career, to an independence that will end by wrecking your heart. I don't say women have no right to be richer and more famous than their husbands. I only say it's against Nature. Some day, after a few hundred centuries of it, women may adjust themselves to such a state. But they haven't—yet. They can't stand it. It goes to their heads. I've known no less than nine cases where women suddenly grew rich or great, while their husbands remained poor. In every case it spelled unhappiness. The women grew bossy instead of independent, wanted to rule instead of being partners, made their husbands miserable and—in the long run—were miserable themselves. They were miserable because they were playing a part whose lines they didn't know, whose 'business' hadn't been taught them by ten thousand generations of ancestresses. God help their husbands—and, incidentally, God help *me!*"

"There's no use arguing with you," she said. "You're a tyrant, like every other man, at heart."

"A tyrant for wanting us to be as happy and as free as we once were? It's a tyranny, then, that you'll be wise to submit to."

"I wont submit to it."

HE bent over her, his hands resting with infinite tenderness on her rebellious shoulders.

"Dear little girl," he begged, "think what you're doing. Happiness isn't so common that we can afford to throw it away, with our eyes open. Come back with me to the blessed old life. Be true to yourself—to your real self. Be the girl who loved me and who was my mate and who found her happiness with me. Shake off this mania. You can do it if you will. Remember, I'm not asking you to give up your career or to turn your back on the wealth it brings you. I just ask that you'll be my wife again, my equal, not my would-be employer. It isn't too late."

She shook off his grasp angrily, as though trying also to shake off the spell of his plea.

"I *am* your wife!" she fretted. "I—"

"No," he retorted, "I am your husband—*only* your husband."

"What do you want me to do?"

"I'm going to Mexico again, for the Dos Hermanos people. I'll be gone a couple of months, perhaps longer. I was going, anyway, after the Marden trial. But I'll leave Shelp to handle that, and I'll start to-morrow. I want you to come with me. Will you?"

"To Mexico?" she gasped. *"Now?"*

"Why not? The revolution's simmered down. Foreigners are safe there. We'll be alone, together, you and I. We can get acquainted all over again and adjust ourselves to old-time ways and forget this wretched nightmare. Just think, sweetheart! It will be like a second honeymoon, only happier. And when we get back—"

"But Royce!" she protested, half crying. "I can't, just now. I can't! Rehearsals are on, and they need me every day, and—"

"I need you too—more, perhaps, than—"

"And the Midnight Club's dinner to Forbes-Robertson: I've promised to speak at it. And I'm giving that tea for Beatrice Campbell the day after her season closes here. And then my new play—the one I've just begun working on—oh, Royce, I *can't*. And anyhow," she added, "it's so useless and senseless. Wont you be reasonable, please?"

"Yes," he promised, "I will. I'll start for Mexico to-night. Shelp will have word to send you fifty dollars a week while I'm gone. It'll be a drop in the bucket, to you. But it will mean I keep a shred of my self-respect. Good-by. I'll start direct from the office without coming back to—back to your house."

"If you must go, you must," she said suddenly, hardening herself against the illogical cry of her heart, and seeking to beat down his firmness by her own. "I hope you'll come to your senses while you're gone, and not come back still nursing the insane idea of making me commit career-suicide."

ROYCE CHURCHILL did not return from Mexico "in a couple of months." Business kept him there—or he let it keep him there—for almost a full year. Weekly, the fifty-dollar check came to Mavis, the only communication of any kind that came to her from Royce. Much oftener than weekly, her foolish unemancipated heart implored her to drop everything and go to the husband she could not stop loving. And always, though with ever-increasing effort, she scolded her poor heart back to shamed silence by telling it how unreasonably and brutally Royce had behaved to her; and that if she should yield now to this crazy whim of his, he would know he was her master and would coerce her as such for the rest of their lives.

No, firmness alone could bring him to see the error of his ways and fetch him back, duly repentant, to her feet. But the months went on, and Royce did not return to murmur the humble apologies that she was forever coining for him in her mental rehearsals of the home-coming scene.

The man who wrote "The Senator" and had all the playgoing world at his feet could never duplicate that success or write one other play which was not a failure. And he died a heartbroken failure. The playgoing world once adored Harrigan. And later it unanimously refused to go to see him act. The same fickle playgoing world has picked up and rapturously crowned many another newcomer whose special form of originality tickled its fancy for the moment—only to cast him into the discard as soon as his particular brand of entertainment began to pall.

The playgoing world had paused for an instant to laugh in babyish glee at the cobweb wit and daintiness of Mavis Churchill's plays. Then, without warning, it announced that she was a bore. And not even in stock could she draw a hundred-dollar audience.

Mavis in dumb horror saw the swift decline of her vogue. She noted, too, that while she was still accepted and even welcomed among her theatrical friends, she was no longer lionized. Managers fled from her as from the plague. One of them, cornered,—the second-rater who had grown rich on her first two plays and who had gone broke on their two successors,—told her, in a fit of ugliness, how Royce had financed her first play and made possible her short meteoric triumph.

Being a wise woman, Mavis forestalled disaster. At first sign of a slump, she collected all her royalty-savings and her husband's weekly checks and invested them. She purchased with this sum a block of preferred stock in a gold-mine whose owner—her manager's own brother—assured her on his word of honor that it could not possibly pay less than forty per cent dividends. It was the chance of a lifetime. And she took it. A few months later the gold-mine suspended operations, for the very excellent reason that no one could locate it—not even the Federal authorities, who were noisily interested in its promoters' mail-circular campaign.

It was when the numb-stricken Mavis confronted her manager with his brother's dishonesty that he, in revenge, told her of Royce's share in her success.

And, cashing that week's check and pawning a handful of jewelry,

Mavis Churchill took the next train in the general direction of Mexico City.

"I HAVEN'T come to whine for mercy," she told Royce very bravely, after she had sketched a pitiful little picture of her financial collapse. "I haven't even come to ask you to let me go back to you—on your own terms. I've just come to say there isn't anyone on earth, except you, who wouldn't have thrown in my face, that day, the fact that you gave me my start, and to—"

"Why,"—he laughed uncomfortably, —"no white man could have done that."

"I'm afraid a great many near-white women could," she sighed; then she went on with her confession: "And to tell you, dear, that I'm sorry, just that I'm sorry, and ashamed to look at you. Not that it does any good to say it now. But it's true. And I wanted to say it—not to write it. To *say* it! That's why I'm here...... You've grown so thin, Royce! So old-looking!" She broke off.

"I've—I've missed my boss," he said, very simply. "That's all: I've missed my boss. No, not my partner—my *boss*. Lord, but it's good to have a boss again!"

The Night of the Dub

THIS tale's introduction could be shortened and made simple to a degree by dropping unwieldy verbal portraiture for the apt art of the movies.

For example, on the snow-glare screen might be thrown a "flash," or a "still," of a youth with colorless hair and homemade features, absorbedly busy, conning a seed catalogue. This might be followed by the pulsate caption:

Homer K. Twitty, Commuter; Twenty-four-dollar-a-week Clerk in Brokerage House of Ganz, Ganz & Sons.

After the audience's record holder for slow reading had had ample time to master and commit to memory this announcement, the genius in the box might screen another "still"; this one depicting an aggressive-jawed and portly man of thirty, clad in due servility to next year's most advanced styles, thoughtfully passing a few yards of ticker tape through his gloved fingers. The Iris Fade-Out of this attractive glimpse might be followed—or preceded—by some such lucid explanation as:

Reggie Ganz, New Head of Ganz, Ganz & Sons.

Thus, in four brief stills or flashes, everyone in the darkened auditorium would at once become familiar with the two protagonists' personalities and chief traits, and would be thoroughly prepared for some such later gem of photoplay rhetoric as:

"Whom do you suppose would credit such a lie when you would reveal it to them?"

The screen is mightier than the pen; and it clears—in one glad stride and two captions—the ground over which the typewriter must plunk tediously for six pages. Wherefore—

Homer K. Twitty was not even a cog in the great minting machine known to fame as Ganz, Ganz & Sons. He was merely one of the numberless drops of oil that kept the cogs duly lubricated. Yet he was a reliable little drop. Between the ages of thirteen and twenty-seven he had mounted dizzily from wastebasket guardian to the afore-hinted twenty-four-dollar-a-week clerkship.

Being reliable, he would always have a job of some kind. Being reliable, he would always need one. His special oil dropper was the second of the three employee-jammed outer offices of Ganz, Ganz & Sons. Here, like Theseus in Æneas' vision, he "sat, had sat, and"— presumably—"evermore would sit."

Beyond him, amid roseate clouds, loomed the inner office, the shrine toward which all good clerks' upward steps were bent; the goal of attainment which outer-office workers viewed with dimming hope as the toil years slowly ground their optimism down to hardpan drudgery.

For the rest, Homer K. Twitty was of the type so eagerly sought for by life's stage director to enact such stirring roles as Second Citizen, or Voice in the Crowd, or Confused Noise Without. He was not a shining light. He was not even a danger signal. He was a dub.

All this in the offices of Ganz, Ganz & Sons, on Wall Street, Manhattan.

But there was compensation, and it lay to westward—twenty-two miles to westward. To reach this Promised Land, Homer daily plodded to ferry or tube, crossed the river, rode in the second car behind the smoker for sixty-seven minutes—except when he chanced to miss the express, in which sad case the trip was eleven minutes longer— and detrained at Pompton Plains.

But it was no dub who stepped importantly down from the train. It was a Wall Street man. Therein lay the compensation, Wall Street being like a successful operation, or a conscience victory, or a stormy scene with the boss—in that the farther away from it one travels, the more important and glow-inspiring it becomes.

Not that Homer had laid claim to greatness. He had simply announced, when first he moved to Pompton Plains, that he was in the brokerage house of Ganz, Ganz & Sons. And Pompton Plains had done the rest. It was passing sweet, after a lubricating day of dubdom, to have fellow commuters beg him to tell the inside reason for some Wall Street antic that had smeared itself on the evening papers' first page. It was even sweeter to be chosen unanimously as arbiter in every petty financial argument. Sweetest it was to be asked:

"Why don't you bring Reggie Ganz out with you, some night, to one of our duck-pin tournaments?"

Reggie Ganz! Homer had stood in the presence of the great man just four times in all his life. Twice, when the head clerk had sent him shivering into the inner office with accounts the boss had asked for; once when Ganz had passed him in the corridor and had made him the proud bearer of a message to the office manager; once when Reggie, shooting through the outer office in a rush for a train, had stumbled over Homer's wastebasket and had courteously asked the basket's quaking proprietor why in hell he didn't have sense enough to keep the aisle clear!

To be just to Homer, he had not bluffed—to any criminal extent—when Pompton Plains had sought to thrust Wall Street renown upon him. To all requests for tips or for the secret reasons for some stock flurry, he always made curt and truthful answer:

"I don't know anything about it."

A reply which convinced his worst enemy that he knew all about it. To the suggestions that he bring Reggie Ganz out to fair Pompton Plains for a session of the Duck Pin Bowling Club, or for some other local orgy, he ever replied, with equal curtness and veracity:

"Ganz is a pretty busy man. I'm afraid he wouldn't be able to spare the time."

Nevertheless, at heart he thrilled with the importance thrust upon him. And, to prevent his fame from ebbing—there was always his wife. Bertha Twitty knew, to a penny, what pay Homer received. She knew he was merely one of a swarm of subsidiary clerks in an immense brokerage house. All this she knew—with her mind. Even as, mentally, the average mother must surely realize that her only son is not a choice blend of d'Artagnan, Socrates and Sir Galahad.

Yet, as a mother drapes the combined mantles of those three worthies over her slack-jawed boy's narrow shoulders, so did Bertha endow her clerkly spouse with all the glories of a fictional Wall Street man. She was a truthful soul, this brown-and-drab little woman. Yet—well, she was a childless wife, who must perforce have an idol. And Homer K. Twitty was the sole available candidate for the pedestal. A poor, blind candidate, perhaps; but the only one in stock.

Social life in the pretty suburb of Pompton Plains waxes gay to an extreme when the summer boarders have departed, and when, like hibernating bears, the commuters must rely upon themselves alone for pabulum. And the bright center, round which revolved the winter gayeties of Homer K. Twitty's set, was the Pompton Plains Thursday Night Duck Pin Bowling Club.

There were but eight members of this exclusive club—all men. But they had injected a jolly feminine atmosphere into the functions—and disarmed wifely remonstrance at lonely home evenings—by adjourning once a month, after the game, to the house of some member, whither the wives of the seven other members had preceded them, and completing the night with a dance and with a supper revel. The fare ranged in variety from Welsh rabbit to stewed oysters and cocoa.

It was Mr. J. B. Threbble, president of the club, who on one such Neronic night broached the plan that leads this story by slow steps from introduction to action.

"Say!" exclaimed Mr. Threbble, a third glass of sparkling lemonade mounting like *aqua vitæ* to his fecund brain and there suddenly begetting an inspiration: "Say, people, what's the matter with our doing this, sometime? What's the matter with our doing this? Listen, now. I got an idea. What's the matter with all of us doing this? What's the matter with our having a real blow-out? Hey?"

Mrs. Spencer Belding, hostess of the evening, bridled at the implied slur upon her delicious hot coconut cake and seltzer lemonade. But Mr. Threbble was too excited to notice. He expounded with growing eagerness:

"Listen! What's the matter with the whole crowd of us going to New York some evening—you girls meet us there when we quit work—and getting dinner at some good restaurant, and then take in a swell show and—and maybe get a bite of supper somewheres afterward, on our way to the train; and then catch the one-ten home? Hey? How about it, everybody?"

Probably when Columbus played his apocryphal trick with the

nonauthenticated egg the hypothetical group of scientists gasped in silent amaze for a second, before breaking out in wild acclaim of the unique if asinine stunt. Certainly the assembled members—and their wives—of the Pompton Plains Thursday Night Duck Pin Bowling Club stared in awed bewilderment at the speaker for several consecutive seconds before their ravished vocal powers returned. Then everybody talked at once.

Mr. Threbble's plan was so alluring, and so feasibly simple withal, that his seven fellow members could have kicked themselves for not having thought of it long ago. As for the wives, they were unanimous in their plaudits. Seldom have sixteen people been so thoroughly unanimous in indorsing anything. After that first check at the magnitude of the scheme there was not one dissenting voice.

At last the tumult and the shouting died and the gathering resolved itself into a committee of the whole, to go into executive session on the topic of ways and means. Here, as was but to be expected, there were a few minor clashes. But the universal optimism wave easily splashed over and through these. And the thing was ordained.

Bit by bit, during this committee meeting, Homer K. Twitty crept out of the ruck and well to the front, passing even the inspired Mr. Threbble himself. For as the theme took on a tinge of high finance— as regarded assessments, dues, the division of the outlay for dinner, theater, supper, and so on—all eyes turned by instinct upon the Wall Street magnate, whose long experience in handling such details as mergers, pools and reorganizations had fitted him above all other members for such a task as this.

Modestly Homer accepted the burden. A few deft if shameless questions gave him a precise knowledge of the sum that might be relied on to capitalize the venture. This total, with the aid of a pencil and an envelope back, was applied to the probable outlay, which was duly and by inches whittled down to meet the subscriptions.

"Here we are," was Homer's final masterly summing up: "Total assessment, sixty-four dollars—that's you men's eight dollars per. Get that amount in your minds. Sixty-four dollars. Total assessment."

He was very much the steel-cold Wall Street financier now. Even Bertha—who had seen him cry, that time he mashed his finger so cruelly in the china-closet door—felt just a little awed.

"Dinner comes next," he went on. "No; carfare from the place we're to meet to the restaurant. That's a nickel each, or eighty cents in all."

Mr. Threbble's lips worked rapidly in calculation; then he nodded assent.

"Dinner, next," proclaimed Homer. "Now I take it we want a real feed. The kind we can date time from, eh? Well, there's lots of good places where they serve a corking dinner for one dollar and twenty-five cents. Of course there's dozens of good dinners cheaper," he hurried on, steamrollering an objection from prudent Mr. Spencer Belding, the evening's host. "But we're doing this thing only once, and we want to do it right. So let's say one dollar and twenty-five cents per. That's a total of just twenty dollars. Exactly twenty dollars and no cents. And two dollars for the waiter—ten per cent, you know—making twenty-two dollars. I'll pick out a place not too far from the theater," with a conciliating glance at Mr. Belding, "so we can walk there from the restaurant and save eighty cents that way. Now good seats for a good show will cost two dollars per. That makes—"

"There are plenty of nice vaudeville places," objected Mr. Belding, "where they only charge—"

"That makes a total of thirty-two dollars for the tickets." Homer frowned him down. "Then, on the way back, we can stop at a restaurant near the theater and get some dandy fried oysters and coffee all round. That'll be thirty cents more apiece; and a nickel each to the waiter—a total of five dollars and sixty cents. Then—"

"With such a swell dinner, what do we want to load ourselves up with supper for afterward?" protested Mr. Belding.

"Oh, let's go the whole thing!" enthusiastically suggested his wife. "We're doing it only once. And I—"

"Then," continued the auditor, "five cents apiece—carfare to the ferry. That's eighty cents more. I'm not counting in railroad fares. We men have our own commutation tickets and you girls all have ten-trippers. So the total expense of our grand outing is due to be just exactly—exactly—sixty-one dollars and twenty cents," he ended in triumph; adding, as a bright afterthought: "Which leaves us two dollars and eighty cents in the treasury toward next year's spree, if we decide to make an annual thing of it!"

"Why not rebate the two dollars and eighty cents, pro rata, to the members?" ventured Mr. Belding.

But nobody heard him in the gust of approval over Homer K. Twitty's financial achievement. On the crest of this applause Homer was unanimously chosen treasurer of the expedition, and was further honored by popular assignment to the responsibility of picking out the restaurant and the theater. He felt much as though Reggie Ganz had turned over to him the entire yearly profit of the firm and had bidden him invest it in whatsoever manner his judgment might dictate. It was a fearful responsibility his fellow club members had thrust upon him. But in his own sanely self-confident heart Homer knew himself equal to it.

"Shall we say—shall we say eight weeks from to-night?" he asked. "That'll give us plenty of time. I'll pick out the show and buy the tickets to-morrow. You know, in some of these New York theaters you have to get tickets a thundering long time ahead. Nobody's got any engagement for eight weeks from to-night, have they?" he ended jocularly, as though naming a date in some post-historic period.

No one had.

All the way to town next morning Homer K. Twitty conned the theatrical proclamations in his newspaper. After an hour's careful perusal and comparison he decided that the show most favorably and also most extensively mentioned in the advertisements was Miss Manhattan. The management not only conceded, in print, that Miss Manhattan was far and away the Brightest, Bulliest, Best Show in

New York, but it backed the claim by brief excerpts from the works of competent metropolitan critics, as published in no less than six leading dailies. This seemed to clinch it.

At noon, instead of lunching, Homer took the Subway at Wall Street for Times Square; whence, by the help of a telephone directory, it was no feat at all for a seasoned cosmopolite like himself to locate the desired theater. Five minutes later he was the owner of no less than sixteen ochre pasteboard oblongs entitling the holder to sit in any or all of sixteen contiguous seats in Row N of the theater's orchestra section on the night of January sixteenth.

A little to his annoyance, Homer learned that all seats in the first seven orchestra rows were two dollars and a half apiece instead of the advertised two dollars. Also, that no block of sixteen seats could be procured, even fifty-five days in advance, in any part of the orchestra farther forward than the fourteenth row. Not even a frank statement that the tickets were for the annual frolic of the Pompton Plains Thursday Night Duck Pin Bowling Club could change the harsh verdict. Still, by way of balm, the courteous box-office man assured Homer that the seats he had just bought were in the very middle of the house and were in every way highly desirable.

On the return walk to the Times Square Subway, Homer was pleased to find no less than three restaurants that advertised a truly Lucullan dinner for a dollar and twenty-five cents. All were within comfortable walking distance of the theater. So was at least one quicklunch emporium.

Homer endured, almost unterrified, the office manager's clever sarcasm as to his ten-minute tardiness in returning from lunch. He had proved worthy of his own self-confidence in arranging the forthcoming revel. And he was just a little proud of himself.

Reggie Ganz, at precisely the moment when his least-considered clerk was listening to the office manager's rebuke, was burrowing both arms into the sleeves of a seven-hundred-dollar fur overcoat, assisted by two reverential hat boys. He had just risen from luncheon. And he had risen conqueror. He had been host. His guests had been four fellow alumni of Harle University, who, with himself, had been appointed as entertainment committee for the forthcoming Harle Alumni Reunion.

Reggie, in undergraduate days, had not been wholly a success at Harle. He had brought thither nothing but money—of which he was inordinately and volubly proud—and a financially shrewd brain, which did not prove a popularity asset. He had seen poorer and less brilliant youths "make" one fraternity after another, to which his cleverness and cash could not win admittance for him. Class offices had also passed him by. He had all but failed of ingress to the Harle Club after graduation.

Ten years had spun along. Reggie had risen fast in the finance world. He had won a score of worth-while successes. Yet the memory of his college mediocrity had always rankled. Those same ten years had softened and materialized and turned rational the idealistic under-graduate standards of his classmates. Men who once had snubbed Reggie Ganz gradually discovered that he was decidedly well worth cultivating. His popularity grew—not only in the world at large but also in the Harle Club, to which he had so barely gained entrance, and in the Harle Alumni Association as well.

Yet the faintly bitter taste of that old memory never quite left him. He longed avidly for a feat that should destroy it. Money gifts of vary-ing hugeness to the university had scarce half-achieved this. But those gifts, together with his business prominence, at last won for him a place on the Entertainment Committee, in whose hands was placed every detail for the mammoth gambol planned by the Association. It was a foothold. And Reggie Ganz proceeded to improve it. To-day, at this first meeting of the committee, he had secured for himself the chairmanship. He had also persuaded his four slightly bored and easy-going and overbusy colleagues to depute to him the bulk of the initiative in organizing the reunion spree.

From the luncheon be drove direct to a theater; summoned the house manager to his presence, and, check book on knee, proceeded to buy out the whole house for the night of January sixteenth. He furthermore arranged for the decoration of the place. And he departed thence with a strong letter of introduction to the company's manager. For Reggie had wonderful ideas as to Harle lines, gags and interpolated song verses, and he yearned to pass along his commands for these, without further delay. One trivial discord alone marked the harmony of his interview with the house manager. That followed on a consultation between the latter and the box-office man. After which the manager said apologetically:

"I thought I was playing safe, Mr. Ganz, in promising you the whole house so far ahead. Six weeks is as long in advance as we generally have any sales at all—except to a few speculators, and we can always fix them if we have time enough. But it seems somebody came here an hour ago and bought sixteen seats in Row N for the night of January sixteenth. I don't understand it. The man here tells me he doesn't think the buyer was a speculator. He said something about a social club with a queer name, like The Duck Hunters of the Pampas Plains, or—"

"Never mind!" interrupted Ganz. "Get rid of him. Offer him a bonus on his tickets or change them for some other night. If you can't do that, let him and his fifteen duck shooters come to the show, and I'll buy 'em out or explain why they can't come in. Duck hunters are usually good sportsmen. They'll understand and clear out. Leave that to me if you can't lose them any other way. You go ahead with the rest of the business."

During the fifty-four days that followed, Reggie Ganz toiled and planned and bullied and coaxed and spent money with both hands in a way which, by all rights, should have crowned him the fictional Napoleon of Wall Street if he had lavished half as much cash and effort in the improving of his own brokerage firm. Under his fierce manipulations the amorphous germ known as the Harle Alumni Reunion took on clearly defined and most attractive shape.

The theater decorations were to be a masterpiece of three great decorators' skill. The seating arrangements—minus sixteen—were little short of sublime. A former President of the United States, three Cabinet members, the president and the president emeritus of Harle University were to fill a lower stage box. The storage room under the auditorium was fitted as a bar de luxe.

The chorus of Miss Manhattan was rehearsed, to tears and hysterics, in the Harle Marching Song, which was to close the performance. The first comedian and his feeder were pat with the fifteen Harle gags written by Reggie Ganz. The second comedian had learned and blasphemously relearned the two interpolated Harle verses in his topical song. And—crowning achievement!—the prima donna had been lured, by managerial cooings and Ganz jewel gifts, into substituting for the words of her wonted entrance song an original lyric laudatory of Harle. This song had been written by Reggie Ganz himself. It was the capstone of his lifework. It represented all that was best in lyric poetry, almost as fully as Swinburne and Tennyson, in reverse conditions, might have stood for the last word in financial juggling. The song began somewhat like this:

> *Come, boys! On this festive night*
> *Let's forget each brawl and quarrel.*
> *Let's unite for dear old Harle!*
> *Come, boys! View in mem'ry's light*
> *Those happy days gone by.*

Then followed the refrain—a pretty thing, copies of which were to be placed in every seat, so that the "Come, Boys" could join in, more or less intelligently:

> *For with joy and with pride*

We do stand side by side.
  Now and forever
    Old Harle sticks together
In bonds of true friendship so tried.

And there was more of the thing—five verses more. One or two of the verses would have sounded just a very little more congruous in a barroom than in a theater. Not that they were an absolute or unforgivable kick in the stomach of decency; but they were, at the very least, what professional entertainers vaguely term "club stuff."

Reggie was justly proud of his song. He had laughed very loudly indeed, no less than four times, while he dictated the final polished copy to his stenographer. He had also prided himself on his delicacy in sending for one of the office's male stenographers for the job. You see, Ganz was always a gentleman.

At any rate, he was a "perfect gentleman"—which amounts to almost the same thing.

A Broadway restaurant's entire second floor had been requisitioned for the supper that was to follow the show. And here again Ganz' genius shone like a day star.

Reggie was draped majestically athwart an angle of the theater's bar de luxe—having looked upon his work and having seen that it was good—half an hour before the scheduled rise of the curtain. A hundred fellow alumni were honoring the bar with their presence and warming up for the performance. In the cavernous foyer above, two or three hundred more Harle men were lounging in loquacious groups, acting as a volunteer reception committee—a committee swelled every minute by newcomers.

Then, into the glassy pool of harmony, plumped the stone.

An usher, dispatched by the house manager, winged a downward flight to the bar and there sought out Reggie Ganz.

"Excuse me, Mr. Ganz!" he broke in on one of Reggie's best-told anecdotes. "Mr. Comyn sent me to ask you whether any women were asked to this party. He understood you to say it was stag."

"Women?" grunted Reggie. "Women? What women? Who?"

"There's eight of them up there in the foyer," reported the usher, "along with eight men. They all have tickets. They were starting to go

in; but Mr. Comyn got them to wait while he sent for you. He says—"

"Women?" snorted Reggie. "Good Lord! The notices all said 'stag.' If any of the boys have brought wives tagging along—Here! I'll go up there with you and straighten it out. That song of mine and some of the gags would sound sweet to a bunch of women, wouldn't they?" he appealed to one of his lieutenants as he departed.

The foyer—aflame with Harle colors—was nearly full of jostling, babbling alumni. One knot in the center had apparently taken a running start for the gambol, and was blissfully singing an under-graduate air, replete with those fearsome close harmonies technically known as "barber shops." In a far corner, herded in a pathetically out-of-place covey, were eight men in business clothes and eight women whose costumes were irreproachable in subdued neatness. In brief, and to end the killing suspense, that lucky corner held the flower of Pompton Plains' beauty and chivalry; in other words, the Pompton Plains Thursday Night Duck Pin Bowling Club—and wives. Particularly "and wives."

The eight women, as I have hinted, were endued with clothes chosen for serviceable decorum and for church wear—the sort of toilet a self-respecting suburbanette should ever wear to a metro-politan function if she would make certain not to commit the crime of conspicuousness or be mistaken for a Sinning Sister. Yet, in this jocund assemblage, the eight were just now attracting more notice than would a pony ballet at a directors' meeting—a fact whereof they were horribly conscious.

It was the climax of Homer K. Twitty's annoyances—this delay. His vexations had begun nearly two months earlier, when his proud announcement that he had bought seats for Miss Manhattan had been right sourly received by his fifteen prospective fellow revelers. In the first reaction from the dash of enthusiasm that had pledged them to the expedition they had been prepared to cavil at anything. It appeared that none of them wanted to see Miss Manhattan—even those who had never heard of it.

Mrs. Hinkle—a literary lady who wrote Social Whispers for the Pompton Plains Palladium—had been told the piece was immoral; immorality, of course, being in inverse ratio to length of skirt. Mr. Belding had read that its prima donna was the heroine of a fascinatingly shameful divorce case. Others of the circle contributed similar patches to the wet blanket.

Mr. Threbble glumly declared he would greatly have preferred to see the all-star revival of dear old Pinafore. Whereat the entire remaining fourteen at once decided that they, too, would infinitely have preferred to see the all-star revival of dear old Pinafore; in fact, they would rather go to that than to any other show in town. But, of course, it was too late now.

The dollar-twenty-five dinner brought the next serious jar to Homer's nerves. During the soup course Bertha had seen a woman at the next table toying with a Vienna roll. And she noticed that she herself had neither bread nor butter. She called Homer's attention to the deficit. Homer, as master of ceremonies, gravely chided the waiter for negligence, and ordered rolls and butter all round. Then Mrs. Hinkle was so pleased with her casserole squab that she asked for another helping, as did her husband and Mr. Threbble. The dinner took on a belated gayety, which it sporadically maintained until the bill was presented. Then followed gloom, for an extra charge was made thereon for bread and butter. And the three extra portions of squab were appraised at no less than forty cents each.

Thus the twenty-dollar dinner cost twenty-four dollars and forty cents—completely wiping out the two-eighty nest egg for next year's outing and putting a one-sixty crimp in the five-sixty supper fund. Nor was the waiter at all grateful, or even gracious, at sight of his princely two-dollar tip.

Then came the walk to the theater—a promenade marred by a scurry of rain and by the fact that no one had an umbrella or rubbers. And then, as Homer K. Twitty was marshaling his disgruntled convoy past the theater's door man, came the inexplicable halt and the request to wait. Cranky, bewildered, volubly complainant, Homer's fifteen convives huddled in their assigned corner, dividing their time between angry questionings of their guide and scared glances at the hilarious throng of men who surged and eddied through the foyer.

Homer could make nothing of the mystery. He was returning from his third fumingly fruitless interview with the ticket taker when he saw a heavy-set man in evening dress bear threateningly down upon the marooned fifteen. Even as he recognized Reggie Ganz he heard the boss' hectoring voice demanding of poor little Mrs. Threbble, whom Ganz had instinctively singled out as the smallest and meekest and shabbiest member of the party:

"Now then, what are you ladies doing here? This theater is engaged for the night by the Harle University Alumni Association; and—"

"You'll have to ask Mr. Twitty about all that," spoke up Mr. Belding right sourly, as Mrs. Threbble visibly shrank into herself at the experience of hearing herself addressed by a strange man. "He's supposed to be managing this affair. He—"

"Managing what affair?" railed Ganz, on whom the phrase "Managing this affair" had much the same effect as might a rival's battle crow on a pugnacious gamecock. "Managing what affair? Who?"

"Homer K. Twitty," ventured Mr. Threbble conciliatingly. "And we are the Thursday—"

"Twitty?" growlingly repeated Ganz. "Twitty?"

The name sounded familiar. And as he glared about in search of its bearer he discovered that unhappy creature at his elbow. At once Reggie understood why the name had had an accustomed ring. And now that something tangible had appeared out of the muddle, the great man's brow cleared.

"Oh, it's you, is it, Twitty!" he bullied. "What's the meaning of all this? Speak up!"

"Why, Mr. Ganz," faltered Homer, involuntarily cringing from long habit at the crack of the driver's lash, "I—we—that is—"

"Mr. Ganz?" cheerily exclaimed Mr. Threbble, catching eagerly at the name. "Not Mr. Reginald Ganz, of Ganz, Ganz & Sons? Good! That's mighty good news! We've heard so much about you from your friend, Mr. Twitty, here, that we almost feel as if we—"

"Twitty!" boomed Reggie, unhearing and heedless of the audible flutter of relief and admiration from the group at mention of the puissant Wall Street name. "You people will have to get out of here. Your seats were sold to you by error. We have taken over the whole house. I'll personally make good to you on the price if the management won't. Hand them over! There are forty men waiting a chance to buy them in."

He stretched out his ample white-gloved hand with the gesture of a victor who receives the conquered city's keys. The glower was gone from his rubicund face. This last obstacle was to prove no obstacle at all. Providence mercifully had put the missing tickets into the shaky fingers of one of his own slaves. Being nearsighted—except in the eyes—he did not remark that Homer K. Twitty's face had flared beet-red and was now yellow-gray. Neither did he trouble to observe that Homer K. Twitty's slightly recedent chin had crept forward below a suddenly compressed mouth.

For the first time Homer K. Twitty, invertebrate Wall Street clerk, and Homer K. Twitty, Pompton Plains finance captain, had met. The meeting was a clash, compared with which the fabled battle of Jekyll with Hyde was a listless slapping bout.

Reggie Ganz was the boss. The Big Boss, at that. The Big Boss of Ganz, Ganz & Sons. In which capacity he stood second only to God in the control of his employee's destiny. The Big Boss had just given Homer an order—an imperative order. The whole ignoble army of wage mendicants know, to a man, that disobedience to an order of the Big Boss is the automatic death sentence of the job.

Behind Homer, in this foyer corner, were assembled his social universe, his home, his personal future. He had heard the multiple wordless gasp that had greeted Reggie Ganz' sharp command—the command whose voice and wording were those of master to servant. Assuredly not those of a magnate to his equal and business chum.

Homer's beloved edifice of neighborhood prestige was tottering above its shaken foundation stones. At any minute now it was due to collapse into unrebuildable ruin.

Worse, far, far worse, his adoring wife was looking on with widely incredulous eyes—he could feel their scared gaze—while her hero was kicked from his pedestal and was rolled ki-yi-ing into the gutter. Homer might henceforth dodge the new contempt of his old admirers; but he must live for the rest of his days with his pitifully disillusioned wife.

In that single brief instant he mentally drew up the debit and credit sheets, balanced them, and noted the result. And, acting on what he read there, he coldly proceeded to commit job suicide. Not that the act did not scarify him to the inmost soul; but he did it on the principle that makes a fire-trapped hotel guest shoot himself rather than burn to death.

"Hand them over!" repeated Reggie. "I have no more time to waste."

"Mr. Ganz," answered Homer K. Twitty, marveling at the steadfastness of his own dead voice. "I make allowances for your bad temper. It has let you forget that I'm a friend of yours. But you can't ride over me like this. I bought these sixteen tickets for the Pompton Plains Thursday Night Duck Pin Bowling Club—and wives. I paid good money for them. They entitle us to see this show. These ladies have come all the way to town to see it. And they're going to see it. If that fellow who takes tickets won't let us in I'll call a cop to make him do it. Get me?"

Balaam, of old, is credited with some momentary surprise when his saddle ass undertook to argue with his master in human voice. But it is doubtful that the ancient prophet's amazement excelled Reggie Ganz' at this unbelievable language from an outer-office clerkling. For nearly a second it struck Ganz speechless. Reggie improved this tiny interval of silence in trying to stare his revolting serf out of countenance. But Homer K. Twitty's desperation-glazed eyes met his boss' scowl without a flicker of dread. His job was lost. He knew that. And, being without hope, he was very naturally without fear, since neither of those two counterbalancing traits can exist for a moment without the other. Vaguely Homer wondered at his own stark bravery.

"Get me?" he repeated hoarsely. "I bought these tickets. They entitle me to sixteen seats in Row N. And I'm going to use 'em!" He yearned morbidly to add "You big stiff!" But he refrained, through notions of delicacy toward the palpitatingly listening women of the party.

From the corner of his bloodshot eyes he noted the tense eagerness of the fifteen delayed revelers as they listened to this verbal combat between the two Wall Street giants. Already his sacrifice was almost worth while.

Twice Reggie opened his mouth to speak, but only gobbled. He, too, was aware of the regard—the grinning regard—of friends. His hard-won prestige seemed at stake. And something told him that mental prowess, not mere bullying, must be his cue.

As Hercules held Antæus high in air, that the giant might be deprived of the Earth's reviving force, so Reggie now proceeded to detach Homer K. Twitty from the dowdy women before whom the little man was showing off. His hand almost lovingly on the rebel's shoulder, he drew Homer out of earshot of the rest.

"Look here, Twitty," he began in a bluffly friendly manner: "you'll do me a big favor by letting me have those seats. Hand them over, like a good chap. I'll pay you for them, of course. And I'm sorry to inconvenience your party. But—"

"You needn't be sorry," said Homer doggedly, "because you're not going to inconvenience us at all. I'll see to that. We're going right in."

He made as though to turn back to his friends. But Reggie detained him—resisting with difficulty an impulse to grab his collar and shake him.

"Hold on!" pursued Reggie. "These ladies with you—I suppose they would hardly care to hear some of the jokes and one of the songs that are to be pulled off here to-night? The stuff is pretty raw, in spots. Not quite the sort of thing to bring respectable women to, you see."

Homer's heart slumped to his kneecaps. This was the ultimate blow—the climax of the evening's failure. After fighting his party's way into the contested seats, the ladies were to be insulted by jokes and songs for which they would everlastingly blame him! He was responsible for the choice of the show. Well, let them blame him! Let them! He wasn't going to back down now.

"That's up to you, Mr. Ganz," he heard himself say. "If you choose to subject decent ladies to an indecent show—you and the rest of Hale University—I can't stop you. We're going in."

Reggie had a vivid mind picture of the attitude the better element of the alumni would take toward those cherished gags and verses if the spiced quips were delivered in the presence of several patently good women. It would not redound to his own personal credit or skill at management.

"Wait!" he begged, again detaining the peripatetic Homer. "One moment, please. I—"

"And while I'm waiting," flashed Homer, "please take your hand off my shoulder. I hate to be pawed."

"Twitty," said Ganz coldly, "I think you forget yourself."

"Maybe I do," growled Homer. "Let it go at that. What was it you wanted to say to me? Speak up. I'm in a hurry."

Whereat Reggie Ganz took the next to lowest step an employer can take.

"Twitty!" he cooed persuasively, "just oblige me in this, like a good sportsman, and I'll see you don't suffer for it next pay day."

"Good-by!" was Homer's brusque retort to this lure.

And Ganz proceeded forthwith to the lowest step of all.

"If you can't see your way to obliging me in this, Twitty," he said somewhat deep in his throat, "next pay day may be your last with Ganz, Ganz & Sons."

"Is that so?" sneered Homer, white-mad. "Is that so? Well, Mr. Reggie Ganz, of Ganz, Ganz & Sons, your—your face don't fit you!"

Yes; it was bitter repartee. As bitter as it was scintillant. But the bully had brought it on himself by his dirty threat. Homer, at heart, was dazzled and dumfounded by his own suddenly discovered genius for brilliant retort. Not wishing to spoil the effect by anticlimax, he snapped "Good-by!" once more and turned toward his staring friends.

A little to his astonishment, Ganz did not smite him to earth; nor did the lightnings of heaven punish his boss-blasphemy. Instead, Reggie choked back a whole mouthful of words and barred Homer's return route.

"One minute now, Twitty," he urged. "I don't blame you for being hot under the collar. I was a bit caloric myself. And I'm sorry I spoke as I did. But surely, between two business men, there must be some easy way of settling this. Let's talk it over sanely and see whether we can't get together."

"Get together!" The catchword brought back to Homer a scene—reported by Reggie's discharged stenographer to a clerk who went to the same Christian Endeavor Branch with her, and repeated, in turn, by the clerk to Twitty and several others—a scene wherein Reggie Ganz had used that same phrase in the same wheedling tone to a man whose stock he wanted for the control of the C. G. & X. Line. And, with the recollection, a sublime idea popped full-grown into Homer K. Twitty's blazing mind.

"Get together!" he rasped as nearly as possible in the tone of an admired Wall Street demigod. "Get together, hey? Now you're talking! What's your proposition? Make it brief."

Reggie should have been past all faculty of wonder by this time. Yet he stood gazing open-eyed at the worm transformed to a dragon.

"Well," he began uneasily, "since you've cornered me, I don't mind giving you double money for that set of seats."

"Double money!" scoffed Homer. "Forget it! Look-a-here, Brother Ganz; when you wanted to get control of the C. G. & X. for your principals you paid through the nose for the blocks of stock you had to buy in. And you've got to do it now! See? I own sixteen shares of Theater, Preferred. Here are my sixteen stock certificates. See? Now you've got to have those shares if you're going to control this performance. See? You've got to have 'em! And you offer me a measly 'double money'!"

"But listen, man alive! I —"

"I've been listening!" harangued the inspired Homer. "I heard your offer. And I turned it down. Now it's up to you to listen while I put my terms. Get that, Mr. Ganz?"

"Well?" replied Ganz. "State your fool terms, then. What are they?"

"I—I don't know yet," confessed Homer, trying to think and talk at the same time. "Wait a minute."

"I've no time to wait!" snarlingly protested Ganz. "The curtain goes up in ten min—"

"I've got 'em!" proclaimed Homer. "I've got 'em! Now listen! You'll have the manager, here, phone and reserve four boxes—boxes, you understand—for tonight's Pinafore performance—boxes that hold four people each—right close to the stage. That's the first thing. Then you'll send for four taxicabs to take us there."

"And, of course, you'll want supper afterward?" suggested Reggie in elephantine sarcasm.

"I—I hadn't thought of that!" exclaimed Homer. "But you can bet we will! Thanks! Supper for sixteen, after the show. And taxicabs to take us there and afterward to the ferry. Four of 'em! And no measly hand-out supper, either! A swell feed! At—at—"

Homer racked his fevered memory for the name of some impossibly fashionable supper resort. The Waldorf-Astoria occurred to him. But he was not certain a regular hotel's restaurant would be open so late as eleven o'clock, and he did not want to risk Ganz' contempt by asking.

"Delmonico's!" he said suddenly, falling back on a name he had heard from babyhood. "A supper at Delmonico's. Not less than two dollars a head, either."

"Is that all?" patiently queried Reggie.

"Not quite," answered Homer, emboldened by the other's unwonted meekness. "You spoke pretty raw to me just now before my wife. I want you to come back to our crowd with me now and be introduced to her, and say you're an old friend of mine. That's all!"

For perhaps half a minute Reggie Ganz stared inscrutably at the bargainer. His own eyes were dull, but not with stupidity. It was the look that always stole over them when he was sizing up an opponent. With all the criticisms of his many and various faults, Ganz' almost uncanny power of reading human nature had never been questioned. Presently he said:

"Taxis to theater; from theater to Del's; then to the ferry. Four four-seat boxes for Pinafore. Supper at Del's. Introduction to Mrs. Twitty. That's all? You're sure?"

"That's all!"

"You're on!"

Homer fought to keep his face impassive. His was a once-in-a-lifetime victory.

"Now that's settled," resumed Ganz. "Just hand over those sixteen seats, will you? I've paid a gilt-edged price and I want them."

"No," refused Homer, recalling another anecdote of the Street; "I guess I'll hold them as collateral. You see, something might slip up or you might forget part of your contract. And then we'd all come back here and use 'em. You can put other folks in our places till then if you're a mind to. But I'll just hold on to the seats."

"Huh!" barked Reggie. "How do I know you'll keep your share of the bargain, then? Why should I trust you when you won't trust me?"

"Because you've got to, I guess," said Homer simply. "Come on, now, and meet the wife. Then you can send for those taxicabs and phone to Delmonico's, and have the manager, here, phone to reserve the four boxes."

Homer K. Twitty next morning accorded a groan and a bleary succession of blinks to the whole-souled clangor of his alarm clock. It was cruelly hard to get up and go to work after such a night. Such a night! From the moment Reggie Ganz—game loser!—had bowed before Bertha and said how glad he was to meet the wife of his dear old friend—from that moment until the four taxis deposited the returning revelers at the ferry, barely in time to catch the one-ten A. M. train, the evening had been one of inconceivable radiance. Never in all the annals of Pompton Plains—to say nothing of the comradely annals of the Thursday Night Duck Pin Bowling Club—had there been such an Occasion.

Homer's very sweetest memory of it all was a little speech Mr. Threbble had made just before the party broke up. After a whispered consultation with the other men Threbble had cleared his voice and said—Homer remembered every golden word:

"Ladies and gentlemen: I know I am speaking for you all when I tender a vote of thanks to our fellow member, Mr. Homer K. Twitty, for the happy time he has given us to-night. Without Mr. Twitty's financial genius, ladies and gentlemen—and without his close friendship with Mr. Ganz—such a night as this night would have been impossible. And at no extra cost! I think I am betraying no confidence," Mr. Threbble had concluded roguishly, "when I tell you that, on my resignation next month, the name of the next president of the Pompton Plains Thursday Night Duck Pin Bowling Club will be that of our distinguished fellow townsman, Mr. Homer K. Twitty!"

And everybody had rapped applaudingly on the table. Great was Homer K. Twitty! But now next morning had come. Last night had been the Night of the Dub. Today was the Day of the Boss.

Homer was of two minds about going to the office at all. More dignified it would be to drop out of his job without going in person to be fired. But highly needful it was to clear his desk of the belongings he could ill spare. As he drearily shaved at the bathroom window he heard a rug beater in the adjoining yard enlivening his castigating labors with song. And the burden of the thump-punctuated ditty was "Last Night Was the End of the World!"

Reggie Ganz fared officeward that morning with a reluctance as great as Homer's, but from a wholly different cause. Ganz merely disliked the thought of banishing a glorious dream by a day of work. His head ached, and his mouth was dry and furry and full-flavored. But in his heart was a great peace. In his ears still tinkled the sweet echoes of a thousand-voiced banquet chorus whose words set forth in no uncertain terms the statement that he, Reggie Ganz, of Ganz, Ganz & Sons, was "A-jolly-good-fellow-which-nobody-can-deny."

Also, his song had been sung and resung, not only at the theater but afterward at the banquet. A dozen fellow alumni had chucklingly jotted down its words at his dictation. More than one prominent man, during the meal, had been spirituously moved to declare that no one but Reggie Ganz was a fit candidate for next president of the alumni body. Reggie's happily aching head was fairly abuzz with adulation. His thick shoulders were sore from slaps of good-fellowship.

Up the steps of the Ganz Building he made his way. And at the outer entrance he all but collided with a pasty-faced man who was emerging with an enormous paper-girt bundle under his arm. Homer K. Twitty had sought to take time by the forelock by clearing out his desk and departing before the Big Boss' arrival.

Despite this, now, as last night, he had nothing to hope or to fear from his employer. And he met Reggie's dreamily happy eye with the profound calm of a Yogi. Starvation might lie waiting round the corner. At the very best, temporary joblessness was his certain fate. But at any rate, this particular Big Boss could no longer hurt or help him.

"Hello there!" hailed Reggie, stopping short.

"Hello!" was Homer's gruff reply; and he added: "I'm in a hurry."

"Have a good time?" went on Reggie.

"Yep. Fine! Did you?"

"Did I?" repeated Ganz. "It was One of Those Nights! Where are you going?"

"To leave this stuff at a Subway package stand and then look for a job."

"A job, eh?" queried Reggie. "What's the matter with the one you had? Couldn't you get on with the Boss?"

"Nope!" said Homer in like vein. "We quarreled over a stock deal. And I quit—to keep from getting fired. So long!"

"I don't blame you," sympathized Reggie. "Rotten place to work— the outer office. But, queerly enough, I've been thinking I could find something to do in the inner office for a chap who has brains and sand enough to hold up his own boss for his own terms. Want to come in and take a look at the new job?"

"Th-thank you, sir!" bleated Homer K. Twitty, panic-fear rushing back into his soul along with the surge of golden hope. "Oh, thank you! And—I'm sorry I spoke so rude to you last night."

But, by grace of one remaining shred of self-control, he said it all to himself, and not aloud—gallantly mustering up strength to vocalize the two stranglingly careless words: "You're on!"

The 101st Man

JEAN WYTHE put one foot sidewise on the edge of the chair-seat behind her, sat down upon it and let the other foot swing loosely floorward. This maneuver is technically known as "sitting on one's foot." The average man could not compass it without giraffic awkwardness and a possible fracture of the ankle. Women do it by instinct; and they do it with more or less grace.

Jean had chosen a deep leather chair in the library, in front of the big log-fire. The fire this afternoon was not a mere luxury, for outside, the November weather was doing all sorts of horrible things.

It was good to sit thus, tucked away in the depths of the old chair, listening to the screech of the wind and snow. Doubly sweet to Jean was the knowledge that there were at least a dozen relatively important things she ought to be doing at this very moment, and that she did not intend to do one of them. Instead, she planned to idle for a drowsy hour in front of the fire—to blink at the flickering flamelets, to hear the snap of the sparks—just to be at peace and very, very happy.

Jean had been happy—ever and ever so happy—for nearly three years now. Yet she had never wholly grown used to her own happiness, or to the fact that hers were the treasures of a beautiful home, a covetable social position, all the money she really cared to spend—and a husband who loved her almost as ardently as she adored him. Every now and then—after the fashion of a child who takes out its tin-bank hoard and counts it over, penny by penny—Jean liked to steal away, all by herself, to sit and brood blissfully over her sweet fortune. This was one of those dreamy times.

But pleasant solitude was not to be her portion to-day, even here in the storm-isolated library. A furry shape presently detached itself from among a pile of couch-cushions, yawned cavernously, stretched itself fore and aft and then mincingly advanced toward the fireside chair. The intruder on Jean's privacy was a half-grown mass of gray fluff, with enormous gold-and-black eyes and a tail the size of a fox's. In brief, it was her Persian kitten Saladin.

Saladin, after the manner of cats,—and women,—did not approach its goal in a direct line. It paused to inspect corners of rugs, made endless detours around chairs, affected to see peril in perfectly familiar pieces of furniture—and by a circuitous route at last reached its mistress' side. Jumping up into Jean's lap, it purred thunderously, laying back its furry ears and rubbing its icy nose in rapture against her idly caressing hand, greeting its mistress with a succession of the whistling squeaks which Persian cats alone can compass. Then, lazily stretching itself at full length athwart the woman's knees, the kitten disposed itself for a nap.

For a space, the muffled yell of the storm, the intermittent crackle of the fire-logs, and the diminuendo purring of Saladin alone broke the room's twilight stillness. Jean began to nod. Her long-fringed lids drooped ever so little.

EVEN the opening and closing of the front door did not trouble Jean's calm. She knew her husband would not come back from the office for another hour; and she had left word for chance visitors, that she was "not at home." So she woke, with an actual start, at a step in the hall and the rattle of the library doorway's curtain-rings. Turning her head to see which of the servants had disturbed her peace, she discovered a man, hat in hand, standing on the threshold of the library.

Jean got to her feet, peering through the half-light at the unannounced visitor.

"Good afternoon, Mrs. Wythe," the man greeted her, coming a few steps forward. "It's a vile day outside, isn't it? I'm afraid my umbrella and raincoat are making a bottomless lake in your front hall."

Jean stood looking at him, a perplexed frown wrinkling her pretty forehead. The kitten, rudely disturbed from its doze, gathered itself from a sprawled bunch on the hearth and leaped to the mantel-shelf, where it perched, glowering at the interrupter of the room's peace.

"I'll draw a chair up to the fire, if you don't mind, and warm myself," went on the stranger, at evident ease with himself and with the situation.

He moved forward as he spoke, and held out his hands to the blaze. Long hands, they were—long and white and shapely, with the look of an artist's—strong, capable hands too, in spite of a flaring three-carat diamond that marred the ring-finger of one of them.

The man himself, as the firelight now revealed him, was slender, of middle height and middle age, smooth-shaven and of simple, almost ministerial garb. His face was lean and ascetic. His gray eyes were totally without expression of any kind.

JEAN was still looking at him in unfriendly perplexity. He seemed so thoroughly at home, and yet without any outward indication of impertinence or bravado.

"Your card was not brought in to me," she said at length, lamely enough. "If you wished to see Judge Wythe, he is at his office. And I—"

As she spoke, she turned toward the bell. The visitor checked her with a slight but decidedly imperative move of his hand.

"Please!" he said with a sudden firmness.

She hesitated. The man continued:

"I know Judge Wythe is not at home. I spent an hour with him at his office this afternoon. In fact, I have come directly from there."

"But—"

"As I climbed the steps, here," he went on, "I saw the glow of firelight from these library windows. I took the liberty of peeping in—for which I crave your pardon. I saw you sitting by the hearth. I told the servant at the door that I had an appointment with your husband, at this hour. I was shown into the reception-room across the hall. As soon as the servant was gone, I came in here."

"If you have an appointment with Mr. Wythe—" she began.

"I haven't," he assured her. "That was what might be called a needful lie. I never tell needless lies. They spoil one's skill for the other kind."

"I am not receiving, this afternoon," said Jean stiffly. "I don't care to ask why you have intruded on me like this. But you will please go, at once."

"I always humor a pretty woman's whim, when I can," he replied, "but this time I can't. I put myself to some slight trouble to pay you this call. And it is decidedly important to me—perhaps to you as well. So you'll forgive me for refusing to go?"

By way of answer Jean crossed to the electric bell at the far side of the room.

"You are ringing for tea?" he asked pleasantly. "Though I seldom eat between meals, I'll be glad, on a day like this—"

"I am ringing to have you shown out," she replied, vigorously pressing the bell.

"'Shown out' is the polite way of saying 'thrown out,' isn't it?" he asked. "But whichever it is, it wont be done to me. May I introduce myself? I am Joel Fordyce."

HE paused. The name meant nothing to Jean, however. She still stood beside the bell, impatiently awaiting a response to her ringing.

"I see you don't read the papers as closely as you might," he went on, after waiting politely for her recognition. "Let me try once more to stir your interest. I am here to talk to you about Jeffreys Lander, Mrs. Wythe."

He spoke quietly; even ingratiatingly. There was no threat in his pleasant voice. The expressionless gray eyes did not so much as seek hers. Yet, on the instant, Jean's face went rigid as a death-mask. Her slim body stiffened. Wide-eyed, lips parted, she stared at her unbidden guest.

At the same instant a manservant appeared at the doorway, in answer to the bell's repeated imperious summons. For a second Jean stared dully at the inquiring servant. Joel Fordyce had not turned from his placid contemplation of the fire.

"You rang, Mrs. Wythe?" queried the servant, wondering at the pause.

"Yes," answered Jean in a voice astoundingly like her own. "You may serve tea in here, this afternoon."

When the servant had departed, she walked straight over to Fordyce, her muscles tense, her brave eyes level and challenging.

"Well?" she demanded sharply.

"Well?" he retorted, with a smile that began at his lips and never reached his eyes.

"Would you mind sitting down?" he added. "I talk more easily sitting down. And as long as you are standing, I—"

Without a word she sat down—*not* on her foot this time. He seated himself at the far side of the hearth, and his blank eyes again began to study the embers.

Jean moved impatiently in her chair and seemed about to speak. The action broke off Fordyce's contemplation of the fire, but he did not yet speak.

He reached out to the mantel instead, and ran his sensitive fingers along Saladin's silken fur. As a reward for this kindly advance, the Persian kitten made a lightning-quick motion with one fluffy paw— and a triple line of scarlet marks appeared as by magic on the back of his white hand.

FORDYCE surveyed with mild interest the red scratches on his hand-back.

"Animals don't take to me," he said apologetically. "I don't know why—unless, perhaps, because I don't take to them. It's that way with some people, and just the opposite with others. There was Jeff Lander, for instance. All animals loved him. Dogs and cats—and women."

Jean winced, ever so little, through her aspect of stark terror. Just then the servant came in with the tea. Jean busied herself with the cups and the bubbling silver water-kettle until she and Fordyce were once more alone together. Then she whirled upon her guest as fiercely as had Saladin.

"What do you want of me?" she demanded. "Tell me!"

"Tell you?" he returned. "Certainly. That is why I came here. It is a rather long story. But I'll cut it as short as I can—for both our sakes. Mrs. Wythe, have you ever chanced to hear your husband speak of the Fordyce Pool Bill?"

"Yes," she said coldly, "I think I have. What has that to do with—"

"That is *my* bill," he told her, a little thrill of pride creeping into his low-pitched voice. "It comes up at the Capitol, day after to-morrow. It would have every show of passing both Houses, by a comfortable little margin, too, if it were not for Judge Wythe."

He sipped reflectively at his tea; then he went on:

"Ordinarily, we'd be strong enough to laugh at a single obstacle like that. But this year the reformers are thick, at the Capitol. And your husband is their ringleader—or, rather, he's their bellwether. They trot along meekly—the silly sheep—in whichever direction he cares to lead them. Judge Wythe is against the Pool Bill—and that bill means something pretty close to life or death to me and to the interests I represent in the legislature, Mrs. Wythe."

He paused again. She did not speak.

"I've been to your husband this afternoon," he resumed. "I've used every argument I could. He's dead set against my bill. He can't be made to see what a benefit it will be for—for the best interests of the community, if it goes through. He ended our talk by practically ordering me out of his office. So I came to *you*."

"Why?"

"To get your help, of course. Everybody knows how crazily in love your husband is with you. He'll do everything or anything you ask him to. Why, wasn't it you who got him to put through that silly Widows' Pension Bill, even after he'd publicly said it was unconstitutional? Just by playing on his sympathies and his sentiment, you did it. Well, if you could do that, you can do this. Will you?"

"YOU are mistaken," she said. "I don't know anything about politics, and I don't care anything about them, except as they interest my husband. I happened to read about the Widows' Pension Bill, and then I asked questions about it and I found what a splendid thing it was. And I told Judge Wythe how I felt about it, and why. I made him see the *human* side. That's all."

"That's all," assented Fordyce in high approval. "And that's all you need to do about the Pool Bill. I can tell you, offhand, that it will benefit twice as many people as ever the Widows' Pension Bill did. Say so to your husband. Tell him your heart's set on his withdrawing his opposition. Cry a little, if that will help. Oh, you'll easily be able to make him think as you do, about it."

"But my heart *isn't* set on it," she protested, bewildered. "I don't know anything about the bill, and I don't care anything about it. Why should I interfere? And"—with a renewed gust of impatience—"what has all this to do with—"

"With Jeffreys Lander?" suggested Fordyce. "I'm coming to that:

"Mrs. Wythe, before I went to the State senate—before I went into active politics at all—I was associated at one time with Barney Cranfield. You may have heard of him. Or, again, you may not. His place was closed, for good, when the reformers first began to bleat, about three years ago. He and I ran the most exclusive gambling-house in the State. Some of the best men in this city used to play there. One of our regular patrons was a big, jolly man-about-town, a man that everyone liked a lot. That was just the trouble with him. Everybody liked him too much—which is the next worst thing to having nobody like you. He was Jeffreys Lander."

AGAIN the twinge of pain contracted Jean's lips. This time the man saw and gravely noted it.

"Jeff Lander was one of the most lovable chaps I ever met," said Fordyce. "I seldom allow myself the luxury of liking a man as much as I liked Jeff. That was why it was a real sorrow to me, the night he tumbled over dead at Cranfield's and—"

"He didn't!" she denied wrathfully. "He was found dead in his own rooms one morning."

"He was," assented Fordyce. "Barney and I and two of his friends carried him there. It was kinder, for his sake—and for ours—not to have the story go out that he died at Cranfield's place."

"Is that true?" she asked. "Did he—"

"He died at Cranfield's—almost at my feet, as we were chatting at the buffet. 'Valvular disease of the heart,' the coroner called it afterward. Luckily it was late, and everybody on that floor had gone. The poker-players upstairs never knew anything about it, and so we could hush it up and get him home.

"After I'd helped undress him and lay him on his own bed, I was arranging his evening clothes on a chair, when a note tumbled out of the pocket. It hadn't any envelope on it. I guess it had come that evening just before he started for Cranfield's, and he'd read it and stuck it in his pocket, meaning to tear it up afterward. I found the envelope in his wastebasket and put the note back into it. Then—well, more from sentimental memory of Jeff than for any other reason—I kept the note. I've still got it."

"The note?" she quavered, all but incoherently. "The note he got the night before he died? But—"

"I didn't want the reporters or any other busybodies to get hold of it," he said. "That's why I took it away with me. Then, as I said, I kept it as a memento of Jeff. Lately, though, I've thought of a much better use for it."

"You stole a letter written to a man who couldn't defend it from you?" she blazed in abhorrence. "You robbed a dead man?"

"Robbed him?" repeated Fordyce, a shade of resentment ruffling his perfect self-possession. "Robbed Jeff? That's no way to talk, Mrs. Wythe! Jeff Lander had won nineteen hundred dollars from us that night. I was in a tight corner, just then, for lack of ready coin. But every cent of that nineteen hundred was found by the coroner, in Jeff's wallet, next morning. That ought to show you the sort of man I am."

"You might at least have destroyed it!" she told him.

"I never destroy a letter," was his terse reply. "And I never write one."

"Then give it to me!" she commanded. "And let *me* destroy it— if—if it was *my* letter," she added less assuredly. "Perhaps it was some other note he received that evening."

BY way of answer Fordyce drew a folded sheet of paper from an inner pocket. He opened it wide and held it so the firelight could fall on the page. Then, in slow and unemphasized monotone, he began to read aloud.

"'Jeff, dear,'" he read, "'this is good-by. A good-by I am writing, because I have not the courage to speak it. If I were foolish enough to tell you my decision, face to face, I know there would be a terrible scene. You would try to prove I am wrong in breaking with you. And perhaps you might succeed. So I am writing, instead.

"'Don't think this isn't hard for me. It is—bitterly hard. But it is *right*. That is why God is giving me the strength to do it. When I met you, you know how desperately poor and unhappy I was. Mother had to have the care and comforts that only money could give her. And I had no money. I tell you this again—not as an excuse but as a fact.

"'You loved me. When you told me your wife had been hopelessly insane for ten years, and that the doctors said she could live only a few months longer, I believed you—just as I believed you when you said you would marry me as soon as you should be free.

"'I cared for you—as much as a girl of eighteen can hope to care for a brilliant man of the world who is double her own age. And Mother's life could be prolonged and made so happy by the money you were willing to give me for her. I never touched one cent of that money for myself, Jeff—not a cent of it. That was why I kept on working when you said it was silly of me to work.

"'You have a wonderful power of persuading people, Jeff. You've often convinced juries of grown men that wrong was right. Is it any wonder you were able to convince an ignorant girl of eighteen? And honestly, I always believed you were going to marry me as soon as you could. *Honestly,* I did. That belief was my only rag of self-respect. And you'll never know how desperately I clung to it.

"'When Mother died, last week, I told myself I couldn't take any more money from you. Two whole years had gone by since you'd said your invalid wife had only a few months to live. So I made some inquiries about her. And Jeff, *why* did you lie to me? You have no wife. You never were married. There was not one word of truth in what you had told me.

"'I didn't have actual proof of it, till to-day. And to-day I am writing to tell you good-by. I have no right to blame you. I suppose it is fair for a man to lie to a woman. Men seem to do it—even men who would bite out their tongues sooner than tell a lie to another man.

"'But I can't see you any more. And now that I look calmly back at our two years together, I see I never really loved you. Oh, yes, I used to think I did! But real love can't live without respect. And I know now I never respected you. How could I? I wanted to. But always the shadow of your wife came between us—the wife whose death you were discounting, for love of me. And now that I know there wasn't any wife,—that you lied to me,—why, I know, too, that I never could respect or love you.

"'I am offered a position as secretary to Judge Wythe. I am going to accept it. In work, I am going to drown memory. No one knows I have been anything to you. The way is clear for me to atone. And I have a right to happiness, if I can earn happiness. Men, who are a million times worse than I, live happily, even without repenting. And I *have* repented. In horror and black grief, I *am* repenting. I—'"

THE monotonous reading was broken by a gasp of physical pain from Jean. Numb, stricken, breathless, she had sat in a terror-trance since Fordyce had begun to read. Now all at once the merciful numbness passed.

"Stop!" she shrilled. "You sha'n't read any more! You *sha'n't!* You have no right! I—I—"

"There's only a few lines more, anyway," said Fordyce, "and there is no need to go on with them. I only wanted to prove that I had told you the truth, and that I—*know.*"

"Yes! Yes!" she murmured. "You know! You—you will give me the letter? Why, you *must* give it to me! It is my life! It is my happiness! No one but yourself knows anything about—"

"Not even Judge Wythe?" he queried.

"My husband? God forbid! It would kill him."

The man's thin lips relaxed. His expressionless eyes were the only part of his face that did not show genuine relief.

"Good!" he said. "I was pretty sure of it, but there was always the chance—and everything depended on that."

"I don't understand you!" she exclaimed vehemently. "But if you think I should have told my husband, you are mistaken. In storybooks a wife is always supposed to, but in real life, why should she? From the hour I entered Judge Wythe's office as his secretary, up to this very minute, I have lived as blamelessly as ever mortal woman lived."

"Of course, of course," agreed Fordyce soothingly. "I know. And—"

"And," she stormed, almost beside herself, "he has no more right to my past than I have to his. My present and my future are in his hands, as his are in mine. But one sin of my girlhood—almost of my childhood—is not going to wreck both his happiness and mine. I repented. No *man* could understand how utterly I repented. And I paid!"

HER voice and words had unconsciously waxed melodramatic, but the fierce sincerity behind them softened their theatric bombast.

"There! There!" crooned the man. "Don't go getting hysterical! I—"

"When Judge Wythe asked me to marry him, three years ago," she continued, unheeding, "I told him he knew nothing of my past. He just laughed and put his hand over my mouth and told me he didn't want to know anything about it. I suppose he thought I dreaded to tell him about some harmless early engagement, or a kiss or something like that. But I took him at his word. I—I loved him so! I couldn't bear to lose him. It meant too much to me. And—and I *had* atoned! Mr. Fordyce, give me that letter!"

"Mrs. Wythe," answered Fordyce in the same vein, "give me the passage of my bill in the legislature on Wednesday."

"What do you mean?" she asked, bewildered. "What have I to do with—"

"You have everything to do with it," he replied. "As soon as that bill is passed and the governor signs it, I shall return your letter to you. *Now* do you understand?"

"No," she said in blank perplexity, "I don't. I can't see how I—"

"Can't you?" he interposed. "You got your husband to work for the Widows' Pension Bill. Make him withdraw his opposition to mine. You can do it. You can do anything with him. Will you do it?"

She did not answer at once, but sat leaning forward, her hands tight-clinched on her knees, peering at him through the flickering light. He waited tranquilly for his proposition to sink into her comprehension. In perhaps half a minute she spoke; with an almost grotesque blend of curiosity and awe, she asked:

"This is what is called 'blackmail,' isn't it?"

"It is anything you choose to call it," he replied, unabashed. "Personally I like to think of it as a plain business proposition—a matter of straight bargaining. Will you do it?"

"You would—you would really sell my happiness—you would spoil my beautiful life?" she stammered. "You would do all this to a woman who never harmed you or anyone else? Why, you *couldn't* do such a thing, Mr. Fordyce! No one could. My husband doesn't know. He doesn't suspect anything. He thinks I'm—I'm wonderful. He's told me he thinks so. He's told me, again and again. He doesn't know I'm not. He doesn't—"

"A husband is always the last person to find out these things," philosophized the gambler. "I've noticed that. If a hundred men know

a woman's gone wrong, her husband will always be the hundred and first. His number is easy to get. It's One Hundred and One. It's queer, but it's true. This time only one man knows. It's up to you, whether the husband shall be the second or—"

"Or the hundred and first man?" she broke in harshly. "I understand! It is—"

"No," he contradicted with a show of patience, "you don't understand. In either case, I'm not going to spill this story broadcast. What would be the use? Judge Wythe isn't running for President. And there's no other position or office where a man is hampered by his wife's past or where that past is any good for political or personal capital. It would only give me the reputation of a he-gossip, if I ran around blabbing the yarn. And nothing would be gained. No, Mrs. Wythe, you don't need to worry your pretty head over that end of it, at all. The man can't even divorce you, in this State, for what happened before you married him. He—"

"As if I cared for that!" she disclaimed hotly. "I don't mind what the public knows or doesn't know about me, so long as it doesn't affect my husband. And when this letter has made him hate me, it wont matter to me whether he divorces me or not. It's *he* that I'm thinking of—the husband that loves me and trusts me and looks to me for his happiness. You're planning to break *his* heart, not mine! And it's *his* happiness I'm going to fight for."

"I'm not going to break either of your hearts," he said, toying idly with the folded note, "unless you force me to. All you have to do is to wheedle him into withdrawing his—"

WITH the swooping plunge of an angry cat, Jean threw herself forward, caught the note from his idle grasp, flung it into the fire and, with bungling, vigorous pokes of the tongs, began to thrust it deep into the red caverns between the logs.

Joel Fordyce made no move to recover the ravished sheet of paper. He sat, quite coolly, watching it burn.

Jean, marveling at his inertia, glanced from him to the crumpled and half-burned paper. Then she saw why he had taken his loss so placidly. An unconsumed corner of the sheet was still in view, between the blazing logs. The letter was not written by hand, but typed. She wheeled on the man in new fury.

"That was not my letter at all!" she accused.

"Of course it wasn't!" he admitted. "It was my typewritten copy of it. The original letter and its envelope are here in my inner vest pocket. Did you suppose I'd hold a letter like that where you could grab it? I knew you'd try to. Any woman would."

"You haven't the original at all!" she declared.

The same mirthless smile touched his lips and died there, still-born. He did not even trouble to deny the charge. And his silence told her what no wealth of protest could have made her believe—that he had spoken the truth.

"Will you persuade Judge Wythe to withdraw his opposition to the Fordyce Pool Bill?" he asked again presently. "If you will, I'll mail the letter to you the day the bill is signed."

"Is—is—you say the bill is for the public good?" she faltered in surrender.

"It sure is," he responded with an actual approach to eagerness. "You can gamble on that: The Judge hasn't got the rights of it. That's all. When he finds you're set on its going through, he'll make inquiries and find out he's been all wrong. Let me tell you, Mrs. Wythe, you're one wise little woman. And I hope you'll keep on being happy."

"I've told you," she protested drearily, "I'm not doing this for my own selfish happiness. I'm doing it to keep my husband from becoming the hundred and first man."

"But nobody else knows. There are no hundred other men, in this case."

"The idea is the same," she said in dogged misery. "You would have wrecked his life for—"

"For wrecking my bill," supplemented Fordyce. "Yes. That's business. And I don't mind telling you it's a little more than business. The Judge spoke to me to-day as if I'd been a yellow dog, and he ordered me out of his office. It isn't on the free list to do that to Joel Fordyce. It would have eased my loss a mighty big lot, if I could have smashed his home life for smashing my bill. But I don't let business get gummed up by personal feelings. And I'm glad it's turned out as it has. And"— with a tinge of the ever-present vanity of his type—"I'm glad I've been able to handle this in a gentlemanly way. The crowd nicknamed me

'Gentleman Fordyce,' you know. And I always try to—"

"I *didn't* know," she interposed in sullen contempt. "And I didn't know the underworld had such a cruelly ironic sense of humor. Now would you mind going? I am very tired."

She rose to her feet. The gambler's pallid face reddened a little above the cheek-bones, and he seemed about to speak. But he checked himself and with a nod moved toward the hallway. A swish of damp air smote him. At the same moment the front door slammed shut. A man's big voice boomed in apparent reply to a servant: "In the library, is she? All right."

JEAN and Fordyce looked at each other in alarm. Both recognized Judge Wythe's voice. Both realized the complications that might follow should the Judge walk in on them together or meet the visitor on the way out. There was no time for words. There was no need for them.

Fordyce, professionally quick-witted, was first to recover himself. In two silent strides he had reached the shelter of the window's alcove curtain. So swiftly did he hide himself, and so dim was the light in the room's far corners, that he seemed rather to have vanished into space than merely to have stepped behind a portiere.

Jean, her heart thumping in her throat, walked unsteadily forward to greet her returning husband.

Judge Wythe was a big man, with a big manner—a manner that went with his size and his voice. He seemed to bring into the tensely still library a sweep of outer air and of clean winds.

"You're home early," Jean heard herself saying as he caught her to him in a bear-hug and kissed her.

"Yes, I am," he laughed. "I got homesick. The wind was raising Cain, and the sleet was scratching at my office windows. And I got to thinking how snug and warm and cozy it would be to sprawl in my big chair in front of the fire, with you. So I cut work and came home. And"—with a sigh of tired contentment—"it's all just as I knew it would be! I wonder if you know what home means, baby? It means just—you!"

He sank luxuriously into the deep leather chair, his feet to the blaze, and drew her down to a seat on his knees, holding her to his broad chest with one arm, her head on his shoulder.

"This is life!" he muttered restfully. "This is the real thing. It isn't what happens at the office that makes a man's day. It's what happens afterward. And we—"

"Dear!" she broke in on his joyous musings, "tell me—tell me about the—the Fordyce Pool Bill! It's a good thing, isn't it? A benefit to—"

"Huh?" grunted Wythe, his relaxed body tightening. "A good thing, eh? You must have been reading the editorials in the *Apex*. That's the only paper in the State with the chilled-steel nerve to indorse it. And it's owned by the Fordyce crowd. 'A good thing?' A *good*—"

"Aren't you prejudiced?" she asked timidly. "I've heard that it is a—"

"Listen to me, little girl!" he interrupted. "I'll tell you about the Fordyce Pool Bill in just a mouthful of words. If you still think I'm prejudiced, you can ask any other white man of your acquaintance or read about it in any reputable paper. You'll get the same answer."

"But I've heard—"

"THE Fordyce Pool Bill," he went on oracularly, "is a measure to legalize race-track gambling in this State, to enable gaming-houses to run wide open, to allow race-track and poolroom betting. Those aren't the exact provisions of the bill, in so many words. But that's what it amounts to. Every lawyer, from the district attorney down, who has studied the bill, agrees that its passage would open the door to an era of law-protected gambling such as this part of the country has never known. As a by-product, it would mean that a thousand families would starve, because the breadwinner would be throwing away his wages at the track. It would mean an army of boys and young men sent to prison for robbing their employers. It would mean a new lease of life to all the red-light places we've tried so hard to wipe out. A good thing, eh? Why, the whole decent element of the country, in the legislature and out of it, has been fighting that bill, tooth and nail, for weeks. And, please God, we're going to down it!"

"I—I—" she stuttered, aghast. "Are you sure, dear? You're *sure*?"

"Sure?" he echoed. "I should say I am! The clique of temporarily unjailed crooks, who keep Fordyce as their handy-man at the Capitol, have spent hundreds of thousands of dollars in pushing the bill. It would be a good thing—a decided benefit—to *them*. But it would be a curse to everyone else in the State. That's gospel truth, Jean—not just my personal opinion, but the truth. Can't you see it must be?"

"Yes," she said in an oddly hushed voice. "I can see it. And—thank you for telling me."

With no warning, she began to cry—not daintily or picturesquely, but as a frightened, heartbroken child cries.

"Sweetheart!" cried Wythe, aghast. "Why, *sweetheart!* What is it?"

"I—I won't do it!" she sobbed incoherently. "I won't! I won't! I won't even *try* to! I—"

"Do what?" the dumfounded man asked. "Try what? What is the matter, darling?"

"I think I can tell you in fewer words than your wife seems able to," said Fordyce suavely, walking forward to the fireplace.

"What the blazes are *you* doing here?" thundered Wythe, getting to his feet as Jean sprang up tremblingly to confront the gambler. "Who let you in? And what do you want?"

HIS manner was as savage as a kick. As he spoke, he moved closer to the gambler, as though to throw him bodily out of the house. Fordyce did not flinch. In one hand he held a letter.

"I had the pleasure of calling on Mrs. Wythe, this afternoon," he said, unperturbed. "In fact, we were still chatting when you came home. I came to ask her to intercede for us in the matter of my bill."

A wordless snort from Wythe interrupted him, but he continued, without pause:

"I thought I had gained her promise. It seems I was wrong. I am sorry, for all our sakes—especially, for yours, Judge. Here is something that belongs to you."

He handed Wythe the enveloped note he held, at the same time moving with aimlessness between the husband and wife. The Judge mechanically took the letter, but he did not glance at it.

"You came here—*to my house?*" he growled. "You intruded your filthy self here—to beg my wife to intercede for your filthier bill? You mangy cur!"

"I am sorry," said Fordyce, unmoved, "sorry to have to do this. But the account is a rather long one, and it needs paying. May I trouble you to glance over that letter?"

Jean collapsed into a chair, without a word, and sat huddled there, her face in her hands, a pathetic little heap.

"I'm not interested in anything you could bring me," said Wythe angrily, and still without looking at the envelope he held. "Here! Take this thing back! And get out!"

As he proffered the note, his eye chanced to rest on the superscription.

"This is in your handwriting," he said, turning to the crouching woman. "It is—"

HE paused, reading the envelope's address. Then he stood very still for a moment. The red anger died from his face, the blustering rage from his manner, and he became cool.

"This letter," he said quietly, without drawing it from its envelope, "was written by my wife. It contains something that you thought she would not wish me to know. You held it over her as a means of making her use her influence with me, to let your bill pass. Failing in that, you wish to stab me with it, in revenge for my killing the bill. I am right, am I not?"

His judicial composure and the logical inferences he had drawn, wrung a glint of unwilling admiration from Fordyce. Jean looked up—hopeless, apathetic—into her husband's face. But there she could learn nothing.

"I—I love you!" she whispered, oblivious of Fordyce's presence.

She reached out and timidly patted Wythe's free hand.

"I *do* love you, dear!" she whispered again in the same lifeless tone. "Always, you must remember that. Always! Read this letter, now. And when you've read it, I'll go. I—I love you!"

Wythe did not so much as look at her. His quiet gaze still gripping the gambler's, the Judge continued:

"I infer that this letter tells of the unhappy relations that once existed between my wife and the late Jeffreys Lander. You have brought your goods to a falling market, Mr. Fordyce. I knew that whole story five years ago. I was Jeffreys Lander's personal counsel. He told me all about it a month before he died—and he rightly placed the blame where it belonged. He wished to make legal provision for my wife. For her sake I persuaded him not to. I gave her a post in my office instead.

"And now, sir," he ended, gingerly dropping the unopened letter into the embers, "kindly leave my house. I should very much dislike to soil my hands by touching you."

The gambler, after the manner of his kind, was an ideally good loser: Without replying, he turned and departed.

Not until the closing of the front door reached the silent library did Wythe move or speak. Then, stooping over, he gathered the weeping woman to his breast.

"Little girl!" he murmured, his lips to her flushed, hot forehead. "Little girl of mine, don't cry like that! It makes me feel like a criminal, to have you cry."

"You—you knew—all the time?" she gasped brokenly.

"Not all the time," he corrected her, "—only at first. After that I forgot. Even at school, I was never any good at remembering ancient history. Won't you let me help you to forget, too?"

"You—you married me," she cried, unbelieving. "You married me, knowing, all the time—"

"Knowing, all the time, that my life would be as empty as my heart, if I didn't," he told her. "If you could forget, I surely could. Together we'll make even more of a success at forgetting. I wonder how soon dinner will be ready. I'm half starved."

The Crippled Doughnut

THE day's joys or woes, its hopes and grouches, may, or may not, start originally from the hand of destiny. But they are invariably delivered to us by the hand of a man in gray—a man who receives twelve hundred dollars a year (and no pension) for distributing, in epistolary form, rapture or gloom to his fellow-mortals.

The first morning mail had brought Jere Misk, of the famous real-estate firm of Misk & Bros., a letter for whose receipt he had long and frantically been yanking a handful of political wires. It arrived in a long envelope with a Washington departmental imprint. The envelope held a short note and a shorter official statement. Jere glanced first at the statement. It certified in formal phrase that the accompanying relic was a part of the twice-sunken battleship *Maine*. Misk smiled comfortably and opened the letter. It ran:

Jeremiah Y. Misk, Esq.,
999 Broad Street,
New York City.
Dear Sir:
In compliance with the requests of Senators Byng and Wipfenhaage and of Mr. Justice Meagley, the Bureau of Navigation is to-day shipping to you at the above address one of the few relics of the Maine still available for such purpose. A certificate of genuineness is herewith enclosed.
The Secretary directs me to say he is unable to grant your application for the eagle figurehead of the battleship in question—first, because such a souvenir would not lie within the gift of the Department, second, because the Maine had no eagle figurehead. Her bow was adorned only with the conventional shield and scrolls.
The Secretary regrets his inability to accede to your wishes, but hopes you may find the accompanying relic suitable for your purpose.
Respectfully, etc.

JERE MISK leaned back in his swivel chair and allowed himself the luxury of a second after-breakfast cigar—for this was an Occasion—another Misk triumph. It was as complete in its way as had been his swinging of the triple deal that put him at the head of the potent real-estate organization of Misk & Bros.

And to Titus Snider, lowliest vassal of his sales-force, he had owed the inspiration whose success this letter and certificate crowned. Snider had told the boss of certain pretty Labor Day ceremonies at Pompton Lakes—five miles to the north of Titus' own home-village of Pompton Plains—when a relic from the *Maine* had been unveiled. And listening in idle amusement to the garbled story, Jere had begotten his great idea. He had recently undertaken a branch real-estate deal whereby a square mile of rolling Long Island farm-region was to be made to blossom like the fifth proposition of Euclid and whereby, in short, a new suburb was to spring to life under the hauntingly sylvan name of Misk Manor. Great is the man who can make two mortgages bloom where none bloomed before. Great was Jere Misk—real-estate overlord. Already, at Misk Manor, no less than three semisolid streets of bungalows and villas—Queen Anne front, Mary Ann back—crowned the genius of the promoter.

But the geometric village green between the station and the country club still had a décolleté, almost undressed, look. It was a look that could be changed to one of rare historic beauty by the erecting of a roughhewn granite pedestal in the Green's center—a pedestal duly inscribed by means of a raised-letter bronze tablet and capped with— well (memory flitting back to Titus Snider's tale), say with some such precious national relic as the eagle figurehead of the martyr-battleship *Maine!*

It would be a godsend to Misk Manor. It would give the suburb columns of free space in the New York papers. It would be a shrine for sight-seeing motorists. Briefly, the plan was in every way worthy of the brain that evolved it.

JERE began at once to work his political pull. At once, too, he found obstacles. Even the most docile Congressman warned him that the giving away of *Maine* relics was frowned upon by the Government, and that except for a few trivial bits of wreckage, the battleship in its entirety was presently to be resunk in solemn form—a form not to be marred by the further denuding of the dead warship.

All of this meant nothing—less than nothing—to Jere Misk. In spite of warnings and of snubs, he had hammered away on his quest. And to-day he had the fruits of his labors. As ever, when he set his whole heart and energy on a thing, that thing became his. That was the way to thrash the world into submission—nerve, bulldog tenacity and more nerve. The Government had surrendered. He had won. The relic was his.

He was sorry it was not to be the eagle figurehead. A giant eagle would have looked fine atop the rough granite monolith. But that was only a detail. One of the grim steel gun-turrets would be every bit as impressive—a gun-turret pitiably racked and twisted and scarred by the explosion. Or even—

"Hey, Snider!" he boomed gayly as Titus pattered past on the way to his own cubby-hole niche. "Snider! Come back here! Just take a look at this, will you?"

He shoved the letter and the certificate at his salesman. Titus glanced over them with polite rapture. He did everything politely— this tidy little commuter who sold real estate for Misk and could find no buyer for his own home.

"Landed 'em!" exulted Jere. "I landed 'em! I told you I'd do it. They know better down there than to say no too loud when the right man up here wants 'em to say yes. In the nick of time it is, too. I'll have them start in work on the pedestal to-morrow, and we'll have the whole thing all ready for unveiling by Labor Day. That's the right day for it—Labor Day. The last day the whole city goes out of town. I'll have Senator Wipfenhaage and some of the Governor's Island crowd down for the ceremonies, too."

"It's a pity you couldn't have the eagle," prattled Titus, handing back the two sheets of paper. "What are they going to send you instead of it? This certificate don't say. And by the way, Mr. Misk," he continued roguishly, "coming to New York in the train this morning, I just happened to—"

"It'll be a rush job—for such a big pedestal—of course," Misk rumbled on. "Especially a monolith—I'd better have Hinkle telegraph to—"

"On the train this morning," pursued Titus, "I—"

"Just chase into the outer office and send Hinkle here," ordered Jere, unheeding. "That telegram ought to be rushed."

He turned to his stenographer and began to bark forth a staccato volley of dictation.

AN hour or so afterward, armed with two long sheets of figures, Titus set forth to Jere Misk's private room. Perhaps, after securing the boss' signature to the sheets, there might be time—and favorable chance —to ask advice as to a plan of his own. It was a nebulous plan to put Pompton Plains on the map by means of some sort of Labor Day exercises such as should draw visitors to the place. He had no definite ideas for the celebration. But Jere Misk was certain to have. Jere fairly exuded ideas. Titus nursed a secret yearning to be mayor of his own suburb, and the engineering of the right kind of celebration would go far toward boosting his ambition.

As he reached the door of Jere's room, Titus came to a jarring halt.

Inside the sanctum, apparently, a steam calliope was running over a pack of bloodhounds. On the instant, the glass door flew open. Out scampered a putty-faced office-boy, clutching in one hand an express order-book which was still virgin of Mr. Jere Misk's desired signature. Jere himself followed the escaping youth to the doorway and stood there, brandishing something and continuing to make truly terrifying noises.

All at once his eye fell on the quaking Titus. And on sight of a sympathetic audience, his clamor redoubled. To Snider, who was musical, it sounded like something awful from an opera—not the "Carmen" (or Garden) variety of opera, but one of those Strauss things where the orchestra and the singers battle to outracket one another. Jere Misk sounded like winners and losers combined, in such a cacophony contest.

Titus' rabbitlike stare wavered from his liege-lord's empurpled tangle of features to the object Jere was clutching so spasmodically in one upthrust hand.

The thing was an ellipse and brownish-yellow of hue. It evidently had once been a circular hoop of brass, perhaps fifteen inches in diameter, with something like a hinge at one side and a U-shaped catch at the other; the brass was an inch or so in width. But now the former circle was battered into a crude oval, irregular and distorted and bumpy of contour; the metal was tarnished and stained.

Misk was gripping one sagged curve of it as though, by sheer force of hate, his stubby fingers would bite their way through the discolored brass. From the oval dangled a few shreds of jute. Under Misk's convulsively uplifted arm, Titus could see an open packing-case on the desk beyond the doorway.

SNIDER'S guinea-pig astonishment was balm to the bellowing Misk. And it lured the great man to lucidity. He choked back the torrent of wordless sounds and groped gobblingly for coherent speech. Titus took advantage of the momentary lull to point at the crooked oval and to ask with respectful solicitude:

"Whatever is that, sir?"

The artless query pushed Misk's wrath once more past the power of speech. Titus, thinking no doubt to dissolve anger into radiant smiles, pointed once more at the thing and said wittily:

"It looks like a crippled doughnut."

"A crippled doughnut!" sputtered Jere. "That's what it is, all right. A crippled doughnut! And only a crippled dough-brain could have thought of that name for it. A crippled doughnut! Sent to me with the compliments of the United States Government. Lord! I'd give a year's income if the State or the National Committee would send a man around here to-day for campaign funds. I'd jam this crippled doughnut down his throat. Lord, but—"

"But what *is* it, Mr. Misk?" bleated Titus. "An infernal machine? Or—"

"Snider," replied Misk with a sudden icy and elephantine access of irony, "this crippled doughnut was one of the deadlight-rims of a ship's galley. A galley is a kitchen—a measly kitchen. A card in the box says what the thing is. And the card says the ship was the *Maine.* A generous government has rewarded my services to my party. A group of disinterested friends at Washington have recognized my many favors to them by clubbing together and presenting me with this priceless relic of the *Maine.* I had not dared to hope for anything more valuable than an eagle or a gun-turret. But they have made me their life debtor by lavishing *this* on me. This measly, dod-gasted crippled doughnut!"

"He-he-he!" dutifully tittered Titus Snider, misreading the grin of fury that ripped at Jere's overfull lips.

The grin was blown violently outward and into space by a chunk of lurid language that surged up from Jere's bursting heart and which rattled with deafening force about Titus' quivering ears. Thinking over the scene, long afterward, Titus always liked to bolster his tottering self-esteem by telling himself Mr. Misk could not possibly have meant more than one-tenth of the sulphurous terms he applied to his horrified listener. But just now the little man stood dumb, panic-smitten, and let the fusillade of abuse bang about his bent head.

Presently, for utter lack of breath, Jere checked his harangue and glowered about the office. Instantly six avid auditors ducked behind their desks. Jere turned on his heel, stamped back into his room, slammed the *Maine* relic into his wastebasket, crumpled the certificate viciously into a ball and flung it after the crippled doughnut; then he jammed on his hat and departed for his club, to breathe forth afresh his torrid griefs for the benefit of the little group of earnest drinkers whom, even at that early hour, he found rallying at the bar.

Not for weeks did he wax cool enough to admit that perhaps certain governmental departments may harbor a sense of humor—or a sense of divine justice—or a sense of fitting rebuke—or perhaps a choice blend of all three.

Misk Manor went without its promised historic landmark, and Labor Day in that paint-new suburb went unmarked by any more solemn event than a ball-game of ten languid innings between the Commuters and the Stay-at-Homes.

BUT, so philosophers tell us, nothing in nature is really lost. Presumably, this applies to crippled doughnuts. Titus Snider sat numbly at his desk for a full hour, head in hands, trying not to repeat over and over to himself some of the worst of the names Jere had called him. Then the inspiration-germ that had led Misk along a shining path to such bitter disaster fluttered from the private room into the cubby-hole niche and blithely burrowed its way into Titus' word-dazed brain. It took a long time for the germ to take root and grow in that abuse-sterilized soil. But minute by minute it did grow.

At first Snider found himself visualizing the greensward at Misk Manor, with the relic-crowned monolith surrounded by a cheering crowd. Then he recalled the scene at Pompton Lakes on last Labor Day, when a broken ventilator of the *Maine* had been unveiled. Next he pictured the blank stretch of grass across the road from the court-house and the Methodist chapel at Pompton Plains. Next—

JUST before noon, Titus Snider tiptoed into the private room of Mr. Jere Misk. The room was empty. In the big wastebasket still lay the crippled doughnut. Wedged between the basket-edge and one side of the oval was the tightly crumpled certificate of genuineness.

All the world over, wastebasket contents are free salvage. Sinlessly, almost piously, Titus Snider lifted from its abode of disgrace the twisted ellipse that had once been a deadlight-rim in the galley of the *Maine*. He did not think of it, now, as a crippled doughnut. In his heart he referred to it as a holy relic. Also he jettisoned and smoothed straight the wad of paper that was the certificate. Balm had stolen into his scarified soul. And there are better and shorter and more spectac-ular ways, after all, for winning the mayoralty than by rising through the successive offices of pound-master, school-board, chairman and borough clerk.

No longer did Titus need to plead with the boss for a Labor Day idea. The idea was at hand—it was in hand.

The next week's issue of *The Pompton Plains Palladium* contained an announcement that Titus Snider had public-spiritedly

secured a priceless relic of the *Maine,* that the exact nature of this relic was to be kept as a surprise until the moment of unveiling and that *The Palladium's* editor would gladly receive subscriptions for a field-stone pedestal whereon to erect the aforesaid pricelessly precious relic. A facsimile of the governmental certificate was published on page 2.

The date for the unveiling was set for high noon on Labor Day.

On the patch of ancient common, newly christened "The Green," a heap of field-stones daily took on a nearer and nearer approach to pedestal-shape. Evening after evening Titus returned from work, paused only to bolt a hurried dinner and change his wilted collar and then sallied forth on his nightly subscription hunt.

NIGHT after night Mrs. Titus Snider racked her brain for some cunning mode of attack whereby she might hope, Delilah-like, to lure from her spouse the revelation of the exact nature of the relic.

For, as *The Palladium* said, Titus told no one—not even Tillie, his own professionally trustful little wife—what the mysterious relic really was. His reticence was due only in part to a love for dramatic suspense and to his experience with Tillie's hopeless struggles to keep a secret.

In his calmer moments—and they were few enough in those troublous days—Titus recognized the unheroic appearance of the relic. He even recalled his own thoughtless words about a crippled doughnut. Displayed prematurely to the gaze of Pompton Plains, his treasure might possibly lack impressiveness. Mounted on its pedestal and revealed to view by a tug of the unveiling string, grasped in the moist palm of little Greta Wetherwolks (four-year-old daughter of our genial assistant freight-agent), it would flash forth as a surprise. Even a crippled doughnut, under such inspiring circumstances, could not but have an impressive appearance.

Knowing Tillie's zeal for ferreting out the truth,—and acting on an impulse worthy of *Dupin* himself,—Titus clamped a brand-new padlock on the door of the windowless third-floor storeroom and stuffed the door's keyhole with chewed paper. After that he brazenly took the deadlight-rim to the attic where, from the time of spring cleaning until fall, Tillie never set foot—on account of a squatter wasp-colony. He hid it behind a disused easy-chair and descended to the porch with the sinister certainty that the relic was as safely hid as though it were in a deposit-vault.

Naturally, all this happened while Tillie was at church.

On her return home, unerring feminine intuition led Tillie straight to the storeroom. Four times in the following week Titus was obliged fussily to renew the chewed-paper keyhole plug. And the new padlock's bright surface was scored and marred by scratches from the

entire bunch of household keys. But the lock held firm. And the dark store room guarded its secretless secret with due fidelity.

HALF the night Titus Snider had lain awake, ever and anon rising from his couch to scan the fickle sky for signs of rain. A dozen times he congratulated himself that he had decided to wait until gray dawn to set the relic in place on its pedestal, instead of affixing it there the night before. Under cover of darkness, vandals or nonsubscribers might well have stolen it. And he was glad he did not have to add to his weather-worries this extra fear.

"Up rose the sun, and up rose Emilie"—so Dan Chaucer has averred. Both Emilie and the solar orb, on Labor Day morning, would have found Titus Snider up and around a full hour ahead of them. Yes, and they would have heard him greet the dawn in a manner not unworthy of Jere Misk's crippled-doughnut outburst. Here is the chronology of the morning:

Titus lurched to his feet from a troublous dream, to hear his alarm clock chant the tidings that four-thirty had come. Instantly he was awake and tensely ready for the Day. At five, by prior double-rate arrangement, the two masons were to meet him at the pedestal and were to cement the relic to the proud base. After this Titus was to veil the ellipse in four yards of white cheese-cloth, test the unveiling-string, leave the village constable on guard and then return to bath and breakfast.

He therefore attired himself with stark haste in an elderly fishing-suit, postponed his shower and shave and hied himself to the attic. As he passed the padlocked storeroom door, a twinge of pity for Tillie jarred across his exultance. It had been a shame to trick her like this. She was a dear little thing. But he would make it all right with her somehow or other.

He was glad she still slept. Perhaps, after all, she need never know of his deception. This too was an inspiration, and a kindly one, withal. Titus paused long enough to unlock the storeroom door and push it open. Thence, on the feet of silence, he sped on toward the attic.

A MINUTE later Tillie was roused from slumber by a sound like that cleverly explained in stage directions as *Confused noise without.* Then, in a trice, the confused noise was no longer without but within—within her peaceful bedroom, and hammering a hideous alarm upon the chaste portals of slumber.

Tillie sat up, uttering a birdlike screech. Before her blinking eyes, her tidy little husband was doing a very creditable war-dance amid the tangling rugs. Also he was polluting the sweet morning air with language that accorded but ill with the rustic loveliness of the dawn. Making allowance for the difference in size and training and lung-capacity, he was no ignoble copy of Jere Misk.

"Titus!" squealed the scandalized Tillie. "Titus!"

Thinking of nothing more appropriate to say, she sought once more to stem the cataract:

"Titus!"

But on raved the dancing Titus. Tillie wanted to stop up her ears. But she feared she would miss something. And truly, for an amateur, the exhibition was well-nigh worth while. Titus kept it up more than two minutes, and except for the screeches, he scarcely repeated himself once. Then through his wife's panting expostulations broke his fierce demand:

"What in blue blazes did you do with it? Speak up!"

"With—with what?" she gasped timorously. "Oh, Titus, I don't seem to know you at all when you're like this! What *is* the matter, dovy?"

Dovy waved aside the love-term, cooing blasphemously the while, and then again demanding:

"What did you do with it?"

"With what?" once more asked poor Tillie with equal originality.

"With the relic, of course!" he wheezed. "It's gone! What's become of it?"

"I—I never saw your old relic," she averred tearfully. "How could I, when it was all locked up like that? If a burglar's broken in and—"

"What would a burglar be doing in our waspy attic?" stormed Titus. "What would he want of an easy-chair that has lost its easy, and with a lot of—"

"THAT wasn't a burglar," she wept. "That was Gustus Pape. He—"

"*What* was Gustus Pape?" hotly interrogated the dizzy Titus. "What's Gustus Pape got to do with the relic? What are you talking about, anyhow?"

"It was Gustus Pape," she sniveled. "It *was!* He—"

"He stole my relic? How'd he know where it was? Who gave it to him? Tell me, now!" thundered Titus the Terrible.

Tillie quailed at his voice, but none the less she made shift to reply:

"I'm not talking about your relic. I don't know anything about your nasty relic. Why should Gustus Pape take your relic? Who said he did?"

"You just said—"

"You asked if a burglar took that easy-chair, and I told you Gustus Pape took it, and you said—"

"Put it into words!" pleaded Titus, bewilderment turning away wrath as thoroughly as ever did a soft answer. "Put it into words, won't you, Tillie? What about Gustus Pape, first of all? We'll never get anywhere at this rate. The relic's gone! *Gone,* d'you hear? And—"

But Tillie was not listening.

"It was just a surprise, to please you," she whimpered. "Just as you said, the relic was kept a surprise to please me. And I thought you'd be so glad."

"Tell me!" sputtered Titus.

It was all he could think of to say. And luckily it was enough.

"I wanted so to help," she began, "because you were so worried about that last eight dollars and a quarter that no one would subscribe for. Well, when you told me last night that it had been turned in without any name, and that most likely it was that old Mrs. Slater, down at Little Falls, who did it—well, all the time I thought I'd die of laughing. For it was *me*."

"What was *you?*" implored the reeling Titus. "And where does Gustus Pape come in, with—"

"It was Gustus Pape," sniffingly pursued Tillie, while Titus groaned aloud. "You know how I hate the sight of him—ever since he cheated me so on those agate-ware things he traded in for my house-gown with the spots on it. And he's a blackmailer too! Look how he made poor Mrs. Geddes pay him two dollars a week for ever so long, for not telling on her about—"

TITUS' piteous groans brought her waveringly back toward the thread of her narrative.

"Just the same, he *is* a blackmailer and a rascal too," she said. "But when he stopped here last Monday and asked if I had anything to trade for cash, I thought about the Pedestal Fund and how worried you were. So I took him up-attic and sold him a lot of the truck we were going to burn anyhow, and some ginger-ale bottles down-cellar and some—"

"Did—you—sell—him—a—brass—thing—shaped—like—a—kind—of—doughnut—of—some—sort?" Titus checked her in a measuredly slow but terrible voice.

"I—I—why, there was a funny thing tucked away behind the easy-chair," faltered Tillie confusedly, awed by the fearsome tone of her lord. "A—a funny thing—made of brass. A lamp-frame, I guess. Anyhow, it wasn't any good and—oh, Titus, what ails you?"

The room shook with a yell that could not normally have come from so frail a body as her husband's. Horror had for once made Titus

Snider one hundred per cent vocally efficient.

Presently he was able to explain. And shortly thereafter, Titus and his wife were weeping in abandoned unison. Tillie was heartstricken when she learned the enormity of her well-meant deed. She even forbore to chide Titus for his storeroom deception and devoted herself to soothing his helpless sorrow.

At last, when the agony had spent itself, Titus began to remember that he was a resourceful real-estate magnate—also that his local prestige hung on a frayed thread. He conjured up the gathering crowds on the Green at noon—the slow change from enthusiasm to impatience—last of all, his speech of apology. And at this climax of humiliation his soul snappingly rebelled. The timorous rat, cornered, is a deadly foe.

"Phone over to Garvey's and have him come around here in a rush with one of his machines!" Titus suddenly bade his wife. "No, not here—to the Green. I've got to go first and tip those masons and get them to wait for me. Tell Garvey I'll be waiting for him there. Have him hustle!"

"You're—you're not going to do anything desperate, sweetie?" quavered Tillie, wiggling her hands limply in the air.

"I'm going to find Gustus Pape," sternly announced Sweetie. "I'm going to find him, whether he's in his junkyard, or whether he's at Hopatcong or Madagascar, or jogging his jingly old rattletrap cart across the old plains of the Sahara. I'm going to find him, and *I'm going to get that relic.* I'll buy it from him if I can. If I can't, I'll murder him and steal it from his widow. But I'm going to get it back here in time for the ceremonies. Gimme the housekeeping cash," he commanded, writhing into his coat. "I may not have enough money of my own to buy it if he's such a blackmail crook as you say."

GUSTUS PAPE—modern development of Robin Hood's jolly scoundrel-tinkers, who roamed the muddy highroads of muddier medieval England—was setting out in quest of mingled pleasure and profit. Forth from his high-fenced yard he drove into the holiday streets of Paterson.

Titus Snider, in describing the Pape equipage as a "jingly old rattletrap cart," had grossly flattered the vehicle. The cart seemed held together—or approximately together—by some mysterious force of gravitation, rather than by any visible means. The same comment might almost have fitted the horse that drew it—an animal built neither for endurance nor speed—an animal occupying the same place in the equine world as did the cart among Paterson's privately owned rolling stock.

But the battered sleigh-bells on horse and on cart jangled none the less blithely for that. Nor was there aught but joy in the equally battered heart of Gustus Pape. The junk-man did not troll forth a lilting carol as he fared from his yard to his daily toil. But that was because his mouth was quite full of a choice brand of eating tobacco.

As Gustus Pape steered his veteran palfrey—or palfrey emeritus—out into the street-traffic, he was subconsciously aware of an insistent if incoherent voice that swelled above the holiday clamor. And almost at once that same voice drew his closer attention. For it was calling upon him by name. Gustus Pape checked his steed's snail-like prog-ress and looked around. From an antique livery automobile a small man of large gestures was clambering. The next moment the excited newcomer was diving into the junk-yard and mysteriously beckoning Gustus to follow.

The junk-man flowed earthward from his perch, leaving his neolithic horse and cart to the perils of the highway. He sidled into the yard in the wake of Titus' furiously beckoning finger and cautiously shut the gate behind him.

"MORNIN', Mister Snider!" he greeted his visitor effusively.

"You bought some junk from Mrs. Snider last Monday," said Titus, repeating very fast the wily speech he had been rehearsing for the last forty minutes. "Some attic-junk. Well, I've got sentimental feelings about that junk. We've had it a long time. You paid eight dollars and a quarter for it. I'll pay you twenty dollars for the lot. And I'll load it into the car and take it home. Be quick hauling it out, please. I'm in a rush to get back to Pompton Plains for a celebration we're having there at noon."

"Now—that stuff was worth a lot more than twenty dollars to me," ruminated Gustus, his hand wandering pensively over his furry chin. "On fair profit, I'd say it had ought to be worth—"

"Well," growled Titus, "just how much?"

"Now—pretty near thutty dollars, anyhow," decided Gustus after painful and visible mental absorption.

"Here's thirty dollars," returned Titus, dredging for a handful of rumpled bills. "Get the stuff out of your barn for me as quick as you can."

"Now—it ain't exactly in my barn," objected Gustus. "Matter of fact, it ain't anywhere, so far's I know. I shipped it with a whole swad of stuff to Bayonne, yesterday, to the Rummage Sale at Oberteufer's. That's the furniture, of course. The reg'lar junk went to the—"

"The regular junk?" interrupted Titus. "The—the—"

Then he threw away the useless mask.

"Do you remember a brass thing?" he asked throatily. "A brass thing—a thing shaped something like *this?*"—with appropriate digital gestures—"a kind of twisted brass thing—like—like *this?*"

Again—and for eons of precious time—Mr. Pape ruminated. He even helped the process of thought by a new bite from his trouser-hidden quid.

"Now—it seems like I do," he said at last—a long last. "Seems I do kind of remember it. It was the only bit of brass I got from your house. All snarled up an' bent-like!"

"Is it here?" gasped Titus, his mouth very dry—his hands very moist.

"Now—I'm sorry, but it ain't. That is, not exactly," lamented Gustus Pape. "You see, I kind of made an all-around clean-up Tuesday an' yest'day. The furniture an' such went to Bayonne, an' the bottles to the fact'ry. An' all the brass an' iron an' things like that—why, that contraption of yours is most likely brass-filin's by now. It went to Communipaw to the—"

TITUS smote his breast. Mr. Pape halted in his narrative to gaze on him in real wonder.

"That settles it!" burbled Snider. And his heart was dead.

Disregarding Gustus Pape's interested queries, he turned and plodded heavily toward the street.

Within a step of the gate he stopped abruptly. Something bright had caught his eye. And the eye flashed an impression to the grief-

sodden brain. In apathy's place blazed the last-ditch brilliancy of the desperate.

"What's *that?*" croaked Titus Snider, pointing a crooked finger at an object huddled against the fence.

"That?" echoed the puzzled Gustus. "Now—that's an eagle, of course."

"I know," Titus answered. "But where did it come from? A battleship?"

"Battle-nothin'!" was the scornful response. "That was one of the four eagles on the courthouse cornice. The cornice got all busted in the thunderstorm Wednesday. The eagle was so bad knocked out, 'twasn't no use to fix it up. So they sent it around here along with the mess of lead from the cornice."

Titus was surveying the eagle with a look of dawning and frightened hope. The bird was of lead, and it was gold-leafed. It stood perhaps three feet high on a shaky base of cast iron. One wing was quite gone. The head was twisted to a rakish angle that gave the noble fowl an aspect of mingled craftiness and imbecility. The gold-leaf still glittered bravely here and there in sheltered valleys of plumage. But for the most part it was dulled and fused by the electrical storm.

Still the thing was an eagle. Anyone could see that—an eagle that had seen hard times—an eagle that might well have been the victim of a submarine explosion. And despair was just then making Titus Snider play far above form.

"How much?" he asked as carelessly as his throat and banging heart would let him.

"Now—that's a mighty valu'ble lump of lead," said Gustus. "An' lead's scarcer every day—then all that gold-leaf too. It—"

"How much!" rasped Titus deep down in his chest.

"Now—" began Gustus, continuing after a second look at the grim little face. "Thutty dollars—just to you."

AN hour afterward, Titus hobbled up the front walk of his own home, lugging over his shoulders a huge burlap bag whose m a n y - a n g l e d contents seemed almost to crush him

to earth by dint of weight. Tillie was at the door.

"I got it back," he panted, breathless from speed and effort. "At least I got something better—the eagle figurehead."

He did not say of what the thing was a figurehead, and his adroit evasion cooled his rising conscience-pangs. If Tillie chose to think— if Pompton Plains chose to think—that this disreputable eagle had been the figurehead of the *Maine* and not of the Paterson courthouse's southeast façade, that was no affair of his. He had suffered too much to let mere conscience rough-ride him now.

Within a half-hour the constable was shooing the curious to a respectful distance, while Titus and the two masons scramblingly lifted the Bird of Freedom to the top of the five-foot pedestal and into the downy bed of concrete prepared for it. Then it was that Titus espied, on the bent iron base of the eagle, the dim, yet wholly visible stamped legend: HALCYON MOLDING CORPORATION, 1911.

For an instant this meant nothing to the tired but exultant relic-collector. But somehow the sight of one date recalled to his memory another. And the other date was February 15, 1898—the date of the sinking of the *Maine.* Not waiting for a trowel, and only making certain that the busy masons were not observing him, Titus slapped a handful of wet concrete athwart the damning legend.

"Leave the smudge of mortar like that," he bade his coworkers as he helped them adjust the cheese-cloth veil. "It'll give it a rough, rugged look to go with the field-stone pedestal. Statuary oughtn't ever to look too tidy. I read that in a piece about a foreign sculptor called Mr. Rodin. Leave it the way it is. We got two hours to spare. I'll leave the cop to watch things, and I'll chase home to get dressed and shave myself. Thanks, boys. You've fixed it on fine."

PEACE crept back to its rudely jogged nest in the heart of Titus Snider. And with peace entered pride of achievement and the bliss of popularity. The trio took up so much room there that poor conscience was crushed to death and passed away without a moan.

The monument had been duly unveiled in the presence of a vast throng of nearly two hundred people. Not less than nineteen automobiles were parked in a semicircle behind the pedestrian spectators. And their horns had squawked vociferously and almost in unison as the veil (after only two easily remedied hitches) was rent away from the relic.

The fourteen Boy Scouts had saluted at precisely the right moment. And at approximately the same instant the Firemen's Band had struck up "The Star-Spangled Banner," with the jute factory fife and drum corps chiming in scarce half a beat behind.

The Reverend Mandeville Preakness, in behalf of the Borough, had thanked Mr. Titus Snider in sounding periods for his beautiful and patriotic gift. And Mayor Threbble had added a few well-chosen words as to real-estate values in lovely Pompton Plains. Then Titus had made his own brief and perspiring speech—a graceful speech, yet full of feeling and strength. He had spoken of the *Maine*. He had spoken of the figurehead. Yet he had scrupulously refrained from saying in so many words that this dissolute-looking eagle *was* the figurehead of the *Maine*. So murdered conscience had not come to life and bitten him.

And now it was all over. He shook hands with the Reverend Mandeville Preakness, with the Mayor—whose successor was to be himself—and with the editor of *The Palladium*. Then he stepped down from the six-inch dais—smiling in patronizing tolerance at a farmer who timidly opined that he'd always s'posed a battleship figgerhead was some bigger'n that eagle—and shook hands with admiring friends who surged about him with congratulations and shoulder-slaps and words of heavenly praise of his exploit.

Tillie, it was true, would need a little talking to, to make her understand how he had miraculously chanced upon the eagle figurehead of the *Maine* in the course of his early morning quest of the crippled doughnut. He felt he had been a bit too sketchy in explaining the phenomenon to her—also that he had not laid enough stress on the need for silence as to the substitution. But he knew Tillie. And he was confident he could make everything satisfactory.

THROUGH the clustering crowd he worked his modest yet conquering way. Some one bellowed:

"Three cheers for Titus Q. Snider!"

And the response was not at all bad—either in volume or in spirit. Some one else—a nameless Mark Antony to the Labor Day Caesar— then "did offer him a kingly crown" by howling raucously:

"Three cheers for the next Mayor of Pompton Plains!"

The cheers, if less ecstatic than the first trio, were hearty enough to send the blood sizzling and humming through Titus' whole body.

It was the very proudest, gladdest, mightiest moment in all Titus Snider's life. His ears vibrated with the joyous buzzing in his head. His eyes blurred from wild happiness. He strode on, oblivious—drunk-

enly rapturous.

He came to a halt only as he realized he was walking into the slowly dissolving phalanx of parked cars. The check brought him to himself. His clearing vision alighted on the automobiles in front of him—and on something else.

Sandwiched between two haughtily scintillant flivvers was a ramshackle cart in whose shafts slouched a mangy wreck of a horse. On the cart's high seat was perched a man—a miserable man — a thing of shreds and patches—a man who was looking down upon Titus with a subtly and speculatively gleaming eye. One orb was closed in a wink, giving to the junkman's face an evil cast that sent vague tremors of fear through the erstwhile jubilant Hero of the Hour.

Titus stared back blankly, his soul whispering to him of dire peril— tales of the junk-man's local repute swishing through his memory. Before he could turn coldly away, Gustus Pape leaned forward and cooingly asked:

"Now—can I speak to you—just a minute—Mister Snider?"

The Dubess

IT WAS Dirck Barry who coined the name. If Dirck had been hired to compile a brand-new dictionary he most assuredly would have included the word in it, much like this:

> DUBBESS— common noun. Feminine of Dub. The female of this species is more deadly dubful than the male. Example: Hester Gregg.

Now there was no more chance of anybody's asking Dirck Barry to compile a new dictionary than to think a new thought. So the term Dubbess circulated by oral report alone. In spite of this limitation, it stuck. Presently nearly everyone who knew Hester Gregg by sight was referring to her by her Barry-given title rather than by her name; which would have hurt Hester horribly if she had known.

Her father was perhaps the foremost numismatist in America. Also, he was a close runner-up for the long-distance Egyptology championship—if such a championship exists. Her mother had not an equal, of her own sex, in the mastership of ethnology in all its branches. Hester was their only child and she had been brought up at home.

In the triune family circle the Greggs never chatted. They conversed. For small talk they had about as much use and aptitude as has a heavyweight pugilist for ping-pong.

Of laughter, though—genial and hearty laughter—there was a lavish plenty among the Greggs. As when, at nine, Hester pointed to a crude sketch of the hawk-headed god, Horus—part of a hieroglyph triptych copied by an amateur Egyptologist and sent to Professor

Gregg for inspection—and innocently asked whether it was a picture of Ptah or only of the cat god, Bubastis. The professor's study rang with Homeric mirth at this unconscious quip. And, later, a tableful of learned dinner guests echoed the merriment. Yes; for all their erudition, the Greggs were not without a fund of humor and jollity. And Hester, as I have said, was brought up at home.

At fourteen she had a long and troublesomely slow convalescence from typhoid. During her tiresome weeks of getting well Professor Gregg laid aside all his weightier interests and duties and devoted himself to entertaining the sick daughter he adored. Doffing his garment of erudition, he was her constant playmate. And what a gayly carefree time they had of it, to be sure! For years afterward, at intervals, both of them would laugh in fond happiness at the very memory of those convalescent days.

For one thing Professor Gregg livened the sick child's boredom by inventing a game whereby, in contest form, she mastered and memorized tables of logarithms. She grew so proficient at this giddy sport that soon she could repeat yards of gloomy logarithmic tables backward.

As she grew a little stronger, logarithms palled. But the ever-resourceful professor was ready with a new game, even more amusing. He and Hester tackled plane geometry, according to a system of the professor's own. They sought playfully to catch each other in errors, and they chuckled gleesomely over their alternating victories.

By the time Hester's typhoid-shaved hair had begun assume ringlets she and her jocund father were playing a tensely exciting game based on the mazes of the binomial theorem. And Hester had learned to make puns Greek.

No, it was not pathetic; for there was no unhappiness connected with it—or perhaps, for that very reason, it was pathetic. Father and daughter keenly enjoyed the brain exercise. To the girl's inherited mentality there was a positive thrill in the sport. And she had known nothing different. That was the crux of the thing.

All children look on their parents as gods and are we content with the life at home until they go to school—until elsewhere they meet other children. Then begins the painful eye-opening—a million times more painful for the dethroned gods than for the disillusioned devotees. Then, too, begins the process of Individualism, which makes its victims a pride to themselves and a pest to the aforesaid dethroned gods.

Hester had never gone to school. She had been taught at home, this being one of the Gregg maxims of education. There were no children of her own age in the rural district where stood the professor's rangy old house—none with whom her parents would let her associate. So she grew to womanhood—or, rather, to nineteen—calmly happy in her superscholarly environment, her sole touch with the outer world formed by the occasional scientific visitors to whom the Gregg house was a shrine.

She grew up wondrous pretty and winsome and sweet of voice. Of course she did not know how to dress. But neither did her mother. And the latter's choice of clothes for her seemed to Hester the last word in fashionable elegance.

When she was nearly twenty her father accepted the professorship of Egyptology and kindred themes at Harle University.

At Harleville the social life of the town centers round the college; and the members of the professorial set are the arbiters of local society. Hester Gregg, all at once, was plunged headlong, but gleefully undismayed, into the real world.

According to time-sacred custom, Professor Gregg's official advent at Harle was marked by a huge and formal dinner party at the president's house. Not less than sixteen Harle professors and their wives were numbered among the guests, as well as four of the trustees and a full dozen of the town's younger set, on whom the ægis of Harle approval rested.

These junior guests—ranging in age from eighteen to thirty—were invited on Hester's account. A veranda dance, as small and informal as the dinner itself was large and ceremonious, was to wind up the evening. This, again, was to launch the new professor's daughter, in due and ancient form, into Harleville's social waters.

One or two men of this faculty-hallowed younger set had chanced to see Hester from afar, as the Greggs debarked from the train, and again as she sat curled up behind a brown little book on the brown little side veranda of the new Gregg home. They had found her deliciously easy to look at. And word went forth that the latest professor had a daughter who would make that brown veranda not only popular but populous in the spring twilights. Not one invited guest from the town dodged the president's dinner; not even Dirck Barry, who usually displayed positive genius at eluding such functions.

Hester was athrill at the prospect of her first dinner party. She had read of these affairs in the pitiably few bits of light literature that had come her way—flashily frivolous tales by Thackeray, Trollope, Jane Austen, and the like, which Professor Gregg tolerated in his library for the pleasure of any fellow scientist's nonscientific wife who might be his guest.

Hester had read of dinners—dinners unlike those at which her father had been host at his own board. And now she was actually going to attend one.

Lest she prove less entertaining than those around her, she was at pains to brush up on several of the topics that had been found especially enthralling at her father's table, as well as upon themes she thought out on her own account for the occasion. She even rehearsed scraps of scintillant repartee, which would have done credit to Evelina or to Maria Edgeworth's sprightliest heroine. She looked forward to the ordeal with nervousness, but with no fear at all. And the nervousness was of a decidedly happy kind.

Hester had a brand-new evening dress, too, made for the festivity and designed under her mother's own eye. It was the prettiest and most expensive dress Hester had owned in all her nineteen and three-fourths years. It was of changeable silk—a very thick and handsome material splendidly serviceable, with endless wear to it. It had shrewdly reddish lights. But its prevailing color was gray—a harsh gray that our Elizabethan ancestors termed "hodden."

Also, it fitted. Indeed, it fitted with a closeness that in arm and shoulder, vaguely suggested the skin of sausage. It was just too high in the neck for evening wear, and just too low for a decorous street gown. It was in no way ridiculous, or even ugly. But—well—Helen might easily have averted the Trojan War by wearing it when first she met Paris.

Hester's soft dark hair was drawn wavily back at either side of its central parting, and was piled in a big knot, too far forward for Psyche's and too far back for Madame Récamier's. A man would have wondered subconsciously what was the matter with the coiffure. A woman's fingers would have itched to rearrange it.

Her full young throat was encircled by a coral-and-chased-gold necklace—an heirloom from her father's grandmother. The necklace, like the dress, was just a little tight.

But, as she looked at herself in the long glass of the dressing room, before going downstairs under her black-silk-swathed mother's convoy on the night of the dinner, Hester fairly caught her breath at sight of her own elegance. It was the first time she had thought much about dress. And the first thoughts were blissful.

Another girl sat in a far corner of the room, waiting impatiently for a white-capped maid to unbutton her street shoes and ensconce her feet in a pair of dancing slippers. Hester, in the glass, shyly but critically appraised the fluffily white costume of the girl and the almost rowdy fluffiness of her hair. The rather low cut of the white dress forced a tiny gasp from Hester. She wondered whether the girl had not forgotten some part of her carelessly intricate attire.

Just then Mrs. Gregg took her daughter's hand and led her downstairs—into the world.

There were quite a million people gathered in the drawing-room, and at least a hundred thousand of them were looking at Hester when she came in. A rush of color ran up over the debutante's classic little face at the survey, and her eyes waxed big and softly lustrous. A horse blanket and a blue wig could not have spoiled her beauty at that minute.

Dirck Barry gave a

grunt of heartfelt satisfaction, as of one who, after years of hope-less waiting, finds his life goal. And almost at once he had wriggled through the press to a post of vantage beside Hester. The moment he was introduced to her he proceeded to cut her out of the herd with all the skill of an exhibition cow-puncher, and to corner her in an alcove.

"If I'd been born lucky instead of saintly," he was saying to her when she came out of her daze, "I'd be treating myself to one large hope that Mother Prexy is going to let me take you in to dinner. But, anyhow, there's the dance afterward. And—"

"Which of the ladies is Mother Prexy?" asked Hester, interested in locating the bearer of so quaint a title.

"Mother Prexy?" echoed Dirck. "Why, it was she who introduced me to you! Didn't you know who she was? The one, there, with the homemade face and the features that show such bad teamwork. She is—"

"But I am quite certain you must be in error," corrected Hester. "That lady is Mrs. Gatenby, the president's wife; the hostess of the evening."

"Yes!" assented Dirck, bewildered. "I said so. Mother Prexy—Prexy's one remaining wife. When I was ten years old I fell in love with her; and I made up my mind to marry her when I grew up. I've never forgotten it."

"*Ne tum quidem veterum immemor amorum?*" queried Hester in a shy attempt at small talk.

Dirck, who had not opened a copy of Tacitus in ten years, and whose Latin, at best, had been fragmentary, blinked dizzily.

"Come again!" he invited.

"Indeed I shall," promised Hester. "It is all so charming and bril-liant that I shall accept as many such invitations as I am fortunate enough to receive."

From the blankness of his erstwhile ardent face she realized he had misunderstood her, or else that she had in some way misunder-stood him. She was slightly dashed by the obscure blunder; but she rallied her analytical mind and went back to the point of divergence to locate the break.

"You deemed yourself in love with Mrs. Gatenby when you were ten?" she prompted. "And you still remember it? I do not wonder. She must have been a comely and statuesque woman in those days. She is still of fine presence. I think, with that rich auburn hair and—"

"Yes," said Dirck absently. "I remember her when it was gray. I've known her a long time, you see."

Again Hester had a feeling that she had not quite understood. She was not able to go on with her effort to unravel the verbal problem, for the last belated guest came downstairs and dinner was announced. Clem Hathaway darted eagerly to the alcove to claim his hostess-given privilege of taking Hester in to dinner.

Dirck, to his own surprise, felt less grief than he had expected to in his failure to have the lovely newcomer for a dinner companion. And he felt less elated than he could understand when he found that his own place-card enthroned him directly upon Hester's other side at the table.

During the passage from alcove to dining room Hester put herself through a sharp mental reorganization. Somehow or other she had not done well in this brief conversation. She and Barry had apparently been talking at cross-purposes—just like that farcically droll couple in Aristophanes; only in real life it had been confusing rather than funny.

She must keep her wits awake; and she must speak slowly enough for her dinner partner to grasp the meaning of her every word. It would never do to let these new friends misjudge her, or brand her as rattle-brained and lacking in power to follow a rational trend of talk.

Wherefore, by the time she shook out her table napkin she was gallantly ready for the next bout. She recalled one of the topics she had prepared for dinner talk; and, with perfect distinctness and self-possession, she asked Hathaway:

"What is your personal opinion of Meyer's Claim?"

"Whose claim?" stammered Hathaway, who had been marshaling his own forces, with gay confidence, to the attack.

"Why, Meyer's, of course," responded the surprised girl. "Professor Meyer, you know. I refer to the manifestly absurd claim of his that Petrie is wrong and that fully four hundred years elapsed between Egypt's thirteenth and seventeenth dynasties. Or"—she caught herself up—"perhaps you do not consider it absurd. I really had no right to term it so, except that it is my father's contention. And it was Ruthven's too. I should be interested to hear any good sound argument to uphold Meyer."

She paused, expectant. Clem Hathaway was a fast-rising young banker in Harleville, and was clever, withal, at his profession. But his chief knowledge of Egypt was based on the brands of cigarettes he favored.

"I'm afraid I don't go in much for high-brow stuff," he said in cowed apology. "I'm sorry. But—"

"Clem's a wizard at all that sort of lore," cruelly announced Dirck Barry from the far side of Hester. "He pretends he isn't; but that is just his modesty. Me, now—I'm a dunce! All of my education I can ever remember is something I heard once about Euclid."

"Euclid?" echoed Hester, glad to find something in common with one of these puzzling persons. "Euclid the Megarian or Euclid the Alexandrian mathematician?"

"Search me!" dazedly replied Dirck, reeling a little under the query. "I don't know which one. I never knew there was a whole nest of them. I mean the one who wrote the geometry. And the thing I heard about it that I remember," he went on, "was this: The third book of Euclid is the most interesting of the lot. Because it's so much more impassioned than any of the others."

"Euclid?" gasped the dumfounded girl. "Impassioned? Why, you must be momentarily confusing him with Anacreon! Or perhaps you have unconscious reference to the third fragment of Sappho. Surely not of Euclid! Geometry is merely a true science. Not—"

"No," insisted Dirck. "I'm right. Perhaps when you studied Euclid they gave you a copy with the racy bits left out. But—"

"Perhaps," agreed Hester with quick tact.

She realized that this solemn-faced youth had made a most ludicrous and laughable classical error. And she was at much pains to keep her face straight as she foresaw how her learned father would roar over the inexcusable blunder when she should relate it to him on the way home. She did not yet see how a college-bred man could have made such a mistake. But she must not let Barry know she had detected it. It would be unkind to set him right, here in public. Perhaps later on she would do so.

"I hope you are going to like Harleville, Miss Gregg," broke in Clem Hathaway, noting her flush and fearing she had seen through

Dirck's clumsy teasing. "There is an awfully jolly set of people here. At least we think so. Won't you try to agree with us?"

"I shall not have to try," answered Hester; "for I know I shall agree with you. I am looking forward so zestfully to mingling with them! Perhaps they may even permit me to join their debating clubs or their research classes—or whatever the favorite forms of recreation are."

"You must surely join our Pythagoras Greek-root League first of all!" declared Dirck, overhearing.

Hester's face brightened at the prospect. A dozen questions as to the nature of this society with the interesting name were rising to her lips when Clem Hathaway cut in, with a suddenness that seemed to her all but rude, and changed the subject.

"I'm sorry, Miss Gregg," he said, glowering savagely at the grinning Dirck; "but we are a pretty frivolous lot here, I'm afraid. We oughtn't to be, of course; but we are. Won't you try to come down to our level, since we can't come up to yours? You see, there is plenty of high-brow intercourse of sorts among the faculty crowd—especially the older ones. But we younger people seem to get more fun out of dancing and golf and tennis and the theater, and all that, than from the intellectual things. Won't you please try to like those low-brow things too?"

"Certainly I shall!" promised Hester in genuine relief and in some regrettable anticipation. "I was so afraid you would find me sadly stupid and backward, living, as you do, in the very heart of learning: and I am glad to hear you can unbend. I should love, in particular, to dance. I never learned any of the modern dances; but I am certain I could acquire them if anyone would take the pains to instruct me."

"Oh, the modern dances aren't everything!" Hathaway assured her. "People say the old ones will come back. And one can waltz to a 'hesitation.' We'll do that to-night if you'll let one."

"I—But the waltz is a modern dance!" insisted Hester. "I read so in Pessy's History of the Dance. It was in vogue in France—at least a modification of it—as the *valse,* as early as 1795. And as the *volte* it was danced during the reign of Henri Trois. But it was not introduced into England until after the beginning of the nineteenth century; and not into this country until about 1830. So it is really a modern dance. And I don't dance any of those modern dances—the waltz and the raquette and the varsovienne and the schottische and the polka, and the rest of the new ones. I have read of them, of course. I know all their names. But I never had a chance to learn them. As a matter of fact, the only dances I know at all well are the Dance of Isis—which my father taught me when he was reconstructing it from a papyral palimpsest at the museum—and one of the Eleusinian dances. I learned that myself, from—"

"The most popular up-to-date dance here this season," gravely spoke up Dirck Barry, "is the Post-Chautauqua Dip. It is very simple: A couple stand at opposite ends of a long room and curtsy to each other to the tune of Old Hundred. Very simple but graceful; and quite beyond reproach from a moral ground. It—"

He broke off, squelched by the scowl in Clem Hathaway's brooding eyes. This time Hester noted the scowl as it flashed athwart her on its way to silence Dirck. And she saw the laughter-distorted faces of two girls who had been listening from across the table.

All at once she knew she had been making herself ridiculous—though she did not at all see why or how—and that Dirck Barry had been making fun of her. Also, that Clem Hathaway had been trying to make things easier for her. She wanted to cry.

Clem, reading her very transparent thoughts, began to talk volubly and banally to her in a monologue, the only value of which was that it did not call for any answers.

All round her was a hum of voices that seemed to blend into a single buzzing note of animated good-fellowship which was sprayed with splashes of laughter in many keys. The younger folk were evidently on terms of gay comradeship and bubbled with talk. The girls, in their low-cut dresses, were jabbering merrily, and about nothing, with men who loved to hear and abet their chatter.

Hester's mother was talking earnestly and enthrallingly with the professor of ethnology—a man so meager of body that his frame scarcely covered his giant intellect and threatened to leave his mentality improperly exposed.

The rest of the oldsters, whether in general talk or in dialogues, were at their ease. Everybody, indeed, was at ease and happy—except Hester Gregg. Hester was finding her new world a strange and icily lonely place.

She began to study the other girls under cover of Clem's flow of vapid talk. And as she scanned them her own dress grew less elegant and up-to-date in her eyes. She did not know why. Also, in contrast with these girls' frothy flow of gossip and badinage, her plans for the preparing of worthy topics of table talk appeared not unlike the carrying of a trench mortar to a humming-bird hunt.

She felt all lost and confused. She was thoroughly at home in no less than three dead and three modern languages. In numismatics, in ethnology, in Egyptology, she had few equals among amateur scholars. She was a natural mathematician. She had a splendidly developed analytical mind. With no conceit at all, she now knew herself to be the mental peer of any of these people—or, indeed, of ninety-nine people out of a hundred. Yet what did it all avail her?

One saphead had made a fool of her. One self-confessed low brow—whatever that might mean—was talking to her through sheer charity alone.

Hester was aware of a rising surge of wrath, which not only engulfed herself but spattered over upon the heads of the father and mother who had, until now, been flawless and whom she blamed fiercely for her own social ignorance. With anger came returning courage. Girding herself afresh, she listened with flattering interest to the almost foundering Hathaway, and laughed loudly at several cryptic bits of general-conversation badinage that were tossed hither and thither across the table.

When the dancing began Hester had another relapse. The strains of music set her aquiver. So did the sight of one filmily clad damsel after another melting into the black-cloth arms of partners and swaying off into the rhythm of a dance whose steps were an insoluble enigma to the poor bookish outlander.

Man after man came up to ask her to dance. Man after man she refused, because she had merely learned differential calculus instead of the fox trot. But her beauty led several of these applicants to sue for the privilege of sitting out dances with her.

Not until the awful evening was nearly over did she note that the same man never asked to sit out a second dance with her. Before his dance was at an end, her partner would begin to look vague and troubled, and to answer her at random when she forgot herself and indulged in some ethnological jest or quoted a snatch of Greek or

Hebrew. The moment these men could decently get away from her, they did so. And—except Clem Hathaway—they never came back.

Hester noted, too, that most of them were brought up to her by Dirck Barry. Dirck so dearly loved a joke he could not bear to say good-by to it.

At the last—Clem having been forced to leave early—she sat quite alone, on a very uncomfortable but mercifully shaded veranda bench. On her face was riveted a painful smile of gayety. In her heart were tears and hot indignation. Once or twice she smoothed furtively the folds of the thick changeable silk which had seemed to her so exquisite and which she was slowly learning to detest. The prized coral necklace, too, began to dig into the creamy column of her throat as that throat swelled with the effort of gulping back sobs.

She had looked forward so rapturously to this wonder evening! All her days, like the Lady of Shalott, she had dreamed of the glorious world of real life and of the fellowship of youth. Now for the first time she was in that world. And now for the first time she was lonely and downright miserable.

"Why aren't you dancing, dear?" she heard Mrs. Gatenby's well-meant voice in her ear at last. "I hoped you'd have such a good time; and—"

"I'm having a delightful evening," said Hester. "I cannot dance any more, I fear, because I have hurt my foot."

Thus did Hester tell her first lie—or, rather, brace of lies. Truly this was a night of first things!

At once Mrs. Gatenby bustled off to a knot of men to bring someone back for the solitary guest to talk with. Miserably Hester watched the hostess stop in front of the group. Miserably she watched the group melt—all its component parts drifting in some other direction than her own. Mrs. Gatenby charged toward a second knot of young people, still bent upon her hospitable mission of charity. Midway, as she passed Hester's chair, the girl sprang up to intercept her.

"Oh, please do not discommode yourself on my account, Mother Prexy!" she blurted out, trying not to cry. "I prefer to remain here alone. I—"

She stopped, with a gurgle of horror, as she realized what she had called her hostess.

And a murderous hatred for Dirck Barry flamed into her heart. With it came a cold resolve for vengeance on the man who had made a butt of her throughout the evening and who was responsible for the atrocious thing she had just said.

All night long, in her severely mannish bedroom, Hester Gregg lay, wide-eyed and in anguish. Story-book heroines in such vigils are supposed to be dry-eyed in their grief. Hester was not. She cried a great deal at short intervals, from the time she discarded her loathed thick silk dress until dawn.

But ever, as the night wore on, her hatred for Dirck Barry hardened and strengthened. And all through the next day, and the next, it grew, until it was a miniature mania. Hester forced herself to go over and over every guying word and deed of his, her reveries always culminating with the memory of that hideous Mother Prexy break which had completed the wreck of her evening.

She understood, at length, how Medea and Electra had felt; yes, and Orestes, too, and a hundred other classic vengeance seekers. Like them, her once placid thoughts ever centered on revenge. And, at the last, like them, her primitively original young mind hit upon a plan.

At its dawning this plan seemed to her well-nigh absurd. She would have termed it melodramatic if she had had any knowledge of melodrama. But as she dwelt on its charms she became more and more intrigued by their glitter. Presently the plan no longer seemed foolishly impractical. Its very lure made it take on the guise of feasibility.

Hester Gregg had been taught to think everything out from her own angle. She had no real-life precedents to go by. Having suffered no defeats at the hands of the world until the night of the dinner, all things had seemed to her possible. Most things still seemed so—especially this odd plan of hers.

She had the little brown veranda to herself all the time nowadays. In the dressing room, after the dinner dance, Dirck Barry had coined the term Dubbess and had affixed it to her. The name had spread. Hester's local repute and title were instantly established; wherefore the emptiness of the veranda she had so happily fitted up for flocks of guests.

Her first caller was Clem Hathaway. Hearing by chance of her ostracism, Clem proceeded to break that ostracism to the best of his ability by going at once to see the Dubbess. Which, somehow, was Clem's way.

He was tremendously popular in Harleville. He called at comparatively few houses. This naturally added to the prestige of such calls as he bothered to make.

To Clem's surprise Hester greeted him with a cordiality that was almost vehement. As she led him out on the veranda she interrupted a bromidic comment on the weather by saying abruptly:

"Perhaps it is an instance of telepathy that you have come here this evening, for I was beginning a note to you asking if you would call."

"Why," stammered the mildly astonished Clem, "that was mighty good of you, Miss Gregg! I—"

"You see," she hurried on, "I am anxious for help. I need and desire it very much. And I know of no one else but yourself who would consent to help me, or who would be able to. There is no reason why you should do so. I appreciate that. But you were very kind to me at Mrs. Gatenby's dinner. So I ventured to hope that you might do me an even greater service—out of the charity of your good heart."

Clem Hathaway listened in genuine bewilderment to the stiltedly dictioned preamble, noting its wording less than the undercurrent of almost fierce appeal in Hester's voice.

"Fire away!" he bade her with an effort at lightness. "Whatever it is, I'll be glad to be of use. But you're wrong about my ever having done you any kindness. At least if I did I can't for the life of me remember it. What was it? I'm a vain chap, and I like to hear my pretty virtues rehearsed. You say it was at Mrs. Gatenby's? What—"

"You tried to shield me from Mr. Barry's flights of cruel wit, for one thing," she said. "And you talked to me when no one else would. And—"

"Miss Gregg!" he exclaimed, dreadfully embarrassed.

"You did!" she affirmed. "And I am going to ask you to do even more. If you do not care to I shall not be offended at your refusal. Let me tell you the service I seek."

Drawing a long breath of nervousness, she forestalled his interruption by launching at once into her theme.

"I am very unhappy," she began simply, as though stating a series of premises in logic. "I am unhappy because I am alone in a town full of young persons. I am alone because I am so different from all those young persons. I am different from them because I talk differently and think differently, and because my clothes are not like theirs, and because I do not know how to dance. Those, I think, are the chief reasons for the divergence.

"I want to know if you will teach me the language of young persons of their sort; and if you will teach me how to dance some of their peculiar dances; and if you will advise me what variety of clothes is most becoming to me. And—and all that," she finished lamely as her rapid-fire utterance failed her in face of the daring favor she was asking of this half-stranger.

For an instant, as Hester hurried through her plea, Clem had an overwhelming desire to laugh. Then, unbidden, something choked him; and her earnestness and misery sifted through to his very heart, in spite of the stark absurdity of her proposition.

He tried to disclaim any ability along the lines she attributed to him. He sought to say something which should put her at her ease and soften that wistfully wretched look in her big eyes; but the right words would not come to the embarrassed man. All he could see was her appealing gaze boring into him. And his ears were full of the desponding throb of her voice.

So, in his confusion, be decided to temporize. With this diplomatic end in view, he swallowed twice and then heard himself saying vapidly:

"I'll send a phonograph and some dance records round in the morning. We'll have our first dancing lesson to-morrow evening if you like. And I'll send you my copy of George Ade's Fables in Slang too. Don't try to talk as he writes. But graft his style on your Lindley Murray vocabulary. Ade is a grand counterirritant for Jane Austen. I'll send you one or two other books that'll help. And—if you don't mind my correcting you—I can help in that way too."

"Yes," she urged. "Yes. If—"

"For instance, you just spoke of 'young persons.' You don't need to speak of our crowd as 'the bunch' if you don't want to; but, at that, it's better than the young-persons talk. You'll excuse my telling you? You asked for it, you know. . . . A few vaudeville shows would help, too—those and some live literature; the sort that isn't written by men with Ph.D. or F.R.S. after their names, but by men who have been living while the scholars have only been thinking. As for dress, I'd be no good to you there. I don't think any he-man would. But my mother could help if you'd let her. She has lots of taste."

Then he, too, stopped short, amazed at having spoken so and at having committed himself to such a task. It was the very last thing he had expected to do or say. Not even the eager gratitude of Hester's words and the almost slavish adulation of her eyes could wholly calm his self-ruffled composure.

But, being in for it, he did not turn back. And that, also, was Clem's way. Besides, the bizarre nature of the task appealed to his slumbering creative instinct. The zest of tutelage was already upon him. So it was settled, and the tuition began.

Her mind trained to wrestle with hiero-glyphics, with Greek roots and with higher mathematics, it was a joyous and increasingly easy task for Hester to absorb the teachings of Clem Hathaway. Presently both tutor and pupil were enthusiastic over the unique task. Not even the dancing lessons filled Hester's soul with such wondering joy as did the books and magazines Clem brought her. They did all manner of things to her classical trend of thought and to her vocabulary.

But the crowning bliss was the tactful instruction by Mrs. Hathaway in dress and in the wearing of clothes. Hester had not dreamed that her monthly allowance could compass such miracles of taste in

the way of hats and gowns as the outfit which began to adorn her
wardrobe.

With all her heart and intellect she threw herself into every branch
of her new education—an education, by the way, which brought Clem
perforce to the Gregg house on an average of four times a week. The
frequency of his calls had much the same chance of escaping notice in
a town like Harleville as would the presence of the Statue of Liberty in
a three-car garage.

It was two months after the beginning of her studies when Hester
ventured to make a personal test of her
proficiency. The Faculty Club gave its
annual dance. Thither, under Clem Hathaway's escort, fared the Dubbess.

It is only in books that the arrival of
any guest at a dance—any nonintoxicated
guest—"creates a decided stir throughout
the crowded hall." But Hester Gregg's
advent at the Faculty Club dance caused
the focusing of many a pair of eyes on
her. And into those many eyes crept an
admiring wonder as they inspected the
apotheosized butt of Dirck Barry's humor.

The girl's dress was simple; but it had
the perfection of simplicity. So had her
loosely piled hair. So, too, had the quietly
assured poise of her manner. Her dancing was graceful. The exertion of the first
dance brought an adorable color to her
face. Her eyes were alight with glad excitement.

Dirck Barry beheld with dropping jaw. Dirck had been away from
Harleville on business for his law firm for more than a month, and had
returned only a day or two earlier. Thus the metamorphosed Dub-
bees burst upon him as a revelation. He had not even had a chance to
hear the gossip as to Hathaway's countless calls upon her.

For a time Dirck was smugly content to view Hester from afar and
to speculate. True, she no longer dressed like the girls in Volume One
of Little Women. And she certainly could dance! Moreover, there was

an air to her.

But, with acute memories of her mental processes and type of conversation on the night she had won her title, Dirck did not crave to come to closer quarters. Long since he had tired of the joke.

Expectantly he watched the men who, drawn by Hester's beauty, sought dances with her. He had so much enjoyed guying men who, similarly drawn, had sat out single dances with her at Mrs. Gatenby's! But this time he noted an odd difference: The same men came back—and back—and back. With a feeling-out process, Dirck finally sounded one or two of them. Then, to clear up the annoying mystery, he pocketed caution and went over to ask Hester for a dance.

She welcomed him with undisguised pleasure and was prettily regretful that her card had not a single blank left on it. To be greeted as an old and warmly liked friend by a girl so lovely and so manifestly popular was as incense to Barry. And when Hester persuaded the chagrined Clem Hathaway to forgo one of his own dances in Barry's favor Dirck felt like a conqueror.

But he was none the less dumfounded by the utter change in the former Dubbess' speech and manner. Assuredly she was not the same girl who had afforded him such refined delight on the first evening they had met! There was not one outward trace left of the pedantic little prig of that night.

Clem was sore puzzled and hurt when his pupil begged him to sacrifice his supper dance as well to Dirck. Hathaway had fairly glowed with pride at Hester's success. And in the very acme of his pride she was cutting dances with him for the sake of a cad who had made her a laughingstock!

The more he mulled over it, the less offended and the more sharply unhappy did Hathaway become. Wherefore, on the drive home, he tried to be unusually natural, to keep Hester from guessing at his hurt, and thus from marring some of her triumph-evening's joy. His only allusion to the ache crept into his good-by words to her; and they were in such form that he was sure she could not guess what it had meant to him.

"Well, Miss Prize Scholar," he observed with ponderous lightness, "here endeth the last lesson. You are graduated with honors. To-night proved it. There will be standing room only, on the veranda after this.

And I am getting too old to shine in a crowd. So it's lucky you don't need a postgraduate course. If you'll let your discharged tutor give you one final tip though: Don't ask a man to give up his dance to some other man. It isn't the thing to do; and it is apt to be misunderstood. Not that it mattered a single bit in my case!" He hurried to soften his rebuke. "I was only the school-teacher; and I was glad to let you dance with anyone you happened to prefer to me. I was there only professionally, you know. So you could have cut all your dances with me and not have done the wrong thing. But don't try it with other chaps. You don't mind the hint, do you? You know you asked me to be sure to tell you whenever—"

"When you say there'll be crowds of men here," interrupted Hester, who did not seem to have absorbed more than the first half of his carefully framed harangue, "and that you are too old to be in the crowd, it—it's a joke, isn't it? It doesn't mean you won't care to come here at all after this, does it? Now that the lessons are over? Please! It doesn't mean that, does it?"

Before Clem could answer—before he could brace himself against the queer little childish appeal in her tone—her mood had shifted; and she went on gayly, without waiting for a reply:

"Oh, it's awfully late! Almost as late as it ever gets to be. And you said you had to be at the bank at nine. I'm keeping you up till all hours and letting you catch cold by standing out here with your hat off. I'm so sorry! Good night! And—thank you a million times!"

Clem drove home in the graying dawn even more perplexed than Dirck Barry had been, and infinitely more unhappy than ever he had dreamed he could be. Hathaway angrily resented his own unhappiness; the more so because he could not in the very least understand it.

He fancied a course of absence from Hester might bring him back to his normal nonhurtable self, and for a full week he forced himself to follow this self-imposed martyrdom. At the week's end he went to call on his former pupil. Four other men were adorning the once desolate veranda. Dirck Barry was apparently more at home there than any of the rest. Two more men dropped in while Hathaway was there. Clem did not stay long—merely long enough to load up with a fresh supply of heartache, which kept him away from that part of town and from all Harleville social life for nearly three weeks.

Then he called once more on Hester. This time there was no one with her on the veranda but Dirck. And a blind imbecile could see that Barry's unresented air of proprietorship had driven away all less-encouraged competitors.

Hester was very cordial indeed to Clem; but always her eyes and her talk would stray to Barry. Clem spent a hideous half hour with the two; then departed, unhindered.

Perhaps it was the ease wherewith Barry had just routed so formidable a man as Hathaway; perhaps it was the open favoritism Hester had shown toward himself during Clem's tragically short call; perhaps the hour was ripe and the tender lure in the girl's eyes was no longer to be resisted. In any case, as Hathaway's springless footsteps died away down the still street, Dirck crossed suddenly to where Hester stood at the veranda rail, gazing through the summer dusk after the departing guest.

"Little wonder girl!" whispered Barry, coming up behind Hester and drawing her slim body back into his eager arms. "Little wonder girl, you've put the Indian sign all over my heart! You've got to marry me, Beautiful! You've just *got* to!"

For the barest instant she shivered in his clasp and made as though to shake herself free; but only for that mere instant. Then the adoring swain felt her relax and lean to his embrace.

The great eyes that looked so timidly up into his in the June twilight were luminous and worshiping.

"You darling!" panted Barry in ecstasy. "You glorious sweetheart of mine!"

But when he would have kissed the radiant upraised face the girl's timidity got the upper hand of her courage. She buried her face in his coat front, whispering in fear:

"Not yet! Not just yet! Please!"

And his kiss landed somewhere between her left ear and the soft knot of hair at the nape of her neck.

Nor could he win the lips he yearned for. He pleaded; he urged; he tried masterful cave-man tactics. But always she eluded him; and always came that coquettishly frightened whisper:

"Not yet! Not just yet!"

"Then when?" he cried at last in loverly exasperation. "When?"

"Not—not till our engagement is announced," she faltered. "If we're still engaged, then—" She checked herself, and added, in adorable doubt: "We *are* engaged—aren't we, Dirck?"

"Engaged?" he exulted. "Engaged? Show me the man, from the Kaiser up, who dares to say we aren't. You can bet we are, sweetheart! That's the surest thing and the wonderfulest thing in all this world."

He sought to prove it by kissing her; but again she eluded him, reiterating:

"Not till our engagement's announced. Please!"

"Then when will you let me announce it?" demanded Barry, starkly eager.

"Not till—till you want to kiss me," she murmured bashfully.

"That means this minute," he vowed. "Listen! Do you mind if I tell the men over at the Faculty Club on my way home? And, if you like, I'll drop in at the Palladium office to-night, too, and tip off the Social Notes man there. And to-morrow mother and the girls will be round here to call on you. Is that announcement enough?"

"Ye-es," she said consideringly; "I think it is. Will it be in to-morrow's Palladium, do you suppose? Or will they wait till—"

"If I could I'd make 'em run off a special ten P. M. edition to-night," retorted Dirck deliriously, "and then be here on your doorstep at ten-one for my kiss. Oh, girl of mine, how did you ever manage to make me so crazy about you? I've been just daffy over you from the first minute I set eyes on you!"

"The first minute?" she repeated dreamily. "That very first evening?"

"That very first evening!" he declared.

Hester sighed long and contentedly.

Next morning's Palladium informed all and sundry of the engagement between the junior partner of the law firm of McEntee & Barry and the daughter of Professor Maximus Q. Gregg, of Harle University.

Several hours before the Palladium went to press various men who had been spending the evening at the Faculty Club had carried the same tidings home to their wives, having obtained it from a no less reliable source than the exultant Dirck himself.

By breakfast time the story was common property throughout Harleville. Perhaps the only household of any social importance which did not discuss it at the morning meal was that of Professor Gregg himself. The professor did not take the local morning newspaper, choosing that method of punishing its editor for advocating the much-mooted three-year undergraduate course.

Clem Hathaway was not hungry, anyhow, that morning. And when, midway in his breakfast, he came upon the engagement announcement on the fourth page of the Palladium he unconsciously decided that eating is a needless and sickening habit.

Just as he was leaving his rooms, leaden-footed, for the routine of the day, a telephone call stayed him at the threshold. From the far end of the wire came an unhappy little voice, which hailed him in tremulous excitement.

"Oh, I'm so glad I caught you before you went to the bank!" Hester exclaimed as he made a thick and incoherent reply to her shaky greeting. "I'm in such a lot of trouble! Won't you help me?"

"Pardon me," returned Clem with awful stiffness; "but isn't Dirck Barry the man you ought to be calling on now for any sort of help you may want?"

"No!" wailed Hester. "He's just the man I ought not to! Have you seen the Palladium? Isn't it horrible? A dozen people have been calling me up to congratulate me. What am I to do?"

"Perhaps an etiquette book would give you a better idea how to answer them than I could," suggested Clem. "Why not just say 'Thank you—yes; I am very happy!' and let it go at that? It is a harmless answer to a congratulation."

"But I'm not engaged!" she made reply—"not the very least bit. That's the horrible part of it. I've just telephoned to the Palladium to say so. And father heard about it on the way to college. He came straight home. And now he's gone round to the Palladium himself. And after that he is going to the Faculty Club to deny it. And then he is going to interview Dirck Barry.

"I never dreamed dad could be so nearly humanly angry as he was when I told him it wasn't so and when he found that Dirck had announced it at the club. I'm afraid he isn't going to be one bit nice to Dirck. And the Palladium is going to print a retraction to-morrow and say it got the story from Dirck Barry himself, and that I deny there is a word of truth in it."

She stopped to wait for an answer from Clem. But it was a long time coming. And at last it came in the form of a wild burble of:

"I'll be there in ten minutes!"

It was a very calm and self-controlled Hester who awaited Hathaway on the little brown veranda; not in the least the tearfully distracted damsel his telephone talk had led him to expect. Hester read the bewilderment in his look and said demurely:

"We're on a party wire, you know. And the three other families on the same wire get so much real pleasure in listening and then in reporting! I couldn't let the chance slip. And one of them is Dirck Barry's aunt too. I always know when she is listening, because I can hear her parrot swear. Dad just phoned from downtown. He seems to have had a very terrible conversation with Dirck. He says Dirck is coming straight up here, in spite of dad's forbidding him the house. So we haven't much time."

"I—I don't understand," sputtered Clem. "What's—what's it all about? I am at sea. If you and Barry aren't engaged, how did he have the criminal nerve to—"

"But," she asked in sudden solicitude, "since he has gone all round announcing that he is engaged to me and since I'm denying it—well, won't it make him just a little bit ridiculous in Harleville?"

"Ridiculous?" cried Hathaway. "Why, he'll be the joke of the town!

He'll never be able to live down such a thing or explain it. People won't stop laughing at him and guying him for five years. He'll never stand it. He'll move away. See if he doesn't! But"—hotly—"before he goes someone ought to thrash him for dragging your name into such a thing. He must be insane! You're certain you didn't give him any reason to think—to imagine—to—"

"Yes," she said contritely; "I'm afraid I did—just a little. You see, I was engaged to him."

"You—you were!" babbled Clem; but she went on:

"Yes; just for a few minutes—long ago. As long ago as nine o'clock last night. Then, as soon as he went home, I sat down and wrote him a note breaking the engagement. And I mailed it to his office, so he'd be sure to get it before noon today. But that part of it is a secret. Nobody but you is ever going to know that I was engaged to him at all. He—Don't look as if you were going to fall apart!" She broke off to command the wretchedly staring and dumbstricken Hathaway.

Clem tried to speak; to make his miserable thoughts stop revolving like Catherine wheels. But Hester gave him no time to marshal his words. Her manner took on a sudden change—a change that would have done credit to Electra herself if the vengeful Atrides had been brought up with a Persian kitten instead of an Argive dagger for a plaything.

"Do you remember that night I met you at the president's?" she demanded. "The night you were the only man who didn't laugh at me or shun me as if I was a dangerous maniac? Do you know why they did that?

"Dirck Barry started it all. He would send them to talk to me, and then make fun of me with them afterward. He made me make a fool of myself at dinner. He made me do and say things that turn me cold when I let myself think of them. He stamped me before everyone as a bore and a freak. And a bore and a freak I'd have been as long as I lived here—and as left-alone as Robinson Crusoe too—if you hadn't put me on my feet. And I'd have owed it all to Dirck Barry.

"I had plenty of time to think it out before you came to the rescue. It may sound silly to you; but I made up my mind that some day I'd make Dirck Barry as ridiculous and as ashamed as he had made me. And—and I honestly think I've done it. Honestly, I do! It was a perfectly vile way for me to do, I suppose; and I'll probably be more and more disgusted with myself every time I think of it. But he did need it!"

Still, the man sat gaping, dazed. She continued, with a queer hardness in her tone that stung him:

"A man can't understand; but any girl would. Men aren't wallflowers. They can always go somewhere or other for a good time. A girl has to wait till the good time is brought to her. If it isn't brought she never has it. And Dirck Barry kept it from being brought to me. He did it because that was his idea of being funny. Well, this engagement plan was my idea of being funny.

"The people who don't laugh him out of town will cut him for a cad. They did much worse to me. They all kept away from me. I came here, just a kid, with no more knowledge—except book knowledge—than a three-year-old baby. And I looked forward to everything—the way a baby looks forward to Santa Claus' visit. I thought it would be heavenly to have girl friends of my own age and to meet men who were not old enough to be my father.

"I meant no harm. I was doing the very best I knew how to make a good impression. And Dirck made the men laugh at me. And he must have told the girls I was impossible, too, for none of them came to see me. I used to wish I was dead. My chief amusement, those first evenings, was to sit alone on this porch and see how long I could keep from crying."

"Lord!" ejaculated Clem, momentarily finding his tongue in a gust of indignant pity as he pictured the scene and recalled, at the same time, Dirck's witty term of Dubbess.

"The longer I sat here," pursued Hester, "the worse I hated Dirck Barry; and the harder I prayed for a chance to punish him. Then came my idea. I couldn't work it out alone, so I got you to help me. Now you hate me! Don't you? And we're enemies! And I'd rather be enemies with anyone else in the world. Honestly, I would—Clem!"

With a start, as of a man coming out of a dream, Hathaway realized she was no longer speaking; also that her eyes were slowly filling with tears as she looked at him.

"Yes," he said heavily, and through no volition of his own, as he continued to stare in dull fascination at the girl's brimming eyes. "Yes;

I suppose we are enemies—you and I—if you say so. And that means I'm a better Christian than ever I expected to be; for, God knows, I love my enemy!"

He spoke with no emotion at all. But, the bungling words once out, he seemed to know, for the first time, what he had said. And he looked apprehensively at Hester, as though hoping she had not understood. She tried to speak again—in the forcedly hard tone of her earlier confession. But, for some reason, her sweet voice began to play all kinds of tricks with her as she answered irrelevantly:

"Do you see that red smudge back of my left ear? I did that, rubbing off the nearest approach to a kiss that Dirck Barry was able to give me. I washed it till it burned. . . . It—it must be nice to be kissed by someone whose kisses you don't have to rub away afterward. Even the kiss of—of an enemy must be—"

She got no farther; for—luckier than most conjecturers—she found herself able to prove, at that very moment, the truth of her own theory.

Presently a ring at the front door jarred the experimenters back to sanity.

"That must be Dirck Barry!" said Hester. "I'm too happy to talk to him now. You go and see him—won't you, dear? And—explain! Please do! It ought to be very easy. Why not just tell him the Palladium printer must have made a blunder in setting the announcement and used the name Barry by mistake for Hathaway? I'm quite sure that is the sort of joke to make Dirck Barry laugh happily and forget his troubles. . . . Did anybody ever tell you how cunningly your hair curls over that cowlick, Clem?"

The Cross-of-War Man

THE hero of this story—for the first few paragraphs—is "Spike" Brenner. He does not appear in the rest of the tale at all, though his work runs through to the end of it, piling up big and bigger results.

Spike was one of a host of minor cameramen and general utility roustabouts in the employ of the Meagher-Royce Film Corporation. He was on duty in France, at some distance back of the line, with the cohort of Meagher-Royce workers whose job it was to photograph genuine war-films for the delectation of stay-at-homes.

Marching troops, trench-scenes, devastated towns, the firing of camouflaged long-range guns, transportation episodes—all that sort of thing the Meagher-Royce men duly pictured. And the reels went back to America, where thousands of film-audiences gazed on them with enthusiasm.

One of Spike Brenner's immediate superiors went under with enteric fever. Another broke his shoulder in a shell-hole fall. A third was on leave in Paris. Thus it came that Spike was detailed to grind the camera-crank when Marshal Joffre visited a certain base hospital for the purpose of pinning war-crosses on several wounded soldiers.

Brenner's flivver broke down on the way to the hospital, and he did not reach the wards until the Marshal was about to decorate the very last man on the list of *Croix de Guerre* recipients.

Hurriedly placing his camera, Brenner focused it on the cot where lay the gallant soldier who was about to be decorated. The man in the cot looked at the camera in mild surprise as the crank began to turn.

Then all at once Brenner noticed that Marshal Joffre was not approaching that particular invalid at all, but a man in the adjoining cot. And hastily Spike swung the focus upon this second cot's occupant.

The second invalid saw the camera-eye bent upon him and peevishly flung one arm across his face to hide from view. Perhaps in civilian days he had done something which rendered the broadcast publishing of his portrait unadvisable. Perhaps, like so many other Cross-recipients, he felt a strange bashfulness about being photographed. In any case, as the camera-crank began to turn, the soldier's face became wholly invisible.

Marshal Joffre smiled amusedly down upon the shrinking hero and affixed the glorious decoration to the breast of his pajama suit. Then the Marshal leaned over the bed with outstretched hand. The soldier at once forgot his shyness in the honor of shaking hands with the army's idol. But by this time Joffre's broad left shoulder was between the camera and the invalid's face.

When the film came to be developed, its two successive exposures represented a man lying on a cot looking straight at the camera, then, apparently, the same man modestly shielding his face from public view while Marshal Joffre smiled down upon him and pinned the Cross to his breast. The last few feet of the film showed the man shaking hands with the Marshal—his face invisible, but the rest of him well in sight.

Brenner was only mortal. He dreaded the call-down that must be his if he confessed that he had arrived at the hospital too late to get at least one good picture of the presentation of the Croix de Guerre. So by a very little manipulation the second picture was made to represent a continuation of the first.

In due time, the film was shipped, along with many more, to America. It was labeled:

Joffre Presents Coveted French War-Cross to Wounded Hero in Recognition of Gallant Deeds on Field of Battle.

Brenner belatedly made inquiries as to the man in the cot next to the Cross' wearer and learned that he was an American noncombatant named Leigh who had been employed as an assistant superintendent in some dock-construction work near Brest, and who had been stricken with typhoid.

Brenner was sorry his own job's safety forced him to thrust unmerited fame upon the man. But presently, being busy, he forgot all about the matter. And here, with a more or less graceful nod of farewell, Spike Brenner drops permanently out of our story. At the same time the scene shifts to the western shores of the gray Atlantic.

WILTON LEIGH was not a warrior. He had no desire to risk his very comfortable life by exposing it to shot or shell or gas. Therefore he did not enlist when the surging wave of patriotism smote his little North Jersey home-town of Cadman. Perhaps he was a coward, perhaps not; certainly he was selfish. At all events, he did not enlist.

Yet fearing the obloquy of the men and girls he knew, especially of the girls he knew, be did not care to proclaim himself a slacker. So he managed to get a safe and fairly well-paying job in one of the construction companies which had contracted to build docks and storehouses for our government on the French seaboard. Leigh did not tell the nature of his new employment. He merely said he was going to France, "on service." And he vanished.

Two weeks later several Cadman people received postcards from Leigh announcing his safe arrival at a French port. A month after that he came down with a light attack of typhoid. And in another month he was invalided home as too weak and inert, from his illness, to be of further present use to his employers.

Back to Cadman came Wilton Leigh—very pale and thin and haggard. He was curt, to the point of rudeness, when people asked if he had been wounded. He was starkly noncommittal. As a result, a hundred varying stories of his adventures flew through the little town. He was a man of mystery.

From out the ruck of rumors presently emerged the facts that he did not have a military bearing, as had the rest of Cadman's citizen-soldiers, that he showed no familiarity with places named in letters from the front, that he had not consulted the local doctor as to the treatment of his presumptive wound and that several letters which had been addressed to him during his absence in care of the American Expeditionary Forces, had come back to their senders.

Cadman, in general, began to look with sour suspicion on its returned townsman. Almost the only exception to this order of suspicion was Rena Frost. Rena was a grave-eyed girl, with ideals. And for a year or more Leigh had worshiped openly at her shrine.

Not until he came home, pallid and emaciated, from France, did she show the slightest sign of smiling on his timid suit. Since then, her preference for him had been undisguised. The stories she now heard hurt her—the more so because she could not get Leigh to say anything that might disprove them. Even to Rena he would not speak of his overseas experiences.

She tried to believe that his silence was due to a brave man's modesty, and with her heart she did believe it. But sometimes her logical brain would call her heart a credulous fool—which brings us to the point you have all been waiting for—the evening at the Cadman Motion Picture Palace.

THURSDAY evening was the time chosen by the better people of Cadman for patronizing the movies. On that night there were finer pictures, and more of them, than on any other. And it was the night of the weekly Meagher-Royce films, which preceded the five-reel "feature."

Every Thursday evening Leigh took Rena Frost to the movies. The choice of evenings was hers, not his. She had a morbid eagerness for the war-films and used to scan keenly the pictured faces of American troops in search of Leigh's. She had done this from the day she had received the postcard announcing his safe arrival in France. On that day, too, she had moved his photograph from an obscure corner to the very center of her dressing-table and had swathed its frame in a little silken American flag.

To Leigh himself the Meagher-Royce film-showings meant little enough. He had been half delirious the time the camera-man had invaded the hospital, and he had only the vaguest remembrance that a photographer had leveled the lens at him. He did not know why it had been done. He had not associated the matter with the movies at all, never before having seen a motion-picture camera. He was not certain, in fact, that the queerly shaped machine had been a camera, or anything but a part of his fever delusions.

On the way to the Motion Picture Palace that Thursday evening, as they strolled along together slowly through the sweet summer dusk, Wilton Leigh got up his courage to propose. He did not do it in the way he had so carefully rehearsed. He did not do it dramatically or even eloquently. He did it very badly indeed. But he made himself perfectly intelligible—which, in a proposal of marriage, is probably the main object.

Rena heard him out. There was an adorably soft flush on her soft cheek, and a softer light lurked behind her grave eyes. Yet when he came to a floundering halt, all she replied, was:

"You say you care for me. Love and trust mean the same thing. Won't you tell me what your life was, in France? I am not asking you from curiosity. I am asking, because everything that concerns you should concern me too. Will you tell me?"

And Leigh, knowing her as he did, had not the courage to slay her possible love by the sordid truth. Miserably he made answer:

"I can't, dear. I *can't!*"

She shivered a little and drew away from him as they walked. Her face had lost its flush and was as white as the face of one who suffers fierce pain. But her sweet voice was steady as she said:

"If you can't trust me with your past, you surely can't expect me to trust you with my future, Wilton."

"But sweetheart," he began wildly, "I—"

"I don't think we'd gain anything by arguing about it," she interposed very gently, yet with utter finality.

And reaching the theater just then, they mechanically went in.

THE place was full, and the two had trouble in finding good seats. As they seated themselves, the Meagher-Royce announcement was flashed on the screen.

To-night Rena did not follow the various scenes with her wonted interest. Her heart seemed queerly tight. She had a babyish desire to cry. She gave scant enough heed to the pictures of a ship-launching in California, to a Red Cross parade led by the President himself, to the inspiring sight of thousands of American troops marching along a muddy French road, with Old Glory flying. She noted with but half her brain a flaring caption that read:

*Joffre Presents Coveted French War-Cross to Wounded Hero
in Recognition of Gallant Deeds on Field of Battle.*

Then, not only from Rena but from a full hundred people in the dark theater, went up a wordless gasp of utter amazement. On the pictured hospital cot was stretched the helpless body of Wilton Leigh! Sharply outlined in the strong light, every detail of face and figure was unmistakable! He was looking straight at the audience. His eyes were sunken and tired; his cheeks were hollow; his hand, on the coverlet, was claw-like, in its thinness.

The picture told its own story to the hundreds of dazedly excited spectators. There lay their townsman, Wilton Leigh, in a French war-hospital, sore stricken. They recalled the caption, which had described him as a wounded hero, about to be decorated by no less a personage than the adored Marshal Joffre.

Tense, with lips parted and bodies thrust forward, the audience stared. Rena Frost, scarce knowing what she did, groped in the gloom for the real Wilton Leigh's hand as it lay clenched in his lap, and

pressed it worshipingly and remorsefully in her own warm little grasp.

The man in the picture suddenly realized that he was the camera's target, and that his receiving of the Cross was about to be depicted for the benefit of an admiring public. With a gesture of annoyance he flung his arm across his face, his hand nervously opening and closing. Then Joffre approached the cot, smiled down in fatherly pride at the stricken young warrior, bent over him and pinned to the pajama breast the splendid Cross of War! Then the Marshal stretched forth his hand in fraternal greeting and fellowship to the man he had just rewarded, and the invalid gripped the hero-hand with eager deference.

That was all—but it was enough!

From the whole audience burst a wild salvo of handclapping and frantic stamping. Through the din came yells of:

"Leigh! Wilt Leigh!"

Some one called for three cheers. And they were given with a rapturous vehemence that shook the house. For nearly three minutes the pictures went unheeded. The audience was mad with enthusiasm. And through the racket ran an undertone of shame—shame that they had so misunderstood and censured their one local hero, that they had so cruelly mistaken his modest silence concerning his gallant exploits. The same modesty, they now saw, had led him to cover his face that the world might not witness the reward of his battlefield prowess.

The uproar seemed to frighten Rena Frost. Hastily she had withdrawn her shyly proffered hand from Leigh's, and she sat bolt upright, breathing very fast.

Leigh was too dumfounded to note her agitation. His brain was in a whirl. If the screen-caption had announced a picture of "Wilton Leigh, President of the United States," he could not have been more aghast. The thing did not make sense; it was crazily impossible. Yet, there it was.

By superhuman effort Leigh forced his dizzy brain back to sanity. He tried to find a clue to the gross blunder. And seeking, he gradually found it. He remembered, now, the queer camera, with the hand-organ-crank attachment, that had been trained on him at the hospital. He remembered, too, that the camera-man had almost at once shifted its focus to the bed next his own. Yes, and well he remembered the man whose bed it was. For he and the cot's occupant had spent nearly a month side by side.

The other was a Frenchman who had often kept Leigh awake, at night, by snoring. And Marshal Joffre had come to the hospital to give the Frenchman the Croix de Guerre. He had come there the same day the camera had been turned on Leigh. The mystery was no longer a mystery. Leigh understood what had happened. It was really quite simple. He could visualize the unshaven camera man, hurrying into the ward and starting to photograph the wrong man—then shifting the lens to the right one.

By the time the matter was clear to Leigh, the thrilled audience was beginning at last to quiet down. But through the gloom man after man in the near-by seats was silently thrusting forward an earnestly admiring hand toward the new-made hero, seeking the high privilege of shaking the hand that had done such magnificent deeds of warfare.

Into Leigh's bewildered heart glowed a mighty joy. Through no lie of his own he had cleared the rankling stigma from his name and had established himself forever as a hero. Again he was popular with the men and women who had grown up with him. More—he was their idol, the man of the hour. And it had all come about without his having had to earn the distinction in that hell of battle-peril. It was his without so much as the asking.

But all this adulation was as nothing, to Leigh, compared with the effect the revelation must have had on Rena. He had felt his heart die within him, when she had refused to marry him unless he would first tell her what had befallen him in France. He loved her with his whole selfish soul. He knew her high ideals; and he knew how far short of those ideals he fell. Yet now—

"Shall we go?" he whispered to her. "Pretty soon the lights will blaze up. And I don't want to meet this crowd—tonight. Let's get out before they can see us."

Rena nodded assent and left the theater with him.

They did not speak until they had come out into the dusky village street. Then Rena said, her sweet voice a bit shaky:

"Will you come home with me, before we say anything about—about what we just saw? There's so much—so *much* to say! And this isn't the place to say it."

Leigh understood. And he tingled at the knowledge. Assuredly

the street was not the place, as she had implied, for her to tell him how sorry she was for her earlier cruel judgment of him, and for the love-scene that must interrupt that dear avowal.

Neither Leigh nor Rena spoke, until they turned into the yard of her home and climbed to the deserted veranda. There, amid the shade of the vines, Rena turned and faced him.

Leigh had looked forward, avidly, to this perfect moment, and its anticipation had gone through him, like the breath of God. Nor had conscience troubled him. If Rena had been tricked into giving him her love—well, it was not he who had tricked her. His hands were clean. And unhesitatingly he could seize the bliss which fortune had so amazingly flung at his feet.

As Rena faced him there, he took an ardent step toward her, his arms half extended. She did not move, but stood looking up at him, her great grave eyes luminous in the half-light. For an instant his own happy eyes reveled in the beauty of hers. Then, through no volition of his own, his step faltered and his arms dropped limp to his sides.

Her look had seemed to go clear through to his soul. The man had an odd feeling of standing on holy ground. And his love flared, for once, high above his selfishness.

With something like a groan Leigh moved away froth the silently waiting girl. In his heart was waging a battle as fierce as any in France. And it waged the more deadly, because it was not only himself and his happiness, but thirty years of selfish habit that he was fighting.

He knew, too, that it was not he who was fighting against this terrible alliance. It was merely his love for Rena Frost that was holding out, against all that made life dear.

"Rena!" he said abruptly—his voice harsh, his words jerky. "Listen! I won't have the nerve to say it if I wait any longer. I wasn't the man who got the Cross. No, it isn't modesty; it's the truth—for once. It was the Frenchman in the right-hand cot from mine—the one who snored so. The photographer made a mistake. He began to take a picture of me, and then he turned the camera on the other cot. I suppose he pieced it together, so it would all look like the same picture. But it wasn't. I was there, with typhoid. I wasn't in the army at all. I was a sub-boss in a dock-construction job. I never was within fifty miles of the front. That's all. Good-by."

THE girl had listened without interruption and without moving, while he blurted out the breathless confession. Nor had that strange look in her eyes changed—the look he had read, in the deceptive light, as hero-worship. But now, as he moved heavily away, she stayed him.

"Wait," she commanded, her own tones muffled and none too steady. "Why did you tell me this, Wilt?"

"Why?" he repeated, dully. "Because I'm a fool, I suppose. There doesn't seem to be any other reason. You could never have found it out, if I hadn't told you. And now that I *have* told you, you despise me. I—I didn't mean to tell. I didn't know I was going to. But—well, your eyes kind of made me feel as if I was in—in church. And—I found out, all at once, that I'd rather not have you at all, than have you when I hadn't won you, fair.

"I was a fool. Let it go at that. I'm not going to see you any more, Rena. For one thing, I couldn't. For another, I wont be here. I'm all well again now. And, tomorrow I'm going to Paterson, to enlist. There isn't a chance in a million that I'll ever get the Cross. But I'll be able to know I'm not giving you and everyone else the double-cross. I'll be a *man,* for once in my life."

"One minute!" Rena checked him as he finished his disjointedly muttered speech and turned again to go.

He paused at the top of the veranda steps, looking back miserably.

"What is it?" he demanded crossly. "I can't stand much more. It isn't easy to—"

"I want you to know something," said Rena very slowly. "In fact, I want you to know two things, before you go away. The first is this: as soon as I saw that man, on the screen, throw his left arm over his face, I knew it wasn't you."

"You knew—" said Leigh.

But she went on, unheeding!

"You see, the little finger of his left hand was gone at the first joint. I don't suppose anyone else noticed. The hand showed for only about a second."

Leigh stood agape. She resumed:

"I wanted you to come home here with me, because I had just a faint hope you might tell me the truth about it. It was such a *faint* hope! And I knew, if you *didn't* tell me the truth, I'd loathe you. And I was—I was *sick* with fear about it. I couldn't even speak. I—"

Her voice faltered, and fell silent. The man still stared at her in dumb wonder. Drawing a long and quivering breath, Rena continued at last:

"That was one of the two things I wanted to say to you, Wilt. The other thing is: I think you have won the Cross—and won it splendidly, too—in this past five minutes. And when you come back from France, well—well, I'll be right here, waiting to say yes, to any—to any question you may happen to ask me, Wilt!"

The Final Crop

HALSEY GRAINGER had made good. He was not a millionaire, or an adored leader of men, or President of the United States. The chances were against his reaching any of these heights. Yet considering his start, he had covered more ground than has many a man who wins the Presidency.

Halsey's father, Clay Grainger, was a farmer who strove to scratch a living from sixty acres of hillside rock and sand in the most mountainous stretch of mountainous Duneka County, Kentucky. The original American Grainger had been a very gallant figure indeed. He was the fourth son of the Duke of Kensington and had taken up a huge grant of land in Virginia early in the seventeenth century. For two hundred years thereafter the Graingers had been a mighty clan in the South. Clay's grandfather had come over the mountains into Kentucky with Dan'l Boone. And bit by bit the fortunes of the Kentucky branch of the

ancient family had slumped.

To all outward appearance, and in speech, there was little enough to distinguish Clay Grainger from any of a thousand other down-at-heel mountaineers. But a flash of the Grainger pride of race must have lingered somewhere in his lanky carcass, for when his tow-haired mountaineer wife died, leaving him alone in the cabin and in the world, except for the couple's ten year old son Halsey, Clay held an auction of his few salable effects, and with the proceeds sent his boy to the county seat of Duneka, to school. The next year, by selling half his land to a coal company, and mortgaging the rest, he sent Halsey to the East, for still more education. Thereafter, until the lad finished school and college and law-course, Clay somehow managed to keep on mailing him enough money for expenses. The sum was pitifully small. But by working in offices or behind counters during the summer, Halsey made it cover the slender costs of his education.

AS soon as he was admitted to the bar, Halsey came back to Kentucky to practice law. He settled in the thriving county seat some forty miles from his father's farm. There he sought clients; and there he found them. He was a good lawyer, a persuasive pleader. By an odd throwback, some of the ancestral Grainger manner and personality were his. Moreover he knew the mountaineer nature in all the phases of its queer secretiveness and its mingled simplicity and cunning. He could do more with mountaineers, in the witness-box, than could almost any other counselor in the State, and they flocked to him with their intricate cases.

Within three years Halsey had made a name for himself at Duneka and had piled up a goodly practice too. With his earliest money he sought to pay back his father for some of the latter's sacrifices of the past fifteen years. But Clay would not accept the offer—declared the farm brought him in enough to live on in comfort, now that Halsey no longer needed so much of his scanty revenue.

The old fellow would not even consent to leave his hillside cabin, to live at Duneka with his worshiped son. Halsey understood why Clay refused to share his pleasant Duneka lodgings, and the knowledge hurt the boy cruelly. He knew his father's inordinate pride in this lawyer-son of his; and he realized that Clay feared to mar his boy's success and social career by the presence of his own illiterate and uncouth self at Halsey's home. In vain the youth tried to shake Clay's decision. The old man had full share of the traditional Grainger stubbornness, and every atom of that stubbornness forbade him to share his son's home and money.

Halsey's two closest friends at Duneka were Judge Wirt and the Judge's daughter Sibyl. To the Judge—directly and indirectly—he owed many a plump bit of legal business. To Sibyl he owed the most tremendous sensation of his whole life—the sensation of falling deliriously and irrevocably in love.

ONE evening five years after he had begun practice, Halsey was dining with the Wirts, on the Judge's return from a circuit-tour. Halsey had accompanied him on the tour; and several interesting cases had been assigned to the young lawyer—cases wherein the judge had power to appoint counsel for the defense. There was little money, of course, in these assignment-cases, but there was reputation, and useful training too. On the following day a court-session at Duneka itself was to complete the circuit.

The judge, soon after dinner, went away to his study with a bagful of papers that bore on the next day's trials. Left alone with Sibyl, whom he had not seen before in a month, Halsey Grainger summoned courage to plead his most important and nerve-racking case, before an audience consisting of supreme referee and jury alike, all combined in the person of one dainty and big-eyed girl.

Quite simply, and with no effort at eloquence, Halsey told Sibyl he loved her, that he could support her in tolerable affluence—and that he was not worthy to touch one of her pink little finger-tips. He went on unflinchingly to remind her that his father was a "poor-white-trash" mountaineer farmer, but added the oft-repeated assertion that Clay was the best father and the finest man God ever made.

Sibyl was the most divinely merciful court of last resort before whom a scared young lawyer could hope to plead a life-and-death case. She granted every single clause in Halsey's plea—notably his imploring request that she marry him within the next three months. And then Halsey—as brave now as a whole jungleful of lions—sought out Judge Wirt in the study and brazenly asked the Judge's consent.

To his amazement Judge Wirt did not seem in the least surprised at the thunderbolt of tidings which Halsey brought him. He behaved like a man who had expected to hear that news for a long time. And he was not at all like the heavy parent in plays or in novels. He was actually cordial in his welcome of the young aspirant into the sacred Wirt family. But as Halsey was departing to tell the eagerly waiting Sibyl what a splendidly reasonable man her father was, the Judge called him back.

"I'm sorry to break in on paradise with a matter of sordid business," said Wirt, fumbling with the papers strewn on his desk. "But there's a case I want to assign you to, a case that's first on the docket tomorrow morning. The fee won't be worth the work, as you know, and it looks like a pretty clear case against your man. But it will add a little to your pull with the mountaineers, and it may even attract notice in several other quarters. These picturesque cases often do."

"That means it's moonshine," said Halsey.

"Moonshine it is," assented the Judge. "They've laid Old Misery by the heels, at last."

"No!" ejaculated Halsey in quickened interest. "Old Misery, eh? He boasted he could never be caught. Who got him? And how did—"

"Here are the papers in the case," answered Wirt. "Look them over at your leisure. Misery's in the courthouse jail. You might drop in on him, if you like, on your way home, if you think you can get anything out of him. He has refused to employ counsel, and he sits mum all day in the corner of his cell like a caged badger—so this note from Fallon says. You have a way of your own with these mountaineers. Perhaps you can get him to talk. Not that it's likely to do him any good! There's enough evidence against Old Misery, first and last, to send an archbishop to prison."

HALSEY bore to Sibyl the tale of her father's consent to their marriage. Then ensued an extremely heavenly half-hour, ended all too soon by Halsey's rising to go.

"I have to stop at the courthouse," he explained to the reproachful-eyed girl. Your father has assigned me to a case for tomorrow, and I ought to get a word with my client to-night. There's no use in waking up even a criminal out of a sound sleep. That's why I am leaving here so disgustingly early. Besides, after I see him, I have these papers to go over."

"Who is the man?" asked Sibyl, with all a newly engaged girl's painful interest in the business affairs of her betrothed. "What has he done? You said he's a criminal, didn't you? What was he arrested for?"

"Moonshining," replied Halsey, answering her last question first. "Running an illicit whisky-still, you know."

"Yes," said Sibyl dryly, "I think I know. My father is a judge, and I am a Kentucky girl. You needn't waste time explaining to me what moonshining is, dear. Next you'll be trying to explain what blue-grass looks like. You're going to clear him, aren't you?"

"No," he returned glumly. "I'm afraid there's no chance of that. He's an old offender, you see. A dozen times in the past few years the law has almost had him, but he has always slipped clear, till now. He runs a still back in the mountains ten miles or more beyond Dad's farm. It's an inaccessible place, at best. And Old Misery has had plenty of friends to tip him off to any raid, and give him time to hide. He's probably the most notorious moonshiner in Kentucky to-day. He supplies hundreds of mountaineers with booze. But he won't supply any more of them. He—"

"What did you call him?" asked the girl. "Old Something-or-other, wasn't it?"

"Old Misery!" said Halsey. "It's a nickname the revenue officers gave him, after a temperance orator made a speech about him, down at Breckenridge, I believe. The orator shook his fist at the line of mountains where the old scoundrel's still is hidden and shouted: 'He is distilling human misery! Misery! *Misery!!*' The title stuck to him. I don't know his real name. No one seems to, except his mountaineer friends, and they won't tell. They're a close-mouthed lot, those mountaineers. They call everybody outside their own hills a foreigner, even if he lives in the same county with them. They even look on me as more or less a foreigner, because I've left there. They'll talk freely with me, up to a certain point. Then they shut up like clams. Dad himself does that. I asked him, once, who Old Misery is. And he was just like everyone else I asked. Said he'd never heard of such a person and that some foreigner must have been guying me. They're a strange lot, the best of them!"

AS Halsey entered the courthouse jail a little later, he felt a twinge of real curiosity, and asked to be taken to Old Misery's cell. In his childhood he had played with other "poor-white-trash" boys, throughout the mountain region of his birth. These children's fathers had often come to the Grainger cabin. Old Misery might well be some former neighbor of the man now assigned to defend him. The situation had an odd piquancy for Halsey. He prepared to enjoy it to the full.

The turnkey led the way down a corridor of stone lined on either side with barred cells. At the farthest cell he paused, turned up the low-flickering light just outside the grated door and began to fit a key into the lock.

"Hold on!" whispered Halsey. "When you've unlocked that door, just swing it open and let me go in. Then shut it after me and go away. Come back in about an hour and let me out. I know these mountainfolk. The sight of a jailer will always strike them sulky. If I go in there alone, the prisoner may believe me when I tell him I'm here to help him."

The turnkey nodded, and pushed open the cell door. Halsey stepped quietly in, and the iron gate shut behind him. The turnkey, after a careless glance through the bars, plodded away down the corridor.

The cell's only furniture was a hinged bunk and a deal chair. On the bunk lay the prisoner, face down. Curled up there, in the uncertain light, he looked a mere bundle of rumpled butternut clothes.

He seemed to be asleep, but he was not. For as the turnkey's tread died away, he raised his head from the circle of his arms and sat up. He evidently thought he was alone in the cell. And at sight of his visitor he started violently.

For perhaps fifteen seconds Halsey and the captive glared motionless, blank-faced, aghast; at each other. Then Halsey found his voice in a strangled cry of:

"Dad!"

Clay Grainger made no response to the greeting, but his sallow face turned to the greenish-gray hue of a corpse's. His eyes, though,—sick with anguish as they were,—did not flinch or waver. And Halsey, in all the horror of the moment, paid subconscious homage to the thoroughbred quality in the ancient Grainger blood.

All at once the numb dismay that had gripped Halsey fell away. With a gasp of relief he strode across to his father and gripped him by both hands.

"Lord!" gasped the lawyer shakily. "You gave me the shock of my life! It's bad enough as it is, but not a millionth as bad as I thought it was. I—I actually thought you were Old Misery! I thought it was *you* who had been moonshining! I'm ashamed of it, but I did. I ought to have known better. Now tell me how in blue blazes they ever made the fool blunder of locking you up. If Old Misery is a friend of yours and if you let yourself be arrested so that he could have a chance to get away again—"

"I'm the man they call Old Misery," interposed Clay Grainger, his mountaineer drawl in odd contrast to his son's excited tones. "I'm the man. It ain't a mistake. Only—only I'm kinder sorry you had to find it out, sonny boy."

Halsey slumped helplessly into the chair, and his mouth fell ajar. Clay continued:

"I was hopin' you wouldn't ever know. That's why I've allers tried to keep it dark. That's why I give my name as Ben Gary when they brang me here to the jail. It's right ornery for you, to know your dad's

goin' to be a jailbird for most of the balance of his days. I'd fixed it so you'd be told I had gone over to Tennessee, ile-prospectin', for a spell—so's you'd never know what had become of me. Tell me, how'd you find it out, anyway?"

The old man's tired voice had droned slowly on, with occasional brief pauses, but with no interruption from his son.

Paralyzed, dumb, his brain in a sick whirl, Halsey Grainger was gaping up at the prisoner. Clay looked into Halsey's bloodshot eyes with something like timid apology in his own burned-out gaze.

"I'm sorry," he murmured as Halsey still stared speechless, "plumb sorry, son. If I could 'a' got at my rifle, when they cotched me, I'd 'a' put a ball into my worthless head an' kep' you from findin' out. But they jumped on me so sudden-like, I couldn't. That's what I'd allers 'lotted to do, if ever I got cotched. An' I had it fixed with two of the boys to bury me as Ben Gary an' then to tell you your dad had died of lung-sick or mountain-fever or suthin'. There ain't nothin' I c'n do to make up to you for the blank shame I'm puttin' on you. If there was, I reckon you know I'd do it. But we c'n keep other folks from findin' out. So you won't be disgraced none in public. Jest a few of the folks back home, knows—not any foreigners."

HALSEY had not even been listening. Into his memory had flashed, inconsequently, the last words Sibyl had spoken as he bade her good night:

"I'm going to be at court to-morrow, in the very frontest seat I can get. Just think! I never heard you argue a case. And it's high time I began."

Halsey visualized it all—the girl's flushed and eager face in the courtroom, the shriveled figure of his father crouching beside him at the counsel-table, Judge Wirt's classic profile, the throng of onlookers.

All of Halsey Grainger's rainbow hopes faded into ashes. His engagement—well, he had little trouble in forecasting Sibyl's attitude toward him when she found out who Old Misery really was. Judge Wirt too! And the profitable group of Duneka society, folk who had been added so laboriously to Halsey's growing list of clients. The bright career was at an end—at an end just at the very gateway of perfect happiness and of increased success. He was henceforth only

the upstart son of an illiterate criminal.

A gust of hot anger blazed up in him. Turning fiercely on his father, he demanded: "Why did you do it? *Why?*"

"Why?" echoed the old man in genuine surprise at the question. "Why, for money of course. It was the only way I could make any money. The farm is pow'ful poor ground. You know that. It was all I could do to keep out of the poorhouse, by what I made on the farm. I jest nach'lly had to have money. So I picked out the only way to get it."

"Money!" railed Halsey, indignation sweeping him along. "Money! If you wanted money, you had only to come to me for it. You can't have forgotten that I've begged you, time and again, to let me pay you back what you spent on my education. You can't forget I've tried in every way to force money on you—that I've begged you to come to live with me. If pride made you refuse help from your own son, it ought to have kept you from becoming a lawbreaker. Is it nothing to you that I have always loved and honored you above all the men in the world—and that now I must see you in a place like this, that I must find out my hero and ideal is a criminal? And you did it for money you didn't need!"

"I needed it bad enough," argued Clay, cringing away from his son's outburst, but speaking in the same apathetic drawl, "I needed it. I had to have it. I—"

"Then why couldn't you have come to me for it?" challenged Halsey.

"Come to *you* for it?" echoed the old man in dreary wonder. "Why, sonny boy, you was as hard up as I was. You was a schoolboy, back East. You hadn't a red cent but what I kep' sendin' you. It was for *you* I had to have the money, not for *me*. The farm had allers kept me alive. But it wouldn't pay for my son's eddication."

"For my—for—it was for my education you—you did it?" stuttered Halsey, aghast. "For—"

"What else?" queried the father in mild wonder. "When your ma died, she asked me would I try to get you some of the chances we-uns hadn't never had. She set a pow'ful store by you, she did. So did I. I promised her. An' I kep' my word. Us Graingers most gener'lly does. I sold things, and I sent you to school. I sold more, and I kep' you there. An' at last there wa'n't nothin' more to sell. An' you kep' writin' from the East, sayin' how fine you was gettin' on at school an' college an' all that. I hadn't the heart to make you give it up. An' I knew how glad your Ma would 'a' been, too. So I figgered I must keep you there. An' I done so."

"I—do you mean—" began Halsey, then stopped.

CLAY GRAINGER went on: "There wa'n't nothin' more to sell, an' the farm was mortgaged up to the rooftree. I couldn't raise anything more on it; an' nobody would pay me the face of the mortgages to buy it. I had to get money or else you'd have to give up the eddication that was makin' you so happy—an' that your ma had been so sot on your havin'. The only money, thereabouts, for an uneddicated cuss like me to make, over an' above farmin', is in moonshine. I'd allers turned up my nose at moonshiners—me bein', as you might say, a law-abider, by nature. Nor yet I wa'n't a drinkin' man, nor I never have been. But it was moonshinin'—or else sendin' for you to come back home an' mope the rest of your life out as a farm-boy. An' I chose moonshinin'. I'd do it again, too."

"Dad!"

"I would," reiterated the tired old voice. "I would so. I'd do it again. It was worth it. I hated it, like it was toad-pie. But I done it, because it was for my boy. Ev'ry penny I got out of the still, went to you. I never tetched a cent of it for myself. I went hungry, now an' again. But that was how I kinder eased my conscience for bustin' open the law—me that had allers respected the law. I reckon there's two laws—God's law an' the United States Rev'nue Reg'lations. I couldn't keep 'em both an' give you your chance in life. So I kep' God's law an' looked after my boy at the expense of Uncle Sam's Rev'nue Laws. Not that I'm tryin' to excuse myself none!" he added almost defiantly.

Halsey made as though to speak; but Clay rambled on:

"At that, I wa'n't able to pay, in a lump, for all the cash you had to have to finish law-studyin' an' get your start here. For there ain't a fortune in moonshine—not in these parts, there ain't. But there was parties who would loan me a tidy lot of money on future bar'ls of moonshine. I borrered the money. An' I've been workin' an' moilin' ever since, to get it paid off. I was on the very last of it when I was nabbed. Principal *an'* int'rest. Another half-hogshead would 'a' put me square with the world an' let me live again like I useter.

"Now," went on Clay, "don't let's waste no more time talkin' about *me*. You're lookin' all tuckered out an' sick. Best go home an' get some sleep. I'm pow'ful sorry you had to find out, sonny boy, but there needn't anyone else know. You won't be shamed before the neighbors. An' where I'm goin', it'll be fine to think of you as bein' so rich an' respected an'—"

"Dad!" broke in Halsey with a cry that was half a sob.

He caught the old man's meager body in his arms and gripped it close to his breast in a hug that Clay found as blissful as it was rib-crushing.

"Listen to me!" exclaimed Halsey, winking very fast to clear his eyes of an irritating moisture. "We're going to fight this thing out shoulder to shoulder, you and I! You got into this to give me an education. And I'm going to use my education to get you out of it! If I can't get you out, I'll rob a bank or do something else that'll put me along with you in prison. From now on, we're going to buck every game together, you and I, Dad. That's settled."

THE trial of "Benjamin Gary, *alias* Old Misery," for the crime of making and dispensing illicit whisky was well under way. Sibyl Wirt, in the front row of courtroom benches, looked with pitying interest at the bent body and ghastly face of the prisoner. In the preliminary stages of the trial, she thrilled with real pride at the calm authority of her lover's manner. Yet the love she bore Halsey made her note with anxiety that the nervousness of his position had robbed his face of every trace of color and had made it drawn and haggard. Pallor and tenseness gave him a ludicrous resemblance to the prisoner himself. Sibyl, glancing from Old Misery to Halsey and back again, was more and more struck by the all but uncanny likeness between the two.

In cross-examining the prosecution's witnesses, Halsey took a line of procedure which brought a crease of perplexity to Judge Wirt's brow and set the prosecuting attorney to whispering with his assistant. The counsel for the defense made no effort to shake the witnesses' testimony, or to confuse them, or to seek for personal bias on their part against the prisoner. Instead, he confined himself to questions whose answers showed how little drunkenness—and poverty due to drink—existed in the part of Duneka County where Old Misery had plied his lawless trade. He brought out the fact that a large percentage of Old Misery's whisky had gone to mountaineers who were afflicted with malaria and with similar ailments, for which distilled corn-juice was an immemorial neighborhood specific. He elicited testimony of frequent instances in which Old Misery had given whisky, free of charge, to sick men and women who could not afford to pay for the needful remedy.

WHEN the prosecution rested, Halsey caused further surprise by announcing that he should call no witnesses, not even the prisoner. And presently he arose to address the jury. Tersely he outlined the crime of moonshining and the penalties therefor. Then, speaking at first haltingly, but with increasing ease as he forgot himself in his cause, he continued:

"I have shown you that the pursuit colloquially known as moon-shining is contrary to the laws of this State and nation. As an officer of the court I am sworn to uphold the law, not to palliate its breaking. As to the manufacture of whisky in general and its undoubtedly deleterious effect on mankind it is not my province to speak.

"You have heard from the lips of the prosecution's own witnesses that the whisky alleged to have been distilled by my client was used far the most part for the alleviating of illness. I mention that, to show not only the effect but the chief intent of my client's alleged trade. That trade is an offense against the written law. I hold that—as he is said to have conducted it—it is no offense against the *moral* law.

"Many a gross violator of the moral law is protected from punishment by the clauses of the written law. Is it wholly unfair, then, that a technical violator of the written law should receive mercy, on account of the moral law he has so stanchly upheld?"

Judge Wirt looked more puzzled than ever as he sought to follow the purport of the dull preamble.

"My client," resumed Halsey, "is accused of turning his corn-crop into whisky instead of turning it into bread. His miserable mountain farm brought forth a wretchedly poor crop of corn, at best. Yet on that farm he has raised something better than bread, something far better than the whisky he is charged with distilling from his sparse handfuls of corn—as you shall see.

"The true purpose of all food-raising is to produce God's final crop—man.

"Man is the crop which God wants produced—the Final Crop for whose nourishment all lesser crops are raised and garnered. An uneducated man is a crop-failure. A man whose education and upbringing make him an asset to his community and to the world at large is the supreme crop in all God's broad harvest-field. Whether by means of bread or by whisky, the farmer who can make his corn bring forth the right kind of man-crop has done his highest duty.

"And such a farmer is my client. He has turned the proceeds of his poor land into the making of a man—not so worthy a man as many of yourselves, perhaps, gentlemen of the jury, but the highest type of man that the material at hand would permit. My client has had no advantages. Some of you might classify him as a crop-failure. And you would make the error of your lives, in so classifying him. Though advantages were denied him, yet he resolved to pass along the blazing torch of education and of progress which he had not been permitted to hold in his own feeble grasp.

"He denied himself the veriest necessaries of life—he sold the household goods and mortgaged the home he loved—in order to educate his only son and to fit that son to take his place in the world—a place that had been denied the father.

"The sum was not sufficient. Sooner than turn a promising final crop into a failure, he swerved from the path of the written law and invoked the aid of Heaven's first law—*necessity!* He continued to nurture that final crop, at the cost of his own safety, by the manufacture of illicit spirits.

"By the letter of the written law he is guilty. I admit that; so does he. And he stands ready to pay the penalty, if need be. He is content to have done his life-work—to have harvested at last the crop which his Maker sent him into the world to harvest. He is well content with that crop—content with the son he has educated on the results of his technical crime, the son who (thanks to him alone) is able to do a man's part in a man's world.

"He is content, I say, with that final crop of his. But I am not content with it. Nor shall I rest content until the son has paid the debt to his father, even as the father stands prepared to pay his debt to the law.

"Poor land produces poor crops. Parents of a poor moral type produce ignorant and diseased and criminal children, as their crop.

"My client has produced a crop which the community has honored with its endorsement. Could a criminal have raised that crop? Should the farmer who raised that crop—whether on bread or on whisky—be rated as a criminal and be punished as such? At worst, is not his offense merely nominal, to be penalized nominally?"

For the first time Halsey Grainger turned his terribly earnest gaze away from the jury, and as though by chance faced Sibyl.

"The crop my client raised, on his barren hill-farm," he said simply, "is myself."

"Gentlemen of the jury, the prisoner is my father. And the man who says I am ashamed of him—*lies!*"

THERE was a sudden new rustle in the courtroom. For as the old man had begun to protest, Sibyl Wirt had risen from where she sat and had passed unopposed through the doorway of the railing which divided the spectators from the participants in the trial.

She crossed to where Halsey Grainger sat. Stooping, she kissed the astonished lawyer full on the lips. Then, sitting down beside Clay Grainger, she slipped her hand into the prisoner's hard palm and looked serenely up at the Judge.

Now, Duneka is in most respects a thoroughly up-to-date county seat. Yet in local juries and elsewhere may sometimes be found a little of the old leaven of individuality left over from pioneer days.

The jury's foreman now rose from his seat and passed down the double line of his eleven confreres, whispering as he went.

"Judge, Your Honor," he announced huskily, "if it please the Court, we, the jury in this case, have unanimously decided—after careful and exhaustive study of the testimony—that the prosecution, through its witnesses, has wholly failed to establish any real proof of moonshining against the defendant. We therefore beg to bring in an unanimous verdict of Not Guilty. We're willing to be polled, if you doubt my word."

Then some hysterical person cheered.

And during the next few minutes Kentucky was disgraced by the applause which greeted a gross miscarriage of justice.

Tidy Emotions

SHE was a woman of tidy emotions. From birth she had been so. Her emotions were as untried as were the six-month colts that frisked in her father's paddock.

One of these colts, perhaps, was a future Derby-winner. One was destined by nature to be a carthorse, one a roadster, one a delivery-wagon steed. But at six months no expert on earth could tell with absolute exactness which fate was to befall any special colt of the group.

So it was with the untested emotions of Valda Moore. Brought up carefully,—half the year on her father's Kentucky estate, half the time in his Chicago winter home,—she had need for no deeper or wilder or shallower or more chromatic emotions than has a hothouse rose. And until—if ever—there should be need for them, Valda kept those emotions of hers just as tidy and unrumpled as she kept the drawers of her bureaus and the general appearance of her room.

Much is written—generally by wifeless or daughterless poets—concerning the virginal fresh neatness of a young girl's room. More young girls' rooms look like chicken-runs than like stage boudoirs. But Valda Moore's room was an exception—like Valda Moore's emotions.

A college senior with a homicidal football record, a first lieutenant of the regular army, a college professor, a Wall Street man, a professional heart-denter—all these, from time to time, had sought to stir a ripple, or perhaps a storm, on the placid surface of Valda's emotions. This, before she was twenty-two—for she was very lovely. Each and every suitor had scored a pitiable failure.

She did not flirt with her wooers. She was not cruel to them. She met them simply, with a well-bred calm which merged into a luke-warm surprise when they grew violent in their entreaties. And within three years after her debut she had unconsciously won a repute for kindly but icy indifference.

After that she met Lloyd Sherwin.

As a matter of fact, Valda had met Sherwin a dozen times before. But during their earlier acquaintance he was the husband of another woman—which, of course, made Valda view him through blinders. Moreover she knew, and diffidently admired, his gloriously magnetic wife.

Sherwin was a corporation lawyer. He was still several years on the ideal side of forty, and he had a great deal of money. For the rest, he was big of shoulder, well-groomed, brilliant and polished of manner, and good to look on. He and Adele, his wife, had been married nearly ten years. They were a strikingly handsome pair, and popular withal. Comparing Lloyd's polish and Adele's glowing Southland warmth, some one had once nicknamed them "Steel and Fire."

At last—quietly and with no open recriminations or explanations on either side—the Sherwins separated. A divorce of convenience followed. No one knew any of the details. No public blame tainted the name or the popularity of either of them.

Adele went out to California to live with her brother, whence presently came word of her marriage to another man, a former Chicagoan like herself. Sherwin went on a South American exploring-tour and in due time returned to Chicago and to his old social life there.

And six months after he came back, his engagement to Valda Moore was announced.

Everybody was surprised—perhaps Valda most of all. She did not quite know what had happened to her emotions—whether they were still undisturbedly tidy or whether they had become like other people's. And not being given to self-analysis, she did not investigate.

She had not at all expected to marry Lloyd Sherwin. She had not known she was in love with him. She had not had the faintest idea that he was in love with her. After his return to Chicago, it merely chanced that he and she were more and more often together, that she met him everywhere she went, and that half insensibly she grew to realize the quietly dominant charm of the man. But she was breathless with amazement when he said to her, one night, in a perfectly self-possessed way:

"I am a battered, shopworn, middle-aged divorced man. You are probably the most glorious girl God ever dreamed of making. You would be throwing yourself away, if you married me. Will you throw yourself away, Valda?"

For the tiniest fraction of a second she had a hysteric impulse to laugh at the whimsically adoring words spoken so calmly and with a subcurrent of mastery. But before she could conquer or explain the impulse, she found herself saying with equal calmness:

"No. I won't throw myself away. But—it won't be throwing myself away."

AFTER which they kissed each other,—not at all as movie heroes and heroines kiss,—and it dawned upon Valda that she was engaged.

She did not know whether or not she was in love with this man, so much older than herself, whose polish and cleverness and magnetism so impressed her. She had read much of love; she had heard much of love; but the actual symptoms were strange to her. She did not know whether she had them or not. Yet she was pleasantly happy, and just a very little bit thrilled. Thrills were new to Valda—even polite little misses-and-children's-size thrills.

THE engagement was short, and it was enlivened by all sorts of social excitement and the sublime task of trousseau-gathering. After that came an egregious church wedding and a more or less seasick yachting cruise and a final settling down to married life de luxe in a bijou house—all before Valda had wholly recovered from the first blank and blinking surprise of finding herself engaged.

Little by little, though, as the weeks danced on, she began to gain a clearer perspective. Marriage was no longer a profoundly novel experience to her, but a plain workaday fact; and she was able to take account of stock. Like many another bride, she learned she must get acquainted all over again with the man she had married. The Lloyd Sherwin she had seen for only an hour or two a day, during the engagement, was of course a totally different man from the Lloyd Sherwin who lived in the same house with her, and whose hopes and plans and habits were her own. And she began to study her husband.

The more she studied him, the fonder of him she became, and the more she rejoiced that she actually belonged to him. For this reason she fell to studying not only Lloyd himself, but his tastes—more especially his tastes concerning herself. Some of these tastes pleased her; others vaguely perplexed her; others she did not like. But one thing on which the couple heartily agreed was Sherwin's keen admiration for his wife's beauty. Each did everything possible to foster that particular taste.

For example, of all the various dresses in Valda's pretty trousseau, the gown that met Sherwin's fullest and most eager approval was a black velvet dinner costume cut with a severe simplicity that was little short of genius.

In this dress, Lloyd vowed, his wife was more exquisitely lovely than in anything else she wore. Valda was mildly astonished at his praise. She herself did not care particularly for the black velvet dress. Its plainness did not appeal to her. She had been overpersuaded by the dressmaker, against her own judgment, to buy it. Lloyd declared she must henceforth have a succession of black velvet gowns as closely resembling this first one as shifting fashion would permit.

The only ornament he would sanction her wearing, with the black velvet, was a thick rope of pearls that had been his wedding gift to her. The combination of pearls and sable velvet, he told her, formed a veritable symphony, with herself as its inspired theme.

For her own part, Valda greatly preferred a flame-colored evening gown that was the pride of her trousseau, and which seemed to swathe her slim body in pulsant fire. But Lloyd did not care in the least for this beloved garment of hers. He appeared almost to dislike it. So with a sigh Valda meekly substituted for it the black velvet—and the pearls—whenever Sherwin was more than usually anxious to have her appear at her best. To her own astonishment she did not grieve over this and other cases in which she was forced to yield her wishes to Lloyd's. Indeed, she was aware of a subtle joy in bending her will to his. And this (though there was no one to tell her so), was love—a love that has no place in a galaxy of tidy emotions.

Because her love for her husband was growing more and more whole-souled every day of her life, Valda sought to make herself in all ways what she thought he most desired her to be. She took her cue from the black velvet and pearls as much as from Lloyd's own polished self-control.

That, apparently, was the sort of woman he liked—the calm, gravely sweet, distinguished type of woman, gently sympathetic and statuesquely ornamental, either devoid of any gripping intensity or else with that intensity in perfect control—not necessarily frozen but completely self-possessed.

She found it an easy role to play—for it was her natural self, her tidy-emotion self of a lifetime, the self Lloyd had fallen in love with. She played it as convincingly and naturally as a one-legged and hump-backed man would enact the role of a cripple. And she knew it was pleasing to Lloyd. In his look and manner she saw he approved—which made her very happy, indeed—for almost three whole months.

But as time went on she was vexed to find herself less and less satisfied with her chosen role. For a while she did not know why. Then one morning she understood. She was passing behind Lloyd as she came into the breakfast-room where he was already seated at the table. Her light tread made no sound on the rug. He did not know she was in the room.

The sunlight was striking athwart his hair and bathing his classically regular face in gold. Looking at him, Valda felt a throbbingly swift yearning to steal up behind him and gather his head ever so tightly in her arms and to kiss him again and again.

Now this craving impulse caused as wild a stir among her array of tidy emotions as though the minister's wife, at a conference of the Women's Temperance League, should suddenly clamor aloud for a Scotch highball. Never before had Valda felt the remotest inclination to do so undignified a thing as to bestow a fiercely loving caress upon her correct husband. At least, she had not known of any such inclination. But now she realized that it was the one thing she most wanted to do—that she wanted to throw her arms about him, to have him strain her ardently to his heart—like lovers at the theater or at movie-shows. And she wanted it more than ever she had thought she could want anything in all the well-ordered routine that she called life.

For a moment she stood there looking down at her husband, the blood surging oddly through her, her hands tight-clenched, her eyes suffused and aglow. She drew a deep quivering breath and took a step forward.

Then her shadow fell across the tablecloth. Lloyd glanced up, caught sight of his wife and punctiliously sprang to his feet to welcome her. In a manner as courtly and as emotionless as an eighteenth-century marquis', he placed a light good-morning kiss on her lips and then went around the table to draw back her chair.

On the instant his greeting sent her flying back to her black-velvet-and-pearl pose, and relieved the momentary panic-scattering of her tidy emotions. But when Lloyd had gone to his office for the day, the memory of her queer impulse returned. And again Valda took mental account of stock. Hitherto it had never occurred to her to wish or to expect in her married life anything different from the smoothly tender chivalry of her husband and her own unruffled demeanor toward him. This new phase bewildered her.

She could not understand why she had wanted to clasp Sherwin's head in her arms and hold it tight to her breast while she kissed the handsome unlifted face. She could not understand why she yearned for Lloyd to shatter his polished attitude and to embrace her roughly, and to mutter fiercely adoring love-words to her. It did not fit in at all with her scheme of life. She was ashamed of the craving, and she tried to crush it. But it was stronger than she.

A psychologist could have explained to her that she was not by nature a woman of tidy emotions—that she was merely a woman whose emotions had seemed tidy because they had never been disturbed, that she was a one-man woman, and that the one man had at last awakened her—that her choice of the flame-colored dress had been a sign of subconscious awakening. But as usual there was no psychologist at hand to tell Valda these simple truths. She remained in the dark, but she remained there, resentfully, not placidly.

From her dressing-room window, as she stood brooding, she happened to glance down into the street. The bay-window commanded an oblique view of the house's area gate, which was hidden from the sidewalk. A grocer's delivery-man—big, young, ruddy—stamped down from the walk to the gate and rang the bell. With suspicious suddenness the Sherwins' pretty housemaid answered the summons.

The man set down the basket he carried and entered into a voluble conversation with the maid—a conversation so voluble as to imply long and interested acquaintance. He bent lovingly down toward her as they talked. And the maid gazed up at him with all her honest little soul in her eyes.

Presently he caught both her hands in his and bent closer to her flushed face. The maid drew back. The man threw both his strong arms about her, lifting her bodily from the ground and pressing her to his broad chest. There was a brief moment of halfhearted resistance on the part of the damsel. Then with a fluttering gasp of happy surrender, she let her arms steal shyly about his red neck and lifted a transfigured face to his kisses.

Valda drew back from the bay window—not in disgust or in amusement, but with a feeling she had no right to intrude longer on the sight. Her heart was beating fast. Then and there her tidy emotions died a complete and unlamented death.

She sat down in the nearest chair, her big eyes fixed intently on nothing. And she sat thus motionless, for nearly an hour. At last, out of the daze, came coherent thought and a steady resolve.

Surely she had as much right to embraces and to the unchecked utterance of her great love as had her grubby little housemaid! Surely her own beauty and charm were as great as her maid's! Why, then, should not Lloyd clasp her to his heart as the delivery-man in the dirty white coat had clasped the servant? Must life be all ice and reserve? Were black velvet and pearls the only suitable combination in the universe? Was there no place, in the scheme of existence, for flame-colored dresses or flame-colored emotions?

Fiery rebellion at her lot, the lot that had once seemed so comfortable, flared up in her. She had a right to happiness—the same right as was claimed by that spooning couple in the areaway. And there was no reason it should not be hers.

Always, Valda had heard that an open understanding, between two people who love each other, is the one solution to marriage's myriad pitfalls and misunderstandings. She took a swift resolution that she at once would have such a talk with Lloyd. He would understand; he was certain to understand, even if she stated her case awkwardly, and stammeringly—as she was quite certain she would.

The resolution taken, she felt happier—happier than ever before, and in a totally new and unsettling way. She even sang a little as she moved about the room, dressing for lunch.

Then her song trailed away into startled silence, and her eyes lost the mystic new light that had glorified them. She halted in her leisurely task of dressing, and into her face crept a look of acute distress. Into her mind had come, by chance, the memory of a stray phrase —a phrase she once had heard long ago, and at the time had scarce thought of. The phrase was "Steel and Fire."

And her mind cast back to the time she had heard it. A group of women had been speaking of the separation of Lloyd Sherwin and Adele, his first wife. One of them had said:

"What else could be expected of 'Steel and Fire'?"

The words had meant nothing to Valda. Now they meant everything. Never had she been jealous of Lloyd's earlier wife. Jealousy has no place in a set of tidy emotions. But now Valda's emotions were no longer tidy. She discovered she hated the woman from whom Lloyd had parted, whom he had chosen from all the world as his wife, before ever he had met Valda.

Back went her mind again, this time to a visualizing of Adele, as she remembered her. The older woman had been dark, sensuous, all but voluptuous—torrid of soul, starkly demonstrative in her affections.

That was the type of woman whom her steel-bright husband had selected for a wife, the type of woman, therefore, that he preferred to any other. The reflection cheered Valda just at first, for it would make her own talk with him easier and more probable of success.

Then came the after-reflection: that was the type of woman he has chosen—yes; but it was also the type of woman with whom he had found life insupportable. Emotional, too demonstrative, Adele had lost her hold over him. Valda wanted to keep that hold, forever and ever. How could she hope to do so if she should declare to him her wish to be treated as Adele had wished to be treated? Would not that turn Lloyd from her, as it had turned him from his other wife?

Valda had never asked Lloyd—nor had he volunteered to tell— any details as to his life with Adele, or the causes for their estrangement and divorce. From childhood she had been singularly free from feminine curiosity. Moreover an innate delicacy had kept her from inquiring into a subject that her husband so studiously avoided.

She had merely been certain that the fault of temperament had all been Adele's. And that same fault of temperament Valda herself had just now been in danger of committing..... No, henceforth, she must content herself with a black-velvet-and-pearls attitude, with no tinge of flame-color in it.

The battle between her new and her old self was fiercely waged that day. But in the end her old self—outwardly, at least—conquered. When Lloyd came home that evening, she greeted him with her usual pleasant coolness. But now it was as forced as once it had been natural. And Lloyd's courteously correct kiss stung her to reasonless anger.

Sherwin, in some occult way, appeared to sense the inner change of her bearing toward him and her gust of illogical wrath, or else her impulse begot impulse. For as she stepped back, he put both his hands on her shoulders with an almost boyish eagerness and made as though to draw her to him. For a flash of time her heart leaped in response to his unwonted warmth. But instantly, on the heels of the thrill, came memory of the demonstrative Adele, the woman who had been fire, and who had been unable to keep her husband's love.

At the reflection, Valda's yielding body stiffened. Indeed, it drew away ever so slightly from the lure of Sherwin's arms. An expression, too rapid in its flight for Valda to read, flitted across the urbanely smiling mask of Lloyd's face. His outstretched arms dropped gracefully to his sides. At once he was his usual self. The momentary impulse of affection seemed to have passed from his mind.

But it did not pass from Valda's. She felt strangely alone and bewildered and heartsick. All through the early evening she battled with her longing to tell him she craved to be as other loved wives, that she was growing to detest her rôle of theme to a symphony of black velvet and pearls. And always it was her love for him that held her back from speaking—that and her dread lest he find her as distasteful as he had found his first wife.

It was at nine o'clock that the explosion came—explosions are prone to occur when people think they have fought Nature into submission—nature being the craftiest and most unbeatable enemy known to mortal fighter.

Valda and Lloyd had dined at home, but at ten they were due at a dance. At a little before nine Valda went to the library safe to get her pearls. For she was wearing black velvet, and the pearls as usual were to play their symphonic part in the completion of her ball-dress.

The library safe was set deep in the wall behind a hinged panel of bookshelves. Valda swung back the panel, twirled the combination on the fretted little steel knob and opened the outer safe door. She had a flat drawer at the bottom of the safe for her own use—for the deposit of her jewelry and papers. This she now pulled out and began a search for the pearls she had grown to detest.

They were kept in a white satin box which usually lay at the very front of the drawer. To-night they were not there; nor were they anywhere in the compartment. Valda was sensible of a shock of fear. Then the startled frown vanished from between her brows.

She had broken the catch of the necklace a week earlier and had given it to Lloyd to leave at the jeweler's for repair. The previous day he had told her he had brought home the pearls and had put them in the safe.

Lloyd, from the beginning, had made it a foolishly punctilious point of honor never to open the safe-drawer he had given his wife. He had, half laughingly, explained to Valda that such a compartment ought to be as sacred to its owner's exclusiveness as any box in a safe-deposit vault. She had thought the notion rather silly, but quite in keeping with her lord's ideas of personal ethics. Now she realized he must have put the pearls elsewhere in the safe. And as she did not at all share his quixotic punctiliousness, she proceeded to rummage through various other compartments for them.

In the third pigeonhole she came upon the white satin case. She took it out. Then she began to close the compartments she had opened in her quest. In the smallest of these was a thin packet of letters held together by a very much attenuated rubber band. As Valda shoved shut the drawer, a corner of the packet was caught against the top. The action of closing the little compartment pushed the package into a rumpled mass.

Valda was instantly aware of what she had done. Her orderly soul rebuked her for her carelessness. She opened the drawer and took out the packet to smooth it flat again. The rotted rubber band had snapped. The letters—there were four of them—lay loose in her grasp. They were not enveloped.

Valda recognized the bold, sprawly handwriting of Adele—a chirography she was forever coming upon in flyleaves of the Sherwin books, and which was thus too familiar to her to be mistaken for anyone's else.

A month ago Valda would have put the letters away with a sense of guilt at having touched them, and without a second glance. But now the fire of jealousy blazed up to her very brain. Lloyd, then, had not forgotten his earlier wife nor ceased to care for her!

With a quick intake of breath she cast away reason and sense of honor. Opening the single folded sheet of the first letter, she read it.

My wonderful man-without-words:
The day has been as black and as bitter as ice. For it has brought me no word from you, my god-man. I am aching for the mighty grip of your arms, for the heavenly pain of your lips crushing mine. Every hour is a shackled year, until I—

Lloyd's step on the stair above made Valda start up as from a nightmare. She laid the letters in their compartment, put back the pearls where she had found them and opened again the flat box assigned to her own use.

"Dear," she called unsteadily,

"my pearls aren't in this drawer. Where did you put them?"

"Oh," Sherwin answered, quickening his pace, "I forgot to tell you. I'm sorry. I put them in another compartment. Wait a moment."

SHE rose to her feet, her brain awhirl, and turned to face the doorway through which he must presently come. Before her eyeballs were dancing the madly impassioned words she had just read—the words of a woman who had poured out a wealth of hot adoration upon this man who preferred black velvet and pearls to flame! And a hatred of her own part seared into Valda's soul like white-hot iron.

In the doorway stood her husband—immaculate in dress and in bearing. His masklike face wore a look of polite regret at his carelessness in not telling her where he had put the detestable pearls. Facing him, her cheeks pulsing with high color, her eyes ablaze, her body swaying, stood Valda.

"It was abominably careless of me to forget—" suavely began Lloyd.

But at sight of his wife the civilly apologetic words were stricken from his lips. He stared open-mouthed, the dark color surging into his own face, his icy mask shattered. Then in one stride he had cleared the distance between them and had caught Valda to him.

For a second her escape-efforts were futile against the power of the ardent arms that imprisoned her and of the lips that sought hers. But almost instantly Sherwin was aware of her resistance. And releasing her, he let her shrink out of his reach.

The man's face was working. When he spoke, no one could have recognized in his roughly panting voice the wonted careful diction of Lloyd Sherwin:

"I've frightened you!" he said harshly. "I've disgusted you! A man can't be a block of granite forever—not when he loves a woman as I love you. He can't remember every minute that he is married to a framework for black velvet and pearls, and not to a flesh-and-blood woman. I won't offend again, I can promise you that. I've never done such a thing before. You know I haven't. And I could have kept a curb on myself to the end of the chapter too, if you hadn't looked—"

"You speak as if you were blaming *me* for it," she flashed, scarlet with unreasoning anger. "It was not my fault. I—"

"I know it wasn't," he half groaned. "Nothing is your fault. You haven't a fault, not one single redeeming fault. Let it go at that."

"It *wasn't* my fault!" she raged on, unheeding. "I've tried to be the way you want me to be. I'm going to try to keep on being the way you want me to be. It used to be easy. Now it's impossible. But I'm going to do it. Only—don't make it a million times harder by—by doing as you did just now."

She was crying, fiercely, hysterically. He gaped at her in amazement.

"What do you mean?" he demanded, his voice harsh and shaky. "What do you mean by—"

"You sneered at me for being a 'framework for black velvet and pearls!'" she sobbed. "Whose fault is it? Who made me wear them? Who wouldn't let me wear my flame-colored—"

"A flame-colored dress—on an iceberg!" he broke in. "Do you wonder I didn't like the combination? If there had been flame within the flame, I should have fallen down and worshiped you. But to swathe *you* in flame-colored silk is like—is like putting *papier maché* food in front of a starving man. Oh, I'm talking like a brute! Try to forgive me. I won't lose my grip on myself again. And don't think I'm not proud of you, as you are; and that I don't love you more than all the whole world. When I begged you to marry me, I knew what you were. I knew you were perfect. I knew you were so perfect that you'd be mine only as a wonderfully inspired statue could be mine. And I forced myself to be content. I even pointed out to you the adornments that would best suit such a statue. Won't you forgive me, if I can't quite always forget that you aren't a *woman* as well as a statue—that I yearn, sometimes, for a wife to love, as well as for an idol to adore? All my life I have craved that. And it has never been granted to me. And now I know it never will be. So I'll be content—I *am* content—with what I have. I—"

"You have no right to speak so!" she blazed back at him. "And I am *not* a statue. I'm a flesh-and-blood woman, and a woman who loves you, and whose whole heart cries out to be loved as other women are loved. If I loved you less, I shouldn't have shrunk away from you. But one woman lost you by showing too clearly that she worshiped you. And I—"

"One woman?" he repeated, dazed. "What do you mean?"

"I mean Adele!" she raged. "She let you see she loved you—that the days were as 'bitter as ice' away from you—that she longed for the 'mighty grip of your arms'—that she—and all that. And yet you say you never had such love from any woman! Oh, I don't understand you, Lloyd! I *don't!* I—"

She checked herself, held by the blank dismay in his face. Presently he spoke. And now all the excitement was gone from his voice and manner—and all the life too.

"I wish I didn't have to speak of this," he said heavily. "I've tried not to. It seems disloyal to a memory. And yet it would be worse than disloyal to you not to speak. I—"

"I don't—" she began, frightened.

But he went on, in the same dead voice:

"When I married Adele, I was a blindly infatuated boy. I got my eyesight back quickly enough. I got it back when she explained to me, very carefully, in our first and only quarrel, that she had married me because I had money and social position of a sort, and because she had not."

"Oh!"

"She told me, frankly, she never had cared for me and never could care for me. There was nothing for me to do but make the best of it. If, on the surface, I grew hard and cold and indifferent,—as people have told me I did,—it was only an armor to save me from heartbreak. And I was forced to wear it so long that it grew to be a part of me. Or I thought it had grown to be a part of me, till I married you. And since then—since then—"

A RUSTLE of velvet, sweeping quickly across the polished floor, broke in upon his miserably faltering speech. Before he could guess her intent, Valda's lips had silenced the man's confession. With a great wordless cry he gathered her into his arms. And for a space there was silence—a golden, heaven-born silence. Then—

"But if Adele didn't love you," came a question whose tones were muffled somewhere in Lloyd's shirt-front, "if she didn't love you, how could she have written you those letters—those love-letters?"

"Love-letters?" echoed Sherwin, a note of perplexity tinting the boyish rapture of his new voice. "What love-letters? She never wrote me a single—"

"Those letters in—in the littlest compartment of your safe," explained Valda, too happy to feel ashamed for her prying.

"Those?" returned Lloyd. "Those were the letters that gave me my divorce. They weren't written to *me*. I never had a love-letter written to me in all my life—worse luck!"

"If—if you keep holding me so tightly that I can't get to the desk," she laughed, shyly, "I'm afraid you'll go on never having one written to you, sweetheart!"

The Winner

by Albert Payson Terhune

THIS is the thrilling story of a horse-race—and of other things. It is preceded by a masterly essay on the horse. You may skip the essay if you want to, though it is the truest and most original thing in all the story.

Foremost among the million lies that have lived so long as to be taken for gospel truth, is the theory that the horse is the noblest and most sagacious and bravest of animals, and that he is man's best friend.

He is man's best friend, perhaps—or was, until rubber tires supplanted ironshod hoofs. But that was no credit to him, any more than it is to the credit of your tub or your razor or your shoes that they serve you well. They don't do it on purpose. Neither does the horse. As for the horse's loyal nobility and brains: Breed and train a horse and make him your closest friend for ten years. At the end of that time, any stranger can come along, knock you over the head and then jump on your horse and ride away. The horse will carry him wherever the man wants to go; nor will the steed come back at your call, any more than he would stand up for you when the thief overpowered you. Any mongrel cur, any alley cat, will show more loyalty and sagacity than will the noble steed, you see, when it comes to standing by his master.

As for courage and "horse-sense:" Your horse will shy violently at sight of a twisted newspaper at the roadside. Even a cow has the wit to know that scrap of paper is harmless. Yet your horse is not only afraid of it, but shies just as affrightedly the tenth time he passes it, as the first. He hasn't a doodlebug more sense than that.

Your horse knows what three simple motions of the reins mean. He knows enough, at those motions, to turn to right or to left or to halt. He may even be wise enough after long experience to know which of several stalls in the stable is his own. He also has been taught that a chirping sound or the order "Giddap" means he will be flogged if he does not increase his speed.

The foregoing are all the things the average horse learns, in a lifetime of training and practice. And during that time any unusual sight or sound will throw him into a spasm of terror. So much for the wisdom, the courage, the loyalty, the nobility of man's "best friend!"

The horse is big. He keeps his mouth shut. He has the gift of looking stately, when he is really only foolish. So he gets away with it. And in spite of this honest exposure of his cowardly stupidity he will continue to get away with it, to the end of the chapter.

(Let me spoil still further the effect of this brilliant essay by confessing that, in my very late teens, I cried, unashamed, at the grave of the glorious saddle-horse I loved.)

THE same lying glamour has always been cast about horse-races. One reads of the magnificent thoroughbreds, straining every nerve to win, thundering down the stretch, with a human comprehension of all that hangs on the result of the contest; of their proud joy in victory and of their noble grief in defeat. One reads all that, usually in the same story wherein the losing jockey is inspired to victory by a long look at one sweet and tensely white face in the grandstand.

The fact of the matter is, a bunch of half-developed colts are tortured to excess of speed by the whips and spurs of their jockeys and go careening thus frantically around the great circle, looking for all the world, from the grandstand, like a clump of hunched-up and crumple-legged patent toys surmounted by writhing jumping-jacks. As for the mad yearning to win: what animal, from the hippopotamus down, would not run his level best, with a welting whip flailing his back and shoulders and a double pressure of sharp steel digging into his under-ribs? Yes, and the jockey who, during the climax of a race, should take the time to exchange a long look of understanding with a white-faced girl in the grandstand, would probably end the happy day in a bed in an emergency hospital.

Apart from these trifling defects, the average racing-yarn is true enough.

Horse-racing has been called "the sport of kings." Probably the term started in the days when kings were about the only people who could afford to play the races without having to tap their employers' tills for the means to gratify their zest for true sport. There may be people whose interest in a horse-race can center on the track itself, rather than on the betting ring. But there are not enough of them to keep the grass off the race-tracks, in States where the anti-betting law is rigidly in force.

Which ends the essay and brings us by prosy degrees to our story.

WHEN Peter Farren learned, from his trainer's telegram,—sent collect,—that his racing mare Calyx had died in giving birth to her first colt, he realized he had lost something like nine thousand dollars' worth of horseflesh and gained in return a two-day-old leggy monstrosity that might or might not sometime be worth nine thousand cents.

Farren was busy, just then. His farm was far away, and the season was early winter. So he waited until the next May before taking the two-hundred mile trip from his city activities to the mountain region where so much of his income went into the so-called "improvement of the breed."

At sight of the defunct Calyx's six-months-old colt, Farren was pleasantly impressed. He liked the youngster's points and bearing and his shyly friendly ways. And sentimental memories of the purses Calyx had won for him, made him more than ordinarily inclined in favor of this, her only offspring. He indulged himself in dreams of the colt's future and of Calyx's possible legacy to her adored old master (whom the mare had not known by sight) in the shape of this coming Suburban winner.

Farren gave special orders as to the baby's upbringing. He had already lavished upon the colt the name of "Calliope"—not through any knowledge of the Muses or from association with the shiny music-chariot that hoots such classics as "This House is Haunted" and "I'm Longing for You," in circus parades, but in recognition of an age-old horsy custom.

The youngster's dam had been Calyx. His sire had been Leopard II. Taking the first syllable or so of each name, Farren had evolved "Calliope." And he had done it with less straining of intellect than most race-horse reamers must undergo.

Some months later, Farren received his trainer's professional opinion on Calliope's promise as a racer.

"He's a dawg," pronounced the trainer with perfect frankness. "A dawg. A hound-dawg, at that. He's got the laigs. He's got the wind. He's got the bar'l. But there's a chunk of yeller where his heart oughter be. Nobody knows has he got any speed or not, because, as soon as you commence to push him, he lays down. An' then, if you sail in to wallop a bust of speed out of him, he blows up, like he was a Zep'lin. I figger he's the original missin' link between an armored tank an' an aviator. When he ain't creepin', he's goin' up in the air. His hide an' his hoofs," finished the trainer in a belated attempt at condolence, "might be wuth a little suthin', for sole-leather an' glue."

PETER FARREN did not relinquish his early hunch as to Calliope's future until he had proved by personal inspection that his trainer was not only a truthful but a conservatively truthful man. Calliope, under his owner's eye, performed prodigies of rank incompetence.

"There ain't a race-horse in America," declared the trainer enthusiastically, as he and Farren walked back to the stables, "there ain't a race-horse in America that gives promise of doin' better than this Calyup of yours—between the shafts of a garbage cart."

"That's the answer," gloomily assented Farren. "You've tried him with the dope, of course? How does he work, under that?"

"I didn't try it on him but once," said the trainer. "That was enough for any man who ain't a hawg. It acted on him, grand. First, he tried to canter up a telephone pole. An' then he went to sleep."

"I'll sell him," announced Farren, with the air of one who abandons a great hope, yet thinks to save something from the wreckage. "I'll sell him. There's ways."

A day or two later, tiny news items began to sprinkle the sporting pages of divers metropolitan papers. They dealt with the surprise which Mr. Peter Farren was preparing to spring upon followers of the sport, in the shape of a truly wondrous two-year-old, Calliope by name, which had been bred by Farren and had shown such phenomenal speed as to warrant the owner in saving him up for a "killing."

Among various people whom these items interested was Ralph Glenn, a young man who loved horses and who knew nothing about them. Glenn was making fairly good money in the law, and he had inherited a few thousand dollars from his father. He had recently decided to make horse-racing his life-fad, to such extent as he could comfortably afford, and no more.

Thus, he had broken into the racing game with a modest string of three horses—two of them selling-platers. He had won an obscure race or so, on off days, at second-rate tracks. He had lost a tidy bit of cash, of course, in pursuing his jolly hobby. But he had not lost more than he could afford to. And he found the fun well worth the price.

NATURALLY, Ralph Glenn had ambition—oddly enough, the very same ambition that hits every small-way horseman. He yearned to breed or else to develop a colt which should amaze the whole racing world and win turf immortality for himself and for his worshiping owner. You see, Ralph had read many racing stories and had not yet had enough experience to class them along with the works of the well-known Baron Munchausen.

So he continued to dream his beautiful dream. He even taught Sibyl Garth to dream it with him. Sibyl Garth was the girl who went faithfully to the track with Glenn, and whose practical knowledge of horses was almost equal to his own.

Glenn chanced upon one or more of the news-squibs anent the wonderful and hidden colt Calliope. Ralph was a clever youth. He flattered himself he could read between the lines and could see there what must escape the notice of duller horsemen. By all these veiled accounts, Calliope must be a marvel. In fact, he must be just such a colt as Ralph had yearned to develop and win fame with—and *for.* Presently other men would begin to think. And one of them would snap up this paragon. There was no time to waste.

Indeed, other men were already thinking—horsy men, at that. One of them had summarized the sentiments of the rest, when he had looked up from a perusal of the sporting page and said yawningly:

"I see where Pete Farren is pulling that old wheeze about a world-beater colt hid up his sleeve. Most likely the skate was born with only three legs. Well, there's a sucker born every minute, and there's ten amachoor hoss-buyers born, to every reg'lar sucker. Pete's liable to unload, all right, all right."

RALPH GLENN made a visit, by appointment, to Farren's stock farm. There the man who loved horses, and didn't know them, came into close contact with a man who knew horses too well to love them. And the inevitable ensued.

Glenn departed thence, the glad owner of Calliope. Farren remained behind, to celebrate the receipt of Glenn's check for $1,900. Which sum was a bare $1,800 above Calliope's present true cash value.

Farren wished he might have done better in the sale. But he felt he had played a four-flush hand to its limit. You see, he had had to be very upstage, and refuse to let Ralph have an exhibition of the brute's speed.

"I'm not selling him as a racer," he announced, when Glenn approached him. "I'm not guaranteeing he can run. All I'm guaranteeing is that he's sound in wind and limb—there's the vet's certificate to prove it—and that to the best of my knowledge and belief he hasn't got a single ugly trick. As I tell you, I'm not selling him as a racer. My men, here, have been trying him out on the sly; and some nosy stable boy must have tipped off the papers. I'm not saying what time he made or that he made any time at all. All I do say is that if I hadn't dropped so much coin in Butler Munitions, I wouldn't be selling out my string here, in a hurry, for what I can get. And I wouldn't be selling my colt, Calliope, for all the money coined, till I had a chance to see if he could run in public the way he can run on my own track. But I've got to sell him, 'as is.' You've heard the price. It goes as it lays."

Once more Ralph Glenn prided himself on his shrewd power at character-reading. He saw through this astute turfman, as through glass. He read Farren's vast underlying faith in Calliope's prowess and the grief that a wrong turn of the market forced him to part with the "dark horse" he had so carefully been "saving." It was a chance of a lifetime. And Glenn, while heartily sorry for poor old Farren, grasped blissfully at that chance.

FOR weeks thereafter Ralph scanned the papers in vain for any mention of the forced sale of Farren's stable. Failing to find such announcement, he inferred that some new investment had put the semi-bankrupt on his feet. And Ralph rejoiced the more at his own good luck in getting Calliope at the psychological moment.

But as time went on, he rejoiced less and pondered more. In his first zest of possession, he saved Calliope for a fairly important stake race at a Long Island track. There were eleven horses entered for the event.

Calliope did not finish first. He did not finish eleventh. He did not finish at all. Something happened to him, no one knew what. He made the barrier comfortably enough. He was even among those present, at the quarter. Indeed, he was leading, at that point.

Then, for no reason at all, he slumped into a hand-canter. His jockey's whip began to do harsh things to him. Whereat, Calliope did some spectacular bucking and finished by rolling clean over. He did not fall. He let himself down, deliberately; and wallowed. The rail and the stand were so much entertained by his quaint performance that they almost missed seeing the race's finish.

Calliope's next three races were of the same general type as his first, and Ralph Glenn was fairly dazed by such ill-luck. He and his new colt were fast becoming the unsalaried Charlie Chaplins of the racetracks. Ralph had optimistically entered Calliope for no less than four good races for the next few months, including the classic event known as the Island Handicap, second in importance only to the Suburban.

He had entered the colt for this classic in the first flush of owner-ship, eagerly urged thereto by Sibyl Garth. Now he felt doubly a fool, as the list of weights were made known. And he told Sibyl so. Calliope carried bottom weight, and was scheduled, in the early betting, at odds too deplorable to print.

RALPH and Sibyl motored down, one morning, to the Long Island stables where Calliope and Ralph's three other horses were quartered.

"What's the matter with him, Bud?" demanded Sibyl of Clymer, the jockey, who was exercising the colt for their delectation. "He is beautiful. And he has such splendid lines, too. And, as long as he *does* run, in any of his races, he makes grand time. Only he always shuts up again almost before he gets into his stride. What ails him?"

"What ails the big Mamma's boy at school, when he lets a kid half his size larrup the head off'm him, in a scrap?" snorted the disgusted jockey. "Well, the same thing ails this mutt. He's got the goods. And he's got nothing else. He's a cur. He lays down, at the first tussle. He's scared to death, scared to run, scared to do anything but fall to pieces.

"Why, miss," went on Bud Clymer, warming to his theme, "that Calliope is the measliest coward you ever run up against. He's yellow, clear to the middle of him. He's scared at everything. Watch right now, how he's shaking and trying to bolt, because you shook out that handkerchief of yours! He can run, all right. And he did it, just this very morning. If he'd run a little farther, he'd have caught up with himself, going around the track a second time."

"But," ventured Sibyl. "If he—"

"Oh, it wasn't in a tryout!" the jockey forestalled her. "It was when he was having his morning exercise. The boy had just got on him, when along comes a kid, with one of these 'mouth sirens.' The kid let out a long hoot with it, just as he passed behind Calliope, and it scared the skate to death. He gave one bound and put his head down and started off. If we'd had a watch on him, we could have claimed something like a training record. It was a mile before the boy could bring him in. And yesterday a lad comes into the stable with an auto-tire slung over his neck. Calliope got a glimpse of it and near tore down the side of his box, to run away. And he bolted, two days ago, when a couple of dogs got into a scrap, out there in the infield, a half-mile away from him. And again yesterday, he shivered all over and looked like he'd faint, when he saw a sheet tumble off the rack. It's the same in a race. As soon as he finds out he's racing, he slumps. His coward legs give out. And the whip only puts him into a panic, so that he rolls, or else rears till he falls back. Oh, he sure is one rotter, that Calliope colt!"

SYBYL drew Ralph away as soon as she could get him to stop listening in morbid fascination to the tale of his dream-horse's worthlessness.

"Listen!" she commanded. "You're not to look as if Santa hadn't left you any toys at all! You're not to. At least, not yet. Not until the Island Handicap is lost."

"Lost?" he mocked, savagely. "It's as lost now as ever it will be, so far as I'm concerned. I'm going to 'scratch' Calliope, of course. I thought you understood that, without my telling you. I've been made a laughingstock for the last time."

"Perhaps you have," she assented. "Or perhaps you haven't. Would you risk being one, just *once* more, if I begged you to? Or wouldn't you?"

"Oh," he grunted, his sour tone at merry variance with his words, "if it would make a hit with you, I suppose I'd keep on racing Calliope till Doomsday and let every grandstand on earth laugh itself sick at me. But why do you want me to? If—"

"Because," she answered. "I think there's one chance in a million that we can win the Island Handicap. And the odds—even against Calliope—aren't as large as a million to one. Not quite. Besides, good, kind Mr. Peter Farren owns Roisterer. Don't forget that, Ralph. And don't forget that Roisterer is the favorite, either, and that the papers say that it has been the hope of Mr. Farren's fair young life to win an Island Handicap. Remember—"

"If it's just the same to you," interrupted Glenn, "I'd rather not remember anything at all about Farren. He took my money as easily as if I had been a blind beggar. Every time I see him in the stand, laughing himself pink in the face at Calliope's antics, I want to commit mayhem on him. He—"

"But aren't there better things than mayhem?" she urged, soothingly. "I mean, aren't there better ways of teaching crooks the error of their sins than by—by—"

"Than by beating them up?" he supplemented. "Maybe. But I don't know any such ways that would give me the solid satisfaction I'd get from just one smash at Pete Farren, with my right, to the jaw."

"Don't you?" she queried sweetly. "Don't you really know of any better ways, Ralph? Then I'm going to teach you one. Listen—"

FOR the scenic setting wherein that year's Island Handicap was staged, and for the aspect of the crowd and the stately beauty of the parading horses, I refer you to any of the stenciled newspaper accounts of any big race-meet for the last ten years.

To the surprise of everyone,—even of the mirthful Peter Farren,— Glenn did not "scratch" Calliope. All were pleased. For now refined humor was certain to mingle with thrills, in the big race.

The Glenn colt carried "bottom weight." And the gorgeously tempting odds, chalked up by the bookies, seemingly lured only two people into taking advantage of the rich bargain. Those two were Ralph Glenn himself and Sibyl Garth. And neither of them plunged deeply.

Another surprise was the news that Bud Clymer had consented to ride Calliope. Bud was not a world-famed jockey. But he knew how to ride; he had a cool head and a good pair of hands. He liked ridicule no more than do most mortals. And it seemed incredible that he should ride a colt he himself had so often denounced as a joke.

But Sibyl Garth had a mighty persuasive way about her. And Ralph Glenn, backing her judgment, gave Bud a pleasantly thick wad of bills in advance payment, along with certain of the weirdest instructions ever passed from owner to jockey. Bud had a sense of humor. He also had a sense of cash. Whether the oddity of Glenn's racing orders or the pledge of a Monte Cristo winner-fee decided him, there is no sense in arguing.

Ten horses paraded before the stand and eventually passaged up to the barrier, for the fourth race of the day, the Island Handicap.

As Farren's Roisterer—carrying top-weight and a renowned jockey—moved past the stand, there was a ripple of applause. Roisterer carried too much of the spectators' money not to merit some ovation. When Bud Clymer piloted the already-scared Calliope past the stand, a ragged howl of laughter went up. The unexpected sound all but made the craven horse bolt for the paddock. Bud looked red and sheepish, not to say disgruntled. But he was honest, in his way, and he vowed to stick to the crazy deal he had made.

There were fewer false starts than usual. As the barrier at last was raised, no earthshaking roar of "They're off!" swelled forth, to be heard for miles. That well-rehearsed and carefully dictioned din exists only in newspaper and novelistic reports of races. Still, there was a very creditable burst of noise as the horses clattered away from the barrier.

THE race meant nothing to Calliope. He was a fool. But experience had taught him that it could not last longer than a few seconds, as far as he was concerned. Presently the strangely moveless boy on his back would begin to urge or to guide or in other ways to pester him. Then Calliope, as usual, would drop to a sullen canter. At further urging, he would rear or roll. Then he would be led away to the comfort of paddock or stall. And he prepared to put his program into effect.

Meanwhile, he had gotten a good start and was traveling at a gratifying rate of speed. And so he and his rider came to the quarter, with only two horses ahead of them, and with the skillfully nursed Roisterer bowling along at ease nearly two lengths behind. At this point something happened which drove from Calliope's pinhead brain every idea of his prearranged program of quitting.

From close behind his flattened ears, a hideous and soul-shaking sound burst forth.

It started nowhere and it did not end at all. It arose, from a shrill squeal to a shriek of earsplitting awfulness.

A steadier and saner horse than Calliope has been frightened by a lesser noise. The rabbit-hearted colt went quite crazy from terror. All he knew or cared to know—was that he must get away from that horrific sound with all the speed he had.

Eyes shut, he bolted. Fear put unguessed strength and swiftness into his appalled body. Heretofore, when he had bolted, his rider had sought, with might and main, to bring him in. But Bud Clymer sat as still as a rock. Only the deftly muscular hands were at work,—both of them,—to keep Calliope on the course and to maneuver for such openings, and like advantages, as his mount's whirlwind speed rendered possible.

It was not a race Calliope was pursuing. It was a runaway. The average horse, in running away, cannot make as good speed as can the steed which is guided. That has been proven by countless captures of bolting saddle-horses by mounted policemen. But Calliope's was a super-runaway. Stark terror lent to his limbs a maniac strength. He was not merely scared. He was insane. The awful screeching sound, that rose and fell so gruesomely, was a sentient demon that chased him, refusing to be left behind.

EVERY sinew of Calliope's powerful young body was strained to the breaking point in a mad effort to run away from the sound. Its shrillness pierced his delicate eardrums like a brace of white-hot needles. Its unearthly stridency robbed him of every idea except panic-fear. And all the time, so deftly that Calliope did not realize it, Bud Clymer was doing the cleverest bit of guidance possible to a cool-headed jockey.

Blind,—madness hurling him forward,—the colt was running as no sane horse could force himself to run. The fact that he carried lighter weight than did any of his competitors lent speed to his wild flight. Bud Clymer sat as if he were cemented to his saddle. He had not so much as drawn his whip. A whip of scorpions could not have given to Calliope the incredible burst of speed that the mysterious screeching sound was evoking. Terror made him forget his own limitations, even as terror will make a stout and rheumatic man put to shame a college track-record—when an angry bull is following at top speed just behind him.

The colt was oblivious of the length of the race. Under the spur of such mortal fear, he would run as now he was running until he should fall dead, or until the harrowing screech should cease.

Across the finish-line, Calliope whirled. And as he did so,—a full quarter-length ahead of Roisterer, his nearest rival,—the hideous sound ceased.

Bud Clymer spat out the little tin disk he had held between his teeth and lips throughout the race, and on which he had been blowing incessantly until his lungs ached. The fifteen-cent "mouth siren" had done its work, even as Sibyl Garth had hoped it would! The tin disk rolled unnoted into the dust of the track, while Bud braced himself with all his might and sawed at the runaway's reins.

Calliope was brought down to a lurching canter with comparative ease. At the cessation of the horrifying screech enough of his terror had departed to let him realize that he was exhausted and breathless and wabbly, from such exertion as he never before had known. He was glad enough to slacken his pace and, presently, to let himself be turned about and ridden at a shambling walk back to the scales.

THE grandstand rose to him as he passed. But for his dizzy fatigue, the spectators' ecstatic racket must have made Calliope bolt once more. He had never had the wit to know he was a laughingstock. Nor, now, did he guess he was a new-crowned king in Horsedom. Calliope was still a fool—a craven fool. But soon his tiny brain would begin to work again. Then, he would at once associate the very feel of the racetrack with the fright he had undergone. And it would require three men and a derrick to drag him onto the course again—to say nothing of making him start in a race. For the first and the last time in his worthless life, Calliope had gone all the way around a track before a crowd.

Through the press of chattering people, Peter Farren lunged his heavy way. He was bound for the box where sat two idiotically exultant young people—a man and a decidedly pretty girl. The girl saw him coming and delightedly announced his approach to her escort.

"Didn't I say he'd look you up, the first minute he could?" asked Sibyl, in triumph. *"Didn't* I? And here he comes! It's all turning out just as I knew it would! And now, if you'll only remember what I said about—"

"Don't worry!" replied Glenn. "I'm ready for him. But, oh, you *are* a wonder, sweetheart! First, you prophesied that Calliope would win a race he couldn't possibly win; and next you prophesied I'd be buttonholed by a man who has been dodging me ever since he stung me for nineteen hundred dollars with a hundred-dollar skate! He—"

"I didn't prophesy that Calliope would win," she protested. "I only told how he might have a *chance* to win. As for Mr. Farren—it wouldn't be human nature for him to keep away from you, now."

Sibyl, as usual, was right. Farren could not have kept away from Glenn, just now, if he had tried to. Nor did he try. Farren's mind was topsy-turvy with the need for a quick readjustment of his ideas as to Ralph.

Up to the last half-hour he had looked on Glenn as the very easiest of easy marks. Then Calliope won. And all Farren's notions underwent a violent change. His own sublime crookedness made the affair perfectly simple to him.

Glenn had secretly trained the unpromising colt into a world-beater, had hired a jockey to make the brute ridiculous in one or two minor races, and thus caused the bookmakers to chalk up unheard-of odds against him for the Island Handicap—and had doubtless cleaned up a fortune.

And this was the colt,—this marvel,—which Farren had sold for a paltry nineteen hundred dollars! A craving to repossess the paragon surged hot in Farren's heart. He had bred Calliope. The owner of a great horse is tenfold more honored if he can also boast that the horse is a result of his personal judgment in breeding. Farren foresaw himself the turf hero of the year, if only he could persuade Glenn to sell.

GAINING his way to the box, he complimented the modest Ralph right fulsomely on the victory, and forecast many such triumphs for the peerless Calliope.

"Oh, I don't know!" deprecated Ralph. "He may never win another race. I shouldn't be surprised if he didn't. Anyhow, he won't win one for *me*. I'm through with racing. I was only waiting till I could quit ahead of the game. I'm better at the bar than on the turf. I begin to see that. So, I'm going to put up my little string for sale. It's almost a pity your bad turn on the market should have left you so hard up, Mr. Farren. Otherwise I might let you make an offer for Calliope, before he goes to the auction block."

Farren fairly gobbled with rapture. So thrilled was he by the prospect of buying in the mighty Calliope, that he threw old customs to the winds and asked eagerly:

"What's your rock-bottom price for him?"

"Let me see," mused Glenn, ruminatively. "He cost me nineteen hundred dollars. In keep and fees and training and all that, he has cost me perhaps another six hundred. And I am entitled to a shade of profit, besides. Especially from you. Shall we call the price three thousand dollars?"

Farren stared, agape. The winner of the Island Handicap offered for sale at a measly three thousand dollars! At first, he was certain Glenn was trying to be funny. Then he saw the younger man was in earnest. And a cold sweat came over him, lest some other turfman learn of the idiotic terms and begin to run up the price before Farren himself could seize the golden gift the gods were dangling before his bulging eyes.

"That is your final price?" he asked, trying to keep his voice steady.

"It is," returned Glenn, rising as though to start for home.

Farren blocked his way; feverishly hauling forth a dense roll of bills.

"Wait!" blithered the bemused turfman, shelling money shakily from the wad. "Here you are! Three thousand, just! Here! I'll scribble a memorandum of sale; and this lady can witness your signature. I'll—"

"Remember," cautioned Glenn, as Farren began to write hurriedly on the leaf of a betting book, "remember, I'm not selling him as a racer. I'm not guaranteeing he can run. I'm selling him, 'as is.' Let this lady bear witness to that, too."

FARREN scarce heard, and heeded not at all. Assuredly he did not recall the words as his own. His corkscrew-shaped soul was in a ferment of rapture over his new gulling of this young imbecile who could not keep a treasure when he had it. Three thousand dollars! Farren tore out the leaf he had scrawled on and passed it over to Glenn for signature.

"I figure I am netting just about five hundred dollars on that deal," Ralph confided to Sibyl, as they left the grounds. "And that five hundred belongs to the genius who taught me how to twist a liability into an asset. We're going to stop at a first-class jeweler's on the way home, and invest it for her. I meant what I said, too, about dropping the racing game, dear. And I'm going to stick to my word. I'm going to break that resolution just once, though: I'm going to throw over every bit of business and come to the track—the first day Farren enters Calliope for a race!"

Human Interest Stuff

HAPPINESS, to Jeff Titus, had become a fine art. It had become so when he married Eve Wallace, a little wisp of a city girl who had come to the Kentucky mountain hinterland to cure a set of weak lungs—and who had not only wedded but well-nigh civilized the lanky young mountaineer.

Happiness had remained a fine art for Jeff, up there on his bare hillside farm, with Eve. It had remained so, for the most part; ever since his wedding. And now in a single breath happiness had taken a place among the lost arts.

The "single breath" had been supplied by a sour east wind which had smitten Eve as she stood in the shack dooryard waiting for her husband's homecoming. She was thinly clad, and she was in a perspiration from working in her flower garden. Her lungs were still weak. The east wind did the rest. By night she had a heavy cold. The third morning pneumonia flung out its flaming red No Surrender signal in each of her fever-scorched cheeks.

And life, to Jeff Titus, all at once became a horror.

A frightened anguish gripped him by the throat and shook him to the bewildered soul as he crouched night after night beside the slab bed where tossed and muttered the delirious little wisp of a woman who was at once his mate and his saint.

Eve was so tiny, so fragile, so good! It wasn't fair that this bullying unseen spirit of illness should torture and harry her and sap the life of her—while the man who right blithely would have been burned to a crisp to please her, sat helpless at the bedside, unable to do a thing to drive forth the damnable visitant! Jeff Titus dwelt upon the theme of his own impotence to save her; he swore venomously, and in the peculiarly hideous diction of Kentucky mountaineer blasphemy.

There were doctors, of course, in the county seat of Duneka, thirty-two miles away. But they might as well have been in Germany, for all the good they could do the sick girl. Jeff could not desert Eve to go in quest of such a physician. Nor could he send one of his mile-distant neighbors. He knew that. It would be of no use.

Those city doctors had no convenient means for getting over the thirty-odd miles of half-inaccessible trail to his hinterland farm. Assuredly none of them was going to make the journey on foot or on

mule-back, leaving his town practice for days, at the behest of a hill-billy who perhaps could not or would not pay for the sacrifice.

Meantime, Eve was growing worse, steadily worse. Even the ignorant Jeff could see that. So too, apparently, could the only sharer of his day-and-night vigils—a huge and leonine dog which lay pressed close to the far side of the bed, and which all Titus' commands could not keep out of the sick-room.

This dog, Robin Adair, was the joy of Eve's heart—or he had been, when her heart still could hold joy and not merely fever and delirium. One of Eve's ragged hill-billy admirers had given the dog to her in the old days, when Robin was a roly-poly mass of tawny-brown fluff no bigger than a Persian cat.

The dog had grown into a shaggy giant. A passing seed-catalogue man had told Eve he was a collie—a breed of which she had heard, in a vague fashion, as emanating from Scotland. And she had named him Robin Adair after the hero of a Scotch song her mother had been wont to sing. He was Robin, for short. When she had married Jeff Titus, she had brought her beloved collie to live at the mountain shack.

From the moment his mistress fell ill, Robin had not once willingly stirred from her bedside. Drinking little, eating nothing, the great dog had lain there, his sorrowing brown eyes fixed on the small white figure in the big slab bed. But of late he was beginning to vary the vigil by low-voiced whines from time to time. And once or twice his huge body quivered as if in physical pain.

It was on the dawn of the fourth day that Robin got to his feet with a leap, and pointing his heavy muzzle skyward, set the still room to reverberating with a yell that was nothing short of unearthly.

Jeff, starting from his daze of misery, made as though to throttle the brute that had broken in on the invalid's unresting rest. Then, remembering Eve's affection for the collie, he contented himself with picking Robin up bodily and bearing him toward the door with the intent of putting him out of the house.

The door, before Jeff could reach it, was flung open from outside. On the threshold stood a ramrodlike figure in rusty black. The caller was the Reverend Ephraim Stair—Methodist circuit-rider for the up-State counties, and a man whose brain and heart had long since made him the blindly obeyed autocrat of his scattered mountain flock.

What's wrong, Titus?" was his wondering greeting as his sharp old eyes flashed from the man with the big dog in his arms to the eternally whispering little form on the bed. "I heard a scream, as I was riding past, and—"

"Oh, parson!" gasped Jeff in babbling relief, dumping Robin on the puncheon floor and gripping the circuit-rider by both hands. "For Gawd's sake, *do* suthin' fer her! She acts like she ain't goin' to git well none!"

Loud through the mountains were the praises of Stair's medical lore. Many were the tales of sick folk he had cured, when the old women had given them up and had begun gruesomely relishful preparations for the funeral. Jeff Titus clutched at his unexpected presence as at a life-belt. Half in superstitious awe, he glanced at the dog whose providential din had made the clergyman halt in his brisk ride from one county seat to the next.

Meantime, Stair had crossed to the bed, and on his knees beside it, was examining the stricken Eve. Jeff came up behind him, standing awkwardly and with open mouth, in expectation of some miracle.

But no miracle was vouchsafed. Instead the clergyman asked one or two questions as to the illness' course, felt the patient's pulse and her torrid cheek, then ordered his host to go and fetch in his saddlebags.

"My medicine-kit is in them," he explained. "And you can stable my horse, too. I'm going to stay."

"She—she's goin' to git on all right now you're here, ain't she?" pleaded Titus ingratiatingly, pausing at the door.

"Get my saddlebags!" was the noncommittal retort. "Jump! Then you can heat some water. Wait! Before you go, open those windows. And leave the door open. Isn't this poor child having enough trouble in breathing without your sealing the room hermetically?"

"Sick folks hadn't oughter be let have cold air tetch 'em, I've allers heard," Jeff defended himself, nevertheless obeying. "It gives 'em—"

"It gives them life!" retorted Stair. "Now get those saddlebags!"

Next morning Eve was perceptibly worse: the breathing was more labored; the fever blazed higher. And this in spite of Stair and his ceaseless ministrations. Stark despair tore at the husband's throat.

Following Stair, as the circuit-rider left the room for a moment to wash his hands at the pump, Titus demanded fiercely:

"She's a-aimin' to die, ain't she? Spit out the truth, man! I got a right to hear it!"

"I can't say," answered Stair, taking no offense at the furious manner. "She is in the midst of the crisis now. That is the turning-

point in such cases. If she rallies from that—Meanwhile we can only hope—and work. It is in God's hands. She—"

"In Gawd's hands!" mocked Jeff wildly. "In *Gawd's* hands, hey? You're Gawd-a'mighty fond of blattin' 'bout Gawd, parson! But I take notice He ain't a-doin' nothin' fer that pore sick gal of mine, in yonder. Why ain't He? Where is He, anyhow, if He cain't—"

"He is *here,*" answered Stair very quietly. "Here, and in that delirious girl's room, back there. He is wherever His children cry out to Him in sorrow and pain—just as, in your inmost heart, you are crying to Him now. If His children are too deaf or too scared or too noisy, in their grief, to know He has come at their call, then the fault is with their own stupidity, not with the all-pitying Father, who is carrying them through the ordeal."

He pushed past the mouthing Titus and went back to his post in the sick-room.

On the second morning Eve was in a heavy sleep. Her once-parched forehead was moist. Stair with a jerk of his thumb motioned Jeff out into the dooryard. On his withered face was the glow of a conqueror. Harshly, as if in doubt of his own self-control, the circuit-rider said:

"The crisis is past. She has turned the corner. I think she will live. The rest depends on nursing—on building her up. You may thank God, if you care to. Or if you still think He hasn't been here—"

"If He ain't," choked Titus ecstatically, "He sent a damn' fine sub— meanin' no disrespec'. I—I reckon, parson—I reckon you-all knows how small I feel 'bout blabbin' like I did. An'—an'— Oh, you're dead *sure* she's a-goin' to live? There—there ain't—there ain't nothing I c'n say! But—but—"

Incontinently Jeff Titus bolted around the side of the house and out of sight into the woods. When he returned an hour later, he was carrying a half-armful of kindling. Circumstantially and at some length he explained to Stair that he had spent the entire hour in looking for it. Stair accepted the explanation in grave credulity and forebore to glance toward the high-piled heap of kindling in the woodshed.

At noon Eve woke. She was very weak, very tired, very thin and big-eyed. But she was alive. And in Jeff's heart there was something that made him yearn to howl aloud in rapture and roll on the grass, and to join the church all over again, and to thrash some mythical man for speaking mythical ill of Ephraim Stair, and to turn over his farm and his savings to foreign missions, and to get very drunk indeed, and to buy Eve a gold watch.

Being a Kentucky mountaineer, and a Titus to boot, he contented himself with grinning down upon her and grunting:

"Feel better? That's nice. Be all right, pretty soon, now. Reckon I'd best be gittin' in some more wood, b'fore it rains again. So long!"

Robin Adair, like his master, knew Eve was on the way to health again. But being only a dog and not a mountaineer, Robin did not sneak out of the house to hide his emotion. He stood beside the bed, wriggling all over with puppyish joy, and wagging his plumed tail frantically every time his mistress looked at him.

ONE evening a few days later the two men were smoking together in the dooryard before turning in. Eve had been made comfortable for the night and was asleep.

She had gained a little ground, but her convalescence was maddeningly slow and uncertain to Jeff. The horror of the past fortnight or so had left him nerve-shaken. In spite of all Stair's assurances, he could not throw off his fear for her safety.

"She has been through a terrible illness," patiently explained Stair for the hundredth time. "Her body and her mind are exhausted. She lies there like that because she is resting. She is resting because nature is making her rest. She is steadily getting better. Bar accidents, she is practically out of danger. Her strength is beginning to seep back too. It would come back faster, of course, if she could rally her tired mind to some great interest in life—something that wouldn't tire or excite her too much. It would help Mother Nature along. An interest in life is a wonderful aid in convalescence. A bit of unexpected good news, for instance—"

"Good news, hey?" mused Jeff, his bony hands supporting his leathern face as he cogitated. "Good news? H'm!"

"Yes," returned Stair, "that, or something pleasant to look forward to. When she's well enough, you might take her to Duneka, or somewhere, for a little outing. Tell her so. It may brighten her to—"

"Nope," dissented Jeff. "It wouldn't. I tried, to-day. Told her she must git well right smart now, so's we c'd have a ja'ntin', somewheres. She said she was so tired, she reckoned she'd jest stay quiet to home a spell. It didn't brace her a wee peckle. Funny, too, 'cause jest before she was took sick, she an' me was projectin', a hull lot, on a trip we was plannin' to make. She'd got her heart real sot on it—'count of suthin she'd read into the Duneka *Chron'cle.* The fall County Fair is on, to Duneka, this week, you know. An' the *Chron'cle* told how they're lottin' on holdin' the State dawg-show there the fourth day of the fair. That's the day after to-morrer. The *Chron'cle* said there was to be real silver cups offered fer best dawgs of a lot of breeds. Collies was one of the breeds it spoke about."

"Well?" asked Stair in no special interest as Jeff paused.

"Wal," went on the mountaineer sheepishly, "you-all know how much store Eve sets by Robin, here. She thinks he's jest the finest dawg on thisyer planet. She was a-sayin' there couldn't be no finer dawg in the collie bunch, at the show, than what Robin is. An' she was honin' fer us to take him down there an' let him git a chance at that silver cup. Wal, whatever Eve hones fer, she's a-goin' to git—if it's gittable an' if I'm in reach to git it fer her. So I 'greed we'd take Robin to the show. She was all het up over the idee of a-gittin' that 'ere cup. An' she was a-sayin' how grand it'd be to have the paper print Robin's name as winnin' it, so's she c'd send a copy of the paper to her folks down Looeyville way, an' all that. Wal, that's all there is to it," he ended with a loud sigh.

"Why is that all there is to it?" demanded Stair with sudden inspiration. "Why can't you take the dog down to the show yourself, if he really has a chance for the cup? That cup, and the notice in the paper, would do more to stir Eve up and to renew her interest in life than any other good news I can think of. And it'll be something to look forward to. Go ahead and do it!"

"Good! Oh, good!" exulted a feeble little voice in the room behind them.

EVE had waked during their talk. And in her tones, as she applauded the plan, rang the first interest she had shown since the beginning of her illness. Stair, listening, shut his thin lips on a belated objection that had come into his mind while the mountaineer was applauding his chance suggestion.

It had just occurred to the circuit-rider that if Robin should not be adjudged worthy of the cup, the disappointment was likely to do the invalid more harm than a week of nursing could counteract. But it was too late to voice that warning now. Eve had heard. Eve was pathetically eager over the scheme. And kicking himself mentally for his own impulsiveness, the clergyman held his peace.

He knew nothing about dogs, from a show standpoint—and mightily he hoped Eve's estimate of her pet might be correct. But he doubted—more and more, he doubted. Collies fit to win silver cups do not often find their way into the mountaineer cabins in the Kentucky hinterland.

Timidly, Stair sought to wet-blanket the venture. But again he was too late. At last Eve had the desired interest in life, an interest that threatened to bring back her fever. The dog-show virus is potent, as any exhibitor can testify. It has a mystic lure. Jeff, once he grasped the idea, was swept off his feet by it.

THE fall County Fair at Duneka had begun its fourth day. That day's star feature was to be the "all breeds" dog-show, to be held in the Agricultural Building.

A gratifying number of dogs was benched in the main hall of the Agricultural Building early on the morning of the show. Two stewards were busy receiving the fast-arriving entrants, assigning to them their places in the double aisles of wire-partitioned and straw-littered "benches," and assessing late-comers the usual extra fees for "post-entries."

To these grievously overworked functionaries, in the thick of their labors, appeared a lanky farmer of the true mountaineer type. He was clad in store-clothes that sat on his angular figure as might a clinging directoire gown on a washboard. By a rope the hill-billy led a large and shaggy dog whose rough, tawny coat had been washed and brushed until it shone like bronze and fluffed out like the hair of a Circassian beauty.

"Collie dawg," announced Jeff, "owned by Miz Jeff Titus. Entered for the silver cup."

Patiently the stewards explained to him that a dog must be entered for one or more of the show's regular classes, and that the coveted silver cup was to go to the collie adjudged best in the whole show. They also informed Jeff that as his was a post-entry, it would cost him an extra fifty cents to exhibit his dog. He was told that in addition to this it would cost him a dollar for every class in which he might enter Robin.

As most of this was Greek to the puzzled exhibitor, one of the stewards asked if the dog had ever before been shown, and on receiving a negative answer, took one look at the uninterested Robin and suggested he be entered for the novice class alone.

As soon as he could be made to understand that a dog winning the novice class would stand as good a chance for the cup as would any other, Titus paid over his money and led Robin to the stall in the collie section corresponding to the number the steward had tied to the dog's collar.

After mooring Robin's rope to the ring in his wire-partitioned bench and getting him some water, Jeff had leisure to take in his odd surroundings.

Dogs—dogs—dogs! Everywhere dogs, more dogs than Jeff had known existed—of all breeds and sizes, from Peke to St. Bernard. The iron-girdered roof was reëchoing with their clangor. They were barking or yapping in fifty different keys, but all with the same earnestness.

Jeff saw that each breed had a bench-section to itself. In the center, to which the bench aisles converged, were two wood-and-wire inclosures, in each of which were a low central platform and a corner table and chair. On the tables were neat piles of red and yellow and blue ribbons alongside a record-ledger. Handlers were everywhere busy making their pets ready for the judging.

Crowds of onlookers had already begun to filter through the aisles. Jeff heard some one say that the judging was about to begin, and that collies were to be among the first breeds shown.

His general curiosity sated, Titus fell to examining the dogs which were to be Robin's competitors, and at once his mountaineer scowl merged into a grin. Here, forsooth, was nothing wherewith the splendid Robin need fear comparison.

Why, of all the nineteen collies on exhibition, there was not one within three inches of Robin's height, nor one which bore any real resemblance to him. These others were strongly slender chaps, with thin heads and tapering noses and tulip ears and slant eyes. Whereas, Robin's mighty head was almost as broad and heavy as a Newfoundland's, his ears were pricked like a wolf's, and his honest brown eyes were large and round. No, he most assuredly was not in the very least like any other collie entered in the show—or in any exhibition of thoroughbreds since the birth of time.

Poor old Robin Adair was probably more collie than anything else; he may even have been a shade more than half-collie. But in his veins ran also the mixed blood of many another breed, Newfoundland predominating.

"Look over there!" Jeff heard a dapper collie-handler in a linen duster say in guarded tones to a woman who was sifting talcum powder into her gold-and-white collie pup's fluffy coat. "Over at Bench 89! What is that thing, a dog—or a hippopotamus?"

As the woman turned to observe the luckless Robin, Jeff Titus strolled across to the man who had called her attention to the dog. His eyes mere glinting flares behind their lowered lids, and his lips twisted into something which looked like a smile and wasn't, he said softly:

"Beggin' you-all's pardon, mister, what was you a-happenin' to call my dawg?"

The man in the linen duster gave one glance at the leathern face peering down so intensely into his. Then shakily he made reply:

"I—I wasn't speaking of your dog, sir. I was speaking of the dog in the next bench to his. I—I read the number wrong. Yours is—a—a grand—a grand—collie, sir."

He gulped, and sped down the aisles on a new-remembered errand somewhere. Jeff turned back to Robin, his mind freed of its momentary angry doubt.

The collie classes were called a few minutes later. The first to be judged were, as usual, the male puppies. Jeff, watching the performance of the entrants, saw how the judging was done. First the dogs were made to march around the ring. Then, in ones or twos, they were placed on the platform while the little tweed-clad judge studied them and felt them all over. After that, the judge wrote certain numbers in the ring-steward's book and handed to the owner of the winning dog a blue ribbon; a red ribbon went to the owner of the second best, and a yellow ribbon to the third.

Every one of the several collie classes, it seemed, must be judged in that same deliberate way before the winners of all classes could compete for the rosette, the acquisition of which meant also the winning of the silver cup. Jeff began to chafe at the needless delay which must ensue before Robin could receive his merited prize.

Then, directly after the judging of the puppies, came the novice class. Along with only two other entries, Jeff Titus led the majestically unconcerned Robin into the ring. As he passed, a titter swept the quadruple line of railbirds outside the inclosure. Robin did not so much as look about him to locate the cause of the mirth. These fool city-folks were always laughing at nothing.

Nor did he note the glare, almost of horror, which the little tweed-clad judge bestowed upon Robin as Eve's adored pet paced into the ring. The judge eyed him with much the expression one might expect to see in the visage of a Supreme Court justice who has been asked to hand down an official opinion on a Gilbert and Sullivan paradox.

"Walk your dogs, please!" rasped the judge.

The parade started; Robin paced unconcernedly at his lanky master's side. As he was not a thoroughbred, his nerves were not of the hair-trigger order. The racket and the crowd and the new surroundings did not excite or terrify or make him profoundly miserable as they did some of the high-strung collies about him. Jeff observed this calm demeanor and was proud of his dog's bearing.

The parade was halted. The judge motioned Robin's two competitors to the platform, squinted at them for a moment, ran his hand over them, stood back and studied them—then handed to the owner of one a blue ribbon and to the other a red. The third-prize yellow ribbon he tossed back onto the steward's table. Then he motioned the trio from the ring.

The winners of the first and second prizes departed with their collies. The steward chalked up the next class on the blackboard. But Jeff Titus did not leave the ring. Eyes bulging, cheeks slowly turning from tan to brick-hue, he strode over to the judge.

"Look-a-here, you!" he rumbled in a blend of wrath and dazed incredulity. "What's the meanin' of this-yer? Are you aimin' to double-cross me? My dawg's wuth ten of them ornery critters. He's a heap bigger'n an' huskier, an' he's purtier to look at, too! What the blue blazes do you-all mean by treatin' him thisaway, you hard-biled shrimp? He—"

With much dignity the little judge turned his back on the angry Titus and started across the ring. But before he had gone two steps, Jeff was once more confronting him.

"Look-a-here!" snarled Titus, striving to keep himself in hand. "I ain't goin' to lay down under no frame-up! You judged crooked, with my dawg. I c'n prove it. Even if you didn't have the sense to see he was the best of the hull bilin', you was bound, anyhow, to give him the yaller ribbon fer third prize. An—"

"I was bound to do nothing of the sort!" rapped out the exasperated judge. "I am here to judge collies, not dinosaurs. I refuse to countenance the claim that your dog is a collie by giving him a third-prize ribbon, even in a class of three. So, in this class, I have deliberately withheld the third prize. Your dog is not a collie. The Lord alone knows what he is, but he's no collie. That's all. Clear out!"

The little judge had all the bristling pluck of a rat-terrier. And he needed it in facing this lean giant in whose slit-eyes the murder-light was beginning to smolder. Jeff half extended one windmill arm in the general direction of the judge's throat. Then he checked himself.

IT was going to be bad enough to slink home with no cup, but it would be tenfold worse to go to the hoosgow for mayhem. He pictured sick Eve's grief over such a disgrace, and his clenched hand dropped again to his side. Fighting with his temper, the mountaineer wheeled about and led the disqualified Robin out of the ring and back to the bench.

A sweet mess he had made of everything, he and that parson, up yonder! They had wrought on Eve's hopes and had made her so gloriously confident that her dear dog was going to sweep all before him and win the cup! She was lying at home this minute, her big eyes shining with anticipation, her vivid mind picturing the triumph-scene at the show. How confidently she would be waiting for that cup!

Jeff had sought so enthusiastically to work out Stair's theory of a "good news" cure! And how was the experiment to result? He must go home on the morrow and tell Eve not only that he had no cup to show her, but that the judge had actually refused Robin a third-prize ribbon, on the ground that the dog was a mongrel! What effect was that news going to have on a sick woman whose swift recovery depended on her spirits?

Knowing Eve as he did, Jeff was ready to believe it would undo most of her hard-won convalescence. And at the very least, in her weak state, it was certain to make her cry. Jeff would rather have faced a machine-gun nest than make his gallant little sweetheart cry. He began to swear, very softly but very, very zealously. And then his resourceful mountaineer brain unlimbered and went into action.

Presently he arose from the bench, patted Robin absent-mindedly on the head and slouched off toward the end of the hall, where, in a high glass case, were displayed the prize cups and the other trophies.

Long and minutely he scanned the glittering prizes, especially the cup engraved "Best Collie." And he spelled out the printed legend over the case—which proclaimed that the cups were supplied by the long-famous jewelry firm of Pinkus & Bernstein, of Republic Street, Duneka, Kentucky.

TEN minutes later, leaving Robin to shift for himself on his bench, Jeff was hiking toward the business streets of the mountain metropolis. He paused, for a space, at the bank, where he had a carefully scraped-together little account, and he drew forth a goodly share of that sum. Thence he made his way to the jewelry-store. After a half-hour of dickering, he emerged from the shop, bearing a bulky parcel.

Returning to the Agricultural Hall, he seated himself once more on the narrow bench beside the exultantly welcoming Robin, and proceeded to unwind the tissue wrappings of his package. Robin looked on in mild curiosity. His sense of smell had already told the dog that the parcel contained nothing of vital interest to him. Yet because he had been lonely and a little worried by Jeff's long absence, Robin evinced a polite concern in the undoing of the wrappings.

The last layer of paper was removed. To the dog's view was exposed a huge and gleaming silver cup, a cup with much chasing on its polished surface and with three handles and an ebony base. It was at least double the size of the cup offered by the committee for best collie.

"See that?" questioned Titus, holding the trophy aloft for Robin's inspection. "Forty-one dollars, that set me back. An' it'd 'a' been a heap more, only it was a left-over. Robin, if that cup don't tickle her suthin terrible, I'm a clay-eater. You-all won this yer vase to-day, Robin, by bein' 'best collie.' Jes' keep a-rememberin' that. I ain't never put nothin' over on her b'fore. You-all knows that, Robbie. But—I reckon it's wuth doin', this yer time. She—"

He paused in his low-pitched confidence to the blinking, sympathizing dog. Two men had halted just in front of him. One of them was carrying an apparatus which movie-camp memories told Jeff was a camera.

It chanced to be a moment when no less than two "Winners' Classes" were on in the show-rings. Accordingly the ringsides were banked deep with onlookers, and this secluded section of the aisles was wholly stripped of spectators. That was why Jeff had ventured to bring forth the cup from its wrappings. The sight of the two keenly interested men set him to scowling in dire embarrassment.

THE chairman of the dog-show committee was also one of the chief stockholders of the Duneka *Chronicle*. Wherefore the dictum had gone forth to the *Chronicle* city-room that the show was to be played up big, in both morning and evening editions. And the paper's best descriptive writer, one Graham, had been assigned to do some "human interest" stuff about it, in addition to the sporting editor's regulation account.

Graham was a good reporter, and he had a genius for human-interest yarns. But of dogs he knew little, and of dog-shows he knew even less. Yet gleaning such information on the subject as he could, he had set forth for the show this morning, taking along the paper's sole photographer.

Pausing near the front entrance to accustom their ears to the frightful din and to take a snapshot of the trophy-case, the two newspaper men had wandered down the first aisle into which their non-enthusiastic feet had chanced to stray. There, suddenly, Graham saw one of the human-interest bits for which he was always hunting.

Midway in an aisle labeled COLLIE SECTION sat a tired man, a typical mountaineer, beside a huge collie. And to the civilly interested dog the mountaineer was exhibiting pridefully a silver cup larger than any in the trophy-case. He was talking to the dog too, in a confidential whisper, evidently telling the collie what a splendid victory he had scored and how proud of him his master was. Here was human-interest stuff if ever Graham had seen it!

"Cup for best collie in the show?" asked Graham of the scowling hill-billy.

"Yep!" snapped Jeff Titus defiantly.

"Good boy!" exclaimed Graham, seeking by effusive geniality to break down the mountaineer's surly reserve. "He's sure one peach of a dog! What's his name? And what's yours?"

"His name," said Jeff with perilous courtesy, "is Robin—Robin Adair. He b'longs to my wife, Miz Jeff Titus—up Keytesville-way. She's sick, to home. I'm showin' him fer her. Got any more questions to pester me with b'fore—"

"Would you mind holding up the cup a second?" wheedled Graham, scribbling with a chewed pencil on a doubled wad of copy paper. "So! Thanks!"

Still defiantly, Jeff had held forward the cup for inspection, his free arm around the majestic Robin's shoulders. The camera clicked. Titus did not hear it, through the noise of a hundred barks and yelps. Besides, he was focusing his indignant attention on this slick-spoken opponent of his.

"Wal?" he demanded truculently. "Anything more you-all wants o' me? He's our dawg. An' he's good enough fer us. If you-all don't like him none—"

"But I do!" effused Graham. "A great dog, Mr. Titus! And"—his eye running along the collie section—"he must be close to championship standard, to have beaten all of these beauties. I'd like to ask you—"

"I ain't got nothin' more to say!" growled Jeff, half rising, and his yellow eyetooth began to show under his up-curling lip. "An' if you-all is aimin' to start trouble 'bout this yer cup—"

Graham was not aiming to start trouble. Not at all did he like the new expression, nor the voice, of this sulking hill-billy he had sought to patronize. With a signal to the photographer he moved rapidly away, continuing his progress down the aisle.

JEFF glared after him. If the man were going to inform the committee that Titus had bought a cup when he had not been able to win one, why, let him do it. Jeff wasn't going to run away. So he held his ground, feeling very wrathful, but somewhat scared. He restored the cup to its wrappings. It would be handier to carry in that way, should he be ejected from the show on account of his fraud.

But no one ejected him. Except that people paused now and then, through the course of the day, to stare amusedly at poor Robin (and to straighten their faces in comical haste as they encountered Jeff's glower), no one molested Titus.

At four in the afternoon Jeff's raw nerves could stand the strain no longer. Untying Robin from the bench, he led him to the entrance of the hall. There he sought the superintendent of the show.

"When c'n me an' my dawg git outen here an' traipse home?" he asked.

"No dog is supposed to leave the building before ten o'clock to-night, when the show ends," replied the superintendent, adding with a cryptic glance at Robin: "But I don't think I need hold your entry to those rules. Go when you like."

The cup under his arm and Robin at his heels, Jeff departed. He had come to town on muleback, the dog running alongside. Even at the best pace he could scarce hope to get home very much before midnight. He had come to Duneka on the preceding day and had planned to stay until next morning. But already his imagination was afire with the thought of bursting in on Eve that very night, with the glittering trophy. So he bent his steps toward the stable where he housed his mule.

ACROSS the fair-grounds from the cityward gate a bevy of

barelegged newsboys was scampering with armfuls of newspapers—copies of the *Chronicle's* two afternoon editions. One of them ran past Jeff.

Jeff's keen mountaineer eyes chanced on a dark blotch near the bottom of the swaying sheet's first page. With an unbelieving gasp, he stopped short in his tracks and bawled to the fleeing newsboy to come back.

The boy returned, holding out the paper. Jeff snatched it from him, riveting his incredulous gaze upon that dark blotch on the front page. The blotch, at close range, resolved itself into a two-column cut—a picture of Robin, lying majestically at full length in his bench, his trustful gaze fixed on the lank man who squatted beside him and who held aloft an ornate silver cup!

Above the cup ran the caption: "A PRIZE-WINNER AND HIS PRIZE." Beneath the picture were the lines:

"Mrs. Jeff Titus' Robin Adair: Winner of Cup for Best Collie in Show."

Doubled, in single-column space under this, was one of the two-stick "human-interest" stories with which Graham was wont to strew the *Chronicle's* pages. Jeff's fascinated eyes tore themselves from the picture and caught a glimpse of his own name midway of this explanatory yarn. He read the sentence containing the name, then the next line or so. Slowly and painfully he spelled out:

> Mr. Titus exhibited the dog for his wife, who is ill at their Keytesville home. With characteristic mountaineer modesty Mr. Titus refused to sound his splendid exhibit's praises. When congratulated by throngs of admirers who paid homage to the peerless Robin Adair, Mr. Titus' sole comment on Robin's sensational victory was:
>
> "He's good enough for us!"
>
> Robin Adair was good enough for the judges, too, and good enough to win over one of the finest aggregations of high-bred collies ever shown in this part of the South.

The brief story switched back to the human-interest note—to the man's evident rapture in the triumph of his sick wife's pet, and his shy pride in the magnificent cup. But Jeff read no more just then.

Whirling on the impatiently waiting newsboy, he demanded thickly:

"Gimme all them newspapers you're totin'! An' then scuttle off an' fetch me a dozen more! Scat!"

Again he stared in idiotic bliss at the smudged two-column cut. What did it matter to Jeff Titus that the picture and its erroneous caption were to be "lifted out" of the next edition, and that Graham was to incur the sharpest call-down of his career for the break he had made?

Not three copies of the *Chronicle* a week made their way to Keytesville. And even should the next day's full account of the dog-show reach the Titus region, no mountaineer in the State would possess the technical show-lore to decipher the cryptic "summary of wins" and thus learn of Robin's defeat.

No: in the mountains, the printed word was accepted as gospel fact—by those who had education to read it. And its pictures were accepted as such by those who had not bothered to master the effete arts of reading and writing. Jeff was going to take home enough papers to go around the whole sparse neighborhood, in addition to those which were to be mailed to Eve's people at Louisville and to any other distant kin or friends of hers.

Not in the very least did Jeff Titus understand the meaning of this newspaper tribute. Nor did he bother his overwrought brain about it. He had the required "good news" for Eve. He had printed and pictured proofs thereof. If this didn't help along her tardy cure, by leaps and bounds—

"I ain't never lied to her yet, Robin!" he informed the prize-winner as they ambled homeward at dusk over the purpling miles of hilly trail. "Nor yet I don't aim to now. We'll walk in on her, with the cup. An' when she asks, all pleased an' tickled-like, 'Why, whatever is this yer fer?' we'll jest stick a copy of the newspaper up in front of her. I'm bettin' the R'cordin' Angel is due to strain his pore ears till they ache him, if he 'lots on ketchin' *me* tellin' a lie to that Gawd-blessed gal!"

The Unmarrying of Veeder

CRAIG VEEDER was swimming. He was swimming away from matrimony.

It was a long swim, but a queer exhilaration kept him going. The same exhilaration made him forget that the West Indian waters contain sharks of every respectable dimension and of keen appetites for white meat.

To a casual observer (such an observer would have needed a night-glass plus a searchlight), Veeder would have seemed merely a luckless man battling for his life against long odds, in the midnight waters of the Florida Straits, eighty miles southeast of Key West, and some ten miles off the northwestern Cuba coast.

But casual observers usually see things wrong. Perhaps not one such observer in a thousand would have changed places, just then, with Craig Veeder. Yet assuredly Craig Veeder would not have changed places with one observer in twenty thousand. He was swimming away from matrimony.

At twenty-seven, Veeder had been meshed in wedlock's net. He had not known he was meshed. He thought it was he who had done the meshing; for he had had the very deuce of a time in winning Reina Burr—the very deuce of a time. It had been one of those touch-and-go courtships wherein the man does not feel really secure of his victory until (in reply to an intoned query from a man in gray whiskers and white surplice) the girl has said: "I do!"

Craig had been making his way in New York's business world, at a pace all but phenomenal for so young a man. He had graduated from boarding-house to hotel and from hotel to bachelor flat and Jap servant, all in seven brief years of Napoleonic labor.

Then he had met Reina Burr.

Reina was a home-body of a damsel who kept house for her old parents and who kept it with a daintiness and exquisite efficiency that did queer things to Craig's heart. You see, Veeder had lived, home-less, ever since his mother's death. And after seven years of boarding-house and hotel and hit-or-miss bachelor-flat life, there is a positive magic about a real home, and especially about the woman who is the keynote of that home.

More lonely and homeless youths have been ensnared by the sight of a pretty girl setting a table or pouring tea or fussing over a chafing dish than by all the professional sirens or brilliant talkers since Ninon de Lenclos. And so it had been with Veeder. His home-loving and home-lacking heart had gone out with a bound to the charming little home-maker from the very first. And he had laid instant siege to her affections.

Craig had tried to make it a whirlwind wooing. But in a soul as methodically neat as Reina Burr's, whirlwinds have scant place. Reina was not to be taken by storm—which redoubled Veeder's longing to win her. And so he laid siege, in due and ancient form.

Several things during the courtship might have warned him, but a man whose brain is in condition to assimilate warnings is seldom the man who goes a-courting. For example: Reina and her mother came to tea, once, in his bachelor apartment. Craig and the Jap had spent hours in trying to make the flat shipshape for the visit. A score of interesting pictures and other trophies had been cached, safely out of sight. The rooms had been rearranged and swept and dusted and aired; and they were full of flowers and soft lights, for the Occasion. Yet the moment Reina and her mother entered the cozy living-room, the girl halted and sniffed the blossom-laden air.

"Whew!" she complained laughingly. "What a fearful smell of tobacco, and—and of drinks too! I don't see how you can breathe in it all day!"

Ten minutes later he had seen her pass a furtively exploratory finger across the edge of the chimney-piece and then examine the pink digit for dust-traces—which, of course, she found. And he caught her frowning at a whitish ash-smudge on the rug under the tea-table.

He felt ashamed of his own nonobservation and of his Jap's incompetence, and he fell to dreaming blissfully of a spotless home, with this angel of home-making to preside over it.

A few months later, Craig and Reina were married.

Reina used to tell Veeder's bachelor friends, very merrily indeed, that she had "taken him, out of pity," in order to remove him from the pigsty surroundings in which she had found him living. The bachelor friends laughed dutifully at the joke, but it did not incline them the more warmly toward matrimony.

The Veeders had not been married a month, before Craig first began to feel the galling of the chain. No, Reina was not a shrewish comic-paper spouse. She was a loving and winsome wife, who adored her husband and strove to make his home happy. That was the trouble. Reina's idea of a happy home was an orderly home.

And in her eyes an orderly home was a home where all was in order. There must be no ghost of tobacco-reek noticeable anywhere in the rooms. To spill a half-inch of cigarette-ash on chair or rug was as reprehensible as to spill the same quantity of ink or vitriol thereon.

Furniture had its own appointed places in the house; and the careless leaving of a wall chair near the bay window or the shifting of a table to a less sunny corner—these were deplorable deeds which must be commented on and corrected, if the home were not to degenerate into such another pigpen as the bachelor flat had been.

Also, if a great idler of a man should throw himself wearily on the library couch, it meant just that much more trouble to the poor tired little housewife, who must afterward smooth out the couch and beat up and rearrange the pile of crumpled cushions.

These were but a few of Reina's myriad safeguards against defilements of divers sorts—defilements which ranged from the tracking of mud into the front hall to the wiping of horrid razor-blades on the very newest guest-towels in the third-floor bathroom.

She did not rail at Craig for committing all these atrocities. She just looked pained, or else she spoke in the kindliest correction—which made Veeder feel far more like a vile sinner and a rough-neck than would all the scolding on earth, besides robbing him of the privilege of getting good and mad.

There were other things, too: when a man had a sweet home and a loving little wife waiting there for him, what was the sense of his spending a whole evening every week or so away from that home? When the aforesaid home and wife were eager to welcome him, how could he be so silly as to want to stop, for an hour or more, at his club, on the way from business, and then come in all redolent of tobacco and stomach-destroying cocktails? These faults were set right as tactfully and as gently as were those of Craig's non-housebrokenness in the matter of furniture and razors and ashes.

But terrible is the final power of gentleness. It is fifty times as formidable as a tirade or tears. It is the ultimate victor in every marital duel.

And so it proved, with Craig Veeder. By the third year of his married life, he had ceased to be a mere man and had insensibly become a Husband—even as a corruptible young politician might cease to be a Representative and become a mere Congressman.

Scarce realizing his own gradual change, he learned to leave furniture where he found it, to steer well clear of the most tempting cushion-strewn couches, to do his smoking at the office or on the street and never where it could taint curtains or smudge the rugs. He learned to follow the line of least resistance, by eschewing the once precious twilight hour of cocktails and chat at the club, and to come home at once from work. He learned that there is absolutely no sense or excuse for a happily married man to spend a single evening a week with a lot of rowdy men when there is a dear little wife at home who is only too glad to go with him anywhere she may choose, and who is worrying herself sick whenever he is out late by himself.

Oh, Craig learned a whole lot of useful things, without so much as realizing that he was learning them! The chain was full-forged and welded into place before he realized how fast it could bind.

And so his six years of wedded existence had dragged along. Only one night in all that time had he and Reina been apart. And that was the night she had to go on ahead of him to the bedside of her mother, who was dying. Only two evenings had the couple spent asunder in the past three years. Both of those were when actual rush of business kept Craig at the office until twelve.

Unconsciously, as time went on, Veeder had adapted himself to all this, as might the once-wild ox to his routine of stall-and-plow. Long since, Craig had become a Husband. And outside of business hours he was nothing else—which brings us by prosy and needfully long degrees to our story.

It was at the end of the sixth year of their married life that Craig Veeder's nerves went bad from a too-long strain of work. His doctor ordained for him a sea-voyage. To the worn-out man the prospect of lying in a deck-chair for fourteen hours a day, for an indefinite number of days, was a pure delight.

But Reina could not see it that way. She was an abominably bad sailor. Even a rowboat trip across a mile-wide inland lake was enough to lay her up for the day. She had been to sea only once in her life. And it was months before she had recovered from that. There are a few such people—folk to whom water-travel is not only a torture but a physical mishap. Reina was one of them.

Yet the doctor's orders stood—and the mandates of two consulting specialists backed them. And because she loved her husband, Reina at last consented to his making the journey without her. Craig met her surrender halfway.

He arranged to go through the West Indies in a touring steamship which would carry him at a leisurely pace to Nassau and Havana and Porto Rico and Kingston, and would enable him to debark at Miami, there to take a train home and thus shorten his absence from his waiting wife. In this fashion he could have eight or more days at sea and yet be gone from home less than a fortnight. And he went.

UNDER the mystic healing of the ocean, Veeder's racked nerves at once began to heal. He slept like a dead man, for more than twelve hours of each day, sometimes snoozing in his deck-chair, sometimes in his bunk. To his amazement, he discovered a new interest in food, and tobacco once more tasted like something besides dead leaves.

To his equal surprise, he felt ridiculously like a schoolboy on vacation. There was no gently protesting voice to chide him awake when he chanced to snore. There was nobody to look on in mute reproach when he took a second helping of some indigestible dish or when he lighted one cigar from the butt of another. There was no one to make him ashamed of piling his stateroom's upper berth high with a disorderly array of clothes—of smoking in bed, of strewing ashes in regal fashion all over the stateroom floor, or on the deck around his chair.

It was a queer feeling to be free—to be absolutely free, to know that the chain had fallen away and that the galled spots were beginning to skin over. With a twinge of shame at his own disloyalty, Craig found himself reveling in it all. As he grew better, he even sat up one night until the approach of dawn, in a smoking-room card-game.

As the night waned, the battle waxed fiercer. Veeder left the table at two o'clock in the morning nearly three hundred dollars ahead of the game. And there was no one to reprove him for this, his first card-night in four years! He was magnificently free.

Off Cape Hatteras, that tossing graveyard of so many anti-seasick resolutions, the ship's leisurely southern progress had become still more leisurely, by reason of bucking the five-mile-an-hour urge of the purple-blue Gulf Stream. Two days later, dodging the Gulf Stream by running close inshore, the vessel passed so close to the drearily monotonous east coast of Florida that Veeder could read with naked eye the historic sign of *"Welcome to Our Ocean!"* and could study the Palm Beach bathing suits. That same day, the recurrent schools of porpoises that butted playfully through the ever-bluer waves off the weather bow were varied by skittering swarms of flying fish which skimmed like tiny gray-and-white airplanes over the nearer waters. And a gray-green sea-turtle spun clumsily astern in the steamer's wash.

Thenceforward glowed the drowsy warmth of half-tropic seas, and Craig Veeder felt new life seeping into his nerve-tired body. He was getting well. He was getting well fast. And always increasing, was that odd sense of newborn freedom. He had been a Husband so long that he had well-nigh forgotten how to be anything else. But he was learning, every hour. And the knowledge was as strong wine to his groove-held brain. He was gloriously happy. He began to look back with wondering disgust at his own sheeplike meekness in wasting so many golden years in the endless routine of home-to-office and office-to-home. It was wonderful to be free—to be alive once more, to be a man among men, not merely a Husband. And growingly he hated the very idea of a return to his six-year bondage.

Twice more, during the southward voyage, he varied his deck-and-berth drowsing by night sessions in the smoking-room. There were three over-rich South Americans on board who fancied vastly their own prowess at poker. There was also an American tobacco-man who was on the way to inspect a new Porto Rico plantation. These four were inveterate poker-players; and they welcomed Craig Veeder to their table. And whether by reason of his long abstinence or by greater prowess, Craig was a steady winner at these poker-sessions.

ABOUT midnight, after the third evening of such play, Veeder left the smoking-room. He was comfortably tired. The night was hot; and the smoking-room was stuffy. Craig walked the deck alone, to fill his lungs with the sea-air and to lure drowsiness to his poker-excited system.

He had made something of a killing at the green table this evening. Indeed, with his two preceding nights' winnings, he had gleaned a little more than eighteen hundred dollars. This, with fifteen hundred dollars in bills; which he had brought along for the expenses of the trip, swelled the ready money in his pockets to nearly thirty-four hundred dollars—a foolishly large sum to carry loose, as he now realized. He decided that next morning he would stow the bulk of it in the purser's safe.

The phosphorus was glinting eerily along the swirls of foam churned up by the motion of the ship. Leaning over the rail, Veeder watched it in idle interest. Then a memory of earlier seafaring days reminded him of the swish and eddy of phosphorus in the immediate wake of a steamship. On a night like this, and in waters like this, such a display would be well worth the seeing.

Craig walked aft to the ladder connecting the promenade deck with the second-cabin quarters. Descending, he reached the second-cabin deck and went along its deserted expanse to the after rail.

There he leaned over once more to watch the flame-play of the phosphorus—so bright that it seemed to cover the wake with a tossing mantle of fire-blue. To the left, some ten miles across that sleepily rolling waste of star-strewn ocean, lay the low green downs of Cuba, with the bumpy knobs of the Matanzas hills far behind them. Havana itself was not twenty miles distant.

His foot on the rail, and looking down again from his effort to see the outlines of the coast, Veeder began brooding on his own near-by return to the slavery of home-life. With strange fierceness his very soul rebelled at the idea. His brief taste of freedom had made him drunk with the joy of it. And within a week or so he must return to serfdom. He must return, healed in health, but hotly resentful in spirit, to the career of a Husband.

And he would find it harder than ever to get back into his wonted ways of neatness and routine and meek submission after this taste of freedom. But soon, as he well knew, he would slip into the old groove and be once more a plodding bondslave to the daily grind. And all the time the world of gay freedom would be stretching out its arms in vain to him. It was not fair! He hated the thought.

Veeder saw the phosphorus break into a hundred scattering sparks as a porpoise dived through the blanket of pale blue flame. He leaned farther outboard to watch the pretty phenomenon. There was a simultaneous lurch of the light-laden vessel as a lazy groundswell caught her amidships. The lurch added the fraction of an inch needful to make Veeder lose his precarious balance athwart the rail.

OVER he went. As he threw out both arms in a vain attempt to clutch at something which should steady him, his heels came in fleeting contact with the stern gunwale. By instinct, he kicked with all his strength, and hurled his body sideways; at the same time shouting at the top of his lungs. The kick and the sideward lunge carried him clear of the thrashing twin blades of the propeller. But the wake-eddies sucked him far down under the surface, where for an instant, he spun like a teetotum in the milk-warm foam. Then his head emerged; and he made a futile clutch for the spinning rope of the taffrail log. He caught for it by mere guesswork and instinct. And he missed it.

Then—he was panting and sputtering, alone in that star-splashed expanse of warm ocean, ten miles from land and with the lights of the departed ship dwindling into distant and blurring specks.

At such times a man's mind is popularly supposed to dwell on every detail of his past life. This it does not always do, as many a nearly drowned survivor can testify. Yet it is certain that the brain, in a crisis of that sort, works along one abnormal channel or another—as did Craig Veeder's.

For one thing, Craig found, to his own mild surprise, that he was not in the very least frightened. Never had he been less nervous or alarmed. It seemed to him the most natural and commonplace thing imaginable that he should be swimming along, with no special effort, ten miles from shore and with all his clothes on.

Yet, quite as calmly, he realized that he was at the crossroads of life. Good swimmer as he was, it was quite possible that he might lose his strength or miss his direction, and so drown, before he could reach shore. Somehow this possibility did not trouble him at all. He had a feeling he was not going to drown. And a newer and far more powerful emotion swept the very thought of this out of his mind. For, Veeder was smitten by a veritable inspiration.

He would be missed, on board, before the ship could make port. He would be found gone. It would be supposed, of course, that he had fallen overboard and had drowned. Word to that effect would be cabled home. He was officially dead.

That meant he could enjoy his new-found freedom as long as he might choose to. It meant the shackles were stricken forever from his limbs. He was a free man. Through no sin of his, he had been lifted out of serfdom. With a new name, he was at liberty to start life afresh—a new life of glorious and unhampered freedom.

Not only was he free; but he had, in actual cash on his person, no less than three thousand, three hundred and some dollars, wherewith to enjoy that liberty and to make his new start. To not one man in a million is given such a chance. Craig thrilled at his own good fortune.

Then he thought of Reina. But in that period of strange mental aloofness he could not summon up an atom of remorse at the picture of her desolation. His will was made in her sole favor. She was well-to-do in her own right. She would not suffer, financially, by his passing!

Gladly would he have spared her the anguish-shock of learning he was dead. But this, as he understood, was quite beyond his power. Before he could reach shore, his absence from the ship must be discovered. News thereof would be sent north at once by wireless—by cable from Havana, at latest. In either case Veeder would not be in time to intercept it.

He could not spare Reina the horror of hearing he had been drowned. She must hear that, in any event. And the first of her grief would be past before a denial from him could possibly reach her. Since she must suffer the primal agony of his loss, he could afford to let her go on grieving for him as dead. After all, it was not as though some brute had spilled ashes on her newest rug.

She was still under thirty. She was good to look at; she was childless, and comfortably rich. There would be plenty of men eager to console such a widow. Perhaps among them there might be a man who did not mind living in a home that was kept as cheerlessly neat as a new bandbox.

Craig Veeder turned his mind exultantly toward the future. He was swimming shoreward, and every long, easy stroke was carrying him just that much farther away from matrimony. If every stroke were also carrying him nearer to death—well, let it go at that! There were, perhaps, worse things for a tired man than death.

That morning Veeder had changed into a Palm Beach suit, summer underclothes, white silk shirt and socks and white buckskin shoes. Such a costume, apart from the shoes, which Craig now proceeded to kick off, is almost as easy for a strong man to swim in as is a bathing suit. Veeder was about to discard his coat too, but he remembered

in time that a goodly portion of his money was in that garment's inner pockets. So he kept it on.

After an hour of desultory swimming his unaccustomed muscles began to tire. He turned over on his back, to rest by floating. As he lay thus, he heard a drowsy voice raised in a droningly monotonous minor-key Spanish song. Treading water, Craig upreared his head to look about him.

There, drifting lazily in his general direction, was the patched sail of a Cuban fishing-smack.

Veeder squandered a goodly slice of his remaining strength in a bellowed hail which brought the steersman's minor-key ditty to an abrupt stop and wrung from the interrupted singer a highly spiced volley of frightened patois Spanish oaths.

Three minutes later Craig Veeder was crawling wearily aboard the smelly boat and was explaining in very bad Spanish to its gaping occupants that he had tumbled off the deck of his own yacht, which had cleared Havana that afternoon. He said he was Bruce Hawarden, an Englishman, connected with the British consular service in Cuba, and that he dreaded the laughter of his colleagues, should the story of his silly misadventure become known. Wherefore he offered his rescuers two hundred dollars to set him ashore in Havana and to keep their mouths shut.

How much of his yarn the fishermen believed, he did not know or care. But they took one look at the wad of wet money he flashed on them in the lantern flare, and they gave eager consent to his request.

Two hundred dollars in one lump is an all but mythical sum to a ragged Cuban fisherman. And the boat-folk made no further cavil at carrying out the wishes of so princely a passenger.

THE sun was just shoving over the edge of the eastern sea-line when the fishing-smack crawled around the promontory, under the lightsome shadow of Morro Castle and nosed into Havana harbor. Craig Veeder, his clothes rough dried, his feet in a huge pair of disreputable slippers lent him by one of the boat-men,—stood in the prow and stared open-mouthed at the glory revealed to him. Perhaps there are more beautiful stage spec-tacles than the entrance of

Havana harbor at sunrise. But Veeder had twice crossed the world without seeing such. In a trance of wonder he stood drinking in the splendor of it all, while the boat slouched across the bay in long tacks to its anchorage below the Malecón.

In another hour the castaway was climbing a flight of slippery green stone steps onto a landing-stage which faced a grand-opera-scenery plaza. His voyage was over. His new life was ready to begin.

Out in mid-harbor to westward swung at anchor the white ship from which he had fallen overboard less than eight hours earlier. Recalling the vessel's schedule, Veeder knew she was due to sail at noon. That meant he would be in no peril of recognition from any of his fellow-tourists. All he need worry about doing, by way of safe-guard, was to remain under cover for another few hours. This he proceeded to do.

Hailing a closed jitney, Craig drove to an outfitting shop at the lower end of the Obispo, which he remembered from an earlier visit to the island. There he bought new clothing and hat and shoes. He filled his pockets with fat black oily cigars (which would have cost him from twenty-five to thirty cents apiece in the States, and which he purchased here at a price lower than would have been asked for certain brands of Connecticut cigars at home) and was driven to an obscure little hotel a stone's-throw from the Custom House.

On the roof of his hotel he breakfasted greedily on various native delicacies. After that, a three-hour nap, in a room with a stone floor and glassless windows and a ceiling twenty feet high, took away from Veeder the last traces of the night's fatigue.

At noon he fared forth from his hiding-place. A glance seaward told him the ship had gone. He was safe from exposure. With three thousand dollars in his pocket, he could launch out and enjoy his non-marital holiday.

The next twelve hours were one continuous delight. Craig wandered aimlessly through the O'Reilly and the Obispo and the kindred alley-wide streets that bristle with atmosphere. He reveled in the glimpses of mantilla-draped señoritas and in the franker views of ebony women who stalked abroad with thick cigars clenched between their jaws. He was waylaid by scores of little children and cripples who sought to sell him twenty-cent chances in the next drawing of the government lottery. He loitered to listen to vendors singing the praises of their wares to the tune of some new ragtime melody, or stood aside to let sugar-cane carts brush past him in the narrow byways.

Then, turning to the town's center, he dined in hungry luxury at the Inglaterra and thence wandered forth into the newly lamplit Prado—a show street which is transformed into a magic vista with the oncoming of night.

It was late when he got back to his hotel, and the day had tired him. Simple as had been his amusements since he landed in Havana, yet their accompanying sense of freedom, of perpetual liberty from his olden shackles, had given them an impetus which had told on his new-healed nerves.

VEEDER tumbled into bed, utterly worn out. But tired as he was, he could not sleep. He lay wide-eyed until the silences were broken by the before-daylight round of the clattering garbage-brigade, thence until the Cabanas bugle announced the dawn—and until the sleeping city was bustlingly astir with shout and rumble and with the clangor of innumerable bells.

The longer he lay there, the unhappier the man became. He was dumfounded by his own growing unhappiness. It was so illogical, so senseless, so foolish! Here he was, free, with plenty of ready cash and with the world of fun ahead of him. His dream of years had come true. The cramped surroundings of home were forever put behind him. The world of adventure, of jollity, of life and of women and of laughter, lay awaiting him. He had his heart's desire. The shackles were stricken from his soaring wings. And he was beginning this new life of his in a city where, if anywhere in the world, a man can have a good time.

Veeder told himself all these things. And the oftener he repeated them, the more wretchedly unhappy he found himself. And with his personal gloom now merged a feeling which presently eclipsed it. By this time, hours before this time, Reina must have received word of his death. While her cur of a husband had been idling away a jolly evening in this holiday city of the Antilles, Reina had been lying in the darkness, sobbing her heart out, in anguished grief for the death of the man she worshiped—had been whispering through her sobs a prayer to his spirit to come back to her and to listen to her heartbroken love-words!

The thought was like white-hot iron to the miserable man's soul. Freedom to him meant endless tragedy to Reina. He saw that now. She was a one-man woman, if ever one was. And he had wantonly deserted her.

He began to recall little pretty ways of hers, the childlike loving inflections of her dear voice. How bright and clean and comfortable she had kept his home, too! Not many wives would have slaved like that for a thankless and unappreciative husband! And how had he rewarded her love and her work and her sweet comradeship?

All at once Craig Veeder realized what was the matter with him, what had been the matter with him all night. He was homesick—hideously homesick!

He was missing Reina. He was missing her terribly. He was not enjoying this thing he had so blatantly called freedom! It might be all right for some men, for men who had never known anything better. But it was a sorry, shabby substitute for such a home-life as had been his for six heavenly years!

Now that he knew just what ailed him, Veeder stopped worrying. Things were as bad as they could possibly be. So there was no earthly use in mulling over them any longer. As soon as the cable-office should be open, he would send a message to Reina. And he would follow the message by the first available home-bound boat. This being decided, he fell into a deep sleep of fatigue. Nor did he awaken until long after noon.

WHEN he had bathed and dressed and eaten, Veeder made one more effort to revive his former yearnings for freedom. He would not cable Reina. At least, he would not do it until he had time to let his mood of remorse shift back if possible to that gorgeous holiday feeling of yesterday.

Still battling with himself, he made his way again to the center of the city. Crossing Central Park, he headed for the Inglaterra. Perhaps, somewhere in that cream-hued and arcaded Spanish block, there might be a cable-office. It would do no harm to inquire. At the Inglaterra desk or at the Telegrafo or at the steamship office between the two hotels, he could assuredly get full information as to the sending of cables. And he could buy a copy of the Havana *Post,* for the morbid pleasure of reading the news of his own death.

His step quickened. Through his self-imposed indecision, he knew he had made up his mind. He knew that life without Reina was worse than no life at all. He knew he was going to tell her so, in that cable-message, if it took half his cash to do it. He knew, too, that he was going to book passage aboard the *Mascotte,* for Key West, on the very next Florida-ward voyage of that snub-nosed gray-and-red straits ferryboat.

His pace quickened to something like a run. Out of the glare of yellow sunshine he bolted, like an accelerated rabbit, into the cool shade of the Inglaterra's lobby. And there, on the threshold, he collided with a white-clad woman who was coming out.

Craig mumbled a plea for pardon at his awkwardness and made as though to hurry on at the same blind speed. But at an exclamation from the white-gowned woman he halted in his tracks and blinked owlishly down at her.

The woman was Reina.

She did not seem at all surprised to see him. There were no signs of tears in her friendly upraised eyes.

"Why, Craig!" she was saying in loving welcome. "Where have you been all this time? I began to think you hadn't gotten my cable."

"Cable?" blithered Veeder, his face a mask of stark idiocy. "No. No cable."

"But I sent it, four days ago," she protested. "It ought to have been waiting for you when your ship touched here yesterday morning. I can't see why it wasn't. And"—a shade of perplexity clouding her level gaze—"if it wasn't, I can't see why you happen to be here, and not on your way to Porto Rico. I—I cabled that I was coming down by train to Key West, to meet you here; and that I'd get in on the *Mascotte* this morning. I did. And you weren't anywhere. I was just going out, to—"

"But—" sputtered the bewildered Veeder; then he strangled and stood staring in dumb wonder.

Reina flushed. Something more potent than mere perplexity, this time, clouded her upraised eyes.

"Oh, Craig!" she faltered. "Don't laugh at me! It really wasn't funny at all. It was awful. I stood it just as long as I could. And then I had to come. I couldn't be away from you any longer. I *couldn't.* I got to missing you so hard that it hurt like—like an ulcerated tooth, Craig. I couldn't stand it. All the seasickness that ever happened was better than that. So I came."

"But I don't—"

"The house seemed like a vault or a—an empty church," she went on. "Oh, sweetheart, when we get back, I want you to promise solemnly that you'll spill ashes on every rug we have, and roll over on every couch and do all sorts of things to the furniture..... And now"—with an effort at her wonted cheery calm—"come and show me what Havana looks like. I haven't had any eyes for it, till I found you."

"I haven't either," lied Craig, deliriously happy. "But we are due to find out mighty soon. Come along!"

The Dub of Peace

THIS is a historical romance—what the photo-play phrasewrights term "period stuff." Its action dates back to those hazy old years before 1912, when the world was young. That was the Payasyougoic Age; not to be confused in any way with the Neoflushic Period, which set in with the war. It was the dim era when office boys were still willing to begin the climb on five dollars a week. Shipping clerks wed and inaugurated families on eighty dollars a month or less—often less.

Good sirloin steak in that æon cost twenty-two cents a pound, and ice-cream sodas an extreme and war-taxless price of ten cents each. Sugar cost five cents a pound in quantities as limitless as trouble.

Bread and butter were still as much a chargeless feature of a restaurant meal as were water and pepper. Ali Baba's forty playmates had not yet imported from France that vile word, *convert.* Check rooms were in their infancy. A seaworthy business suit could be acquired for twenty-five paltry dollars. Frugal youths could court on twenty dollars a week and marry on eighteen.

Aged men still creep among us who can recall those wonder days. Yet this windy foreword may be needful to explain one or two price quotations, and so on, in the tale that is to follow, lest ultramodernists should imagine its scene laid in Utopia.

When the Gentlemen's Sons Association of West New York canvassed for patrons to its annual outing and games at Meissner's De Luxe Park, above Tarrytown, Old Man Ryle was coerced into buying two tickets. Not that Old Man Ryle yearned for such a strenuous day as was promised for the association's outing. He was past the age for that sort of thing—long past it. Indeed, he was past the age for any but a serene vocation. That was why he had accepted the job of night watchman at the Cavverly works.

Nor was it his way to lavish his wealth on tickets which he could not use. But this particular brace of tickets had been urged on Old Man Ryle by Buck Kevitt, and people had a way of doing what Buck asked them to. Not that Buck was winsome or magnetic or in any sense alluring. But he was not a nice chap to run counter to.

He would not have resented Old Man Kyle's refusal by a belt on the jaw or by any similar method such as had made his ticket canvass so supreme a success. But he was wholly equal to slipping into personalities that would have made Ryle yearn in helpless, senile fury for a flash of his own vanished fighting power.

It is easier to pay out good money than to be insulted loudly and luridly in the presence of the rest of the night shift, and Old Man Ryle paid. Then he conferred the tickets on Hy Becker, the tally boy, who had been tactful enough to remain silent as to the discovery of a cached mattress whereon Ryle was wont to repose when his night-watchman duties grew wearisome. And Becker, who had another date for the Sunday of the outing, passed along the two tickets to the first man he chanced to meet. This first man was Gil Manton, a shipping clerk in the Cavverly works.

Gil Manton, by the way, is the hero of this yarn, and a less heroic hero could not have been found in all the Cavverly employ. Gil was a big, slow-moving chap; long rather than tall, and weighing close to a hundred and eighty. He had piano-mover shoulders and lean thighs and deep chest and smoothly lank muscles, all of which sagged; nor was he ill to look on.

His build had won the mild interest of Pop Glyn, the one-time pork-and-beaner who had charge of the rudimentary gymnasium rigged up for the athletic members of the Gentlemen's Sons Association in the disused Number-Eight smelting shed of the Cavverly works. The association numbered its full roster from among the two thousand Cavverly employees, Buck Kevitt, head porter of the works, being its perpetual president.

Pop Glyn eyed Gil's goodly but neglected proportions with approval the first day Manton came to work, and he extended to him the full privileges of the gym. Being lonely and sociable, Gil dropped round to Number-Eight shed that evening. He had done a bit of calisthenic work in the Y. M. C. A. gymnasium of his home town up state, and he looked forward now to invigorating half hours on the parallel bars and with the chest weights to draw out the kinks of the day's hustling.

But the Cavverly gym held no such effete and mollycoddlish fixtures as these. In tiers on the slab wall hung bunchy and sweat-blackened twin boxing gloves in varying stages of decay. These and two fighting-weight punching bags and a medicine ball were the gym's only equipment. The concrete floor contained a twenty-four-foot ring with frayed canvas ground padding, and a wrestling mat whose coco fiber was stamped and rubbed to iron. Between these main appurtenances was space for two or three pairs of men to box or to wrestle while more important bouts might be in progress in ring and on mat.

The gym did not impress Gil. Still less was he interested in it when he found that four-fifths of its habitues went there to box or to settle grudges with five-ounce gloves, and the remaining fifth to wrestle. In vain did Pop Glyn point out to him the joys of these evening pastimes. In vain did the old third-rate pugilist relate the time-crusted custom of the works which decreed that any two Cavverly men who had a violent difference of opinion must settle such dispute in the gym ring and in the presence of so many of the rest of the workers as might care to attend the bout.

Glyn descanted loudly on the joys of such finish fights, and on the splendid effect they had on the morale of the force in keeping down permanent ill feeling and hold-over grouches. A square scrap, and the quarrel was at an end. Gil Manton was not interested in this fight custom any more than in spending his spare evenings being slugged in friendly boxing bouts or slung round a germ-ridden wrestling mat, and to Pop Glyn's open contempt he did not drop in at the gym again. He even refused during his one visit to put on the gloves. He explained very politely that he had taken boxing lessons at his home Y. M. C. A. for one term, and then had given up the sport because he hated it. Boxing did not appeal in the least to Gil. It was too much like real fighting. He could see no joy or sense in letting some roughneck punch him all over the northern half of his lazy body with a stinging or numbing glove, and he took even less pleasure in punching the other fellow.

He was a peace-loving chap, was Gil—a big, gentle, friendly, nonassertive boy who preferred any day to knuckle under sooner than to start trouble. He was not a coward in the common sense of the abused word. He simply was averse to any form of brutality. He went on much the same principle as the child that sneaks out of taking a dose of castor oil—not that the oil is dangerous or terror-inspiring, but because the very notion of it is sickening. So Gil passed up the gym evenings, and for a space mooned gloomily round his boarding house at night. Then in time Kitty Ryle, a stenographer in the export department, quarreled fiercely with Buck Kevitt, who had been wooing her in desultory fashion, and she deigned that day for the first time to notice the shy friendliness of Gil Manton.

After his initial stammering delight in the aloof maiden's new cordiality, Gil took to calling at Old Man Ryle's flat twice a week, and once he escorted Kitty as far as Coney Island. He was very, very happy. It seemed wonderful to be so happy. Out of his eighteen dollars a week he began awedly to lay aside from two to five dollars as a secret house-furnishing fund, and at least once a week he bought fifty-cent seats for Kitty and himself in the orchestra section of that refined local palace of vaudeville, the Olympium. After the show always there was supper at Walker's Elite Restaurant—Tables Reserved for Ladies—and seldom did the feast include anything less lavish than fried oysters and ice cream. The check often did hideous things to a whole dollar bill, but Gil Manton was no piker.

It was to this unheroic hero that the tally boy gave the pair of dollar tickets to the Gentlemen's Sons Association's annual outing and games. From his casual experience with the Gentlemen's Sons, and especially with their doughty president, Buck Kevitt, Gil felt no impulse to attend their picnic. He was minded to pass along the undesired tickets to someone more keen about such affairs. But it chanced that he called on Kitty Ryle, and this shifted everything.

"Dad must be losing his mind," the girl happened to say in the course of their desultory chat. "He told mommer and me at supper that he bought a couple of tickets for that outing next Sunday, and then that he gave 'em away. Here I'd been crazy to go to it, and the only reason I hadn't asked him to get a ticket for me was because I didn't like to make him hand out so much money, now that he's only got his night-watchman pay. But he ups and buys two tickets, and then never even gives his own family a look-in on 'em."

Gil was groping ruminatively in his inner coat pocket, eyeing her with an expression he deemed merrily anticipatory, but which seemed to Kitty merely an uncomprehending simper. Buck Kevitt had never been so dense. The girl smoothed back a frown of impatience and moved forward her batteries to a less masked position.

"Of course," she explained, "I could go and buy a ticket for myself, I s'pose. But I couldn't go there alone very well. And if I was to buy two tickets and take mommer with me—well, two big soft dollars out of a fourteen-dollar pay envelope is a lot for just a Sunday's fun, isn't it? Still, I'm kind of disappointed, and—what you got there?" she broke off with coy inquisitiveness.

Farmer's satin is an admirable material—for the price—but it has a nonskid surface. Hence it had been the task of more than several seconds for Gil to find and draw forth the two tickets that reposed far down in his inside pocket. He had meant to produce them with a flourish, but they stuck, and he had to yank them out. In the effort the corner of one of the tickets was torn. The other ticket fluttered floorward. Gil retrieved it and handed the pair to Kitty.

"Well, of all the wizards!" she cried in gleeful amaze. "Why, you must be a mind reader, Gil Manton! You've got that blindfold lady at the Olympium last week beat a mile. Thanks ever so much! But how sly it was for you to let me go on grouching away like that and never—"

"I thought maybe you'd kind of like to go," lied Gil happily. "That's why I bought 'em."

"Annual Outing and Games of the Gentlemen's Sons Association of West New York," she read raptly from the uppermost ticket's scarlet lettering. "E. J. Kevitt, President. At Meissner's De Luxe Park, Sunday, May Thirty-first. Admit One. Gents Assessed."

She laid down the passports to paradise and glanced archly at her smugly grinning adorer.

"Now that you've asked me to go there with you," she said with the air of imparting a deep confidence, "I'll tell you a secret. I had another chance to go. Another gentleman asked me only this noon— honest."

"Yep," said Gil fatuously; "I'll bet there isn't a feller at the Cavverly that wouldn't be tickled to pieces to have a swell girl like you go there with him. Yep."

And he relapsed into mooningly admiring silence. Irritated that he was not more keenly piqued at this hint of rivalry, Kitty went on: "It was Buck Kevitt."

"Huh?" queried Gill, his reverie of worship departing.

"You needn't turn up your nose!" rebuked Kitty, misreading the bothered aspect of his wide face. "Lots of girls are crazy about Buck Kevitt. He's just a head porter, of course. But he makes good money, and he sure knows how to spend it. Besides nobody'd dare look cross-eyed at any lady Buck was escorting anywhere. He's a terrible fighter. He used to be in the ring for a while, you know, till the Horton Law took away all the big money from the fighting game. It's sort of thrilling to go to places with a feller who could lick anybody else there and who's aching for a chance to do it. A girl'd be as safe with Buck escorting her," she went on for the pure bliss of watching her pacific swain writhe, "as if she had a comp'ny of the Nashn'l Guard along."

Gil's mind went back miserably to the scene which had inspired this feminine stab. He and Kitty had been coming out of the Olympium one night after the show, and a clumsy man in the crowd had trodden on the hem of Kitty's dress, tearing off a yard of the flounce. The stranger had then departed without so much as a word of apology, and Gil had replied to Kitty's hot question of "Are you going to stand for that?" by mumbling something about its being an accident and that there was no use starting anything. The girl had not spoken to him all the way to the restaurant.

"You see," she went on now, "I and Buck had a tiff. And he said things that any real gentleman oughtn't to said. I told him never to speak to me again, and he didn't till to-day. He can stay mad longer'n anyone else I ever saw. But he was waiting for me when I went out to lunch this noon, and he said he'd like to be friends again and would I go to the outing with him? I told him I wouldn't and I wasn't going to it at all. Won't he be just raving, though, when he sees me there with you?"

Gil was staring at the luckless tickets with much the air of grieved horror that might have been his had one of them bitten him. Well did he know of the warlike prowess of Buck Kevitt. The former mixed-ale fighter's name was one of terror throughout the foundry force of the Cavverly works. Though Gil himself was seldom brought into more than momentary personal contact with the roughneck head porter, he had winced in sharp aversion at the man's snarling attitude toward himself—an attitude born partly of instinctive dislike and partly of Pop Glyn's contemptuous report of Gil's aversion for the gym exercises.

Gil's imagination began to race. He could believe, in every detail, Kitty's forecast as to the way Buck would take her presence at the outing with another man, especially with one of the white-collar force, a clerk whose pay was far smaller than Buck's own.

"Maybe we'd have a nicer time down to Coney Island next Sunday," hazarded Gil. "I just as lief sell back these tickets and take you down there. I read in the paper where it told about a swell new stunt they've got at Luna. I guess we—"

"We're going to the outing," was Kitty's chilled-steel retort, "unless you'd rather I'd go there with Buck." Which somehow seemed to cut off all chance for repartee or argument.

His feet very cold and his palms very wet, Gil said good night and plodded homeward. Glumly he wondered as he lay awake why he had not taken up Kitty's taunting suggestion that she go to the outing with Buck instead of with himself. That would have solved the whole rotten

problem. Yet far down within him some strange voice fairly shouted that he would rather have been torn asunder by Kevitt's grappling-hook hands than to submit to such a thing, and the peace-loving youth wondered unhappily at his own perilous decision. It was not like him. He could not at all understand himself.

The outing that year was one of the most successful in the long bright annals of the Gentlemen's Sons Association. The day was clear and hot. The crowd was a record-breaker. The baseball game stretched into the twelfth inning. The sack race was the funniest ever run off. The beer was of heavenly iciness. The caterer had outdone himself—and there was a moon on the way home.

Also there was dancing, not only at the De Luxe Park pavilion during the day, but on the broad moonlit deck of the excursion boat on the return sail; and the band for the most part had remained sober enough to discourse reasonably rhythmic music for this wind-up dance.

Buck Kevitt had had a wakeful day. As president of the association and chairman of the entertainment committee and in divers other badge-adorned capacities he had been in fifty places at once. There had been endless minor details to arrange, problems to solve, people to bully, no less than three fights to stop and to refer to the proper future gym night; two recalcitrants to punch into Chesterfieldian courtesy and the association's erratic cashier to check up at short intervals. Thus by almost no maneuvering at all Gil Manton had been able to keep himself and Kitty out of the head porter's busy ken, and to put a living screen of several hundred revelers between him and themselves.

But on the homeward boat ride Buck relaxed. His work was done. His outing's triumph was assured. He could afford to enjoy the return trip after his own fashion. His temper and nerves grumbling a bit in the moment of reaction from a twelve-hour strain, he sought the soothing influences of the dance deck.

There at first glance toward the maze of swaying couples under the multiple strings of electric light his unbelieving eyes focused on Kitty Ryle. The girl of his alternating choice was fox-trotting with another man. She had refused Buck's olive branch invitation to the outing, and here she had attended it after all with someone else; not merely with someone else, but with that gangling snide of a shipping clerk who had shied at the brutality of the Cavverly gym.

Buck was tired—or as nearly tired as his tough body ever became. He owed himself some let-down from the day's long official self-repression. It was too late to mar the success of the outing by setting a bad example to other Gentlemen's Sons, and his jangled temper craved egress.

As the dance music ceased, and as the dancers were clapping for an encore, Gil Manton was aware of a large and assertive pair of shoulders which butted roughly between him and the gayly applauding girl. The band leader, his baton poised to signal the encore, dropped his stick and stared. People all round became similarly interested, for Buck's sudden action had but one meaning, and that meaning was as clear as day to the initiated crowd.

Gil took an uncomfortable step backward to give the cleaving shoulders more room. The shoulders resolved themselves into a broader back. The back was toward Gil. Buck was facing the fluttered Kitty.

"Well?" he questioned, his voice bull-like in its rumble.

"Oh, h'llo, Buck!" airily returned Kitty. "Where you been keeping yourself all day? "

"I been working like a dredging machine," he made answer, "so's you c'd have a fine time with this big piece of cheese here. What else'd I be doing? I wasn't good enough to come along with you, so you picked up this thing the cat brang in and took it along instead of me."

Turning from the indignant girl, he spun round on Gil.

"Heard what I called you, didn't you?" he demanded. "Huh? Well, it goes, and some more like it. Anything to say?"

Gil had nothing to say. He shuffled back from the undershot jaw that followed him up. He wished he had never come on the wretched outing. He tried to wish he had never met Kitty Ryle. But he could not quite accomplish that—and vaguely he wondered why.

"You're standing all over your feet," pursued Buck in berserk mirth. "Give 'em a rest a minute. I'll learn you how to do it."

Deftly he drove his elbow into Gil's quaking stomach, and in the same move set his heel behind Manton's. Back went Gil under the stomachic impact. By reason of Buck's heel his feet could not follow the rest of his body, and he sat down extremely hard in the middle of the dancing floor.

A guffaw of Homeric laughter from the Gentlemen's Sons greeted this quaint bit of repartee. One or two of the girls squealed, but there was more of excitement than of fear in the cries. Kitty flamed brick red, then went bone white, and she stared down eagerly at her reclining escort.

Gil noted the tense command in her look. He made as though to scramble to his feet. Buck grinned and stepped merrily toward him. Gil let his muscles relax. Kitty gave a little stifled gasp and turned away. Buck left his victim and ranged alongside her.

"Hey, there, p'fessor!" he summoned the band leader. "Cut loose with that ongcore spiel of yours! I and this lady friend of mine want to dance. C'm on, Kit!" he added as he caught her arm.

The girl tore free from his loving hold and ran almost sobbing toward the cabin. At the entrance she glanced back for an instant. Gil was still sitting in the middle of the floor. She worked her way to the bow of the lower deck and was one of the first dozen on shore when the boat docked. Nor could the shame-sick Gil or the ardent Buck find her to claim escort rights for the rest of the journey home.

So ended the annual outing and games of the Gentlemen's Sons Association, and so ended Gil Manton's bright dream of love. Yet Gil did one brave thing. He did it the very next evening. He went to call on Kitty. He had much to say, though he had not the remotest idea how to say it. He was saved any trouble of pleading, for Old Man Ryle met him at the door.

"Got onto your poor feet again, hey?" was the host's greeting. "Last I heard about you, you was giving 'em a rest and cluttering up a dance floor with the rest of you. But —"

"Can I see Kitty, please?" interposed the red and fidgeting Manton.

"Not unless you got X-rays behind them fearless little eyes of yours, you can't," was the calm reply. "Not unless you can see through two walls. Because Kitty said if ever you came here again you wasn't to be let in. That's her say so, not mine. But I'm not saying I blame her none, at that. You sure made plenty small of her, last evening, from all I hear. She—"

The old man checked himself, struck by the utter misery in the caller's stricken face. He eyed the unhappy Gil, speculatively for an instant, then resumed:

"What the blue blazes are you made of inside, anyhow, sonny? I heard about your looking sick when Pop Glyn asked you to the gym, and how you said you didn't get any fun out of watching folks slug each other, and I thought maybe it might be a joke. When I've heard how you always got out of the way when Buck Kevitt bawled you out at the works I figgered maybe you just wasn't int'rested in rough-house stuff. Lots of he men ain't. So I kept making excuses for you, because I kind of liked you. You got nice pleasant ways with you, and you never shut me up when I got to yarning. Like some does. Then—"

"Thanks," faltered Gil, humbly grateful for even this tempered weed of praise.

"Then," pursued Old Man Ryle, unheeding, "Kitty come home last night crying. I couldn't get a word out of her. Nor yet her mommer couldn't either, except that if ever you dared come here again you wasn't to be let in. That got me bristling up along the back, and I was figgering on doing a stunt at warpath work—old as I am. But she shut me up, and she said I'd best save my dander for some mouse that might get fresh round the flat, because it'd be wasted on a cuss like you. This morning when I finished at the works I hung round a spell, and I got the right dope. Ev'ryone was making cracks about it, and for once ev'ryone was telling the same story. Gee, but I'd hate to be you—to have to face all that!"

Gil had slumped against the door jamb. He seemed to have lost a foot of stature and fifty pounds in weight.

"Say," lectured Old Man Ryle, "I never was half your size or build, even when I was a youngster. But in them days if a guy had shoved in between me and mommer yonder, and had upset me and made toad pie of me right where she could see it—well, if he'd been Jim Jeffries and old John L.

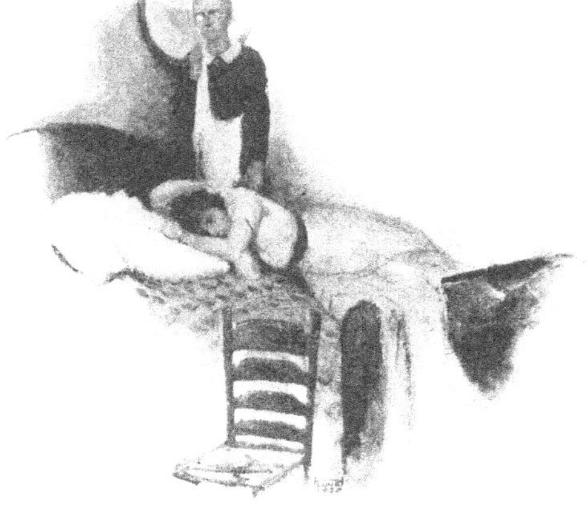

Sullivan mixed, d'you know what I'd 'a' done? Do you? Do you know? Well, here's what I'd 'a' done—I'd 'a' gone straight up into the air like I was a Rooshan candle, and as I passed by him on the way down I'd 'a' bit his ear off. Then I'd 'a' sailed into that feller with all fours—butting too—and I'd 'a' kep' at him till the undertaker got one of the two of us. That's what I'd 'a' done. I'd 'a' done it, not because I was a bearcat or a soocide—I'd 'a' done it because mommer was sure worth it, and because I'd 'a' knowed she wouldn't ever let me within hailin' distance of her again if I hadn't. It's the same with Kitty. It'd be the same with any girl. She—"

"But if you'd only let me see Kitty for just five minutes!" pleaded the anguished Manton. "Let me see her and explain—"

"'Splain what?" challenged Old Man Ryle. "'Splain you was thinking of something else when Buck stood you on your head and walked off with her? Nothing doing, sonny! I'm not hindering you from seeing her. The good old days when a dad was able to say who should and who shouldn't see his girl—those days is in the discard, if they ever happened at all outside of a measly book. It's Kitty that's saying she won't see you, not me.

"When you get to my age, and when the knowledge is too late to be any use to you, you're li'ble to learn one or two things about women. One of 'em is that a woman's got no use for a loser. Another is that a woman's got still less use for a man that makes her look like a fool in public. Another is that she's got the least use of all for a feller who acts like a rabbit when he'd ought to act like he was a man-eater. Think all that out, and figger for yourself how much chance you got of keeping comp'ny with Kitty, or even of getting her to look sideways at you. If I was you—"

Gil Manton drew a deep sigh that sounded more like a gargle, and his wilted stature straightened. His spirit seemed to rise with it from beneath the whiplash of his wordy old mentor's tirade. His eyes were still sick and stricken, but they met Old Man Ryle's for the first time that evening, and they met them with level directness.

"You're right," he said huskily. "I'm all you say. I'm a mouse and a rabbit and all the rest, and I can see you're right about Kitty's not wanting to speak to me again, but she's going to, for all that. She's going to speak to me. Not now, but by and by. I—I guess even a rabbit sometimes runs up against something in life that makes it worth while for him to stop being a rabbit. Kitty's the only thing that makes it worth while for me. Are you going to work now?"

"Not for near an hour yet," answered the puzzled Ryle. "Why? What's that got to do with—"

"Then put on your hat and come along," adjured Gil, his voice thick, his long hands clenched and quivering. "Come along. It'll interest you, and I want her to get the true story of it from you. Don't go pestering me with questions. I need all the nerve I've got to keep me from running up a tree."

It was a banner evening at the Gentlemen's Sons gym in Number-Eight shed. The desultory bouts and bag punching were shelved in favor of no less than three fights—bred of the outing—which were scheduled for settlement. Wherefore the big shack was jammed, and tobacco smoke and sweat hung heavy.

Buck Kevitt was in his glory. As master of ceremonies he was dictating the order in which the bouts were to occur and was choosing seconds for the six nervously scowling amateur warriors.

"I'm refereeing all three," he concluded his Napoleonic oration, "with Pop Glyn's leave—or without it. He's due to be busy enough with the dead ones, without having to—"

"If you're refereeing the bouts," spoke up a quavery but blustering voice from near the thronged doorway, "the bouts will have a crook and a fool for referee."

The hum and jostle of the crowd died to instant silence, followed by a multiple gasp and a craning of necks. Then it was that Gil Manton strode unevenly forward from the threshold, with Old Man Ryle pattering in his wake, the wondering athletes parting their ranks to make way for the courter of destruction. At sight of Gil there was a roar of reminiscent laughter. But it ceased at once, choked back by amaze at the poltroon's bellowed insult to the paladin.

Buck had spun about at sound of the affront as whizzingly as though the bumpy concrete flooring had turned to white-hot iron, and his heavy jaw fell ajar as he recognized his insulter. Taking quick advantage of the spell, Gil walked up to the bemused Kevitt, declaiming as he came.

"Before you referee any other fights, are you too much of a coward

to put on the gloves with me—or to fight me without 'em? Are you?"

The hush was broken. The room was in a gleeful uproar. That the mouse should be challenging the lion was wholly delightful—as joyous as it was incredible. The Gentlemen's Sons were not psychologists. They did not waste gray matter now in trying to explain the impossible. Time enough for such academic speculations over dinner pail or workbench or forge or desk next day. For the moment it was enough to revel in the unbelievable. Buck Kevitt's blank stare melted to a smile of pure happiness.

"You're on!" he said briefly. "The other bouts can wait. Last I saw you, you was setting on the floor. I s'posed you was there yet. I didn't figger you'd have the sand to get up without me saying you could. Who wants to handle this pile of slag?"

"I'll take his corner," spoke up Old Man Ryle as one deep in a dream. "And I'm telling you to your face, Mister Kevitt, that you'd be a better sport if you'd cut out that line of talk to a lad who's got the gall to fight you. C'm over here, Gil, me boy, while I find you some gym shoes big enough to park them fine roomy feet of yours in."

It was just nine minutes later that Gil Manton bobbed under the single rope and squatted gawkily on a rickety stool in the southerly corner of the ring. He was clad in sneakers and running trunks—volunteered loans from two of the gym's regulars. His jaw was set, partly to keep his teeth from chattering with nervous hysteria, partly by the rigidity that somehow had encompassed his whole loose-jointed frame since the sudden reaction of his cowed mind under the tongue lashing of Old Man Ryle.

"Keep your hands limber, son," commanded his second, wrestling to induct the neophyte's stiff and chilly fingers into a work-worn five-ounce glove. "And keep your head cool, so long as you can keep it at all. That course of Y. M. C. A. boxing lessons you was speaking about—they'll have taught you enough to stave him off for the best part of a round anyhow. Don't carry the fight to him. That's his meat. Box him. Use your left lead and your footwork—if you've got any footwork. Keep him off you as long as you can. He can't spar. He always bores in. That's his game—infighting—and that's where he always gets 'em. Don't let him corner you. Don't try to stand up to him. Keep moving. Keep your left out. Don't use your right except for blocking. If you do, or if you try to swing, you'll let him right in at you. Maybe you can land one or two if you do like I say. Maybe—gee, who knows but maybe you'll last out a whole round if you have luck!"

Gil tried to assimilate this cheering counsel, and tried not to look at Buck, who had just vaulted into the ring and was doing a double shuffle on the rosin patch.

Pop Glyn swaggered to the center in dual capacity of referee and timekeeper. He rattled off a condensation of the Queensbury rules, to which no one listened, then glanced at his watch and yelled: "Time!"

He had to hop briskly aside to avoid collision with Buck Kevitt, who came out of his corner with his wonted professional bound. Gil was on his feet almost as quickly, but with a galvanic jerk which spoke of an uncertain brain forcing unwilling muscles.

Gil would not let himself think. He had not let himself think since that unaccountable mad impulse had seized him on learning that Kitty was lost to him by his cowardice. The idea, full grown, had flashed into his mind that there was this one chance in a million to win back his old sweet standing with her. Urged on by it he had made his crazy resolve; since when he had set his teeth and had thrown his thinking apparatus and his imagination out of gear and had prepared to do violence to all his beliefs and desires and nature.

As he faced the shifting and feinting Buck, the novice instinctively threw himself into the first posture learned during his boxing course. He had not been an inept pupil of his Y. M. C. A. master during the few months he had been prevailed on to keep up his sparring.

Buck did not follow his usual custom of beginning the fight with a whirlwind rush. That could wait for a minute while he should try out his queer opponent and show him up for the benefit of the bunch. He had a magnificently developed sense of humor, had Buck. He shuffled, feinted ponderously with his left and then pulled his right quickly aside an inch or two as if for a head swing.

Gil was not drawn out by this double maneuver, either into covering or leading. He continued to stand stock-still in Position A of The Complete Boxer. The crowd chuckled its appreciation of its champion's jest and of his opponent's dull nonresponse.

Buck remarked sweetly: "She must be tickled to pieces to think what a swell scrapper she's landed!"

As he spoke he feinted again and stuck his jaw invitingly forward. The antic was prettily provocative, and for so good a judge of distance was not especially rash. But Buck's mental calculation of the big shipping clerk's loose-jointed reach went wrong by something less than two inches. At the scoff and at its accompanying gesture Gil's long left arm shot forward, and behind the blow he flung his whole weight.

It was a crazily bad bit of boxing. Had Buck side-stepped, Gil must have fallen prone from his own gawky momentum. But Buck was expecting anything rather than such sudden aggression on the part of his stiffly set foe. Indeed, he was thrusting forward his body along with the derisive jaw. And speedily he learned the folly of underestimating even the rankest amateur.

Gil's wild lead smashed full into Buck's wagging jaw. It met the slight forward movement of Buck's shoulders. It sent Kevitt's head snapping back at a breakneck angle and drove his body back with it. Floorward tumbled the unprepared professional under that haphazard blow. His head was the first thing to hit the canvas. It smote with a resounding thump. The redoubtable Buck Kevitt lay there inert and asprawl, while Gil stood dazedly above him, and the crowd milled and muttered and Old Man Ryle did a breakdown of rapture at the ringside and Pop Glyn mechanically began to count off the seconds.

At the count of four Pop Glyn's numerical labors ceased. Buck had sat up, blinked dizzily for an instant, had taken one upward look at the wonderingly elated Gil and was scrambling to his feet. Nor did he wait to recover his balance or to rise to full height before whirling into Gil like a blend of a wildcat and a cyclone. Before Manton fairly realized it, Buck's knees were off ground—the enemy was at him.

Mechanically Gil struck out at the oncoming flash of battling humanity. His left fist was lucky enough to catch Buck on the side of the chin and to stay his charge for the fraction of a second. Gil used that brief moment of grace to follow up with his right and to land a glancing blow under Kevitt's ear.

Both punches had strength behind them, if not science. But both together failed to bring Buck to more than the briefest staggering halt. Then he was inside Manton's windmill guard and all over him. The rest was slaughter. Not that Gil quit. With that odd second consciousness of his he wondered why he didn't quit. He wondered still more why something in him was waking to a crazy zest for this brutal contest. This same something made him hit out wildly and furiously with both fists, disregarding the awful punishment he was enduring. But such of his blows as landed did scant damage, and in the flurry of battle he quite forgot his scarce-learned boxing maxims. Thus despite his fiercest efforts he was turned at once into a chopping block.

Buck was raging to wipe out the knockdown—first of its kind he had incurred in this gathering of his satellites. He could have ended the fight at a blow, but before delivering that knock-out he was minded to make his foe pay for what had just happened. He spent the next two minutes in administering to Gil the most scientifically cruel beating in his power.

Then a second or two before the end of the round he blocked with pitiful ease a swing from the groggy and bleeding boy, set his own broad feet and gauged his distance. He stepped swiftly in and struck. It was a right half hook to the jaw. When the bell rang for the beginning of the second round Gil was still lying limply athwart his stool, mouth open, eyes aquiver. Old Man Ryle was vainly pouring cold water over him and thumbing his supraorbital nerve.

It was fifteen minutes before poor Gil Manton came to his senses. Then after sitting for a few moments with his head in his hands he got

groggily into his clothes and refused his second's proffer of an escort home.

Next day Kitty Ryle suborned an office boy to carry a note to the shipping department for her and to deliver it in person to Manton. The note read:

> "I think you're just fine. Come round and see me this evening. Dad told me about it. Dad thinks you're just fine too. Come round early."

Presently the office boy brought the note back to her unopened. He brought with it word that Manton was not working to-day and that he had telephoned at nine that morning resigning his job. When Old Man Ryle—urged thereto by Kitty—called at Gil's boarding house that night he was told that Manton had given up his room and had left town. Nor for a long year did West New York hear of him again.

Buck Kevitt, oddly enough, lost little prestige from having been floored by a novice. He had scant difficulty in making most of his devotees believe that the knockdown had been a bit of hippodroming on his part to amuse the spectators and to con the palsied Gil into fighting instead of standing petrified. It was so fully in keeping with the rest of Buck's chronic ring wit that it passed muster with the bulk of the Gentlemen's Sons. Yet Kitty Ryle and her father still cherished a sadly proud belief in Manton's exploit.

In his heart Buck knew he had been knocked down—fairly knocked down—and into that for at least two or three seconds he had been in no condition to get up again. The memory bit deep into his vanity. Nor did the knowledge that it had been a fluke and that he had been criminally off guard lessen the sting. The only consolation he could find was in the recollection of the merciless beating he had given the dub for the two minutes following his fall, and that the fright of that beating had sent Gil flying to parts unknown rather than to stay and chance future bullying from his conqueror.

As time went on the memory of Gil's fluke knockdown rankled the deeper. The boob had shattered Buck's flawless record by punching him off his feet. Never again could Kevitt find joy in his own proud boast that no opponent had been able to floor him. Thus—he had heard somewhere—did Jim Jeffries brood in growing wrath and shame over his chance knockdown by Jack Munro; until the stain was removed by a later and definite ring victory over this first man who had been able to send the heavyweight champion to earth.

Buck yearned unspeakably to wipe out his own 'scutcheon blot in some such spectacular way, and as he realized the utter futility of such a craving he waxed the angrier. This Manton, this white-collared, mealy-mouthed peace lover, had floored the great Buck Kevitt, and he had got away with no worse punishment than a brief licking. Buck took to scanning street crowds with morbid eagerness in the daily slighter hope of seeing Gil. It was a real pleasure to picture what he would do to the dub if ever he should happen across him. Buck made a truly cave-man attack on Kitty's heart during the first weeks of Gil's absence, and the reception he met was as of ice mingled with vitriol. Nor did this soften his obsessing hate for the absentee. The next annual outing and games of the Gentlemen's Sons Association came and went. As before, Buck was the heavy-handed genius who steered the affair to its wonted success. As before, the day's revelry left a choice assortment of grudge fights to be settled the next evening in Number-Eight shed. The ramshackle gym was filled to the walls. Each and every window sill was a reserved seat for at least two spectators. The reputed virulence of the forthcoming bouts had drawn even Old Man Ryle to the works a full hour before his time to go on duty.

As Buck's truculent eye roved over the crowd during his usual announcement of the evening's program his gaze grew fixed and his hectoring voice trailed off into a grunt. From his soap-box dais in the center of the room he caught sight of a face that rose somewhat higher than the ruck round it, and a hot thrill stirred the orator's soul. Breaking off in his announcement he leveled a thick thumb at the man whose presence he had marked. At his gesture scores of glances were turned on the newcomer.

Gil Manton sustained the multiple stare with bashful uneasiness. He shrank back a step as if to get out of range of Kevitt's rigid thumb.

"Along about a year ago," proclaimed Buck gratingly, "a poor white-livered dub went nutty right in here and thought he could handle his fists well enough to keep him warm. It didn't take me more'n a couple of punches to cure him, and he lit out. He was so scared he kep' on running and didn't ever stop. The schoolmarms used to tell us the world is like a orange. Well, this feller kep' on running a whole year, and at the end of the year he's gone clean round the world and got back to where he started from. It's a cinch he ain't going to be let stay here with he men, not even long enough to get his breath back. So, if you'll all just watch me, I'm going to start him round the world on his second lap."

He stepped from the box and bore down upon the unlucky pacifist. The crowd, grinning and expectant, made way for him. Old Man Ryle, from the far end of the gym, sought to shoulder his way to the new arrival. As he wiggled feebly through the press he heard Gil's voice raised in scared pleading.

"You leave me be!" begged Manton, backing away from his advancing tormentor. "I'm not doing you any harm. This gym is open to all the Cavverly employees, isn't it? Well, I got my job again this afternoon. I was lonesome, so I dropped in here to see some of the folks I used to work with. I'm not bothering anyone. Let—"

"Yes, you are," blithely denied Buck, coming within arm's length. "You're bothering me a whole lot, and when a feller bothers me I'm li'ble to wake up real wide. I—"

He ended his speech with a sudden grab for Manton's collar. Gil dodged the grasping fingers and cowered as far back as he could among the close-packed Gentlemen's Sons.

"Quit!" he pleaded. "I never did you any harm. I'm lonesome and I came back here to—"

Buck gained his grip, shutting off further whining entreaty. With a mighty tug he pulled his victim off the ground and brought the wriggling body, face down, across his own quickly bent knee. His free hand hurtled aloft in the preliminary gesture of the oldest form of castigation known to mankind. But the calloused palm did not reach its inviting mark. Even as the first guffaw burst from the onlookers in their reading of Buck's intent, the limp body squirmed free with eel-like speed. In what seemed the same motion Gil was on his feet, and the friendly timidity of his look was lost in a sternness that turned his face to many-angled flint.

Buck, leaping up in pursuit of his elusive prey, was met with a short-arm jab delivered with perfect accuracy and scientific force. Gil's left fist had connected with the head porter's mouth. Down went the unprepared Buck on the broad of his back, with two loosened front teeth as a souvenir of Manton's return.

"I came here again," cried Gil hotly as he stood aside for the dazed man to rise, "I came back here, hoping to get decent treatment. I've always tried to be good friends with everybody. You men looked down on me before because I hated to fight. Then I fought. I fought the best man here. He licked me, but I fought my best. That ought to have given me a square deal. It didn't. He began picking on me the minute he saw me to-night, and you other men egged him on and laughed at me. I came back, hoping for a square deal, but I was ready for a crooked one in case I got it. Have you had enough, Kevitt?"

Buck had regained his feet long before the blurted speech was finished. But he stood still, glaring at Manton instead of attacking. For the second time this dub had floored him by a fluke. It was in Buck's heart to fly at him wild-beast fashion and mess him into ribbons. Then came saner judgment.

A rough-and-tumble scrap here in the middle of a cramping throng would do no manner of justice to his grudge. To wipe out the effect of this second knockdown there must be a definite and drastic punishment, a beating that should pass down into gym history and efface the dual fluke. Once let him get this lucky stiff into the ring!

"Because," continued Gil, somewhat hampered by the vehement pump-handling and back-patting of a gleeful little old man who had just reached his side, "because if you haven't had enough, and if your streak of yellow isn't wide enough for you to hide behind, just strip and get into the ring with me. We'll run off a return match for last year's."

It seemed to Buck far too good to be true. He dared not trust himself to speak lest he might scare the coward into repenting of his suicidal challenge. With a nod he turned and led the way to the lockers.

As Gil stepped out of his clothes Old Man Ryle well nigh dropped the sweat-stained trunks he was proffering. Clearly did the oldster recall the loose meridial flesh and the sagging shoulders and half-flabby muscles of his forlorn-hope principal of yesteryear.

Surely this new-stripped body could not be the same as the ill-developed hulk of that other gym night!

The shoulders and limbs were clean as a statue's, but they had a gaunt ruggedness that could be imparted to no statue made of any lesser stone than granite. The chest span was arched like a massive bow. The arms hung light and alert instead of dangling. Their long muscles were still flowing rather than bunchy. But below the shoulder blades, where the chief power of every blow has its source, the muscles stood in smoothly swelling ridges. The eye was level. The once slackly deprecatory jaw was square. The neck was a rugged column. The torso tapered down to the loins as might a hungry wolf's. The legs were lean and lithe. Every atom of the frame was in perfect coordination with the rest.

Pop Glyn, at sight of the nude athlete, forgot his impartial twin office of timekeeper and referee. Fairly dancing up and down in front of Gil, the ancient pork-and-beaner chortled:

"Ye did it! Ye did it! Ye did it after all! That night when ye came sneakin' to my place, all beat up and bloody from Buck's maulin', and got me to give you the name of the place and the note to him, I'd 'a' bet my pay env'l'p' agin a rusty spike that you was bluffin' or crazy. Even when you lit out—"

"I don't blame you for not believing me," said Gil with a reminiscent twist of the mouth. "Nobody with eyes open would have done it. The first six months was hell. Maybe you think it's a cinch to act as chopping block for Tom O'Roon's string of pugs, and to work as handy man round the place at the same time. I started to clear out of there a hundred times, but I stuck.

"I don't know why. Yes, I do, too, but it wouldn't interest you. And by and by it began to come easier. I'd been training the same as his reg'lar pugs, and when I quit Tom offered to put me on his string. He tried me out in two prelims over at the Broadway and in a final at the Greenwood. But—but, Lord, how I hate to fight!"

Buck purposely had loitered over his own disrobing—to give his opponent every chance for ring ague by reason of a long wait. Now emerging from the locker angle he vaulted into the ring and seated himself in his corner, studiously and sneeringly refusing to glance across at Manton. Such scornful ignoring of an enemy was a favorite ring ruse in that day.

Thus it was not until he left the corner with his long-practiced bull rush at the call of time that he favored Gil with so much as a glance. And then, intent on his own plan of campaign, he took no stock of the other's make-up.

Buck's line of battle was carefully thought out. He was not going to put this novice to sleep with a single punch. He was not going to put him to sleep at all. He was going to gauge the force of his blows to a nicety—in such way as to keep Gil in the ring as long as possible. In this manner he would be able to administer a truly murderous and spectacular beating, and to continue administering it until Manton should no longer have the strength or the nerve to withstand the unceasing smashes.

Such a thrashing was certain to spell a hospital term to the victim—not a mere few seconds of senselessness. This fight was due to pass down to posterity in the annals of the association and to increase tenfold the terror of the victor's name. It was a sweet thought.

Head down, Buck charged out of his corner and made for his man, preparing to slug him to the ropes in one rush and to keep him hanging to them under a shower of punches until the ever-lax referee should force him to desist. But Gil was not there when Buck arrived. With perfect ease Manton side-stepped, and as Buck lunged past him he drove his left to the wind with a thud that could be heard in every cranny of the long shed.

Buck wheeled and was at him in black fury. Again the shipping clerk's left shot to the wind and the right to the heart, even as Buck was still turning. Dancing back from a second rush, Gil suddenly set himself, and by dint of reach planted a left-hander to the jaw with a fervor that snapped his foe's head back. Buck tore in for the close-quarters work that was his forte. Again Gil was not there, but shifted gracefully to the left and accompanied the move with a ripping right uppercut to the heart.

By the time this sort of thing had continued for the best part of three minutes Buck had wholly cast aside his plan to give Manton a prolonged and spectacular beating. Thus far he had been able to land scarce half a dozen effective blows in all, and none of these had served to slow up Gil's speed. In return Kevitt had received a series of jolts that were doing fearful things to his self-control. Gil had been playing chiefly for the heart and wind—two particularly vulnerable points to a man who is not in the pink of training. A surge of nausea was rife within Buck's cosmos from the repeated shaking up of these indignant centers.

Buck could not understand anything that had happened. It did not make sense. But he did realize that the fellow had picked up somewhere an annoying gift for sparring and for foot work, and was making a fool of him before his leal admirers. It was time to end the farce—high time. With this in view Buck tore in again, disregarding two jarring counters, and drove his left ragingly for the jaw. To his amaze Gil this time did not block or duck. He stood stock-still, his leanly powerful legs braced, his body forward, and let the terrific blow reach its mark.

The impact's sound was like that produced by banging a blown-up paper bag on the table. The force of it sent a shock through Buck's whole body. Gil went backward a full three feet, but landed square on his toes and in perfect balance. He laughed aloud—a, genuine, infectious laugh.

"Gee!" he exulted. "That the best you got? And that's the bush-league punch I've been scared of for a year and more! It's a love pat, to the kind Sharkey and the rest used to hand out to me when O'Roon made me take them on for a round or so at the training quarters. If that's your best —"

The signal for the first round's end cut in on his pæan. He sauntered back to his corner, leaving Buck blinking dully after him in midring. In the corner Gil was met and embraced by an elderly maniac who could not keep both rheumatic feet on the ground for the fraction of a second. Mere spoken words were not for Old Man Ryle in this moment of heavenly bliss. After the manner of the Icelandic skalds in like divine dementia he burst into falsetto squeals of song. He chose by inspiration a London-Prize-Ring saga that had been a loved battle hymn in his own distant and warlike youth:

Slug him in the kisser! Biff him on the jaw! Slam him to the ropes! Sling him on the floor!
Bust his teeth and eyeballs! Hornpipe on his bones!
Whale him till he —

"Shut up, you wild Irishman!" laughingly ordered Gil, disengaging himself from the frenzied embrace. "You're singing down my throat! Get busy with that towel, can't you?"

He smiled pleasantly across at Buck. Kevitt had slumped down on his stool and was eying him with blank disbelief in his own senses.

"Time!" hooted Pop Glyn after an agonizingly impatient scanning of his watch.

Buck, his arm still vibrating with the mighty and ineffective jaw punch, plodded stupidly forward—this time to meet an opponent who was everywhere and nowhere. Gil was all over him, slipping past Buck's ever-slower guard, eluding counters or taking them as they came. To heart and to wind, however eagerly protected, poured his whalebone blows. He was tireless.

As though scorning caution or the saving of energy against so puny a foe, he forced every step of the fighting.

Halfway through the sixth round Manton paused for the first time in his blithe task of undermining Buck's powers. Kevitt stood swaying and reeling in front of him, the knotty arms a-sag, the jaw hanging, the neck too weak to carry the bullet head erect, the lax body swaying to and fro like a hobbled elephant's.

"You're standing all over your feet," said Gil in tender concern. "Give 'em a rest for a minute. I'll learn you how to do it."

He placed his flat palm on the center of Buck's heaving chest and gave the stricken man a playful push. Kevitt's wabbling legs gave way. The beaten fighter sat down hard in midring. Manton, without a backward glance at him, strode to his corner, pulling at the strings of his wet and shapeless gloves as he went.

"Shoo the crowd off!" he begged the tearfully delirious Old Man Ryle. "I want to get into my things in a rush. I've framed up a date. I've been framing it up for a year."

The night watchman risked a fine for reporting late to duty that night, for he insisted on accompanying Gil to the flat, urging that he would stay there only a minute, but that it was necessary for someone to go along who could tell the tale better than Gil would have the pluck to tell it.

The minute was only a bare half hour. Half an hour after that Kitty examined for the twelfth time the purplish lump on Manton's jaw. In order to get a better view of it she was obliged to sit on his knee.

"Promise me," she commanded, tyrannical in her new proprietorship, "promise me you'll never let anyone wheedle you into a fight again as long as you live! It—it's horrible! Promise!"

"Sure!" assented Manton with a sigh of pure relief. "Only—only what a hit you could have made with me, girl of mine, if you'd just happened to ask me for that promise a year earlier!"

Females of the Species

WHEN the three boarded the past-worthy and makeshift steamship Farragut at the Carib Isles Company's East River pier, not one of them knew the others by sight or by name.

Not one of them knew by experience that Fate or Life or Chance (or any of the other trillion nicknames for God) can sometimes take hold of a smug and superupholstered and veneered human machine and strip it to its running-gear.

Hector Dallam was something or other in a Broad Street brokerage house. Office-labor had never paled him, or stooped one of his wide shoulders lower than the other. He had money enough to play at work and to work at play. A nasty little attack of "flu" had given him the excuse for a two months' rest from business and for the lazy West Indian cruise he desired. Hence his presence on the Farragut.

Nedda Burns was celebrating her recent graduation from Vassar by a similar trip. Nedda's health needed no upbuilding. She was a basketball star, a crack swimmer, and all-round athlete, and was glowing with magnificent health and youth and vitality. She was gloriously alive, and she had a dark and flashing beauty that did queer things to men's blood-pressure. She was making this trip for the sheer fun of it, and to meet her father, who had gone ahead to Havana for the races and was to join the cruise there.

Celia Thayer was a mere wisp of a girl, pale gold of hair and gifted with a pair of soft brown eyes two sizes too big for her flower-face. Nature and inclination had cast this shyly demure little lass for the role of home-maker and of inspired housekeeper. The death of her mother had forced her out of the home and into the unyearned-for job of school-teacher in her native Connecticut River town. A year of inhaling chalk-dust and of bending over scrawly exercises had given her a settled cough. And this ailment she hoped to shake off somewhere in the tropics.

Nedda and Celia were forced to share a stateroom aboard the overcrowded little steamship. Perhaps no two more totally dissimilar people have ever been thrown together as cabin-mates. Yet, by the second morning out, a friendship had sprung to life between them.

Hector Dallam chanced to be one of their four seat-mates in the dining-saloon. At the first meal, they did not so much as glance in his direction. At the second, they acknowledged with the briefest of nods his perfunctory bow. At the third, Nedda assented politely to his assertion that the air was growing decidedly warmer. Celia, shrinking from the stranger's boldness, secretly envied Nedda's fearless reply.

On the third day, at dinner, the three talked quite freely together. At least, Nedda and Dallam talked freely, and Celia listened with a pleasant decrease of her early New England reserve.

After dinner, Hector went to the smoking-room for a mildly thrilling evening of poker; and the girls sat on the moonlit deck neither mentioning him nor thinking of him.

Just before dawn, a howling tropical hurricane, coming from nowhere in particular, smote the (one-time) good ship Farragut as a boy's shinny-stick might swat a lump of rotting ice—and with just the same effects.

But, first, the gale carried the helplessly wallowing vessel miles and miles off her course and off the trade-lines of any South Atlantic boats. And the first tentative smash of the wind put her patched-up wireless out of commission.

The captain and his officers had had ample time to prepare the boats before the end came. But there was not an ample supply of boats to prepare. Nor was the weather propitious to their launching.

Yet boat after boat was lowered, usually with safety, into the boiling froth of waters. Nedda Burns and Celia Thayer were assigned, with two other women and a baby, to places in the last of these. Two sailors manned the undersized craft—hardly larger than a dingey. The men passengers and such of the crew were not detailed to rowing duty were provided with life-belts and permitted to go through the farce of trying to fashion a raft.

Into the smother of waves settled the little boat that held the girls and their fellow fugitives. The two sailors tugged gruntingly at the oars—to put the dingey's nose into the wind and to get under way in the track of the vanishing boats which had preceded them. Dusk was beginning to settle down. The boat leaped and twisted crazily under the counter-efforts of wind and oars.

Thirty yards away from the Farragut's tilted sides, the two rowers cried out in mortal terror. For an instant, fear paralyzed their oar-strokes. With a drunken lurch, the ship had dug her stubby prow deep into the water. Up went the stern. And with a sound of rending that roared forth above the racket of the storm, the Farragut broke in two. A rain of blackish and sprawling bodies poured forth through the rent and from the vertical sides of the decks. And the smitten ship was gone.

The suction-wave swelled out from the whirlpool, hillock-high. It caught the dingey, turned it upside down, spilled out part of its human cargo, then righted it, and left it almost awash with water, full in the trough of the sea.

Celia had been clinging with both hands to a thwart which she had gripped instinctively as the hill of suction-wave rushed down at them. And Nedda had been clinging to Celia. Thus, the two had not been swept overboard, but were rolling helplessly in the swash of water which half filled the boat.

Celia struggled to her knees and, with a battered tin, began to bail. Nedda, in the same instant, seized one of the two remaining oars and wrought with all her athletic young power to head the tossing craft into the eye of the gale.

Presently, a sudden jar and tipping apprised them that some one was trying to clamber aboard. And they saw one of the two capsized sailors wriggling weakly over the stern-sheets. He collapsed into the splashing bottom of the dingey.

"Here!" called Celia shrilly, as she went on bailing, "take that other oar and help her keep the bow into the wind!"

Dully the man obeyed. For a space, the three worked gaspingly and with all their might. Then Nedda, kneeling in the prow, cried aloud, gesturing with her head at something that bobbed in the water a few yards to starboard.

A man, worn out and buffeted, but still swimming gamely, was trying to reach the reeling boat. Celia braced herself and held out one fragile hand to help him. As he caught her fingers with a tug that almost pulled her out of the boat, she saw he was Hector Dallas.

He put his hands on the gunwale; he worked his way to the stern and, with one last struggle, hoisted himself aboard. Exhausted as he

was, he wasted no time in rest, but took the oar from Nedda's wearied grasp. Then he and the sailor bent their remaining strength to keeping the dingey's head into the wind, while the two girls bailed until they no longer had the strength to stir their aching arms.

An hour or so later, one of the confusing crosscurrents which lace the West Indies seized the boat in its frolic-clasp. The wind had fallen as suddenly as it had risen. The four dead-tired castaways let their cranky little craft take its own course.

And so, through the night and half of the next day, the dingey slapped along, borne on the breast of the current.

At noon, Gryce, the sailor, roused himself from an animal apathy to yell raucously and to point to leeward. Low against the pulsing horizon lay a yellowish spit of land.

The two men jumped to the oars and rowed with all their might. By two o'clock, they were within a furlong of the dirty yellow beach, and could see beyond it a huddle of dreary looking palm trees and the roofs of one or two buildings.

"There are houses!" exulted Nedda. "That means there are people—civilized people. It means—"

"No!" growled the sailor, who had turned to take a long look at the land and whose face now lost its first glint of hope. "No, it don't neither. No folks there. We won't starve. That's one thing. But there's no folks. And nobody's li'ble to touch here for another year or more—if they do as soon as then."

"How do you know?" demanded Celia.

"I been here before," he answered, taking up his interrupted task of rowing. "Twice before. This here is Calamity Island. They named it that because it was such a measly place. This island was leased, back in 'Ninety-eight, by the Keene-Varden Line, for a provision and outfitting base for their freighters. Their reg'lar liners never came so far east. They put up them corrugated iron huts and that big storehouse, and kept a bunch of roustabouts here to help load. Cap Seeley was in charge. Freighters used to put in here for food and outfit stuff. For water, too. Good fresh-water spring, back among them mangy pa'm trees. I was here a couple of times when I sailed on their freighters. When the war came, the men was all took off and most of the stuff in the storehouse. But a feller told me they left quite a passel of it here so's to have it ready when the line started runnin' again. But the war put it on the blink, and now it's bust up for good, I heard. So there'll maybe never anyone touch here. There ain't enough stuff to make a spesh'l trip worth while. Besides—"

A long roller, ground-swell from the dead hurricane, interrupted his homily by lifting the dingey without warning and hurling it, broadside on, against an invisible sand spit some hundred yards off shore. The cranky boat upset, spilling its passengers incontinently into four feet of milk-warm water on the landward side of the narrow spit. As the quartet floundered sputteringly to their feet, the same wave, receding, bore away with it the overturned dingey.

Before any of the four could recover breath and self-possession enough to look round for their eccentric boat, it was far out of reach.

Wading through the gradually shallower warm water, the two men and the two women made their awkward way landward.

The next three days were filled, from dawn to dark, with work. The men had no difficulty in smashing with stones the padlocks on the doors of huts and storehouses. Then came the task of inventorying and bringing forth, to use, the stacks of provisions and blankets and canvas and slop-chest articles, the cleaning of the huts, and rendering them once more habitable dwellings.

The girls were hardly less busy. Nedda, rejoicing in her vigorous strength, worked side by side with the men in the hauling-out of boxes and cases and in the fitting-up of the huts.

Celia at once took charge of the kitchen hut. She assumed this duty by her own eager choice. After a year of boarding and school-teaching, she reveled in practising again her cherished art as a cook. Nor was she content with this. It was she who put various deft touches to the living-quarters and to the assembly and dining-hut that gave those barren spots a new and elusive homelike air.

And so passed the first few days—days so busy in arranging for present needs as to leave little chance or time for discussing problems of the future.

On the morning of the fifth day, Dallam rigged up a signal flag from a red blanket, and, carrying along a handful of nails and a hammer, fared to the dune's summit, two miles inland, bent on nailing his distress-banner to the twenty-foot stump of a dead palm that crowned the sand-hill. He left Gryce to finish the task of inventorying the storehouse. The girls, in their own sleeping-hut, were busy, with slop-chest needles and sail-thread, in repairing the rents and other ravages to their dresses.

Dallam had been gone the better part of an hour when Gryce, in the course of his investigation, came upon a small wooden box, hidden, with elaborate carelessness but with much skill, under some bolts of tarpaulin in a far corner of the store house.

Gryce pried open the box with the chipped edge of the stock house's one hatchet. The removing of the lid revealed a top layer of six bottles, each imbedded in a hutch of straw. There were six more in the lower stratum. Gryce pulled away the thatch from one bottle and studied the label. His once mild interest was ablaze. For he had chanced to unearth a contraband case of high-proof whisky—cached there, doubtless, for the private use of the roustabout gang's boss.

It was perhaps an hour later that Celia Thayer looked up from her primitive needlework at sound of singing. And the singer was approaching the hut in which sat the two wondering girls.

Nedda dropped her sewing and ran out into the sandy dooryard to investigate. Celia, conquering a twinge of fear, followed. Coming toward them from the storehouse was the sailor. It was the width of his journey, rather than its length, which seemed to bother Gryce.

As he neared the girls, his brick-red face wreathed itself into a most loving smile. A child could not have mistaken his condition—nor his intent.

"Gee!" announced the sailor joyously. "I was just a-comin' to look for you—an' here the two of you was comin' to look for *me!* Fine an' el'g'nt! I gotta grand plan, dames both. A reg'lar *he* one! I'm—I'm goin' to be king of thisyer des'late desert island of ourn. King of it! An' I'm goin' to elect the two of you to be my queens. How 'bout it? I—"

His maudlin advance had brought him close to Nedda. He finished his sentence by flinging both arms about her. The girl fought, with all her strength and loathing, to free herself from the uncouthly ardent clasp. Celia cried out in wild terror and smote with all her frail force upon the sailor's embracing hands, to loosen them from their amorous hold.

Then—in true dime-novel fashion—came rescue.

Dallam, returning from his signal-raising on the dune-top, rounded the corner of the nearest hut just as Celia's terrified cry changed his swinging walk to a run.

Gryce, to his own dismay, found himself caught by the three and flung prone on the sand, six feet away. Dallam, with second glance at the two panic-stricken girls, followed at a bound and stood over him.

With the quickness of a mad cat, Gryce was on his feet again. He had dropped the bottle. As he leaped up, he whipped from his belt a crooked sheath-knife. And he hurled himself at the man who had blocked his kingly purpose. Dallam was a boxer and an all-round athlete. He had full need of his prowess.

Sidestepping the rush, he struck for Gryce's jaw. But the blow glanced off the sailor's skull. And Gryce was upon him once more. As much by luck as by skill, Dallam was able to grip the sailor's right wrist as the two came to a clinch. And, breast to breast, the men battled, in ferocious embrace, at close quarters.

Up and down the dooryard they raged, sending the sand aloft in choking swirls from under the stamp and shuffle of their flying feet. The girls, chalk-faced, clung close to each other and watched, with wide, dry eyes, the primitive conflict. Twice Dallam lost his hold on the other's wrist. Twice the fast-plying knife cut him, once to the bone. His breath was fast and irregular, and he felt himself tiring.

But a quart of high-proof whisky is not an ideal training diet for a fight. Gryce was slowing down and growing clumsy. With a last surge of fury-driven strength, he wrenched free his captive wrist again and lunged viciously for Dallam's bare throat. But his speed was gone.

Hector caught the plunging wrist in his own left hand, bent and caught, with his right hand, the sailor's trousered right leg just above the knee. In the same motion, he darted in and brought his shoulders under Gryce's stomach. Bracing himself and calling on every atom of his muscle, Dallam gave one mighty heave.

It was an old rough-and-tumble trick. But it served. High in air shot Gryce's writhing body. Then it crashed to the ground, his head striking first. The sailor lay motionless, his neck at an angle which told its own story.

It was Celia Thayer who broke the moment's spell of horror. Stealing forward timidly, she laid a trembling hand on Dallam's arm.

"You're—you're hurt!" she murmured, shuddering. "Come to the hut and let me wash out your cuts and bind them for you."

She turned and led the way. Unconsciously, she was still holding Dallam by the shoulder, leading him as a mother might guide a hurt child, yet with a feverish intensity in her slender fingers that was surely not maternal.

Nedda made as though to follow. But, in the sudden reaction from her multitude of stormily stark emotions, she was aware of a dizziness and nausea that made her sway. Puzzled at her own unwonted weakness, she sat down on a rock and struggled to shake off the spasm. Nedda shrank from letting the bloodily victorious demigod see her sick and trembling. And, though she noted, with a swift dart of pain, the queerly proprietary air which Celia had all at once assumed toward the injured man, she forbore to join the two in the hut until her own nerves and brain should have regained their iron calm.

Dallam was well content to let the tender girl guide him to the shadow and coolness and rest of her hut, and to bring a rickety chair for him to collapse into, while she sought rags and cool water for his hurts.

Celia had found the worst of these—a ragged jab in the left shoulder. She drew away the soaked and rent shirt from the shoulder-wound, and, with cool, competent fingers, she bathed the gash. Then, the wetted bandage still in her hand, she stooped suddenly and kissed the hurt.

The contact of hot, smooth flesh to her lips, the mingled reek of sweat and blood mounted to her brain. Beside herself, she pressed her feverish lips again and again to the wound, gasping brokenly, under her breath:

"I love you! Oh, I *love* you, my god-man!"

Then, in a flash, her lifelong New England repression, her colorless past took possession of her once more. The thought of what she had done filled her with a terrified revulsion. Amazed, horrified, she drew back. She could not understand what she had just done. She could not believe she had done it.

Her panic-stricken eyes ventured to glance toward Hector Dallam's face. And she thrilled with a mighty relief. Under the mingled pain and faintness, the man had swooned.

"He doesn't know!" breathed Celia, in a wave of gratitude. "He doesn't know! God be thanked, *he doesn't know!*"

And, still loathing herself, and marveling dully at the brief revelation of her unsuspected hidden fires, the girl drew back the heavy head and began to splash cold water into the lifeless face.

With a heave of his big shoulders and a look of stupid wonder,

Dallam came to himself. Above him was working a very efficient and emotionless young woman, whose dead-white face and quivering lips were offset by steady hands.

"Thanks!" he muttered dizzily. "I—I'm afraid I—I was mollycoddle enough to—keel over for a second."

"Don't talk," she admonished coldly. "Rest. Sit still. You'll be all right presently."

She was at work again on his wounded shoulder, using all the skill left in her fingers and mind from a war-time course in first aid. But, to her surprised self-contempt, she found that the momentary revulsion of feeling had passed, and that again she quivered to the very soul at the magic contact and the sight of him and at memory of the hero-fight he had waged for her. Swept away a second time by that resistless impulse which had been hers for too short a space to be controlled, she began incoherently:

"You'll despise me! You'll think I'm—"

The hut doorway darkened. Nedda came in. Her dark eyes burning, she stood staring at the confused Celia. In Nedda's smoldering eyes, she read something akin to deathless hate. And it bewildered her.

"Well," asked Nedda harshly, "why should he despise you? And what will he think you are? I heard that much as I came in. Am I interrupting you?"

"Not at all," answered Celia, her nerves brought back to normal, with a jerk by this new shock. "But I was doing the bandage work so bunglingly. I'm ashamed of such a clumsy job. I was just beginning to tell Dallam that he'd despise me for being awkward, and that he'd think I had never profited by any of my first-aid study. Reach me that other length of linen from the foot of the bed, won't you? I'm afraid this bandage will unwind if I let go of it before it's tied."

Thus began a ten-month space of life on the island for two women and one man. Outwardly—as soon as the gruesomeness of Gryce's killing wore off—this life was monotonous enough. All three worked steadily and efficiently to make their odd abode habitable and comfortable and to stay as faithful to civilization as might be. They even whiled away the spare hours by starting various classes for their common self-improvement and to keep their minds from rusting.

This, outwardly.

But inwardly, all manner of things were occurring. Here, on the island, day by day, conventions grew fewer and more difficult to maintain. The slave-whip of civilization sounded fainter and fainter. The never-silent voice of Mother Nature—that awful and insistent voice which has not once wholly been stilled since the birth of time—came louder and more imperatively to the ears of all three.

Besides youth and nature, and the fact that life was stripped to its running-gear, another element still more powerful wrought upon the two women. They had stood by and had seen this man fight for them at risk of his life. They had seen Dallam conquer and slay the beast who menaced them. And they had dressed his wounds.

In such conditions, it was next to impossible to remain commonplace. Yet all three strove bravely to remain so. Hence the elaborate courses of mental improvement—a pathetic appeal of the trio to their olden and vanished god, Conventionality. But, like Baal, this god was "sleeping or on a journey."

Dallam, with the merciless and nonromantic logic of his sex, saw the inevitable future in all its phases long before either girl willingly let her mind dwell on the theme. Being a man, he reverted, at heart, wholly to type. He knew now there was no reasonable hope of rescue, despite his carefully renewed signals on the dune-crest. He knew that only in superpolite fiction do a man and a maid dwell together in Platonic aloofness for years on a desert island. He foresaw the certain climax.

Yet, being a man and not a brute, he would not force the issue. He was not in love with either of these women—in the sense of the word that he had been brought up to understand. Gladly would he have accepted one or both of them for mate, here where time stood still and where conventions were but ghosts.

But he shrank from bringing their pleasant relations to a climax. He knew women. He knew these two girls were clean and high-minded, and that they were without experience with the realities of life. He noted the instinctive fight they were making to live up to their early precepts of refinement and culture and the decencies of existence. And, he was not willing—yet—to shatter this pitiful fabric they toiled so hard and so unconsciously to keep intact. Wherefore, he waited—being, as I have said, a man and not a brute. He was not yet thirty.

As for Celia and Nedda, each girl had long since discovered, to her amazement, that she was overwhelmingly and romantically and jealously in love with this strong, well-bred, attractive man.

Each, womanlike, guessed the other's secret while guarding furtively her own. Each looked on Dallam as an assuredly prospective suitor for the hand of one of them. Certainly not for them both. That idea never once entered the clean mind of either woman.

They felt he must inevitably fall in love with one of them, soon or late. And secretly they began to angle for him, not realizing at all that they were angling.

For example, Nedda made full use of the athletic prowess and powers of comradeship and outdoor gifts which had turned the heads of a dozen callow youths in her college days. Her strength and her beauty were aids which she employed as unconsciously but as freely as does the wooing oriole.

Celia instinctively played on the man's domestic impulses. She evolved and cooked a thousand dainties for his delight. She kept his sleeping-hut and the assembly hut not only in spick-and-span neatness but redolent of a genuine home atmosphere. In all matters of creature-comfort, she studied and forestalled his slightest need.

She had fought down and conquered the wild, primal impulse that had overwhelmed her as she had dressed Dallam's wounds. At least, she had it in check, not consenting to realize that it was daily becoming more and more dominant.

Thus, each according to her kind, the two girls strove for the favor of this man they had learned to worship. And so, for months, the odd duel went on, its intensity and stark eagerness increasing so gradually that neither girl was aware the increase. The process of stripping to running-gear had been imperceptible as are all nature's processes. But all those processes are irresistible and relentlessly sure. For, patient as nature is, she never carries patience past a certain point.

That point was reached, one morning, when the three castaways had been living on the island a little less than eleven months.

Dallam had just set off to the dunes on his monthly inspection of the signal-flags. Nedda had been eager to go with him on the long and breath-taking climb, which was too much for Celia's delicate lungs and muscles. But it had been her turn to-day, to do the scant weekly washing for their community. And she had lacked the courage to beg Celia to take the turn for her.

So, sullenly, she gathered together the bag of soiled raiment and prepared to draw the needful spring water for the irksome task. The bag over her shoulder and the big tin pail swinging from her free hand, she crossed to the sleeping-hut which she and Celia shared.

Of late, a queer constraint had crept into the once close relations between the two girls. By a sort of mutual consent, they avoided each other as much as they could in their forcedly cramped surroundings. But, to-day, Nedda was obliged to go to the hut where she knew Celia was at work. She had left there one or two of the garments which were to go into the washing-bag, and now she went thither to get them.

She had left Celia sweeping out the hut. But as she crossed noise-lessly through the soft sand and reached the door, she saw Celia had laid aside her broom and was sewing. The sight roused Nedda's curiosity.

The trio's clothes problem had became exigent. Long since, the light garments they had been wearing when they were cast ashore, had gone to pieces. They had been forced, thus, to fashion clothes out of blankets and bolts of sail-cloth and of such few remnants of mate-rial as they had found in the slop-chest contents of the storehouse. The result, in spite of Celia's best skill, had been picturesque rather than beautiful. And Nedda wondered on what manner of garment her rival might now be working.

On Celia's lap was piled a mass of soft and gay-colored cambric. A second glance would have been needed to recognize that it repre-sented many fragments of the material—handkerchiefs, underclothes and so on—deftly sewn together and fashioned into a waist. Along the front of this waist the girl was now sewing tiny opalescent sea-shells in which holes had laboriously been drilled by a needle.

Nedda, unnoted, slipped away from the threshold and out into the glare of sunlight. She was shaking as from a palsy.

For perhaps five minutes longer, Celia wrought at her dainty, grotesque sewing. At moments, an elusive smile played athwart her soft lips, and her eyes would grow big and luminous. Again she would shake her head impatiently and frown.

The spool of thread tumbled from her lap, jarred thence by a vehement headshake. It rolled wabblingly across the uneven floor and brought up against the far wall. Celia gathered her work in her arms and left her seat, going in quest of the errant spool. She picked it up, paused a few moments to adjust her pale hair by the help of the hut's one flawed mirror, and sat down on the side of the bed, near the looking-glass, instead of returning to her chair.

She stitched away for perhaps another two minutes. Then a shuffling noise made her glance upward. She looked just in time to see one end of a roof-joist slip from its mooring.

Down crashed the ninety-pound joist, end first. Its point smote full upon the edge of the chair which Celia had so recently been occupying. And its weight and impetus crumpled the rickety seat to match-wood.

Celia shuddered a little as she realized what she had escaped by her chance move to another part of the room. Then, choking with the dust raised by the fall, she wondered perplexedly how such an odd accident could have occurred.

The hut's tin roof had been rotted to worthlessness and had grown to be hardly more protection than a sieve against the torrent-rains of the tropics. So, months earlier, Dallam had torn it down, and, with Nedda's strong help, had substituted a thatch whose foundations were a dozen heavy joists, on which lighter sticks were laid transversely to hold the thatching.

The joists had been fitted into nicked grooves, but had not been nailed in place. So heavy were they, and so scarce and precious were nails, that such further fastenings had not seemed needful. It was strange that, on so still a day, a joist could have been jarred loose.

Even as Celia was pondering the mystery, Nedda Burns came running into the room.

"I heard a racket here," she began, as she crossed the threshold, "and I—"

Her voice trailed off as she noted the joist and the wrecked chair. Her face was a brick-red, and her eyes were furtive. Also, in the instant before she had let herself look upon the ruin, her gaze had been fixed on Celia in something akin to horror. Her teeth began to chatter, as from a chill.

"It was lucky I had happened to move from there," commented Celia, picking up a broom and beginning to sweep away the drifts of dust and splinters. "If I hadn't, there might not be much more left of me than is left of our one chair."

She spoke lightly, to mask the sense of shock the mishap had caused her. But her commonplace words and placid diction seemed to spur Nedda to anger. Her wrathful eye fell on the makeshift waist that lay athwart the foot of the bed. Celia noted the inspection, and she flushed.

"Pretty, isn't it?" she asked, trying to make her soft voice sound natural. "I saved a bit here and a bit there, out of the rags, till I had enough. And I dyed it with that half-bottle of cochineal we found in the storehouse. It—"

"Yes," said Nedda dully, as she fought back the pangs of ever-increasing rage; "it's pretty. It must have taken ever so much work, too. Let's hope Hector will appreciate it enough to make all the trouble worth while."

There was a more than subacid note in her voice. And Celia flushed hotly.

"That seems rather an unnecessarily nasty thing to say, doesn't it?" she asked. "I dress for my own pleasure—not for Hector's or for yours. At all events," she went on. "I don't sulk like a cross schoolchild when I have to do a morning's work that keeps me from trapesing off to Signal Hill with him."

She bit her lip with vexation that she had been goaded to make so coarse a retort. But the thing could not be unsaid. And, for the first time, the ever-thinning veil of pretense was ripped from between the two women. Nedda's glowing face was ablaze. For a moment, a score of fiercely resentful words seemed striving for precedence at her full young lips. Then, with a tremendous effort, she choked them back. And her face grew cold and set.

She crossed the hut and faced the other girl. When she spoke, it was with a grating calm that gave no hint of the struggle whereby it was attained.

"I'm sorry you said that, Celia," she began. "And yet, in a way, I'm glad, too. For things couldn't have gone on any longer—not a day longer. I knew that when I saw you at work on this—this thing."

Celia had shrunk back in her chair at the outset of the other's speech. But now, bracing herself, she met Nedda's eye with a steadfastness that knew no flinching.

"I used to tell my pupils," she said, as Nedda paused, uncertain, "that conventionality was the finest anchor in any storm of doubt. But I never heard that an anchor was of any special use after the ship was wrecked. You are right. It's time to speak. I'm sorry. But it is. What are we going to do?"

Nedda's brows contracted. Through her towering anger, she seemed at a loss for words. Again it was Celia who came to the fore. Striving to speak primly, she said:

"What you are trying to tell me is that we both—we both—both—care—for Hector. And only one of us can marry him. It's—it's horrible to have to talk this way. But we can't put it off any longer. If he is in love with one of us—and, of course, he must be sometime, or maybe he is now—if he is in love with one of us, how can—how can he marry the one he is in love with? I mean—there isn't any minister or justice of the peace or—or even a Bible on the island. So, how can he? Oh, I've wondered and puzzled over it till—"

"I think," interrupted Nedda, her voice still cold and grating, "I think that's a point that can be taken up when we come to it. The way matters stand now, we are both in love with him. It's more than just 'in love,' too. It's something I didn't even know existed. Something fifty times stronger than we are. We must find out just one thing—find out which one of us he wants. Everything depends on that. *Everything*. Till we find out, nothing else matters. Nothing else in all this world matters to *me!*"

"We can't go on as we've been going," reiterated Celia. "We can't. Another month of it will drive me crazy or make me kill myself. I—"

"Another month?" flashed Nedda. "Another *minute!* I know how you feel. Except I've never wanted to kill myself. But I've wanted to kill you, again and again, when he seemed to—"

"Nedda!"

"I have!" insisted Nedda, unashamed, in her reckless fury. "And, more than that, I've tried to do it."

"Nedda!"

"I fought against it a hundred times," raged Nedda. "But to-day it got the best of me. I always knew it would sometime. I always knew it would. And today it did—when I saw you making that hideous waist. It's just the kind of thing that would attract a man. I wanted to rush in and strangle you. But I was afraid he'd see the marks on your throat. So I pushed the end of that roof joist from outside till it—"

"*Oh!*" panted Celia, aghast.

She crouched back against the wall, staring bemusedly into the distorted face that confronted her. So, for a space, the two women stood. Then Nedda turned away and busied herself with clearing up the wreckage.

There was a long silence. It was Celia who spoke at last.

"It was not *you* who tried to kill me," she said, her words stifled by the horror of what Nedda had confessed. "It was something else. The 'something fifty times stronger than we are' that you spoke of just now. But since you aren't afraid to kill, perhaps you aren't afraid to risk death?" She paused, then hurried on. "Here is one of the million plans I've been shaping over and over in my mind when I couldn't sleep. It seems less crazy than any of the others I've thought of. Will you listen to it?"

The other nodded dumbly. Celia drew a long, quivering breath, steeling herself to her task. Then she said:

"We both love Hector. If I can judge you by myself, you would risk your life, blithely, for a bare chance of making him care for you."

"Yes!" cried Nedda, almost hysterically. "Oh, yes! *Yes!*"

"He can marry only one of us," pursued Celia. "I feel that he couldn't help falling in love with one of us—and of saying so, too—if the other one of us wasn't here. I—"

"Yes!" cried Nedda again. "I don't just feel that—I *know* it! He—"

"Good!" agreed Celia. "Then I propose that one of us leave him and one of us stay here and—and—marry him."

"But how can—"

"I've thought it all out," continued the droning voice. "Oh, hundreds of times! And I've prayed for the courage to say it to you. But I'd never have dared to, if—if you hadn't just done what you did. It's so simple! And it's the only solution—the *only* one. Are you brave enough to draw lots with me? Are you? And let the winner take Hector? Then let the loser—go away."

"'Away?'" echoed Nedda, puzzled, as she glanced out over the oblong patch of fire-blue sea. "But where is there to go? There's no—"

"Yes, there is," denied Celia quietly. "Out there. Where you were looking. To walk out there, to-night. To walk on, until there is no more walking—and—"

A gasp from Nedda broke in on the dully voiced plan. For an instant, the two girls—white and tense and wide-eyed—continued to gaze on each other. Then, through the stillness, came the far-off tread of running feet.

Thus, on his return from the dunes, Hector Dallam ever ran back to the noonday meal, working off his mighty vitality in strenuous exercise. The girls would have known and thrilled to his returning step among a million. At sound of it, Nedda shook off her daze.

"Yes!" she exclaimed, hoarse and shaking with emotion. "Yes; I agree! It's worth the chance. It's worth every chance on earth. We'll draw the lots, now—before he gets here. And, to-night the loser will—" She finished the sentence by snatching up two of the wood-splinters at her feet. "These will do as well as anything else. Will you hold them, or will you draw? If—"

"Hello!" broke in Hector, pausing on the threshold at sight of the two girls and their unwonted bearing. "What's up? I'd have been back sooner, but I spent half an hour studying that fog-bank a few miles offshore. It seemed to me, once or twice, when bits of it lifted, that I almost caught the shape of some sort of ship far out in it. But I was mistaken. I'm always imagining such things. So I came back to lunch. The fog is lifting, too—What happened to the floor? And what's happened to you girls?" He broke off in his recital.

"Nothing's the matter, Hector," replied Nedda, lying confusedly. "One of the joists caved in, and we were going to draw lots to see which of us should clear up the mess. That's all. We—"

"No," calmly denied Celia, "that is not true. We were just going to draw lots to see which of us should die to-night and which of us should—stay—with *you*, Hector."

She spoke as expressionlessly and fast as a child going parrotlike through its lesson. And, contrasting her unbelievable words with her flat tone, Dallam gaped in dumb wonder.

Having made her avowal, Celia stood mute, waiting for the man to speak. But he only eyed her in amazement, and then looked stupidly from her to Nedda. It was Nelda who took up the tale and shattered the eternity-instant of silence.

"She is right," assented Nedda, her rich voice vibrant, her dark eyes gleaming. "It's come to that. We can't go on as we have been going, Hector. Both Celia and I understand that. One of us most go. So we—"

"But why?" stuttered the man, hardly grasping the drift. "Why? We've lived here comfortably, so far. And we—"

Then he saw the light in Nedda Burns' face. And, all at once, he understood. A hundred times he had interested himself in wondering when and just how their artificial wall of civilization was going to crumble under the ever-increasing pressure on it. But now that the crisis had burst on him, with all its strange revelations, it found him

unprepared. And he was aware of a twinge of dire embarrassment and self-conscious shame.

From one to the other of the tense faces, Hector stared with bewildered incredulity. This time, it was Celia who broke the uncomfortable pause. The constrained flatness was gone from her tone, the repression from her manner. Through her eyes and her voice, the girl's spirit glowed forth like a white flame.

"Now that you are here," she said, "there is no need, perhaps, for us to draw lots. Though I think the fate of the loser must be the same. Yes; it surely must be. Hector, it is for you to choose. It is always for the man to choose. I—I love you. I ask no more in life than to serve you and to make you happy so long as I shall live. I—"

Nedda broke in upon the panted avowal.

"She doesn't know what love is!" she cried. "Her soul is as pale as her hair and her skin. She is not the mate for a giant like you, Hector—

for a man whose blood is red and whose veins are hot. Look at me—
look at me, Hector! I'm your mate! Your *mate!* Can't you hear my heart
and all the fiery body of me calling to you? It—"

"I love you," Celia kept repeating softly, her adoration alight in
her swimming eyes. "I love you, Hector. I—I love you so wholly," she
continued, the blood surging scarlet into her brow and cheeks and
suffusing her white throat, "so wholly that there can't be any life without you. So wholly that, even if you couldn't choose between us, I
would be content to—"

"My arms are waiting for you, Hector," breathed Nedda. "They are
waiting for you and aching for you. There can't be any second choice.
Nothing but *you*—or else the sea out there. I belong to you. I—and I
alone! And I—"

Her wild speech broke down in a tempest of passionate weeping.
Celia pressed forward, her arms outstretched.

"I am all yours, Hector," she pleaded. "All of me. My lips were wet
with your blood the day you fought for us. That kiss sealed me to you
for all eternity. Take me for your own. Let me—"

She paused, startled by the swift murder-flare that dried the tears
in Nedda's great eyes. But, rallying fearlessly, she would have gone on,
had not the hysteric contraction of her throat made her pause to fight
for breath.

"Good God!" blithered the man.

To steady himself and to try to think clearly, he strode to the doorway and stood gazing unseeingly out across the glittering expanse
of ocean. The fog was gone. The horizon was as clear as the inshore
waters. The waves and the white beach-sand gave back pulsating hot
eddies of light. And, looking dazedly out, Dallam was aware that his
blank eyes were subconsciously focusing themselves on something.

A wild yell from him brought both the frenziedly pleading girls
to his side in astonishment. Mouthing, dancing, gesticulating, he
pointed seaward.

Two miles offshore rode a white steamship at anchor. Midway
between ship and shore, a boat was dancing along as fast as eight oars
could drive it through the calm blue water.

When the boat made its return trip, the three castaways were huddled in its stern. From over the ship's rail peered down hundreds of men and women—inquisitive tourists from the States: men clad in Palm Beach suits and buckskin shoes and silken shirts; women bedecked in all the glory that Fifth Avenue shops offer to folk of cash and leisure who are about to tour the West Indies.

The two girls stared up at the ranks of untanned faces and ultra-fashionable garments. Then they faced each other in sudden mortal shame—shame that these denizens of their former world should behold them, tattered and bronzed and clad in their hideous make-shifts, and accompanied by a man whose shaggy hair and grime and rags and unkempt beard made him look like a masked-ball Robinson Crusoe.

Their self-humiliation was as nothing to their mortification that these outsiders should see them in Dallam's scarecrow company.

Miserably, they hoped everyone would understand it was no fault of theirs they had been cooped up on the island with such a creature.

Civilization was cracking its fearful slave-whip over the castaways' cowering heads, once more. And with Civilization, as ever, trod her twin-sister, Shame.

There was a glorious moon, that evening. The sea stretched out as smooth as a plain and as bright as the Milky Way. The Obispo liner, Maria Santa, was continuing her lazy jaunt through the West Indies, along the new route that had brought her, on her maiden trip, within sight of the island's signal-flag. The deck was comfortably full of promenaders and of people lounging in steamer-chairs. Dinner was finished. Somewhere a band was playing a dreamy waltz of other days. The music floated out across the warm miles of moonlight water like a caress.

Nedda Burns and Celia were idling happily in deck-chairs, surrounded by a little group of supercorrectly dressed men who were pleasantly eager to learn more of their adventures. Thanks to other women passengers, the two girls were dressed once more in the habiliments of fashion.

Hector Dallam, shaven and shorn and clad most conventionally in borrowed dinner clothes, strolled past. At his side was a gay and pretty young widow, who, on the strength of a bowing-acquaintance in New York, had just annexed him as her own. As he passed the two reclining girls, Dallam glanced away from the widow's fascinatingly upraised eyes long enough to bow to his former island-comrades. His bow was thoroughly courteous. But it held not a fragment of personal interest. And, at once, he bent both his gaze and his thoughts again on the woman who had taken him in tow.

Thus, he did not observe how exceedingly slight and frigid were the nods wherewith Nedda and Celia returned his civil greeting. The two had acknowledged his salute—since decency obliged them to.

But, instantly, both of them turned away and began to talk very fast indeed to the men beside them, as women do when they seek to cover up the sudden intrusion of life's ugly but necessary facts.

The Whiffet

ONE day Michael Ponder, solid and gigantic head of the solid and gigantic packing firm of Ponder & Brothers, roared just a shade too loudly and more than a shade too offensively to the boyish clerk who had been transferred from the shipping department to the inner office.

This because of a letter he accused the youngster of putting into the wrong file. And the clerk, Calvin Bryce, so far forgot the abject humility due to his huge employer as to wheel on the giant with a snarl of:

"Look here! Neither you nor any other man on two legs is going to swear at me and get away with it!"

For an instant Ponder glowered down on the stripling who, pale and with just the faintest tremor, clenched his fists and stood defiantly meeting the august glare. The office force stopped work, breathlessly waiting the curt command for Bryce to go to the cashier and get his pay.

The word of discharge was not spoken. From behind his glower Ponder was scanning the revolted serf. He noted the clenched fists, the steady eyes, the unflinching little body. But, presently he also noticed that unconquerable vestige of trembling. And the reluctant admiration which had begun to replace his scowl changed to something like disappointment. He turned away into the private office, calling back over his shoulder, with indulgent contempt:

"You mangy little whiffet!" And the glass door shut behind him before Bryce could retort or could fairly grasp the meaning of the taunt.

Thereafter Michael Ponder never again swore at young Bryce.

Indeed he ignored him for the most part; except to pause once on his way through the room to jerk a disapproving thumb at the shiny elbow of Calvin's coat and say:

"You seem to have forgotten the office rule, Bryce, about the staff presenting a neat and well-groomed appearance. A new suit is cheaper to get than a new job in these hard times."

But throughout the whole half-acre main building of the plant seeped the story of Calvin Bryce's brief clash with the boss; and of the latter's grinning epithet of "You mangy little whiffet!"

And from that day on Bryce was cursed with the office nickname of "The Whiffet." Having been conferred by the mighty Ponder himself, the name stuck.

Now one dictionary defines "whiffet" as follows:

> An insignificant person who assumes a manner of importance.

Which assuredly makes the term a misfit for Calvin Bryce. In the first place, he was not insignificant, despite his mere five feet four of stature and his hundred an twenty-odd pounds of fleshless weight and his retiring ways. Nor did he assume a manner of importance or any other manner.

Cal was thirty-three years old; and he not only was married but had a daughter of twelve. It was because of this wife and daughter that his brief blaze of wrath against the bullying Ponder had been followed so quickly by an involuntary shudder—a thought of the loss to them, should his revolt cost him his job. It was also because of them that his office suit was shiny and that he had worn it for five seasons.

If heroism consists of sacrifice and of long-enduring struggle, bravely borne for the sake of others, then assuredly The Whiffet was a hero. And there are a million similar heroes in the wage ranks to-day—men who endure with outward calm a course of bullying and hectoring and overwork from office bosses in order that their own dear ones may continue to be clad and fed. If such folk be heroes, there surely must be an equally superlative term to describe the boss who, knowing the conditions, harries the voluntarily shackled wage slave because of his helplessness.

All of which is extraneous to our story but is the wisest thing in it.

At high school Cal Bryce had won the interscholastic featherweight boxing championship of Midwestburg, his home city. He was a natural-born boxer, not only in physique but in brain and coolness and pluck. There was great wiry strength in his seemingly meager frame. And without having the slightest trace of brutality in his make up he loved a square fight above all else.

His local prowess caught the notice of a fight promoter in Midwestburg, who added the lad to his string, while Cal was working his way through business college after graduation from high school. And, for a year or so Bryce forged rapidly ahead in the fight game. His manager foresaw the featherweight championship close ahead and predicted for Cal a second Terry McGovern career.

Then, at twenty, Bryce met Celia Marsh, a substitute schoolteacher of his own age. Two months later he married her.

Celia thought pugilism was one degree worse than burglary. And before she would consent to marry him Cal had to promise most solemnly to give up his loved profession and to look for some less debasing form of work. It was a fearful wrench to his ambitions and desires. But if Celia had told him she would marry none but a one-armed man he would right blithely have cut off either arm.

Thus, while they lived on his ring earnings, he found a petty job in the packing house of Ponder & Brothers and threw all his energies, if not his heart, into mastering the new and uncongenial work.

By the time he was earning a living wage there, the bulk of his fight savings had vanished. Marrying and furnishing a flat and settling down to housekeeping—these are not on the free list. The remainder of his hoard went during Celia's long illness after Baby Mildred was born.

The next eleven years had been made up of days of utter drudgery and of the pleasantest kind of home life. All the couple's ambitions centered around little Mildred. She was their idol, their one life-hope, the only child fetish of their home.

They vowed to give her every advantage, although like most of the rest of us they were not wholly clear in their own minds as to what "advantage" really means for a child. They did not appreciate that often the greatest "advantage" which can be given the child of poor parents is a rigid training in economy and in unselfishness and in the sharing of family deprivations—all of which go to the building up of iron character and of true greatness.

Cal and Celia themselves had had this upbringing. And they had profited thereby. Yet they resolved that their adored child should have everything which they themselves had missed in the way of fun and social life and education and comforts. And they kept their resolve.

Public school teaches far more than is contained in its mere curriculum. Yet, from the first, they decided against public school for Mildred. She was sent to the costliest private school which her parents could afford. Celia took to turning and revamping her own old dresses. Cal's clothes began to take on the shininess that was henceforth theirs. But Mildred went to school, dressed as tastefully and as expensively as any girl there. Whereat her father and mother rejoiced in the sacrifices they were making.

When she was twelve they took her from the first private school and sent her to another. This second establishment was patronized by the loftiest families in Midwestburg. It was Celia who chanced to hear of its rarefied existence and who persuaded Cal that Mildred ought to go there.

"You see, dear," she reasoned as Cal scratched his head bewilderedly over the cost estimate she had scribbled, "Mildred is beginning to grow up. It is time she made friends who can be of real use to her in later years. It's different with a boy. But a girl like Mildred must start out by knowing the right people. She'll form friendships at Mademoiselle Cretin's School with girls who will some day be social leaders. They will invite her to their houses. She will become one of their set. She will meet eligible men there—men of wealth and social rank who—"

"Oh, hold on!" expostulated Cal. "The baby's only just twelve. She—"

"She can't begin her upward journey too young," retorted Celia. "I only wish we had known about Mademoiselle Cretin's School five years ago."

That month Mildred went to the new school; and that month Cal stopped buying lunches and began to carry a surreptitious sandwich to the office, instead. But that month, by Providence's mercy, his pay was boosted four dollars a week. And nothing cracked—noticeably—under the strain.

Almost at once, the couple learned that membership in Mademoiselle Cretin's School was like marriage and automobiling, in that the initial expense is the lightest part of it. There were myriad details of extra cost that neither of them had dreamed of. There were a million-and-one little expenditures, all of which were proven needful—expenses that ranged from class pins to school-dance dresses. Also the everyday type of clothing worn by Mademoiselle Cretin's gilt-edged pupils needed much living up to.

Then it was that Providence once more intervened in Cal's behalf by getting him a chance to balance the books for three successive neighborhood stores in the evenings, and to compile some dry statistics for a report which one of his superiors was making out for the Ponders. This meant several hours of nightly toil after a nine-hour day at the office. But it also meant a thimbleful of extra cash to go toward meeting the new expenses.

It was three months after his spat with Michael Ponder that the back-breaking straw was added to his burdens. Cal came home one evening to find Celia and the little girl in a glow of ecstasy. Through their volleyed explanations he gleaned the ensuing vital facts:

First, that there was a secret society in Mademoiselle Cretin's School. Second, that it was known by the mystic name of "Sigma Sigma." Third, that it was ultraexclusive and admitted to membership only a chosen few of the school's pupils. Fourth, that those few comprised daughters of the richest and most socially prominent families in Midwestburg. Fifth—and all-important, that the always popular Mildred had that day been elected to the sacredly secret clique and that it was quite the most wonderfully advantageous thing which had ever befallen the Bryce family or could ever be hoped to befall it.

Duly, though less understandingly than they, Cal rejoiced with his wife and daughter. Duly he listened to Celia's dazzling forecasts of Mildred's future. Then came the catch in it all. And he realized why Celia's blond face had worn that glint of nervousness beneath her air of rapture as she had told him the news.

Briefly, the initiation fee to Sigma Sigma was one hundred dollars. The darling little jeweled fraternity pin would cost another twenty-five dollars. Total, one hundred and twenty-five dollars. In other words, more ready cash than Calvin Bryce had had lying loose at any one time in the past ten years.

Cal said so—blunderingly yet frankly. Then Mildred burst into shrill weeping and raved loudly that her parents were the meanest people in the world and were always skimping her and spoiling her fun and grudging her everything—and how could she face the girls and tell them her stingy father wouldn't even let her have such a measly sum?

Celia shed a few tears, too, and looked at the miserable Cal with dreary-eyed reproach.

Cal jammed his well-worn hat down over his ears and stamped out of the house. He wanted to be alone—and to think. Every word of the silly, spoiled child's had cut him on the bare heart. He was fairly writhing. Even Celia had eyed him as though he were to blame in not being able to reach out and snatch one hundred and twenty-five dollars from the atmosphere.

He tried not to remember the scene at home, but to cast about in his sorely harassed brain for some miraculous way to get the sum which apparently meant present bliss and untold future social advantages to his worshiped daughter.

He might of course borrow it from the office, or seek to, and pay it back at the rate of five dollars a week out of his salary. But a gleam of intelligence deterred him. As things now were it was hard enough to save rent money from his tiny week's pay. Moreover it gave a chap a bad name to be known as an office borrower. The boss was supposed to frown on such transactions, though they gave him fuller power over the men thus involved.

No, there was no way to get the cash. Incidentally, there was no way to make Mildred believe her adoring father was a not miser who cared nothing for her. Bryce squirmed at the thought.

Then, on the instant, he saw before him the solution to his whole problem.

He had come to a halt in his aimless strolling and was standing idly in front of a lighted store window. One corner of the window contained a cardboard sign, put there at billboard rates.

The sign set forth the stirring news that the Baldy Todd Burlesque

Company was to appear at the Olympic Theater that week. The bulk of the space was taken up in announcing the show's "added attraction," in the shape of "Tug" Brindell, featherweight champion of the Middle West, who would give an exhibition with the punching bag and box three rounds with his sparring partner.

At the bottom of the card, in red letters, was an announcement that the champion stood ready to box any and all amateurs of one hundred and twenty-two pounds or under, at the end of each performance; and that he would pay one hundred and fifty dollars to any such who could last out four rounds against him.

Calvin Bryce had seen this sign a score of times on fences and in windows during the past week. It had meant nothing to him, except to stir old and buried memories. For Tug Brindell had been a Midwestburg boy like himself and had had his start in Bryce's home town. His present scintillating career might well have been Cal's own, if it had not been for Celia.

Now, for the first time, Bryce found himself scanning the one-hundred-and-fifty-dollar offer with a queer little thrill. At last it had a personal meaning for him.

In his day, he had been as good a beginner as had Tug Brindell. And his one recreation outside his home, this past thirteen years, had been his thrice-a-week hour of hard exercise at the Y. M. C. A. gym. There he had not only kept himself reasonably fit by calisthenic work but had boxed with the instructor and with fellow clerks.

Thus, at thirty-three, he was far suppler and in better general condition than are most business men of his age. True, for the past three months he had let the gym lapse because of his night work. But he was confident he was in more than tolerable shape for a short bout.

In any case, he was certain he could ride out four rounds against any man of his weight. All he need do was to cover up and keep out of his opponent's way as much as he could and trust to old-time skill and stamina and craft to enable him to avoid a knock-out.

The store into whose window he was peering chanced to be a grocery. Cal stepped in and asked leave to weigh himself on the back-room scales. To his annoyance he tipped the beam at one hundred and twenty-eight. This, after making allowance for his clothing, whose weight he knew to within a few ounces.

The Baldy Todd show was to begin its engagement at the Olympic three days hence. That meant he must get rid of six pounds in seventy-two hours. To a fat man or even a large man the task would have been more or less simple. But Calvin Bryce carried not a pound of soft flesh on his slim body. There was but one certain method of losing six pounds in three days. Namely, to "dry up."

Drying up is an expedient often resorted to by those who for some cogent reason must lose much weight in a short time. It is not a pleasant nor a healthful nor a strengthening process. It consists in depriving the system of all forms of moisture. No food containing liquid properties must be eaten. No drop of water must be drunk, so long as nature can do without water. Most vegetables, all fresh meats, tea and coffee and other beverages, in fact everything which moistens the inner man, must be avoided.

Nature, ever craving water, uses up such moisture as the body contains; and when liquid is denied she begins with the fats and similar easily consumed secretions. As a result the weight decreases at an amazingly rapid rate. But so do the stamina and the strength which depend so largely on the secretions thus dried up.

Frank Erne, in 1900, sought this means of bringing himself down to the weight required for his battle with Terry McGovern. And almost before the fight began he was beaten. Nature is a cruel dame, who permits no one to tamper, unpunished, with her world-old rules.

Nevertheless, Calvin Bryce took this one short cut to the required one hundred and twenty-two pounds and to the one hundred and fifty dollars cash. He was confident he could make the weight and that he could do it with none too much loss of strength or of speed or of endurance. And he rejoiced mightily at the chance which fortune had thrown in front of him. But prudently he said nothing to Celia of his plans. He explained his change of diet to her on the grounds of indigestion. And forthwith he began the drying-up process.

The fact that Tug Brindell was a Midwestburg product filled the Olympic on the opening night of the show's engagement. As the stupidly tepid performance ended Brindell's manager came out on the stage, repeating the champion's offer of one hundred and fifty dollars to any one-hundred and-twenty-two-pound "amachoor" who could stand against the redoubtable Tug for four rounds. His call for volunteers was answered almost before it was voiced.

From a second-row aisle seat Cal Bryce scrambled up the runway onto the stage. In one hand he clutched his trunks and fighting shoes. Ten minutes later he was facing Tug Brindell in the center of the improvised ring and the manager was calling "Time!" for the first round.

With something of his olden battle joy Cal came up to the fray. He felt splendidly fit. Before his eager vision danced the one-hundred-and-fifty-dollar prize money. In his memory loomed the sulkily tearful child he had left at home. He had no fear of recognition from any one in the audience. The disreputable old Olympic was not a resort likely to be favored with the patronage of the severely correct office force at Ponder & Brothers'. Nor would any of his colleagues expect to see the meekly taciturn Whiffet in the role of gladiator. To add to his security, Cal had given his name to the announcer as "John Tebbins."

True to his plan, he backed away from the encouragingly dancing Brindell and continued to give ground before the other's careless rushes. Almost from the start the champion saw this opponent of his was no novice who had picked up a smattering of fistic skill from streets or gym. Such volunteers he was used to. And with such he usually played for a couple of rounds before addressing himself to the easy task of deleting them. This for the amusement of the audience.

But here was a different proposition. This supposed novice was shifty and catlike and graceful and he showed in every motion the mark of the professional. Moreover, such of his counters as landed were of a backbone-jarring quality and were delivered with consummate science.

Fierce anger blazed up in the heart of the money-loving Brindell. Here opposed to him was that bane of all professional sports men—a "ringer." This was a seasoned ring warrior who was seeking to annex the proffered one hundred and fifty dollars—and perhaps to outpoint Tug or even to knock him out.

Brindell abandoned his grin and his amused self-confidence and began to fight. Into Cal he tore, battling with every atom of force and ferocity in his perfectly trained body. Cal met him, foot to foot, with blow for blow, when he could not side-step or retreat. And the crowd roared itself hoarse at the outsider's splendid showing.

But the end was inevitable.

Tug Brindell was twenty-three years old and he had kept himself in the pink of condition. Cal was ten years older—this in a game where every year after twenty-five is a terrible handicap. For thirteen years he had taken only mild exercise. For the past few months he had gone without lunches or at most had eaten a mere sandwich at noon. For years he and Celia had skimped their daily fare on behalf of the money needed for Mildred.

For the past few months, too, he had been working nearly every evening and late into the night, after his office day. For three days he had tortured his system by the enfeebling drying-up process. None of these things tend to ring success.

During the first round Cal held his own— almost more than held his own. But as he went to his corner at the call of time he was aware of a wabbliness of knee, a heaviness in the arms, a shortness of breath, a sense of fast-increasing weariness. He had shot his bolt. And he knew it. Yet, confident of his power to ride out the three remaining rounds, he came back with a vim for the second period.

This time the men did not meet in mid-ring. Almost before Cal had stepped forth from his corner Brindell was upon him. With a succession of short-arm blows he drove Bryce back against the ropes, giving him no chance to escape.

Nor did he trouble himself now to elude or block most of Cal's counters. Certain of his ability to avoid a knock-out so early in the bout, he bored in, savage with rage and eager to put out this ringer as quickly as possible.

Gallantly Cal met the whirlwind assault that he could not beat off. Momentarily weaker and slowing down, he could no longer avoid the champion's whalebone smashes as easily as in the first round. Such of them as got through to his face or body began to distress him more and more. To the audience he was still putting up a slashing battle. But he knew himself gone.

Slipping aside once from Brindell's ceaseless rush he drove his left to the champion's jaw with all his remaining strength and snap.

But luck was against him. For as he delivered the blow his braced left toe slipped ever so little on the ill-resined canvas. And his fist struck glancingly, instead of flush, on Brindell's chin point. Thus a possible knock-out was spoiled.

Yet the champion's head snapped backward under the impact and the champion reeled—dizzily. Starkly eager to take advantage of this one chance before his own waning powers should fail, Cal threw caution aside and jumped for his man. As he did so Brindell straightened from the assumed dizziness, blocked the flailing right fist that sought his jaw, stepped in with lightning speed and uppercut his adversary.

The blow caught Bryce under the jaw point, lifting his feet clean off the floor and then atoned for this bit of levitation by stretching his entire body in a huddled mass on the canvas.

It was a mighty blow and delivered with all Brindell's fearful strength. The champion stepped back, while his manager, who also served as timekeeper and referee, prepared to go through the seem-ingly needless formula of counting the victim out.

At the count of six Cal Bryce shook convulsively. At the count of eight he was lumbering blindly to his feet. The audience bellowed and stamped encouragement to the plucky loser. Still gripped by fury, Brindell rushed in to finish the swaying and defenseless man. But, as he struck, the call of time checked the slaughter.

Back to his corner Cal Bryce groped his way. He was beaten—hopelessly beaten. That crashing blow to the jaw had taken from him his last hoarded atom of speed. And untrained and dried up as he was there was no earthly chance of his coming back to anything approach-ing recovery in the sixty seconds of rest.

Yet, out of his corner at the call of time he made his uncertain way. His head sang from the jaw smash. His body was as heavy as lead. His limbs all but refused the commands of his dazed will power. He dizzily hoped to be able to keep out of Brindell's way until he himself should have more time to get back his vanished speed and hitting power.

But Brindell willed it otherwise. He had no intention of sparing this professional who had rung himself in as a novice and who had tried to fool and belittle the champion. As before, he rushed from the very instant the round began. In less than ten seconds he recognized that Cal was of no further menace to him. Brindell knew he could end the fight at any moment. But still rankling at the trick attempted on him, he planned to make the trickster pay full price. Wherefore, during the next two minutes his scientifically driving fists played havoc with his foe. He administered such a beating as sickened even his elephant-hided manager and made three women in the audience faint. Then, setting himself, he smote.

Cal had kept on his reeling feet, taking the awful punishment and essaying with uselessly hanging arms to fight back. Now, at the finishing blow, he crumpled and pitched forward on his face. Nor did he come to his senses until, some minutes later, he found himself lying on a table in one of the dressing rooms.

Promptly at nine, next morning, a truly hideous creature limped into the office at Ponder & Brothers' packing house and sat painfully down at a desk. From the astounded roomful of fellow workers arose a gasp of incredulous horror. The newcomer had some of the general characteristics of The Whiffet. But a second and closer glance was required to make certain of his identity. Tug Brindell had done his work with scientific efficiency.

Before the first excited voice could be raised in query the door of the private office opened, and Michael Ponder came into the room with a handful of papers. Halfway to the farther door the giant halted. His careless eye had fallen on Cal.

For a moment he stood blinking. Then abruptly he turned back into his private office and shut the door behind him. Immediately the buzzer on Cal's desk sounded. With leaden heart and reluctant limbs Bryce got up and prepared to obey the dread summons.

Into the sacred private office he limped, shoulders back, head up, face a battered mask.

He had been looking forward with wage-slave terror to this meeting with his employer—the employer who demanded that his staff present "a neat and well-groomed appearance." All night Cal had worried over it. Almost he had been tempted to report sick and stay home all day to listen to his wife's tearful reproaches. But he knew it must be many days before his face could hope to return to normal. And there was no sense in putting off the evil hour.

He found Ponder awaiting him on the middle of the gaudy office rug, hands behind back, legs apart, shaggy brows puckered. And at sight of the disapproving wonder in his chief's glare Cal abandoned the well-rehearsed lie about a trolley car accident and resolved to spit the truth at this smug-faced hulk who ruled his financial destinies. He would not stoop to lie to him. The man wasn't worth a lie.

"Bryce!" Ponder was intoning severely. "What is the meaning of this outrageous appearance? How dare you come to the office in such—"

He got no farther. Forgetting the propriety of waiting in servile courtesy for the great man to finish speaking, Cal Bryce was at him with the truth.

Blurting out his words from between swollen lips, he told his story. Briefly, concisely he told it. He began with the need for raising one hundred and twenty-five dollars and he told what that need was. Then he went on to the means he had employed to get the money and described sketchily the fight with Tug Brindell. Not once pausing for breath he hurled the entire, terse narrative into Ponder's fat face. When he came to an abrupt end he stood with shoulders still squared to take his ignominious sentence of discharge.

But for a full minute Ponder did not speak—still staring cryptically at the battered clerk. Once before had the boss stared thus at Cal. And at that time, behind his flash of defiance, Bryce had trembled ever so little. But now he felt no tendency to tremble. He had withstood three rounds of Tug Brindell's murderous onslaught and he was in no mood to shrink from a mere job destroyer.

At last, when Ponder still kept silence, Cal put all to the test by asking a favor which he had been leading up to when he told the story of the fight. It could do no harm to ask it, even though it were refused.

"I should like," said Bryce, doggedly, "I should like to get off at noon to-day. The off time can be docked from my pay of course," he added from wage-slave habit.

Ponder grinned.

"It'll do you no harm to get to bed and stay there till you're more like a human and less like a devastated sector," he said with massive wit. "Chase along, at noon or chase now, whichever you like. Stay in bed till you—"

"I wasn't asking time off to go to bed, sir," rasped Bryce, honesty still riding his tongue. "I want to go to a Turkish bath and get suppled up a bit for to-night."

"To-night?" echoed Ponder, adding, "So that you'll sleep better?"

"No, sir. So that I'll fight better," answered Cal, simply.

Ponder's plump jaw drooped.

"What's that?" he blithered. "Fight better? What d' you mean—'fight?' You've sure had your dose of—"

"Don't you see?" interrupted Cal, impatient at the man's stupidity. "Brindell's only going to be at the Olympic two nights more. That means I've only two more chances at the one hundred and fifty dollars. I—"

"You wall-eyed fool!" yelled Ponder, aghast. "You don't mean to say you're going up, again, for such a beating as you got last night? You're stark crazy, man!"

"Maybe," assented Cal. "Or maybe not. Anyhow, I'm not due to find such another quick way of making the one hundred and fifty dollars. So I've got to take every advantage of *this* chance. Besides—I've been thinking it over and I believe I can maybe do it. Either to-night or to-morrow night. You see, I've had experience, now, in his way of fighting. And I'll know better how to keep out of his way. If he hadn't fooled me into going in to finish him when he played groggy, I'd never have got that haymaker that took all the steam out of me and I might have lasted the four rounds. No, this time I won't let him fool me. I'll stall and keep away. Maybe I can last out."

For another long minute Ponder blinked owlishly at the bruised and cut and swollen face. Then he said:

"I suppose you know he'll hurt you ten times harder than last night—now that you're just one big bruise?"

"It's worth the try," said Cal, tersely. "Can I go back to my desk now? If I'm going to the bath at noon, I'll have to hustle to clear up my work. Thanks for letting me have the half day, sir. I'll be on the job at the usual time to-morrow, of course."

That night, as before, Cal Bryce was the first man in the Olympic's noisy audience to scramble up the runway in response to the call for volunteers. And, as before, he faced unflinching his opponent's hurricane rush.

The bout was a hazy dream, afterward, to Bryce. He realized that Tug Brindell was forever forcing the pace, that the champion's blows shook him like an earthquake and hurt most unbearably as they smote his aching ribs and face. Three times Bryce was knocked down.

And all three times he took advantage of the full count of nine, before heaving himself to his feet again.

Every second of the bout was agony. Every second he forced himself to endure the onslaught as best he could, waxing more and more hopeless of withstanding his merciless opponent for another round.

But he fought on.

At the end of an eternity, the fourth round began. At the end of countless eternities it ended—with Calvin Bryce still on his reeling and staggering legs. By some miracle he had escaped a knock-out and had remained fighting to the end. He could scarcely believe his own good luck.

Hustling into his clothes and clutching tightly the fifteen dirty ten-dollar bills the champion's manager had so grudgingly handed him, the bleeding and exhausted little man turned his swollen face homeward.

At the same time a glumly scowling Tug Brindell slouched into the Olympic's "star" dressing room and confronted a huge and obese visitor who sprawled on one chair with his big feet on another. The visitor hauled from his pocket five fifty-dollar bills and passed them across to the sullen Brindell.

"Here you are," said he. "You sure earned 'em. Thanks."

Stuffing the money into his pocket, Brindell grumbled:

"I wouldn't 'a' done that for any man alive but you, Mr. Ponder. I'm not forgetting you gave me my ring start and my first backing. And I'm not forgetting how you helped me out when I sent you that hurry call for cash when they cleaned me in N'Orleans. I'm a grateful cuss. And I done what I done, to-night, because it was *you* that asked me to. But it don't do a champ no good to have it known that an amachoor stayed the distance with him. It don't—"

"So you said when I put this up to you," interrupted Ponder, the grin still playing on his fat jowls. "And, once or twice to-night, from the wings, it looked as if you were going to double cross me. If you had—"

"That's no way to talk!" said Brindell aggrievedly. "Not to a white man. You told me to give him everything he c'd take, but not put him out. And likewise I done it. I had to make some sort of a showing, didn't I, before that crowd? They'd 'a' hollered 'fake!' if I'd—"

But Ponder was not listening. He had broken into a noiseless chuckle that shook his whole enormous body. Speaking rather to himself than to Brindell, he exulted:

"The Whiffet's no whiffet at all. He's a hell-cat. I had a suspicion he was, that time he talked back to me, a couple of months ago. But then I saw he was shivering. And I figured he was a bluffer. But after the things he told me to-day—and the way he scrapped, to-night—say! It's worth a good many times that two hundred and fifty dollars to me to know I've got a man with all that gameness on my staff. He's thrown away—in the piker job I stuck him in. To-morrow he's going to start climbing upward. And if he's the man I know he is, he's due to climb plenty high—with Michael Ponder giving him the boosts he needs. Thanks, again, Tug! You've done me a big favor. But don't go gassing to other folks about my being a patron of boxing. I've always kept it dark. It hurts a man's business name. Good night!"

Calvin Bryce—looking as if a fire truck had twice run over him—walked lamely into his flat. Mildred was in bed and asleep. But Celia had sat up for him. She forbore to question or to scold. There was something maternal in the loving arms she passed about his aching body as she laid her cool cheek against his puffed and feverish face.

Cal, with a tired air of triumph, fished out the money and laid it in her lap. At sight of it she smiled—a rueful little smile.

"You poor boy!" said she. "I could have saved you all this horrible experience tonight, if you had come home for dinner—or if I had known where to find you. I could—"

"What do you mean?" he asked dully.

"Oh, it seems some famous sociologist—I forget his name—delivered a lecture at Mademoiselle Cretin's School this morning. And he explained his theories so simply and so fascinatingly that all the girls not only seem to have grasped his meaning but they went wild over him. Of course it is only a phase. But for the moment they are daft about economy and 'unearned increment' and all that sort of thing. Mildred came home fairly bubbling over with enthusiasm. On the strength of his teachings, the Sigma Sigma is disbanded, as 'criminally capitalistic;' and I understand that most of the girls have gone home resolved to lecture their rich fathers on the subject of 'hoarded wealth.' "

"But—"

"Even Mildred. She wanted to sit up to tell you how wicked you and I are—not to divide all our 'surplus earnings' with the poor. She—"

A gust of laughter from Cal broke in on her amused homily.

"That's just what we'll do!" he declared, merrily. "This one hundred and fifty dollars is 'surplus earnings.' And we're going to divide it between two poor people named Celia and Calvin Bryce. And we're going to insist that they spend it on some really up-to-date clothes for themselves. They sure need them. Hurroo for sociology!"

Beauty

KURT MASSON inherited from his American father enough money to buy him butterless bread for life. From his Slavic mother he inherited a dreamy distaste for needless work and a love for the Beautiful. This beauty love was a creed with Kurt; perhaps a monomania.

When his parents died, one within a month of the other, Kurt waited only long enough to wind up their slender estates. Then he turned his back forever on the mid-Western town of his birth and came to New York to live.

It was not the lure of adventure or of profit or of crowds or a metropolitan urge which dragged Kurt Masson to the rackety and overthronged little tongue of top-heavy land between the North and East Rivers. These things meant little to him. But something else meant everything.

New York, he had heard his discontented mother say, was the home of American art and beauty. Paris, London, Munich—these and the other foreign art centers whereof she had sighed—were all too far away and too uncertain for Kurt's lean income. New York was at least within striking distance of his birthplace.

Kurt's first month in Manhattan was a daze of wonder. For the only time in all his twenty-seven years his beauty-starvation was fed. And from that same feeding it waxed insatiable.

For hours he would stand looking down lower Fifth Avenue at the white arch framing Washington Square's mass of green, with the clean of the blue sky above it all. For miles he would plod dreamily, glimpsing narrow vistas of sunset water at the ends of the cañonlike side streets. Riverside Drive was paradise to him—not for the amorphous lines and architecture of its buildings but for its glorious sweep and curves and spaces and for the shipping-dotted river and the elephant-hued cliffs on the Jersey shore.

Jostled and sworn at he would stand entranced in the rush of Park Row, an ache of delight in his throat as he watched the shimmer of the Woolworth Tower through early-morning mists.

Much that he saw was ugly. Much that was banal struck him as exquisite. But to him it was wonderful. For his background was the mean town of his birth, with its soft-coal murk and the pompous squalor of its newness.

After the first month Kurt paid scant heed to New York's outward charms. For he had found the art galleries and the museums. And there he went quite mad. For three solid weeks he haunted the Metropolitan Museum of Art, drunk with the glow of its Sarollas and Titians, shivering in vaguely raptured awe at dim old masters with greenish flesh tints and *oscuro* backgrounds.

The supreme thrill he had thus far known was when, in an aimlessly enchanted wandering through the Metropolitan, he chanced upon the Benvenuto Cellini chalice. He stood before it, bareheaded, moveless, mute. Its glory hurt him as with physical pain.

Presently, with the true discoverer fever, Kurt widened his field of exploration to include the Hispanic Museum. He skimmed the surface of its delights in a single day. And then he went on to the International Museum. He went no farther, then or on later days.

In the Ceramics Room of the International he came to a stiffening halt—as he had done before the Cellini chalice—and for a like reason. There, in a central case—the room's other art treasures skillfully made to lead up to such a climax—stood a single small vase. It stood on velvet. Beside it was the antique and strangely wrought copper casket which once had held it.

Kurt gazed at the vase until his eyes ached. Exquisitely slender and graceful in its aureate beauty, it was carved and chased with figures which seemed to float, rather than rest, on its burnished red-gold surfaces. A gleam of gems, here and there, twinkled like meadow fireflies among the dancingly floating figures and around the daintily curling lip.

The beauty worshiper had an absurd craving to kneel in obeisance before such unearthly loveliness. Compared to it the Cellini chalice seemed to him coarse and unwieldy. He trembled with the wonder of the creation.

Then at last he turned to the guard who sat boredly at the far end of the Ceramics Room and who was eying the visitor with drowsy truculence.

"Can—will you please tell me its name?" asked Kurt, pointing reverently at the vase. "I didn't get a catalogue. The number is seven hundred and—"

"That's the Maximinian Amphora," said the guard ungraciously. "Costliest thing in the museum. That's why *I'm* stuck here. The room wouldn't need a reg'lar guard, else."

He spoke as if he harbored a grudge against the Amphora for imprisoning him in so gloomy a corner of the museum.

"It—it is very wonderful!" breathed Kurt. "You're a lucky man to be able to sit here and look at it all day and every day. It is—"

"I'd rather look at a tripe sandwich and a bottle of decent beer, for a change," grumbled the guard. "It don't look like such a much, to me, that thing don't. Folks comes in here and raves about it and stands google-eyed over it. And it's gotta go back into the big safe every night, like it was the national debt. But it's just a gold jug to me. I've seen prettier on the 'Your-Choice-For-Three-Dollars' counter, down at Kriegstein's. But—"

Kurt's genuine shudder and expression of horror seemed to grate on the guard's temper.

"Anyhow," he defended himself, "I ain't paid to throw fits at sight of it; nor yet to answer fool questions about the thing every time a bird comes in here that's too mean to pay for a cat'logue. I—"

Kurt broke in on the blaspheming of beauty by stalking from the room. He went down to the main corridor's entrance and bought a gray-paper catalogue from the attendant there. Riffling the pages he came upon what he sought.

He glanced impatiently over the verbose account of the gift of the Amphora to the Emperor Maximinian by an Egyptian potentate whose ancestor had looted it at the sack of Babylon—the loss of it until the eighth century, A. D.—its recovery and its preservation as an heirloom in a noble Italian family—and its nineteenth-century sale to an American multimillionaire for seven hundred and seventy-five thousand dollars. The catalogue's description continued:

> The Maximinian Amphora has been tabulated among the five most precious art treasures extant. Ordinarily, it would have been placed in the Gem Room. But the donor expressed a wish that it remain in the Ceramics Room, in company with his priceless Egyptian and Etruscan and Babylonian collection of pottery. In accordance with his desires it has—

Kurt read no farther. He would as soon have thought of wasting time in studying the chemical compound of chromo coloring during a sunset as of poring over this dry-as-dust account of the Amphora when the Amphora itself awaited his gaze. And back he hastened to the Ceramics Room.

He stayed there until closing time. And he was back at the museum next morning before the great bronze doors of the institution were open. Kurt did not try to analyze his emotions of hypnotic rapture as he stood, hour by hour, drinking deep of the beauty of the Amphora. He studied its every chased figure, its every softly gleaming gem, its marvel of symmetry, its intoxication of form and hue. Each angle of inspection brought out some new loveliness.

His beauty-starved youth was atoned for. He had found the most beautiful thing in existence. And for the time he was content to gaze on it in tireless adoration and to revel in its myriad phases of new grace and color.

The guard had glared coldly on him, the first day. On the second, the old fellow favored him with an open scowl. On the morning of the third, as Kurt came into the room, the guard whistled to a page boy who was loitering in the corridor.

A few moments later, Kurt Masson turned impatiently to find a thin little old man close beside him. In this off season, visitors to the Ceramics Room were comparatively few. For such of them as had paused to admire the Amphora, during the past two days, Kurt had been aware of a cross antagonism. And he had eyed them with scarcely more favor than the guard had bestowed on him.

Kurt glanced annoyedly at this fragile, little old gentleman, in rusty black and skullcap, who had stopped beside him. And now he noted that the newcomer was looking, not at the Amphora but at him. He moved a step aside. The old man smiled up again into his face, in friendly fashion.

"I was told you had spent the best part of two days here," said he pleasantly. "And I left word to be sent for if you came back. Why have you been studying the Amphora so long? Are you a collector?"

"No," said Kurt, in dull resentment of the breaking-in on his exalted mood.

Then, urged on by the other's air of friendliness, he blurted out boyishly:

"It's the most—the most perfect thing I ever saw or ever dreamed of. I—I can't keep away from it."

The little man's terrierlike watchfulness, behind the smiling mask, melted away at the unquestionable sincerity of the reply and the shining eyes of the speaker. As Kurt drew back, ashamed of his own gushing outburst, the other nodded entire comprehension.

"I understand," said he. "It is not given to most people to worship beauty. At least, to worship it in that way. You are one of the gifted few. I congratulate you. And you could not have found a worthier object for your worship. I gather you are not a New Yorker? Perhaps you might be interested in seeing some of the documents that trace the history of the Amphora. I have them in my cabinet. Including the parchments written in post-classical Latin. Would you care to see them?"

As Kurt still gaped, embarrassedly, the man added:

"My name is Renier. I am curator of ceramics, here. Would you care to come to my office and see the data on the Amphora? I have a little time free this morning."

Thus began a queer acquaintanceship between two men who had not one solitary thing in common except their mutual love of beauty. It was as though an untrained child with a natural ear for music should have struck up a friendship with Caruso.

For Gerard Renier was one of the world's foremost scholars and antiquaries. In his cubby-hole office, on the third floor of the International Museum, he was a central figure in the lore of the ages. He knew the history and exact whereabouts of every art treasure along his own line of work. From all over the globe collectors and antiquaries came to him or corresponded with him. To the public at large he was unknown. In the realm of ceramics and other branches of the antique he was as famed as Schliemann.

At Renier's feet, figuratively, sat Kurt Masson, neophyte. He haunted the International Museum. He scanned the papers and parchments Renier let him see. And, ever and again, he would return to the Amphora, to study it and to devour its beauty. His obsession for the treasure waxed instead of waning with the passing of the days.

The guard, long since classifying him as a fellow freak of old Renier's, let him severely alone. Other museum attendants accepted his presence as natural, since so often he passed in and out in company with the curator.

Kurt could not tell just how or when his enjoyment of the Amphora merged into an insane craving to possess it. So far as he could tell, the craving was born full grown.

At first he shrank in horror from the vagrant idea of stealing the prize. Then, bit by bit, he ceased his useless struggle to escape from the longing. The Maximinian Amphora was the most beautiful object on earth to him. And he hated to share its beauty with a horde of sheep-like sight-seers and musty old collectors! It was not fair. The thought was racking his brain, night and day. At last, he gave himself up to it.

Then, with a coolness which amazed his wontedly impulsive self, he set to work at making his plans. And again he was astounded at his own resourceful cleverness. He was in no hurry, now that his mind was fully made up. He could afford to take his time.

One morning a sluicing rain swept the streets clear of pedestrians and left the International Museum with scarce six visitors in all its vast expanse. Kurt, climbing the stairs, glanced in at Renier's cubby-hole office. The old gentleman had been confined at home with a bad cold, for several days. Kurt had been almost certain the sick curator would not venture forth in such weather. Yet he looked in, to make sure.

Thence he strolled across to the closet where the various electric appliances of the third floor were grouped. Here was the night watchman's time clock. Here, too, among other things, were the switch and clock of the fire alarm, which was turned on for practice test at three o'clock every Monday afternoon. Its dial was now set for three.

After a glimpse at his own nickel watch, Kurt dexterously set the dial for ten-fifteen.

Then he strolled on down the deserted corridor to the statue niche just on the hither side of the Ceramics Room. Behind the statue group he slipped. There, without an atom of outward or internal excitement, he stood, waiting.

Three minutes later the corridor reverberated to the clanging of the fire alarm. Out from the Ceramics Room dashed the guard and sped down the corridor in search of the blaze.

On almost the same instant, Kurt sped into the room and up to its central case. Unlocking the case's door, by means of a bunch of keys he had taken from Renier's desk, he drew forth swiftly, yet with reverent fingers, the Maximinian Amphora and its ancient metal container.

He had ample time to slip back into the statue niche before the muttering and disgusted guard returned from his fire quest. As the guard entered the Ceramics Room, Kurt walked quietly to the back stairs and descended to the basement, where he let himself out of the building by means of the service doorway at the rear.

He knew the Amphora itself had not been visible from the corner where the guard was wont to sit. And its case was not in any way disturbed. There was every chance that the guard might not think to look for the lost treasure itself until closing time.

Should Bates, the curator's assistant, happen in there before then, so much the worse. But, in either event, Kurt himself was free of the building; and the Amphora, protected by its copper covering, was nestling safe in his voluminous breast pocket.

He went to One Hundred and Twenty-fifth Street. There he boarded a train for New Haven. At New Haven he disembarked, took a second train to Springfield and there, again alighting, took a third train for Boston. He left this last train at the Huntington Street station and made his way to a cheap hotel whither, a week earlier, his scanty luggage had preceded him. Next morning, he took second-cabin passage on a boat which chanced to be sailing that day for England.

During the seasick voyage he had time and ability to think. He did not regret what he had done. Indeed, the knowledge of his possession thrilled him as had nothing else. The season was early winter and he had his cabin to himself. Thus, he could while away the endless hours by staring raptly at the Amphora. It was his. Not his to look at in company with every one else, but all his alone.

He could feel no compunction at the theft which had brought him such bliss. Whom was he robbing, if it came to that? He was robbing no individual, certainly; only a bodiless and soulless corporation of rich men and the equally bodiless and soulless city of New York. No one person would be the poorer for what he had done. Beautiful things were for those who could appreciate them. And surely no one else could appreciate the Amphora as did he.

Nevertheless terror began to gnaw at him. It was a terror that increased almost to panic as the days at sea wore on. The Amphora had been valued at seven hundred and seventy-five thousand dollars—clear back in the middle of the nineteenth century. Presumably it was worth at least a million dollars by now—although Kurt hated to think of mere sordid cash in connection with such loveliness.

That meant the police of the two continents would be on the look-out for it. Every port, by this time, would be watched. His own absence would be noted and his love for the Amphora would be recalled. His description was probably in every police station on earth. It was a miracle he had not been recognized and seized at the Boston dock. It was certain he must be caught the instant he should set foot in England.

For all the meticulous carefulness of his plans, this part of the matter had not occurred to his unbalanced brain. His sole thought had been to get the Amphora and then to escape from New York and from all probability of capture. He wondered why this most obvious of dangers had not entered his mind until now. If only he had had the sense to go to some small mill town—say in New England—and find work and stay there for a year or two! He was courting inescapable capture by going to England.

Then, when his system could hold no more terror and worry, he grew stolidly calm. Scratching through his luggage, he got out an old revolver of heavy caliber which had belonged to his father. This he stuck in side his trouser band as he left the ship at Liverpool.

His mind was made up. At the first touch of a hand on his shoulder, at the dock, he would whip forth the pistol and send a bullet through the Amphora, in its resting place over his left breast—and thence to his heart. The heavy-caliber bullet would still have power, after wrecking the fragile vase, to kill him.

There was a crazy sublimity about the idea of perishing with his treasure which stirred Kurt to the very soul. As calmly as he had stolen the Amphora he walked down the gangway to the pier. He was ready for anything.

But nothing happened.

No, nothing happened. The customs men glanced perfunctorily through his bags. Then he was allowed to move on, unmolested, through a yellow fog, to the London train. If there were grim sleuths scanning the passengers, none of them seemed to find the haggard and shabbily dressed young man worth stopping.

Through his relief and the slumping nervous reaction Kurt was aware of a sudden contempt for the vaunted power of the law. He had stolen something worth nearly a million dollars. He had given the international police more than eight days to head him off here. And not one of the force had had the wit to recognize him by any description cabled from New York.

Kurt had no immediate plans. His sole desire had been to put himself and his beautiful plunder as far as possible from capture. This, apparently, he had done. He was free and in a foreign country, safe from pursuit. He could afford to loaf around, for a while, till his wrenched nerves should recover; and then he could shape his future.

He took a small room in a lodging house in the Battersea district and prepared to enjoy life in London as he had enjoyed it during his first weeks in New York. But here he was disappointed. His visits to the British Museum and National Art Gallery and to other oft-read-of shrines left him cold.

Beauty in such places had no longer the power to grip him. For, in his breast pocket, bulged the most beautiful object on earth. Compared to the Maximinian Amphora everything else looked to him tawdry or vapid. He stopped going forth to seek the beautiful and resumed his old custom of sitting for hours staring at the Amphora.

It was during his third week in London that he met Selena Marsh.

She was an undernourished girl in the early twenties, willowy of figure, red-gold of hair and with red-gold glints in her big eyes. For the rest, she was unhealthily pretty and was possessed of a certain lazy charm which Kurt had not the sense to tabulate as a blend of indolence and lack of force. She was studying art in London; and she had come from southern Missouri.

Kurt met her at her first meal in the smellily damp lodging house. They were seatmates at the single long basement dining-room table. Neither of them could recall, afterward, how they happened to fall into talk. Both were Americans. Both were exiles. Both were art lovers. Both were young. The rest was logical.

Never into Kurt's life had come such a woman as Selena. The girls back in his own mid-Western home town had been hearty, tremendously normal, devoid of mystery. Somehow they had never appealed strongly to him. He had gone through his twenty-seven years without a single serious love affair; not even the one mad boyish passion for an older woman which serves so finely, in later years, as inoculation against susceptibility. Hence, his heart and his imagination were fallow soil for such a woman as Selena Marsh.

She appealed to his twisted admiration for beauty, for intellect, for poise. Her graceful body, her soft-voiced, slurring Southern intonation, the cryptic set of her pale face, the weary appeal in her gold-red-flecked eyes—all these wrought mightily on the man.

At first he did not know what had befallen him. He thought of Selena merely as a congenial friend in this city of strangers—as a link with home—as the only woman who had never bored him or been bored by him. It was only when he realized that he was sometimes letting a whole day go by without so much as a glance or a thought for the Amphora, that he understood.

Then he greeted with incredulous ecstasy the knowledge that he was in love. He told himself he was in love with the one woman alive whose beauty and grace and mystic charm paralleled the Amphora's. She reminded him of the Amphora in a thousand wondrous ways. He recognized that, now; and he believed it was this similitude which first had drawn him to her.

Love of woman ousted every other love, every other desire, every other thought in his tumbled cosmos. And, once admittedly in love, Kurt Masson wasted no time in beginning his campaign of ardent wooing. And, to the rest of the lodgers, this affair between the two lank and shabby Americans became a topic of rare amusement.

It was during a walk through Battersea Park, one drippy winter afternoon, that Kurt ventured to put his worship into words. A little to his surprise, Selena was not startled or in any way upset by his agonizingly stammered declaration. She heard him out, making no effort to draw away the long-fingered hands he had clutched. Only when his words began to repeat themselves and when he was wholly tangled by his pleading oration did she answer.

Then, with the slow Southern speech he loved, she made reply:

"I like you, right well, Kurt. I like you a heap better'n any other boy I ever met. I don't mind saying that. I—I reckon I really truly love you. I—"

Nor did she resent the wild exclamation of bliss wherewith he interrupted her cool avowal. She did not even protest when he caught her to him with a half sob and kissed her upturned wet face over and over again.

Kisses were no astounding novelty to Selena. Indeed, she was enough of an epicure to note that most of Kurt's struck her damp face glancingly and with none of the art of long practice. Also, a furtive glance around told her there was nobody, just then, in sight along the wet pathway where they stood. Yet, presently, she drew away from him, cutting in on his flood of awkward love words.

"No, no, boy, dear!" she chided. "Not here, in public. Besides, we've got to talk sense, you and I. You didn't let me finish what I was telling you. My, but you're a cave man!" she added, straightening her slanted hat.

Kurt could have knelt on the wet earth and kissed her galoshed little feet. He contented himself with gaping, fishlike, at her, and gurgling broken sentences. Never had he been so thrilled. Compared to this, his possession of the Amphora was a cold and trivial thing. And his mad joy was climaxed by her calling him a cave man. He ceased to gobble and waited, breathless, for her to go on speaking. He had not long to wait.

"Listen, dear," she continued, the slurringly soft voice unruffled. "Kisses and Romeo talk are gorgeous things. But they aren't all there is. Let's be sensible, you and I. I take it you want to marry me?"

Another gobbling interlude and a threatened return to cave days. Selena nodded comprehension and said:

"Then there's a lot of things to settle, first, before we go committing ourselves to any engagement. Don't look like I'd slapped you, boy. We've got to be sensible. You want me to marry you. I'd like mighty well to. I don't mind telling you that."

Dexterously—almost as though with skill born of practice—she averted another avalanche of words and cave-manliness; then she proceeded:

"I haven't got a dollar in the world, except just enough to get me through this year at the conservatory—and then my fare home. And there's no fortune coming to me from a rich uncle or a missing will, either, Kurt. I—"

"But—"

"Quiet, deary! If I can't make a living, back home, as a painter, I'll have to get a store job. That's the best I can look for. That—unless I marry a man who's been pestering me to marry him for two years. He's head of the biggest hay-and-feed business in our part of the State—and he's near fifty and his nose whistles when he breathes hard. I'd hate to marry him. But maybe it'd be better'n clerking in a store. Sometimes I remember how his nose whistles and I think I couldn't marry him on a bet. Then, when the eating is so bad, back yonder at the boarding house, or when the professor tells me I'll never be a painter—well, at those times, I think: Maybe, yes. Then, *you* came along, Kurt. And, since then—well, boy, I've told you all about *me*. Now, s'pose you tell me some about *you*?"

She paused. More than once, during her cool recital, Kurt had tried vainly to interrupt. But, now that she waited, silent and expectant, he was at a loss for words.

"I—I don't quite understand," he faltered. "You want me to tell you about me? What shall I tell you? Shall I tell you you're the gloriousest girl the Lord ever made—and that I love you more than—"

"No," she interposed. "Tell me all those things, afterward. They'll be right sweet to hear, I expect. But, just for now, don't tell about loving me. Tell about having the right to."

"If you mean, is there any other girl—" began Kurt ardently.

"I don't. I mean, can you support a wife? Can you, Kurt? You don't look any too flush. But I don't judge folks that way. It isn't safe. What I mean is—you've asked me to marry you. Can you take good care of me, if I do? Can you give me the nice things I love to have and the kind of a home I want and—oh, and all that? I don't want to seem grasping or mean, Kurt. And I'm not. But I've been hard up too long to care about staying broke till the end of the chapter. I got a right to ask these things. And if you care for me the way I want you to, you'll answer me, straight."

For an instant the man winced, as might a musician at some hideous discord in a Beethoven symphony. Then, haltingly, he replied:

"I've got between seven hundred and eight hundred dollars a year from my father's estate. I've got no profession or business. I used to work in his store till he died. Then I sold out the business. I—"

"That's all you got?" she demanded, her voice less dreamy than was its wont.

"That's all, in real cash," he confessed. "But if you'll marry me, I'll work my fingers to—"

"'To the bone—to provide me with every luxury,'" she quoted, with a sigh. "And you'll 'devote your whole life to my happiness.' I know. It's sweet of you, boy. And you'd do it. But you'd fail. If you were to start in, now, at twenty-seven, to learn some business, it'd be years before you could make even a piker living at it. In the meantime, if we married, we'd spend those years starving on your seven hundred a year. And if we didn't marry till you could afford to, I'd be wasting my years in working; and I'd be old and worn out before you could make enough for us to live on. Don't you see, boy dear?" she added, a note of tenderness in her slurring voice, as if she sought to teach a lesson to some defective baby. "Don't you see how unspeakable and impossible it would be? I don't want to be horrid. And this hurts me a heap. But I'm—"

"You mean you won't marry me unless I'm rich?" he demanded harshly. "You mean you're too selfish, too petty, too heartless to stand a pinch of poverty for the sake of the man you love? Lord! I didn't think any woman in real life could be so—"

"I think," she broke in icily, "I think that'll be about all. I'm not used to being called names or to being hollered at. Good-by."

She turned away and struck off through the mist at a faster gait than usual. Kurt made no effort to follow her. He stood, in a daze of horror, staring after the thin figure until the murk swallowed it. Then, with a shake of his whole body, he came to himself.

A queer, resistless rage possessed him. So this was woman's love! He had laid his heart and his life at her feet. And she had not even trampled on them. She had turned them over, exploratively, with one toe—and then had walked off. All she wanted was a rich husband—a Crœsus, like that old hay-and-feed slob, back in Missouri, who whistled when he breathed hard!

She was worse—why, she was worse than that *Camille* woman he had seen the night Mr. Renier had taken him to the theater! That was it. She was worse than *Camille,* without *Camille's* excuse that she deserted her lover for the sake of his own future and his family.

What had *Armand Duval* done when *Camille* threw him over for a rich man? *Armand* had gambled until he had won a whole wad of money. And then he had slammed that money in *Camille's* face. That was what *Armand* had done.

Oh, if only Kurt Masson could do the same thing! If he could stamp into Selena's presence, loaded down with wealth, and say to her: "You wouldn't marry me, because I was poor. Look at me *now!*"

Such hysterical daydreams were fruitless things. They—

Or, were they?

A flashing idea seared the furious man's brain. And the more he thought it over, the more luridly desirable it grew. His new obsession had driven out all others. This was no daydream. It was within his grasp—at a price. No price—not life itself—was too high.

Nor would he fling the fortune in her face. He would marry her with it. That was better!

In less than three hours Kurt Masson was on his way to Antwerp.

Back in his memory flickered a discourse of Renier's—a talk of the Antwerp jewel experts and professional antiquaries—especially that active minority of them who were willing to buy stolen goods at fair prices. Kurt even recalled the name of one of the foremost of these—a name which Renier had spoken with contempt in detailing the fellow's unsavory services to certain museums and collectors.

On the morning of the second day after leaving London, Kurt sought and obtained private audience with Pieter Culp, in the latter's private office. He did not stop for preliminaries. Striding up to the table, behind which lounged the swarthily obese expert, the visitor drew tenderly from his breast pocket an ancient copper receptacle of rare workmanship and odd shape.

This Kurt opened. From it, with reverent fingers, he took the vase he had stolen from the International Museum in New York. At sight of it, Pieter Culp's politely interested face froze. Kurt set the vase on the littered black table. Its mellow radiance seemed to brighten and beautify the whole musty office.

But, after that first sharp glance at the vase, Culp turned his red-rimmed eyes resolutely from it and fixed them on the caller. "Do you know what that is?" asked Kurt, his voice dry and crackling.

"Yes," returned Culp in excellent English, but without trusting himself to glance again at the treasure. "I know what it is. That is the Maximinian Amphora. It is supposed to be in the center of the Ceramics Room at the International in New York—a city I have never had the good fortune to visit. What then?"

"I—I want to sell it," croaked Kurt, trying to steel himself against the almost horrified stare of the red-rimmed eyes. "It was bought for seven hundred and seventy-five thousand dollars in—"

"In 1858," supplied Culp. "By Hiram A. Craig. And bequeathed by him, along with his ceramics, to the International Museum. It—"

"I want to sell it," said Kurt again. "If it was worth that sum, in 1858, it must be worth more than a million dollars, to-day. What will you give me for it?"

"Huh?" grunted Culp. "Me?"

"Don't haggle, man!" cried Kurt, his nerves fraying. "Name a price. Then we'll have something to go on. I'd—I'd rather cut off my right arm than have to sell the Amphora. But something has happened that will make life unlivable for me unless I can get at least a part of the money it's worth. How much? Name a price, I tell you!"

"A price?" repeated Gulp solemnly. "Not one counterfeit penny! Take it away!"

"I told you I'm not in the mood for haggling!" raged Kurt. "Make me an offer or I'll take it elsewhere. I—"

"Haggling?" scoffed Culp in loud scorn as he leaned forward. "Take it elsewhere, eh? Good! Take it to every merchant in Europe! Then take it to every thief and fence and pawnshop! If you find one fool who will advance you a penny on it—or who will so much as keep it as a gift—then you can have my bank account and one of my ears, as forfeit!"

There was no mistaking the angry genuineness of the man. Kurt stood dumfounded, irresolute. Before he could speak, Pieter Culp resumed—this time with a return of that ill-fitting solemnity where-with he had first greeted the sight of the Amphora.

"Listen to me, you poor novice," said he. "That is the Maximinian Amphora. Its value is well above five million francs. But it could not be sold for a clipped copper. Are you too much of a dolt to see that? The Maximinian Amphora is as well known as the Eiffel Tower or Brooklyn Bridge or the Great Pyramid or the Taj Mahal. It is known to every art collector on earth. They all know its history. They all know where it is supposed to be on exhibition."

"But—"

"You stole it," went on the measured tone. "You stole it. You or another. It was stolen from its place of honor in the Ceramics Room at the International. Doubtless to the heartbreak of my saintly friend Renier. Who would dare take it—even as a gift? No dealer, no collec-tor, no receiver of stolen goods would dare be found with it in his possession. That possession could mean but one thing. It would be a passport to prison."

Kurt stiffened. Pieter Culp's slow voice continued:

"An art treasure or a jewel may pass through a hundred hands. But when it reaches a museum it is forever at the end of its wanderings. The museum is the tomb of art treasures. They can go no farther. Their travels are done. They have come to rest. Every one knows where they are. If ever again they are found elsewhere, it means they have been stolen—and that the police of the world are ready to seize the thief. Now—unless you are even more a dunce than you look, you will see why I refuse to deal with you and why I bid you take that thing away from my establishment, at once. Go, please! You do not wish me to call the police, to have you ejected. I shall not hesitate to do so. My own hands are clean. Go. Take it with you, you bungling amateur criminal!"

There was no need to seek farther for a purchaser. Kurt Masson knew that. And in a daze of misery he returned to London.

As he let himself in at the Battersea lodging house, his landlady chanced to be mounting the stairs. She turned and beamed down upon the returned lodger.

"Welcome back, Mr. Masson!" she hailed the glum youth. "It's good to see you. Enjoy yourself?"

He made no reply but took fresh hold of his valise, in order to mount the stairs. Rebuffed, the landlady smiled. There was acid in the smile.

"Your friend, Miss Marsh, has gone," she said, peering avidly down to note his certain chagrin. "Left yesterday. Gone back to the States. Her mother came for her. And a gentleman—a fine-looking elderly man. Her mother told me he'd brought her all the way across the ocean to persuade Miss Marsh to go home and marry him. Seems he's been in love with her for a couple of years. Quite romantic, I'm sure. Like something out of a cinema. Well!" ended the landlady lamely, as Kurt continued to stare at her in owlish vacancy. "She went."

Slowly, springlessly, like a very old man, Kurt mounted to his room. There he drew forth the Amphora and stared fixedly at it. Dully he wondered how he had ever brought himself to risk a long prison sentence by stealing such a thing. Then he fell to remembering Gerard Renier's friendliness to his lonely self and the wise old curator's foolish trust in him.

Kurt looked back on the whole adventure as a sobered drunkard might listen to the tale of his own last-night spree. He was sane now. Much had happened to make him so.

Gerard Renier sat, doubled over as usual, at the messy desk of his cubby-hole office on the third floor of the International Museum, in New York. He looked up from a pile of morning correspondence in many tongues to see a man standing in front of him.

Kurt Masson had entered the little room soundlessly and had shut its door. At sight of the ghastly faced man Renier lifted his own sparse, white eyebrows in civil inquiry and leaned back in his chair. He gave no other sign of greeting; and no sign whatever of surprise.

Kurt drew forth the copper case, opened it and laid case and Amphora on the desk in front of the curator. Renier scarcely glanced at the returned treasure.

"So you've brought it back?" he queried, breaking the silence for the first time. "Why?"

Kurt swallowed hard, then burst forth: "There it is! Take it! Now ring up the police! I won't try to get away."

"The police?" repeated Renier in mild wonder. "The police? Why the police?"

"To arrest me for stealing this!" snarled Kurt. "Don't play cat and mouse. I'm ready."

"Ready for what?" pursued Renier. "My dear young man, there is no need for all this melodrama. I am not going to have you arrested. Why should you suppose I'd do such a thing? You stole that vase. Is there any need to tell the whole world about it? Is there any need to admit to the public that the International Museum can be robbed by any amateur crook? Is there?"

"Do you mean—"

"I mean a museum is supposed to be safeguarded in every way against all possibility of theft," explained Renier patiently. "If it were known that any one could come in here and steal whatsoever he might choose to steal—why, every kleptomaniac and souvenir snatcher in New York would make our lives a burden. That is why we did not notify the police when you stole this. That is *one* of the reasons," he corrected himself gravely. "We said not a word to any one outside."

Kurt could not speak. He blinked at the calm little man at the desk.

"There was another reason why we did nothing," said Renier, picking up a letter he had been reading. "It would hardly have added to the public's enjoyment of our museum's exhibits if we had confessed that the supposed Maximinian Amphora on view here, all these years, was only a clever tinsel copy of the matchless original. It—"

"*What?*" babbled Kurt, unbelievingly.

"Mr. Masson," exhorted Renier, "use your own intelligence. Is it likely that the original Maximinian Amphora—one of the five chief art treasures extant and valued at nearly a million dollars and a thing so small—would have been left in a glass case, in a room guarded by only one man, for any clever thief to steal or for fire to destroy? Wouldn't any sane board of directors have ordered the Amphora kept in the innermost compartment of the museum's safe—and a plausible copy made of it for public view? A copy, we'll say, whose cash value is something under twenty-five dollars? Think it over. The theft of such a copy comes under the head of petit larceny, at worst. Now, perhaps you see why you were not followed?"

But Kurt Masson saw nothing. Blindly, he was groping his way from the office and from the building.

Bates, the assistant curator, came into Renier's cubby-hole in response to a summons from the electric buzzer. He found his chief bent over his desk, both hands clasped worshipfully around a golden vase. At sight of what Renier was caressing, Bates cried aloud in joyous amaze.

"It's come back! It's come back!" he exulted. "Thank God, it's—"

"Yes," breathed Renier, shaking with emotion. "It's come back at last, by some utter miracle. He brought it back, himself. Who says prayers aren't answered? He—"

"Brought it back himself?" echoed the assistant. "You don't mean he—"

"Just that. And I sent him away believing he had stolen only a cheap copy of it. Do you suppose"—in answer to Bates' wide-eyed stare—"do you suppose I was going to give him the satisfaction of remembering he had laid his miserable sacrilegious hands on the real Amphora? I've stripped him of even a thief's self-esteem!"

The Punch

AT the back of many a motion-picture Moorish Palace is the "lot's" garbage dump. At the back of Crescent Hill wiggled Coogan's Alley.

Get the geography aright. Above the big, black city soared the classic summit of Crescent Hill, garlanded with garishly beautiful houses set in acres of superornamental grounds. And, at the Hill's base, to the rear, Coogan's Alley twisted its malodorous way toward the railroad tracks. The Alley and the alleys that kept it company formed the squalid back yard to Crescent Hill.

Michael Brian's house was the second biggest on Crescent Hill. Michael Brian's estate flowed away on every side from the house. To rearward, halfway down the hill, the grounds took an abrupt dip in a shamefaced fashion and came to a jarring halt against an eight-foot board fence which separated them from the Alley. A mercifully thick evergreen hedge, at the verge of the dip, masked the Alley from the rarefied view of the house.

Claude van Rensselaer Brian, aged ten, had ever been forbidden by a series of nurses and then of governesses to pass beyond the evergreen hedge, in his thin-legged tours of the estate. First, because the dip was too steep for safe foothold. Second, because Alley squalor was no sight for a perfect little gentleman to gaze upon.

And Claude Brian was as close to perfection in the matter of gentility as his fadedly pretty mother and a corps of overpaid assistants could make him. This, despite the surly opposition of his two-fisted sire, Michael Brian, lumber king.

Michael had run away from his wharf-side home at the age of ten. Perhaps it was a throwback that made Claude run away at the same age. But the harsh, red blood of Michael ran through his spindling son's veins, diluted with the thin and chill azure blood of Michael's purple-born wife.

Wherefore, instead of running away to the lumber camps, as had his father, Claude merely wiggled through the evergreen hedge, then slipped and stumbled down the steep embankment, brought up with a jounce against the rotting slab fence and, in an access of courage, crawled through a two-board gap and into the Alley.

How much farther his feeble spurt of adventure-spirit might have lured him, nobody knows. For, at his second experimental stop along the Alley, he came face to face with Tessie Glynn.

Tessie was eight. She had a thin little face and thinner little legs and a pair of black-fringed Irish blue eyes two sizes too big for the rest of her. Her calico dress was faded and indeterminate of color. But it was clean. Tessie's clothes were always clean. So was Tessie, herself. No one bothered to reason why. It was as much a part of her "different" ways as were her queer daintiness and her queerer air of good breeding.

As she rounded a twist of the Alley and beheld the velvet-clad little outlander, Tessie came to a wondering halt. Then she smiled friendlily and demanded with glad excitement:

"Where's the movie being took?"

"What movie?" asked Claude.

Once he had watched the shooting of a few stray "exteriors" along the crest of the Hill. He was athrill at the prospect of another such sight.

"The movie you're in, of course," answered Tessie, viewing with real admiration the dark-blue velvet suit, the wide and snowy collar, the silken hose and buckled shoes and scarlet bow tie. "Where are they shooting it? I was in one, once. Ma got two dollars, just for letting me tumble down in front of an auto and have a man catch me and carry me away from it. The auto was standing still," she added, with reluctant yielding to truth. "Where's your movie being took?"

"I haven't got any movie," said Claude a little crossly. "I—"

"Is it a fancy-dress party?" insisted Tessie. "I saw one in 'All For Her Child.' The kids was togged up, like you are and—"

"Stop that!" broke in Claude. "You're making fun of me. You stop it! I don't like to be made fun of."

There was a shake in his reedy voice. Tessie noted this and his flushing face with wondering interest.

"You don't mean your folks rig you up like that all the time?" she asked. "Where d'you live, anyhow?"

"Up there," said Claude, with a homesick yank of the head toward the hill behind them. "I'm Claude Brian. My father's Michael Brian. The lumber king, you know. I guess you've heard of *him,* all right. He's the—"

"H'm!" mocked the girl. "I'm Tessie Glynn. My father's Aloysius Glynn, foreman over to the bottling works. I guess you've heard of *him,* all right. Do you honest wear them things all the time?"

"Pooh!" bragged Claude, the primal male stirring him to boastfulness in the presence of this big-eyed child. "I have much handsomer clothes than these. These are the kind I wear when I go for a walk on week days. I've got—"

A screech, piercing and rapturous, interrupted his catalogue of treasures. From around the corner had swaggered a youth of perhaps his own age, fiery of hair, snubbed of nose, pale of eye and baptized in freckles. The new arrival was barefoot. Certain frank apertures in his garb proved that his sole costume consisted of ragged knickers and an unclean shirt.

Like Tessie, he had halted in amaze at sight of Claude. Unlike her, he had voiced his astonishment in calliope fashion. Now he bore down on the loftily contemptuous heir to the Brian hoard.

Around and around Claude he walked, pop-eyed and marveling. And ever, as he gazed, his wide mouth stretched wider in a grin of dawning ecstasy.

"Pug" Beasley was a globe-trotter. Though he honored Coogan's Alley by making it his home and headquarters, yet the adventure-lust often carried him far afield. He knew every fire house in town. He knew the glories of Crescent Hill. He had traveled many miles on those sturdy bare legs of his. And he had used his pale-green eyes. At a glance he had tabulated Claude. But it took him several moments to realize that the gilded young patrician was actually standing unguarded in the Alley.

Claude Brian watched the convolutions and the grin of this intruder with growing resentment.

"What are you laughing at?" he asked haughtily.

"Nothin' much," chuckled Pug. "Say, Tess, like a reel pretty ribbon for your hair? I'll blow you to one."

With surprising deftness both Pug's grubby paws shot toward Claude's neck. Before the visitor could guess what was happening or could raise his own pipestem arms in instinctive defense his flowing, red silk tie was unfastened and jerked from under his wide collar.

"Here y' are, Tess!" declaimed Pug, proffering her the flaming gift. "An' if they's any other part of him that makes a hit with you, put a name to it an' it's yours. How 'bout it?"

In the expensively denatured soul of Claude Brian surged up a gust of wrath.

"You miserable little gutter boy!" he shrilled, advancing on the bandit. "Give me back that, or—or I'll slap you! Give it back, I say!"

Pug greeted this horrid threat with a squeal of terror. He did a very creditable tremble and proceeded to go down on his knees in the mud, pleading:

"Aw, spare me life, big feller! Have a heart! Don't bust me in two with a slap! I—"

"Then," decreed Claude judicially, "give me back my tie and ask my pardon for—"

He got no further. Pug was no longer kneeling. He was rolling over and over, with howls of unrestrainable laughter. Claude's reddening face went purple! This gutter pup was making fun of him! He was making fun of him in the presence of the big-eyed little girl. Claude Brian, the aristocrat, was mocked by a ragamuffin!

In fury he sprang forward and kicked viciously at the rolling body on the ground. His patent-leather toe came in painful contact with Pug's stomach.

On the instant, the helplessly laughing alley boy was transformed to a compact fighting machine. Pug had won his way with his fists in Coogan's Alley and elsewhere to the very top of juvenile pugilistic fame. Not a lad within two years of his age could stand against him. He was a natural-born fighter. And, never before in all his eleven years, had any one—except his own father in moments of bellicose drink—dared to kick him. This had been done, now, by the sissy boy from the Hill—and in the presence of the only girl on earth whose high opinion Pug craved!

Like a ragged whirlwind, he was up and at the astounded Claude. The latter saw him coming just in time to aim a punitive slap at the lowered red head. The slap went wild. Pug's fast-flying fists did not. One of them caught Claude amidships, doubling him like a jackknife. The other opened one or two well-filled veins in his nose.

It is hard to double up when one's nose is propelled backward. It is harder to remain upright when one's stomach is punched. Claude was agonizingly conscious of those two warring impacts. Before either pressure could prevail, one of Pug's iron fists was slamming his jaw. The other landed square on the bridge of his nose. This latter blow, when rightly placed and heavily enough delivered with bare knuckles, is good for two black eyes. Pug was an expert in its delivery.

Claude sat down very hard indeed on the ground. He was gasping and blubbering. Around him danced the victorious Pug. The whole battle had consumed but the merest fraction of a minute.

Now, Tessie, recovering from the suddenness of it, rushed in between conqueror and conquered. Catching the gurgly and breathless Claude by the shoulder she hoisted him to his feet. Merrily Pug danced back to the fray. But with her free hand Tessie shoved him off.

"You've pretty near killed him, Pug Beasley!" she chided. "Be ashamed of yourself, you big brute! A poor little feller like him! He—"

"He's taller'n what I am," Pug defended himself, curiously meek under her push and her sharp rebuke. "He's—"

"You leave him be!" commanded Tessie. "You leave him be or I won't ever speak to you again."

"All right!" grunted Pug in disgust. "He can chase home, for all of me. But there ain't any one else, but you, that I'd leave him go for. Get that! An' if he snoops around her ag'in, jawin' with you, I'll dern near kill him. Let him get *that,* too."

"I'll let any one speak to me that I want to!" flashed Tessie.

"No, you won't, neither," called back the departing Pug over his shoulder.

"Why won't I, smarty?" she challenged.

"You won't, 'cause you're *my* girl," responded Pug sheepishly.

Then he fled, his ears crimson, his head down. Pug—otherwise Francis Xavier—Beasley, was far braver in war than in love.

Tessie, after an indignant "Huh! Is that so?" turned her attention to the bleedingly disheveled and gasping Claude.

"Did he hurt you so awful bad?" she cooed. "Here, lemme wipe your face. The blood's all running down to your—"

Claude Brian tore free from her solicitous grasp and made a blind dive through the broken palings of the fence. Thence, flinging himself against the embankment, he swarmed, crablike, up its muddy sides and past the evergreen hedge. He was hysterical, in his pain and impotent fury. Through the swelter one odd memory stood forth in torture: he had been thrashed in the presence of a girl! The knowledge was unadulterated anguish to his bruised soul.

Michael Brian was smoking a cutty pipe in the sanctuary of the sunken Italian garden behind his hotellike mansion. By his wife's wish, he no longer smoked a pipe where outsiders could see him. Especially a cutty pipe. Cutty pipes are vulgar. But, now and then, coming home early, he would sneak down to the sunken garden's shelter, for this contraband joy.

To-day, as he sat puffing, a truly fearsome little creature burst into the sunken garden, by way of taking a short cut to the house's back doors. Michael blinked twice before he recognized the bloody and torn and mud-slimed child as his wontedly spotless offspring, Claude van Rensselaer Brian. Then he reached out a hamlike hand and arrested the weeping youngster's flight.

"For the love of the Lord!" exploded Michael the inelegant. "You look like something the dog drug home from the swamp. What's happened to you?"

Now as a rule, Claude stood aloof from his thick-necked father, having unconsciously acquired some of Mrs. Brian's aristocratic contempt for the man. But to-day he discovered all at once that he stood in sore need of sympathy—of sympathy from one of his own sex, at that. In sobbing gulps he told of his adventure. He told it very badly. But Michael understood. Claude ended the lachrymose recital by blubbering:

"I wish Pug Beasley was smashed into a billion pieces! I wish—"

"Hold on there, sonny!" broke in Michael. "That's baby talk. If ever you wish a cuss was smashed into a billion pieces, don't stand around saying so. Go to him and smash him into those same billion pieces. If you can't, don't wish it. Get busy and put yourself into shape to *do* it. You took that thundering big licking, eh? Didn't you lift a hand to help yourself?"

"Yes, I did!" declared Claude. "First I kicked him. Then—"

"Kicked him?" echoed Michael, scowling. "Kicked a man in a stand-up fight? Son, that's—"

"It was before we began to fight," explained Claude, sensing disapproval and seeking to clear himself. "He was lying down, laughing at me. And—"

"Angels and principalities and powers!" groaned Michael. "You kicked a chap that was down? What sort of mill waste have I fathered, anyhow? I—"

"Then," pursued Claude, "he ran at me with his fists and I slapped him. He—"

"Slapped him!" repeaed Michael, in mortal misery. "Saints in glory! *Slapped*—Here, you! Listen to me! Don't you know how to hit a blow? Double your fist and slug me. Here! In the face. Do as I tell you!" he ordered as Claude hesitated in surprise at the queer command. "No, don't double it, with your thumb inside your fingers. That's a woman's way. One good punch would bust your thumb and put you out of commission. This way. See? That a son of Mike Brian shouldn't even know how to bunch his fist! Now then, *hit!* Right here in the middle of my face. Put your shoulder muscles behind it and—hit!"

Thus coached, Claude smote with all his frail force at the outthrust features of his sire.

"Well," commented Michael, "you hit me. I know that, because I saw you do it. But if I'd had my eyes shut I'd not have known if it was a fist or a leaf that skittered down my cheek. If you hit the other boy like you hit me, I don't wonder he could down you. Any one could. Lord! That a boy of mine shouldn't even carry a punch! That's what's the matter with you. That's what's been the matter with you, all along. I see it, now. You pack no punch. And when a man packs no punch he may as well put up the shutters, for all he'll ever amount to. For the punch is the index to the mind and the soul of him, as well as the body. He—"

Claude, recovering some of his wonted sense of superiority, gave the mutteringly unhappy man a cold glance of disfavor and began to move off toward the house. He had seen his mother do this on such rare occasions as Michael ventured to reprove her. Michael Brian made no move to check the departure of the bedraggled little figure. Instead, he sat glowering moodily after it, champing his battered pipe-stem and mumbling disjointedly under his breath.

That night, in the Brian house, there was a terrible scene. For once, Michael emerged victorious from the conflict with his wife. Nor did he allow a consistent course of tear-stained cheeks or even the dread "silence cure" to rob him of the fruits of his victory. He was in deadly earnest. And, for once, in his own home, he had something he deemed worth fighting for—something too important to be lost by tears or by threatened nerve collapse or by any others of Mrs. Brian's choicest weapons.

News of his sorry success reached Coogan's Alley almost as soon as it reached the thither stretches of gilded Crescent Hill. Tessie Glynn was coming home from school, one afternoon, when she beheld Claude standing in mid-alley, just beyond the gap in the fence.

He was not the beauteous visitor of a week before. Not only because one of his eyes was still slightly swollen and because of blue-green marks under both of them, but because his hair was cropped short and his meager body incased in a simple, gray tweed suit. His stockings were of ribbed wool; and he wore wide-toed shoes.

"I—I've been here, three times, this week," began Claude haltingly. "But you weren't here. And I didn't know where you live. I—"

"Why, hello!" she hailed him, recognizing with some effort the shorn and nonornamental youth. "I didn't know, first off, it was you. I—"

"I wanted to tell you," said Claude valiantly, "that you can keep that red tie of mine. Because I'm not wearing those things any more. My father won't let me. And he's making me go away to boarding school, to-morrow. So I—I kind of wanted to say good-by, too."

"Boarding school?" asked Tessie, tasting the new phrase and failing to classify it. "What's that?"

"The kind of boarding schools I've read about," said Claude, "must be rather nice. But this isn't that kind, father says. It's a school that's run by a man who used to be an athlete or something. It's for boys that need to be toughened, father says. They sleep outdoors and they have to box and swim and ride horses and do all sorts of rough things. I think I'll hate it. My mother hates it, too. She's terribly unhappy. She says she never saw father like this, before. I heard her tell him she thought he must be going insane. And he said, no, he was 'going sane, and it was high time.' I—I thought I'd come down here and say good-by to you," he finished lamely.

"That was nice of you," she made shy answer. "And I'm awful sorry how Pug Beasley treated you. I haven't spoken to him since. And I'm not going to—ever."

"Pooh!" scoffed Claude, wriggling uncomfortably. "That was nothing. I—I didn't try as hard as I could. I didn't like to, you know, when there was a girl looking on. That's how he came to—to get just a little the best of me. He—"

Tessie's sympathetic big eyes shifted in worry to something behind him. Claude turned. There stood Pug Beasley. Pug had a way of appearing, whenever Tessie was near by. His bare feet had brought him in silence to the two. To-day no grin adorned Pug's square little face. His light eyes were ablaze and his wide mouth was set. Ignoring the flinching Claude, he addressed Tessie.

"That's why you wouldn't speak to me, hey?" he rasped. "That's why you made a snoot at me when I tried to give you the candy? Stuck on this sissy, hey? Gee, but he's sure goin' to get his, this time!"

Wheeling about, he sprang at Claude, head lowered, fists pumping. Claude did not slap. Certain long and unwelcome harangues from his father, this past week, had taught him better. Instead, he doubled both fists with meticulous care. And, drawing his right arm far back, he prepared to launch a lethal blow at his charging enemy.

If Pug had had the consideration to await the attack, Claude's blow might or might not have landed. But before the Crescent Hill boy had finished drawing back his arm Pug's hard-driven left had caught him on the mouth. And Pug's other fist had followed it to the nose.

Under the dizzying pain, Claude forgot his father's instructions. He yearned to flee. He was horribly afraid. He had been horribly afraid to set foot in Coogan's Alley. Yet, even as he had come thither three times in a week, at imminent risk of meeting the murderous Francis Xavier Beasley, so now he held to his ground—what there was of it to hold. He had come there because of Tessie. He stayed there for the same reason.

Forgetting to hit, he fell back on first principles. As Pug ran into a tussling clinch after delivering his two unblocked punches, Claude buried the fingers of his own left hand in his foe's shock of hair. With the nails of his right hand, he assailed Pug's freckled face.

Long and deep were the furrows he dug into his adversary's uncomely countenance. And long and shrill was the fury yell they evoked. In a second Pug had jumped back from the clinch and was tearing into him with a volley of punches, to face and to heart and to wind. The rest was slaughter.

Dimly, from the ground, Claude at last looked up through puffed lids to note that Tessie had hurled herself bodily on his conqueror and was shaking Pug by the shoulders with all her wiry young strength.

"I'll tell the cop on you!" she cried fiercely. "I'll have you arrested. You've killed him. He—"

"No, he hasn't!" sputtered Claude, staggering dazedly to his swaying legs. "Keep out of this, Tessie. I'm not licked yet. I can—"

"Good!" roared a mighty voice from behind the palings. Michael Brian was surveying the scene through the fence gap, with manifest rapture.

"Good!" he boomed again. "Son, it was worth following you here! You've got something besides mouse blood in you, after all. Only don't draw your hand 'way back, again, before you hit. I—"

At first sight of the grown-up, Pug Beasley had taken to his heels. He knew Michael Brian by sight and by fame. Tessie stayed where she was; supporting the tottery Claude and gazing with level, unafraid eyes at the mountainous man.

"If—if he hadn't run away from me—" blustered Claude feebly.

"Shut up!" ordered Michael. "Don't spoil the first real thing you ever did. This is the little girl you told me about, eh? I don't blame you. What's your name, sis? Where d'you live?"

Tessie answered with no embarrassment or boldness. Michael nodded approval.

"I'm going to drop down for a chat with your dad, some day," he promised cryptically. "A kid like you deserves a chance. Besides, I owe you something, for putting a backbone into my boy, here. Son, chase up to the house and wash. Better dodge your mother. She's liable to throw another hysteric if she sees you like that. And, say! I told you to punch. Not to scratch."

Thus it was that the mandate of a cruel parent snatched Claude van Rensselaer Brian from a home of wealth and great refinement and tossed him into a camp school where, for the first few months, his life was torment. Nor, except for a single month each summer, was he allowed to bask again in that home's rarefied atmosphere for a full six years.

During each of his brief vacations Claude made surreptitious visits to Coogan's Alley—visits fraught with a tinge of that same old mingled dread and incitement. But, during none of these short slumming rambles did he chance to meet either Tessie or Pug. Boylike, he forbore to make even the most roundabout inquiries as to either of them. Yet both remained vividly clear in his memory. Never, in boxing, did he fail to visualize Pug as his opponent. Never, among the few girls he met, did he fail to find himself contrasting them with the big-eyed and thin-faced child whose queer charm had made him brave the Alley's terrors.

Then came Harvard and two supplementary years at Oxford—both university experiences being triumphs for Claude's mother over the earthborn father who craved to see his son succeed him in the lumber business. Old Michael's one ray of light, during these years of higher education, was the news that Claude had gone in heavily for athletics. He had won the middleweight boxing championship at Harvard and had won a similar honor at Oxford.

Michael thrilled at this double achievement. It compensated him, fiftyfold, for the fact that Claude seemed fated to win no scholastic glories.

"Never mind his not getting red hoods and white sheepskins and the like," he consoled his grieving wife. "I've got men in our shipping department who are crawling with college degrees and languages and such. They're maybe none the worse for 'em. But it's a cinch those things don't bloat a pay envelope. It's the punch does that. The punch and the brain behind it. And if these boxing goes wasn't won for foot-work, Claude's got the punch. Let him alone."

Mrs. Brian died early in her son's second year at Oxford. Michael's grief was quite bearable. Yet, in deference to her wishes, he suggested that the boy stay out his term at the university.

When at last Claude van Rensselaer Brian came home for good, Michael observed him long and keenly. The spindling body had knit to strong compactness, by reason of years of ceaseless athletics. The shoulders were a joy. Yes, and the eye was steady. But, dropping his appraising look to mouth and chin Michael noted a comely softness of outline about each that did not reassure him.

"Those boxing bouts, now," he interrupted the boy's gently modu-lated account of the homeward voyage, "the ones you won the cham-pionships on—how many rounds, each, did you need before you knocked out your man?"

"Knocked out?" repeated Claude, with his pleasant laugh. "Why, there were no knockouts, sir. In such bouts—except in case of acci-dents, of course—the decision is given on points. It is a matter for skill, not for slugging. It—"

"Grmph!" exploded Michael, his hopes collapsing. "Next you'll be telling me you used six-ounce pillows or—"

"No, sir," corrected Claude. "Eight ounce. Six-ounce gloves are never used any more, I believe, in collegiate contests. They are too light and they bruise too hard."

For a long time old Michael sat in glaze-eyed silence, peering at his graceful son from under bristling brows. Then he spoke, once more interrupting Claude's entertaining account of the icebergs sighted on the home voyage.

"At the Number Two Mill," said he, "I've fitted up a gym for some of the younger men. They have boxing bouts there, every Friday night. I put up prizes to make it worth while. And I'm apt to drop in there on Friday evenings. Men work better under the Big Boss' eye, you know. Pretty lively bouts, sometimes. Four-ounce gloves, of course. We've turned out one or two fair professionals from that gym."

"Yes, sir?" asked Claude in mild interest. "Perhaps you'll take me down there some time to watch the bouts."

"Sure. The best young fellow we've got there, now, is named Beasley—Pug Beasley they call him. Began in Number Two as a tally boy and worked his way up. *Slugged* his way up, if you like. Remember him?"

The old man was speaking with elaborate nonconcern. Yet his heart warmed as Claude's soft chin tensed and his eyes darkened at memory of an ancient wound to pride.

"Remember him?" echoed Claude. "I do! He gave me my first licking. And my second licking, the next week. He—"

"He's ready to give you your third," craftily suggested Michael. "I happened to tell him about your winning those two bouts. He just laughed. But when I was moving away I heard him say to a chap there: 'I'd need just one round to show that mamma's boy what boxing is like.' It kind of peeved me to hear him say that and get away with it. I was wishing then that you'd have the sand to drop down there, some night, and try a bout with him. But I s'pose it's too much to expect. He's too clever with his hands for an amachoor like you. He—"

Michael paused. He saw Claude was not listening. Before the returned wanderer's mental vision arose the picture of Pug's pitiably easy victory over the poor little rich boy, while the little girl with the big eyes looked on at the victim's humiliation. Vividly clear arose the memory. And with it came an unworthily babyish yearning to salve his own self-respect by wiping out the score. It would be sweet, if petty, to trounce the heavy-fisted proletarian by dint of brilliant prowess and to square the twelve-year-old account.

"To-day's Thursday, isn't it?" said Claude presently. "If you'll get your tally-boy Paladin to the gym, to-morrow night, I'll be very glad to put on the gloves with him."

"All right," agreed Michael with ill-acted reluctance. "I'll see what I can do about it. But if you get scared, between this and then, I'll feel like a fool to have to call off the match. Six rounds we usually make it. That too long for you?"

"No, sir," returned Claude stiffly.

"By the way," went on Michael carelessly, "remember little Tessie Glynn?"

"Why, yes. I've often wondered what became of her."

"I got kind of interested in her future. Sent her to business college and gave her a job in my office. Last week I made her my personal stenographer. She's all right. Good blood, back there, somewhere. Well, I'll send for Beasley in the morning and tell him about the match."

In the morning—perhaps in order to see that Michael did not forget—Claude paid his first voluntary visit to his father's suite of glittering offices in the Brian Building. And, Michael being elsewhere in the suite, he went directly to the private office.

His name cleared a way for him past a hedge of secretaries and guards. So, unopposed, he stood at last in the doorway of his father's big room, watching the bent head of a girl who wrought with lightning speed over a typewriter. The closing of the door behind him made her raise her head in inquiry.

Claude stared eagerly at the flushed face and the deep-blue eyes with their black Irish fringe. Tessie had changed tremendously. Her face was no longer thin, though even yet it had not quite grown up to her eyes. The elfin charm was still there. But with it was something more—something that made Claude prolong his stare past all bounds of courtesy.

"Have you still got the red silk tie?" he asked.

He had not meant to greet her like that. And he was relieved to see a glint of mischievous response in the black-fringed eyes. But at once the dancing glint died.

"Good morning, Mr. Claude," said Tessie, rising and coming forward to greet him. "Your father told me you were back. I suppose you'll be coming here to work, in a few days, won't you?"

"To work?" he repeated, puzzled. "I—why, I never thought of that. I—I suppose I must do something, pretty soon. Every man's supposed to, isn't he, in this country? But the lumber business, I think, doesn't appeal to me. My mother was anxious for me to go to law school. But—"

"Excuse me," she put in primly. "I didn't mean to be rude or ask questions. I supposed of course you'd follow your father in such a grand business as he's built up for you. But you know best."

"No," he denied. "I don't know at all. I haven't even thought. It hasn't appealed to me. By the way, how did you happen to recognize me? Haven't I changed in any way from the gangling kid in the Fauntleroys?"

"Not in your eyes. It was those I saw, first."

"I hear Beasley's working for my father, too," said Claude. "In fact, I'm to meet him, to-night. I hope, for his sake, you didn't fulfill your threat never to speak to him again. No, I don't, either!" he interrupted himself, on odd impulse. "I hope you did. Did you?"

"Of course, I didn't," she laughed.

In the laugh was a quality which Claude read for confusion. And, for some unaccountable reason, he resented it. She was so dainty, so pretty, so self-possessed! Why should she show confusion when he asked her about a guttersnipe like Pug Beasley? And why—a million whys—should Claude find himself caring the snap of his finger about it, either way? He frowned, portentously. Then, through no volition of his own, he heard himself blurt out the query:

"Will—will you go to lunch with me, today? I want to talk over old times and to—"

Again her laugh cut him short. But this time there was no hint of confusion in it. Nothing but amusement.

"Of course I won't," she answered. "Why should I?"

"Yes, and why shouldn't you?" boomed Michael from the door-way. "Isn't the boy good enough to eat with? He's guaranteed safe and kind. Run along with him, like a good girl, Tessie. It'll keep him out of mischief."

"You'll please take notice, Mr. Claude," said Tessie gravely, "that I'm lunching with you only because it is my employer's order. I've had orders I liked better."

"By the way," urged Michael, "steer him off of sweets and fried things. He's due for a terrible beating, to-night. And I want him to stay in some sort of condition, till then."

"A beating, sir?" asked Tessie in wonder. "Surely you're not going to punish him for—"

"No. Pug Beasley is. I've just seen him. He's going to box with my boy, at the gym. He—"

"Oh!" cried Tessie sharply. "Please not, Mr. Claude! He's the hardest hitter and the—"

"There, there!" interposed Michael. "Don't go making the poor lad any scareder than he is! Now run out to lunch, the two of you."

Luncheon, that day, was a long meal, though neither Claude nor his guest ate much of it. Course after course was dallied over or sent away almost untouched. But if there was scant eating, there was much talking. For some strange reason, the two found themselves gabbling to each other as freely as if they had been friends for a lifetime.

And, when Tessie left the office, at five, Claude chanced to be strolling past the employees' entrance. Nothing would do but he must walk home with her. And seldom had the mile journey been traversed in slower time.

Claude returned to Crescent Hill by way of Coogan's Alley, where Tessie no longer lived. For several minutes he stood near the gap in the almost collapsed fence, to view the scene of his two long-past battles with Pug. Then, as he turned homeward, he mumbled, half aloud:

"She can't care—she surely can't care for a thug like that. Then why did she laugh that queer confused way when I asked her about him? She—her eyes make me feel just a little bit as if I were in church. I—I wish I wasn't so glad of a chance to beat up that roughneck. It's not sportsmanly. But—but I *am* glad. And I hope dad tells her about it, to-morrow."

The low-ceiled gym shed of Number Two Mill was stuffed to suffocation that evening. Claude, followed by his father and a roustabout, came out of the impromptu dressing room to find Pug Beasley already lounging in a corner of the ring. Pug's face had changed not at all in the twelve years since last Claude had seen him. But the shoulders were as wide as a steam radiator and the massive chest sloped gracefully down to a small waist and lean thighs. If his arm-and-back muscles were bunchier than true art and the best speed demand, they were at least formidable.

Claude crossed the ring to shake hands, in affable patronage, with his opponent. He noted the bunchiness of the muscles and the heaviness of the legs. He knew these spelled mere hitting force and seldom go with swiftness or skill. He was a little sorry for the honest fellow. Then his memory conjured up their earlier meetings and his heart hardened.

The bell sounded and the bout was on. Beasley advanced from his corner with crafty slowness, his guard well up, his head low, his feet shuffling. The handshaking, by rule of the gym club, had occurred before the ringing of the gong. With professional caution Pug approached the ring's center.

Claude did not wait for him to arrive at that center. From his corner, with the speed of light, he dashed straight into the fray. Ducking Pug's outthrust left with ludicrous ease, he flashed in, playing a tattoo on heart and wind; then, stepping back from a proffered clinch he planted a flush left-hander to Beasley's jaw.

The audience purred and shuffled with approval. This was boxing. Not for nothing had Claude trained that supple body of his for years; and studied under the best glove masters of two countries. His work was a pleasure to watch.

Pug, irritated at his own humiliation, put down his head and rushed. But Claude was not there. As Beasley charged past the spot where Claude should have been awaiting him, a right-hander to the heart jarred him. As he wheeled, Claude delivered a left and a right to the face, then danced out of the way once more.

And so on, for the rest of the round and for the round that followed. Claude van Rensselaer Brian was treating Number Two Mill gym to the best exhibition of scientific sparring its frequenters had ever witnessed. Deft, lightning quick, tireless, tigerishly powerful, he bored into the clumsy Pug, landing at will and escaping with entire ease the slow counters and leads of his foe.

It was beautiful boxing. But, as old Michael noted with increasing annoyance, it was not fighting. Blow after blow pattered to Beasley's jaw. But they pattered. They did not crash. The heaviest of them had not the force to do more than shake their recipient.

"What ails him?" grumbled Michael, to himself. "He's got the strength, back in those long panther muscles of his. But he don't know how to throw it into his hitting arm. It's the same old trouble. He hasn't the punch. That'll bar him everywhere, unless—"

He broke off in his maundering pessimism. Beasley, as usual, had made a clumsy effort to get to close quarters. And, as usual, Claude danced back. But, grown overconfident, he had allowed himself to be fought into a corner. There was no sea room.

Before Brian could side-step to safety or even clinch, Pug Beasley had set himself and struck. The smashing blow hammered through Claude's carelessly artistic guard and to the jaw.

The referee, with an apologetic glance at old Michael, began to count out the gallant young heir to the Brian lumber interests. As in a thousand other fights, the punch had discounted mere science. A half minute passed before Claude van Rensselaer Brian emerged from dreamland to find the roustabout throwing cold water over him and the battered-faced Beasley thumbing his super-orbital nerve.

"It's the punch," said old Michael, as they set forth for home. "You had everything but that, and he had nothing but that. You could do everything to him except put him out. And he couldn't do a thing to you, but put you out. You're due to go through life that way, son. Tessie says you don't like the idea of coming in and learning the lumber business," he ended, with irrelevance. "That's a job that calls for a punch, too. How's your poor head—so much of it as he didn't knock off?"

Next morning, Claude did a very brave thing. He went to his father's office and, walking up to Tessie's desk, said with forced gayety:

"Well, I got my third licking from Beasley, last night. It was even more conclusive than the two others—except that you weren't there to see it. He—"

"Your father told me you made a beautiful bout of it," she comforted him. "He never saw prettier sparring, he said. You couldn't be expected to stand up against a man like Pug Beasley. I begged you not to, you know. It's a shame he hurt you so."

Perhaps there is a living man who could endure without agony of shame such tactless condolence from a girl of whom he has been dreaming and thinking all night. But Claude was not that man. He went red and tried in vain to think of something appropriate to say. All he could compass was a blurted:

"I'll meet him again, any time he likes. Even if I can't beat him, another time I may be able to keep clear of a knock-out."

"You shan't fight him again!" exclaimed Tessie vehemently. "You shan't! Even if I'm not able to keep you from doing it, I can make him promise not to. And I shall."

There was something in the proprietary way in which she spoke of Beasley, that turned Claude's dire mortification to red rage. Glowering, he strode away. Nor, for at least an hour, did he regain enough composure to come back and ask Tessie's leave to call that evening. Thanks to this delay, he missed a brief chat between his father and the girl, when Michael came into the private office, ten minutes after his departure.

"You're one grand girl, Tessie," approved Michael when she recounted the scene with Claude. "And it's working out, grand. Let me know when you think things are ready for the last act."

Three days later, old Michael stood on the sidewalk near the employees' entrance of the Brian Building. He was pulling his gloves on and looking up and down the street in search of his car. It was a few minutes after five in the afternoon and employees were trooping out of the building in batches and then in driblets.

Suddenly and with much surprise Michael beheld his son and heir standing unobtrusively in an angle of the outer doorway. Thus had Claude stood, every evening, until he could see Tessie approaching down the hallway. Then it was his wont to hurry to the sidewalk and, rounding the corner of the street, to meet her by happy accident.

Now, at sight of his father, the swain was aware of some embarrassment. Yet he stood his ground. Michael bore down on him.

"Run up to my office, that's a good lad," adjured Michael, "and fetch me that roll of blue prints off the top of my desk. I just remembered I'd forgot them. And I want to go over them, to-night. If I go back, myself, I'm dead sure to catch some of the outer office's late shift sneaking away early because they think I'm gone. On the top of the desk I left it. If you can't find the roll, ask Tessie where she's put it. She's working a bit late, this afternoon."

Galvanized into willing action, Claude sped upon his errand. And, entering the building at his heels, old Michael picked up an anteroom phone and sent a curt message up to his private office. Then, taking the next elevator after his son, he ascended thither, himself.

Blithely Claude hastened along the upper hall and into the huge outer office. Recalling subconsciously what Michael had said about the late shift, he grinned. For not a living soul remained in the place. The private office door stood ajar. And as he crossed the main room toward it he heard voices.

The voices were loud and excited. Mechanically Claude checked his own stride, as he heard and recognized them. Tessie was saying, hysterically:

"I won't! *I won't!* I—"

"Cut out the shy stuff!" interrupted Pug. "You been giving me the go-by, long enough. And I been waitin' a chance to see you where half the county won't come buttin' in on us. You hit me in the face, just now, when I tried to kiss you. That's gotta be paid for. I get that kiss—and I get it, *now!*"

There was a gasp—a shuffling—a muffled cry from Tessie. But before the sounds registered themselves fairly on Claude's senses he was over the threshold and in the private office.

Beasley had seized Tessie around the waist with one mighty arm. With the other he was brushing aside her fiercely protesting hands from her face. Claude waited for nothing more. Something seemed to give way inside his hot brain. With a yell he leaped at the man.

Beasley, with instinctive fighter-lore, loosed the girl and spun around to face the avenging youth. The two came together with a shock that set the desk furnishings to hopping.

Beasley flung his bunchy arms about the other, seeking the under-hold. Claude tore free and drove his left fist into Pug's face. The blow set Beasley caroming against the center table with an impetus that knocked over that massive piece of mahogany and sent him rebounding toward his opponent.

That smash to the face was a revelation to Claude. For the first time in his life his brain and his whole body had coordinated in a blow. The force of it hurt his arm and his back. Through the red fury which possessed him he was dimly conscious of the novel bodily and mental sensation and he thrilled to it.

Culture fell away from him, as a garment. Back in his cosmos snarled the spirit of forty generations of two-fisted men who had been his father's forbears. The vile affront to Tessie—the girl's pitiful helplessness as she had struggled in the grip of the brute—all this had laid bare the silken-swathed primitive human in him. Not that he knew this or cared. Just now, all he asked was a chance to tear apart the man who was lunging toward him again.

Not troubling to guard, he received on the mouth a glancing right-hander and then hurled himself at Beasley; with an avalanche of short-arm smashes he drove Pug before him, the length of the room, and banging against the wall. In the rush two chairs and a filing cabinet went by the board.

At the far wall Pug rallied enough to whip across a left counter to the jaw and a jab to the wind. Their impact turned the delirious Claude sick. But they did not slow him down nor abate his aggressiveness.

Foot to foot, almost chest to chest, the two exchanged thudding punches that echoed through the room as accompaniment to their grunted breathing. Then, under the rain of punishment, Pug ran into a clinch. Wheeling, Claude tore free again, at the expense of the more ornamental parts of a two-hundred-dollar suit. And, with a whistling intake of breath between broken teeth he dashed in for more close-quarters work. His fists flying, his body crouched forward, he rained rib-cracking blows on Beasley, taking, unflinchingly, heavier punishment than he would have deemed it possible for mortal to withstand.

Tessie cried out in terror. Old Michael, without shifting his own fascinated eyes from the battle, laid a gently authoritative hand over her mouth.

"Watch him slug!" breathed the old ruffian. "Watch the way he gets the back and the shoulders of him into it, every time. Glory be, he's got the punch, at last!"

"Oh!" wailed Tessie, her voice muffled by reason of the number nine hand over her full lips. "Oh, they'll murder each other! Pug will kill him. He—"

"Pug will make him alive!" corrected the crowing old voice. "Pug's earning his five hundred dollars to the queen's taste. Shut up now, dear, and let me watch it in peace and contentment."

Bleeding, their clothes in ribbons, the men warred on, up and down the wrecked room. Claude's long-studied sparring knowledge clung to him as sketchily as did the remnants of his suit. He used it, mechanically, to add scientific force to his punches; but not once did it deter him from letting a smash land on him if, by taking the blow, he could land a harder.

Pug's rugged strength seemed unabated. Though he could not send home one effective blow to his faster adversary's three, yet he was doing frightful damage with such punches as scored.

One of these caught the ever-attacking Claude over the heart. Claude swayed and retreated a step, for the first time in the bout. Tessie caught her breath in terror. Pug sprang greedily forward to follow up his advantage. As he charged, wide open, he had a momentary view of his enemy straightening from the brief slump and setting himself.

Then, with all his new-found dynamic strength, Claude struck.

Long experience in distance judging and in aim guided his blow. Flush to the jaw point whizzed the left fist. And, almost simultaneously a right swing followed it true to the same goal.

Pug Beasley wheeled halfway around, under the dual impact. Then he fell—forward. He fell across Michael Brian's sacred and immaculately furnished desk, face downward, among papers whose aspect was not improved by a baptism of blood.

Thus did Francis Xavier Beasley suffer his first knock-out—Pug Beasley who, five years earlier, had left the Brian employ for the climb which had recently made him middleweight champion of the State and who, by dint of heavy subsidy, had been lured into giving his services to his ex-employer and backer, at the gym and again at the private office.

Old Michael hurried forward to lift the fallen professional. But, midway, he was stopped.

He was stopped by a hideous and brutalized creature with bloodily distorted face and indecently few clothes. A youth whose swollen mouth and chin had, by some miracle, taken on a new hardness of line.

"Hold on!" roared Claude, gripping his sire detainingly by the shoulder. "He can wait. Something else can't. I want a job. D'you hear? I want a job. Fix it up for me, first thing to-morrow. I—"

"A job?" bleated Michael, the crafty, in badly done repugnance. "You don't mean you want—"

"I mean I want a job!" reiterated the hoarse-voiced ruffian. "A *job*. If you won't give me one I'll get it somewhere else. You don't suppose I'm going to keep a wife on my father's cash, do you? Give me that job!"

Appendix

Publication information
for the stories
in this book

A Lightning Change

Lippincott's Magazine, July 1901
Front text:
A Columbia Collage Tale
Author of "Columbia Stories," "Dr. Dale," "Syria from the Sadde," etc.
Seventh in the Series of College Tales

A Park Row Galahad

Lippincott's Magazine, September 1902
Front text:
Author of "Dr. Dale," "Columbia Stories," etc.
Edits:
A boyish stride replaced his former slouching gate
...was changed to:
A boyish stride replaced his former slouching gait

A "pas seul" is a dance for one person.

Drunk or Crazy?

Argosy, March 1910
Front text:
Goward's idiotic investment, and the stir it caused in Jeweler's Block.
Edits: The following line was printed as:
"To tear a hole in that $2,00?"
It was edited to read:
"To tear a hole in that $2,700?"

Back to the Wickiup

Argosy, June 1912

A Knight of New York

Top-Notch, June 1 1912
Front text:

(A COMPLETE NOVEL)

Edits: The name of a theater was used in this story only twice. It was spelled "Hyperion" and "Hyperior." The latter was changed to "Hyperion."

The Sights They Missed

Top-Notch, December 1, 1913

Front text:

(A COMPLETE NOVEL)

Illustrator not credited, but opening-page illustration is initialed.

Edits: The word "enveloped" in the following:

Nor was he astonished to see several stamped and postmarked enveloped flung with elaborate carelessness...

...was changed to "envelopes".

Cephas the Paladin

Popular, Febuary 15, 1914

Front text:

In which there is for hero a pig—a month-old porker so rawboned and stunted that not even the most optimistic of farmers could have hoped to sell him. But he had the heart of a Paladin

Edits: The second reference to the character Ophido was spelled "Ophida." This was corrected to "Ophido."

The Fate Chaser

Popular, October 23, 1914

Front text:

Author of "An Amateur War Lord," "Cephas the Paladin," Etc.

The flight of Halil Ben Ismail from the bazaars of Syria to the bazaars of the Pan-Universal Exposition in America to escape from Azrael, the angel of death. A noteworthy story of a Mohammedan's experience in the land of the infidel A tale that will cheat you of a tear and tease you to smile.

Edits: The italicization of non-English words in the published version was inconsistent. A few words were italicized for this edition, for better (though possibly not perfect) consistency.

The "Other Man"

Green Book, March 1915

Illustrated by Charles Dean Cornwell

Front text:

A SHORT STORY BY THE AUTHOR OF "WHOSE WIFE?"

Original captions:

Page 173: "After all, what's the use? I'm as good as a dead man. We spend our lives lying to each other; why should we spend our deaths doing it?"

180: Since afternoon he had sat thus. But Claire had not arrived.

181: Horace Steell, seated in the dark niche of the Mercer Hall veranda, smoked an endless succession of cigars.

185: At a table, under a single thick-shaded electric burner, sat a bearded man, filling in a certificate. Among the bedside shadows knelt a woman who wept in frightened, strangled sobs.

A Post-Marital Engagement

Blue Book, June 1915

Illustrator not credited.

Front text:

Two men and one woman—and a situation develops which is handled in a unique and vigorous fashion by this most able of our newer writers.

Author of "Whose Wife?" "The Man Who Went Wrong," etc.

Money Makes the Marriage Go

Blue Book, October 1915

Illustrator not credited.

Front text:

When Royce Churchill's wife Mavis acquires a big income of her own, a surprising situation develops. Mr. Terhune handles it with his usual skill and power.

Author of "Whose Wife?" "The Greater Radiance," etc.

Note: The publisher could find no definition for the word "bithely," but did find it used, so it was left intact.

The Night of the Dub

Saturday Evening Post, March 31, 1917

Illustrated by Gordon Dingwall

Original captions:

Page 227: "Of Course There's Dozens of Good Dinners Cheaper. But We're Doing This Thing Only Once, and We Want to Do it Right!"

231: "Never Mind! Duck Hunters are Usually Good Sportsmen. They'll Understand and Clear Out!"

234: "The Notices All Said 'Stag,'" Snorted Reggie. "If Any of the Boys Have Brought Wives Tagging Along—"

241: "I Heard Your Offer. And I Turned it Down. Now it's Up to You to Listen While I Put My Terms."

The 101st Man

Green Book, May 1917
Illustration by William Oberhardt
Front text:
THE STORY OF A WOMAN WHO LIVED DOWN HER PAST; AND OF THE DRAMATIC SITUATION WHICH REVEALED TO HER THE MAN WHO HAD HELPED
Original captions:
Page 257: She did not answer at once, but sat leaning forward, peering at him. In perhaps half a minute she spoke: "This is what is called blackmail, isn't it?" "It is anything you choose to call it," he replied, unabashed.

The Crippled Doughnut

Green Book, August, 1917
Illustrated by Fontaine Fox
Front text:
JERE MISK, THE DEMON REAL-ESTATE DEALER, GETS HIS VASSAL, TITUS SNIDER, INTO AN AWFUL PICKLE
Original captions:
Page 270: Titus Snider sat numbly at his desk, trying not to repeat over and over to himself the names Jere had called him.
271: Wastebasket contents are free salvage. Sinlessly, almost piously, Titus Snider lifted from its abode of disgrace the twisted ellipse.
273: Half the night Titus Snider had lain awake, ever anon rising from his couch to scan the fickle sky for signs of rain.
274: The room shook with a yell that could not normally have come from so frail a body as her husband's.
280: Titus was surveying the eagle with a look of dawning and frightened hope. "How much?" he asked as carelessly as his throat and banging heart would let him.
281: Titus hobbled up the front walk, lugging over his shoulders a burlap bag.
283: One orb was closed in a wink, giving the junk-man's face an evil cast... Titus stared back blankly, his soul whispering to him of dire peril.

The Dubess

Saturday Evening Post, August 17, 1918
Illustrated by Edward L. Chase
Original captions:
Page 289: She Fairly Caught Her Breath at Sight of Her Own Elegance.
300-301: Hester Gregg's Advent at the Faculty Club Dance Caused the Focusing of Many a Pair of Eyes on Her.
304: At the Week's End He Went to Call. Four Other Men Were Adorning the Veranda.

The Cross-of-War Man

Green Book, January 1919

Illustrations by L. Pern Bird

End text:

"THE FINAL CROP," another of Mr. Terhune's exceptional stories, will appear in an early issue.

Original captions:

Page 316: From the audience burst a wild salvo of hand-clapping. Through the din came yells of: "Leigh! Wilt Leigh!"

319: As Rena faced him there, he took an ardent step toward her. Then his arms dropped limp to his sides. Her look had seemed to go clear through his soul.

The Final Crop

Green Book, February 1919

Illustrations by Hawthorne Howland

Front text:

Author of "Dollars and Cents," "The Years of the Locust," etc.

End text:

THERE will be another of Albert Payson Terhune's vivid and dramatic stories in an early issue of THE GREEN BOOK MAGAZINE.

Original captions:

Page 323 (top): "Old Misery has plenty of friends to tip him off to any raid and give him time to hide. He's probably the most notorious moonshiner in Kentucky."

323 (bottom): The original Grainger had taken up a huge grant of land in Virginia early in the seventeenth century.

325: Sibyl was the most divinely merciful court of last resort before whom a scared young lawyer could hope to plead a life-and-death case.

330: The prisoner raised his head from the circle of his arms and sat up. For perhaps fifteen seconds Halsey and the captive glared, motionless. Then Halsey found his voice in a strangled cry.

332: "If I could 'a' got at my rifle, when they cotched me, I'd 'a' put a ball through my worthless head. But they jumped on me so sudden-like, I couldn't."

Tidy Emotions

Green Book, May 1919

Illustrations by J. Allen St. John

Edits: The line of one column, on a 3-column page (page 96), seems to be missing and unaccounted for. The original text reads:

"You have no right to speak so!" she

statue. I'm a flesh-and-blood woman,

and a woman who loves you, and whose

The text inserted between the words "she" and "statue," in this edition, are not the words of Albert Payson Terhune. They are the publisher's best guess.

Original captions:

Page 343: She stood looking at her husband, the blood surging oddly through her. She drew a quivering breath and took a step forward.

349: Opening the folded sheet, she read it—too crazily jealous to feel shame.

351: She was crying, fiercely, hysterically. "What do you mean?" he demanded in amazement. "You sneered at me for being a 'framework for black velvet and pearls!'" she sobbed.

The Winner

Blue Book, August 1919

Illustrator not credited

Front text:

AN engaging story which has to do with the sport of kings, and with a lady who knew how to turn a liability into an asset.

End text:

"SHEEP IN WOLF'S CLOTHING," another of Albert Payson Terhune's stimulating stories, will appear in our next issue. Along with it will be notable contributions by Edison Marshall, Frank Packard, I. K. Friedman, Edgar Jepson, Clarence Herbert New, H. Bedford-Jones, Gladys Johnson, Chester Crowell and many other clever writers.

Human Interest Stuff

Red Book, November 1919

Illustrations by Frank Stick

Front text:

Here is another of those splendid stories about men, women and dogs—

Original captions:

Page 371: Meanwhile, Eve was growing steadily worse. Even Jeff could see that. So too, apparently could the only sharer of his vigils—a huge and leonine dog.

374: The circuit-rider said: "I think she will live. You may thank God if you care to. Or if you still think He hasn't been here—" "If He ain't," choked Titus, ecstatically, "He sent a damn fine sub.'"

380 and 389: No captions in source.

Note: Terhune used this title for at least three distinct stories. There is the one included in this volume; one in the June 11, 1927 issue of Cosmopolitan; and one in The Terhune Omnibus (1937), an anthology later retitled The Best-Loved Dog Stories of Albert Payson Terhune (1954). Where or if this last story had appeared previous to its publication in the Omnibus is not known by the publisher of the

APT Readers. It was used as the basis for a 22-page comic book adaptation, written by Rodney Schroeter and Illustrated by William Messner-Loebs, and published in 2012.

The Unmarrying of Veeder

Red Book, December 1919

Illustrated by R. L. Lambdin

Front text:

Here's a story of what every woman—that is, married woman—knows, but that Mr. Veeder had to experiment to learn.

Edits: The following:

he dined in hungry luxury at the Inglaterra and thence wondered forth

...was changed to:

he dined in hungry luxury at the Inglaterra and thence wandered forth

Original captions:

Page 392: Caption, illustration 4: Reina and her mother came for tea, once, in his bachelor apartment. "Whew!" she complained. "What a fearful smell of tobacco!"

400: Three minutes later Craig Veeder was crawling wearily aboard the smelly boat and was explaining in very bad Spanish that he had tumbled off the deck of his own yacht.

401: The fishermen took one look at the wad of wet money Veeder flashed on them, and they gave eager consent.

402: In another hour the castaway was climbing a flight of slippery stone steps onto a landing-stage which faced a grand-opera-scenery plaza.

The Dub of Peace

Saturday Evening Post, July 24, 1920

Illustrated by Harold Lund

Edits: The first part of the last two lines of the story were partially blanked out on the available source. The words published in this book are the editor's best guess. The last two lines of the source material are:

you' ??? st happened to ask me for that

??? ar earlier!"

Original captions:

Page 413: The Outing Was One of the Most Successful in the Long Bright Annals of the Gentlemen's Sons Association

417: "Kitty Come Home Last Night Crying. I Couldn't Get a Word Out of Her. Nor Yet Her Mommer Couldn't Either"

420: "Before You Referee Any Other Fights, are You Too Much of a Coward to Put On the Gloves With Me?"

423: It Was a Right Half Hook to the Jaw

Females of the Species

Cosmopolitan, September, 1920

Original captions:

Page 436: A man, worn out and buffeted, but still swimming gamely, was trying to reach the reeling boat. Celia braced herself and held out one fragile hand to help him

440: Up and down the dooryard they raged, sending the sand aloft in choking swirls from under the stamp and shuffle of their flying feet. The girls, chalk-faced, clung close to each other and watched the primitive conflict

452-453: From one to the other of the tense faces, Hector stared with bewildered incredulity. This time, it was Celia who broke the uncomfortable pause. "Hector, it is for you to choose. I—I love you. I— " Nedda broke in upon the panted avowel. "She doesn't know what love is!" she cried. "Look at me—*look* at me, Hector! I'm your mate!"

The Whiffet

Popular, February 20, 1922

Front text:

Author of "The Feud," "Sant-El-Klaus Najib," Etc.

The Whiffet was named wrong. He was just plain hell-cat—or he never would have lasted those second four rounds

Beauty

Popular, July 20, 1922

Front text:

Author of "The Writer-Upward," "Sant-El-Klaus Najib," etc.

Almost anything may be carried too far—even a love of beauty

End text:

Mr. Terhune will have another short story—"The Punch," in the following number.

The Punch

Popular, August 7, 1922

Front text:

Author of "Beauty," "The Writer-Upward," etc.

Man needs an incentive, just as powder needs a match, before he can really get himself across.

General Notes

The contraction **won't** in several stories was spelled without an apostrophe. This seems to have been the convention of the time, not limited to one magazine title.

The word **ain't** was also used without an apostrophe (very odd, as a word like sha'n't was used with both).

The apostrophe was inserted in both, for this book.

In the source material, the opening line of a new chapter often starts with a drop cap. When that first line is dialogue, many magazines also dropped the opening quotation mark. The Publisher simply does not like that, so in this book, such lines start with an opening quotation mark.

Several longer stories were broken up into chapters, headed by Roman numerals. For at least one, the opening was not headed by a Roman numeral I in the source, so it was not included here.

Appendix B

Terhune Letters

The following correspondence, related to APT's inquiry about the movie rights to one of his stories, were purchased at auction at the Windy City Pulp and Paper show in 2005. Most are file copies of letters sent out; unsigned carbon copies on onionskin paper.

```
                                          "Sunnybank,"
                                          Pompton Lakes, New Jersey,
                                          September 1, 1915.

    R. H. Davis, Esq.,

            c/o Frank A. Munsey Co.,

                8 West 40th Street,

                    New York City.

Dear Davis:-

        On January 14, 1911, you very kindly gave me the dramatic

rights to my story, "The King from Boston" (January "Scrap Book," 1911).

I understand this does not include the moving picture rights.

Can the latter rights also be granted to me?

        If by any chance your generosity in the matter could be

stretched to cover "40 Ali Babas and the Thief" or "A Complete Tweed

Suit," I should be still deeper in your debt.

        May you be where rose-leaves shall fall upon your tomb!

                            As ever,
```

RHD

September 3, 1915.

My dear Terhune:-

I beg to acknowledge yours of the 2nd, which
I have turned over to our business department with the recom-
mendation that every consideration be given you in the matters
referred to.

I don't know just how far "Forty Ali Babas and
the Thief" or "A Complete Tweed Suit" have gone in the direction
of the movies, but Mr. Brophy, in whose hands these matters
rest, will give you all the information.

Believe me,

Ever sincerely,

GEJ

Carter —

Terhune says
Davis released
dramatic rights of
"The King from Boston."
Our [illegible] not shew
it. [illegible] if any corres.

Not in 1912 to 1915

On the reverse of the above:

The Evening Times
PHILADELPHIA

JDB   September 14, 1915.

Messrs. Nicoll, Anable, Lindsay & Fuller,
61 Broadway,
New York City.
                    Attention of Mr. Mortimer Boyle.
Dear Sirs:-

          On November 2, 1910, we purchased from
Albert Payson Terhune a story entitled "The King
from Boston". This story was published by us in
the January, 1911, Scrap Book. We hold a receipt
from Mr. Terhune reading as follows:-
                    "By endorsement of this check the
               payee acknowledges payment in full
               for the following: One story
                              entitled
                    "The King from Boston"
               which the payee has sold to the
               drawer with warranty of authorship
               and ownership, and with authority
               to copyright and all other rights
               whatsoever therein. Any alteration
               of the above clause makes this check
               void."

          Under date of January 13, 1911, Mr. Terhune wrote
to us as follows:-
                    "I have received a request to use the
               plot of "The King from Boston", which appeared in
               the January "Scrap Book", as the basis of a comic
               opera.
                    I shall be greatly indebted to you if you
               can secure for me the rights to this story.
                    I do not suppose anything tangible will
               come of the scheme to make an opera of my story,
               but every chance seems worth taking."

          We replied under date of January 14, 1911, thus:-

                    "Replying to yours of January 13, requesting
               all dramatic rights in your story "The King from Boston",
               which appeared in the January Scrap Book, I beg to inform
               you that it is a pleasure to grant that request. This
               letter can be used as an acknowledgment of our surrender
               of said dramatic rights. It is understood that all other
               rights are still held intact by The Frank A. Munsey Company."

          Did our release of the dramatic rights to Mr. Terhune also

convey to him the moving picture rights? My understanding is that under

The letter on the previous page continues, on the back
of the onionskin carbon copy:

Messrs. Nicoll, Anable, Lindsay & Fuller.   -2-   September 14, 1915.

the provisions of the old copyright law the dramatic rights
included moving picture rights and that our release of the
dramatic rights did also give him the moving picture rights,
although we might point out to you that in his letter, Mr.
Terhune specifically stated that he wanted the plot of "The
King from Boston" as the basis of a comic opera.

        Will you be good enough to advise us on the matter
at your earliest convenience?

                Very truly yours,

                Assistant Treasurer.

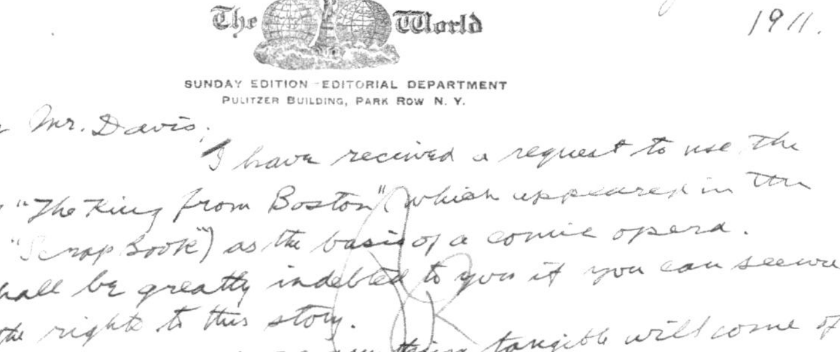

The World

SUNDAY EDITION – EDITORIAL DEPARTMENT
PULITZER BUILDING, PARK ROW N. Y.

January 13
1911.

My dear Mr. Davis:

I have received a request to use the plot of "The King from Boston" (which appeared in the January "Scrap Book") as the basis of a comic opera.

I shall be greatly indebted to you if you can secure for me the right to this story.

I do not suppose anything tangible will come of the scheme to make an opera of my story; but every chance seems worth taking.

Very truly
Albert Payson Terhune.

RHD   January 14, 1911.

Albert Payson Terhune,

  The World,

    Pulitzer Bldg., N. Y.

Dear Mr. Terhune:-

    Replying to yours of January 13, requesting all dramatic rights in your story "The King from Boston," which appeared in the January Scrap Book, I beg to inform you that it is a pleasure to grant that request. This letter can be used as an acknowledgment of our surrender of said dramatic rights. It is understood that all other rights are still held intact by The Frank A. Munsey Company.

    Sincerely yours,

9/14/15 Noted on cards.

JDB   September 14, 1915.

Mr. Albert Payson Terhune,
Sunnybank,
Pompton Lakes,
New Jersey.

Dear Sir:-

Mr. Davis has referred to me your communication
of September 2 in regard to moving picture rights. I
shall give you some definite word on the matter in the
very near future.

Very truly yours,

Assistant Treasurer.

CS

Nicoll, Anable, Lindsay & Fuller,

Cable Address: Nalaf

De Lancey Nicoll.
Courtland V. Anable.
John D. Lindsay.
Thomas Staples Fuller.
Cornelius J. Sullivan.
Courtlandt Nicoll.

No. 61 Broadway

New York September 17, 1915.

The Frank A. Munsey Company,
    8 West 40th Street,
        New York City.

Gentlemen:-

    We are in receipt of your three communi-
cations of September 14th, 1915.

    In regard to the story by A.P. Terhune
entitled "The King from Boston" we would state that
your letter surrendering your dramatic rights acted
as a release of the moving picture rights.

    As to the Merriefield matter, if all the
receipts in your possession expressly state that
the stories are sold with the copyright and all
other rights, the moving picture rights belong to
you. We note on the itemized list of the stories
you have purchased, that in two cases the moving
picture rights have been sold. We assume by this
that you hold receipts similar to the one described,
but have parted with the moving picture rights.

    In the Mohican Company matter, it is not
necessary that an entry be made in the minute book
whenever the Company signs a lease.

             Very truly yours,

             Nicoll, Anable, Lindsay & Fuller

The stamp at left is on the reverse
of the above letter.

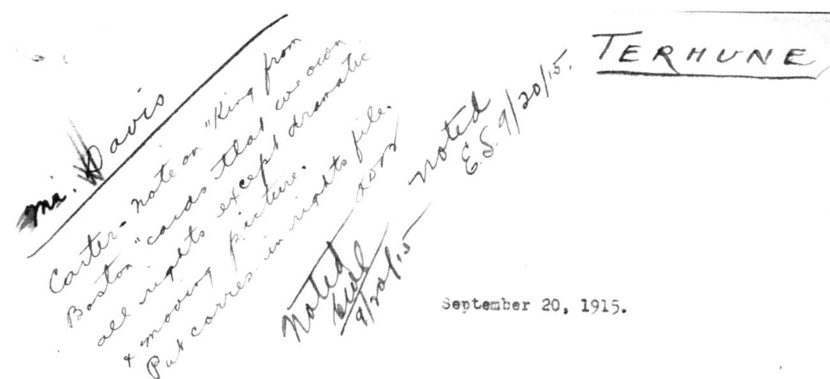

September 20, 1915.

Mr. Albert Payson Terhune,
    Sunnybank,
      Pompton Lakes,
        New Jersey.

Dear Sir:-

Referring again to your communication of September 2, regarding moving picture rights.

We find that our release to you on January 14, 1911, of the dramatic rights of your story "The King from Boston" conveyed to you the moving picture rights.

We cannot release to you the moving picture rights of "Forty Ali Babas and a Thief", as they have already been disposed of by us to a moving picture house.

Nor can we surrender the moving picture rights of "A Complete Tweed Suit", owing to certain "movie" connections that we have.

Very truly yours,

Assistant Treasurer.

JDB/ST

Appendix C

How this Book was Made
by Rodney Schroeter

Why I'm Writing This

I hope others decide to preserve old fiction, carefully edit it to remain true to its source, and make it available for interested readers.

I have encountered numerous e-books obviously created by scanning and— nothing else. The scanned images were converted to text by an OCR (optical character recognition) program, but otherwise "untouched by human hands." Or, more appropriately, untouched by human minds. Such texts are a mish-mash of special characters where letters should be; punctuation missing where it should be; new paragraphs where none should be; one monolithic block of text where several paragraphs should be.

It takes a special personal integrity to salvage fiction from an old magazine and want to preserve it as it originally was (minus the obvious errors).

I am here describing the procedures that I use to create my anthologies of public-domain fiction for two reasons.

The first is to help others who would like to do the same.

But that first reason might never happen. In fact, I would be relieved if it does not. I truly hope that, on publication of this essay, I am bombarded with communiques indignantly asking, "Why do you do things so old-fashionedly? There are much better methods to accomplish this."

And that is my second reason. Undoubtedly, I have established my procedure (presented here in excruciating detail) and have locked into it, blithely unaware of any alternative. (Or, if I know an alternative, I have been unable to make it work.)

I hope people contact me with those better techniques, even for a single, isolated step of this scan-to-book process.

A brief summary

I am writing this in the last half of 2017 / early 2018.

I scan pulps or other magazines. (I find some magazines on the Internet, and process those slightly differently.)

To prepare for more accurate OCR, I edit the scanned images with Adobe Photoshop.

I convert the images to text via OCR with Nuance Omnipage 18.

The text is saved in WordPerfect format, and then in RTF format.

The resulting RTF text is brought into Adobe InDesign.

The text is edited on-screen. In another window, I view the original scanned source page for comparison.

With InDesign, I create the documents needed for:

— a print book

— an ebook

I proofread a printed copy of the book.

I submit the final book files to Ingram-Spark.

Scanning

I have a Brother printer/scanner that I selected specifically for the size of its scan surface, which is large enough to scan a whole piece of original comic art (but not quite wide enough to scan a vinyl LP cover). I can scan two pages at once. I weigh the pulp down with several heavy textbooks (likely on InDesign and Photoshop). The scanner bed is also large enough to scan a full magazine page, the size of Country Gentleman or Saturday Evening Post.

For this example, I've scanned pages 90 and 91.

For pages without illustrations, I scan at 300 dpi. Illustrated pages are scanned at 600 dpi. During the final submission process for the book, Ingram-Spark raises a warning flag that all interior art must be at 600 dpi.

I scan in color and save the two pages as 90_91.tif.

Why in color? I'm going to convert it to black & white, so why make extra work for myself?

OK, I was once advised to scan in black & white. But for whatever reason, I could never get that to work ("work" in the sense that the end result would go through OCR well). There are undoubtedly some simple settings that would save me time. As I say, let me know about them.

I save the scan as 90_91.tif.

About the software I use

In 2009, the year I was mostly unemployed, I was asked by an officer of the Wisconsin Writers Association to come on board for the purpose of creating books. They wanted to add some prestige to the organization by starting a WWA Press.

I knew nothing of making books. But I had contact with several small publishers at the Windy City Pulp and Paper shows. One publisher I'd done proofreading for composed his books with Word-Perfect. His books are of excellent quality. Another used Adobe Creative Suite.

I decided to go with InDesign, part of the Creative Suite. I had one false start; I bought InDesign alone, without Photoshop and the rest. Wrong move, based on incomplete knowledge.

I bought Creative Suite 5.5. I was fortunately able to use my wife's teaching ID to get a discount. Also fortunately, I upgraded to version 6.0, before Adobe went to a subscription-only version (which I consider economically suicidal; but I am not privy to their financial statements).

I took two InDesign classes at a private training company in Milwaukee; the first, an intro course; the second, some months later, on creating ebooks. Otherwise, I trained myself. I have several thick books on Creative Suite or InDesign alone. These books are excellent, if you spend the time and go through the exercises.

I knew just enough to assist an editor of a local newspaper to convert from paste-up composition to using InDesign.

I became competent enough in InDesign to create two projects for WWA: an anthology, A Wisconsin Harvest Vol. II; and a comic book based on an Albert Payson Terhune story, Human Interest Stuff, written by myself and illustrated by William Messner-Loebs.

2015 would see the end of my involvement with WWA, as new

leadership was no longer interested in a WWA Press.

Processing the scanned image

In Photoshop, I:

— Open 90_91.tif.

— Save As 90_91_bw.tif (doing this first avoids the all-too-common error of revising it, saving it, and overlaying 90_91.tif; after a 2-decade career in Information Technology, my view is Save All Versions).

(A "TIFF Options" pop-up appears for me. Under "Image Compression," I select LZW, which a friend told me is a lossless compression, making the resulting file smaller.

— Convert 90_91_bw.tif to grayscale. (Image / Mode / Grayscale)

— In (Image / Adjustments / Levels), I:

(See Figure 1 and 2.)

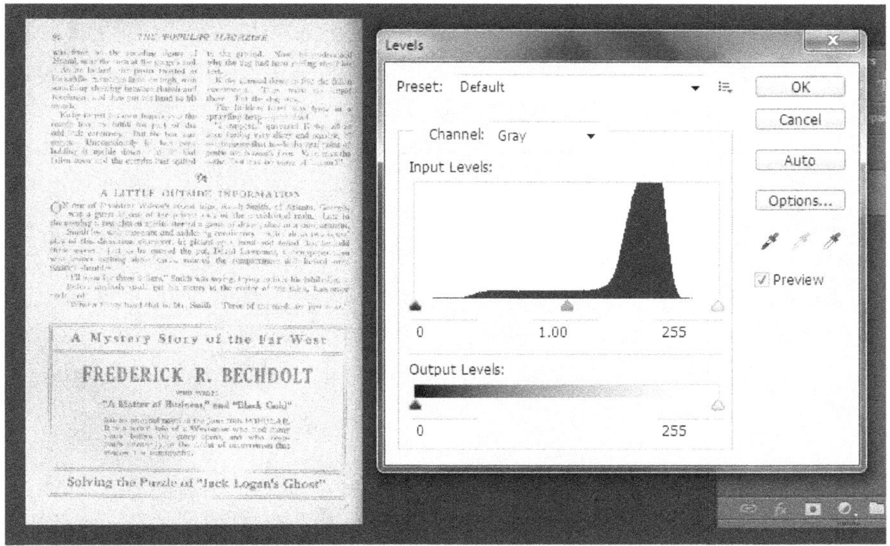

Figure 1

— Slide the white thing to the middle of the big black hump (making the whites whiter)

— Slide the black thing to the left-most hump (making the blacks blacker)

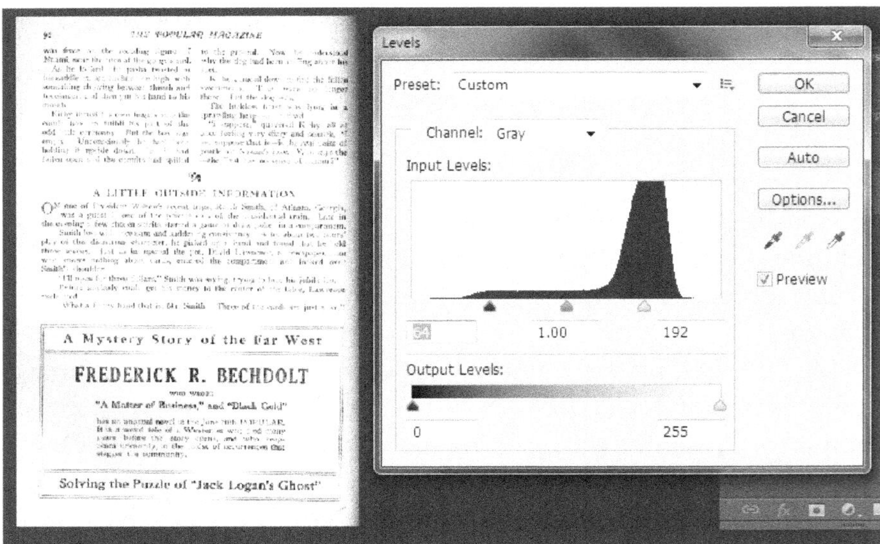

Figure 2

— Leave the gray one (for midtones) alone.

(As you see, I don't know the technical name for some of these tools, but can describe them unambiguously enough.)

I select the page with the Crop Tool. I use the guide lines that come up to see if either or both pages are lined up horizontally (see Figure 3). This is necessary, because OmniPage needs vertical columns of text to scan. (Unless there's a way to define a rhomboid text column in OmniPage; if there is, I imagine manually setting such columns would be extremely tedious, so straightening them out in Photoshop is the

Figure 2

way to go.)

If I have a 2-page spread, more likely than not, the two pages will not be aligned with each other. So I have to save them separately:

90_bw.tif

91_bw.tif

With the Crop Tool, I

— Align the text.

— Crop margins as tightly as possible.

I enlarge the page. With the Eraser Tool, I get rid of every stray mark that it is practical to erase. Any little dot can be interpreted by the OCR process as a period. Any small line can become an extraneous quote mark, or mutate a letter and word into gibberish.

This process could go on forever, because there is an endless number of specks, if you keep magnifying the page. At some point, I stop.

The pulp's spine margins are sometimes dark. If they're too dark, I will, in Photoshop:

— Select the darkest area with the Rectangular Marquee Tool.

— Cut it.

— Create a new layer.

— Paste in Place on the new layer.

— Use (Image / Adjustments / Levels) to lighten the dark, but not so much as to obliterate the letters.

When 90_bw.tif and 91_bw.tif are edited to my satisfaction, I move the original color scan, 90_91.tif, to a directory called "_processed."

When I don't scan

I have found some magazines on the Internet. This saves hundreds of dollars in buying the original magazines. Quality of page images varies. But I'm surprised by how well this process works with such files. There are some differences in processing; pages found online can sometimes be saved in .pdf format, as opposed to the scanned .tif. But much of the subsequent processing is the same.

OCR

I open Nuance OmniPage 18.0.

I found it easiest to work with three windows open:
— Thumbnails
— Page Image
— Document Manager
I also have the 1-2-3 bar visible at top.
I (1-Load Files), find and open the .tif images for that story.
I (2-Automatic), which performs the OCR.
A note on this: I'm glad I discovered the Document Manager window, as it tells me what processing has taken place on which pages. The results of OCR would sometimes drop an entire page, leading me to suspect it had not been selected. Or whatever.

The OCR Proofreader window comes up, but I'm not ready for that, so I close it.

I click on each page in the Thumbnails window, and check the corresponding Page Image. What could you find here?

— A page of 2-column text that has been scanned as if it were one column. I have to adjust manually.

— Portions of the page that should not be interpreted as text. A picture. A heading. A footer. A big blob of crap. Though, if I've done my job in Processing the Scanned Image, there should be no extraneous blobs of crap, anywhere.

If any page contains anomalies that need manual fixing, I select all pages in Thumbnails and (2-Automatic) again. The program will protest, "Hey, some of these pages I did already!" Nonetheless, (2-Automatic) again.

Now it's time for OCR Proofreader. (This comes up automatically if you did another (2-Automatic); if not, find it under (Tools).

I cannot decide which is worse, this step, or converting scanned pages to black & white. If you have a long piece to use OCR Proofreader on, allot a block of time sufficient for the purpose. If there is any way to stop this process, save what you've done, get out of the program, and then come back and start where you left off, then—as with most software programs, when you want something truly practical—the documentation for this procedure is deviously hidden. I suspect the software developers, confronted with a wish-list item like this, would respond in the usual way: "Huh? Waddaya wanna do that for?"

If you are prone to road hypnosis, take a break from the OCR Proofreader. About once every five minutes to flush your mind out should be good. The process is spell-binding. Mind-numbing.

With the Document Manager open, you know how far along you are (as in, you only have 137 items to review). That's important for my sanity.

OCR Proofreader is finished at last. Time to (3-Save to Files):

Filename: mag_name_dt_dt_dt.wpd

Save as: Text

Files of type: WordPerfect

Formatting level: Plain Text

File options: Create one file for all pages

Page range: All pages

Oh, by the way. Anything denigrating I say about this OCR software is strictly peripheral. Overall, I am overawed by how well it actually works, and consider OCR in general and Nuance OmniPage specifically to be tremendous boons to civilization.

Proof / correct in WP

Early in this process, I would proofread / correct the text in Word-Perfect. I found the next steps to work better.

Sequence of steps, in processing the text vs. the graphics, is optional.

Oh, yes. About WordPerfect. It is so superior to Microsoft Word, that I consider the fact that Word is used more widely than WordPer-fect to be one strong datum supporting my view that our civilization is in decline.

Create RTF

Because InDesign is not yet advanced enough to place WordPer-fect files, I remove all tabs and save the WordPerfect file as an RTF file.

Filename: mag_name_dt_dt_dt.rtf

Bring RTF into InDesign

To keep things consistent, I have an InDesign file called

Generic_6x9_Paperback3.indd, which I copy as (given the above example) 1914 01 01 Top-Notch.indd.

In this member, I have a box with several instructions:

— Place text onto first page.

— Select all text.

— Set para style to Body Text (which is up to you to define).

— A plus sign might be OK; it might indicate italics and other formatting was brought over (it usually is not, for me).

To keep the pages consistent with how they're defined in the Master pages, I

— Create a 2nd page (blank).

— Apply Master to both pages.

— Flow text onto 2nd page with the Shift key down. All pages needed for the rest of the text will be created.

Run script

I set up a script which will reformat or correct the most common errors. Designing a script is a logical challenge, as you can write a command line that makes some corrections, and have those same corrections undone or sabotaged by a later command.

Trial and error (experimenting on a disposable file) will help you sharpen this tool into optimal use.

Proof / correct in InDesign

I open 90_bw.tif in Photoshop and size the window to take up half the screen, with text enlarged enough to be legible.

I open book.indb and open story.indd. I size the window so it takes up the other half of the screen.

I read story.indd, comparing it to 90_bw.tif as needed. I constantly check 90_bw.tif for italics, small text, or other formatting which didn't carry over to story.indd.

Some items get lost with perplexing frequency:

—" (em-dash and close quote; many dialogue lines end this way in pulp stories)

I or I'll (it just disappears)

Things to watch out for:

There's a tab where a space should be; messes up all formatting

Type > Show Hidden Characters

This is one reason WordPerfect is so superior to Microsoft Word. WP has Reveal Codes. (Did Word ever evolve to the point of having anything comparable?

It seems best to insert a blank line with a style, rather than hitting <ENTER> twice.

As I proof, I right-click on a red-underlined word that is legitimate, and Ignore All. This is a good idea because if you leave the screen littered with red-underlined proper names and colloquialisms, you will much more easily miss something that you don't want to ignore.

I proof a page from one story here; a page from another story there. The idea is to scramble the plot of each story in my memory. I want to proof each page out of context as much as possible. I recently heard of an editor who will proof/edit the first time by reading a book paragraph by paragraph, backwards. The idea is, while proofing it the second time, one won't be tempted to think, "Yeah, I know what this says," and to lose one's concerted attention on it.

Isolate graphics

Pages with graphics have been scanned at 600 dpi.

I bring each such page into Photoshop and crop away the text.

I adjust the Image / Adjustments / Levels as needed.

Pages in pdf form, which I find on the Internet, are brought into Photoshop and processed similarly, though the quality of images is usually not as good as those I've scanned myself.

I place a graphic on the page where it actually takes place. Believe me, the source magazines sure didn't do that. They opened the story with an exciting picture that sometimes came quite late in the story.

Second proofreading

When the book is pretty much complete, I have a copy printed off at actual size. I mark this up as needed and make corrections.

Creating a book with InDesign

I'm still in the puttering stage of creating books with InDesign, so I won't go into detail. Many tutorials are available regarding the technology of creating a book.

Regarding the esthetics of designing a book, that's quite different.

I began a new career in the newspaper business relatively late in life—age 59. One of my tasks is to compose pages. After four years of doing this, I realize I will always have much to learn. But I am pleasantly surprised with how well I'm doing.

I never took classes in graphic arts theory. But I did observe the comics, magazines, and books that passed through my hands. I must have processed those observations to the point where I was not totally lost when I started composing newspapers.

There are a lot of things I still haven't mastered. Such as using master items effectively. I learned computer programming before the concept of inheritance, and I'm not sure I'm able to think with that mindset. Sure, I get what inheritance is. But I find attributes always coming from the wrong source.

Try as I have, I cannot seem to successfully generate a good Table of Contents.

I'd really like to tag a picture, and in the Appendix, use the page number that picture is on as a variable, and have it plugged in. "The caption for the illustration on page n is:" And if the page the illustration changes, due to adding or deleting preceding pages, n would change in the Appendix as well. Something tells me that should be possible. (If you know how to do it, please don't just say, "You simply have to do a flux capacitation." Tell me in detail what the steps are to perform a flux capacitation, including what menu items I have to click, what settings I have the change, etc.)

With InDesign, I create the documents needed for:

— a print book

— an ebook

To create an ebook, I copy all files I used to make the book, and revise them. You have to do things a little differently. At least, I had to. And I soon found the files for the book will be quite different from the files for the ebook, and if I didn't save the book files, I'd regret it.

The first time I successfully changed the book files into a workable ebook, I worked for three solid days on it.

I submit the final book files to Ingram-Spark. After paying a one-time fee (as I write this, it's $49), the book can be printed on demand. It is listed with, and can be ordered from, Amazon, Barnes & Noble (my personal preference), and a couple dozen other online booksellers I'd never heard of before.

If I want to order some books to sell myself, I pay for printing and shipping costs. If I buy 50 copies of the book within a certain time, that $49 is refunded.

Ingramspark.com has details on how the company works. I am quite satisfied with them. With the present volume and its companion, I will have utilized their resources to create eleven print books, and not quite that many ebooks.

The Flood Fighters
A novel first serialized in Country
Gentleman magazine in 1920,
published under a pseudonym and
not reprinted until now.
By Albert Payson Terhune

In Treason's Track
A novel of the
American Revolution
by Albert Payson Terhune

The Woman Tamers
Six essays on
heart-breakers of history
by Albert Payson Terhune

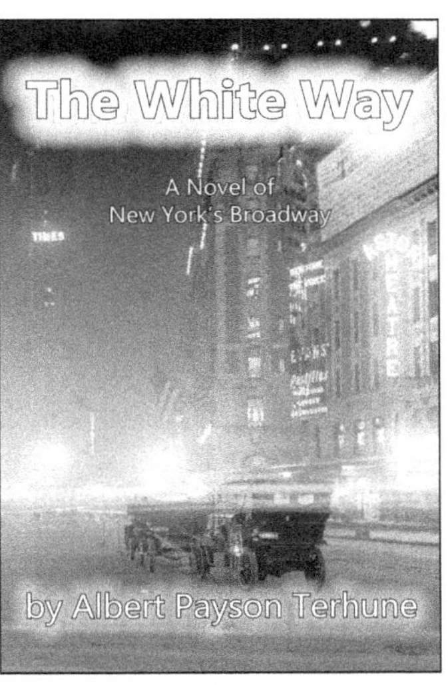

The White Way
A tale of New York's Broadway
by Albert Payson Terhune

An Albert Payson Terhune Reader II
27 stories by Terhune from pulp magazines of the 1910s and 20s,
featuring all original illustrations
by Albert Payson Terhune

Books are available from the major bookstores online,
as print books and as e-books.